To: Park view North

med - surg

by y. Braudstetter md
auther of

JOE'S TRIAL

Coming from Moses Brand

The Trap

Joe's Trial

An almost true story

Moses Brand

Published by
Big B publications
211 Eddy St, South Bend, Indiana 46617
In conjunction with AND Books
702 S. Michigan Ave, south Bend IN 46601

First printing February 2000
10 9 8 7 6 5 4 3 2 1

LIBRARY OF CONGRESS CATALOGING-IN-PUBLICATION DATA
Brand, Moses
  Joe's Trial/Moses Brand
  ISBN 0-942520-12-2
  LIC card number: 00-190040

printed in the United States of America
by Wayne Johnson, Dexter, Michigan
Designed by Yuval Brandstetter

Publisher's note

This is a work of fiction. Many characters may resemble actual persons, but they are all fictitious. The places are real but the events depicted are also fictitious. The historical context of the fictitious events depicted in this book has been kept as accurate as possible. Although none of the events in this book actually happened, they are all possible given the state of the technology.

Big B

In memory of those
who never made it back from Lebanon

For my family who are a source of constant inspiration, especially
my wife, who tolerated the long days and nights
of medicine and writing

In appreciation of my mentors
at the Children's Hospitals

For Sam Gross who always believed in me

To Linda, she knows why

Joe's Trial

JOE'S TRIAL

Chapter 1

DOCTOR JOE

The 4 year old child was panting and crying and sniffling all at the same time, eyes wide with fright. The exam room was strange, scary, with a smell reeking of Hospital. Worse, his mom appeared to be as scared as he was, maybe more, and he didn't know why. Only a few hours before he had gone for a doctor's visit to his pediatrician's office, that bright cheerful place with the big fish-tank, the colorful fish and the little sunken castle. He had his favorite panda bear with him as he always did when going for shots and that place was not really scary even if he *did* have shots. But this place was huge, and terrifying, with strange sick kids with no hair in the playroom, and he wanted to go home *right now*. This scary blond nurse was trying to calm him down in a low soothing voice, but he was not going to go quietly. He took a deep breath and screamed in the highest pitch he could muster "**Mom I want to go home**" over and over again.

Doctor Joe stepped into the room, closing the door softly behind him. He looked at the screaming child and took in the familiar tableau, the small procedure room, the white walls, the wash-basin, the gleaming steel equipment racks, the exam table and the frightened mom holding on tightly to her child's hand. He smiled his most reassuring smile at her, practiced hundreds of times in similar situations and said:

"Hi, I am doctor Joseph Bergman, and I am the Pediatric Oncology fellow, are you Mrs VanLeiden?" He extended his hand. Mutely she took his hand by the fingers only, noticing a wedding ring on his left middle finger. "Doctor Oppenheim from Appleton called me a few hours ago and said that we have a little problem with....he glanced at his clip-board with the new sticker on a scribbled page "Robert here." He turned to the child who had stopped screaming and looked at the newcomer with huge round eyes. "Can you tell me about it?"

As the story, variations of which Doctor Joe heard two to three times a week, came forth, Joe busied himself with examining the 4 year old. He worked quickly top to bottom, noticing the pallor of the conjunctiva, the quick moving eyes, the supple neck, enlarged lymph nodes, the spleen that protruded 5 centimeters below the costal margin, and the multiple bruises on the shins and above the knees. Mrs VanLeiden talked about the tired-ness that overcame her usually active child, the refusal to eat, the vague complaints of leg pains, the initial doctor's visit where the child was given some iron syrup, and finally the appearance of the bruises on his fair skin, without any playful activity to explain them away. She was recently divorced and Bob was her whole family nest. Joe let her tell her story with little interruption, knowing most of the information from Dr Oppenheim.

When he was done he said: "Mrs VanLeiden, you already have an idea that we have to do some tests to help us figure out what is going on. We will do everything under Conscious Sedation so that Bob here will feel the minimum of pain. will you let me do those tests?"

She nodded, his courteous reasonable voice doing the trick of inducing calm to tense situations, she couldn't place his accent though, it was not a Midwestern one, that was certain. He did not even appear American but he did not fall into any of the usual categories of foreigners. He must be from the East Coast she decided in her mind. Karen, the charge nurse, produced the standard Informed Consent sheet and a Bic pen and she signed it.

Joe then turned his attention to little Bob. "Versed" he said shortly to Karen. She handed him the small syringe. He squirted a tiny amount of the clear liquid into the kid's nostril. After a short while his new charge's eyes turned sleepy and he prepared for the IV.

Having established an intravenous line with a minimum of fuss he prepared the Bone Marrow Aspiration tray and the Spinal Fluid tray. The door opened again and Mark Haily, the medical student, came in. Joe, without turning around, said:

"Mark, will you please take Mrs VanLeiden to the parent's Lounge? It's at the end of the corridor, and come back here."

Mark opened the door again and led Mrs VanLeiden softly to the room marked Parent's Lounge where there was a coffee machine always ready with coffee of indeterminate vintage. He turned and almost ran back to the procedure room - he didn't want to miss the initial workup of a new Leukemia.

The Pulse Oximeter was already beeping quietly, the green screen showing a strong pulse and saturation of 98%. Joe had the green mask on and was prepping the puncture site at the hip-bone crest with Betadine. As he swabbed the skin in concentric circles he took the opportunity for some teaching.

"What did I give Robert for sedation purposes?" Joe asked, sounding didactic.

Mark was ready for that one "Versed" he said.

"Why choose this medication?" Joe countered.

Now I am in for it "because it is short acting and because it induces amnesia - I think" Mark replied.

"And what is the main danger?" Joe continued the quiz.

"It may decrease the respiration" ventured Mark.

"Very good, so please give Robert zero point two milligrams to keep him where he is" Joe grinned and prepared the Jamshidi needle. Mark watched as Karen tensed her hands on Robert's back and legs under the blue sterile wrap. Mark observed Joe closely. He was just under six feet tall, powerfully built with wide shoulders, long arms and a tremendous grip. There was just a suggestion of fat around his middle and stout legs with size 14 shoes. Mark estimated Joe at 220 pounds. He had the obligatory pair of round glasses, definitely not Armani, resting on a shelf above the straight unremarkable nose, and green-brown eyes. It was a typical doctor's face except for those weather-beaten eyes. With a short twisting motion Doctor Joe inserted the needle into the bone. Bob twitched and whimpered. Joe used the 10 CC syringe to pull just a little bone marrow, which came frothing out. The sudden vacuum in the syringe forced a quick cry of pain from the child, and Doctor Joe quickly spread the drops on the glass slides prepared in advance. He turned back to the needle and slowly withdrew 15 more CC into syringes prewashed with Heparin. Gently the needle came out and the wound was covered with heavy gauze and tight adhesive bandage.

Next came the collection of spinal fluid. Joe marked the space between the vertebrae with his gloved thumb. After prepping the proposed site with Betadine Joe concentrated on the 2.5 inch needle. With a swift jabbing motion he inserted the needle right on the mark and advanced it until he felt the 'pop' of the Ligamentum separating under the pressure of the needle. The steel stylet came out and clear fluid issued from the hub of the needle. Joe handed the sterile plastic test tubes to Mark as the fluid came up to the one centimeter mark. Finally he connected a small syringe to the needle hub and pushed in the first dose of chemotherapy right into the spinal canal. He pulled the needle out and quickly laid his small patient's head down to facilitate the movement of the chemo towards the fluid bathing the brain itself. Mark watched the proceedings in quiet fascination. Karen, for whom this was the routine, watched with proud approval, she needed to protect every patient from bumbling doctors and this patient was in good hands.

Doctor Bergman rose from the metal stool and collected the tubes. On each pre-stamped sticker he wrote the destination because each sample was essential to the process of diagnosis and prognosis. Generally he could leave routine samples for the lab distribution system, but these samples were too valuable to allow casual treatment - he believed in no one when it came to initial diagnosis of Leukemia, the hopes and grief of people were totally dependent on the content of these tubes so he preferred to take them himself. Little Robert began to shift and move and then to cry, and Joe knew it was safe to leave him to Karen. Leaving the procedure room, Mark and Joe walked quickly up the corridor to find Mrs VanLeiden sobbing into the Kleenex provided by one of the parents who inhabited the room while their children received chemotherapy. The Parents lounge was shadowy and lit only by one lamp so that another parent could catch a nap in the corner settee. Joe just touched her shoulder and told her that the procedure went very well and that Bob was waiting for her. Then he turned on his heels and strode out, already intent on the next stage.

Mark found that he almost has to run to keep up with Doctor Joe. Not that he appeared in a great hurry, but his steps were long and his butt was moving like the long distance walkers Mark saw on TV in the Olympics. Mark also noticed a strange arm position that Doctor Joe always assumed when setting a quick pace, elbows held and 90 degrees and with relatively little vertical movement.

They reached the stairs at the end of the corridor and Joe just kept on the same momentum down the stairs taking them two at a time. Joe distributed the tubes to the various labs and kept the Last to the end, The HematoPathology lab. The glass slides he has made he gave to the tech on call to stain with Wright Giemsa stain. This would take about thirty minutes and in the mean time Joe and mark headed for the big double-headed microscope.

Joe pulled a small cardboard envelope and extracted two glass slides which came from Dr Oppenheim, along with the new patient. Mark had never seen the blood picture of a new leukemia. He did see many blood films in previous rotations but felt apprehensive of facing a blood film with such consequences. Most of all he feared disapproval as would project from Joe if he did not see whatever it is that needs to be seen. More than anything Mark wanted to win doctor Bergman's approval, and the only way to win it was through knowledge and understanding of patients and the diseases that brought them to the Children's Hospital. Not that Joe ever censured him, but upon hearing either incorrect information or worse, coverup, he would raise his left eyebrow, drop the right, purse his lips slightly and start pouring out the straight dope with the appropriate references. Mark quelled his apprehension and applied both eyes to the double lenses. Joe first looked at the field under low power, chose a good spot, dropped one drop of oil on the glass slide and rotated the lense to the 100 power enlargement.

They came right into his field of vision, blue stained, evil, killer cells, each one as menacing as his identical clone. They filled the field from end to end, leaving no room for normal cells. He looked at them, fascinated by the sight of the Enemy staring at him through the lens.

"Mark, please tell me what you can see" said Doctor Bergman.

Mark took a deep breath "I see leukocytes ..."

"Hold it" commanded Joe, "start from the beginning, from the general appearance of the field and then work your way to the description of the Blasts."

"All right, the field appears to be well stained, the cells do not seem to be overlapping. The red cells appear normal with a discoid shape. The leukocytes are uniform with no variability. each has a large nucleus and granular cytoplasm er... "

Joe smiled, this was very good for a first effort and continued "the cytoplasm is abundant with secondary and primary granules, and one can discern Auer rods in each of them. So what do you think we have here?"

Mark was lost, his brain ground to a halt, if Joe had asked him his own name he would not remember it that very moment. A few seconds of complete bewilderment overcame him and he felt his face flushing, and then the coin dropped; The word 'Auer' clicking that safelock that he felt his brain was locked in, and he blurted "Myeloblastic Leukemia" through a dry throat.

He then lifted his eyes to see Doctor Bergman grinning at him. Joe landed his paw on Mark's shoulder with a convincing slap "good, good" he said and Mark winced just a little. Joe was different, he gestured freely with his hands and occasionally landed a hearty cuff. On the other hand he was the best teaching Fellow in the Service. Joe then proceeded to talk about the methods of further diagnostic means and the strengths and limitations of each laboratory.

By and by the 30 minutes were up and the Bone Marrow slides were ready for viewing. The picture was more complex but the essential finding was the same-Myeloblastic leukemia, a disease with only intermediate chances of cure. The final diagnosis would rest with the laboratory results that would only be available the next day. It was time for the most difficult task of all, facing Mrs VanLeiden and telling her the bad news. Despite 6 years of experience in either watching, or performing the terrible job of transmitting horrible news to parents Joe never got quite used to it, and dreaded again and again the inevitable "Is he going to die, Doctor" question. He became aware that Mark was huffing and puffing behind him as he ascended the steel staircase to the seventh floor just like he descended it, two steps at a time. He slowed down somewhat and controlled his own breathing as they approached the parent's lounge. He stopped by the housephone and called the front desk of the ward. He asked to send Karen to the parent's lounge. Karen was present during many of these sessions and could steer him away from thin ice.

Joe waited by the house phone and watched Karen walking quickly towards him. Idly he wondered what she was really like behind the professional facade she always displayed in his presence. Actually he almost never saw her participating in the girl gossip that the nurses engaged in as they did their charting at the end of their shifts. She would do the paperwork efficiently and spend the rest of her time with the kids. She would take a pack of cards and play with the teenagers who had incredibly complex limb-sparing operations for bone tumors. She would paint with the Paintbrush on the portable computer with the 6 year-olds with Leukemia, and she would go over the resident's orders with a fine-tooth comb to maximize pain control. As she approached Joe felt the faint stirring of something he thought he had suppressed - and immediately felt the self disgust welling up within. Back to earth, man, he commanded himself and arranged his features in a non-committal not-quite grin.

Karen looked very seriously at him, "This mother is not going to tolerate much, Doctor Bergman" she said quietly, her voice full of concern, soft, Midwestern. "She is alone, divorced, and her own parents denounce her for the breakup of the marriage. He left her with nothing, *nothing*, and they recently moved to a trailer park. Bob is all she has, and her job in the Bergstrom paper-mill. Her coverage is adequate though, they were enrolled in the HMO through her job. What's the word, is it a straight forward ALL?"

She referred to the most common subtype of childhood leukemia for which there was an excellent chance of cure. Joe pursed his lips and shook his head.

"Its probably AML, but I will know tomorrow, they will not do the FACS tonight unless it's an emergency and although he is sick, he is not critical, and all his other parameters are stable" Joe referred to the set of routine lab work obtained from Bob previously. "Let's see if there is anybody in the lounge" He let Karen precede him into the room, her short flaxen hair just brushing by his nose.

They found the small crushed bundle that was Mrs VanLeiden, essentially a mousy 30 year old woman with brown hair, large brown eyes all sooty with tears, crumpled in the corner, where the only lamp cast shadows on her tear-streaked cheeks. Karen lowered herself gracefully beside her on the settee and draped her arm on the thin shoulders. Joe dragged a multicolored Green-Bay chair from the door and faced her. Mark stood unobtrusively at the doorway.

Joe felt the tightening of his breath, the choke in the throat and said: "Mrs VanLeiden."

"Mary, my name is Mary" She said in a small voice.

"OK Mary," said Joe gently, voice low and soothing, "we need to talk about Robert's problem and I have some more information" oh God, oh God, she is gonna cry and ask the inevitable ...

"Is he going to..going to...." The sobs racked her.

I have to do it right now "no Mary, he is not going to die and we are going to try and cure him, and I need your help to do it. He will need you to be strong for him" his voice hardened somewhat, kinda military thought Karen, "and we will give you all the help you need, but Bob will need you, now more than ever. Bob will look to you and if you are in despair, he may despair too. Children feel with their parents, and you must remain steadfast for him." Karen thought that Joe spoke above people's heads sometimes, but Mrs VanLeiden appeared to heed, she stopped sobbing and listened intently to the rest of the Talk.

Doctor Joe told her about leukemia, about the effects on children, about chemotherapy (no details yet, the disease subtype was still an unknown) and about the Central Catheter that Bob would need. He wound up the talk with words of hope and encouragement. Karen nodded slowly with approval. There were as many styles of imparting bad news as there were Doctors, but Joe's style was unmistakable, it almost sounded like the Major preparing his company for battle against the real enemy, Leukemia.

Mark was fairly shaken by the emotions in the room, and Joe had to tap him on the arm to break the immobility. They filed out of the lounge and headed for the nurses station. Joe pulled the new chart from the rack and filled in the H and P, in a slanted hand writing. This was only a summary because he intended to phone in the History and Physical directly to the dictation service. He also paged Amanda Carter-Halim, the fellow on call for the night, for whom he covered for the past hours so that Amanda could finish an experiment in the lab. The tissue cultures were finicky and he knew that the work must be completed and could not be finished at 5 o'clock just to suit the accepted knock-off time. Anyway, Home was not much since... He forced his attention back to the page and was just done when Amanda called in.

"Hey, what's up?" her cheery voice came down the line.

"Are you done with your funny cells?" Joe asked playfully.

"Yeah, I just put them to sleep for the night in 5% carbon dioxide, and I won't see them for four days thank the Lord, anything that will bother me tonight?"

Joe launched into a quick check-out monologue while Amanda scribbled the essentials on her clipboard. He finished by describing Bob and his mother "nothing for you to do tonight. Karen is with them now, I see her coming, I'll get off the phone now."

"OK, G'night, come back tomorrow" Amanda plunked down the phone, satisfied with a job well done. You could always count on Joe to help in a pinch as long as you didn't take advantage of him.

Both Michelle and Tommy, the nurses who were usually on the afternoon shift ganged up on Joe with various requests, Can I give Johnny an extra dose of Zofran, he has been nauseated all evening, Buddy has not put out enough urine since three and he is still getting Cytoxan. Joe dealt with the questions curtly and with authority. He knew that most of these questions could have been answered by the resident, but she was new in the rotation and was busy admitting a routine admission. Karen passed by, and filled in her nursing notes. She flashed a smile, and as she was sitting under the clock he saw that it was already eight o'clock, way past her sign-out time. She would have to be back at 0700, man, she was such a concerned nurse. Lastly, Joe looked at the counter in front of the nurses station. He found Doctor Horowitz's phone number posted up and punched his number on the phone console.

"Dr Horowitz residence" came a piping voice, "who is it?"

That must be Debra "Can I speak to Dr Horowitz, it's Joe at the Hospital calling."

The phone changed hands and Joe picked up the receiver "Dr Horowitz, it's Joe here, we admitted a new AML, tonight, the one Oppenheim called you about. The BM and LP are done and the labs are doing their stuff. I don't think you really need to come in" he told the attending physician. Dr Jay Horowitz cross questioned Joe for a minute, verified the lab work, the fluids, the medications, surgery consult for the next day. He trusted Joe implicitly, but anyone can forget an important point or overlook something. He was the attending and he was ultimately responsible.

"How is the research going?" Doctor Horowitz asked.

Joe sighed "it's slow, the statistics take real concentration."

"Keep at it mate" Doctor Horowitz encouraged him. He liked to style himself an Aussie.

Joe placed the handset back and went into the back room where he found Mark buried in a big book. He clapped Mark on the shoulder and said "Mark my man, you need to know when enough is enough, go away. I promise no grilling tomorrow or Monday." Joe went for a Goodwill type of trench-coat hanging in the corner, extracted a balaclava-cap with Yamaha emblazoned on it, "this is a reminder that summer will come and I may ride again" he grinned at Mark, a weird grin Mark noted, the mouth smiled but the eyes did not.

Karen gave her scarf a last wind around her neck before stepping outside. Wisconsinite or not, December was cold and the weather report on the five o'clock news was dismal, temp of 25 and a wind chill factor of 5 degrees.

She thought of waiting for the security escort, but she was a big girl and that escort may take his own sweet time about appearing. She wished for the deep bath she would draw at home and Beethoven on the stereo, and so she pushed the weather-tight door and ventured outside. The wind hit her with her icy claws and she felt the top of her ears recoiling from it but she went ahead resolutely. Overhead there was the overpass which was under construction, which in due course would extend all the way to the parking structure. Right now though, it created a heavy im-penetrable shadow, blocking the yellowish meager light cast by the visitors parking-lot streetlights. Three weeks before, a nurse who came off duty was attacked right there in the parking lot and barely managed to escape. The attacker was never found, and the Hospital announced that Security would provide escort to the parking lots and structure on demand. All that sounded fine, except that as the incident receded in people's mind, Security took a little longer to assist individual nurses and doctors. Karen avoided the shadows and walked quickly on the slick tarmac. A sudden movement in the shadows startled her but when she looked into that spot there was nothing. She doubled her pace, passing between the cars until she reached the door at the foot of the entry to the huge concrete parking structure. As she opened the door she glanced again around her, but only the wind tore at the tip of her nose and loosened the scarf from her neck. As the door closed behind her, the sudden absence of wind made the dark staircase almost warm. She did not see the figure entering the parallel doorway 20 yards away. Karen climbed to the second landing, pulled the door and turned left. The wind whined mournfully between the concrete pillars.

The arm that came around her neck was as brutal as the knee that slammed into her left kidney. Were it not for her scarf she would have fainted there and then. Karen did release a thin eerie choking scream that stopped abruptly as the other hand smacked into her mouth so hard that her lips split against her teeth and she tasted salty horrible blood. She swallowed hard and opened her mouth to bite the hand that was blocking her nose and mouth. All she got was some leather and the other hand tightened around her neck so hard she thought her neck must surely snap. The pain from her flank reached her consciousness and a wave of nausea so strong overcame her that her legs buckled under. The arm around her neck tightened some more and her lower jaw snapped up, catching her tongue, more blood gushed into her mouth. The gloved hand withdrew from her mouth and the man began dragging her fast backwards, while her feet dragged on the concrete. She tried to scream again and as she took a breath a blade flashed in front of her eyes and a hateful throaty voice rasped "Shaddap, shaddap, you bitch or I cut you up." His breath stank, her brain screamed 'This can't be happening to me' and the knife flashed away to the right. The man stopped behind a rusty Dodge van and half turned so she could see the tow bar bolted to the van. She heard the clink of the knife haft hitting on the door handle and tried to wriggle. The blood was roaring in her ears and she choked on her ruined tongue and she knew that she must break loose now or fear of death will paralyze her. Her legs began to beat on the floor and the grip under her chin tightened some more as the man jerked her around so she looked right into the gaping hole that was the back of the van. The smell of Death rushed out of the Maw at her and she gathered her last reserves to lash backwards with her right elbow. Her elbow sank into the loose clothing and she knew the effort was totally useless. Defeat swelled into her mind and then the deathly grip around her loosened so abruptly that she fell and the black tow bar came up and hit her forehead. Blackness enshrouded her.

When Karen came to it was not a smooth transition from sleep to wakefulness. She felt as if she was swimming up through filthy salty sticky fluid and that she must take air soon or succumb. Pain rushed at her from everywhere, her head was exploding and she saw bright floaters in front of her eyes. There were two figures in the muddy picture that formed in her brain and she recorded it in ludicrous slow motion.

The man who attacked her was circling, crabbing sideways, a knife held in one hand and the other hand hanging limply from the extended arm. He was hunched forward, bulbous nose thrust ahead and the black sockets seemed to hold no eyes. His face was covered by a thick beard and the moustache seemed to merge right into it so there was no mouth. The sounds that issued from him were low and guttural and menacing. "Cummon cummon you motherfucker" over and over. Facing him, slowly rotating, was another man, dressed in quite a similar manner, with a black balaclva pulled over his face. He was taller and maintained an upright position. His right hand held an implement with a thin shiny stem, with a brush at the end. Karen took a second to recognize it for what it was, a snow scraper, something every Wisconsinite keeps in the car. This man appeared calm and watchful. Meager light was afforded by an overhead bulb somewhere to the left and silent cars were parked all around. The mournful wind sluiced between the cars and blew up the edges of the coats.

The attacker let out a maniacal shriek and rushed at the man who appeared to stand transfixed. The knife began an arc pointing towards the man's belly. But then the metal handle whipped down hard and the knife hand dropped as if severed. The left hand swung around in a short vicious circle and connected solidly with the exposed neck, the knee came up impossibly high and the bearded face was thrown up and backwards. The knife clattered to the concrete and lay there. As the body of the attacker fell back the man whipped out his foot in a straight kick with the pelvis jerking into the kick. The attacker was almost lifted off his feet and slammed into the big gray Lincoln his head snapping back and forth. He slowly slid off the trunk and crumpled on the concrete. Karen was almost as shocked by the concentrated violence perpetrated on her assailant, as she was by the attack upon herself. She cringed as the man took a quick step toward her. The light was behind him and she could not discern his features. He crouched next to her, put down the deadly snow-brush now bent at right angles. His large gloved hands came around her head and neck and probed gently -"Don't move" he said, the voice low and soothing and cultured. Karen was startled, who was it? Her fear receded and the relief was so great she almost fainted again, despite the pain clamoring for attention from every point in her body. She felt a strong arm cradling her head and another sliding under her buttocks and with a grunt she was lifted and carried to the door of the LeSabre. The man helped her to sit and then pushed her down on the sofa-like seat of the big old car. She found that she could not speak due to the sticky mess inside her mouth. The dome light revealed the holes in the cloth of the front seats. The car smelled of gasoline and oil. She heard the man dragging her assailant off to the side. Suddenly he appeared and rummaged in the front, and came up with some cable ties.

"That should keep him secure for a while." That muffled voice again, where did she hear it before? Those shoulders, she knew them from somewhere.

He appeared again, folded her legs to slam the car door and plunked himself at the driver's seat. "Let's see if the old lady will start" he said and hit the starter. The old V-8 roared into life "She really loves the cold air" he crowed from the front. Karen held her head tightly against the U turns in the parking structure and the pain beating in her temples and forehead. She pushed her right arm against the front seat to keep from rolling. "We are going to the Hospital" he yelled over the engine. Karen almost laughed, they were practically *inside* the Hospital. The sickening turns stopped and the car raced up the straightway and made the street corners much more gently. She lost her sense of direction entirely when the car screeched to a stop and the front door opened. The cold air rushed in again, and he bounded out. And then the rear doors were opened wide on both sides and bright light rushed in. Concerned faces glanced in and a gurney wheeled next to the car. She was gently lifted and placed on the rolling gurney and a large blanket draped over her. Karen found herself shivering violently, unable to stop, teeth chattering like castanets. She looked around for her benefactor and could only see the ski-cap moving behind and along with the orderlies rushing her to the big glass doors. They swished open and the hot air hit her face like an open furnace. The sign said Welcome to Milwaukee County Emergency Center. Karen knew where she was.

The orderlies parted and the cap with the Yamaha came off. "Doctor Joe" she breathed.

Joe gave her a big bright smile, entirely uncharacteristic, and said "not a word now, County Docs will take care of you, I am only a Pediatrician and you are WAY out of my league, must take care of your friend up there" he jerked his thumb backwards, "is there anybody I should call?" She shook her head dumbly, it was Doctor Joe, the senior Pediatric Oncology Fellow, two and a half years and she knew absolutely nothing about him. The way he disposed of that animal, the same hands that inserted an IV into the tiniest of scalp veins .... Karen shook her head and immediately regretted it, it still hurt so much.

Doctor Joe scooted to the back of the county ED and informed the command center of the suspicious character to be found on the second floor of the Children's Hospital parking structure. He looked through the armored glass at the Zoo: That was the name they gave the room into which the dangerous types came in for medical treatment. He guessed that Karen's assailant may soon be there.

He then went back to the ED to find Karen. He found her in one of the back rooms, already drinking a cup of warm chocolate that one of the ED nurses brought her. She managed a wan smile.

"What took you so long?" she asked, trying her hand at some humor.

Doctor Joe took her seriously "I went into the car before you did, I always park on the second level, it's less crowded. Before I could start the car I heard a noise, a scream, but I was sure my ears were playing tricks on me, so I rolled down the window and listened. Then I saw that bastard dragging someone and flashing a knife. I grabbed the only thing nearby, which turned out to be the snow-brush and crawled out. When he turned you around he had his back to me and that was my chance. You did something to distract him" she remembered the ineffectual elbow jab "and then I hit him on the upper arm where he held you. As soon as he let you go I stepped back, hoping that he will run. He did not and attacked me with the knife. He left me no choice but to hit him hard. That Van may have an interesting story. But enough about this, did he do any permanent damage?"

Karen listened to this self deprecating story with disbelief "whadoyoumean hit him hard? From where I was this looked like Bruce Lee Kong-whatever stuff" she mumbled through her lips which were beginning to swell up in earnest now, and her tongue felt wooden and stingy all at the same. "The ER doc - I don't know him - said that nothing seems to be broken and he is gonna order some X-rays and have the Plastics people look at me. Where did you learn this stuff and how come I don't know any thing about you at all? and..."

Joe gently stopped her with a index finger to her lips, not actually touching her. "Listen, I need to skedaddle before the Po-lice start getting their act together. Tell them whatever they want. OK?" He turned around, the long trench-coat swishing, and was out of the room before she could react.

Karen just stared at the door, this was too much for one night.

Chapter 2

Karen

One of her recurring dreams was of a long corridor, she was running wildly, and there were doors on either side, always closed. She was running and screaming "Who am I" and "Let me in" over ad over again and there was never any answer. Karen would have these dreams early morning in the twilight between sleep and awake. Dreams being reflections of day time worries, Karen reflected that this dream summed up her life pretty well, living as she did between worlds.

Karen was born to the best the world had to offer. The delivery suite resembled a room in a good hotel much more than a hospital room. The window looked over Lake Michigan, down the slope of Saint Mary's hill. The walls were papered in a soothing shade of gray and a small cross was over the doorway. The furniture almost resembled that of a hotel, and the nurses could teach most bell-men some courtesy. This was the epitome of private medical care in the richest nation on earth, 1968, the United States of America. The Rust Belt was in its hey-day, and the war protests were something that happened in Washington and Madison, most people did not worry about it.

Her mother, the only progeny of one of the more affluent families in River Hills Village, looked with trepidation between contractions, at the Doctor. Doctor Berkovitz had the worry-about-nothing-my-dear grin, as always. After all, she was a healthy young woman with no puerperal complications. Her husband, an anxious young man from an equally affluent family from Glendale held her hand and worried anyway. They practiced the Lamaze breathing and performed it in earnest when the contractions came and convulsed the young body.

Miriam gaze went to the spot above the door where the Cross was. There was no getting away from it, this was Saint Mary's, it was the best in Milwaukee, and her Doctor who was Jewish, practiced in it. She even married the Cross through her dear husband John, who was Catholic, so the Cross could stay where it was. The religious Jewish couples from the West Side would always take the Cross off the wall for the duration of their stay. In the respite between contractions Miriam mused that the Virgin Mary's real name was Miriam just like herself. She tightened her grip on John's hand as the labour pain came, this time harder than ever, and a small scream escaped her lips as she bore down. John held her head forward and Doctor Berkovitz exhorted her to push just one more time. With the next spasm, the worst thus far, the baby's head came out and Doctor Berkovitz reversed himself and cautioned to stop pushing, and breath. John was breathing for her and she wanted, more than anything, to push the huge thing that was distending her body worse than any thing she had ever experienced. And then came the scream of a baby, lusty, full of life, filling the lungs with air, and her eyes filmed over and she cried tears of relief and joy. John, that reserved lawyer, was crying openly and kissing her hand, and then nurse Buckley placed the tiny bundle on her belly. "It's a girl" beamed Doctor Berkovitz, "and she is perfect." With great effort Miriam raised her sweat-drenched and looked at the tiny face, eyes so blue, mouth already rooting for the breast.

The holiday season was a most confusing time for Karen. There were always two things going on at the same time. At Grandpa Toby's place right after Thanksgiving there was a wonderful big tree, green with red ribbons and a star on top. Karen loved coming in from the cold, stripping her hat and gloves and coat, and hugging her Grandpa Toby and Grandma Jayne and having her curly hair mussed. Then she would scamper away and dive under the Tree, and imagine herself in the forest just like the Sunday walks in the park atop the backpack that Dad stuffed her into. John loved the woods and the paths along the river and took Karen with him every time. But when she visited with her Grandpa Jacob, there was never any tree. She really looked for it because the Tree was in Daycare, the tree was in the Mall, the tree was in front of the big shop Mom called Marshall Fields and it was EVERYWHERE except Grandpa Jacob and Grandma Esther's. So, one Saturday, when she was four years old she asked Grandpa Jacob. She was sitting on his lap and he read her some story from a big book.

"Grandpa, how come you don't get a tree just like everybody else?"

Jacob looked up from the book with the brightly painted pictures and cast a sad look after his daughter, the one who had married a Goy.

"That's because we are Jewish, and we do not celebrate Christmas" he said quietly. He knew this would come up sometime.

"What's Jewish?" piped the little one, looking up at him with those huge heartbreaking eyes.

He sighed, that's the most difficult question anyone ever asks. If one had a single Jewish ancestor 4 generations back that constituted Jewishness in the eyes of the Nazi regime, a sufficient justification to put one in the Gas

Chambers and convert their body fat to soap, and their gold fillings to bullion in a Swiss bank. If you happened to be the progeny of a Jewish Cohen (priest) and a woman who happened to be a divorcee, that barred you from a Bar Mitzva and a Jewish wedding. So difficult. Explain that to a four-year-old. "Jewish means being a member of a tribe that thinks God gave them a special mission, Ohmygod, this is WAY over your head. Jewish means we do things a little different, and we don't have a tree for Christmas."

Karen nodded sagely at that and her attention wandered over to the glass cabinet where shiny cups and other strange implements reflected the overhead light. On Saturdays Grandma Esther always had the light on in that cabinet. She knew though that she must not open it because Grandma Esther was once pretty cross with her when she did get her hands on the delicate porcelain cup Grandpa Jacob used occasionally.

Growing up, Karen was especially bewildered on those Friday nights when they went over to Grandma Esther for dinner. First, Grandpa Jacob was always dressed in his best and had a white cap on his balding pate. Then the table was always set in the same way with large loaves of sweet bread in the middle and wine and grape juice to the side. And the Grace, that was really strange. Instead of being a quiet affair with both hands held and heads bowed just like Dad liked it, Grandpa Jacob sang it loudly, modulating his voice REALLY strangely. Mom would join him half-heartedly, she obviously knew the foreign words, and Dad just stood there mutely, cringing slightly, like he had something bad in his mouth and did not know quite how to spit it out. Karen would look from one to the other and sensed some major tension there, and she sometimes caught grandma Esther looking at her with great pity. Then once the dinner started, everything would loosen up, Dad would become cheerful again and no more strange words and language. With time though she started looking forward to those special Friday nights, the singing, the Special Soup, the special foods and when it was just a plain Friday night at home with Dinner Bath and Bed she would sulk and whine.

"Why can't we have Kiddush at home? I wanna go to Grandma Esther."

"That's because they are Jewish and we are not" Miriam answered firmly, perhaps too firmly, "now let's brush your teeth. I have a surprise for you."

Karen tried to speak through her frothing mouth, "what is it mom, I want a new Barbie, the one with wedding dress, please Mom, Please!"

"Well" said Miriam "this is almost like a new Barbie, mommy is going to have a new baby, would you like it to be a girl or a boy?"

"A new baby! but Mommy where is the baby going to come from?" She was full of wonder, her beautiful face turned up to the light.

"The baby is growing inside Mommy's tummy, would you like to feel it?" Miriam stood in the bathroom and guided her daughter's hands over her belly which was just beginning to lose its flatness and acquire a rotund bulge right above the pubic bone. A female bonding moment. There, was that the tiniest little kick? She was only a third of the way through the pregnancy and she did not even tell John yet. She was afraid that indeed this may be a boy and then things will come to a head. Oh God , dear "Adonoi" let this be a girl like Karen, I don't want to have a fight with John over Identity, Brith, girls are so much simpler.

The pregnancy progressed uneventfully, and Dr Berkovitz performed a Sonar exam, he was so proud of the new machine. All Miriam could see on the scope was a snow storm but Dr Berkovitz swore he could see the heart pumping, and the abdominal cavity and even the cranium. Miriam was afraid to ask him about the sex of the fetus, it was better not to know. Karen was so excited she never noticed her mother's worries. John was busier and busier in the office and sometimes Karen never got to see him during the day and only in her dreams could she sense him coming up to her bed for a kiss long after she was fast asleep. She did see that the moments of shared happiness between her parents grew further and further apart. Mornings were a rush to the office or to a meeting with a quick peck of a kiss to Miriam and a quicker muss to Karen's curls. And then one night there was a fight.

Karen could hear them at it and snuck out of bed, across the landing and shivered right at the bedroom door.

"I never said I wanted another baby" her father hissed, it sounded ugly. "I am not ready for another baby, the diapers, the stink, the crying..."

"You never did any of it anyway, I was the only one to wake up to Karen, you hardly ever changed her, or fed her, and I never asked you too. And Karen never stank either. It takes two to make a baby in case you haven't noticed."

"You said it was safe" John was defensive.

"Well, by the time when you were finally willing, it was not." Miriam was all acid. Karen never remembered her gentle mother speaking in this way and she shivered some more. Her eyes were smarting and her nose was filling up and she turned and ran back to her bed. It was just as well because John stormed out of the master bedroom two seconds later. His feet drummed all the way down the steps, and then the clink of the Scotch and glass, an uncaring clink that almost broke the glass. Karen crept back to he shelter of her Eiderdown, but she still trembled, because when her dad drank he would sometimes spank her for the slightest provocation. The closet was just a peek open and the dark slit appeared to widen slightly and the monster with red eyes was pushing the door open. Before it could come out Karen jumped out of bed and scurried as fast as she could to her mother's room. The door squeaked and Miriam, ashen-faced in the gloom, held her arms out to her and enfolded her into and onto her growing belly. The monster stayed away and she fell asleep secure in her mother's arms. Miriam lay quietly and stared at the ceiling until daybreak.

In the colder climates animals are usually born in the spring, at a time that Nature allows for foraging for food. Although Humans believe that they are immune to the natural order, it is obvious in Wisconsin that babies appear to arrive in the greatest numbers in the Spring. The shoots were just beginning to show on the bare trees, with just a hint of green, when Miriam woke up in the first light of dawn with a weird feeling that she has just wet in her pajama and in fact in her whole bed. Then the cramps hit her like a sledge-hammer, her belly was being twisted and squeezed by a giant hand. She fell back in the bed and winced and bit her lip, and groaned and tried to call for John, and then slowly the cramp dropped in intensity, the sweat rolled down her forehead and into her eyes and through the smarting fog she could see Karen standing at the foot of the bed, mute with horror. Miriam tried to smile, but then the harder truth hit home: **John was gone**, she was alone with her daughter and the next cramp was imminent. She dragged herself out of bed, her pregnancy (now slightly reduced) creating a constant drag, like a tanker in a small harbor. Who could she call, she thought wildly, John has not answered her calls now for weeks, she could not bring herself to call her mother, it was too early to call the Doctor.. then the next cramp began starting from the top and arcing down and she found herself on the carpet and bearing down and huffing the familiar rhythm of the Lamaze. She could feel the head of the baby distending and tearing at her low pelvic insides and she was seized by panic. She was about to scream when her daughter's face swam into view. Karen was not mute anymore. She was holding the oversize receiver to her ear, her face resolute and her right index was dialing the black phone. And then, as the labour peaked, she could no longer hold back the long agonizing scream which escaped her clenched lips. The scream was heard on the other end of the connection, and Jacob Lifshitz swung into action.

Esther went for the phone as Jacob threw on a coat and rushed to the Garage. He hit the wall button to open the double garage doors and wrenched the spanking new 1975 LeSabre door. The new engine roared to life and he gunned the engine, the car was always parked facing out for a quick getaway, one never knew when the Nazis were going to come, old habits die hard. The wheels whined for traction as he twisted the wheel and he avoided the snow-pile from last week's snowfall. This car was GRRREAT. The twisting village roads he knew by heart, and he was soon out of River hills and into Glendale. He crossed Good Hope Road with hardly a side look and zoomed into Green Bay road. A left and a left and he was there, The familiar lannon-stone two story house looking just a little bit unkempt. Karen was looking at him from the second story bedroom.

Jacob overshot the drive, stopped and drove back into the driveway, facing out again. He ran out despite the old pain in his hip and hoped that the door was open. It was not. As his eyes began wandering for a likely hiding place for the key, Karen opened the door from the inside.

"Where is Mom?" he said breathlessly.

"Upstairs" replied the little one, older suddenly then her seven-going-on-eight.

Jacob went for the stairs like the 25 year old he was not and pulled himself mightily up with his left strong hand when his hip rebelled. His Miriam was in distress and he would not let her down. The door was open and the bed unmade and Miriam was by the bed on the carpet and it was all messy over her once-beautiful Marshall-Fields house coat. She was just done with another bout, and her hair was a mess and the sweat was pouring down her face.

"Gott-im-Himmel" he muttered, Jacob always reverted to his childhood mother-tongue when under severe stress. "How far apart are they?"

"Don't know, they seem to come almost all the time. I am sure I'm gonna have the baby very soon." Miriam was regaining some color and confidence. Her father was always a rock of a man, unfailing in his love and support. What a poor substitute John turned out to be.

"Alright, Esther was calling Dr Berkovitz as I left. Let's get you out of this coat and up on the bed." Jacob was alarmed but not frightened. In Treblinka he had been the right hand man of Doctor Menashko, and helped deliver women under the worst of circumstances. Jacob flashed back to the Camp, the filthy huts, the 4 tiered bunks, with half-dead inmates looking on as the unfortunate malnourished women gave birth to wretched human babies, destined for instant death if the Kapo found out. Some of the women died right away, some survived and hid the babies until the inevitable time that the newborn was snatched away, mewing like a lost cat. Jacob was not the Doctor but he had learned a thing or two. Now it was up to him again because his grand-baby was coming, ready or not.

Karen was at the door, all serious and adorable.

"Get me some towels, Karen" Jacob said gently. "If you know where the scissors are bring them too." Karen turned and rushed to the bathroom just as Miriam was gripped in a spasm again. "Breath!" Jacob commanded as he threw back the covers. Jacob had never looked *there* since Miriam was 7 years old but he knew he now must. Miriam arched her back, little screams forcing their way past her lips and then bore down, and Jacob hastily pushed a couple of pillows under her head. Then the Labiae separated and a huge round head seemed to dilate the small structures beyond any imagination, there was no way it could pass through that tiny crevasse. The spasm relaxed and Miriam started heaving breaths again, like a drowning victim suddenly revived. Jacob wiped up the mess with the sheet and threw it aside.

"Here are the towels, Zeide" Karen said in a small voice "and Mommy keeps the scissors up high." She led him to the medicine chest in the bathroom and indeed there were surgical-like scissors there. Jacob grabbed the scissors and opened the hot water full on. Scalding water washed over his hands and scissors. It was time to get back to the delivery.

Jacob gave Karen the job of pushing the pillows under Miriam's head and concentrated on the job at hand. He wondered why the Fire Department or the Doctor or whoever were not there but a quick glance at his watch showed him he had only been there a few minutes. He hoped the head was not too large. He remembered a Paulina Wohcek, who had a Caesarean done because the head was too large despite the cut, she died with a horrible infection two days later and Dr, Menashko was powerless. Jacob was determined to make the cut deep and wide. Miriam quickened breathing alerted him from the instant musing and Jacob was ready. As soon as the crown distended the tortured flesh, flesh unrecognizable as anything resembling Sexual parts, when his daughter's screams and breathing reached their greatest intensity, he slipped the scissors under the edge, along the dark-haired crown , and then CUT, the flesh surprising him with its toughness and tenacity. He expected it to pop with the first application of pressure, but of course those women were emaciated and wasted where this one was strong and robust. As soon as the flesh separated and bled profusely the head almost jumped forward an inch. "Push" he yelled at Miriam, "and it will come." "Raus" he hissed at the baby and out it came with a final burbling groan from Miriam.

"Alright stop pushing, move aside Jacob, I'M taking over" boomed a new voice. Dr Berkovitz gently pushed past Jacob who readily retreated and hastily wiped his hands on a towel. He joined Karen who looked up at him adoringly and held his daughter's sopping hand as Dr Berkovitz, surgical gloves on, pulled the baby, first down to release the shoulder, and then up. A lusty cry of a new born baby filled the room to capacity and Jacob finally broke down and cried as if his heart would break. Dr Berkovitz quickly put a clip on the umbilical cord, and placed the baby on Miriam's belly. Outside the ambulance shut off the wailing siren. The Golds who lived across the street came out anxiously still in their housecoats and rushed over the lawn to the ambulance. Dr Berkovitz busied himself with the delivery of the Placenta and presently it came out with a rich flow of blood and congealed matter. He examined it carefully, there were no tears.

"Did you do the Episiotomy?" Dr Berkovitz addressed Jacob with wonder in his voice. Jacob nodded dumbly, still holding on to his grand-daughter.

"Well, gee, I never... Dr. Berkovitz shook his heads "well you did a good job, but Miriam must go over to the Hospital now, with the baby, what is the Baby, anyway, let's take a look."

Dr Berkovitz gently picked the baby who was already making sucking sounds and looked. "It's a boy, are you gonna have a circumcision or a Brith, never mind that, now let's giddy up and GO. Where are those scissors, I better culture them too."

Miriam suddenly shook herself alert from the thrall she sank into as soon as the baby's shoulder was delivered. "No circumcision, and don't let John near him."

Dr Berkovitz nodded, a pained expression crossing his features. The Glendale fire-department medics came up, and moved Miriam, sodden sheets and all onto the gurney. They tied her with the straps for the way down and Dr Berkovitz carried the baby wrapped up in new towels close to his chest. The baby was rooting, looking for the breast. He appeared robust and Dr Berkovitz had no fear for him. He ordered the Medics to start an IV, and had a bottle of Hartman solution bolused into Miriam's system, who knows how much blood was lost into the sheets and the episiotomy that the crazy, brave old man had made. This was a big baby, and with powerful enough contractions the uterus could conceivably rupture and then God help the poor woman. The Medics loved their siren and soon everyone in the neighborhood knew that Mrs Fitzsimmons, whose husband had left her, just had a baby.

Eight days later a small gathering convened at the Glendale Beth Israel Synagogue. Dr. James Lipkin from Mount Sinai Hospital arrived with his instruments, and a few of the early morning regulars showed up to make up with Jacob the requisite community of 10. After the short ceremony they had some bagels, cream cheese and Lox, but it was not a happy occasion. This Boy was fatherless and his mother, although Jewish by birth, had distanced herself from the community. Jacob Lifshitz stood in as the father and Godfather, and vowed that this boy, named Alexander (why Alexander for goodness sake?) will know who he is, where he is going and who his real people are. Toby Fitzsimmons was there too and the grandfathers acknowledged each other, distantly.

John came back when Alex was four months old. First there were bouquets of flowers, that Miriam threw with anger into the nearest basket. Then there were letters which Miriam did not read and angrily tossed the same way. But Karen did answer them, even though she did not understand what exactly he was saying in those letters. There was a blue box close to the school bus-stop, and she asked her daddy to come back. Miriam understood only later why her stock of stamps was being depleted so fast. John was persistent though, and the next bouquets stayed, and the letters were read.

One Sunday morning there was a knock on the door, which Miriam did not answer.

"Daddy, Daddy you're home!" Karen could not realize that it was six months since she had seen him at home. "Mommy, daddy is here" she screamed shrilly.

Miriam came down the carpeted stairs, sedately, holding on to the baby who was sucking away contentedly on a pacifier. She looked at John, and at Karen who was so happy to see her Dad and was jumping all over him. He looked up beseeching, one eye buried in his daughter's wild hair, and one eye on her. He promised, and she should give him one more chance. After all, he was the father of her children. She turned to the living room and left the door open.

Karen had no idea what transpired between her parents but Dad was back in the house. There was one obvious change. Dad was home much earlier and after school he was almost always there to take her shopping, or ride the bicycle along the river, or play Monopoly during the long winter evenings. He was especially proud of her skating speed and stamina. It was back to uncle Henry and Aunt Jill, and her cousins Laura and Lee. In fact it seemed that as Alex was growing from an infant to a baby to a toddler they were seeing Grandpa Jacob and Grandma Esther less and less. Occasionally she would see her parents hugging and kissing as they did in the past and this made her very happy. She took good care of her baby brother and soon was a dependable baby-sitter. There was no more talk about another baby.

Karen reached puberty and adolescence without any of the histrionics associated with the transition, and became a serious young woman. She developed her skating abilities, rose in the State ranking, and became the under 16 short distance skating champion, and her coach, Kevin Kollen, began looking into the Olympic future. She liked the company of the volunteers of the Glendale fire-department, especially the paramedics, and learned from them as much as she could. The men especially could not resist teaching the beautiful teenager, and telling of their exploits in life-saving.

Alex was 8 years old when Karen noticed he was huffing and puffing when trying to keep up with her up the hill where they watched the small rapids on the otherwise tame river. This was out of character because Alex was usually ahead of her, riding his bike in a sinusoid across the path and making figure-of eights around her, taunting her all the time. She propped up the old Sunbeam on the worn wood bench and waited for him. Arriving on the hilltop, he appeared a little pale and she could see his pulse race in his neck. He flopped down beside her and concentrated on his breathing. Karen knew from the CPR classes she was taking that rapid breathing meant either lack of oxygen, or insufficient circulation.

"Are you OK Alex?"

"Yeah I'M OK, just a little tired" Alex continued huffing. He settled down slowly.

"Is it alright if I take your pulse, just like I did when we played Doctor?" she asked.

Alex smirked "You are too big to play doctor, mom said I should not walk around with nothing on in the house 'cause girls are not supposed to look at the boys."

"She is right you know, people need to have privacy, but all I want to do is count the pulse in your hand." Alex held out his hand and Karen placed her index and middle on the inside of the wrist and immediately felt it going rapidly under her fingertips. She looked at the old windup Tissot watch that Grandpa Jacob gave her for her twelfth birthday (it's my Bar Mitzva watch and I would like you to have it, he had said) and counted as the second hand swept around the face, She counted 142 beats in one minute, and she knew it was much too fast.

"Alex, when we get home we will go to mom and tell them that something is wrong, how long have you been feeling tired?" She imitated Dr Bacharach, he sometimes invited her when he was seeing kids in the County Clinic.

"I don't know, a little while, and anyway, stop it, I'm alright, race you home, don't get chicken on me down-hill, your breaks keep squealing." Alex left the bench, hopped on his BMX, and shot down hill. Karen followed more sedately, she fancied herself looking like the young women in the old BBC series on PBS, that's why she liked the Sunbeams she found in a garage sale, they were antique as was the watch.

Back home, it was a glorious summer afternoon and Miriam was sitting in the swing on the patio-deck and reading Newsweek. Karen parked her bike in the garage and sat by her. Miriam put down the magazine and frowned at Karen. "Something bothering you my darling?" she asked.

"Mom, have you noticed Alex, he looks kinda tired and peaked?"

Miriam knitted her eyebrows "Well yes, he is a little more quiet than ususal and last Sunday he didn't want to go to soccer, but those are normal ups and downs for a kid, why, do you see anything wrong?"

Karen would not be soothed "Mom, something is wrong, he is *really* out of breath, and he looks funny. Can you take him to Dr Bacharach?"

Miriam considered her impassioned daughter "You are turning into quite a little Doc, aren't you, we don't have one in the family, and at 16, we must think about college. All right, I'll call the office for an appointment."

Alex had to be almost dragged into the East Side Doctor's office. It was a typical Wisconsin office, low, unprepossessing outside, comfortable and inviting on the inside, with a huge aquarium that all children loved. The exam room was neatly arranged and Dr Bacharach was his usual cheery self.

"Hi Karen, you are more beautiful every day, its positively a sin. Hello Mrs Fitzsimmons, do you know how good your daughter is with kids? Gee, Alex we haven't seen you for a year at least. Your mom tells me you are a little tired and out of sorts."

Alex shot a venomous look at his older sister, "she is crazy, first she holds my hand then I have to go and get poked. No poking!" He hugged himself and looked defiantly at the doctor. Dr Bacharach smiled.

"No poking just yet, let's get the women-folk outta here and have a man-to-man talk." Karen and Miriam filed dutifully out of the exam room. Karen had watched Dr Bacharach's face as he had looked at Alex, he was concerned, no question about that. She went over to the aquarium and desultorily followed the tropical fish in their unending quest for food.

Dr Bacharach was way more serious when he came out of the exam room, he told the front desk to hold his calls and to send Mrs Fitzsimmons to his office in the back. Miriam was positively frightened.

"Mrs Fitzsimmons" he said without preamble, "I am concerned about Alex, and I do want to do some blood tests. I can either send you to have them done right now at St. Mary's, or I can take them, and call you tomorrow with the results. Please don't ask me now what this can be because that is why I need the tests."

Miriam's fear level rose some more, but she knew that doing things in the hospital would be impossible with Alex. He would scream and raise hell, even simple kindergarten shots were a disaster. "Let's do things here" she decided.

Alex was sulking all the way back. "I'm gonna tell Dad on you how you made me get a poke and for what, just 'cause I didn't feel like playing soccer on Sunday" he lapsed into silence, he suddenly looked terribly pale. John was on a business trip to Chicago and would come back very late. In fact he came back so late that Miriam decided not to tell him anything that night, but sleep did not come easily to her.

The phone rang at the Fitzsommons residence at 10 AM. Gloria at the Doctor's office requested that they set up an appointment at noon and that both parents be present. Miriam *knew* this was serious. She called up John at the office and told his secretary of this appointment. They met in the parking lot, and holding hands tightly they ascended the steps to the waiting room.

"Hi Mr Fitzsimmons, Hi Miriam, the doctor will be with you shortly." Gloria chirped and went back to the phones. Miriam noticed that nurse Beatrice avoided her eyes as she hurried from one exam room to the other. "You can go in now" called Gloria.

John followed Miriam to the small office in the back. The walls were papered light blue and pictures of various aircraft were hanging on the wall. Dr Bacharach walked in with a sheaf of papers. He shook hands with John and Miriam and settled his big frame in the executive chair. He was dead serious. They were frightened.

"I have some difficult news, and its difficult for me too, so please let me talk and then I will answer your questions. Is that OK?" they both nodded, waiting for the bombshell. "Alex has been ill for a fair while and this is typical. He has had some aches and pains, and some bruising that was a little excessive but you put that down to the ususal boy antics, right?" More nods. "Well, all those are signs of his bone marrow, the part of his body that makes the blood components, failing to do it's job." Dr Bacharach spread the sheaf in front of the bewildered parents. "This is a blood count that the automatic machine makes for us and it is very reliable." Miriam and John leaned forward to look at the meaningless rows of numbers, neatly arranged top to bottom, that were holding the doom of their child. "And this is a count we took from Alex at 3 years ago for his kindergarten physical. Look at the HB, it represents hemoglobin. It was twelve point five then, and it is only seven point two now. The WBC, which represents cells which fight infection were eight thousand three hundred. Now its only two point three thousand. Look at the PLT, that represents cells important in blood clotting. It was two hundred thousand, and now it is only forty eight thousand. Something is seriously wrong!"

"But what is wrong doctor, why is it that way?" Miriam quavered.

Dr Bacharach leaned forwards and met them eye to eye "I don't know, but I know who would, and he is the best man in the *world,* and he works right here in Milwaukee. I called him up at the Medical College and he advised me that he would see you anytime."

John was not convinced "Dr Bacharach, don't you think that Chicago would be better, I mean, Children's Memorial... he stopped as Dr Bacharach emphatically shook his head and reached for the big Nelson Textbook of Pediatrics. Karen had seen him browse that book previously, Dr Bacharach was never too shy to drag out the big book and look through it right in front of the patient. It was already marked and he opened it in front of the shaken parents. "See here, this is THE textbook of Pediatrics, and look who writes the chapter" they craned their necks "and see from where? right here in Milwaukee, if this man thinks that Alex would best be served elsewhere he will be the first one to tell you. I want you to see Dr Kammitzer today or tomorrow because this cannot be put off. Do I have your promise you will take him?" Miriam assented immediately, John was a little more hesitant. This was typical of the city which is always described as 'Milwaukee? Oh, it's North of Chicago'. Even the natives feel that somehow some things are always bigger, or better, or more elegant, in the huge Metropolis to the south. Of course, there is nothing further from the truth, since Milwaukee is a city which lacks nothing, and compares favorably with Chicago in every aspect of quality of life, medical care included.

John did not think that Karen ought to come with them but she insisted and Miriam agreed. "First, she is the one who noticed things, and second, she knows so many things that I am sure she could make sense of the Doctor Talk better than you and I." Karen sat in the back of the Olds wagon and played cards with Alex. Alex thought this was a grand day, no school, early June sunshine, and the poking all behind him. Karen was so bad at 21 that he beat her every time. It was not a long drive, Good Hope road east to the 43, then south on the freeway, off to Wisconsin Avenue, past the Marquette University, the Children's hospital had been the same dingy block since 1926. The hospital had clearly outlived its facilities by the Eighties. The age and *smell* of the buildings were powerful deterrents to some of the more affluent citizens of the city. They parked close to the entrance and walked into the old foyer, small, uncomfortable, but prettily decorated with children's art. Soon they were directed to the first floor, and seated in the waiting room. There were other kids there and the Fitzsimmons family looked with horror at the scrawny necks, the white faces, and the hairless scalps, and then John stood up, pale and angry.

"Let's go, this is the Cancer Ward, it's a mistake, I knew we should have gone to Chicago." Miriam was just as frightened, and irresolute, Karen examined her father, he was irrational, and forceful. "ALEX" he almost shouted, Alex was already off to examine the whiteboard with markers, together with a black kid who was scrawling his name in red "We are going, Alex" he was very loud and Miriam rose to calm him. The door opened and a small man with penetrating eyes and economy of motion walked toward them. The receptionist, who had seen this kind of reaction before made a quick call to the man who could deal with a delicate situation. Dr Kammitzer was as good with people as he was with Bone Marrows.

"Hello there, I am Dr Kammitzer, you must be the Fitzsimmons family, and you must be Karen, Dr Bacharach told me I should look for an exceptional young woman and" he appraised her "he is right, as usual. Please come in." Thus he disarmed the scowling John. Karen walked over to Alex and gently disengaged him from his new friend.

The exam room was small and stuffy, and smelled old.Dr Kammitzer had picked up a fresh-faced student who scribbled industriously on her clipboard as the questions and answers came. Finally Dr Kammitzer said "Alex, you know I need to examine you and this room is very small, would you like Mom or Dad to stay with you?" Alex was very interested in the little poodle on the student's stethoscope "I want Mom" he said and so Karen and John filed out dutifully. It seemed like hours until the initial blood tests came back, but then the receptionist called them all to the Doctor's office. John was back to scowling and Miriam was more frightened than ever. Dr Kammitzer surveyed them from behind his desk, hands on the sheaf of paper, in exactly the same attitude of somber seriousness as Dr Bacharach 24 hours earlier.

"First thing first, we must admit Alex to the hospital because his Platelet count is very low, and that may put him at risk for severe bleeding." Alex snapped his head up at that and started edging towards the door. Suddenly Karen could see a flame shaped spot in his right eye, this must be a bleeding, she reported to herself. She was closest to the door so she held Alex gently and gave him a brave kiss on his dear forehead. Her baby brother was sick, but this Doctor will surely cure him.

"Second, I think that Alex is suffering from Aplastic Anemia, which is an illness pretty rare in children, which means that his bone marrow has stopped making cells almost entirely, this is a very serious illness. I know you have a thousand questions and that's OK, fire away!"

Miriam wanted to stay with Alex that night, and then every night. There were tests, and X rays, and transfusions, and counts. They all gave blood. Karen stayed overnight, she met the parents, the residents, the nurses, especially the nurses. She learned a whole new vocabulary, and she took every opportunity to ask for more information. The tests came back and soon they were all at Dr Kammitzer's office again. Karen asked him once about a very strange inscription that was riveted to his desk. She knew those characters, of course, they were the same as in Grandpa Jacob's prayer book.

"That's the Doctor's Oath in Hebrew, as written by a great doctor, the Maimonedes, who lived in Spain a thousand years ago, its as relevant today as it was then!" he told her. He liked this intense young girl who was so concerned about her baby brother, and anyway, she was the compatible donor, she was a partner in the therapeutic effort. And there was always that tribal kinship, understood but never expressed, with the Grandfather, who came at odd hours, played chess with the kid, and pulled out his Psalm book when the kid was asleep to read silently.

"I have some answers and a course of action to propose, and before I make any propositions, I wanted to say that you should feel free to seek any second or third opinion before we do anything." John and Miriam nodded, by now they knew that this was the best place for Alex, however outdated the facilities were, and they were not going anywhere else. "We did not find an etiology, that is a reason or an agent that would cause the Aplastic Anemia. That is commonly the case. On the other hand we can cure him with bone marrow donated by a family member and you are lucky because Karen here is an exact match and the perfect donor for him." John and Miriam turned their awed faces towards their eldest daughter, who actually beamed with pride. "This is a much harder process than you might think, but the available data shows that it affords the best chance for a complete cure."

"What do I need to do, Doctor?" That was Karen.

"With your parent's permission, and only then, we will take some bone marrow from your hip bone, and give it to Alex."

"But are you going to take out a part of her bone, this must be a terrible operation" John was horrified again.

"No, no" Doctor Kammitzer explained patiently, "the bone marrow is not solid. Its really like a gel suspended inside our bones. All we do, under anaesthesia, is stick needles into the bone, and suck out with syringes. There is plenty left over and it renews itself, not that the procedure does not hurt, but usually it means a one night stay in the hospital."

"And what about that terrible disease AIDS, doesn't that come through those needles?" Miriam was concerned.

"We use needles that are single-use-only" Dr Kammitzer replied for the ten thousandth time. He and his whole generation of Hematologists were absolutely thunder-struck, mortified, by the carnage inflicted through their own hands on their Hemophilia patients, by the AIDS disease. Patients they had literally raised from day one, using the best that science and industry could provide in Factor support, were dying off in agony by the hundreds, and there seemed to be nothing they could do beside more research and prayer. It was just like the middle ages and the Black Death, doctors walking through the wards filled with young people they knew, and seeing them to their deaths. The more things changed, the more they remained the same. "We have learned that contaminated blood passes the disease around and since last year all blood donors are screened. But there is never any absolute assurance. In Milwaukee, we have one of the lowest occurrence of AIDS in the nation so I expect our blood supply to be OK" Promises, promises, he thought wryly.

"Mom, dad, I want to do this, I talked with some other brothers and sisters who gave the bone marrow, and I can do it."

The donation of the bone marrow was the easiest part of all, so it turned out to be. The process was like entering a long and dark tunnel of misery with the hope of reaching the light at the end, and that light was murky at best. Long nights, high fevers, midnight doctor consults, days which were no different from nights, new residents rotating through the hellish place, cries of families who realized that their child was doomed, despite all the efforts, and the occasional farewell impromptu parties for those who had recovered and left the unit, never to come back. The nurses were the backbone of the whole complicated procedure, and the attending physicians relied on them implicitly. Karen learned to love them and came to the decision that this should be her role in life, that of the highly skilled nurse. They told her that only a few years back the success rate had been much lower, and kids were getting better all the time. This was a goal worth fighting for, making sick kids better. She confided in Grandpa Jacob, who was very enthusiastic.

"Do you remember how you helped me deliver him?" Karen nodded solemnly "so now he is almost your son, because his new blood will be yours!"

And so it turned out to be. Three weeks after the bone marrow transfusion, Dr Gupta, the resident for the month of August, triumphantly showed Karen a laboratory report.

"Do you know what this means?" he crowed. Karen looked through and read.

Karyotype report

Name: Fitzsimmons, Alexander
Date: August 15th 1985
Specimen: Blood - buffy coat

The specimen yielded 24 mitoses of which 15 were analyzed
The karyotype is 44XX in all mitoses

This a normal female karyotype

Signed
A.F. Bolton PhD
Head of department- Genetics

"I know, I know" Karen said ecstatically "that shows Alex has my blood now, if this was his, then it must read 44XY, I cured him, I cured him" she was almost jumping up and down. Dr Gupta was smiling widely, teeth bright against his dark Indian skin.

"That's right, you did, although he still has a fair way to go, and now since you DID cure him you must go back to summer school and make up everything you were missing."

Alex was discharged with fanfare 15 days later. He was quiet, subdued, pale, but his counts were going up daily and he was getting stronger by the day. He was getting so many medications it was hard to count. Karen and Miriam cleaned up his room so that not a single bacteria could survive. He was back at the outpatient clinic three times a week initially and then less and less often. Then disaster struck.

Miriam allowed a select number of friends from school to visit at home. Andy was his best friend and washed his hands as instructed and never brought any food. He never told Miriam of the pimples that appeared on his belly and were spreading in crops up his chest. Only when Alex broke out with a storm of those pimples did the story come out. Varicella, chickenpox, had always been one of the enemies of patients with compromised immunity, and bone marrow recipients were THE most compromised. Dr Kammitzer was dumbfounded as Alex was brought through the back door, so as not to expose other kids, and was even more horrified to notice that Alex was breathing faster than usual.

Alex was admitted directly to the Pediatric Intensive Care Unit, and the virus spread through his organs like a wildfire. His skin was covered with them, lips and mouth and face. Medications were useless and Dr Kammitzer raged over the phone at the pharmaceutical company that put red tape and FDA approval above the need to try an experimental drug for Varicella. The lungs became whiter and whiter and the fever raged daily. Miriam and Karen and John and grandparents practically LIVED in the cramped family lounge. The virus overwhelmed the little boy and he lost contact with the surroundings. One night he deteriorated some more and they had to put a tube in his throat, and a respirator at his bedside. Dr Kammitzer hung like a shadow at the bed and blamed himself for hinting that some friends could come and visit. The little body became a thing, infiltrated by tubes, collecting oxygen, blood, plasma, antibiotics through various tubes, and yielding urine and blood tests and wires which registered endless data on the screen and lab reports. The Intensive Care crew were becoming dispirited.

Jacob knew he had to take Charge, because no one was prepared to say the obvious. He accosted Dr Kammitzer after hours, as the latter was making his rounds.

"Dr Kammitzer, I am Jacob Lifschitz, Alexander's Grandfather."

"Yes, I have noticed."

"Doctor, I delivered this boy eight years ago at home. I vont you to give me your honest opinion about his chances of coming out of here." Dr Kammitzer returned a mournful gaze at the old man "Don't spare the details."

"The whole truth and nothing but the truth?" he countered, "and are the boy's parents in on it?"

"No, they are not, and they do not dare. But I have been through the death camps, and sometimes death is a relief" Jacob bored into the younger man's eyes.

"All right, I reviewed the literature concerning overwhelming chickenpox infection leading to respiratory failure, after Bone Marrow Transplant. *No survivors*. Now, what are you going to do with this information?" Jacob maintained his gaze, and his eyes misted over, his face contorted, and tears were running down the lined cheeks, small sobs escaped, Dr Kammitzer hastily pulled out a Kleenex from the service shelf but it was soon over. The tears were dammed and the resolute gaze came back.

"I vill talk to my daughter and son-in-law, talk to Karen, and my wife and Toby Fitzsimmons. Then I vill get them all to meet with you and make a truthful decision." He turned and walked away, shoulders bent. Dr Abe Kammitzer shook his head with wonder. Those old geezers were tougher than nails, it was so hard to tell a family that their child would die, especially after you had already pulled him back from the Jaws.

It took Jacob two more days to make the family understand that Alex was already dead, even though the monitor showed some cardiac electrical activity. They gathered around his bed, Miriam and John and Karen, Jacob and Esther, Toby and Jayne. Henry Wilkins, who ran the pastoral services, joined them silently, and prayed. Dr Harvey Sands, attending intensivist, and Lauren Lowes, who was the charge nurse for the day, disengaged the wires one by one, and then turned off the monitor. They had already given Alex the Caloric test and the Anoxia test and they knew he would not react. Dr

Kammiter placed his index on the respirator button, and turned it off. An eerie quiet descended on the little stuffy room, Miriam turned to her husband, buried her face in his shoulder and cried, silently.

"Yisgodal veyiskodash Shmeh raba" Abe Kammitzer's head snapped up, it was years, no decades, since he had heard that tune, the Kaddish, and he thought he was so well assimilated, even his own children were not Jewish. "Be'olma divra kireutei Veyamlich malchutei Viyekarev Meshichei" Jacob's voice was getting stronger, even those in the PICU who had avoided the scene were now drawn back by the ancient words. Dr Abe Kammitzer found himself saying Amen at the prompt, just like when he was a young boy in St Louis. Karen listened and her heart went out to her grandfather who had lost his grandson, She was much taller than him, and as she looked down she could see the tears streaming uninhibited, and the way he moved with the prayer. "Veimru Amen" and they all repeated Amen, Jew and Gentile, all equal before God in the face of death.

John insisted on a catholic service and burial in the Glendale cemetery, Miriam said nothing. Jacob and Esther made no objections.

Karen went back to skating, and threw herself into the training as never before, leaning into the curves and driving herself raw. She became State Champion at 18 and a serious contender for the nationals. But she knew her real destiny, it was her job to help other people with the misery of illness, and share the triumph of cure. Her skating career ended when she collided with one of the male skaters who would not allow her to go past. Her right ankle twisted, then snapped, the powerful ligaments tearing a piece of bone off. That ankle never allowed her to recreate the same efforts, and although she continued to skate she dropped out of active competition.

Karen could never figure out her religious affiliations so she avoided all religion and religious gatherings. She had another faith , the faith of the Healer.

Chapter 3

YAFFO

Mustafa Halim knew that he must soon come to a decision. He had been brewing this for a long time but soon he must decide to be true to himself or just give up. He looked at his daughter Alia, who was arranging her Barbies in the elaborate doll house that Amanda's parents gave her for her 6th birthday. He cringed at the memory of the in-laws visit. He knew they never truly approved of him and initially that did not bother him at all. Especially the arrival of Alia seemed to erase any previous misgivings they had about him. She turned out to be a beautiful baby, a rambunctious toddler and a gorgeous girl. She had her mother's clear skin, a hint of olive shining through, curly black hair falling all over her face which she frequently brushed aside, and startling blue eyes. Mustafa watched her talking to her dolls and building an imaginary story of the pirates coming over to take the beach house and Ken storming over to save them. She belonged to him as much as to her and to them, he raged inside. *His* parents had no chance of seeing their granddaughter grow and learn and charm her surroundings. He turned back to the computer screen and tried to pick up where his thoughts had snatched him, he had to figure out this genetic sequence and find out how to place the promoter where it would activate transcription most efficiently.

Mustafa Halim was born in one of the most squalid and depressing places in the world, a place that hung precariously between the state of death and zombie, a place that had no future and a past of deep rage and futility. The Sabra refugee camp was placed on the west side of Beirut. Mustafa was born there in 1965, right there in the filthy room with his twin sister. He remembered the building which consisted of skinny bare concrete columns, gray thin blocks of concrete incompletely separated by a thin layer of mortar, and the constant din of cars, screaming children, donkeys, and screeching women. The four storey rickety building was always alive with people going up and down the steps, again bare concrete with no guard-rail. The division to apartments was imaginary and there were six to ten people in every room. It was steamy hot in summer and freezing, windy cold in winter. Mustafa was lucky in a way to be the only boy, born after the arrival of four elder sisters. They all doted on him and only later in life he understood how much effort it took to give him things he considered his due as the only son of the Doctor who was the Abu-El -Banat, the father of the daughters, a slightly derogatory term in the local lingo for a man who had no sons.

Doctor George Abu Mustafa Halim was a scion to a prestigious Hamula (larger family) In Jaffa. He had studied Medicine in Manchester in the Thirties and established a successful general practice in his ancient town with Andromeda's rock in front of the small harbor. He felt therefore connected to the British Empire and to it's great Pact with the Arab nations since the days of Lawrence of Arabia. He and his generation looked with suspicion and disgust at the Jewish city of Tel-Aviv rising from the sands north of Jaffa, and expected it to vanish one day into the sands from whence it came. Even greater was their disgust with the British Mandate which seemed to seesaw between the malicious Balfour declaration (which promised the Jews a homeland in the Holy Land) and their commitment to the Lawrence Legacy. As the war in Europe appeared to approach Palestine he joined the activities of the Mufti Hajj Amin El Husseini, who conspired to help the Germans in the war effort against the British. The battle of El Alamein stopped the German expansion into North Africa and began the series of mishaps which embittered him and his whole generation.

As the war ended, hordes of Jewish refugees from the devastated Europe began pouring in despite British regulations and Arab guerrilla activities. The wealthier Palestinians began to emigrate, and doctor Halim suffered a decline in his business, since the poorer patients, those who did not have money to move, stayed behind. Worse, the Jewish city just kept growing, and prospering, with all the accouterments of European life, Philharmonic orchestra, theaters, and movie houses. Some of his patients even went to the new emigrés who were renouned physicians in Berlin and Frankfurt and Vien before the war. A crushing blow was delivered to the Palestinians on November 29 1947, when the United Nations through the connivance of the victors divided Palestine into two states, thereby affirming the Jewish Zionist aspirations for statehood. The final blow was delivered ironically by the Arab states which trumpeted over the radio that as soon as the British mandate ends, they were going to sweep the Zionists to the sea and drown Tel- Aviv in a river of blood. To facilitate that end they called on all the Arab inhabitants to pack up and leave temporarily until the sweep was over. Dr Halim packed his clinic, wife and two daughters into the Chevy Van and drove north through the racked land, the British roadblocks, Naqura, and to a small Hotel in Sidon. He expected to stay in Lebanon, the Riviera of the Eastern Mediterranean, for a few weeks at the most, his wife even cleaned up the small stone house before they left. The vacation lasted a lifetime in which the Arab armies were defeated, a victorious Jewish state was established, and Doctor Halim became a refugee, no better than the thousands who roamed the Sabra camp in search of food, and living off the charity of UNWRA, the representative of the same hated Western Powers who had helped the Jews from the beginning. In fact he never truly believed the Arab countries and their leaders, especially the pompous king Farouq of Egypt. How could they have lost the war to an upstart state when they had the combined might of five armies with Tanks, and Airplanes and Artillery? They must have been in cahoots with the Western Powers and the International Zionism too. He became embittered, and gradually he fell to Hashish, and lost his ability to practice medicine, such that one could in the refugee camp. The fact that he had no sons only served to enfeeble him further. The Jewish state appeared indestructible and Doctor Halim like the rest of his generation, too old to adapt and too weak to fight with Yasser Arafat and the Fedayeen sank into the quagmire of despair.

The unexpected birth of the twins, Mustafa and Alia, brought the first ray of hope to the bleak existence of the Halim family, even though they were born right into the worst, dirtiest, most crowded conditions in the Middle East. There was one thing the Israelis could never do and that was to stop the growth of the Palestinian population. In fact that was the only way to fight the implacable enemy. The teeming camp produced thou-sands of angry Shabab (youth) who had no outlet for their energy except hate for the Zionists. Doctor Halim emerged from the fog of Hashish, and looked at his newborn son and swore to himself that with Allah's help, his son will not become one of the Shabab but continue the fight to liberate the homeland through education.

Mustafa became the object of the all consuming passion to reestablish respect. His earliest memories were of his father, face deeply etched, with a silver beard and almost white hair, scolding him to disregard the noise of the women and girls cooking and bickering in the cramped quarters, and concentrate on the letters in Arabic. He learned the Latin alpha-bet before other children mastered even Arabic letters. He was not allowed to join in the frenzied activity of the other male children who were running up and down the concrete rail-less stairs brandishing imaginary guns, and killing the cowardly Zionist enemy. Through his son, Abu Mustafa Halim (the Arab custom is to call a man after his first- born son) returned to life. He visited the UNWRA clinic and offered his services after years of neglect. He suffered the derogatory attitude of the volunteer western doctors, and even those of the women doctors, who looked down upon their charges from the heights born of their ability to escape this hell-hole any time they wished. He tolerated, and translated, so that he could look through the new books that those doctors brought with them.

1967 brought a new hope. Gamal Abd -el -Nasser, the hope of the Arab world, began a series of moves against Israel that seemed to bring the possibility of liberation closer. Syria and eventually, Jordan, with the reluctant King Hussein dragging his heels, came into the fighting fold. Then came the signs that the West was forsaking their protégée, Israel. First, the French government placed an embargo on military hardware going to the Middle-East. That held up 50 Mirage V fighter aircraft and 6 missile gun-boats. Then came the closure of the Tiran straits, effectively starving Israel of Oil from Persia. The Americans were unable to muster an international maritime force to break the blockade (and maybe they really didn't want to). Through May and the first days of June the airwaves were filled with high expectations of wiping out the Zionists once and for all. Young men went off to enlist with fedayeen brigades. The Lebanese cowards, those who kept the filthy camps bathed in their own open sewers, putrid air and charity food, those that never allowed a Palestinian Doctor to practice out-side the walls of the Camp, they sat on the sidelines and awaited the outcome. If there was anyone Doctor Halim hated more than the Israelis, it was the Lebanese, the Christian minority which ruled through an antiquated system enforced by the French in 1958. Doctor Halim dreamed of a day of reckoning with both the Zionists and the Lebanese and June of 1967 was the closest to redemption he and the whole camp had ever been.

On the 5th of June all hell broke loose. First came the official boastful declarations of Syria and Egypt that their armies were making great strides, then the Jordanians let loose gleeful announcements about the liberation of Jerusalem. The camp went wild with rejoice. But the air was alive with the delta shaped Mirage III aircraft and within a few days the truth came out. The Arab armies were routed, and fled from the Zionists like sheep before the wolf. The whole Arab Might collapsed like a house of cards, like smoke from the Nargillah. Israel ruled Jerusalem, all the way to the Jordan River, all the way across Sinai and the Golan Heights. The Zionists won and they were invincible.

Doctor George Halim was one of the few who were not totally surprised. He had long recognized the Arab propensity for boastful exaggeration and having learned the British understatement and the stiff upper lip he was not as crushed as were the rest of the Camp. He concentrated on Mustafa, he was the Hope for the future. Mustafa went to the UNWRA school and learned early that if you killed 5 Zionists in the morning and 3 more in the afternoon then the total was 8 dead Zionists. He was a good pupil, and one of the few who actually came out of the school with some education. At 13 years of age, when the other adolescents were out trying either to make a meager living selling fruit or stealing cars, Mustafa went on to a school attached to the American University.

Doctor Halim watched the decline of the British Empire and of French influence. The power in the world was now with the Americans. They were rich and they were powerful and they could get things done. Most of the newer medical textbooks came now from America. Doctor Halim re-started his education with Harrison's Principles of Internal Medicine and Nelson's Textbooks of Pediatrics loaned by Dr Harrelson, the volunteer assigned by the WHO to the Sabra and Shatilla camps. They had a loud voice and insisted on being heard and expected everyone to understand English, that is American. They were also the people who had the biggest heart and with the greatest wish to make the world better through the American Way. They had the most ludicrous belief in the written word and could never comprehend the Arab disregard for it. They spent money like crazy on pet projects like the American University and the high school which prepared local prospects for the University. Most of the pupils in school and students in the University were Christian Lebanese, but the administration insisted that other ethnic groups be represented such as the Sunni Moslems, Shiites, Druze and the rare Palestinian, through their notion of Equal Opportunity. Now that was a foreign, wholly American concept that no British could swallow, class-divided as they were. Doctor Halim helped Harrelson with translation, explanation, and swallowed his pride when it was obvious that the camp people treated him like a junior apprentice, when in fact he was senior to Harrelson by a generation. Doctor Harrelson repaid him by talking to Mr Bernard, the principal of the American University high school, concerning Mustafa. Mustafa was accepted and went through High school in the best place available in Lebanon.

In 1975 Syrian forces invaded Lebanon from the East to "help" the Sunni uprising against the Christian Elite. 70,000 Lebanese died in the following 5 years. The country ceased to be a political entity and became a cauldron of fiefdoms, each contested bitterly by armed militias. The Christians had the

Phalangas, dominated by the Jumaiel family. The Sunnis were divided into Leftisit, Centrist, and Rightists. The Shiites, who were the poorest, lowest on the Lebanese totem pole, developed the armed Amal militia. The Lebanese Army broke up entirely since the Sunni, Shiite and Druze rank-and-file would not take orders from the Christian officers, and in fact occasionally killed them. The Palestinian Guerrilla groups vied with each other in committing daring acts such as the hijacking of airplanes, raids from the sea on Tel Aviv and the killing of the guests in the Savoy Hotel. Beirut was ravaged by car bombs and machine gun shootouts between rival militias, Palestinian guerrillas, and various Moslem groups. Israeli commandos staged attacks on the Palestinian-organization buildings. The Syrians played the old game of divide and conquer, using their firepower and armor to enforce submission and then changing sides in the local skirmish and subduing their former ally. The rich Saudis and Kuweities and Egyptians who made the Beirut Riviera equal in glamour and posh to Nice and Cap Ferrat fled with their money and Beirut became a true Hellhole with bombed out buildings and more refugees than citizens. The American University schools, independent of local funding, continued to function.

The vacuum created in the south of Lebanon drew the Fatah to the South to establish in effect the Fatah-Land, a territorial base for attacking the northern towns and villages of Israel. Daily firefights across the border became common-place. The guerrillas would fire Katyushas in the general direction of a village or a town such as Kiriat Shemonah and the Israelis would answer with a heavy artillery bombardment. Guerrillas infiltrated through the heavily wooded hills and rocky outcrops to take hostage a house or a bus or a school and then conducted negotiations until blown away by Israeli special forces, with tremendous loss of life.

In 1978 Israel invaded South-Lebanon with armored columns. The Palestinian Guerrillas ran, preserving most of their personnel and losing most of their weapons. No matter, since the PLO was flush with money forked by the Saudi regime in an effort to keep them away, and the world was full of weapons produced for Revolutionary Movements by the Soviet regime in it's effort to promote Communism and topple America. This was a limited invasion and the Israelis soon retreated. A basic flaw was discovered in the Israeli war machine: The Israeli soldiers never shot civilians on purpose, women and children could walk up to the guns without fear. They were nothing like the Monster Stories told by the old timers about Kafr Kassem where reportedly the Jewish soldiers killed the children and raped the women.

They were human and therefore they were not invincible, they could be killed just like anybody else. As soon as Israel vacated the area south of the Litanni River the Palestinian guerrillas streamed back and reestablished their bases. The mode of reestablishment was simple. The local commander of the Fatah, or the Popular Front, or Abu Nidal, or half a dozen others, designated a building in a town such as Nabatiyah. The fighters took over the basement and placed there the command center, wireless communications, phone lines, arms and ammunition. The floors above were vacated, forcibly if needed, of their tenants, and taken over for the bunks and personal effects of the guerrillas. Local storage was taken over for ammunition depots, Katyusha rockets, and thousands and thousands of land mines. Kids would sometimes steal them and would lose hands and legs playing with the cute toy-like deadly antipersonnel mines. Others would play with the guerrillas, and learn how to work the RPG-7 rocket launcher and even the RPD-11 machine gun. The guerrillas did not have to make a living since the money came down from Beirut in a trickle-down effect, where the top officials who stayed in West Beirut received Saudi and American money from their sponsors (various Islamic charity organizations) kept the lion's share and some of it was distributed to regional commanders who took their share before trickling the rest down. The fighters did not mind. They were mostly illiterate and had lived in the Camp conditions all of their lives. They trained sporadically with exercises up to the platoon level and spent most of their time establishing turf until the order came down to do something.

Most popular was Katyusha Launching. The launcher which looked like a stack of organ pipes (which was the basis for the nickname Stalin's Organ) was usually hidden near a Mosque or in a basement of a school. They found out in the Litanni Invasion that the Israelis never shot at schools or Mosques. The launcher was usually mounted on a back of civilian pickup such as a Toyota or Dastun. The guerrillas would load the launcher with 18 rockets, connect the rockets to the power source and roll out to close-by hill top. They pointed the vehicle in the general direction of a town and fire the rockets. The wildly inaccurate rockets ignited one by one at short intervals and roared off towards the distant green hills of Israel to the cheers of the guerrillas. As soon as the firing was done they scurried away, because the Israelis would triangulate the point and return artillery fire. Any small deviation would land the 155 millimeter shell on an unsuspecting house and new recruits would instantly be available. Life for the local villagers became hellish and those who could - left. Those that remained were the Shiites whose inspiration emanated from Humeini's Hezzbolah, the party of God, which began its activities through the mosques where Israel was bundled with America as the Devil. Doctors and nurses became scarce and the local children began falling prey to Salmonela, Shigella, Brucella and other bacteria. Children who had cancer quickly succumbed to Anemia and Infections. Fatah Land extended towards the Bekaa valley where the guerrilla activities were sheltered by the Syrian military.

Doctor Halim swelled with pride when his son would come home to the camp and show him the arithmetic, history and life-sciences courses he was taking. It became clear the Mustafa was good in biology, chemistry and mathematics. This was the son that he prayed for. He was alarmed one day when Mustafa, a thin youth, came home with a bloody nose and a swollen eye.

"What happened?" he demanded.

"I had a fight today with Ahmed from the Shabiba gang" Mustafa simpered through swollen lips.

"What about? is it about a girl or anything stupid like that?"

"No, Ahmed said that I was studying just like a Zionist instead of getting ready to fight the Jihad. He said real men did not read the American Garbage but trained with knives and weapons. He said that I don't go to the mosque enough and that I am not a Believer."

"We are believers enough" chided Doctor Halim "but why did he hit you?"

Mustafa shrugged "just to see if I could fight back and I really could not. He and his friends fight all the time. They are the Shabiba and they always fight the Tigers of the Jihad gang, Youness saved me from a beating" Mustafa's shoulders slumped and he sobbed on silently. His father draped his ageing arm over the shoulders of the thin youth and rocked him.

"You see" d he said quietly "that is the whole problem. You are almost a man now so I can talk to you. The problem is that these kids waste their energies on these Donkey-Dung fights and are never able to unite against the common enemy. Just like the leaders of the Arabs they cannot really stop bickering so they can fight the Zionists. I mean look at the facts" Mustafa stopped sobbing and dried his eyes and listened with all his heart, he always knew that his father had more brains in his sandals then all the other Kahwah-house loiterers had in their collective head "there are 150 million Arabs and there are only three million Jews. We should be able to roll over them and squash the whole Israel place like a bug. But we have to roll TOGETHER. Instead , the Muezzin calls us to prayer, and then it's Allah Hoo Akbar and the young Shabab goes out to riot, and join the 20 or so groups who recruit them for the fight. In the mean time though all they do is fight each other to establish supremacy of the Biggest Dog in the Camp. At the same time the Israelis keep bringing more Jews into our Land, keep building roads and schools and Universities, and get the Americans to back them. We cannot win the fight with more guns and stupidity, we need brains and leadership. You will learn to be a scientist. You are going to study hard, you will learn how to Plan Ahead, because Ahmed and his friends cannot see further than their own Dung Eating noses." Halim's last words were delivered in loud, sonorous voice, and he found that his wife, the wizened old woman who shared his miserable existence, was looking at him, somewhat like in the old days when they young and happy and were planning their big house in Yaffo, with a view to Andromeda's rock.

Mustafa went back to school. He did not join the frenzy to enlist with the guerrillas and stayed in school. He visited the mosque in the Sabra camp with his father but always managed to slip out before the prayer became a recruitment campaign.

1982 brought the full scale invasion of the South of Lebanon by Israeli troops, armored columns and air force. American F-16s and Phantoms filled the sky with supersonic booms that rattled all the windows that remained in the South. This time the Syrians fought back with their vaunted missile air defense system that had ravaged the Israeli air force in the 1973 war. The Sam-2 streaked skywards and blew themselves apart. The Sam-6 radar screens could not find their targets, The GunDish 22 millimeter guns, always deadly accurate, were completely jammed and their command centers blown by antiradar missiles. Hundreds of missiles flew and none hit the targets. The Israeli airplanes ruled the sky and attacked at will. The Syrians and their Russian instructors (there was a Russian instructor in the Syrian army in every battalion and a veritable Russian city in Damascus) were dumbfounded as the SAM (surface to air missiles) system crashed and burned. The Palestinian guerrillas ran again, with a good proportion of the populance towards their leaders in West Beirut. This time the Israelis did not stop at the 40 kilometers but pushed on inexorably toward the Beirut - Damascus main highway. Sabra and Shatilla camps became even more crowded and congested and food became scarce. The Lebanese Jumaiel Family and the Phallangas came out of the holes the Sunnis had pushed them into, and sought to reestablish their dominance. General Sharon, now a Cabinet Minister, signed a pact with the Christian Militia which nominated Bashir Jumaiel, the rich playboy who looked like a movie star, for President. A day before he was supposed to enter the Presidential Palace a tremendous car bomb exploded in front of the Phallanga headquarters in East Beirut killing Bashir and many of the top echelon of the Phallangists. The Israelis, arrayed as they were on the hills surrounding the City were stunned, thwarted again. They allowed the Phallanga to exact their revenge.

There had been no school for weeks since the Israeli invasion. The influx of people into the camp from Fatah-Land made conditions even worse. Mustafa Halim, now 17 years old with a new growth over his upper lip and a scholarly face, huddled with his family in the fifth floor waiting for the guns to erupt again. Too late, They heard the shrieks of the women in the lower floors. Small arms fire broke out all around and they hit the concrete floor and did not venture to look outside. Strangely there was no heavy artillery or tank shells but only the Ratatata of assault rifles all over the place. Suddenly the door was blown open by a short burst and four Phallanga -style camouflage-clad young men bounded in rifles firing at waist level, the first right to left sweep and the second left to right and the third coming from behind. The air filled with the acrid smell of ammunition and ricochets of bullets and concrete slivers were flying everywhere. Despite the deafening noise of explosive in the enclosed space, the most penetrating sound was the screaming of the women, Alia, the last girl at home, and his mother, their shrieks pierced the din like a knife and tore at Mustafa's ears like no other sound. And then it was quiet, the four Hoods, their guns smoking, taking the tableau of the cowering family, bleeding from multiple cuts due to the flying debris. Mustafa and George Halim came together to shield the women from the malevolent stare of the gunmen. Too late. The gunmen noticed Alia and she was doomed.

The Phallanga who was the obvious leader barked at the Halim men to move aside. Mustafa looked at the unlined young man's face and saw the animal snarl of unholy anticipation. His bile rose and he did not move. The old Doctor Halim straightened his old back and did not budge. The leader raise his rifled slowly, deliberately took careful aim at the old man's knee and fired one bullet. With an agonizing scream George Halim collapsed, both hands staining rapidly with blood seeping through the fabric and fingers. Mustafa looked at his fallen father incredulously and did not see the rifle butt that was swung viciously against his temple. With a burst of searing light, darkness fell.

When he came to, he wished he had remained unconscious, because the evil deed was being done. He was on the floor, his face in a pool of blood and the pulse booming in his ears. His hands were tied behind his back with a clothes line, his father, ashen , was against the wall. The Phallanga hood was ripping at his sister's clothing while the other was holding her up by her long luxurious black hair. She screamed and twisted and moaned and all this served to whet their appetite even more, their hands frantic and clumsy. This was Alia, his twin sister, closest to him in age and spirit, the one who had fed with him, and played with him, and shared little secrets and joshing and running and parental wrath. This was a monstrosity, they were not human, they were... he did not have a suitable simile. His mother was unconscious due to a blow to the head. They stripped Alia naked, and slapped her hard when she resisted and her moans became less and less until they were done with her. She lay there lifeless as the monster pushed himself up from her with a complaint that it was no fun screwing a Moslem corpse. The leader stayed at the door, rifle at the ready and let his men have their fill, the fiendish snarl and curled lip twisting his features. The assault rifles continued in the streets as the battle, the rape, the murder and carnage swept through the camps. Allah was not looking that day.

The leader looked at Mustafa and raised his rifle while the three men straightened out their uniform. Mustafa stared at Death while Death peered at him through the barrel. Then they turned and left the room, their commando boots crunching on the debris. Mustafa wanted to lay there and die with his sister. Death refused the invitation and presently Mustafa found that he could wriggle his bottom and then his legs between his bound hands. With considerable tearing at his wrists he pulled his feet through and used his teeth to free his hands The circulation that returned to his hands stung with pins and needles like a thousand wasps, but he disregarded the pain. He crawled over to his sister and covered her nakedness with a sheet pulled from a mattress. He felt for a pulse at the neck but it was useless, her soul could not stand the humiliation and fled the ill-fated body. Mustafa sat on his knees and ankles and threw his head back and howled his rage and grief and swore that he will revisit his sister's death a thousand times on her tormentors. It was the Israelis who released the Phallanga scourge and they were the true Devils behind her demise. The gunfire diminished as the pillagers swept through.

The Sabra and Shatilla massacre became evident to the Israel Defense Force as it was being performed, and as is true with any large organization there was a lag period between the realization that something was going wrong, and the decision to find out what it was, and then taking decisive action. By the time the Israeli commanders met with the Phallanga allies with a harsh demand to stay their hands, hundreds of Palestinians were dead, thousands injured, and untold number raped. This was the Middle East at it's worst when the humans sloughed off all claims to humanity and became voracious savages. Israel which had always held the high ground of morality was dragged into the deep mud of collusion with the Devil, and has never been able to wash off that stain, in the eyes of the world and mainly in it's own eyes. For the first time a large proportion of the Israeli army started doubting the democratic elected government that sent them to "bring peace to the Galilee." The grand design of creating a new Lebanon more favorable to Israel was wrecked against the hard reality of the Lebanese Morass and Israel retreated without achieving its goals. It has been retreating ever since because the massacre de-legitimized the State in the eyes of its own citizens. Without Israeli support the Phallanga militia collapsed and the Christian-Maronite power in Lebanon came to an ignominious end.

Doctor George Halim and Mustafa Halim brought Alia to burial on the outskirts of the camp. Doctor Harrelson, who had worked himself half to death assisting the wounded of the massacre attended the mass procession that took the girl and a score of other victims to the makeshift graveyard just beyond the camp. The procession became a wild demonstration with the populance goading each other into higher and higher levels of frenzy. "With blood and tears we lost Palestine and with blood and tears we shall take it back" the epithets became more and more incoherent until the final one rang out and the whole crowd ululated it 'Itbach El Yahood" again and again, and again, till it became a unifying mantra "kill all the Jews" over and over again. Doctor Harrelson, whose grandmother was Jewish, heard the crowd concentrate on it's all consuming hatred. Didn't they learn anything, didn't they understand that more hatred was not going to solve anything? Obviously they did not and he kept his thoughts to himself, he came here to help these people and not to judge them. He noticed the exception to the screaming, chanting crowd. Mustafa who was helping his limping father along did not join in the blood-thirsty chant. That young man had aged overnight and acquired a new set to his features. He did not scream with the crowd and in fact appeared disgusted by it. Doctor Harrelson thought that this young man was worth saving because he may choose the path of peace.

Doctor Harrelson had no idea how wrong he was.

Zion Kahalani had a good reason to be satisfied with himself. He had worked for this moment for many years, and had faced disbelief, frustrations, insolvency, and even his wife's wavering confidence. First came the idea, then the calculations, then the small model, then application for a small development grant, then years of engineering work, days and night s of being away from Home because government set up the Science Hatcheries in the periphery of the country. With all due respect, Sede Boker was just a point in the desert which would dry up in an instant if Government did not support it. Once the concept was proved he had to get interested investors, in a country that lagged at least a decade in financial entrepreneurship behind the US and Europe. He produced some prototypes, showed that his product was both cheaper, faster to produce, and customizable in many characteristics such as size, heat-resistance, and degradeability. A decade of work, at least.

But today was the Big Day. The representatives of the Ministry of Defense signed a contract to produce the first batch of casings. As opposed to the metal casings, the composite carbon-based material that Zion used made the casings customizable, easily conformed to any shape and volume, and, when subjected to heat which was high enough, they returned to their native state of Carbon Atoms. The machine, which looked like a giant computer -controlled spider, could make virtually any container for all conceivable contents. Zion would be the first manufacturer of Smart Bomb casings for the IAF (Israeli Air-Force), and possibly for other air-forces. The Americans always kept an eye on their colleagues in Israel. Once the Popeye TV guided smart bomb produced by Raphael became successful, the Americans acquired the line, and produced their own Popeyes. Thus the market for the Composite material casings which Zion's machine produced, might make it into the much bigger market.

Zion was already looking into his next idea. Let other engineers tweak and adjust, He was an Inventor and he had another idea to develop in his new hangar in the Old Yaffo port.

Chapter 4

Ace Pilot

Mustafa stretched back and looked at the screen through half closed eyes. Amanda was in the hospital again and the girl was asleep, angel-like in her own bed, snoring softly. These were the evenings where he could get the most work done on his thesis, in fact on both theses. He kept the second thesis in a secret file, encrypted with an Elyashim encryption program, the pride of Israel's software engineering. The Israeli company was so sure of it's encryption that they offered a prize to any hacker who would crack it. He reflected wryly that it was fitting that Israelis would contribute to their own demise, however indirectly. The problem was Amanda. She was clever enough to see through his plans and so he worked on it only when she was away and then backed it up into the Zip drive, and he kept the 100 megabyte disk in his brief case, apart from the Flip -File box where the rest of the software was kept. A regular Floppy diskette would never hold that much information as he needed for his analysis.

When Mustafa reached the United States he went through the usual battery of examinations and Academic Aptitude testing and English knowledge such as the TOEFL. It is said that most Americans would fail the test administered by the academic institutions to foreign applicants. Strangely enough, the tests reveal the ability of the person to understand English but not to speak it, so that some applicants from various countries such as from the Orient pass the exams with ease but then are impossible to converse with! Having passed those exams with flying colors Mustafa enrolled in college on a scholarship donated by the ALSAC (American Lebanese Syrian Associated Charities) in Memphis. This charity specialized in Cancer Care and endowed major grants in Basic Research. Mustafa chose to major in biology, with an aim to develop an academic career. He applied himself to his studies and did not join the student activities which centered on booze and casual sex. Certainly with his Middle Eastern look he did not blend into the social mix which consisted of the polarized groups of Black and White, Oriental and Hispanic. He shared a room in the dorm with Sundararaman Chandrasheker, from Bombay, who was like-minded about his studies, but allowed himself alcohol which Mustafa did not, being a Moslem. Other than a genuine love of knowledge and perseverance, the room-mates did not share too much, Shaker being the easy going type, and Mustafa being the intense introspective type. Mustafa's immersion in his studies, combined with his secluded lifestyle would have condemned him to celibacy if fate had not intervened. He did not appreciate the lack of modesty in the American women, the open advertisement of sexual allure on the one hand, and hands-off attitude that came with it hand-in-glove. Nor did he appreciate the notion of female equality and independence that American women displayed. On the other hand he could not accept the docile hidden-behind-the-veil, walk-two-paces-behind-the-man qualities bred into Arab women from birth. So at the age when men ache deep in their bowels the pain of unused sperm Mustafa was working off that energy and frustration into his studies.

Memphis is blessed with one of the most outstanding institutions in the world, St. Jude Children's Research Hospital. This institution specializes in the research of, and care for, children's cancer. It is a charity organization, where the entire staff is dedicated to better the lot of children and parents afflicted with Cancer. The Hospital will never refuse a patient due to monetary reasons and draws patients from the World at large. The Ronald McDonald house nearby takes care of the parents as their children undergo the harrowing procedures and treatments. Due to it's special mission the Hospital usually takes on the unusual, the difficult, the mystifying cases rather than the mundane. Doctors and researchers who have completed their training at St. Jude are considered top-notch and carry on the tradition of self-less care of the patients to the rest of the world. Mustafa began his masters at the University of Tennessee in the basement of St Jude in the laboratory of Dr. Roger Cohen, currently looking for the Tumor Suppressor gene that was linked to NeuroBlastoma, a type of cancer that struck especially at young children the world over.

Mustafa Knew of many doctors who had emigrated to the United States from Lebanon and The West Bank. When arriving at the academic institution he expected to see them well represented in the ranks of the research staff. He found relatively few. Most of the Palestinian brethren chose the path of the clinical private medical care. They bought houses, cars, boats, and availed themselves of the best of the material wealth of America. Their sons and daughters went to American schools and soon lost all interest in Things Arab and Moslem, eventually achieving that very American look of self Satisfaction and self assuredness of being part of the Greatest Country on Earth. Mustafa despised them with all his heart.

On the other hand, the Universities and Hospitals were full of Allah-damn-them Jews. They were everywhere! They headed academic departments, professional societies, committees. They had hospitals such as Mount Sinai, Beth Israel, Jewish National Lung hospital. If you were in medical and Life-science Academia you could not avoid the Cohens, Kaplans, Horowitzs and Levins. Mustafa looked hard for some kind of advantage that the Christian Society, especially the southern fundamentalist Christians, may have bestowed on the Jews who were essentially a tiny minority of two percent in this huge country. There was none. And it was not as if they promoted themselves above others. The laboratories were full of Chinese, Taiwanese, Koreans and every other nationality, but still they were exceptional. Through his conversations with other graduate students and PhDs (scientific Doctors) Mustafa found out that the Jewish head honchos sent their kids to Jewish schools which they paid for out of pocket, maintained social networks based on Synagogues for which they paid too, and erected a rich lattice of social and academic endowments for the Research Hospital and other Academic Institutions. Leafing through the Annual Black-tie fund raiser dinner for St. Jude booklet, placed on every table in the Banquet, Mustafa found out the biggest contributors to ALSAC were Jewish businesses!

Mustafa hated them all the more. Their arrogance, their prominence, and their public support of the Jewish Zionist state grated on his nerves. Mustafa hunkered down to his studies guided by the benevolent leadership of Doctor R. Cohen, Nobel Candidate in Biology and Genetics. If it were not for the Cohens' and The Kaplans' contributions, then America would have let the Jewish abomination in Palestine die in 1967, and 1973, and his darling sister Alia might still be alive and his father might still have gone back to the little house in Jaffa of his childhood bedtime stories. Through knowledge he will find a way to make *them* as afraid and horrified as he had been.

Roger Cohen was the complete antitheses to the Old World idea of the Teutonic Herr Professor. He could definitely exert authority but needed to do that very infrequently. He was at an age that, frankly, his best work was already behind him as a young, aggressive, beat-them-to-the-paper researcher. Now he saw his main role as the facilitator of tomorrow's research and tomorrow's scientists. He gave his laboratory personnel the direction, the grand scheme of things, the horizons, the goals. He gave them his enthusiasm for basic research and how it may apply to the real problem of children with Cancer. In a way he saw himself as a surrogate benevolent father to the young generation. If he audited and put his name on a grant application to the NIH

(National Institutes of Health) then it was not to inflate his ego (I got this 2 million RO1 grant, ho,ho,ho) but to enable him to keep more PhD and Masters students in the lab. Being a father figure included looking out for the students in a personal way. He fancied himself a kind of a match maker and prided himself on two successful marriages that came out of his lab, the happy couples being high achieving students. Mustafa would be a special challenge.

When Dr Roger Cohen had looked through the Masters students applications to replace a PhD who had moved on to the NIH, the name of Mustafa Halim made him stop. Looking through the CV it was obvious that this young man was exceptionally bright and motivated. More over he was Arab and Palestinian. Dr Cohen always harbored a slight sense of shame vis-a-vis Palestinians. As a young man, a warrior, a veteran of the victorious American air force, and an accomplished Ace with 15 Messer-schmidt and JU-88 kills to his credit, he had stayed in Germany and Checho-Slovakia after the war. He involved himself in the reestablishment of air-traffic and airports in the shattered continent by day, and with saving the pitiful few Jews who had survived the camps by night. The Germans had wrought a positive selection, by killing all those who were not capable of slave-work. Those who survived were the strongest, most resourceful of all. As soon as the Hershey bars and some good American rations built up their constitution, these survivors took off to look for their vanished families, and having revealed the awful truth, many assaulted the gates of Palestine. Roger Cohen commandeered aircraft, instructed pilots, prepared airstrips, stole gasoline rations to move the desperate survivors to Palestine, avoiding the British blockade which concentrated on the sea routes. Pilot Cohen flew some of those missions himself, with out-of-service DC-3, avoided the RAF skillfully and landed in god-forsaken airstrips, at night, delivering his charges into the hands of the Palmach, who spirited them away into the towns and Kibbutzim of the evolving State. He did that on his weekends off-duty when his fellow flyers were getting laid by German maidens looking for a way out of subjugated, devastated Germany, and into the land of the Victors. He found ways to decommission aircraft so they could be sold for scrap and moved to friendly airfields where they were hangared for future use. It was obvious that if the Jews did establish a State then the Arab armies were going to try and crush it. Air power would be the advantage of the new State. Then, in the middle of a huge deal for acquisition of 4 captured Messerschmidts Roger Cohen was called to his Wing-commander's office.

"Captain Cohen? come in Please."

"Yes sir, can you tell me what this is about, sir?"

Wing Commander Kowalski sneered "Don't be coy, Cohen, I know exactly what you've been up to."

Roger knew the game was up but tried to brazen it out "Sir I have been doing nothing to interfere with the missions of this Wing, and I resent the insinuations."

Kowalski smirked. "No one is here, Jew-boy, to listen to your crap. I have your transfer back States-side and if you move one more inch I will blow your head off, Jew-boy!" Kowalski showed his other hand pointing the snout of a Mauser at Cohen's raging face "you better move your ass outahere, before I finish the Job that Adolf didn't."

Roger Cohen had no choice but to back off, assaulting a superior officer would do no good, and although Kowalski was a classic anti-Semite, he did not represent the USAF in this regard. He turned smartly on his heels and left the room, taking a huge effort to de-contort his face into normalcy. This was a fight he could not win then and there. He picked up his transfer order and quickly got his stuff together in the barracks. The order specified a midnight flight and he had just a few hours to let his Palmach contact know that he could not help them anymore. There was too much to lose at this point by bucking the system, the GI bill had been announced and he wanted to move ahead with his life.

The phone Rang at the Cohen's residence in Cleveland on the 10th of May. Roger was in his sophomore year of college, aiming for Medicine. He was deep into the new realm of Statistics when his mother called him.

"Roger, come down here."

"Who is it Mom, tell them its not a good day, I have a test tomorrow."

he heard some mumbling and then "It's Hayim from the Palmach, he says he's got to talk to you right now."

Roger let out a groan. Ever since his discharge he maintained only sketchy contact with the Habonim (the builders) chapter, "OK, I'll come down."

He picked up the phone "Shalom Hayim, how's life?"

"Enough with the smart-alec stuff Roger, how would you like to be part of History?"

Roger was startled "what's up, is the Old Man going to proclaim a State?" he said, half in a joke.

"Bingo, give the man a cigar, as soon as the British leave he is going to call a Spade a Spade." Hayim, usually dour and pessimistic, sounded triumphant. "We need every pilot we can get, 'cause as soon as he says the words the Egyptians, Syrians and the Arab Legion are gonna come down on us like a ton of bricks. No jokes, Roger, you always said that air power was the answer, we NEED you NOW."

Roger was irresolute. If he were to go he could kiss this year goodbye, and maybe next year. The thought that he might be killed never crossed his mind. He was invincible.

"What am I going to fly?" he asked, finally.

"I *knew* you would ask that" Hayim chortled "you have a Messerscmidt stashed away in Chechoslovakia. A driver is going to be there in one hour. Don't worry about a passport, we have a new one for you."

Captain (ret) Roger Cohen got exactly two hours of instruction on his old Messer before taking off from a deserted airstrip near Brno. The pilots were a motley crew, two were Jewish Palestinian veterans of the RAF. Roger Cohen and Andrew Katz from South Africa were the Machalniks (volunteers from the Diaspora). Their route took them over Austria, along the Adriatic coast of Yugoslavia, and into Greece. They landed for refueling in Corfu and then in Crete. Katz's plane was spewing oil as they reached Crete and they had to leave him with the Palmach operatives there. From Crete it was a straight shot to Palestine but the trick was to avoid the British patrols. The three airplanes landed on the 16th of May, one day after the Proclamation of the State, at Beit Daras, an abandoned British airfield, in the middle of the well cultivated fields southeast of Tel Aviv.

2 of the Messers were in a bad way and only one was considered flyable. The next morning Captain Weizman loaded his machine gun with the one strip of compatible ammunition and waited for the word from Tel-Aviv. The Egyptian DC-3 had been bombing the defenseless city with impunity, for the last two days, and the Egyptian Spitfires were so non-chalant about any resistance that they strafed at will and did not provide cover for the slow bomber. The word from the watchers south of Tel Aviv came that the bomber was observed flying toward Tel Aviv, heavy with bombs. Roger Cohen looked on with longing as the Messer taxied out to the sole runway and lifted off in the warm May sun. His own Messer's machine gun was jammed, and one of the magnetos was not firing, threatening the engine. The other Machalniks were working feverishly to fix both faults. Weitzman maintained radio silence until he pounced on the unsuspecting bomber and

then whooped as the bomber turned tail with thick smoke towards the Gaza Strip, and went down in flames later, weighed down by the bombs he could not release. One of the Spits did turn back and attacked The Messerschmidt. The first dog fight of the new State was joined over the blue skies of Tel Aviv. Weitzman prevailed again, thus laying the foundation for the legendary superiority of the Israeli Air Force. When the Messerschmidt landed in Beit Daras, he was given a Hero's welcome, and the Messer quickly hustled into a concealed hangar because the Egyptian Air Force with it's the British advisors was sure to try and find out from whence came this air power surprise.

Roger Cohen went back to his aircraft because it was soon obvious that the first Messer was in trouble. Just before sunrise he took off, and a short flight took him to a landing strip that did not appear on any map, hastily prepared overnight by the Kibbutz members. The ambush was set.

When the field telephone rang, Micah raised his thumb and Roger knew that Beit Daras was under attack. He jammed the throttle forward and surged out onto the rough runway. He hoped feverishly that no new hole was dug in the ground overnight by a hare or a mole. Rattling heavily the Messer took off, very light, there was was only one strip of ammunition in each gun and he was low on gasoline. Flying high he came out of the eye of the sun and saw the Spits keeping station as the DC-3 made a bombing run on the single north to south runway. The Spit was turning lazily in a circle as the Messer bore down on him from the sun. The Spit did not have a chance, the bullets ripped his left wing and fuselage. It turned over and fell, spinning, into the orange groves. "Well done" screamed Weitzman from below "watch out for the other one at two O'clock." Roger Cohen, Ace Pilot, jammed the throttle again and pulled his stick up savagely. The Messer went into an Immelman loop with Roger sinking down into his seat with the tremendous G-force generated by the maneuver. As he turned the loop he saw the Spit right below him and discerned the pilot looking around wildly for the Messer that had just been there, and had disappeared into the sun. Suddenly the Spit dove toward the ground and hugging the treetops, raced south. This bird was gone but the Bomber was much slower. Roger banked hard and down and tore the air down onto the fleeing DC-3. It was trying evasive maneuvers but it did not have a gunner in the back as did the Flying Fortress. Roger's blood was up, his lust for the fight as hard as if the bomber was German. He followed the bomber closely, getting closer and closer to his tail, he wanted to see this one blacken his windshield. The beep-beep of low fuel reached his roaring ears from afar and he knew it must end now. He stitched the wing with its fuel tank and was rewarded with an orange ball that burst from the root of the wing. He banked sharply away from the blast and headed home to Beit Daras. He buzzed the strip rocking his wings and, engine sputtering with gasoline fumes, landed to another Hero's welcome.

The next missions they flew together, Roger being number two to Weitzman and keeping his tail clean. With the addition of the third and fourth Messer and four P-51's the young air force began to deter bombing raids which became harried and inaccurate. Tel-Aviv command then asked for strafing raids to help the beleaguered ground troops which were taking heavy losses on all fronts.

The order came down to attack Beit Hannun, an Arab village on the main road to Jerusalem. The pilots spread the British maps of Palestine and marked the hilltops which the rudimentary Intelligence service designated as tactical targets. Major Ilan Barda joined them for the briefing. He came by Jeep from Air force Liaison with some new information. Looking down at the map and some ground photos of the village he indicated a large building in the center of the village, near the Mosque which always featured prominently in Arab villages.

"We have information that AbdelKader El Husseini will   be there tomorrow to collect more volunteers for the Fighting Falcons gangs. They are throttling the Jerusalem Corridor and if he can get more volunteers we are going to have one hell of a time in the upcoming offensive." Then he added significantly "if we can take him out this will be a terrific blow because he is the glue that holds them together." The Israeli pilots nodded with assent. The Machalniks were not so sure. To them Abdel Kader was just another name whereas to the Israelis he was an old, and bitter, and successful enemy.

The bomber was a Piper Cub where the copilot threw down hand-made bombs from the open window. Roger and Andrew were to strafe the building prior to the "bomber" to create some panic. He was number one for the strafing run. The flight itself was very short. Only 30 kilometeres separated Beit Daras from the Jerusalem Corridor. Again Roger took the approach from the east, out of the rising sun and from the direction where the enemy expected help rather than attack. He spotted the mosque and with a terrifying roar the Messerscmidt dove onto the white building, machine guns chattering from both wings. There was no defensive fire, which jolted him. Usually they did try to shoot at the strafing aircraft, and this was supposed to be a village with hundreds of armed semi-regulars. Then the doors of the building opened and a river of people in white and black Galabiya and chadors, and little figures, rushed out. Roger realized with horror that these were women and children and older men, no one was shooting back at him!

"Abort Abort Abort" he screamed into his mike, he saw his number two, Andrew Katz, pressing on with the run and the twin stitches of machine gun bullets running through the Mosque plaza, and the people, and the complete bedlam below. He pulled out of the dive heading west and saw the cub over his head as planned. Katz had broken off too and was banking over at low level. "Abort, mayday, these are women and children down there" he broke all rules of wartime communications, "Yaron, Gabi, don't throw the bombs." He circled back and saw the Cub dropping the bombs by hand, mostly they hit the dirt but a few hand grenades lashed together blew up inside the crowd. Roger Cohen, Ace Pilot and doctor to be, was sick to his stomach.

He had to get back to base, he could not waste precious fuel just to observe the carnage. He headed west to Beit Daras, among the green citrus groves, and almost botched the landing, the tail-wheel swinging wildly across the narrow tarmac. Tiredly he pushed back the transparent cockpit cover and threw down his headphones with disgust. The June sun was hot on his face but he felt very cold inside. The second Messer and the Cub landed shortly after. Andrew walked up to Roger who was sitting slumped in the shade of the Quonset hut.

"Hey, what was all that screaming, you nearly blew my ears off" he said with a scowl.

Roger looked up at him, stupefied, "Whadoyoumean what's the screaming, we were shooting at women and children for Godssake, who came up with the damn Intell, where is that Ilan, I am going to break his face." Yaron and Gabi joined them, and the mechanics rushed over to the airplanes to prep them for the next mission. The fuel bowser was pulled by a farm tractor commandeered from one of the Kibbutzim.

"So what's the big deal" said Yaron in his heavy German accent, his next mission was to take some mail and orders and supplies to Kibbutz Negba, which had been under severe artillery attack from the Egyptian forces, now for two weeks, and was virtually starved, "they are Arabs aren't they, they do the same, and worse, to us, look at what they did to the Doctors Convoy to Hadassah Hospital, they butchered them one and all. Let them get a taste of their own medicine."

Roger looked up at him with disbelief. "I thought we were supposed to be people and not savages."

"Wrong" said Yaron lips drawn back in a snarl, "you are either more ruthless or they will eat us up. I am not going to have another Treblinka here." Yaron yanked back his sleeve and showed Roger the tattooed number. "You think I was born with this name Yaron? I was Hans Meizlich from Munchen before they stuffed my mother into the gas chambers just because she was too sick to work, I had to take her body and burn it after processing. The Arabs want Eretz Israel to be JudenRein just like the Nazis, but this time we can fight back, so the hell with you and your American ethics." Yaron rotated on his heels and strode back to the Cub, shouting something in Hebrew.

Roger stood up. "In that case this is not my war anymore. I am an American and not a hired gun, Tell Weitzmann he can find me in the American consulate, if there is one."

Dr Roger Cohen never forgot that moment, when the reality hit him, that erecting a new state meant forceful eviction of the natives. Most of the Palestinians left Palestine at the behest of their leaders, but many fled the advancing Jewish forces, spurred on by stories of ruthless treatment and assaults on civilians. The Arabs believed that the Jews, now armed and unfettered by the British mandate, would revisit on them the massacres perpetrated by Palestinians on the Jewish communities of Hebron and Ezion. Most of the tales were hugely exaggerated but to every exaggeration there is a kernel of truth. Roger Cohen stayed on until the First Cease Fire mandated by the United nations. He left with the American envoys before the hostilities broke out again. Over the years, observing from afar the developments in the tumultuous Middle East, Doctor Roger Cohen remained ambivalent about the Jewish State that he had helped create. When he was able to redress the balance towards the vanquished, he did. Mustafa was a perfect candidate for him to be a recipient of such a guilty conscience, and he took the opportunity to install him into the lab. When Mustafa one day asked him for some control sample he happily bared his arm and asked Amanda to take the sample for Mustafa Halim.

Amanda Carter was the perfect woman of the nineties. She was tall, fair skinned and blue -eyed and did not need any addition of L'oreal to highlight her straight blond hair. She wore her hair long, but tied it into a pony tail. She alternated between contacts and glasses, and preferred glasses, neat, scholarly round frameless, for work, especially on call and in the Lab. Amanda graduated Summa cum Laude from Notre Dame and the Medical school of the University of Indiana, and chose Pediatrics for a specialty. She was bright, popular and earned excellent evaluations in each of her rotations at Le BonHeur and St Jude. She was also very lonely, the fate of many of the brightest of American female doctors and scientists. The contrast is striking: while 95% of male graduates of Pediatric Residency doctors who are male are married and have children, only 55% of the female graduates are married and 60% of them have children, obviously some out of wedlock. These women set high standards for their potential spouses, and the available men do not measure up. Amanda was intent on following the Academic career path, and if she was not fated to be able to bear her own children, so be it. She was not flirtatious, and took sex seriously, and therefore had very little of it because commitment was a dirty word with her contemporaries. Her refuge was Dr Roger Cohen's Lab where she had a long range tissue cultures to grow and study under a variety of growth factors (hormones that help cells grow). Both the children she took care of in the hospital, and the test-tubes, made no demands on her physical attributes of the Good-Looking-Blond.

Her first encounter with Mustafa was when Roger Cohen asked her, the Doctor, to take a control sample and give it to Mustafa . The poke was the easy part, but the blood needed to be in Heparin, and separated immediately so Amanda took the green tube from the office right down to the basement lab. She found Mustafa at the centrifuge, separating other samples. He had his back to her, long lab coat draped against his long thin legs, nice butt though.

"Hi there, Are you Mustafa?"

Mustafa did not turn "If this is the sample can you leave it in the rack, did you mark it for date and time and sex?" He had a fine baritone, with an obvious Middle Eastern accent, but with clear, exact enunciation.

"Sure" she said, somewhat disappointed, she set the tube in the rack, but then did not go but retreated and watched Mustafa turn slightly, pick up the tube with long, bony, fine fingers and place it into the centrifuge. He closed the lid, set the timer and then turned around, looking first at her shoes, then ankles, hose pant legs, and up all the way to her face. It felt almost like a caress. She looked into the long face the deep brown eyes, the fine nose and the thin lips and then he smiled, oddly not showing his teeth.

"I'm sorry, that was rude of me, I am Mustafa Halim, but I guess you knew that, and what's your name?"

Amanda never felt as nonplused as she felt at that moment. Her cheeks were burning, this guy was a couple of inches taller than her, and looked at her without guile at all. Then her composure and self-reliance reasserted itself and she put out her hand, and flashed her smile.

"Hi, I am Amanda Carter, I am a resident in the program, and I do some lab work with Dr Cohen." Mustafa took the proffered hand, it was long fingered, white as fluffy cotton, with just a hint of roughness, no doubt due to the numerous hand washings those hands endured every day. It was a delicious feeling and he let go reluctantly.

"Thanks for the tube, it closes a circle for me, are you here often?"

Amanda was a little more confident, this was more familiar ground and interaction. She had a little time so she told him a little of her background and the Pediatric program, then the centrifuge clicked and slowed, she looked at her watch and was jolted to see that half an hour passed by while she was talking and he was listening without interruption.

"Er, sorry I have to go now, I guess I will see you around, nice to meet you" she ended lamely. She turned to go when he said softly:

"Wait, don't go yet, when can I see you again, and I don't mean around, but deliberately see you?" her heart jumped a little at that.

"Well, my pager is 4224, page me when you are done today and we will see, I am not sure about my schedule, bye" and   she disappeared with another of those pearly smiles, sneakers squeaking down the tiled corridor.

Mustafa turned back to his test tubes. Suddenly the basement appeared much brighter and the future held more than just dark revenge. Of course, Cohen's nucleated cells would help him unlock the door to that revenge but now he did not have to hurry, there was a much sweeter prospect close at hand.

Roger Cohen looked up at Amanda. "So how did it go? Did you find Mustafa?" He was pleasantly surprised at the bright spots that lit up the pretty cheek-bones, the Plan worked.

"Yes I did, and we talked a little bit, gotta go now" and she escaped his probing gaze, he was really a dear. She knew she was going to see a lot of Mustafa Halim.

Chapter 5

Savoy Hotel

They met again on Monday morning for the weekly division meeting. Dr. Horowitz liked to get everyone, the doctors, nurses, fellows, residents, social workers and clerks, at 0730 sharp, to review the events of the weekend and prepare for the coming week. The fellow on call for the weekend or the resident on rotation, would present the new admissions and discuss the patients who had stayed over the weekend. The Bone Marrow Transplant Unit always got major attention because the patients were the sickest and frequently one of them would need Intensive Care Unit services. Joe had been on call and so he sat opposite Dr. Horowitz and presented the patients to the group, referring occasionally to his clip board. Karen, her swollen lips coming down nicely, sat off to the side and listened very carefully, not only for the information she needed for the daily work, but to the voice itself, the inflection, accentuation, the full stops and the commas. Joe modulated his voice almost like a story teller, and the recipients listened to the clear display of clinical mastery, each according to his or her position in the hierarchy. The new intern, exposed for the first time to the proceedings was almost slack-mouthed, probably in despair how she would fit the torrent of information into her overtaxed brain and overloaded clipboard. The gaze she turned upon the speaker bespoke almost of adoration. The nurses were, as usual, less impressionable and more practical, twittering in the background about poor Robert, the new leukemic kid's divorced mom. They were also not as interested in the quotations from the literature and the latest series from the POG (Pediatric Oncology Group) concerning cord-blood transplantation for non-lymphocytic leukemia. Dr Karmodian, argumentative as always, kept badgering the fellows, Joe and Amanda, with questions, and Dr Horowitz took opportunities to enlarge the scope of the discussion regarding the kids with the difficult problems. Karen listened as Joe parried the thrusts, argued his case, even when he was not the one to have made a specific decision, and conceded ignorance when he either did not know, or was unsure about some case report in the extensive literature. To do all that well he needed to be well versed in physiology, statistics, informatics, genomics, hematology and oncology. Under Dr Horowitz's tutelage and authority the discussions remained civilized even when people strongly disagreed about the most proper course of action for a particular patient. Jerry Connor, a 3 year kid transplanted from his brother two months ago, was doing very badly, and needed a respirator to help him breath, a development which caused Joe to look more tired and frustrated than usual.

Doctor Joseph Bergman had arrived from Seattle as a first year fellow. Typically, most fellows went through a three year program, where the first year was almost purely clinical, the second year more time was allowed for research, and the third year was devoted mostly to research with some clinical work mainly as back-up and on call. Karen heard through the Grape-vine that Joe had moved from the University of Washington due to some tragedy, but since he was mostly in the lab now, they did not seem to be in any close proximity for any length of time and so she did not know any more than the rumors. In fact, Joe almost seemed to avoid her, without being too obvious about it. Karen knew that most men found her attractive and if she were interested in socializing, wearing the right dresses and flirting just a little, then the social pressure cooker that is the Hospital and Medical College, with it's constant supply of interns, residents, pharmacists, computer specialists and students, would surely provide her with more activity than she could handle. Joe *did* spend time with interns and residents, male and female, on call and off call, teaching and explaining, and supervising. He was usually animated, big hands busy moving or drawing, although in his first clinical year he had been generally dour. With her and the other nurses, he was much more reserved. Amanda was the exception, as peers they had to work together, and cover for each other frequently, but Karen noticed that Joe always looked straight ahead, always at her face, never letting his gaze stray over Amanda's other features, which Karen admitted to herself, were quite superior. Amanda was almost a advertisement for Female Doctor. No, Joe kept his speech and body language strictly professional, disconcertingly so, wasn't he human? Didn't he notice the sexually loaded looks from nurses and residents?

The meeting drew to a close at 0900, and the people scarfed down the rest of the coffee and the doughnuts that Amanda had brought from the 24 hour Kohl's. The nurses ganged up on Karen who had been absent for three days. They knew of the attack, such news spreads like wildfire, but no specifics. They had grilled Joe about it over the weekend, but he had let on almost nothing. Karen smiled, cracking some of the makeup she had applied to the ugly bruise on her forehead and generally told them that the children with Leukemia and Sickle-cell had much bigger problems. Via her peripheral vision she watched Joe introduce himself to the nervous intern, trying to keep her afloat and ease her into the daily work of the unit. This time, Karen was determined not to let him go with all those unanswered questions. For some reason, it was important to know more about the person who had saved her life, or dignity, or both. Joe would most likely go to the lab in the Pharmaceutical Sciences department. In the mean time since she was charge nurse , she would go ahead and oversee the work. Dr Karmodian, who was attending, liked Formal Walking rounds.

At three o'clock she called Ronny, Dr. Horowitz's secretary, and asked him how she could get a hold of Doctor Bergman. Ronny was used to these requests "why don't you page him?" he asked.

"Because, Ronny, I need to talk to him privately" and she immediately regretted the slip, Ronny let out quite a chirpy laugh.

"Hey good luck to you and the knight in shining armor, I didn't have any luck with him. Maybe you can break that tough armor. He is usually in the Pharm Lab at 2280."

Karen frowned at the phone. Everybody knew that Ronny was gay, but he didn't make passes at the Doctors for godssakes, maybe he did because Joe was so indifferent to the females, be they nurses, doctors, or floor-cleaners, Ronny must have figured him for a brother.

She dialed 2280 and someone answered on the fourth ring.

"Pharm lab, Harriet speaking" a young pretty female voice.

Jealousy, no wonder he was in that lab afternoons and nights "hi, I am Karen Fitzsimmons, I am a nurse at the HOT unit, is Dr Bergman there?"

"Sure, he is here, did you page him?" some kind of careful he-is-mine-now inflection.

"No I did not" said Karen with asperity "can I speak to him?"

"OK, OK, keep your hat on, I'll call him, Doctor Bergman, can you pick up the other line?" click, click.

"Yes, this is Doctor Bergman."

"Hi Dr Bergman, its me, Karen," she felt just a little breathless "can I see you after you are done?"

"What is it Karen, anybody sick in the unit? No one called me after rounds I thought the new intern was OK for a while" he sounded concerned.

"No, no, no one is any sicker, *I* want to talk with you, when are you done." She was very insistent, she could not believe her own ears.

"Are you OK Karen? I mean are you feeling OK? You sound a little strange you know" concern mingled with a chuckle.

You betcha I am feeling strange, butterflies in my stomach like this was a very important conversation "I need to talk to you about the attack and the police" now that should be a convincing lie since it was conceivably true, "Please Dr Bergman!"

"All right, I will wrap it up in 45 minutes, is the cafeteria OK with you?"

Relief, he did not avoid her, "Fine, see you in the cafeteria at" she glanced at the clock "four o'clock." and she replaced the handset. I wonder why I felt compelled to speak from one of the dictation rooms, I have spoken to Doctor Joe a hundred times from the front desk with everybody and their sister listening.

The shift had changed and Karen checked some of the charting. Now that the meeting was set, she felt reluctant to go. What is she going to say, will he be courteously distant, how would she break down the barriers of professionalism, culture, and god-knows-what-skeletons in the closet. She shook out her hair, consciously smoothed her brow and headed to the elevator.

The Children's Hospital main elevators exited into a lobby artfully designed to look like an average home, albeit a big one. Off to one side was the small cafeteria, run by the good ladies of the town, all volunteers. The cafeteria was open at the wee hours so that the residents, ravenous from a night of admissions, bad IV's, screaming children, upset parents, unhappy attending doctors, conflicting medications, could wolf down a doughnut in preparation for the 6 AM morning rounds that inevitably followed a busy night like frozen batteries after a Wisconsin cold spell. But at four in the afternoon the nurses left through the side entrance, and the cafeteria was almost empty, prior to the wave of parents coming after work to see their children. Karen chose a corner seat, her back to the wall, so she could see Joe before he could see her, before he could arrange his features to suit the occasion. Suddenly it was very important to see who the real Joe is.

He came around the building and she could see him through the glass wall, which was one way glass. He was a big man, his trench coat flapping about solid long legs which were pumping away like pistons. He was clutching a briefcase, and his face was purposeful. He rounded the corner, the electric doors whooshed open and the warmth of the lobby blew away the chill outside. As he entered the cafeteria, stripping his ridiculous Yamaha ski-cap, Karen examined his face, and as soon as he saw her he smiled, fleetingly and then the purposeful look came on again. Karen's pulse jumped, he was happy to see her, and the hell with the professional facade. Joe came up, slung his briefcase on a chair and asked:

"Hi Karen, can I get us something?"

She groped for her hand bag and produced a crumpled 5 dollar bill "Yes, coffee and a Danish, the apple strudel."

Joe looked at the proffered money with disdain "don't forget I'm a rich Doc, my treat this time" and he headed for the bar. His exchange with the little old lady there was all twittery and head-nodding and he paid for the two cups and the two danishes with a bill even more grubby than the one she had produced. Joe set the hot coffee in the egg-basket-like carrier on the small table, pulled a chair, seated his big butt comfortably and flashed his grin, the weird one. "Well, miss Fitzsimmons, what's on your mind, is your paycheck not in order?"

Karen smiled at the conscious effort to put her at ease, but she had found her opening gambit. "First, Doctor Bergman, I never properly thanked you for what you did" Joe made a dismissive wave so she hurried on "so now that I am in your debt I insist on knowing where you got that maroon Le Sabre?"

Joe was completely taken aback, surprise mingled with confusion, then laughter took over, he threw his head back and guffawed so hard that the coffee in the Styrofoam cups appeared to ripple, he slapped both hands with tremendous force on his own thighs, and guffawed some more, and wheezed "the car, I can't believe it, wasn't it comfortable enough?" The laughter became less wild, more controlled, the cafeteria patrons were turning their heads back from whence they snapped. "Was the ride a little hard on you the way I took the corners?" He laughed some more until the tears rolled down his face, and grabbed a napkin to dab his eyes, while still whooping with laughter. Slowly he quieted down and said "God I haven't laughed like that for a l-o-n-g time, nobody made me laugh like that in donkey's years" and he dabbed his face some more "sorry, I must sound like a complete idiot, and thanks, you don't owe me anything, I did what I had to do under the circumstances and that's all there is to it, call me Joe anyway, no patients here."

This was a new, free, uninhibited Joe that she had never seen, and she wanted so much to see more of. Laughing, his face shed some deep sorrow that he was imbued with.

"Laugh all you want, Dr Bergman, but I *know* that car."

"Al right " he said, "I drove myself from Seattle in a rented Avis truck, you know the little ones, which can't go more than 55. I took a week so I could think" a dark cloud came over his brow, and then his gaze settled on her again. "I got here on Saturday night and I unloaded into a small apartment in

Glendale. Sunday morning I used the truck to drive around looking for a car to buy. I drove into River Hills and was going up and down the little streets there when I saw the LeSabre parked on the grass with a big 4sale sign on it. There was no phone number so I just walked up to the door. There was a big Mezuzah on the door, do you know what I mean?" he inquired, lifting one eye-brow. Karen shook her head , of course she knew, this was too thick to believe. "This old geezer with steely eyes comes out, sizes me up and says "ya" just like my dad. So I ask him about the car and he says its OK, 20 years old, starts up fine in winter, and is garaged most of the time but he doesn't live there most of the time and he is too old to tinker with it any more, all in a Yiddish accent. So I paid him 175 bucks and he drove it to the apartment, and I took him back. No surprise, he had one of them concentration camp tatoos on the inside of his arm, he gave me a few tips and almost gave the car a hug before he gave me the keys, why are you so interested in the car?"

Now it was Karen's turn to laugh, although she was much more restrained "This was my Grandfather's car, he held on to it for so many years and took me to movies with him, and to day trips with my grandmother, and so when its time to save my life here is the same car again. Zeide told me that it had saved my mother's life once when my brother was born" Karen stopped for a moment, controlled her breathing   "So I guess you know a thing or two about the holocaust survivors!"

Joe nodded "I was born in Israel, that subject is unavoidable and never goes out of style. Look at the latest spat with the Swiss and the Jewish money they have had for 50 years without paying a dime of interest on. The old generation of survivors is dying off and soon the Nazi denial scheme will start working."

"Israel? Are you really from there? but you don't have even a smidgin of an accent, I and everybody figured you were from somewhere East, New York or something!"

"Yeah" Joe smiled at that, "much further east, it's a family trait, languages I mean, my dad was fluent in eight or nine languages, and I picked up the accent when I lived in LA, my father did his Post-Doc at UCLA and we were there for two years when I was a kid. He spoke Spanish with the gardener, which he had picked up in the Pyrenees, and spoke Italian to the restaurant manager on Olympic Boulevard, like he was in Napoli or something. It was hilarious. I speak English and French and some German too."

Karen scowled "*Was,* where do your parents live now?"

Joe sighed. "They are both dead now, why don't we let this go."

Karen shook her head vigorously " No sir, You are gonna sit right here and *talk*, for once I want to hear something personal, something that's You and no medical literature references either" she pointed her finger at him.

Joe looked at her curiously, was about to firm up, refuse, close up the clam-shell, and then he softened, the high forehead smoothed and the slitty eyes crinkled "Yeah, why not, the empty apartment can wait, no Karate today, have you ever heard of the Savoy Hotel?"

"The famous London Savoy? sure, I even went inside..." Karen stopped at Joe shaking his head.

"No, not that Savoy, the Tel Aviv Savoy, 1975, ring a bell?"

Karen didn't know so Joe gave her his version.

Naftali Bergman always said that the difference between a sage and a clever man was that the sage never fell into the hole from which the clever man knew how to extricate himself. So he was the kind of man who planned meticulously ahead, and avoided most of the pitfalls of life. Problem was, the forces that shaped his life were so unpredictable that planning became impossible. The war caught the family in Belgium, three years after they had emigrated from Germany. In 1940, after a lull which the allies termed the Sitzkrieg, the sit-down war, Hitler bypassed the Maginot line and the Blietzkrieg swept through Belgium and Flandria. The Family prepared to flee, but to where? The Wehrmacht was invincible and the British Expeditionary Force folded like a bad accordion and fled across the channel. Joseph Bergman looked hard for a shelter for his family and finally found an apartment with a well hidden attic where they could all fit during the 'Actions' where the Gestapo snatched Jews from the streets and sent them East. Then in February of 1942, shortly after baby Lillian was born, Joseph, who was still plying his trade as a textile broker, disappeared, never to be seen again. Naftali's older brother, Avraham, now the man of the house, held a council. They did not have enough money or space for a permanent stay in the attic. Naftali and Moses would leave with false papers, and walk to Paris, at that time under the Marchal Petain and the Vichy government, and join their cousins. The two teenaged boys joined the countless displaced people of war-torn Europe off the roads and byways, and walked all the way to Paris, a harrowing and dangerous journey, in which a navigation error, a suspicious farmer, bad weather or just bad luck could foil any planning. A few months after having been received by their Parisian relatives the pressure on the Jewish community increased, and in November the Gestapo occupied Paris fully. The yellow Star-of-David tag was enforced, forced registration was enacted and the 'actzions' resumed. By then it was obvious that those who went "East" never returned. Naftali and Moses were on the road again. They disagreed in Lyon, and Naftali stole west to the Pyrenees, but the smugglers would only take rich Jews to neutral Spain, and murdered some of them on the way. He made his way to the Alps Maritimes where an Italian general created, in the bedlam of the war, a small duchy, hospitable to the Jews. The Italians were never really interested in the Jew-killing amok that seized the Germans, and generally protected their Jewish population. Unfortunately, as Mussolini was deposed in July of 1943 the duchy was dismantled and the Jews dispersed again. Naftali, small thin and rather dark of skin, decided his best chances lay with the Italians he had learned to love, and whose language he acquired along with French, German, Flemish, and Spanish, and move down to the Italian northern plains. He was grabbed in Turin, survived a year in jail as a suspected thief, and escaped the prison using forged papers he had prepared, in advance, by walking brazenly through the guards. By then Lorenzo Enzio, as he was referred to in his papers, a young man, enlisted in the German-controlled-but-not-trusted Italian coast guard, where he survived until July 1944. The intensified British and American bombardment of La Spezia convinced him that it was time to go. Again, after meticulous preparation of papers and food, he left the garrison and made his way down the coast towards Rome. He managed to cross the German and the British lines without getting shot, and became an interpreter for the British, with his middle school English and his tremendous capacity for languages. After the war he made his way, again, legally, after meticulous preparation, to Palestine, and survived the ongoing war in Israel. He believed like many others that the whole Jewish entity in Europe had been destroyed, but painfully the survivors reestablished their families. Naftali Bergman fought in the war of Independence and the Sinai campaign. He married Debora, like himself, a refugee from Poland, and with great difficulty they had their only child, Yoseph, after his father who had gone up the Auschwitz smoke stacks.

Naftali went back to his first love, mathematics and physics. He had a lot of catching up to do, but in due course, he made it to a PhD and a Post-Doc at UCLA. The family lived in a small apartment on the grounds of the Weitzmann institute, named after the first president of Israel. May 1975 was their anniversary and Debora booked a room for Naftali and herself at the Savoy hotel, just off the Tel Aviv sea-front, a modest, popular spot for honeymooners. It would be a night for the opera, a walk on the beach and the specialty of the beach, red watermelon with Greek cheese. Joe would stay with his maternal grandparents in Tel Aviv. Yossi, a strapping 15 year old, loved his grandma Fella, she was like a second mother to him.

The Zodiac boat was painted black, and the 7 men lowered it quietly from the fishing boat to the lightly rippling surface. The Mediterranean was still cool and the seven men were dressed in black head to toe, with black balaclava still not pulled down. The weapons and the explosives were stowed in waterproof nylon wraps and inside military-style backpacks. Night had just fallen and they had 6 hours to get to the unsuspecting city over the horizon. Each man adjusted his webbing, water, grenades, six banana clips for the Kalachnikov AK-47, the favorite weapon of the world's leading terrorist or fedayeen groups. The leader had in his possession a map of Tel Aviv with the General Command circled in black. it was only two miles inland from the beach head. He consulted his watch and compass and as they drifted away from the fishing boat. The territorial waters of Israel extended three miles only, so the fishing boats from Lebanon were free by international treaties to ply the route from Sidon to Alexandria. Soon the white wake disappeared and only the ripples breaking against the soft gunwale broke the silence. That, and the heavy breathing of seven men who were going to war against the sleeping enemy.

After a while, their night vision fully adjusted Yussuf Marzouk the Black September leader gave out the order and each man broke out a black rubber oar. They had trained for this mission for months and the physical labour did not tax them. They could not risk the wake created by the outboard. The leader arranged shifts, 4 men working the oars and two resting, he sat in the stern and corrected the course occasionally. Soon the horizon lightened with the artificial lights of the city and the rowing men redoubled their efforts. The red hazard blinking lights on top of the Hilton was readily apparent and the leader corrected slightly south, and then the strip of lights along the Herbert Samuel Drive, just behind the boardwalk, became apparent. It was three o'clock in the morning when the boat scraped bottom and the seven men jumped out. They loaded their packs from the rolling boat, pulled down their balaclavas and Yussuf Marzouk surveyed the scene. He was amazed that no one had seen them so far, but of course the people on land were blinded by the bright lights of the city whereas they were still in the relative dark of the sea. Beyond the 100 meters of white sand which made the Aussie soldiers of yesteryear compare Tel Aviv with Sidney's Bondai Beach, there was a low wall with cement steps leading to street level. The Opera building was on the left and the Ambassador hotel on the right flanked the mouth of Allenby street, the whole area awash in bright lights. From here it was a straight shot to the General Command HQ. Just two blocks to the right of the Ambassador Hotel there was a small side street, poorly lit. Yussuf decided for that street and pounded the sand, feeling like a black fly on a white ceiling, utterly vulnerable, sand sticking to the wet boots. They hit the sea wall and crouched, a car whooshed by on the street and then they rushed up the steps.

Yacov Levy always thought the idea of carrying his Uzi machine-pistol while on leave was ludicrous, but the standing orders were that soldiers and their rifles were inseparable, and the greatest offence one could commit was to lose a personal weapon. It was not a complete waste of course, because the teen-age girl he was dating was impressed as hell by the weapon, as she was by the red Para beret. Vered was a sweet girl and they had been necking and touching and exploring right there on the beach, on the blanket which he had brought for that very purpose, since midnight. The movement that caught his eye was familiar, figures racing across the sand and crouching against the wall, one hundred fifty meters away. He extricated himself quietly from the embrace and whispered "stay low against the wall, don't move." Vered stiffened but did as she was told. Yacov reached for the Uzi, pulled a clip from his A uniform pocket, and slowly inserted it into the receptacle. It clicked into place. The figures detached themselves from the wall and ascended the steps to the street level and Yacov knew with a sudden chill that these were not Israeli soldiers, or some prank, these were Mechablim, fedayeen, terrorists, just like the ones who massacred the children of Ma'alot and Kiryat Shemonah, and Nahariyah. Xcept now they were loose in the middle of Tel Aviv, the soft belly of Israel. He cocked the Uzi, a very noisy act, and rolled over the top of the wall.

The Uzi is not an accurate weapon at any distance above 50 meters. The heavy one pound bolt runs back and forth inside the weapon and the bullets go haywire unless held very firmly. The Fedayeen were running across the road when Yacov Levy opened fire and hit the second from last. Like a cobra, the leader whipped around and released a long burst in the general direction of the incoming fire and Yacov Levy dove for cover behind one of the cement flower pots that litter the boardwalk. The stench of dog-urine hit him hard as he cautiously poked his Uzi and then his head. Another burst made him scurry back. At least the alarm had ben given, this part of the city was mainly a tourist and night-life spot and this early in the morning it was almost deserted. When He poked his head out again he could see them disappearing into a side street, where he knew there were only a cinema, some small office buildings and the small Savoy hotel. The police sirens were closing in fast. Yacov went out on the street and waved his arms at the blue and white. The policeman got on the radio immediately and passed a report to Central.

In a way Yussuf was almost glad that the mission had to be aborted, the prospect of moving through the enemy city was daunting. A few meters up the street he saw a sign, Savoy Hotel. He made the instantaneous decision to hole up in there and from there to make his bid. He ran up the steps, pulled both glass doors and burst into the small lobby. The night clerk face froze into a horrified stare and his jaw went slack, so he shot him right through that stupid open mouth. The slugs picked up the body and toppled the chair and the blood spattered the wall. Strike one for Palestine, Black September will exact its revenge on the Zionists. His comrades rushed behind him, dumped Ahmad on the floor, he was beyond help. Yussuf yelled at them to secure the doors and the side entrance and to bring everyone in the 4 story hotel down to the breakfast room just beyond the lobby. Abbu Allah came back dragging a frightened Arab from the kitchen. The man could hardly walk as his knees buckled with terror. He kept mumbling "Allah hu Akbar" over and over. Abbu Allah threw him down in front   of Yussuf and then joined his comrades as they piled furniture to block the doors.
"Who are you?" Yussuf barked.
"Ya Sidi , my master, I am only a kitchen help, brother."
"I am not your brother you filthy collaborator, do you make food for the Zionists while they pay you in dog-food, where do you live?"
The man was quaking "In Gaza Ya Sidi, but I sleep here to make breakfast, I have no choice, I have 5 children, they must eat, I will help you, I know the place!"
"All right, how many people in the hotel and in which rooms are they?"
The terrified man ran around the counter and lost whatever color he still had at the sight of the young, dead, night clerk. Then he doubled over and puked, Yussuf looked at him with disdain and then put one shot through his temple. He had no use for a collaborationist who served the Zionists. He had had to endure the hardships of refugee camps, the superciliousness and thinly disguised disgust of the Soviet and Cuban Advisors, while this dog of a man was living it up in Tel Aviv. He looked at the blood-spattered guest book.
Nafatali Bergman's sleep was not as sound as would be expected after a

night on the town and going to sleep after 2 o'clock in the morning. They were shooting at him from hill 69, and at the same time the ship was rolling and creaking. He opened his eyes and in the gloom his lovely Deborah was shaking him awake, her hair mussed. Instinctively he reached for the mass of dark brown hair, now streaked with white, as he had done for the last 20 years.

"Naftali, Naftali, wake up, something is wrong."

"Ma kara, what happened?" but he was already getting up.

"I don't know but I think I heard some shooting."

"Nu, nu, you must be exaggerating, may be it's a motorcycle with no silencer, don't you remember our neighbor Yoni and his noisy BSA, the racket..." Naftali's words died as a burst of shots penetrated the walls, coming from inside the building. He sprang at the window to see the last terrorist rushing into the building. "Put some clothes on" he whispered, "let's get out of here."

"What did you see, Naftali?" Debora was struggling into some slacks and jabbed her feet into sandals.

"Mechablim" he barked, " let's get out of here NOW."

Naftali opened the door cautiously, since this was a weekday night the rooms nearby were unoccupied. With Debora running heavily behind him, she had become a little rotund in her middle age, he reached the end of the short corridor, where the EXIT ONLY door led to a fire-escape, going down to street level. Naftali Bergman always knew where the fire-escape was, a legacy of his war-time youth. As he pushed the door the fire-alarm klaxon blared and a deafening shot blasted his ears, and Debora yelled with pain and collapsed behind him with a thud. Nafatali let the door go and turned around to see his worst nightmare come alive, a Fedayeen in a black balaclava pointing his Kalachnikov at him, trigger-finger white, and Debora on the floor, clutching her thigh, blood seeping between her fingers. There was nothing he could do, nowhere to run, his dyspepsia hit hard and he swallowed acid. He lifted his empty hands and waited for death.

The terrorist lowered his gun and pointed it at Deborah, Nafatli screamed "nein" and threw himself across his wife. Now he can get both of us with one bullet, just like the Nazis did, but the bullet did not come. The fedayeen said something in Arabic and Naftali shook his head. "Bring, bring" he repeated in a thick Arabic accent, and a second terrorist came up the stairs and started kicking the doors in one by one while the first one covered them. Naftali took off his shirt, tore his left sleeve and tied it on the flesh wound in Deborah thigh. This could have been much worse. Another elderly couple was brought out, whimpering, and a much younger couple, tourists most likely, joined them on the landing, hands on their heads, totally bewildered.

The population of the small hotel was gathered in the breakfast room, forced to their knees, and what a group it was. Old couples, young tourists, a homosexual couple, two men holding hands in the universal expression of distress, drawing reassurance from each other. Boys recently discharged from the army, flower girls from Holland and a minister from Georgia. Each reacted in their own unique way to the early morning nightmare, the guns, the screaming terrorists, the wailing of the sirens outside, and the knowledge of being trapped in the hands of the world's most ruthless terrorists, the Black September, who killed the athletes in Munich Olympics, who had hijacked numerous aircraft and subjected unhappy bystanders to torture and death. The melee and noise were insufferable until Yussuf mounted the little stage, that typically served the band for Bar-Mitzva and Wedding receptions, and released a short burst from his Kalach. The noise in the enclosed space was overwhelming. He delivered his words into the ensuing silence in clear, if heavily accented English.

"Silence!!!" (too many movies, thought Naftali, he thinks he is some freedom fighter) "You are now in Free Phalasteen, under the command of Yusuf Abu Ammar. We have come back to take our homeland, and we shall take by fire and blood. You will cheer now for Yasser Arafat, chairman of the BLO (Naftali chuckled inside, they absolutely cannot pronounce the letter P) "Anyone who does not cheer will be shot."

"Arafat" a weak response from the crowd, Yussuf lifted his gun, another short burst right above their heads.

"Arafat" this time a much bigger cheer. The terrorists had long since drawn the curtains over the doors leading to the patio behind the small hotel. Sharpshooters would surely be stationed in the buildings behind the hotel. Abbu Allah spotted the two gay men who were now in prayer and savagely yanked the blond ones hair so that he yelped. His boy friend rose with him and was knocked down with the butt of the Kalach, and collapsed, blood welling from his temple. The blond could not regain his footing, and was dragged by the hair to the upright piano in the corner. Abbu allah forced him on the bench and motioned him to open the Brinsmead and Sons upright. The blond shook his head and the barrel was brought directly into his right eye. He looked at the implacable face and turned to the piano. He played, and well, he was a musician after all, and he played 'God save the Queen' and

Abbu Allah's face contorted with rage as he recognized the tune. He raked his weapons sights across the resolute face and the blond was knocked off the bench. Yusuf barked at Abbu Allah to desist, it was good to let his minions play god or devil, but the real tests were soon to come and he wanted them prepared for the real fight, against Sayeret Matcal, those who had stormed the hijacked Sabena and killed his own baby brother Mahmoud. He continued.

"Any signs of disobedience will be treated with the maximum sentence. You will be tied to chairs and will not move without abbroval. One of you will serve everyone else with water and food. You will go for your needs with one of my comrades and will leave the door oben. I remind you that any strange movements will be answered with a shot. The lives of my comrades and of my brothers have not been sbared and I owe you NOTHING. Minister, do you have anything to say?"

The minister, an owlish, bespectacled young man had his hand up. "The Koran teaches you to be just and kind to all people. No one here has done anything to hurt you..."

"Baas" (enough) Yussuf screamed, hysteria building in his voice, "the American Government has been subborting the Zionist obbression of our beable with money, arms, bolitical, at the United Nations. You are my enemy and if you oben your big mouth once more I swear by my dead brother's memory, I will bersonnally fill it with Nabalm and light it, just like you did our brothers in arms, the Viet-Cong!" The rage subsided "You will serve water and food to my brothers first and the brisoners-of-war. Bring the chairs, one by one, and tie each brisoner." The phone at the front desk rang, Yussuf knew it was time for negotiations, and he cast around for a likely candidate to carry out the negotiations. His eye fell on Sarah, a young chambermaid who had stayed over in the hotel prior to he morning shift. He motioned her to get the phone. He left his lieutenants to take care of the prisoners.

Under the gun of the terrorists, the minister brought one chair at a time and used some cloth napkins to tie their hands behind their back and to the metal frame of the chairs. Light filtered through the curtains as the minister and the terrorist guarding him came by Naftali and with difficulty he and Deborah rose from their cramped knees with a sigh of relief. The relief did not last long, because the minister tied Naftali's hands very securely, although not nearly as well as the terrorists thought because Naftali had tensed his muscles to the max, to leave himself some flex. He kept his face as miserable and resigned as possible so as to give the bastard confidence, he was working out all the possibilities, as always. All this was done in perfect silence after the episode with the blond piano-player. This unfortunate fellow had been tied to the piano wheel. They could hear Yussuf screaming angrily into the phone in Arabic, and Naftali, not for the first time, was sorry he had never taken the time to learn Arabic. Deborah was tied next to him and she put in a brave face for him even though her flesh wound must hurt her terribly.

In Israel, the Military, Shabac (internal security), and the police present the political level with the alternatives, and the government ultimately decides how to deal with a situation. The disastrous news of a terrorist take-over of a building in the heart of Tel Aviv, within shouting distance of the general HQ, the banking, shopping, and administration head of Israel (Israel's heart is in Jerusalem, but the money and influence are in Tel Aviv) reached Prime Minister Rabin in his home, only 5 kilometers north of the Savoy hotel, when it was still dark. The Security cabinet, a select number of ministers within the larger cabinet was summoned to a meeting in the General HQ in Hakiria (the citadel) for six o'clock. They all turned up, grim with interrupted sleep, to hear the briefing presented by the head of Aman, acronym for Agaf Modiin, (intelligence service) The deep distrust towards Aman, which had not predicted correctly the Yom Kippur war, was only enhanced by this new emergency, Aman had failed them again. In their once weekly briefings the ministers were used to seeing photos of Syria, or Jordan, or Lebanon, but not of Tel Aviv, which most knew intimately.

Aluf Sagi kept his face impassive as he placed his pointer on the aerial photo, where the sea was to the west, Jaffa was in the south, PM Rabin could clearly see his own apartment building in the north. "We are here" said Sagi in his clear, high voice, "and the Black September unit is here" and he slapped his pointer at the white roof of the building, which looked like a non-descript white square, identical to all the other white-washed buildings along the street. The Allenby Boulevard tarmac appeared very black on the photo. "The whole area has been cordoned off. We know that they are six or seven from Yacov Levy, the soldier who identified and fired at the threat. We are debriefing him extensively right now, his girl-friend too."

One by one, the functionaries rose and delivered their message. Negotiations had been started over the phone, the leader Yussuf Marzouk was using a girl on the phone and demanding the release of all the Palestinian prisoners of war, as he called them, including those who had fled to Israel to escape the wrath of King Hussein during the Black September of 1970. He also demanded safe passage for himself and his group and the Palestinian fedayeen to Khartoum, and that the U.S. ambassador to Israel should fly with them as hostage. The press has been kept away but one could not help the fact that Israel was a free country and the ratio of foreign correspondents to population was the highest in the world. Phone calls from relatives and family were overwhelming the police, and Israel's embassies around the world were unreachable. Special forces sharpshooters and binoculars were deployed on the Shalom tower, the tallest building in Tel Aviv, about one aerial kilometer away, and on the nearby roofs. Both Sayeret Matcal and the Police anti-terrorism unit had been called up and were setting up headquarters in the Ambassador and Bell hotels nearby. Despite the gravity of the events some chuckled, the rivalry between those two elite units was legendary. The building plans were obtained and the most likely place where the hostages would be centrally dominated was in the breakfast room. Then Rabin asked all of them to leave and only the security cabinet and the mayor remained. Rehavam "Gandy" Ze'evi, Rabin's adviser for Terrorism, took a slightly back seat .

Rabin lighted a cigarette "Any suggestions?" he said, voice gravely as always.

"I think we need to find out more about them, and get some input from the government whose citizens are in there" Peres always preferred negotiations to confrontation.

"They are Black September and that means any threat they make they will make good" Observed Ghandy Ze'evi. He was nicknamed Ghandi for his extreme leanness and mournful face.

"And what if they start shooting hostages every two hours like they said?" that was Katzir, the internal security minister "I think we must prepare the Sayeret or police."

"We have already provided both units with detailed drawings of the hotel" said mayor Rabinovitz, "and the neighborhood has been completely evacuated, and can we use the garbage trucks in any way?"

"We need to find out who is in the hotel and contact their families, especially the tourists" suggested Chaim Basock, minister of the interior. Then the door burst open and a young aide ran in.

"They shot one of the hostages" he reported breathlessly.

Rabin rose, shaking off the years since he had been the engineer and chief of staff in the greatest Blietzkrieg of all, the six-day-war of 1967, when Israel had overcome odds of 1 to 10 in numbers, and came away victorious. "I want detailed plans of attack in 3 hours from both Sayeret and Police. Peres, you take on the negotiations personally, promise them anything and everything, do whatever is necessary to keep them happy until nightfall. Ghandy, get me everything you have on these scum. Yallla, la'avoda (let's go to work).

The Georgian American minister whose name turned out to be Joshua Woods, had been run ragged for 4 hours since 4 o' clock in the morning serving the hostages and especially the terrorists. They made him shine their shoes, they made him sing hymns, serve them juice and tea and make them sandwiches. He sat down for 10 seconds when Naftaly saw Yussuf calling Adnan, the one who had shot Deborah, and point him at the minister. Naftali did not like that at all, even less so when Adnan made the minister untie Naftali's hands and took them to Yussuf. The Leader beamed.

"The Israeli and American governments have agreed to our demands," (not on your nelly, Rabin would never knuckle under this quick, thought Naftali) and to show our good faith we are going to let you" he pointed at Woods, "go, right now, but first you must take down the barricades, do not move before I tell you." Adnan and Yussuf trained their Kalachnikovs at the two unfortunates and they proceeded through the doors of the breakfast room, the passageway to the lobby, that smelled by now of old blood, and the glass doors. Outside there was ominous silence. Yussuf picked up the phone and dialed.

"Yes Mr Marzouk" a soothing voice, a professional negotiator, must be a psychologist. Yussuf smiled his best wolf's grin, and Naftali suddenly shivered, he had seen that grin before, a thousand times, on the faces of the Gestapo officers. Those were fair skinned Europeans, and this was a dark skinned Arab, but the expression was the same, blood-thirsty, malignant, devoid of human empathy. Adnan was covering them well, and he was fifty years old, slow, graying, and powerless. Thank god we did not take Yossi with us, I hope he is oblivious of this, I hope....

"Yalla, move, you two, the bastor is going out. No false moves, your wife is still back there, ya Zaken (old man)." Prodded by the guns, Naftali and Joshua Woods started dismantling the profusion of tables and chairs that the terrorists had erected against the glass doors. It was deathly quiet outside. Yussuf and Adnan retreated under the overhang while the hostages worked. Finally the door was free to swing out. Woods smiled tiredly at Naftali and said "here goes Nothing." He looked back at Yussuf who smiled at him from under the overhang, both the guns were pointing down. Woods pushed the door very slowly, Naftali retreated one step and stole a glance at the terrorists.

They had both guns up and pointing at the Pastor's back, Naftali now knew what they had in mind. " RUN" he screamed at the upright back and threw himself on the floor, hurting his chin and his iliac bone. The two Kalachnikovs spouted fire and the Pastor was propelled outside like a rag doll and deposited his body on the steps. Someone outside released a shot which broke the glass door, and Naftali was covered with shards. He put his hands over his head and cried in shame and helplessness and frustration, this is what I have come to in my own home and country, hiding from the Gestapo all over again. Outside someone else yelled "Lo Lirot" (don't shoot) and there was only silence.

"Get up" that was Yussuf. Naftali wanted to just lay there and make him finish the whole damn thing with a bullet, but Debora, his darling, was inside, and probably scared to death for his safety. He crawled over to the passageway, cutting his hands on the glass shards and only rose to his knees when he saw their desert boots. One of those boots drew back and kicked him viciously to the face, but hit his forehead instead. Adnan yelped and uttered an obscenity regarding Naftali's sister. Yussuf was laughing.

"You will bear watching, old man, you are tougher then you look. Go inside and start the Bastor's job."

"Can you understand" Joe was staring through the glass out to the gloom which had descended on the hospital, "can you really comprehend what it is to wait through the whole day, next to the radio and black-and-white TV, for your Mom and Dad to die? I mean the Yom Kippur war was bad, but we in Rehovot did not really feel it and my dad was too old to fight, so he worked in the tank repair shop. This was up and personal, and my grandpa said that I should stay put, and let the police deal with it. He said he had faith in Rabin, he would know what to do." Karen's eyes were riveted on the animated speaker's face, he was not cold or detached, he just had a terrible life and had to deal with it.

"We sat or paced the small apartment all day, and became more and more confused. They said they were letting hundreds of terrorists go, that the worst murderers were to go free just so my parents would be allowed to live. Then they said that the terrorists would allow the paramedics to collect the bodies of the dead and help someone who had had a heart attack."

It was late afternoon when Naftali decided he must try to force the issue. Deborah, although her flesh wound smarted terribly, appeared well, and would weather the storm. While serving Jaffa Select Orange Juice to Abbu Allah he suddenly clutched his breast, dropped the platter, and collapsed on the floor, breathing stertorously. Abbu Allah jumped with disgust and stood over the man who was turning gray in front of his eyes. Debora screamed in Hebrew, then in English "it's a heart attack, he needs his pills, please, please let me go." Asfar, the baby-face fedayeen, responded to a nod from Yussuf who was eyeing the whole thing from the doorway, and cut the napkins. Deborah rushed over, hobbling to her husband, and rummaged in his pants pocket. She came up with a tiny silver box and opened it, her hands shaking. The small Nitro pills (actually, they were SukarZit, a sweetener) rolled out and she forced one under his lip and under his tongue. There was no response, and the breathing became more noisy and terrifying to the hostages who were watching the proceedings helplessly. They started talking and offering advice. Deborah made a fist and banged her husband's chest, ineffectually, then administered some mouth-to-mouth. Slowly the color returned to the sick man's cheeks and his eyes were less glassy. Deborah suddenly rose and hobbled over to Yussuf and fell to her knees and looked up in supplication, however hard that was. This man thrived on his victim's abject need, and she would give him his wish.

"Please, he has a heart condition, he needs a doctor, he needs to go to Hospital. We are not important, please let him go, I will stay here..."

Yussuf was in a good mood. Shortly prior to this episode he had spoken to Aziz Abd El Rahman, a brother who had been in jail for three years, caught in the Jordan River Valley. Aziz told him with glee that he and 250 other brothers were being freed and were about to go to the airport, on a Swissair flight to Cairo. He had heard the others crowing with triumph in the back-ground. Yussuf felt he could be magnanimous to the old man who had behaved very subserviently throughout the day. He dialed the number that Peres had given him for direct access.

Peres put down the phone and immediately picked the secure line to Hakiria. "Yitzhak, someone in there is having a heart attack, and the bastard Marzouk wants a paramedic team, all female, to get him out. This is our chance, I have been softening him up all day."

"Good work Shimon" Rabin was raspier than ever "they are gonna get more than they asked for." Ze'evi beamed from his desk opposite Rabin.

Naftaly was doing worse when they heard the ambulance. Rashid was sent out to check them, and indeed the 4 nurses were female and good looking ones at that. Rashid gave them the nod and they pulled out the gurney from the back of the ambulance. It was eerily quiet and the sun was about to set into the sea, and the white buildings dressed in the rosy glow of the end of the day. The girls had some difficulty rolling the gurney through the shattered front door but once inside, under the watchful eyes of Yussuf, Adnan and Abbu-Allah the gurney unfurled and rolled on four wheels. The head nurse, a rather tall and dark woman knelt by Deborah and Naftali. Naftali managed to open his eyes, and then winked raffishly.

"We got the story from the tourist who had been tied to the piano" Joe told Karen "The gurney broke up in a flash into rifles, the Matcal men screamed at everyone 'lishkav, lishkav' (stay down) and they broke in from everywhere, the sewers, the windows, the stairs. But the terrorists were not totally surprised. Yussuf KNEW my dad was up to something and emptied his clip in the general direction. Someone else pressed the trigger on an explosive device and the third floor of the building collapsed. Both my parents died, this was a very bloody rescue. They were much better in Entebbe the following year. Impressive funeral too. I stayed with my grandparents until I was drafted."

"You must hate them" breathed Karen.

"Hate who?" Joe rejoined.

"The Arabs, the terrorists."

"Well, not really, not every Arab is a terrorist, so I can't place them all in one basket, a sick Arab kid is just a kid." Joe looked at his watch "I bet you got more than you bargained for, how about it if I see you to your car?"

Karen agreed. She would feel much safer with this big, slit-eyed, reassuring man, going to the parking structure, security or no security. They pushed back their chairs and Joe saluted the broad-faced black lady behind the counter. She smiled and nudged her friend, there goes another good-looking couple. As the sliding door opened, the wind blew Karen's scarf away and Joe gently replaced it around her neck. They walked silently to the GrandAm. "Night" Joe said as the door slammed. She looked back to the large figure, and felt the maturation of maternal concern, or fondness, or was it... stirring her heart and belly.

Chapter 6

Marriage

Like all doctors, Amanda had mixed feelings about her beeper. On the one hand it was the infernal B-Beep, B-Beep that woke her up in her call room 3 minutes after she laid her head down at 4 o'clock in the morning following 10 admissions. "Dr Carter, Johnny's temp is 103. Can I give him some Tylenol?" A frenzied search through the checkout sheets, Johnny is someone who was supposed to be discharged in the morning. "Please do, but I am going to come down and look at him." Heave out of bed, quick wash of the face, tie the mussed long hair and down to see the particular kid. That was an easy one, but when the B-Beeps came while doing a difficult procedure with an uncooperative child and surly nurses, then Amanda positively *hated* the thing. Other times it was more benign. "Hey Amanda can we meet for tennis" That used to be Rachel, her room-mate and best friend in Memphis. Those days were long-gone. Now she waited for the beeper from home so that she could speak to Mustafa, at least over the phone she could talk to him rationally, whereas at home he was mostly unreachable.

Amanda preferred to stay in the hospital during her weekends on call as a fellow. Officially, she could be at home and answer call from the HOT unit resident, but since the composition of the unit had become intensely acute with the decision to keep the mechanical ventilation Bone Marrow Transplant patients on the floor, she found the it was more difficult to take call from home and drive to the hospital in the dead of night, than to stay there and handle the crises on site. Add to that the fact that living with Mustafa was increasingly difficult, and it was an easy decision to use the call room, and get some work done on her research. Although her relationship with Mustafa was strained, his relationship with Alia was fantastic, he absolutely doted on her, she had him round her little finger, except when he was really angry. Mustafa told her that he had insisted on calling her Alia after the sister he had lost, and he was a wonderful father. In fact that was the only glue that held her marriage together, she thought bitterly.

It was romantic enough in the beginning. It was her second year in Memphis, and she was working her butt off, in the NICU and the PICU (neonatal and pediatric intensive care units). Every third night was call, and after call the day dragged on like a chewing gum, long and flat and tasteless, eyes grainy with lack of sleep, and mouth with a lousy film no amount of brushing could remove. Mustafa was always chivalrous and considerate, he waited for her call, and would meet her outside, rain or shine, and walk her to her car. Then, on her night off call, they met for a movie, or a quiet dinner, or they would both stay at her apartment reading up and discussing science, or current events and, eventually, each other. It was obvious from the start that he was a devout Muslim, he avoided Pork and alcohol, and Friday he would go to the mosque, which was really a private apartment of the priest or the Imam, as Mustafa called him. He was also passionate about the Arab-Israeli conflict, explaining the events on TV such as continued violence in Lebanon, the Intifada in the West Bank cities of Nablus and Hebron, but he sounded resigned to the sad situation, rather than involved. He quit his apartment and moved to an efficiency in her complex and gradually they grew closer. He never flirted with any of her few friends and Amanda began to suspect that he was really serious about her. Slowly and surely she fell in love.

They came back to her apartment, after an evening of Harrison Ford in 'Frantic'. The Israelis and Arabs were at it again in the Movies. Mustafa was driving his ancient Mercedes which cost him a fortune in fixups but which he refused to get rid off, and it was raining heavily. The parking lot was crowded and there was no open spot anywhere near the stairway which led to her apartment. It was a warm southern rainstorm, with thick heavy globular drops, each weighing a ton. Finally Mustafa found a spot way at the end of the row. He pulled out the golf umbrella from the back seat, opened it with a whoosh, and stepped out, right into the puddle. He squelched around the car to open the door for Amanda who was giggling at the sight of the tall dark man holding the umbrella and getting his butt totally wet. She stepped out gingerly under the wide umbrella and slammed the car door. They took two squelching steps when a gust turned the umbrella inside out, and they were immediately drenched. So they ran, laughing and squealing through the downpour, up the steps, down the open veranda and soon she had the door open, and the carpet filled up with the cascade of warm water. Amanda ran to the bathroom and pulled out a beach towel, colorful Little Mermaids, and threw it at him. Mustafa was still chuckling and mopping his head and face when she came out in her white bathrobe, and the chuckle stuck in his throat with a small intake of air. She looked directly at him and without a word the tie around her waist fell apart and the robe gaped, top to bottom revealing hint of breasts, the perfectly flat belly and the pubic mound, golden haired somewhere in the center of the long, sinuous body. She came right up to him and the towel dropped as he placed his arms under the robe to encircle her, such a small waist. They kissed for very long, deep and explorative moment, and his hands traced the small muscles of her back, the perfect shells of spine. She took hold of his sopping shirt and with a quick move brought it over his head. As he emerged from the brief cocoon the bathrobe dropped to the floor and settled around her long legs. Amanda took Mustafa's hand and led him to the bedroom, it was small, and girlish, with a black and white print of an embracing couple above the headboard, Mini and Mickey and Goofy plush toys on the window sill, and a pink bedspread. The bedspread never had a chance to come off.

Amanda was quite unhappy at the decision to get married in City Hall. Her mental picture of a wedding was that told countless times in movies and TV. The church, the music, the maids, the flowers, the white gown, the tux, the reception, friends and family, and the ride into the sun-set. Mustafa told her that he had no family, that he couldn't possibly have a Christian religious ceremony, and they could not really afford the whole shebang, and he could absolutely not expect her parents to pay for the nuptials. So her folks and sister came down from Niles, Rachel was her maid, the residents, whoever was not on call, came to City Hall, and Roger Cohen represented the lab. It was short and to the point, and later they all went to the Steak and Ale and Roger Cohen sneaked to the manager and had him put it on his Visa. He was such a dear, and there was no way he could predict how miserable the whole thing would turn out to be.

Amanda became pregnant almost immediately. The morning sickness was tolerable and she continued her work into the third year, the senior year of residency. Her academic work continued to be excellent and she published two articles concerning the development of Neutrophils in long term cultures, one of the Articles even got into Blood, the premier journal of the American Society of Hematology. Mustafa was nearing the end of his Masters and they were very happy in their rented apartment. Fridays he was at prayers and meetings a lot, but otherwise it was domestic bliss.

Amanda got bigger and bigger, and Mustafa suggested they ought to have an ultrasound done, to check the baby, he said, but really to check on the sex of the baby. Amanda was afraid of that. Somewhere she had heard of the preference for male progeny in the Middle-East culture. Dr Ansari, her obstetrician, a friend of Mustafa, took the search for the missing penis and testicles very seriously, but finally made a moue and said:

"This is a perfect looking baby, all the major organs are perfectly formed, arms and legs are equal and moving freely and her head circumference matches your dates. I cannot tell you the sex of the baby but it is surely not a boy." Amanda looked up at Mustafa who was watching the ghostly forms on the ultrasound screen as if transfixed. A huge smile broke on his dark face, like the rising of the sun, from his mouth to his nose to his eyes, he tore his gaze away from the screen, and into his wife's eyes and bent down and kissed her so deep, it took her breath away.

"I always wanted a girl, first, " he breathed into her ear, "She is the sister that I lost and I even have a name for her, if you'll agree." Her eyes filmed over and she nodded, speechless.

Alia came into the world on a glorious May day, a robust fair infant with dark blue eyes. Amanda brought her proudly to her graduation party, and shook hands with Dr Richardson, the program director, one armed, since the other arm cradled Alia. She was voted by the faculty and residents as the MVP of the program. If the faculty grinned and smiled at her, then Roger Cohen positively beamed, glowed, this was one of his best accomplishments as a matchmaker and a mentor of young scientists. He pumped Amanda's hand, slapped Mustafa on the back, and tweaked the little girl's ruddy cheek. He hoped, loudly, the motherhood will not stop Amanda from pursuing her academic career.

Amanda had other ideas though. She had long considered what kind of mother she was going to be. She did not have much to compare with because most of her peers did not have stable relationships, much less husbands, much less children. As a Pediatric Resident she had seen them all. The welfare mothers who brought their kids to the ER and disappeared as soon as they were admitted, the stay-at-home devoted mothers who breast fed their infants, knew birth weight, diaper size, sleep pattern and every minute detail. The career mothers who tried to be superwoman, at once breaking through the glass ceiling of corporate structures and breast feed the baby early in the morning before the babysitter came, and late in the evening just before poring over the sales reports. They were tired and harried, vague about detail of how the child became sick, and panicky with guilt when it became necessary to admit a child to the Hospital. And all the variations in between. Amanda thought long and hard and reached two fundamental decisions :

A: She would a full time mother for at least one full year.

B: Alia deserved a bigger family then just herself and Mustafa. She wanted to be near her folks.

Amanda asked Rachel for a favor, to babysit Alia one day following graduation. Rachel was taking a job in Racine, Wisconsin, where Memorial Hospital was setting up an ambulatory clinic, getting ready for the invasion of the HMO's from Chicago and Milwaukee. She reserved a place at The Samurai, a Japanese restaurant Mustafa favored because they had no pork and the wine was Saké, of rice-origin, and there-fore passable by Muslim standards.

They sat cross legged and dipped the Tempura shrimp in soy-sauce. Mustafa was starting a beard which made his dark face even darker. A smile was playing at the corners of his mouth.

"I know you" he gambitted, "you have something important to tell me, are you pregnant again?" and he chuckled.

Amanda smiled, he always knew how to make her laugh, "not quite, but I wanted to talk about the future without having to answer Alia. Are you up to a serious conversation?"

"Sure."

"All right, I don't want to stay in Memphis even if Doc Cohen has promised he has a spot for me in St Jude. I want to move back North and be closer to my family."

Mustafa smile widened. "And what else?"

"I want to stay at home for one year and be with Alia. I want her to have a full time Mama, at least for a while" she paused, "that is not going to help our finances because I still have school loans to pay, but I think its important for her."

Mustafa lithely rose from his sitting position, over the table and smacked a kiss on his wife's forehead "I wouldn't have it any other way" he said softly. Amanda stiff shoulders came down with relief. She knew the financial burden would become enormous and she had prepared for that by skimping throughout her residency and beginning to pay off her loans while other residents reveled in their newfound income with new cars and vacations in Europe. But she knew that as a PhD student and a stay-at-home mother their situation would close to hand-to-mouth. She continued doggedly on "what about PhD positions, I saw a bunch of mail from the whole country, any from the Chicago Area?"

He wagged a playful finger at her "Looking through my mail, eh? take a look at THAT" he was triumphant. He handed her a neatly folded letter

The Blood center of Southeastern Wisconsin

8200 E Wisconsin Avenue, Milwaukee, Wisconsin

Dear Mr Halim

I am pleased to inform you that your application for a PhD position at the Blood Center of SE Wisconsin has been accepted.

Your stipend will be 21,850 $/year

Pending your confirmation we expect you to start August 1 by attending the reception at the Blood center for incoming PhD students.

Your instructor will be Dr Joyce Gillis, who heads the Center of Immune Recognition, to which you applied.

Please do not hesitate to call my office for any concerns you may have.

P.S Gottschalk - Chief
The Blood Center of Southeastern Wisconsin
N.B
Pass, my regards to Dr R. Cohen who recommended you highly.

"I thought Milwaukee might be just the ticket, close enough to Niles, but far enough that we are not too entangled. What do you think?"

Amanda beamed "this is Perfect, Rachel will be close by and I always liked Milwaukee. When are you going to confirm?"

"Well, I have to check with the Imam first" he said seriously.

"The Imam? what's *he* got to do with it?" she frowned.

"He has everything to do with it" Mustafa retorted "I am not going to live in a city in which there is no Muslim brothers and no Islamic community. I know you don't think it's a big deal but it matters to me." Mustafa brow was thunder.

"OK, OK" Amanda was taken aback by the vehemence flashing at her, "Go ahead and check with him, I just hope it works out because this letter looks like a great opportunity, I mean, I have read some of the articles which this Joyce Gillis published in *Nature* and *Proceedings* and they are right up your alley. I mean, suppose the Imam told you that you could not go, then you wouldn't??" She sounded amazed.

"Of course I wouldn't" he was testy, "You are putting Alia's good before your own career, right? and I have to put the good of the Islamic Movement before any personal aspirations and wishes!"

"But,.. but,.." Amanda sputtered "that's not the same thing at all..."

"It's EXACTLY the same thing" he cut her off, forcefully "we all set priorities and my priorities are set by the Movement. I shall ask the Imam tomorrow after the Friday prayer and we shall see. And if he says no, then its NO, and we shall have to consider other locations." He tried to soften his tone, looking at her crestfallen expression. "Look, he is a reasonable man, I am sure he will make the necessary inquiries and make this opportunity possible."

They ate the rest of their meal in Silence.

They left Memphis in late August, and made the 700 mile trek to Milwaukee in the old Mercedes. They stopped in Niles for a couple of days and Amanda, who had initially wanted to stay a few days more hastened their departure when she saw the chill that ran between her father, who ran the pharmacy at K mart, and Mustafa. On the road she had a better chance to observe Mustafa's growing devoutness. He would wake up early for prayers, roll out a small Persian rug, face east to Mecca and touch his forehead to the rug multiple times while reciting his prayers. This he would repeat 5 times a day, without fail. The beard grew longer and thicker and encircled his face. In Niles he excused himself from her and her parents who were doting on their chubby, lovely grand-daughter, and found a Mosque in Schaumburg. He had a list of such Mosques for Illinois and Wisconsin. He told her, gleefully, that Milwaukee's great Mosque was right on Wisconsin Avenue, a mile or so from the Blood Center. It troubled her mildly that their life was being decided by the Omnipotent Imams but She consoled her self with Alia, and the hope that when they had settled down to domesticity, things would go back to normal.

Things never got back to normal. Initially she thought they did. They rented the second floor of a small duplex on Milwaukee's east side, as close to the lakefront as they could afford. Mustafa threw himself into the work, taking necessary courses in Genetics and Statistics, poring over texts of genetic engineering, laboratory manuals and procedures. They enjoyed the long evenings of Milwaukee's end-of-summer with long walks with Alia, initially supine, and then prone, lifting her raven black head up to look at the passing scenery, the tree-lined avenues, the mansions on the lake front, the weekend rummage-sales, and the series of festivals Milwaukee created on the lakefront. The trees began to change color and Amanda welcomed the change of seasons, the fiery colors, and the cold snap which blew in and presaged the colder winter. She noticed that Mustafa seemed to avoid certain streets close to the lakefront and always steered them away from those streets. Then it became a pattern where she would push the pram and discuss the clinical implications of the oncogenic viruses with Mustafa, and then he would change direction sharply and force the pram another way. Amanda would protest mildly and ask why, and he would reply mysteriously that he had his reasons, and they were religious, that the Imam had forbidden his disciples to go on certain streets for fear of spiritual contamination. This struck Amanda as very odd and so, when Rachel came up from Racine on her day off to visit, she suggested they take one of her beloved long walks with Alia in the pram, while Mustafa was at work.

Rachel looked very happy. The Wisconsin 'Gemmutlichkeit', good spirit, was doing her good. A southern girl, she had lived most of her life in Atlanta, and completed her Medical training in Memphis. Racine was exactly the All American town she had been looking for. She was getting involved with another new recruit to the HMO which had set her up in practice, an ophthalmologist, and love was in the air. She acquired a new Corrola and honked once happily when she reached the little house. She hopped out of the car and rang the doorbell to the second floor flat. Amanda waved at her from the window and pressed the electric latch button. It buzzed and Rachel ran up the stairs. Amanda was at the door, proudly holding little Alia to her breast. The girl was nursing like there was no tomorrow, fists clenched, mouth pumping and blue eyes fixed on her mother's face. Amanda led the way to the little sitting room and Rachel watched her hungrily, her womb contracting with baby-envy, maybe soon, if Eric likes me as much as I think he does.

They chatted over coffee and cake. Rachel was bubbling over with excitement and Amanda was more subdued. It's the inner peace that a baby brings, Rachel was sure. It was not. Amanda was bothered by Mustafa's strange behavior patterns.

"Do you know that he won't allow us to walk certain streets?"

"Whaddyoumean does not allow?" Rachel bristled.

Amanda was a little uncomfortable, she was the quintessential American liberated woman, and she let her husband push her around. "Well, he kinda steers us away from some streets, even if we have to walk the long way around. I don't understand it."

Rachel was up. "Let's go, let's see what these places are all about" then she deflated "Is it some kind of a bad neighborhood? dope-pushers?"

"No way" Amanda pealed a laugh "this is not Atlanta, we are talking lakeside mansions, that's what's strange about it."

"Then let's go" with renewed confidence Rachel was on her feet, grabbing her coat and hat. Amanda placed the sleeping Alia into the Kangaroo pouch and then deftly slipped into the straps, closing the long-coat around the precious package.

Stiff wind blew from the lake as they headed East. Amanda loved the wind and the bright golden red leaves it blew around her feet. It was cold but not yet freezing. They walked along the placid streets, quiet now that most people were at work. There it was, the little street that Mustafa always avoided. They turned left into the wind and the street. It was tree-lined with gracious old houses and mansions with prominent 20's style.

"What is this singing?" Rachel suddenly commented.

"Maybe that is what Mustafa is afraid of, let's get closer" Amanda was happy as a lark, finally overstepping some irksome boundary. It was a huge mansion with large grounds, with plenty of cars parked all around. The wall around it was low, inviting rather than deterring. People were scurrying in and out of the building with food trays in their hands, all dressed in their best, both men and women. The structure they entered was like a huge gazebo but the roof was made of branches thrown on top of the lattice. The east wall was open and they could see the barrels of burning coals that were spaced evenly to deter the chill. Families were seated along the banquet tables laden with food and wine and they were singing in a foreign language. Children were running in and out of the gazebo playing hide and seek, the little boys with skull caps and the girls in dresses. It seemed like a major festival except this was just a weekday in October in Milwaukee.

"Can I help you ladies?" Amanda and Rachel turned to look at a middle-aged man who accosted them. He was short, bespectacled, with a long squared beard, a black hat and a dark suit. He looked at the taller women benignly, as if used to the curiosity aroused by the activity in his manor. Amanda warmed to him immediately.

"Yes , we were just walking by with the baby" the man grinned at the sleeping Alia whose face was peeking sideways from the Kangaroo "and we wondered at what's going on here?"

"Ah, the Tabernacle" the man had a mellifluous voice, he must be a singer or something, Amanda wondered "it's the festival of the Tabernacles, it's a Jewish Holiday." Amanda began to understand, Mustafa always shunned everything Jewish. He often mentioned the Jewish influence in America and how America supported the Jewish State because of the all-pervasive Jewish influence. Initially she did not pay any attention, it was all lost in the cloud of love in which she lived, so that little grating things did not register, but she began to pay attention now.

"By the way, I am Rabbi Shneiorson, and I work here, this is the Chabad house." Both women looked puzzled so he quickly explained "it's a house dedicated to Jewish traditions and learning, as you can see we run the best Tabernacle in town" he ended with a peal of laughter and then became serious. "Are we too loud, did we disturb anybody?" A bunch of screaming kids ran by, chasing each other.

"No, no," Amanda quickly informed him "my friend and I were just going by, and naturally we came for the sound of kids, we are kinda new in town."

"Why naturally?" The rabbi was curious.

"Because we are both Pediatricians. This is Dr Amanda Carter and I am Dr Rachel Quesenberry" Rachel broke in.

"Ah, then you better come in and meet some of the best Pediatricians in town, and they are also some of our major contributors, this place runs by the grace of the good people of Milwaukee. Come, come, don't be shy" he urged them in.

Amanda threw a look at Rachel who shrugged, "why not" she mouthed, and they followed the diminutive man into the Tabernacle. The barrels of charcoal created radii of warmth and the rabbi seated them close to one of them and motioned that they should partake of the food. The singing was at its peak, but Alia was oblivious and slept right on. Amanda and Rachel each speared a piece of herring in sour cream with the toothpicks available and surveyed the happy surroundings.

A few minutes later the rabbi returned with two men, one very tall and distinguished looking, bald pate and silver fringe of hair. The other much shorter and smaller, but very much in command. The rabbi had to raise his voice.

"Ladies , Doctors, this is Dr BenTov" and he indicated the tall fellow "and he is a surgeon, chief, I believe of the surgical service at Children's," the tall one nodded benignly "and this is Dr Kammitzer, who does wonderful things with kids who have cancer, God Forbid, I will leave you Doctors to your own devices, more guests are coming, this is a wonderful year," and he bustled off.

Amanda introduced herself and Rachel to the two dignified gentlemen who sat opposite and did their own fishing. Dr Kammitzer was immediately interested in the two Doctors who had graduated from Memphis and St Jude. "Did any of you know Doctor Roger Cohen?" he queried.

Both nodded "I actually worked in his lab and did some tissue culture stuff for him" Amanda added.

"You don't say" Doctor Kammitzer was amazed. "What a small world." Doctor Bentov assented and they fell into a discussion of the St Jude approach to Neuroblastoma stage three.

"Well, I hope you find the time to visit Children's and join the staff, let me give you my card" and he pulled out a small, modest card.

Abe Kammitzer MD
Pediatric Hematology Oncology
PACC fund building
Children's Hospital of Wisconsin

"Call me anytime, we are a 24 hour service" he laughed.

Dr Bentov rose first "it's a pleasure to meet you, I wish you success here and in Racine, there is always room here for well-trained pediatricians, and I better skedaddle, this is a family Holiday."

Both Amanda and Rachel rose too, Alia was beginning to stir and root. Actually Amanda began to worry as to where she would feed her. Can't very well do that in the middle of the street in October. A thickset woman, all dressed in festive colors, approached them.

"Hi, I am Judy Shneiorson, My husband asked me to help you around here, gee what a cute baby, looky here how she is rooting around, she must be hungry." Amanda was amazed at the prescience of these people, talk about Gemmutlichkeit, these Jews must have invented it. She nodded.

"Is there anywhere I can feed her?"

"Sure, sure, come in the house, there are so many rooms in it I get lost even though I live in it, my husband is a teacher at the Yeshivah. The man who built it was some tycoon, he had a zillion servants." She led them into the huge foyer, past a large room where more people were praying in white striped shawls, and into a small secluded room with a massive door of a dated design. It contained two chairs, a small table and the window overlooked the tabernacle in the yard. "Here we are" she huffed and puffed, "perfect for nursing the baby." Alia started to cry her hungry cry and Amanda pulled her out of the Kangaroo, draped her coat on the chair and lowered her shoulder strap. Her heavy breast was already dripping into the bra so she quickly released it and moved the dark brown nipple into Alia's hungry mouth. The baby latched on and began to suck audibly. Rachel looked on with interest. Judy Shneiorson looked on with yearning. Amanda answered with a questioning look.

"The families here all have lots of children, I love babies, but the Almighty, blessed be his name, has not allowed me to have one." Tears welled up in Judy's eyes. Alia came up for air and Amanda brought her to her shoulder to burp. The woman looked on, beseeching, and Amanda handed her Alia to burp. Judy clutched her like the treasure she was, patted her back, tears still welling up and streaming down the apple cheeks, then came a big burp and she handed Alia back for the other breast. Rachel was moved almost to tears herself, but consoled herself that her time was just coming, maybe Eric will propose soon, or maybe she will not wait for his proposal at all and just ask him at point blank range. That sounded even better, let's cut it one way or another.

Judy saw them out. The party was winding down in the Tabernacle and Amanda was more bewildered than ever. What was it in these people that Mustafa detested so much? Beside having their holy-days out of sync with the surroundings (probably because those festivals originated in a land where October was still warm!) they were totally harmless. And the Doctors she met, they were top-notch!! I must get in touch with the Kammitzer fellow, maybe he would have a fellowship spot in the next couple of years. But to avoid them like a Plague? That's ridiculous, I must talk this out with him. It seems such an important part of the man I love and do not know.

They stopped at the Big Boy and both took the salad bar. Alia was awake and curious about the foods she could not eat yet and made adorable baby sounds. The women took turns eating while one of them sweet-talked the baby. After lunch they walked back to the Duplex. Rachel hugged them both, kissed Alia on the forehead and drove the Corrola south. They vowed to return the visit and phone calls.

Mustafa was bubbly that night. He told funny stories about the lab personnel, held Alia and talked to her as if she were an adult, and eyed

Amanda's rear appreciatively, making the appropriate lewd remarks. Amanda was more thoughtful. She breast fed Alia at 10 and put her to bed. They were both in bed, feeling companionable when Amanda broached the subject. "You know, I took a long walk today with Rachel. We had great fun." "Oh yeah, where did you go to?" he asked playfully, his hand stroking her behind. "On Parsons street there is that huge mansion, they had a kind of a party there." she felt the hand stopping the stroking motion, then withdrawing. He sat up in bed and looked down at her.

"They asked us in, they were awfully nice, and they even let me feed Alia in one of the rooms there" she continued, examining his face and reaction. "And why would you go where I forbid you to go?" he asked quietly. She jumped at that.

"Forbid? what is this forbid business? It's a free country and a free city. OK, OK" she lowered her voice, minding Alia who was in the crib right next to the bed "let's stop that right here, why would you forbid me or anyone from going there? I mean what harm are they? Mustafa, we are *married,* I must understand these crazy notions" his face became thunderous, then relaxed.

"All right , I will take this one by one, or as they say back home, kill a Jew and rest." Amanda was horrified and showed it so he continued quickly. "I never told you the full story of why and how my twin sister Alia was killed." Amanda was taken aback. Come to think of it, Mustafa never talked of his pre-American past, as if he had been born an adult in the United States. But then the American assumption is that people are reborn when they leave the old country and reach the Golden Shores, so that their past is irrelevant. They ought to cut the proverbial umbilical cord, disconnect from the convulsions and hatreds, and pursue the American Dream. The fact that the Sicilian Mafia, and the Irish Republican Army among other groups maintain close relations with the old countries and their vendettas does not register on the American mind. And so Amanda expected that her Mustafa was the only Mustafa.

"She was my twin sister, she was *raped* and *killed* in front of my eyes, just because she was an Arab and a Moslem." Mustafa launched into a long description of the camp, the war, The catastrophic alliances, the rape and the murder. Amanda listened intently, and her heart went out to her man who had suffered so much and for no conceivable reason. Alia stirred in her sleep as if she could not take the horrors retold in the quiet Milwaukee duplex. An occasional car drove by, some with heavy Bass blaring from the 250 watt speakers. It all seemed far away, unreal, but then it *was* real, even within Milwaukee, where Geoffrey Dahmer was quietly killing and cannibalizing people and disposing of their bodies into the public dumpsters.

Amanda shook her head as if to clear the hideous web away.

"But what does it have to do with the Jewish Pediatricians who sit in a Tabernacle and sing songs, and take care of the sick kids here?" she questioned. "What does all this have to do with *Us?* I mean we are here, we are starting a family, we have love to sustain us, we can forget the old hatreds and just LIVE together?!!"

"Oh Amanda, Dear wife, you can't just wash all this away. The horror is part of me, and since we are married its part of YOU. These Jews who were responsible for my sister's death! Who sent the Phallanga to do their dirty job, who do you think supported them?! Who paid them?! Who rolled their loans for them so they can buy superior weapons?! Who paid for their training? The same cute *goddamn* Jews you met who were so nice to you. I am filled with shame that my sister reincarnate was under the same roof with them!!" The intensity of his hatred was frightening, venomous, it was almost hissing. "if you value our life and marriage, then stay away from them, associate as you need for academic reasons, or career, but socially, treat them as the scum of the earth they are!!!" Mustafa turned away from his wife, grabbed a copy of Science and left the bedroom. Amanda was soon busy with Alia who was hungry again. She gazed at her daughter and could not believe that a girl who was as dear to her parents was brutally ravaged. Her outlook on the world took a switch overnight.

Amanda understood Mustafa's fascination with Middle East affairs better now, could even agree with some of his radical views regarding the need to resettle the Palestinians in their homeland despite the resistance of the Israelis, and the necessity of using American power to force a settlement of some nature on them. She involved herself very little with the heated discussions that some of Mustafa's friends brought into the apartment but openly discussed the need to plan on buying a house, something that Mustafa absolutely eschewed. When Alia was one year old Amanda picked up a part time job as a locum for Dr Bacharach, an East side pediatrician, and a year later she became a full time physician at the same office, with privileges at St Mary's, St Michael's and the Children's Hospital. In those years Mustafa was drawn deeper and deeper into the Muslim and Palestinian activities, he traveled extensively to various meetings, the minority scientific, and the majority, Islamic. He donated a mighty portion of his income to various charities associated with Hamas, and so with school loans, the travel, and the downtime from work associated with being a mother, they never had enough to buy a decent house. Mustafa liked that just fine. At the subconscious level Amanda understood that as a sign of temporary, non-permanence, and she did not become pregnant again.

When Alia was five Amanda decided that she needed the additional stimulus of academic work, and being already staff at Children's, she secured a spot as a Pediatric hematology/Oncology fellow. The first year passed like a blur, with a flurry of work, seminars, on call, and hard reading. She hardly noticed that she saw Mustafa less and less and that in fact they both acted as baby-sitters for Alia when she was not in Kindergarten.

The turning point was in March 1996. Two years before, the Palestine Liberation Organization, led by Chairman Arafat, signed with great fanfare a peace treaty with Israel. The Islamic Movement condemned the treaty as a sell-out to the Satan, and vowed to step up the Holy war. The Jewish settlers in the West Bank, Hebron and Nablus and Efrat, staged demonstrations and riots directed at the former Hero turned Traitor, Prime Minister Rabin. A small dark-complexioned Yemenite Israeli man, armed with the sanctioning of certain religious leaders, decided that the only way to avert History was to kill the Traitor. On a Saturday night in November 1995 Yigal Amir sat innocently on a concrete street bench, right where Rabin was supposed to exit from a huge peace rally in the City Hall Plaza in Tel Aviv. The secret service Shabac operatives had seen this man a number of times in previous public appearances and he was so typical of the Israeli religious Yemenite, the epitome of Jewish patriotism, that they just nodded and paid no attention. Rabin who had always been contemptuous of his own safety and pooh-poohed the advice of the Secret Service to wear a body armor came down the steps, with the huge support of the Peace Movement crowd still ringing in his ears. Yigal Amir rose from the bench, insinuated his way between the agents and pulled out the Berreta. One shot felled the Agent guarding Rabin's back, and the next two shots were fired into the unsuspecting Prime-Minister's back from a point blank range, the next shot went into the body of the agent who interposed himself between the falling Rabin and the killer. He was seized and broke out with the famous grin, the Deed was done.

With Rabin dead, his one time political opponent turned peace-making-ally Shim'on Peres became Prime Minister. Soon the country was undergoing convulsions of acrimony, self accusations and a boomerang of feelings against the right wing and nationalist religious organizations. The West Bank settlers became pariahs, budgets were slashed and security was relaxed. The Enemy had become US. The threat of Palestinian terrorism receded before the threat of internal strife. It was the perfect time for the 'engineer' Yihye Ayash. His religion was bifold: Hamas type of fundamentalist Islam and the need to kill Jews, the scum of the earth who had swarmed onto the Holy Ground like the proverbial pestilence. That terrorist activity might damage Palestinian chances of achieving speedy statehood made no difference to him.

The bus system of Jerusalem is as predictable as the rising of the sun on the Dome of the Rock. The routes never change and the bus numbers are engraved in marble. As the city grew and spread out new routes and numbers were added but once established they were set in concrete. Everybody uses the bus, old and young, hip and square, Arab and Jew, male and female and child. The old matriarchs shop for fresh veggies at the Mahanee Yehuda open air market and lug it home on the bus. The Rumanian workers did the same. Bus number 57 winds its way through the poor neighborhood of the Katamons and ends at the Central station, at the mouth of Yaffo street. The city was enjoying one of its greatest periods of prosperity as the world poured money at the New Middle East that Shim'on Peres had proclaimed, with Jerusalem at it's center. No one paid attention to the 20 year old Yussuf Marzouk as he mounted the bus together with the pushing and shoving rest of humanity. Yussuf was born after his father was killed at the Savoy Hotel and he had vowed to take with him, Samson-style, many more than his father ever had. He hugged the 20 kilogram charge in his knap-sack and waited for the bus to fill. Bus No 63 was passing alongside his own as he pulled the ripcord, allowing the battery to close the contact and fire the detonator.

The intersection became an Inferno in an instant. The bus was ripped apart and the No 63 bus was heavily damaged. Bodies and parts of bodies flew in the air and stuck to the nearby buildings. The sheet-metal plates and glass shrapnel flew and hit the passers by, ripping eyes, and necks and arms and legs. The diesel fuel caught fire and the stench of burning flesh rose in the air, making those who had been missed by the carnage, retch and puke. Children were flung out of the shattered glass windows of the 63 bus by parents terrified that the fire might consume them too, and they broke arms and legs. Chaos and Bedlam, the revenge of Islam on the Blaspheming vermin. Of course, at least a third of the casualties were not Jewish at all, they were Arab, and Rumanian, and Swedish tourists. All the better. The Arabs should know better than to buy in the Jewish city and the tourists forfeited their life if they toured the Jewish State.

Almost at the same time it was Bashir Mahmoud's turn. Armed with the same device, Mahmoud was deterred from entering the Dizengoff Avenue Mall at the heart of down-town Tel Aviv by the security guards at the main entrance. Instead he waited for the traffic light to change and for the stream of pedestrians crossing Dizengoff Avenue to converge in the middle. The blast took the human bodies surrounding the young assassin, and ripped them into shreds which adhered to windows as far up as the fifth floor of the Dizengoff Tower. The carnage here was not as bad because the blast occurred in an open space and the bodies closest to Bashir absorbed much of it. Still, it took weeks to scrape the last of human remains off the walls and windows. It was a masterly stroke, no one and no place in Israel was safe.

The CNN and the NBC, and BBC descended on the scenes like carrion birds. Hungrily they fed the world live pictures of the carnage, and blood, and ripped up vehicles. Noon in Israel was 4 o'clock in the morning in Milwaukee. Amanda woke up to the crowing and chortling of her husband. It was 0630 and the networks were full of the news, playing again and again stills and video strips acquired hurriedly from local amateur photographers. Mustafa was chortling and beating the table with glee and when he turned to her his dark face all alight.

"See how we are paying them back? The murdering swine, that will show them they are *never* safe. Don't look so shocked, Beirut was a hundred times, a thousand times worse." Amanda stomach churned at the visions of horror played again and again to the tune of smug commentators and Learned Professors of Middle East studies. Mustafa was back at the screen with a murmur "And this is nothing compared with what's in store for them." Amanda could not believe her own ears. Stories of horrible crimes were one thing, but sheer joy at the perpetration of untold misery was too much. Her love turned acidly sour. *I have married a monster and he is the Father of my Child*, and what can I do about it without harming my dear Alia. She opened the child's room, and there she was sleeping like an angel, totally oblivious of the horror without.

Chapter 7

Abduction

Joe felt Helen's arms tighten around his middle and her breasts touched and then hugged his back. He smiled, although she could not see the smile, he knew she could *feel* it. Her Nava bumped slightly against his own helmet and he swept into the tight turn, the front wheel rock steady, following the curve precisely, Helen loved the curvaceous road through the Jerusalem Forest. It was little traveled and Joe always took it if he was not in a hurry to *get* to Jerusalem. The curve ended and he straightened the Katana, dropped a gear, and was rewarded by an even tighter hug. The needle rushed around the Tach, from 6 to 12000 revs, the motor screamed and the bike shot up the incline while the air shrieked around the helmets. The Speedo registered 110 and he shifted up, and let the incline slow them to legal speeds, 55 was so mundane after the high of 110. They rounded the curve and the white sharp peaks of the Alps appeared through the pines. The sign said 'St Moritz 30 Km' and he decided to take a break at the next vista. There was a green bench and he stopped the machine behind it. Helen held his shoulders and stood up on the foot-pegs, swung a shapely leg over the Chase-Harper saddlebags and landed lightly on the grass. Joe pushed out the side-stand, and leaned the Blue Kat on it. He joined Helen on the bench with a bottle of Chianti. She leaned her curly blond hair on his shoulder, his arm went around her oh-so-narrow waist, the whole Italian Northern plain, Lake Como and the cities around it were before them like a huge, colorful table-cloth. He lifted the red wine bottle and slowly took a dainty taste, and put the bottle to her pale lips and made them red with rivulets running down her chin and into her blouse, converging in the cleavage. Joe leaned over the red lips, the sunburned cheeks, the blue-lined eyelids and kissed slowly and gently, savoring the smell of the hair and the clean salty, Chianti sweat on her neck.

Evening was coming down and it was time to go and find a hotel. They were not really ready for the altitude and the cold of the Yellowstone park. Joe could feel Helen shivering through the thin windbreaker. The dark came on very quickly, but soon the blessed sign of MOTEL came around the gentle bend. They stopped in the office for a key and the red Yamaha Radian purred to the cabin marked 42. As soon as the key turned Joe rushed into the small bathroom and turned the red faucet, a torrent of steaming water issued forth and he ran a bath for Helen. She was sitting on the bed, frozen and shivering, hugging herself tightly. Joe tore his shirt off and collected the poor waif into his arms, he could feel his body heat rushing into her cold, goose-bump skin and warming it. Slowly the muscle shivers relaxed and she allowed him to bring her into the bathroom, take her HiTec shoes off, the blouse, bra, the slacks and panties and lower her into the hot bath. The shivering stopped and she heaved a sigh of relief and a wan smile of thanks.

She always slept with her buttocks into his middle, legs drawn up almost in a fetal position, curled up inside the bigger question mark that was Joe, together under the thick blanket. He woke up at first light, a habit ingrained in the Army, and his left hand was on her waist. He could feel the bone under the satiny skin, and he traced the line as far as he could reach, up the iliac crest and down the smooth leg, all the way to the shell-like knee-cap. Then up the same route, over the thigh, over the crest, down to the waist and then slowly up the chest wall, counting each rib. His fingers sneaked over the upper arm and just brushed the breast, the nipple, and then the other nipple. She mumbled softly and pushed her butt right into his middle. The tension in his member was unbearable, it was ready to explode but he waited patiently for her. The light brightened outside, the birds rioted with song. Helen moved some more and suddenly his member was at Heaven's Gate and the small cleft was wet and waiting and all it took was a tiny thrust and a minuscule accommodation and he entered the warm and moist haven. She took his hand and placed it full on her breast and it filled his large hand with softness and love. She was moving her pelvis back and forth, the cheeks of her butt grinding into his pubic bone, his thrusts became more and more urgent and he could feel the final clenching of all his muscles, the rush of come welling up and ready to flood when the telephone rang, loudly, insistently, stridently, not to be denied, someone's life was on the line. His body ached for release but nevertheless he reached for the phone. The sheet was drenched with sweat, Helen withdrew, and only his bursting member, wrenched from the warmth of the womb, and dull ache in his lower belly and his hard clenched balls, were evidence of the dream.

"Dr Bergman, this is Children's, will you take a call from Dr Carter?" That was Sandy, at the exchange. Joe was surprised, it was Sunday morning and Amanda was on call. The tension in his member slowly receded, Helen was gone, existing only in his memory, living and loving in his frenzied dreams.

"Yeah, I'll take it, put her through." That isn't a voice, it's a croak, he thought.

Click, music, click again "Joe, I hate to call you but you must help me."
God she sounded so strained, stressed, upset.
"Anybody sick over there?" He asked.

"No, no, its got nothing to do with the Unit" Amanda was breaking up
"It's Mustafa, he won't answer the phone and I am really afraid, and there is
no one else I can ask for help..." her words tumbled out of the receiver
conveying urgency and fear. Fear of WHAT he wondered, there are a
thousand reasons for the phone not being answered, a child knocking it off
the hook, a malfunction, Wisconsin Bell problems (pretty rare, he admitted
to himself).

"All right, I'll go and check and knock on the door. I hope he doesn't eat
me for breakfast for waking him up. Give me the address again."

"Its 3202 North Green Bay Road, Building B, Apartment 316, you were
there once."

"Yeah I remember," it had been a fiasco, Mustafa would not even
acknowledge him that time, just because Joe had not agreed wholeheartedly
that Israel was a terrorist state run by the International Zionist Council. Joe
always tried to steer clear of the Arab-Israeli conflict with anyone who
appeared Arab or Muslim, but Mustafa had led the conversation there
anyway. Amanda had been miserable, and after playing chess and checkers
with Alia Joe had made himself scarce. So much for leisurely Sunday Dinner
at a colleague's house.

Joe got up, his muscles were sore from last night's workout with the Torah
Dojo Karate class, and his forearms hurt from blocking so many kicks and
punches. At one time he thought that physical exertion, pain, meditation and
exhaustion will keep Helen from haunting his nights, but to no avail, she lived
there, almost as tangibly as when she had been alive, every night, and some
of the days too. It was five years and there was no end in sight. There I go
again, let's move.

The December cold was not as bad as he expected it to be. Get a coffee
at the drive thru in McDonald's, and drive the two miles up Green Bay road
from Silver Spring. His own apartment was not in one of the new and modern
apartment complexes, but rather in a older house which had been divided into
two apartments. His first floor neighbors were in fact the owners of the old
house. He relaxed into the deep cushions of the Le Sabre and drove slowly
in the December morning dark past Silver Spring House and into the
complex. It was spotless and modern and he found the building easily. His
muscles rebelled slightly at the top floor climb, but soon he was in the empty,

long, carpeted corridor in front of the door marked 316. A little plaque said
:

> ### Welcome to our home
> ### M. Halim PhD
> ### A. M Carter MD

He knocked on the door, very politely, and waited. Then a little more vigorously, no response. He looked at the lock, it was a standard round Schlagge pear-shaped affair with a keyhole. It appeared intact. There was a deadbolt but when he pushed on the door it moved so the deadbolt was not engaged. He glanced at his K Mart Innovation watch, it was 0730, no one is awake on Sunday morning unless they are Doctors. He applied his stethoscope to the door, there was complete silence, then the phone jarred his ears, the phone was ringing stridently, but no one would answer. Maybe someone is in trouble in there, carbon monoxide poisoning, who knows. Joe pulled out his Gerber multi-tool and used the knife to chip and peel at the door jamb. He quickly made a tunnel and forced the tongue in. The door was open.

Breaking and entering, that's all I need now, but Amanda will vouch for me. Let's see if anybody needs help here. Kids are usually up early, watching the cartoons. The living room was empty and the TV was off. Kitchen is empty, no sign of a hurried exit. Bedrooms? Empty master, child room neat and tidy. Joe went back to the closet. Big holes on the man's side, clothes had been taken. Suitcase? under the bed? In the storage behind the bifolds? Computer turned off, printer off, disconnected, that's strange, why would anyone disconnect a printer? Ah, he had another peripheral, like a mass storage device interposed, and that's gone. These are signs of a methodical person leaving his home. Notes? Joe looked around for a conspicuous place. Yes, there it is, in a nice envelope, leaning against the obligatory wedding picture. Time to call Amanda, I hope this is not what I think it is, I hope Alia is OK.

"Children's? can you page me Dr carter, for Dr Bergman? Yes thank you I'll wait" Drum the fingers, scratch head, how to tell a woman her husband just left and kidnaped her kid. "Amanda, this is Joe, did Dr. Kammitzer show up for rounds? Good, tell him you have to go right now and that I'll come in later to help him out, no, right now, and drive carefully!"

Milwaukee is not known for its heavy traffic, in fact Milwaukee rush hour is really a rush minute, and for the Chicagoans or New-Yorkers it's a real eye opener to be in a city where you actually *drive* to work rather than *park* to work. On Sunday morning it's a breeze. Still Amanda had to have broken the legal limits, and then some. Joe was waiting for her on the sofa, idly eyeing the computer, when Amanda ran in, her chest heaving. Joe got up to stop her mad rush to the child's bedroom.

"They are not here Amanda, I am sorry."

"But where are they, where is my baby?" she sobbed.

"Look at the mantlepiece, the answer may be there."

Amanda whirled to the mantlepiece, grabbed the envelope, and her hands shook so badly she could not even tear at it. Joe came over and laid a large soothing hand on her thin shoulder.

"Amanda, do you want me to open it?" She nodded, eyes were streaming and sniffling, her nose red.

Joe took the envelope and held it against the light, the outline of one single folded page was clear. He took out the Gerber and inserted the knife carefully. The envelope was slit end wise and he slowly removed the sheet of paper from it and handed it to Amanda. Joe walked over to the computer niche and sat on the chair, and listened to the sobs. The wan light began creeping in. Presently the sobbing receded, she blew her nose, then came and joined him on a chair, her face was puffy but she was back in control. She handed him the neatly printed page.


```
Dear Amanda

I expect you to read this on Sunday morning. By
this time Alia and I are far away, beyond the reach
of the American authorities.
Alia is well and she knows she is going to visit
the Grandfather she had never met. Although born in
America she is a Palestinian like me, and she will
join in the great war against the Jewish Zionist
regime in occupied Palestine and their sponsors in
Washington and New York. She will learn about the
great Arab and Muslim traditions and she will
unlearn the American soft living. She will be a
better person for it. She will find many surrogate
```

mothers in my family, and will become the daughter they had lost to the Zionist savagery.

As for the Zionists, I have learned well in America and my retribution is almost ready. You will hear about it one day on CNN.

I am not entirely heartless, so I'll keep one channel of communications open so that Alia knows she has a mother. I will leave you messages through the Netaddress USA email system. On the computer I established our address as Mustafa and the logon name is Alia 1.

We had our good times and our bad times, and lately it has been all bad. I have no wish to see you or America again, nor does Alia. Forget us and start again with someone else. Do not try to follow us because here I and my Muslim brothers are supreme.

Allah Hu Akbar

Mustafa (signature)

Joe shook his head slowly, the sheer temerity, the arrogance, the complete selfishness and cruelty, dragging a kid to a war-zone on a demented principle. The picture of the wounded coffee-shop owner was back to haunt him. He looked back at Amanda who was losing her composure.

"Joe, what am I going to do?" she asked plaintively. Joe felt it again, the pull of responsibility, and the wish to detach himself immediately from a very touchy and dangerous situation. he looked at the letter again

As for the Zionists, my retribution is almost ready.

His stomach knotted, what retribution, what is he talking about? What kind of retribution can a PhD in Milwaukee concoct? There were enough bomb artists, forest arsonists, ambush layers and rocket launchers in the Middle East to terrorize the whole world, and they do terrorize it. Daharran, Argentina, Lockerby. Alright, this letter makes it my responsibility, if some threat is really there and I do nothing to abrogate it then it makes me an accomplice. He turned back to Amanda.

"What would you do if I were not here now?" He countered.

Sniffle "I guess I'd call the Police."

"Absolutely right, this letter is evidence of kidnaping, this is a major offense, it's their job. Call 911 and report a kidnaping. Meanwhile we will see what we can dig up for ourselves, is there another phone line?"

Amanda's color was coming back, she had something to do, a course of action to stave off the blow of her baby somewhere in the world "Yes, the computer has a dedicated line we used it, Mustafa used it, I hate the damn Machine, for online searches and for faxes and for e-mailing his friends." Amanda took the phone and punched 911.

"Glendale police, how can I help you?" A deep male voice.

"My name is doctor Amanda Carter, I am at 3202 North Green bay Road, building B apartment 316. My husband just took our kid and disappeared... No, he *kidnaped* her.. No I won't calm down, he left a letter saying he is leaving the country... No we didn't have a fight, his folks live in the *Middle East*... 2 minutes? OK I am here with a colleague."

Joe started the computer and used the headphones and the WIN 95 dialer to call the HOT unit. Dr Kammitzer was making his rounds with the resident. Did he need Amanda or himself there? No, the unit was relatively light, no one was crashing, Joe should let him know what is going on as soon as he knew. Outside the Blue and white Caprice with the red blue flashing rounded the ornate post at the gated entry, and headed directly for the B building. Two police officers came out, the man looked slightly familiar, but he could not see his features. They entered the building. Venetian shades and roll-ups were being drawn up all over the complex.

Joe tried to blend into the corner of the computer niche. After all, this was mainly Amanda's problem, it was her child who was kidnaped. They knocked and entered, the policewoman walking right in, the man stayed behind to examine the door jamb. He looked up and scanned the room, and his eyes locked on Joe. He scowled for a second, then his face lit up in a wide grin. He walked over, each step a mile long. Joe rose from the chair, this guy was huge, no wonder the Parking Structure attacker had looked so small when he had brought him in. Joe extended his hand and it was gripped strongly by the huge blackleather paw.

"Officer Wilkins I presume."

"Dr Bergman, pleasure seeing you again, have you beaten anybody else lately?"

"Very funny, how is our friend doing?"

"I am very sorry to report that he was found to be unfit for justice. In other words, he is a Wacko and will not stand trial. He should have been in a nuthouse, pardon my language, in a protective environment, all along. He has something powerful against women, his mother or sister, or the evil witch that abused him. Anyway, the county nuthouse, er, psychiatric protective custody will keep him off the streets hopefully forever." Joe was nodding "He is the exception to the rule they tell me, but I don't believe it." the big policeman's eyes twinkled "No day of glory in court for you." Joe made a moue and lowered the corners of his mouth "I knew you will be disappointed, learn any new Kung-Fu moves since?"

" No, I just practice the old ones some more and stay out of trouble, but I just got in trouble again, that's my knife at the door there, wanna see?" Wilkins nodded and Joe pulled out the Gerber. The police officer handled the tool appreciatively, slid out the plier jaws, pulled out the knife and removed a sliver of wood from it.

"Did you have her permission?" he asked, suddenly official.

"Not really, but you better ask her" Joe replied.

"Let me keep it for another minute" Joe assented. They looked at the female officer who was examining the letter with nylon gloves on.

"Who handled this paper beside you?" She asked Amanda.

"I asked Dr Bergman to help me open the envelope it was in." Wilkins slid the plier back into the tool and handed it back wordlessly.

"OK, we will need detailed depositions" said the woman, her nameplate showed Officer Anne Dorland "you may take your car and follow me." She got up and started to move towards the door.

"Just a minute" said Joe, very conversational, "while we are taking depositions, the kid is being kidnaped, by her father, against her mother's wishes, most likely to a foreign land. We MUST try and stop him if possible." Officer Wilkins was eyeing Joe respectfully, Officer Dorland was more truculent. People usually did as they were told. Wilkins intervened.

"Any suggestions?"

"Well , Dr carter tells me that her husband did a lot of stuff on the computer, give me a few minutes to see what I can dig up, and in the meantime you can start your formal deposition, does that sound reasonable?"

Dorland was about to object but Wilkins cut in. "Sounds OK to me" he shot a glance at his partner and she produced her notepad again.

Joe looked at the screen, there it was, AOL, America Online, the most popular online service in America. He placed the mouse pointer on it and double-clicked. The modem whistled and phoned, the log-on screen came up.

"Excuse me Amanda, do you know his password?" he asked.

"I think it was Alia, but I am not sure" Joe nodded and entered ALIA. The screen showed the broken key and then he was in and presented with the opening screen. Joe chose Travel. He used the same password again and was refused.

"Another password, Amanda?" she thought some more and went blank.

"Let's try PALESTINE" Joe said, and drew another blank.

"Where did his family came from?"

"Jaffa, he told me once" Joe tried, and failed, then he entered YAFFO, the old spelling for Jaffa, and bingo, he was through. The screen for flight reservations flashed:

would you like another reservation?

Would you like to change your reservation?

Joe chose the second on and was rewarded by the line

The reservation you have is final. It cannot be changed or refunded.
Syrian Airlines flight 215
O'Hare December 15 1201 am
arriving Paris Orly 0230 PM
Leaving Orly 0330 PM
Arriving Damascus International 1005 PM
Price adult 1132$ one way.
price child under 10 942$ one way.
Airport taxes applicable.
would you like to make another reservation?

They were crowding him, all three heads at screen level. Amanda started sobbing again, suddenly it was real, her baby was gone to a foreign and dangerous land, her family was destroyed. She turned away and cried, and cried, and crossed to the bathroom and slammed the door and cried some more. The police officers were mute, and pained, this was beyond their worst dreams. They were used to household spats, the mom taking her kids to

grandma and scaring dad a little. The vengeful father spiriting his kid away
to some cabin in the Northwoods of Wisconsin. This appeared devastatingly
final, the child was gone to a country very high up on the State Department
list of countries directly espousing international terrorism. This was WAY
beyond them. Joe snapped out of it.

"Officer Dorland, please go in there and see she doesn't do anything silly
or dangerous. Officer Wilkins, call up your headquarters or whatever and get
the Feds on it. This is a *Kidnaping,* a federal offense. I'll try Syrian Airlines,
maybe they got delayed somewhere." Joe looked at his watch, it was already
1025, if they were lucky, the flight could be delayed in Paris. He
disconnected the AOL, put on the headphones, and called Chicago 5551212.

"What City?"

"I need Syrian Airlines in O'Hare."

Click. "The number is area code 301-265-0135" Joe scribbled it quickly
and punched it into the dialer.

"Syrian Airlines."

"Er, my name is Hamed Habibi" Wilkins' eyes grew wide open with
surprise, the Arabic accent was so authentic he almost felt he was back in
Detroit, certain parts of the city were dominated by merchants and customers
from the Middle East. Joe continued speaking earnestly into the phone "my
cousin Mustafa Halim and his daughter Alia took the midnight flight via
Baris. He forgot some imbortant documents at home. Do you think we can
catch him in Baris and fax him the documents?"

"Just a minute sir" music, "I am sorry sir but the flight from Paris left on
time but he did not board it."

Joe tsked tsked away, "he is very absent minded, my cousin, he is a
Doctor you know, did he leave some kind of a message for me or anybody?"

"Just a minute sir" click, hold, music , two minutes, Amanda was talk-ing
rationally now, telling officer Dorland about her husband, description, her
child, description. "Sir, a message was left for a person by the name of
Amanda Carter with a specific instruction to be relayed to her only, do you
know who she is?"

"Yes, I know and I will but her on the line for you" Joe beckoned Amanda
to the phone. "He knew someone would trace him this far" Joe said, "take
whatever message he left for you." Amanda took the phone and listened. She
said "yes, Yes," a couple of times and replaced the receiver.

"They are going to Fax it over, Mustafa used to receive faxes on the
computer, but I am not sure how."

Joe went back to the Start button, looked for programs and scanned the list. There it was, MaxFax Status. He double clicked it and waited with his cursor on the 'receive' button. The phone rang again, and he clicked it. The computer began receiving the fax. They all craned their necks at the screen. The transmission ended and Joe clicked on the Scheduler on the newest message.

hello Amanda

If you are reading this Fax then you are trying to follow me. It's no use, by now I am unreachable so you can give up. I have Alia with me and I would rather die, with her, then give her up to you or the American Zionist organizations. I warn you, If Alia's life is dear to you then this is the last effort you will make to come after us.

Mustafa

"Son of a bitch, son of a *bitch* ! " The words tore from officer Wilkins' throat and mouth. Amanda started sobbing again, Wilkins pulled out his cellular and walked outside the door. A couple of doors down the corridor slammed, the curious neighbors did not want to be involved. Joe figured it was time to think. He gazed at the silent screen, his face blank, the hubbub around him died down. Officer Dorland decided it was time to make a stand. "Doctors, you did what you could , its time to get to the station for some paperwork. We will get the Feds involved, but the rules must be followed." Joe looked up, his normal voice, the Arabic mimicry gone. "Officers, If you don't mind, I would like to get back to the Hospital and fill in for Doctor Carter. I know nothing more than you know at this point. I can always be reached at Children's or my home phone." He scribbled it down and gave the paper to Wilkins. Dorland was truculent again but Wilkins nodded. Joe fed Mustafa'a parting letter through the scanner and printed a copy. Joe shut the computer down, and the closing trumpet sound was at odds with the grieving mother and the impotent police. He rose from the computer chair and lightly Passed by Amanda, gently tapping her slumped shoulder. Officer Wilkins Joined him on the landing.

"Any relationship to the Pastor at Children's?" Joe queried.

"Sure, he is my old man."

"Sorry, I did not want to presume. Isn't he involved with some Missions to Africa and other locations?" Joe probed.

"Yeah, he was always very big on helping the less fortunate nations, he organized some medical missions to God-knows-where, the floods in Bangla-

Desh, and other places. I was never as anxious to travel, I guess I am not the apple he wanted. " Chris Wilkins laughed self deprecatingly, "I serve in other ways, closer to home." Joe nodded, wheels turning in his head as he headed downstairs and into the LeSabre which had cooled down in the mean time so that the seat was hard.

Karen looked up and smiled with surprise as Joe came on the floor. She glanced at the board and yes she was right, Dr Carter was supposed to be in for rounds. Joe stopped at the counter and looked down into the inquiring gaze. Gee, she is like Helen in her expression, and really unlike her in other ways.

"What's up doc?" chomp chomp she mimed the Wabbit.

"Not good, can you keep a secret?" he said that without a smile.

The grin wiped off her face "anything happened to Doctor Carter?" worriedly.

"You might say that, her husband, took off with the kid" he said conversationally. Her sharp intake of breath was almost like a whistle.

"When?"

"Last night, I am telling you that 'cause she is not going to be here for a while and people will start guessing so we must come up with something, how about a family crisis?"

Karen was doubtful "I guess I can chime in." She looked up at one of the nurses who was coming back from a patient's room. "Let's talk in the dictation booth." She rose elegantly from the chair and Joe found himself admiring the easy, flowing motion, I guess that means I am still human, he reasoned. Nurse Applebee, large, rotund, and maternal, looked on with approval as they disappeared into the dictation booth.

"Mustafa, that's his name" Joe continued without preamble as he leaned against the door, totally blocking the jambs, the attacker really had some bad luck in running up against this man, thought Karen. "Picked up and left the house, with the kid, after some careful planning, probably to the Middle East. He left her this message" and Joe pulled out the folded page from the inside pocket of his huge jacket. He moved away from the door and settled himself on one of the colorful Green Bay chairs. Karen read quickly and the play of expressions on her face was like watching a whole movie, incredulity, then horror, then fear.

"What is he going to do to the girl, and what does he mean..." The door swung open slowly, Abe Kammitzer's small body was hardly a match for the heavy Algoma door and the return mechanism that held it from above. He seemed amused at the strange conference but then the grin wiped off at the grave expressions worn by both his favorite nurse and fellow. Karen handed him the paper and he scanned it quickly. Then he looked up at his disciples' faces, especially at Joe's.

"Are you going to go after him?" he asked quietly. Karen was deeply startled, there seemed to be some understanding between those two.

"On the one hand I am concerned about the girl." Joe countered "as far as I know, he is a good father and will take care of her, but he is taking her from one life to something entirely strange, alien and possibly dangerous, all that against her mother's wishes. The other concern is this cryptic note

As for the Zionists, my retribution is almost ready

"Amanda did not marry some kind of a bomber, or an assassin. This man is a Doctor of Molecular Biology, granted he is a Wacko, but he must be a clever wacko. I mean he anticipated Amanda's direction of search and prepared a response before hand. He also threatened the child, knowing that Amanda will do nothing to jeopardize her baby, and possibly delay getting help or avoid it altogether. This is a dangerous man, who IS going to go after him and where? Who IS going to assume responsibility for this? Who is going to try and bring the Kid back? Who is going to pay attention to this threat to the Jewish nation?" Abe was nodding slowly, Karen was getting wider eyed all the more, that's the way heroes talk, or those that have nothing to lose. As if to continue her thoughts Joe finished "I basically have no ties except to this place so I am asking you for a leave of absence." Joe concluded.

Abe continued nodding. He gazed up into the bigger younger man's slit-like eyes, the sun-etched lines radiating from the corners beyond the scholarly round glasses, the resolute mouth, the straight nose, and then grinned raffishly.

"And if I said 'no', wouldn't you go?"

The slitty eyes crinkled some more. "Sure I would, but I'd rather go with your blessing." Karen noted that he spoke as to a respected parent, strange, but what is he going to do? she made up her mind.

"You guys are all the same. First you cause all the problems, then you think you can solve them on your own" both men turned on her, Joe with incredulity, and Doctor Kammitzer with a knowing smile.

"Do you have any specific ideas?" he queried.

"Yes" Karen was adamant, "we go after him and pull the little girl from him and bring her back home."

"Sounds easy" Joe was deprecating "where is he, who are his friends, where is the girl, how are we going to take her away without her consent and how are we going to get her out of wherever it is, all that without getting ourselves killed and against the wishes of the State Department which frowns on private action, and finally, what about this threat and how we can avert it. Reminds me of some elephant jokes."

"Elephant jokes? Pray tell" Karen was acid.

"Sure, how do you pass the elephant under the door?"

"Beats me."

"First you stuff him in an envelope. After that it's easy."

"Ha-ha" said Karen, Abe Kammitzer snickered, "any more?"

"How do you seat six jewish elephants in one Volkswagen Bug?"

"In an envelope?" Karen arched her one brow, very prettily.

"Two in the front, two in the back, and two in the ashtrays" Joe continued, unflappable. "Any wish I have to go after Mustafa is heavily tempered by the multiple unknown factors in this situation. We have to analyze this problem logically, just like we attack a scientific question, and start by gathering some data concerning this agent, then consider the environment, then study the subject of the disease, then we can try and come up with a plan, to be carried out with the appropriate controls. Data, anybody?" Karen went blank at the rapid fire assault, but then reoriented.

"Yes Doctor, you got your point across, but since you put me in the know, then you must put me in the DO bracket, so that we can pool resources."

Abe Kammitzer shifted eyes in the ping-pong game of two strong personalities, each fiercely independent and confident of their self-esteem. "Shush you two" he placated both of them "this is too important to be made into an Ego match. Joe, you have your leave of absence. Karen, I'll talk with Paula and help you get the time off. What is the first move Joe?"

"I, that is we, have to find out who he is, what he does, his personality, research and movements as far as we can trace them. The first source is logically Amanda, and from there we work back as far as we can." Joe was analytic and impersonal. "If I may assign duties here then you " Joe directed at Karen "should find Amanda at the Federal Building and I should start on Dr Gottschalk."

"This is Sunday, remember?" said Karen.

"Yeah, and on sundays Dr Gottschalk likes to go to his office at the Blood

Center and do the paperwork left over from the week, so let's go downtown. Its already twelve, where shall we meet?"

Karen frowned, eyebrows arching and pretty lines forming on her smooth brow, then grinned "At the Greek Café opposite the Mosque on Wisconsin Avenue, that's appropriate!"

Joe relaxed the tension with a small laugh "alright, lets go."

They all left the small room, Abe Kammitzer to finish his rounds with the resident, Joe went for the stairs and Karen to pick up her coat. The day was bright and cold, and the brown Lesabre seat was hard again. Joe found himself whistling an old "pooh the bear " children's song while driving the old boat, God I am enjoying the call to action. The broad Wisconsin avenue reeled away on either side, the well kept houses, the bare trees, the school, the Mosque, there was the Café, then further down the old Children's Hospital building and the Blood center opposite.

Doctor Gottschalk's study door was open and soft Beethoven Ninth came through. Joe knocked and entered. Doctor Gottschalk looked up at him, and Joe noted another typically Jewish face with the bald pate and the bloodshot eyes of someone who did not get much sleep the night before, behind the thick glasses. Doctor Gottschalk motioned Joe to a chair and continued jotting fiercely on the manuscript spread out before him on the large disordered desk. Finally he crossed over a whole paragraph with a disgruntled "oof", and looked up.

"For once we don't meet in the dead of night" Doctor Gottschalk grinned good naturedly. Indeed, Joe recalled that almost every time they encountered each other it had been for a difficult blood exchange for some poor Sickler with a chest crisis, or priapism. These crises had the propensity to occur at night or to have been postponed *into* the night by indecisive house officers. "So to what do I owe the pleasure of seeing you in broad daylight?"

"Mustafa Halim" Joe answered simply.

"Why, is he sick?" Doctor Gottschalk wondered.

"No, he upped and left with his daughter, to the Middle East, leaving Amanda high and dry."

Doctor Gottschalk was incredulous "this is ridiculous, he is a great post doc, and he was doing excellent research here, why would he leave all that? I mean, we were about to offer him an extension of his position here. There must be some mistake."

Joe pulled out the letter and spread it on the pile of manuscripts . Doctor

Gottschalk read and his expression changed from the incredulous to the stormy. His fist clenched and he banged the desk, repeatedly, with increasing force. He looked up at Joe.

"This is preposterous. The staff here and myself, we treated him well, Hell, we supported him and gave him the best conditions for work and research. And what is this nonsense about Zionist this and Zionist that and retribution, retribution for WHAT... This is crazy. Anyway so he is gone, oh no, you said he took the child with him??? Oy Vey this is TERRIBLE, did you call the Police, did you call the FBI?" Joe just looked steadily at him and waited for the outburst to die down.

"Yes to both. The Police know and Amanda Carter is at the Federal Building right now. How well did you know Dr Halim?"

"Well, come to think of it not really well, he kinda kept to himself and was quiet and he let his work speak for him. I guess he was into the Muslim thing, and would go up the street a couple of times a day. He is not some kind of genius coming up with original ideas but technically he was very good." Doctor Gottschalk was getting defensive "and we produced some good papers. He was better than almost anybody at bioinformatics. I mean if you wanted to come up with DNA sequences for candidate genes then Mustafa is the best resource. He is a Genius at this stuff, candidly" Gottschalk was sheepish "I like paper better and the computer stuff is beyond me, so he is very helpful."

"What was his main focus?" Joe queried.

"Well as you know we are very big on Hematopoiesis, blood formation, and on recognition of major histo-compatibility antigens necessary for successful bone marrow transplants. Mustafa was teasing out DNA snippets that code for antigens specific for populations. You know how difficult it is to find suitable donors outside the family for minorities because even small differences in the antigenic makeup may cause severe rejection disease in transplants" Joe nodded. "So he would characterize the DNA specific to certain minorities so as to find suitable donors for them in the larger population. This is really important work. Do you remember the little Native American kid you guys transplanted from a white donor? He did not have as much rejection as you expected right? That was Mustafa's work." Joe was actually impressed, the rejections and Graft versus Host disease where the donated bone marrow attacked the body to which it was transplanted were the bane of the bone marrow transplanter's life.

"Can we go and see the lab and the computer?" Joe requested.

"Sure, its on the third floor." Doctor Gottschalk heaved himself out of the chair, he was rather heavy, and they both walked to the elevator after locking the study door.

The lab was a typical bench-top affair with instruments, pipettes, bottled fluids, shakers, and the Hewlett-Packard computer which was festooned with cables leading to instruments and peripherals. Joe eyed the computer with suspicion, it seemed like a silent watchman guarding the secrets of the departed owner. At a nod from Doctor Gottschalk he pressed the ON button and the machine whirred into life. Not for long though, after some clicking the dark screen came up with an inscription

C DRIVE NOT RECOGNIZED
A:
Joe pressed the ENTER button. the machine refused to comply
A:
A:
A:

"What does that mean?" Doctor Gottschalk said worriedly.

Joe rummaged in the drawer stack and looked for a disk. He came up with a disk marked SYSTEM and loaded it into the front slot and punched ENTER. This time the machine was more responsive and went quickly through the start-up procedure coming up with.
A:
Joe changed to the C: drive, the main repository of computer memory and the machine was compliant.
C:
DIR Joe asked.
and the machine replied.
There are O directories and O files on C.
"That means that he erased the whole hard drive, which means all the data on the disk is inaccessible or erased, or physically removed."

"OY VEY" Doctor Gottschalk almost tore at his face, vexed, "ALL the work, *all* the data, *all* the sequences, *all* the oligos, this is a catastrophe, what about backups, they are supposed to back up everything important."

Joe pointed at the external Colorado optical drive. The tray was out and there was no disk on it.

"That's gone too. Who was here Friday night?"

"I don't know, this place is open all night for the emergency transfusions and blood matching and what have you, you know the Blood Center is the major supplier of blood products to southeastern Wisconsin. We can try and ask Security but Mustafa practically *lived* here so..."

Joe frowned "why don't you go down and ask the Blood Bank people when did they see him last" and sheepishly "I'll hit the bathroom in the mean time" Doctor Gottschalk grinned, humans are humans, and they still need to go even if there is a catastrophe.

As soon as he Doctor Gottschalk left Joe donned disposable gloves from a nearby box and pulled out the Gerber multitool. He turned the computer tower around and examined the screws holding the cover. He selected the phillips bit from the tool and quickly unscrewed the back. The hard drive, a flat square device with SEAGATE sticker on it was connected via a flat wide harness. Joe disconnected it from the harness and the power supply cables and unscrewed it from the frame. The drive went into a glove and then his coat pocket and the computer tower was screwed back in no time.

Joe took the stairs down and after much back and forth in the old corridors he found the Blood Bank. The large space was sparsely occupied, after all it was still Sunday, and Doctor Gottschalk was earnestly talking to one of the technicians who had stopped the blood matching process. Across the glass divide he could see the recliners for the blood donors. Joe knew those recliners well, since he made it a rule to donate a unit every eight weeks, which was the minimum interval the Blood Bank allowed a donor between donations. The typical male walked around with hemoglobin count of 16 grams per deciliter, and functioned well with 13. Sometimes he would watch a movie while the machines extracted Platelets from his veins. He knew that those platelet donations were critical for some of the bone marrow transplant recipients and the little Preemies in the newborn nursery. In fact, it was well known that the most consistent donors to the Blood Bank were the Hematology doctors and nurses.

Doctor Gottschalk looked up at Joe, sad and concerned.

"Francine tells me that she saw Mustafa leave on Friday afternoon, and that his briefcase really looked heavy."

"Did he say anything, did he look any different?" Joe queried.

Francine, a heavy bodied blonde puckered her brow and pursed her lips. "Come to think of it he *was* different. I mean he looked happy, usually he is pretty dour, and he said goodnight real cheery-like, but nothing else, you know."

Doctor Gottschalk was getting angrier and redder. "He was *happy* to leave here and ruin all the work, and steal all the data? I don't understand that what did we ever do, what did we ever say, or imply, that would make him do such thing..." Doctor Gottschalk was getting breathless. Joe pulled a chair and gently forced him down into it and Francine raced over to the cooler for a glass of water.

"Doctor Gottschalk, this has nothing to do with you, or your conduct or the institution" Joe was very earnest and soothing, "I am sure he had his own agenda *way* before he ever made it to Milwaukee, and now this agenda, whatever it is, has matured, and he is acting on it.You must not make it personal."

"Sure its personal" Doctor Gottschalk sputtered, Francine handed him the plastic cup and he gulped from it and coughed, "I hired him, I directed him, I even gave him some *blood* for goodness sake, for one of his pet projects ..."

"What was that project?" Joe asked quietly, the voice even, the eyes slitting.

"I don't know" Doctor Gottschalk rejoined, "something about trying to figure out how come the its easier to find an unrelated donor for Jewish bone marrow transplant recipients. But that was a little aside, he never discussed publishing any of his results." Joe nodded, this might be a lead.

"Where did he come from?"

"His Masters came from the University of Tennessee, specifically from the lab of Doctor Roger Cohen at St Jude" Joe nodded some more, of course this was the institution where Amanda had trained. He glanced at the wall clock. It was already 2:30. Let's see what Karen came up with.

She was at a corner table for two, looking desultorily at the menu and stealing glances towards the glass door. The tiny vestibule which allowed the outer door to close as the inner door opens, an energy saving device which saved the clients from being frozen by an incoming blast (something European restaurants never learned!), also allowed her to see Joe coming in and whipping off his Yamaha cap. He came in looking perplexed and flopped down on the cushioned red seat, dropping his big awful-looking coat aside.

"Hi there" he said, even more perplexed.

"Hi."

"Anything real pleasant happening today?" He countered, she still had a smile on, she was very pretty, no, beautiful.

"Not really, I just sat with Amanda while they grilled her and made short hand notes to myself, why are you asking?"

"wellllll, you have this big grin like you're the cat who finished off the cottage cheese" Joe said, still perplexed.

"Oh , I didn't realize that" she puckered her brow, then brightened again "I guess I was pleased to see you, does that ever happen to you?" she asked prettily.

"I don't know " Joe said thoughtfully, looking down at his big hands "in fact I don't see why anyone should be happy to see me. All I do is hurt kids with long needles, and tell mothers their kids have cancer which might kill them, and, sometimes ask fathers to give me consent for DNR orders...". Karen's brow became thunder, and she knitted her features and her fists clenched at this discourse "and I scare young residents and interns to death by implying they don't know Jack about medicine. I am sure not happy to see *me* every damned day!" Joe lifted his gaze and was startled at the vehement features staring him down, even when she is angry she is still beautiful, he noted dispassionately.

"That was the stupidest, cruelest speech I have ever heard. Why are you so hard on yourself?" she filtered through clenched teeth, luckily because otherwise the roof might have lifted off. "You never hurt the kids, you always insist on effective sedation, you always give hope to the mothers and you are the only fellow who has the courage to ask the parents for the DNR orders, which saves the nurses from horrible resuscitation of the hopeless. The residents admire you and the interns love you! And you save lives !!" Joe was incredulous, he never thought he could arouse such intense feelings.

"Geewhiz Karen calm down, can't a person be despondent from time to time?" he laughed falsely.

"No, and I never want to hear any such nonsense from you again, what did Dr Gottschalk add to our present knowledge?"

Joe was getting used to those abrupt switches. An older woman, dressed in a Greek costume, Joe guessed she was the wife and co-owner of the café, made a cautious approach to the intense looking couple and eyed Karen with trepidation. She appeared angry enough to throw a plate at her companion, even if he was big fellow with round glasses. But then the calm on the big man's face appeared to induce a sea change in the pretty girl's features and they both smiled at her. She offered them the shiny menus and waited while they both looked at the single large card. Karen was first.

"The Sunday Special please" Karen said, handing the card back to the lady, "and Diet Sprite."

Joe followed suit "same for me but no Bacon Bits on the salad or anywhere, thank you." The lady retreated and Joe took a sip from the cold water in front of them.

"Actually Gottschalk was very helpful. He told me where they had recruited him, which was Memphis, no surprise there, and that although he was technically very good he was not a big contributor on the originality front, and that he had some kind of side show which took up a lot of his time. Also that he was a devout Muslim and was very involved with the Mosque across the street" Joe pointed his finger at the impressive structure which rose majestically, stone steps leading to magnificent doors between kneeling stone camels, it was deserted on a Sunday afternoon, the big day was Friday. "But he was very secretive and no one knew what he was up to. He avoided social gatherings saying the food was not Kosher. Speaking of Kosher here come our soup. I am always hungry even if I am despondent." He flashed his teeth but Karen did not take the bait. She could not understand how this man who was so accomplished in every material way, could have such a low self esteem. It was not low in the ususal sense, he knew the worth of his intellect, but to value himself so low such that no one would be happy to see him?! That was even worse.

Over the Greek salad with excellent Fetta cheese, and black olives and baked chicken, Karen filled Joe up on Mustafa's history as much as Amanda knew it. There was a big void before the College period, as if Mustafa was born full fledged Foreign College Student.

"My conclusion is that Amanda, that is Dr Carter, preferred not to know. She mentioned one time in which her husband talked about some massacre in the Middle East where his twin sister was hurt or killed and that is what prompted them to call the baby Alia."

"Now, *there* is a motive for revenge, did she say anything more?" Joe drowned some pepper with a large gulp of water.

"Not really, they were interested in Mustafa and his relationship with Dr Carter. Were they cold, did they fight, did they have good sex, any money problems, who are his friends, and so on. I must say they did not ask about the revenge business at all."

"Barking up the wrong tree" Joe was laconic and dismissive "the agent, was it a boy or a girl?"

"He was a nice young man" Karen said primly.

"What do you think we ought to do next?" Joe queried.

"I guess Memphis may hold some answers. Go into his records at St Jude's and work backwards" said Karen.

"Good, and what are *you* going to do?"

"Aren't we going together?"

"Not if we want to save time, we have to work in parallel. I have an idea for you. I am sure you know pastor Wilkins."

"Yes, but what about him?"

"Get us an appointment with him and see if he can make us into a couple of medical missionaries to the Middle East, fake IDs of course." Karen eyed Joe suspiciously.

"Any more illegal things?" she asked archly.

"Yes, meet again with Amanda and the nice young man. Then use your feminine charms on him to get you the names of the persons who move in and out of that Mosque." He pointed at the oriental structure.

Karen appeared baffled "why would he know such names? This is not a police state you know!! And secondly what's this about feminine charms?"

Joe was slightly amused. "Why is it if someone suggests you use one of your natural gifts to get some results its considered a vice, and if a man uses his relative advantage of physical strength its considered a virtue? You could probably get a man to help you much better than I could. Anyway, since the Twin Tower bomb blast I am absolutely certain the FBI keeps a good surveillance on active Islamic institutions, just like they keep the Kahane group under tight surveillance." Karen was baffled again "They were a extremists right wing Jewish group whose leader, Rabbi Kahane was executed by an Arab activist."

Karen sighed, pushing the plate from her, half full. "I guess there is much history and hatred to these things I shall never get used to them."

Joe was again amused. "Any time you want to bow out just tell me." Karen glowered at him so he hurried on "but don't tell me off just yet. Do you want to see my Plane?"

Karen was really taken aback "*your* plane? Are you serious?"

"Sure" said Joe "my very own plane, but not really, the bank owns it and I rent it out, but in the books it mine and I can fly it as much as I want."

"Do you really fly it yourself?" this in an almost awe-struck voice.

"Yeah, why not? its like a small car, only it flies" Joe was deprecating.

"OK OK, wise guy, you just spring more and more surprises out of that ridiculous ski cap, lets go and see the Plane."

Chapter 8

TAVASSIM

They called it "Tavas" and it was the most curious army code- name for a combat activity since it was a truism and an oxymoron all at the same time. "Tavas" was the army parlance for a small armed infantry patrol of the hostile country-side. Sometime during the Israeli occupation of Lebanon it became obvious that the usual Armored patrols were:
1. useless
2. essentially deathtraps.

The APC M-113, nicknamed Zelda, is an armored box that rolls on tracks with the main offensive weapon being the 0.5 inch heavy machine gun mounted on top. Combat personnel enter the vehicle via the posterior ramp which lowers flat for embarkation and is mechanically raised to close the box. It is a highly maneuverable in all terrains and is very adept in muddy conditions. The armor is aluminum so as to save weight and the engine is in front. The floor is lined with sand-bags (thereby obliterating any weight savings thought up by the designers, but useful to minimize land-mine damage). The real firepower of the vehicle is in the hands of the four to six soldiers whose torso, shoulder and helmet-clad heads and personal weapons protrude through the top. When the Zelda is in full charge, tracks churning, Galil assault rifles firing in bursts, and the 0.5 bucking away, it is an awe-inspiring, fearful fighting machine. When the same machine is stuck in a narrow, muddy, Lebanese alley, see-sawing back and forth trying to turn a corner, it becomes a death-trap for the crew, exposed to any well placed gunman, or RPG-7 in the hands of ill-trained youth. After taking a number of hideous casualties, the Israeli command came up with Tavasim. Small contingents of 5-6 soldiers would exit the strongholds at random intervals and scour the countryside and villages and towns of southern Lebanon. They would look for terrorist activity, search houses designated by Shabac, and ferret out "initiation points" where explosive devices were waiting for the unsuspecting patrol or transport, or water-wagon. They would walk on foot and control the land through stealth and surprise.

This was the theory.

"Tavas" translates as peacock, and the peacock is the most conspicuous of birds. Tavas was supposed to be secretive and blend with the land. That was the oxymoron, since the Lebanese girls watching the stronghold always knew when a Tavas went out. Tavas activity always included a patrol through a designated village, to show the Flag, as it were. That is when it was a peacock. There was one aspect of military activity that the Israeli Defense planners did not take into account. The Israeli troops were trained on the concept of the "Purity of the Arms" which meant that civilians, women, and children, were not to be harmed. The guerrillas had no such inhibitions and consequently the Israeli army was at a severe disadvantage. Children, schools, and Mosques, were the cover behind which the guerrillas initiated their attacks. Their fear of the armed Tavassim diminished when it became obvious that they never shot at random, and were not a system of terrorism as were the Phallanga or rival Palestinian groups.

Yossi Bergman had changed his colors a few days before. The bus from Tel Aviv discharged a typical student, shorts, sandals, and a blue teeshirt, carrying a small ruck-sack, into the melee of the Safed bus station. A group of individuals, each different but all joshing and back-clapping, in their middle twenties to early thirties, came together. The military truck, a D-500, motor badly abused by the corporal driving it, stopped at the curb and the group climbed into the back with the usual bantering about the lousy army trucks. After 30 minutes of rough riding through the hills of the Galilee, the truck entered a military installation, home base for the 801 Battalion. By this time the civilians adjusted their mind-set, they knew who had a new baby, who started a new business, who got canned out of work and who did not show up for Milu'im, the reserve duty most Israeli men endure year after year after year till they are either too old or too infirm for duty. The 801 battalion was an infantry unit, made of men in their prime, the back-bone of the Israel Defense Force, the likes of which bore the brunt of the failed occupation of South Lebanon. They spoke a multitude of languages, Hebrew and English and Russian and French. The group dismounted from the truck and immediately became a Platoon.

The Advance Detachment had arrived a day before and completed the setting up of the changeover from a bunch of students, clerks, utility linesmen etc.. into a fighting unit. The men got their KitBags with clothes that did not fit but were clean and immediately set about trading them with each other. Webbing, and helmets and coats came out for inspection. Then they lined up for their personal weapons, which were the Galil assault rifle, a hybrid between the American M-16 and the Russian Kalachnikov. Each man checked his weapon's serial number against the list and for the rest of the Milu'im would be inseparable from his baby. The minority signed for the MAG machine gun, a 12 kg pain in the neck that was designed to provide continuous covering fire for the assault troops. The MAG artists would specialize in extracting single shots, shooting from the hip, from a machine set up to fire 600 rounds a minute. They all received their complement of 7 magazines and sat down to the task of cleaning the oily magazines and filling them with 35 rounds each of ammunition. The officers started moving about solving the inevitable problems (hey, this webbing is lousy, where are the good ones?) and assumed the care of their soldiers. The cooks came up with some coffee, the thick ,black stuff in even blacker cans, veterans of many Milu'im. Lieutenant Yossi Bergman, now in olive-green fatigues with epaulets and army boots and the Galil swinging from his shoulder went off to find Headquarters for the Officer's meeting. He settled with the rest of the officers in the group that was essentially his Company on the rough benches painted inevitably in drab green.

What followed was the same old Routine. The Lieutenant Colonel came up to the podium and faced his officers. Matti Cohen was 42 year old and he had seen his share of wars and campaigns. This was going to be an onerous one because anybody not blinded by the Glory of Power could see that this Lebanon thing was one big bloody fiasco. He knew that this army was based on quick action by men of tremendous potential. This was an army that made the old BlitzKrieg a slow-motion affair. It was *not* an army that could occupy a place by instituting a state of Nazi-type terrorism. The truth always came out in the end but now the job at hand was to finish this Milu'im without any casualties. Lieutenant-Colonel Cohen stretched his pointer and slapped it hard on the 1:20,000 scale map spread behind him.

"Pipe down guys. This is Nabatiyeh and we are going to take it over from the 709 Battalion TONIGHT" Everybody craned their necks and started evaluating the Ground. "Yoram Klein , our new Intelligence officer, will give you the Land and the Forces and so on, so Pay Attention."

And so it went for the next two hours. The land, and the opposition, and the Friendlies and the Hostiles, and the Strategic Points, and location of strongholds, and Vulnerable spots, and communications, and Assignments. The men jotted down furiously in their little Koh-I-Noor spiral notebooks and soon it was lunch time and Army Rations and eating straight from the can. Finally the officers dispersed each to their Platoon to brief them about the coming 26 days.

All this was already a few days ago. The 709 Battalion people had whooped with joy as soon as the trucks rolled into the strong holds which were really a house or two surrounded with dirt perimeter walls piled up by the D-9 Bulldozer tractor. They wasted no time at all in signing the APCs and the Jeeps and Command Cars and everything Military to the newcomers, and in the meantime passed along the information critical to survival in this hostile place. "Don't go into that corner shop, even though the VCR's there are dirt-cheap, one of our guys was knifed there pretty bad, but they didn't allow us to demolish the damned place, I guess they want us to use Harsh Words" and "When you turn the corner near the Nabatiyeh cemetery, right in the center of town, watch the fence carefully because they like to throw a grenade at the Jeep, and then run through the graveyard to the Souk and disappear into the alleys. We call that turn Grenade Alley" Then they climbed into the trucks, rolled the tarps up all the way, and the hell with the wind, and pointed their guns at the perimeter. If anyone would even spit suspiciously they would open 360 degree fire, they were not going to die on the way Home.

Lieutenant Yossi checked his webbing, checked the water-bottles, grenades, checked his Topo map, flashlight, nightsight, placed his Gallil across his torso, jumped up and down to hear if anything was clicking and walked out of the bare dark room to inspect his troops for Tavas activity.

They were all ready for him, standing in a loose line, each checking his buddy's load. First he checked their weapons using a flashlight to see that chambers were empty. Then a brief explanation of the assignment, the order of movement. and Open Fire orders. They checked communications ("Yonah1 from Red Tavas how do you receive? Loud and clear you finally changed the batteries" "Go to sleep couch-potato, Red Tavas over and out"). Each of the soldiers had his special load in addition to his personal firearm. Jonathan was the Medic and carried the medical bag. Eitan was Radio, and Kadosh was Grenades. Ami carried the Russian RPG-7 anti-armor rocket launcher found in such quantities in the armories of the retreating Syrian army that there was enough to supply the whole Israeli army. Shmuel (Sam to his friends) carried extra magazines, all packed with ammunition for the Gallil. Satisfied, Yossi started ahead to the east perimeter and waited 15 minutes quietly to let his eyes adjust to the dark. It was three o'clock in the morning and they were a pre-dawn Tavas. Yossi said "Everybody, load and cock and put the safety on." The magazines were rammed in with a slap and the guns were chambered and they all felt for their safeties just to make sure. No one laughed or joked, this was the real thing.

They climbed away from the Company headquarters though the cherry trees and crossed terrace after terrace. This was a bountiful land if it were left alone and not used as a terrorist base, Yossi mused. In fact the cherries of Lebanon were famous in the Middle east. He was Point, as is the custom in the Israeli Army. Tradition dictated that the order to charge was not "CHARGE" as in other armies but FOLLOW ME. This was one of the strengths of this army because personal example was the rule. It was also the weakness of the army because the Junior Officer cadre were decimated in a real shooting war, up to thirty percent of the casualties in the Yom Kippur war were Junior officers. As they neared the houses at the top of the hill, the dogs started barking furiously and they skirted the motley hamlet. Yossi did not consult his map at all. He knew his route by heart. During officer training it was not unusual to be required to learn a 20 mile route based on the topographic map and air-photos down to the last hill, and valley, water-hole and wadi. His night vision became more and more acute and soon he felt as if he was walking in bright moon-light. It is remarkable how much ambient light is present at night.

Light was beginning to show up in the east, which made the immediate countryside darker by comparison. Yossi led the Tavas via a circuitous route to the main road, which was really a narrow ribbon of asphalt winding through the hills, following the natural terrain, as much as the old donkey route did before it was given that thin coat of asphalt. He figured that this particular spot was a great place to ambush the incoming transports, and that was his function, to prevent such side-of-the-road explosive ambushes. The Opposition had a tactic where they would fill a jerry-can with gasoline, attach a TNT block to it and imbed a primer explosive into the block. Then they would swaddle the whole thing in burlap with construction nails and hide it near the road where the road was cut into the hill so that the retaining wall would deflect the blast to the vehicle being ambushed. Then they stretched an electric cord twenty or thirty meters away and above the level of the road, up sun if possible. The initiation point was really a car battery hidden behind a large boulder, where the Fatah, or Amal, or Islamic Jihad, or any of the other splinter groups would place a 17-18 year old with a promise to be a Shahid (martyr) if he happened to die, to initiate the blast. In six Tavasim so far Joe did not find the expected ambush and he dearly hoped that he would not find one for the rest of his tour of duty.

The Tavas spread it's tail quietly and the men started moving in a wide fan, scouring the terrain.

Right where it was expected, the middle man in the 6 person contin-gent stubbed his toe against the truck battery. He stifled his curse and instead crouched. Then they all crouched. Yossi went down on his hands and knees and scooted between the boulders to Ami who had found the Point.

This was a big battery. His hands traced the wires that were hidden in the underbrush and suddenly he turned cold, the sweat that was building in his sodden shirt turning to ice in the dawn cold wind. This meant a firefight, this meant that his crew may be hit and someone may be wounded or die. On the other hand, doing nothing may spell death to the transports bringing food and water and troops.

He quietly told the others to get into an ambush configuration and followed the wires to the road below. It was lucky they ran into the battery because these wires were well hidden. The charge itself was concealed behind a roadside bush below an overhang. This was the proverbial death-trap. Yossi crawled back up the slope and joined his Tavas. They had the Galill bipod out - that would give them better stability for long bursts. The RPG-7 was loaded and ready. The heavy loads were off their backs and they were ready to charge. Yossi pressed the phone to his ear.

"Yonah 1 from Red Tavas do you read" he whispered.

"This is Yonah1, what's up?"

"We found an Initiation Point on hill number 225, ambush is set, radio silence from now on."

"Roger that Red Tavas, giv'em Hell."

Joe knew that the whole section will now come alive, Company roused, Battalion alerted, Division notified. But tradition dictated that he was on the Ground, he was in charge, and additional forces would come in only if he called for them. Otherwise this was his show. All this has happened a hundred times before, mostly the would-be bombers would not show up and the Engineers would be called to dismantle the charge. Joe settled down to wait and see if his quarry would show up. The wind blew colder and he shivered. His thoughts wondered to his cozy apartment in TelAviv, 100 yards away from the warm Mediterranean, medical books, magazines, papers strewn around, and the occasional girl trying her luck in taking Yossi away from Singlehood. Jewish mothers taught their daughters that they aught to marry a Doctor, and some girls were persistent. The men all cocooned in their thoughts and remained alert because the light was coming on fast.

They were four men and they were heavily loaded. One carried an RPD

0.3 inch machine-gun, another, two boxes of ammunition, One had a Kalachnikov and a backpack full of, probably, Grenades. The fourth who kept looking around was the leader. They all wore the uniform thick Islamic-mandated beard, black-and-white checkered Keffieh wrapped around the head and neck, and multi-patch jungle commando fatigues. They were young, devout, and they were going to kill lots of Israelis today. Their watchers on the border had called on the phone (The stoopid Israelis never destroyed the Nabatiyeh telephone exchange) to say that a convoy was heading in the Nabatiyeh direction and no one had seen any patrols nearby. They had had their Blessings bestowed by the Kadi who promised them that if they are killed in battle then they would each become a Shahid and as such would go directly to Heaven filled with beautiful large-breasted women and food and drink no end. They were spiritually ready to fight and die if needed. Lieutenant Yossi watched them from behind a boulder and a bush and agonized how to spread his fire-power best and avoid casualties. He felt the crushing burden of responsibility towards his boys' mothers, wives, girlfriends, to bring them back safely. The anticipation built up inexorably and he waited for the sun to come up behind him and blind his quarry, just like they had planned in setting up the ambush. This was what he had been trained for. His Tavas had practiced this scenario before and each knew his part. The first rays of the sun shone through the haze, the sounds of heavy diesel motors crept up from the distance, silencing the chirping of the early morning birds and it was time to strike.

Yossi snicked the safety off, touched his chin to check for the helmet strap and raised his Galil to eye level then raised himself silently above the boulder. His soldiers, students, shopkeepers, taxidrivers, followed suit. He aimed at the Guerrilla leader who at that very moment swivelled around and looked him straight in the eye through the slit in his kaffieh. The warning cry died in the short burst and the shells spewed from the Galil. The young man appeared to be picked up and slammed back against the boulders behind. He did not fire a shot. The Gallils around him joined the fire and the ricochets were whizzing into the stones and the earth and the people. The other three guerrillas were better hidden and disappeared from view immediately. Suddenly a single Kalachnikov, a different cadence and tune opened up, wildly inaccurate. Yossi stopped his fire and screamed, "Kadosh, shnei rimmonim (two grenades)." Kadosh, the small sun-burnt Yemenite was ready. He twisted the ring, pulled the pin, released the boom and counted 21,22 and threw the grenade like a pitcher. They all hit the deck. The explosion threw dirt and as it did another grenade went the same way. Joe raised his head slowly and a burst of fire exploded just to his right. There was no alternative but to assault. Kadosh and Jonathan both had grenades ready and he signaled them to throw. Yossi changed his magazine, slapped it in, and cocked his weapon.

The four explosions were close together. The damage to the enemy unknown. His heart was in his mouth and the taste of fear was metallic. Yossi jumped to his feet suddenly weightless. His boots were winged. He screamed "**AHARAI** (follow me)" and started running, his Gallil coming up to his shoulder and his finger pumping the trigger for the short bursts, three-four at a time. The black and white Kaffieh was just ahead and the rest of the body was shielded. The sun's rays highlighted everything, the grey basaltic boulders, the eye-slit in the Keffieh, the Kalachnikov barrel jumping up and the fireflash issuing from it. The range shortened impossibly slowly, Then the head blew apart and the brains spattered, and the Kalachnikov barrel pointed skywards. The machine gun was atop the boulder and a lone hardy man was trying to rotate it towards the storming troops. The Tavas was now fully open, feathers spread, spewing fire and they assaulted onto the machine gun emplacement. And then it was over, the Tavas overran the position and the man was draped over the gun, blood slowly pumping from a big hole in the neck. Yossi looked right and left but there was no one standing or hiding and his troops were all safe. He started breathing again and realized that he had stopped breathing right after the FOLLOW ME scream.

Suddenly the road below was alive with Jeeps and command-cars and soldiers who converged on the small hair-pin turn. The Thwap-thwap of the helicopter came over the ridge. Yossi felt like he weighed a hundred tons and his helmet was a dead weight, and his knees nearly buckled under. He turned the safety on and called his troops together. They all looked beat, loosened their helmets off, and observed their handi-work. Four men, creatures in the form of the Lord, were reduced to insignificant bundles of flesh, wrapped in bloody garments. Lieutenant General Matti Cohen, in green fatigues, jumped out of the leading Jeep and stormed up the hill. Behind him, the Engineering bomb-squad approached the explosive device carefully. Matti came up and demanded "any casualties?"

"None sir" said Yossi, finally beginning to grasp the achievement, this group of guerrillas had been the terror of the transports for months. He was awash in relief.

"So what's this?" said Matti and pointed at Yossi's own sleeve. It was sodden with blood and suddenly Yossi felt the sting and pain spreading from his upper arm.

"Oh its probably a scratch" he replied lightly, "Jonathan will take care of it on the spot."

Jonathan, who had emigrated to Israel from South Africa, went back for his medic bag which he had discarded before the battle, and produced the scissors. Yossi sat back on a boulder and looked semi detached as the sleeve was cut and the gash exposed. It was really beginning to hurt now.

"The bullet went through, it needs to be stitched" Jonathan told him breathlessly.

"OK, put a bandage on it for right now, don't exaggerate" Yossi told him off testily.

The hillside was starting to look like a football field after the win of the home team except that everyone was in Olive-green. The helicopter landed nearby and now it was the Aluf (General) who lumbered up the hill, surrounded by a veritable army of senior officers, radio bearers, intelligence etc.. The local villagers came out and watched the Army people milling about and two lines of cars, donkey-carts and lorries formed behind the road-block placed in both directions. His wound dressed, Yossi described the short battle to the Aluf who cross questioned him frequently until he had the whole picture. Other soldiers collected the armamentarium of the dead guerrillas and others picked through their pockets to look for identification and organizational affiliation. They were Islamic Jihad, and they carried orders from Fat'hi Shkaki, the military chief of the Jihad. Yossi left that part to the experts, it was time to extricate his troops from the Victors Hoopla and come down to earth. Major Levy, the grizzled veteran company commander, gave him his nod. Anyway, he felt a little disgusted with the whole bone-picking-after the fact deal.

"All right you couch-potatoes, breakfast is over and its time to continue Tavas, we are scheduled till eleven AM and its only eight O'clock." Kadosh and Eitan looked at him with dismay and started protesting. Yossi steadied his gaze on them and the protest died down.

"Line up for Tavas" they lined up along the road, each checked their magazines, the medical bag, water and grenades. Yossi checked each weapon for safety on, and then he strode down the road. His Gallil soon settled into the usual position, horizontal across the belly, pointing left, right hand resting lightly on the handle, metal stock under the arm, and the left on the barrel, both elbows at 90 degrees. His pace quickened and soon the characteristic swinging gait, butt pumping and arms on the weapon reestablished itself. This was the seven kilometers per hour gait that ate up the distances while the mind flew to other regions. Tavas spread out behind him, emulating the gait and pace of the leader, heads high, scanning the houses that sprouted on either side of the road. Yossi looked back and his chest expanded at the sight of the troops. The job was a stinking job, but the men were 100 percent, and then some. He was proud to be at their head. Now the Tavas was showing the Flag. This village knew what had gone on only a mile out of town and they knew that these guys were not to be messed with. As they walked though the center of the village Yossi could feel the resentment, and the hate emanating from half-opened windows, the dark staircases, and the veiled eyes of the hooded women. All this was a folly and it had to stop - but not today.

The last shop in town was a coffee shop and the old men were already sitting at the low copper tables drinking thick black coffee from tiny porcelain cups. Yossi nodded in a friendly manner and flexed his shoulder which now sported a cut-off sleeve and a thick blood-stained bandage. He turned off the road and climbed the hill behind the last houses towards the trees half way up the slope. It was time for late breakfast.

Even in repose they were not relaxed. They had their Gallils propped across their knees, and pulled out the water canteens. Kadosh fished for some sandwiches from the Grenade ruck-sack. Sam opened a spare magazine pouch and pulled a folded Iraqui Pitah and dug into it with gusto. Yossi sat on a terrace-stone a few meters above and surveyed the countryside from his vantage point. His water-bottle actually contained cold coffee and he relished the sweetness that flooded his mouth. The sun climbed higher and it was a wonderful day to be alive. The extra magazine pouch yielded a chocolate wafer which appeared pulverized, probably due to the early morning antics. He opened the wrapper and gobbled up the wafer dust that spilled out. The breeze was soft, and the cherry trees produced a sweet shadow and everything appeared etched in sharp relief. He saw a young girl on one of the flat roofs hanging some clothes on a line and pulled the eight power binoculars. She came into view, a sinuous figure, her hair uncovered, falling in long wavy black stresses down her back. The hair shone in the sun and he was captivated. Yossi thought of calling the troops to the sight and then felt almost jealous . She was his, if only for a second, across three hundred meters of line of sight. The girl turned and looked right at him, although there was no way she could see him in the shadow. She smiled and talked to someone and then disappeared into the house. Yossi put the binoculars down and suddenly tensed.

The back door of the building which he knew to be the coffee house, the same building on which roof the girl had done her magic, opened, and a man came out. Yossi immediately scanned him with the binoculars and saw a tall man, dressed in a long white Abaya and the Keffieh, checquered in black and white coiled on his head, leaving his face open for inspection. It was a handsome middle-aged face with a handle-bar moustache. He had a grey blazer on and carried a flat copper tray perfectly balanced. The tray returned a blaze of sun light, and there were 7 cups and a carafe of polished copper with a thin spout and a long round handle. The man started ascending the terraces and approached the troops. Yossi pursed his lips and uttered a short whistle. The soldiers looked up from their food, then grabbed their guns and pointed them towards the lonely figure. The young girl appeared on the roof again and cried something. The man ignored the cry and pushed on up the hill. The soldiers spread out in a semi circle.

"What's going on?" Eitan asked Joe who maintained his outward calm.

"Don't know, maybe he wants to offer us coffee."

"Fat chance" Eitan guffawed and was joined by the rest of the Tavas "next he will offer us his daughter, ha-ha." Joe crinkled his mouth but his eyes did not smile, and the slits became narrower. He left his Gallil where it was, a stick resting on a stone. The man came up and passed Jonathan who followed him with his gun barrel, and, short of breath, came up to Yossi. Yoseph Bergman steadied his gaze through those dangerous narrow eyes on the guile-less face.

The man did not speak at all. His deep-brown left hand supported the burnished beaten copper plate and his right held the carafe. He poured a small measure into each of the small white earless cups, thick black hot brew which wafted vapour in the cool air under the cherry trees. The smell of fresh brewed coffee was intoxicating. He looked at Yossi and Yossi looked right back at him. The man placed the carafe in the middle of the plate and took one cup . He sipped the coffee daintily and looked at Yossi again. Yossi smiled hugely and took a cup. The coffee was strong, sweet, and delicious.

"Come on guys, be courteous, take some coffee" Yossi said loudly. One by one, initially with suspicion and then with relish, the soldiers lowered their weapons and came up to the aromatic brew.

"Assiez avec nous, Monsieur s'il vous plait" Yossi's french was high-school stilted but in Lebanon the French influence had been very strong and it was likely that an educated local would understand.

"What is your name?" Yossi continued.

"Je suis Ahmad Abu Rabi'a and I own the Café that you go by every day." Ahmad's voice was quiet, mellow, well enunciated French with an Arabic accent.

"Et moi je m'appelle Yoseph Bergman, Merci Bien pour le Café" continued Yossi "but why? This has never happened to anybody in this sector."

Ahmad paused and looked down to the village spread along the narrow road and haphazardly over the hillside.

"Because your group here is different, you never harass anybody like some other patrols, you leave us alone as long as we leave you alone, and you don't act like you own the place. I thought some common courtesy would be a nice change especially since you are sitting in my orchard, and doing no harm, that makes you my guests." Yossi quickly translated and they shifted a little uncomfortably. Suddenly each of them thought of how it would feel if a strange armed person would start walking around *their* back yard.

"On the other hand" continued Ahmad "I am not sorry you gave the Palestinian Jihad some of their own medicine. Do you have any idea how these people harassed us before you came? They made the women wear Chadors, they beat up on enfants who did not go to the mosque on Friday, they evicted families from their homes to establish bases, we would gladly be rid of them *and* the Israeli army, but Lebanon is too weak to resist occupation by some foreign force" he added bitterly. "If it's not the Palestinians, it's the Iranians or Syrians." Yossi nodded with understanding while sipping his coffee and translated for the troops. It was quite wonder-ful to see how their expressions slowly morphed from suspicion and a little xenophobic fear, to understanding and empathy.

"Monsieur" said Yossi "we have no wish whatsoever to be here and if I am not mistaken no one wants to be here unless as tourists. It's the Government which is making a huge mistake, that is sending us here, and we try to be as humane as we can while here. On the other hand I can tell you monsieur that life in Kiryat Shemona and Nahariah just south of the border was terrible as long as the Fatah was doing the Katyusha work every day, and that's why we were sent" Ahmad listened and sighed.

"Le problem est, monsieur le Capitain, That we are all little people who do not have much influence over the Government, what can you and I do?"

Yossi replied very seriously "first we can do something by being Humans while we are here and Primum Non Nocere as I was taught in Medical School (first, do no harm). Secondly, the citizens of Israel are not going to tolerate this folly for much longer. I expect a withdrawal within a year, see if I am wrong."

A high pitched yell broke through the air, and Ahmad shifted his attention to the roof where his daughter was gesticulating.

"I must leave" he said quickly "don't stay too long, some one may see." Ahmad collected his porcelain cups, each rimmed with coffee granules and quickly strode down the hill, around the terraces. They all followed him, a solitary figure disappearing down the slope and the spell of friendly conversation broke. The Tavas hefted their loads and rifles and groaning they resumed their trek up hill.

They had just crested the hill and started down the other side when the sound of 3 rapid-fire gunshots erupted. Yossi whirled and then his face contorted with rage and he started running wildly back the way he had come. The Tavas wheeled around and followed their suddenly mad leader. Yossi was going down the hill like leopard charging toward his prey, around the trees, over the boulders, over the terraces. It seemed impossible that he would not slip, or stumble and fall, but he did not. The Tavas could not keep up and Jonathan screamed at Yossi to slow down but he did not. He reached the wall separating the house from the orchard and leaped over it with a mighty bound. He soon disappeared around the house. Silence. Then the Shriek of a young woman pierced the air and went on and on with whoops to take more air and shriek some more. The Tavas rounded the corner at a dead run and stopped in their tracks.

Ahmad was lying in the middle of the narrow street, obviously shot at close range, and his daughter was on her knees shrieking her head off. Yossi was at his side feeling for the pulse at the neck and shaking his head, his face a mask of rage and sorrow. "Spread out" he yelled at his immobile troops "someone shot him and they may still be around. Eitan, get Company on the radio."

"Yonah1 from Tavas Red."

"Reading you 5 Tavas Red. over."

Yossi grabbed the mike "we are on the west end of complex 'Yaarit' " he referred to the names given to the village on the IDF code map designated SECRET, "we have a man shot here, send ambulance and reinforcements."

"Who is hurt Tavas Red."

Yossi exploded "What does it matter *who* is hurt, send it right away, over."

"OK, OK keep your cool, I'll call KodKod right now, This is Yonah1 over and out" squeaked the speaker.

"Tavas Red. this is KodKod , who is down?" That was Major Yacov Levy, the Company commander.

Yossi was already busy tearing off Ahmad's clothing to reveal the three entry wounds, one to the chest, one to the belly and one in the shoulder. They were inaccurate even from zero range. He decided that he must move Ahmad away from the middle of the street where any sniper could pick them off, so he and Jonathan quickly scooped the wounded man and dragged him to the shade of the deserted Café. Jonathan opened his medical bag, and spread out the IV fluid bag and started looking for an IV site. Joe motioned to Ami and Kadosh and   Sam to watch for hostiles and felt for the pulse again. It was steady but weak and thready. The girl stopped screaming and watched wide eyed the soldiers taking care of her father. The street was otherwise deserted, everybody else ran for cover as soon as the shots were fired, and Ahmad would have bled to death right there. Eitan answered the call.

"KodKod, this is Tavas Red it's a local."

"Tavas Red, this is their business leave the place immediately."

Yossi took the mike. Jonathan found an IV site in the neck and stuck the Venflon into it. He removed the steel needle and slid in the plastic catheter. He secured it with tape and connected the Saline fluid to it. Yossi said "let it run" and Jonathan recalled that Yossi was a medical student. Yossi was more composed now and replied.

"Kodkod Yonah This is Tavas Red, he was a local contact and there may be other armed hostiles here. We must search the village NOW."

"Roger that Tavas Red, we are on our way, doctor from Battalion will join us."

Jonathan was dressing the belly wound and the chest wound. Yossi turned to the girl. As soon as he turned towards her she jumped up and screamed something in Arabic, short and hateful, and ran off down the street to disappear into one of the bare buildings. Yossi looked after her with a grim face and stopped Ami who moved to pursue her. "Let her go Ami, I guess she thinks we are responsible for her father's injury."

The convoy of Jeeps and Command cars and a couple of APCs roared into view. The drab-grey ambulance with a Magen David painted in red came up and stopped by Yossi and Jonathan. The medics jumped out and under the direction of Doctor Yigal placed the wounded man on the stretcher. He appeared to be stable, loss of blood but no foaming at the mouth. Soldiers were everywhere, running into the buildings and searching for firearms. This was a nasty business of breaking into peoples homes and searching through their property, upturning beds, rolling over sick elderly, and going through closets to look for guns and grenades. Yossi became numb, this was too much for one day, he and his Tavas needed to be relieved.

"Busy morning, eh?" Yacov Levy slapped Yossi's shoulder, right above where it still stung from the early morning assault. Yossi winced.

"Yeah, get us out of here OK?" he said.

"Hey, you earned it, You guys are gonna get the day off, I wouldn't want you to use up all your luck in one day." Yacov gave Yossi his well-used grin. "Go on the second command-car and keep your eyes skinned." Yossi nodded, Ahmad was in good hands and maybe the terrorist who tried to kill him solely because he had carried a civilized discourse with Israelis would still be caught. Not that it made any difference. For each one you got there were a thousand who walked around with a death-wish. This country drove you crazy, so pretty, yet so dangerous, full of people so different, some tolerant, most hateful. Yossi wished he was not mired here with the rest of his generation.

The Tavas folded wings and tail and climbed aboard the open command-car, six hard seats set back-to-back, guns pointing out. One could not let one's guard down even for a second in this bloody country.

This had been the twilight of the Invasion. Yossi had no idea that one day he may need come back to this accursed place. And he was very wrong about the withdrawal. 15 years later the Israelis were still mired in Lebanon, fighting the same war, only the enemies had changed names. If it was not the Fatah, then it was the Hezzbolah, backed by the fundamentalist capital of the world, Iran. But it was all the same. Fanatic Islamic terrorists devoid of inhibitions versus a modern army hobbled by humanitarian principles.

The only beneficiaries of the Invasion were the migrating birds, the Eagles and the Herons and the Ducks, which, from times immemorial, migrate south in fall to their African winter grounds over Turkey and Lebanon and Israel. When Fatah-land was abounding in guns, the birds were shot at and downed for their feathers or to relieve boredom. Once most of these guns were confiscated and the illegal ones kept under wraps the yearly Golden Eagle count which was run by the SPNI in Israel, after long years of decline, began to increase from 1982. The Human casualties continued to mount inexorably.

Chapter 9

DNA games

Science and warfare have always marched hand in hand, especially in the 20th century. Some of the greatest inventions were devised initially for war-purposes, or received their greatest boost from a war. Some of the most notable political developments stemmed from scientific develop-ment. The Zionist movement received a tremendous political boost from the Balfour declaration, a 1917- slip-of-the-tongue delivered by a British foreign minister who enunciated His Majesty's favourable view of a Jewish homeland in Palestine. This declaration was given prior to the inception of British mandate over Palestine, as a special thanks to a Jewish Zionist chemistry scientist, Haim Weitzman, whose inventions were largely responsible for the success of Allied war efforts in the First World War. The declaration caused a paradigm shift in the Jewish populance, so deep, that decades after Britain reneged on all it's promises to the Jews, it was still considered an ally to the Zionist movement. The Palestinian Jewish population as a whole turned to serve the British war effort against the Ottoman Turkish empire, and General Allenby was received by the Jews as a hero. 25 years later Hitler recognized the power of science and established Science Cities, specifically for weapon development, such as Peenemunde, where modern rocketry achieved prominence and the first Jet aircraft were devised. It was just as well that Hitler rejected Jewish Science, such as particle and Atomic physics, causing the pre-eminent scientists of the era such as Enrico Fermi and Albert Einstein to flee to America. The combination of an effective delivery system (the V-2 rocket) and an Atomic bomb in the hands of the Supreme Murderer is un-imaginable.

The development of chemical and biological warfare has paralleled that of other means of destruction, but has achieved much less success. The German army tried the use of low-tech Chlorine gas in the first world war, with limited success. The heavier than air substance simply sank into the fox-holes and the shell craters and could be overcome by low tech masks. Various gases were developed over the years, the most notorious of which are the nerve gases. These gases penetrate the skin with ease, and interact with enzymes of the peripheral nervous system so that the victim is flooded with his own secretions. These gases were never the decisive instruments that the war-lords desired. The effect is dose-dependent, the delivery is variable depending on the atmospheric conditions and the incoming troops who would follow such a gas attack would need the same protection as the intended victims. The gases were reduced to a marginal use as weapons of mass panic against uneducated or unprepared civilian population. The Iraqis used gases against the Kurds, and The AUM Shinrikio used Sarin gas to scare Japanese commuters in the Tokyo underground, killing 12, and injuring hundreds. Israel's fears of Iraqi gas attacks during the Gulf war never materialized. In a situation such as Israel where the Arab population centers are only a few miles away, and the Mediterranean breeze carries gases inland from the coastal plain, it is obvious that any gas attack is bound to affect the Arab neighbours, even as they were dancing on the rooftops at the sight of SCUDS raining on Tel Aviv.

Mustafa had spent countless days in the libraries, and endless hours on the Internet in the search of a weapon. He defined his problem as follows

1. Sensitivity- the target has to be sensitive to the weapon so that the most minimal exposure would maim or kill. The sensitivity to a bomb depends on the distance from the blast, the obstacles to the spread of the blast shock wave etc.. The simple expedient of taping the windows of a house with paper will enhance the destructiveness of an explosive charge placed inside. In chemical warfare the concept of sensitivity is measured as LD 50, the dose which is lethal for 50% of a given population. In biological terms the LD 50 is the number of bacteria (or virus, or plasmodium) that will infect and kill 50% of the hosts. This is a highly variable number, as some people have a much higher sensitivity to certain organisms than others. The appropriate Immunization reduces sensitivity to Measles to almost zero. Atomic weapons are the essence of sensitivity and lethality. If the gamma radiation, or the heat radiation, or the shock-wave will not get you, then leukemia will, a few years down the line.

2. Specificity- how likely it is that the intended victim will be the one actually affected, rather than the bystander. A knife is almost completely specific, hurting only the victim but doing no harm to his neighbour. A bomb is much less specific as many terrorist attacks have shown. Of the 60 victims murdered by the Palestinian Hamas suicide bomb attacks on Jerusalem city buses in March of 1996, fully a third were not the intended victims, that is Jewish civilians, but rather Rumanian workers, East Jerusalem arab shoppers, Arab cab drivers etc... Chemical weapons are notoriously non-specific since

there is no ethnic nervous systems specificity. Waterborn bacteria are attractive since theoretically they may be limited to the water systems into which they are introduced, but actually they are very likely to spread to the population with the lower sanitary standards.

In fact the problem of specificity is so difficult that it proved to be the Palestinian downfall, since the refugees were advised to separate them-selves from the Jewish population lest they be trampled under the tracks of the victorious Arab armies. Atomic weapons are likewise non-specific. An atomic bomb on Tel Aviv (the wet pipe-dream of the Iraqi, Iranian and Syrian regimes) is very likely to kill as many Arabs in Israel and ultimately in the Middle East due to water and soil contamination.

3. Delivery. In order to be both sensitive (or lethal) and specific, the weapon must be delivered precisely to the target. Most of the military research the world over is devoted to the FedEx V UPS problem of fast, accurate delivery. The ship, airplane, rocket, machine-gun and cross-bow are instruments of delivery. The most accurate and fast ones require the resources of the superpowers to develop, and a high level of technical sophistication. Only a handful of countries have the resources to develop and maintain an intercontinental missile, or an advanced aircraft, or an atomic-powered submarine. Precise targeting can be achieved with a Tomahawk Cruise missile delivering an explosive war head through a specific window, and even then it is only as good as the Intelligence report that directed the choice of target. These instruments address the questions of sensitivity and specificity by the choice of warhead, be it high explosive, napalm, or neutron bomb. Even fewer countries are able to deliver a booby-trapped cellular phone into the hands of a specific enemy, such as the "engineer" Yihyeh Ayash (the mastermind behind many of the suicide bombers of city buses in Tel Aviv and Jerusalem) and activate it only when he places it next to his ear.

Gas is very tricky to store and deliver in significant quantities. On the other hand, bacteria and viruses are extremely easy to transport and deliver. Every person or animal in the world is a huge portable storehouse of microbes by his very existence. We carry a veritable zoo of enteric bacteria in our gut, and respiratory pathogens in our throat. And the quantity is not significant since these agents self-replicate. Truly pathogenic bacteria such as Bubonic plague or Anthrax are harder to carry around because they need very precise growth media. These potential weapons require a high level of scientific sophistication, placing them beyond the capabilities of the average rogue regime, which typically abhors scientists.

The ideal weapon, Mustafa surmised, must be lethal, with a minute exposure causing major damage, easily delivered into enemy territory or personnel, and absolutely selective for the target. The last point absolutely stumped him. In order to be lethal any conceivable agent must damage a major body system, and as Shakespeare had lamented 400 years ago "Has not a Jew eyes" and "When you cut us, do we not bleed", in every material way, a Jew is identical to an Arab, or an American, or an Eskimo. Mustafa did not consider the obscure concepts of 'civilian' versus a 'combatant'. The Jewish occupation of Palestine and Jewish control of Jerusalem Al Kuds (the holy) was a blasphemy and must be removed. If the constant harassment, boycotts, bus-bombing, café-blasting, and political maneuvering did not convince them that Palestine was out-of-bounds for them, then another means must be found. One did not have to kill ALL of them. Only a sufficient proportion that would scare them away. From his point of view, the Western nations had foisted the Jews on Arab Palestine, and they should take them back, somehow, or else. Mustafa did not consider that most Israelis did not feel that they had anywhere to go.

His model was the Exodus. The book of Numbers, the second of the 5 holy books of the old testament tells how the Israelites, who were enslaved for 210 years, left Egypt, and were actually hustled out in the dead of night by the ruling Pharaoh. This Pharaoh and his people had withstood painful and expensive misfortunes administered by the Lord, including contamination of the Nile, pest attacks, debilitating illnesses and even a full solar eclipse. The pestilence that finally brought the message home was the death of each and every firstborn, 'From the Prince on his throne to the firstborn of the most lowly slave'. With a tremendous uproar the Egyptian people forced Pharaoh to kick the Israelites to their freedom. THAT was the type of blow that Mustafa hoped to deliver, a knock-out, a solution to the Jewish problem of the Middle-East.

As Mustafa matured in his knowledge of life sciences the goal appeared more and more elusive. Life is made of abundant chemicals which interact in incredibly complex ways. There are 4 main families of molecules which make up life. Proteins, sugars, lipids, and nucleic acids. Generally speaking, lipids (fats) make up the membranes, sugars provide energy, nucleic acids are information repository, and the proteins provide the lattice, movement and the metabolic engines. The functions of sugars and lipids have been under investigation the longest, and they are totally controlled by the presence and activity of protein enzymes. The proteins themselves are complex molecules made up of 20-some building blocks, called amino acids, just as words, sentences , paragraphs, are made up of 20 odd letters. The sequence of the each protein determines its three-dimensional shape, and the way it interacts with other proteins. The most visible example are the proteins that make up muscles. With the app-lication of energy they interact to shorten the length of the muscle and work gets done. The all-important protein sequence is encoded in the Nucleic Acid molecules, DNA and RNA, which reside in the cell nucleus. There are only 4 standard building blocks here, stretched along a doubled sequence. Specific combinations of any three such blocks, encode one amino acid, just as a combination of 5 dots and dashes encodes a specific letter in the Morse telegraph code. A length of DNA which encodes a complete protein is called a gene. DNA can replicate itself exactly with the aid of the right enzymes, and thus preserves the Genetic code of a species and of individuals.

The DNA molecule is at once simple and incredibly complex because the sequence hides, in addition to the genes, many obscure codes, for start, and stop, and redundancies etc.. Learning the sequence of DNA is just like reading a book made up of only 4 letters, with no spaces, paragraphs, or any punctuation marks The advent of computers, statistics and informatics by computer has leapfrogged the understanding of Life tremendously, but to put things in perspective, only in 1997 was the first nucleated organism, all 6000 genes of it, completely sequenced, and the real work of finding out how 6000 genes interact, really begun. However, some sequences are unique to species, and families, and even individuals. Crime laboratories can scoop up DNA from the site, that present in blood, or in skin cells, and prove with a high degree of confidence, that a specific person had been at the site.

Mustafa knew of many poisons, that is chemicals and proteins that adversely affect a life form. For instance, Botulinum toxin is a protein produced by a bacteria, that affects nervous and muscular tissue, and has been a favorite of bacteriological warfare developers. Antibiotics are chemicals devised by molds and later synthesized by humans, that kill bacteria. Bacterial systems are sufficiently different from the mammalian systems, that they can be eaten by the mammal without adverse effect, while still killing the bacteria. Poisoning mammals is much more difficult, because all the poisons known to affect pests such as mice, are equally lethal to humans, since they affect the same metabolic system. That is because the affected proteins are identical across animal species, and the genes' DNA sequences are almost identical. The most important Life-essential protein are the most conserved, that is unaltered, throughout the Life kingdoms, so that a muscle proteins are virtually the same in humans and insects. Although some chemicals may be more detrimental to some   human ethnic groups than others, there is no poison that would uniformly affect any ethnic group.

Add that to the fact that the Jews were NOT an ethnic group, but rather, a amalgam of people who believed in the same set of rules given to them, so they said, by the Divine. Some were clearly of Indian origin, some clearly European, and a huge proportion were refugees from North Africa and Syria and Iraq, kicked out of those countries by the Arab regimes after the 1948 war, in failed effort to cause an inward collapse of the fledgling Jewish state under the sheer number of refugees. Many of them carried the genetic traits typical of their former homes, such as Thalassemia in the Middle Eastern Jews, and Breast cancer in European descent women. Israel is much like the American Revolution in essence, an ethnic melting pot, with a common set of principles and purpose. This diversity became the strength of Israel, and made the concept of a biologic weapon specific to Jews a farce.

Mustafa went trolling through the Internet. Genomics and the com-puter revolution were born together and were eminently suited to each other. Just as the computer basic language is made up essentially of two signals, 1 and 0, and any computer interaction is made up of a specific sequence of these two signals, so is the genetic information made up of only 4 bases. One of the most ambitious scientific programs of all time, carried in true cooperation by all industrialized nations, is the Human Genome Project, the sequencing and understanding of the human genome, all 60-150 thousand genes of it. The rules of scientific Genomics discovery, especially if funded by the US government, include posting the newly sequenced genes on the Internet. Any investigator with a computer and a modem, with access to the telephone system anywhere in the world, may look through the published sequences and compare them with a newly discovered sequence of interest. Some sequences, whose functions are known, are recognized as common to many genes, and confer a specific activity to the encoded protein. Thus, someone who studies a sequence of DNA isolated from a cancer cell , in Memphis, USA, may compare it to a published sequence of a muscle cell isolated in Kiel, Germany. The computer may then look for some common motifs, similar sequences, which may hint at the function of the protein. Mustafa had been doing exactly that through his work at Dr Cohen's laboratory, isolating proteins likely to contribute to cancer, deducing DNA sequences, searching for similar sequences in databases. During his day time job he collected blood samples from volunteers, and potential bone marrow donors, from which he carefully culled those likely to be of Jewish origin. His night time job was looking for a published sequence that designated a cancer or disease linked to the Jewish Genome, if such existed. Upon moving to the Blood Center in Wisconsin he was allowed closer to his quest. His main theme was to characterize the immune specifics of ethnic groups. The science of bone marrow transplant is really the science of immune recognition. Every person inherits from his biological parents a bunch of DNA sequences which code for the Major Histocompatibility Antigens. Those are proteins imbedded in the cell membrane of the immune system cells which allow them to characterize a cell as "self" or "Non self". That is how they know to attack a foreign cell and spare the body cells. After transplant the incoming immune cells are likely to view the new host as foreign and initiate the dreaded Graft Versus Host disease. They will not do that if the host appears to them as "self" and that occurs if the Major Histocompatibility Antigens are identical. Identical antigens can be found in identical twins and in some siblings, brothers and sisters. Since in the industrialized countries the families tend to be small, then 70 percent of the patients who might benefit from a Bone Marrow transplant do not have a donor in their family, and must look for an unrelated donor.

The Eighties and Nineties saw a tremendous growth in the number of Bone Marrow transplant procedures, numbering into the thousands per year world wide. The US navy first developed the capacity to type, extract and store viable bone marrow but soon the technology took off and a national and international repositories of marrow information and samples grew to accommodate the need. Initially these Bone Marrow banks relied on the old fashioned antigenic typing procedure. This method was slow and imprecise. It was soon obvious that for certain populations it was relatively easy to find suitable donors, persons whose Antigens "matched" those of the intended recipient. Since Minnesota is rather homogeneously Nordic, and the number of prospective volunteer donors is exceedingly high, then the chances of finding a donor for a kid of Nordic extraction are pretty high. Similarly, it turned out to be relatively easy to find a match for a Jewish person since the number of volunteer donors who had registered in the NMDP and other banks such as in Canada and Israel is tremendous. On the other hand, finding a donor for a Lac Du Flambeau native Ame-rican is essentially impossible. Such patients necessitate a 'Blood Drive' , collection of hundreds of samples from family and neighbors of the same ethnic group , which, more often than not, fails to find a "match". The advent of the ability to amplify specific strands of DNA and sequence them allowed typing to be precise and automated. On the one hand many more samples could be processed and the pool grew larger, on the other hand the precision limited further the number of true "matches". Therefore certain "mismatches " were allowed with the hope that the harm caused will be minimal. Characterization of Ethnic Flags, as it were, would make the precise typing much more efficient because it would reduce the number of prospective donors to the more likely ones. Mustafa went hunting specifically for the Jewish Antigens, there by to achieve the specificity he required for his weapon.

Years later he conceded failure. The Jewish antigens were a complete mess. Sure, you could find some ordered similarity in Jews of specific East European ancestry, if both parents of the volunteer were distantly related or from neighboring towns in the days when the Czar ordered all the Jews limited to a "pale". But then there were other Jews whose anti-gens did not match at all, from Egypt, from Bulgaria and China. Mustafa's Muslim colleagues sent him samples from every state in the Union and from Canada. In his extensive travels Mustafa met with other PhD's and Post Docs who were doing Genomics and agreed on the Plan, of finding the Jewish Chromosome number six and identifying the Jewish Genome. The major meeting of the Hematology Wold, the annual convention of the American Association of Hematology, served as the annual meeting of the Jewish Genome Project, as they referred to themselves. For the sake of the organizers, the group identified themselves as a discussion group of G6-PD, an enzyme deficiency typical of middle-eastern populations. In reality the Doctors divided the work of sequencing and characterizing pieces of DNA from chromosome number six which had acquired from their Jewish co-workers. The annual meeting was the focal point of data sharing, arrangements for sample transfers, and fund distributions.

The sequencing of DNA, statistical software, reagents, computer time, online time multiplied over two score of researchers cost a lot of money even though the Doctors involved found ways of doing this extra research on their legitimate laboratory time and money and resources. They had to be very careful because some state institutions such as the University of Florida (Doctor Munir Bachamdoun) and the University of Wisconsin (Doctor Haled Rafia) of Madison were monitored by State comptrollers and their expenses were carefully examined. Therefore Mustafa, as the founder of the Group and the originator of the idea, was forced to request funds from the Islamic

Movement. This move was dangerous too because the request for funds opened the Group to the scrutiny of the Imams, some of whom were opposed to Science on religious grounds. Thus Mustafa relied on Aziz Sidky, the Imam of the Milwaukee mosque, a man who had studied Biology before turning to Islamic priesthood, to convince the Council. The additional danger was that the American FBI had made it a habit to watch and monitor Islamic Fundamentalist organizations ever the since the Twin Tower World Trade Center bombing. No one knew if the FBI was able to infiltrate the Council so Aziz Sidky confided the real in-tent of the monies only to a few trusted delegates convened in Chicago, and for the larger council he presented a slightly different version where the DNA work was earmarked to help Arab patients who may need Marrow Transplants. There was no shortage of money, of course, Arab business-men in Chicago Detroit and NewYork were constantly visited by dark bearded men who asked, cajoled and finally threatened, to come up with "contributions", and mosque comers always left some money in the collection boxes. Merchants who declined to contribute soon found their customer base dwindling due to the same dark bearded men activities at harassing customers. But of course, the fund raisers insisted on knowing who the recipients of the funds were, especially if the monies did not go to the traditional recipients, Hamas, The AZ A DEEN battalions, or the funds set up for buying real estate from Jewish owners in Jerusalem, Tel Aviv and Bat-Yam.

Mustafa was a very prudent distributor of funds and essentially knew who spent each dollar and for which DNA sequences. He kept this information encoded on the lab computer, in a secret manner such that if anyone casually looked through the hard drive the files would not be seen. The communications through the Internet were also encrypted and the data was kept in Zip Drive disks, since anyone may pick Internet traffic, with the proper equipment. Data was exchanged on the same Zip 100 disks using Fed Ex, UPS and Airborne. Thousands of manhours were spent, and to no avail. After 2 years Mustafa had to concede to Aziz that so far he had nothing to show for the work and that it may have been a total waste of time and the precious monies of the Muslim Brotherhood.

Aziz was less pessimistic. He suggested a grand meeting of the Group even though the annual ASH meeting was a few months off, and even came up with the funds to fly in some of those PhD's whose sources had run dry. This was a pivotal meeting, held in Fontana, a small resort south of Milwaukee. Aziz was sure that someone would come up with an idea and he was right.

They conducted the meeting in Arabic, interlaced with technical jargon in English. Academically, this was the most elite group of Arab Palestinian talent anywhere, and it was far beyond the capabilities of any Arab country. In fact only in America with its freedom of information, education and travel, could such a group exist.

Mustafa allowed each individual to present the data and conclusions they had come up with, each in his own project. The results were not encouraging, no one had been able to come up with a specifically Jewish strand along the chromosome number six. The Breakthrough came from a completely unexpected direction with the presentation of Doctor Sharki Machlouf, from Toronto. Doctor Machlouf, short, portly, and with a thick moustache looked down on the small crowd with some well-deserved self-satisfaction.

"As you well know" his family was from the Um EL Fahm area, and his parents also made the fatal decision of leaving for England in 1948 'just for a few weeks'. Consequently he had been born in England but remained acutely Palestinian through contact with his larger family in Israel which had chosen to stay and had since prospered. Consequently his English was British, clipped and precise, very useful in Canada. "Toronto has a large Jewish population and considerable portion of the medical research is done by and for Jews. For example in was researchers from Toronto who had first characterized the metabolic defect for the Tay-Sachs disease, ahead of researchers in New York or the accursed Zionist State. I have had the dubious pleasure of collaborating with Professor Aaron Katz of the Toronto Sick Children's Hospital, and I performed some linkage analysis for the Nieman/Pick disease, which is somewhat similar to Tay-Sachs and is somewhat more commonly in Jews of Eastern European Extraction. Professor Katz asked me to participate in a quest for a founder effect of the Cohanim. In short, the Y chromosome determines the male gender, while a double dose, paternal and maternal, of the X chromosome, defines the female gender. A female may be traced back to her mother through the mitochondrial DNA, contained only in the ovum but not in the sperm, and a son to his father by the Y chromosome for which the sperm is the only source. Theoretically speaking, one may trace a founding father through the Y chromosome provided the sons maintained an uninterrupted blood-line. For instance, a founding father effect has been proven for 90 percent of American Indigent natives, regardless if they are Aztecs or Sioux. Professor Katz proposes that Cohanim , the priest class within the Jewish people, are exactly that phenomenon, all descended for the Mythological father named, appropriately enough Aaron, the brother of Nebi Mussa, the prophet Moses."

Doctor Muhamad Dahlan from Kansas City raised his hand.

"Doctor Machlouf, this is quite impossible, the Jews are not any kind of a continuous blood line but rather a hodge-podge of ethnicities. In fact that constitutes part of our claim of Palestine, that the Jews are not a people at all but rather a host of invaders to the Arab Sphere. Jews from Russia look like Russians, and Jews from India look much more like Indians than a German Jew. Look at the last outrage where the Zionist regime took blacks from Ethiopia, named them Jews and settled them in our beloved Al Kuds, holy Jerusalem, I find this direction of inquiry useless and even blasphemous."

Doctor Machlouf took the criticism magnanimously, like someone who knows his critic is wrong. Mustafa was intrigued, because this direction was entirely new, and as such held endless promise.

"Doctor Dahlan, with all due respect, you are speaking from the bottom of your heart and not from the top of your brain. The Jews have been dispersed for twenty five hundred years and have intermarried and been raped and assimilated other ethnic groups into their faith. But the Cohanim have always been apart. Professor Katz tells me than in biblical times they were not allowed to own land because their mission was to carry the teaching of the prophets from the center to the periphery. They were, and still are severely limited in their choice of marital partner, for instance a priest may not marry a women who had been divorced. The son of a Jewish woman is considered Jewish, regardless who is the father, but only a Cohen is determined by his father, who must be Jewish. Professor Katz's premise is that in all Jewish populations, regardless of colour or background, the Cohanim will be related, and that this relationship can be shown through the pattern of the Y chromosome."

Mustafa asked the question on every participant's mind, very quietly "And what is the answer?"

"To be short and to the point, the answer is 'YES', the preliminary results show a founder effect in the Jewish Cohanim. The procedure is generally as follows: You isolate sections of DNA which are known to originate only on the Y chromosome and amplify them. This section is digested , that is broken up, by bacterial enzymes which cut the strand at specific sequences. You analyze this mixture of DNA segments and get this picture or DNA fingerprint." Doctor Machlouf placed a large film on the viewer. The screen showed a pattern of short lines, some thin, some thick and some almost indiscernible. "The pattern is stored in the computer and multiple images are compared. Our initial results show clearly that such patterns, taken from blood samples of Cohanim have much greater similarity than expected . In fact, the chance that this kind of similarity is a product of blind luck are smaller than one to a million!!" Doctor Machlouf was almost breathless, he was sure he had found their Holy Grail.

Doctor Dahlan appeared uncomfortable. He was also a son of the Palestinian diaspora, and had never been to Palestine, not wishing to have the stamp of the hated Israeli Regime on his passport. "So that means that the Jews are actually a people? That their claims to blood lines to the biblical times, to Abraham, Ismail, and Nebi Mussa are all true?"

Mustafa bristled. "And if so, so what!! They are still invaders who stole our land with the aid of the Western Nations and the stupidity of the Arab regimes. All it means is that we have found the Achilles heel, the target for intervention, a target so specific we can hit it without harming our Palestinian brothers. Brother Sharki, have you been able to define by linkage analysis any markers which are absolutely specific for this Cohanim Y chromosome?"

Doctor Machlouf was vindicated. He had not wasted his time and the brotherhood's money on some wild goose chase. Thank Allah for Professor Aaron katz because he, Sharki, would never have come up with this idea on his own "Yes, brother Mustafa, I have a few candidate Sequence Tags which span regions which were simply not found on DNA taken from the general population, or" he chuckled richly "my own Y chromosome."

"Good" Mustafa was curt, the time for self congratulations was over. "I would request that you share this data with all the participants." He rose and addressed the small assembly "each one of you will start transfection trials into stretches of DNA from your own stocks of samples. We must look for Cohanim and take as many samples as we can. We are looking now for a vehicle that will provide us with a high efficiency transfection and integration tool into the Jewish Cohen Y chromosome. Since we are moving from theoretical research to application, I demand absolute secrecy, no phone calls, all the communications encrypted and no specifics until our next meeting in December."

The meeting broke up in good spirits. They had found their target, it was specific. Now they had to come up with a delivery system and the armament. Each of them knew of hundreds of ways to shut down the function of the organism. It was only a matter of finding out which is the most efficient, and try it out on the appropriate Guinea pig, which in this case, was human.

Chapter 10

Mediterranean

She slept all the way across the Atlantic, which was fortunate because the next day was hectic. Mustafa looked around for the Cyprus Air counter at the Charles De Gaul airport and Alia was wide eyed and wondering at the brightly lit, beautifully dressed windows of the shops strung along the corridors of the huge airport. There was a distinct chique difference in the way those stores displayed their wares which the six year old who was used to the more mundane Milwaukee malls picked up on. Mustafa was flush with money and he splurged on a Hermes scarf which was ridiculously expensive, as they waited for the Cyprus Air flight to Larnaca. Mustafa used his American Passport which he knew could be traced, but after Cyprus he intended to disappear. He did not want any official trace of him in Lebanon, because he knew what tremendous pressures the Americans could bring to bear on any government. If on the other hand his whereabouts were unrecorded, the Lebanese could claim innocence and snicker behind their hands.

The plane ride was shorter, about three hours from Charles De Gaul to the Larnaca airport, and still Alia was full of wonder at the whole concept of flight, and she plied Mustafa with countless questions of how the airplane flies, and where they were going (to see your grandma, he replied) and only after they landed and were standing in line for customs did Alia look up at him and said "Dad?"

"What, sweety."

"When is Mommy coming with us?"

Mustafa squatted on his heels and faced his sweet daughter's questioning gaze.

"In a few days, dear."

"How come she didn't come with us?"

"She was busy in the hospital, now let's be quiet until we are done with the Police," and he pointed at the blue-dressed immigration officer, who was stamping the passports of the portly French couple ahead of them with resounding bangs.

Mollified, Alia stood quietly while Mustafa presented their passports to the Blue. The hall was less than impressive, in fact it looked already like the

Middle East, not quite so clean and rather dingy. The officer whose nameplate said Dimitrios Papnopuoulou examined first the passport, and then the face. They matched, although this man looked Arab despite the American urbanity and the American suit.

"Welcome to Cyprus, Mr Halim, are you here for business?"

"It's Doctor Halim, and I am here for the Conference of the Mediterranean Society of Experimental Hematology at the Paphos Hilton." This was a real conference, a way to get scientists to spend their educational allowances for a vacation with some education thrown in. Mexico, Las Vegas and the Caribbeans are full of these conferences, some of them are serious, and many which are tax-sheltered vacations. The immigration officer smiled, this was exactly the kind of visitor that Cyprus needed. He looked at the other passport, then leaned over the counter to glimpse at Alia, what a beautiful little girl, I bet her mother is a Real American.

"Mrs Halim will join us in a few days, for the fun part of the conference" Mustafa smiled at Dimitrios, showing the teeth that had been reconstructed in the US, as his original teeth were as bad as lousy nutrition and hygiene in the Camps could make them.

The officer stamped the passports with the usual gusto and handed them back to Mustafa. "Enjoy your stay, Doctor" and he shifted his eyes to the next in line.

Mustafa had almost forgotten what the Mediterranean sun felt like. Although it was December the early afternoon sun smote his face with a bright dazzling force and he put down the American Tourister hardshell suitcases and just closed his eyes and savoured the Sun. Allah, all those long, dark, overcast Midwestern winters, they were over, over and done with. He was back in the Eastern Mediterranean where he belonged, with the joshing and shoving humanity, honking cabbies and Gyros smell from the open upright pits, and his irksome life of false politeness behind him. It was wonderful. One more stage and he was Home. Lebanon was only 200 kilometers away.

Alia on the other hand was not as pleased, she hid in his shadow and put her hands over her ears whenever one of the taxies in line leaned on his horn to make way. It was a noisy cacophonous place. The taxi drivers hustled around the tourists emerging from the terminal crying "Paphos, Paphos" or "Nicosia, Nicosia." Mustafa waved them away until he was approached by a dark skinned individual, short, wiry, with a hairthin moustache.

"Doctor Bakker?"

Mustafa fixed him with a baleful stare. The man cringed.

"Allah hu Akbar and we are his children" he identified himself, in English. Mustafa replied in Arabic "Allah hu Akbar and Youness is his servant." The man turned and uttered a short whistle. An Opel Vectra tried to cross the traffic, honked a few times, and with a seemingly suicidal rush raced across the lanes to screech to a stop. The driver leaned back to open the back door. He popped the trunk and his partner heaved the suitcases in. Mustafa lowered himself into the car and pulled the dumbfounded Alia beside him. The wiry one jumped in front and pulled the door shut with a thunk and they were off trailing horns of all notes. Alia hid her face in her father's jacket, and then peeked around. As they stopped in a traffic light she pulled hard and stretched up almost into his beard.

"Daddy, daddy, who are theses people?"

"They are friends."

"But they are scary, daddy, where are we going?"

"Don't worry Alia, everything is OK, and also from now on I want you to speak only in Arabic" Mustafa changed his language in mid-sentence.

"Why daddy? And they are going so fast and scary."

Mustafa leaned forward "slow down, the child is afraid" and the car did slow down and did not swerve as violently as before. They were heading south-west and the sun was shining fully into the windshield. The wiry one turned and grinned at Alia. It was a benevolent grin but his teeth were so bad and rotten that she shrank back. She raised herself to her father's ear.

"Daddy, I still don't like them, I want to go home now." Mustafa did not answer and instead directed his gaze into Alia's eyes. She shrank back. She knew that look, she feared that look, when he glowered like that he was implacable. It was rarely directed at her, but now it was. Alia made herself small, and presently Mustafa let her go and went back to scanning the narrow road and the dwindling buildings along it. It was a dry year so far and the trees still looked dusty, and the earth was still dry.

Cyprus is smaller than Connecticut, and once out of town they made good speed to Limassol, only 50 kilometers away. Alia again was wide eyed as she saw the Limassol bay open up with the Cape Gata headland extending from it as they came along the coast winding road from the hills surrounding the pretty port town. Larnaca was a main entry gate to Cyprus, by air and by sea, and so Mustafa and his comrades looked for a less visi-ble port of exit. Limassol is a beehive of fishing activity, with fishing and tourist vessels plying back and forth, protected by the nearby UK naval base. The Opel entered into the narrow streets of the town center and stopped in front of a typical Greek whitewashed house, down by the port. Mustafa and Alia left the car and entered the house, while Samir carried the suitcases inside. The driver then took off for the other safehouse.

"Moshe 1, eich ani nishma?" (how am I received)
"Chamesh Chamesh (five by five)"

Chayim Lapidot was using his short wave SSB radio made by Tadiran Communications, hidden in his apartment in Larnaca. This was a beautiful assignment. He was posted in a pretty city where the living was easy, the English, and Swiss and German girls plentiful, at least in summer, the pubs alive with action and all he had to do was follow up on leads from Tel Aviv. Ostensibly he was a representative of several buyers of agricultural companies in Tel-Aviv, but in reality he was Shin Bet, or Mossad operative. Cyprus was full of Fatah, and PLO and Islamic Jihad people, and he was watching them intermittently. The Cypriot government knew about Mossad activities but since they wished to be on the good side of both the Syrians *and* the Israelis, they allowed these games as long as no one helped the real enemy, the Turkish Cypriot republic confined to the north of the small island. The historic war between the Turks and the Greeks continued, although on a low flame, in Cyprus.

Chayim Lapidot had been following Samir al Hussam, a short wiry pencil-thin moustachioed operative of Islamic Jihad, who had surfaced on the island a couple of weeks previously. The Tel Aviv headquarters said that there was an increased acitvity of Jihad communications, which had receded considerably since Fathi Shkaki was assassinated. He divided the work between himself and Esther Dimor, an ostensible representative of the ministry of health. Today it was his turn and he had followed Samir in his beat up Fiat Uno, which was equipped with almost one way windows. Once Samir had collected a strange duo, a tall man dressed in an American business suit, and a little girl, he set off in a distant pursuit, because this was potentially a new contact.

The Opel never stopped until it arrived in Limassol, and there, in the narrow streets near the harbor he lost it. After cruising the streets for a while he decided that any more cruising might make him too visible, so he parked the car, took his camera and binoculars along and sauntered down to the open air cafés along the waterfront. It was getting cooler as the sun went down and he hugged himself in the nylon windcheater and sipped the strong Greek coffee. He ordered some salad, and thought that life could be far worse.

Chayim Lapidot's patience paid off. The tall man with a small girl, a beautiful little girl, with raven hair and fair skin he noted to himself, were walking on the boardwalk, accompanied some distance away by Samir. The threesome stopped in another café and ordered some food. Chayim pulled out his binoculars and studied the man and what appeared to be his daughter. He was tall, thin, intelligent-looking, with a thick black beard, and the street lights did not afford him enough light for much more. The daughter, who was digging into a large salad was more remarkable, she was so pretty.

Half an hour later Chayim concluded that there was nothing interesting about this. He put the 800 ASA film into the Cannon, and walked by the café where the threesome were having coffee for the men and a juice for the girl, and snapped a picture unobtrusively. The man and the girl were not bothered by the cold. Samir obviously was. Let Tel Aviv worry about that. He had other assignments to follow up on and a new female prospect in Larnaca, an English nurse who had recently come to town.

"A new contact by Samir al Hussam."
"Roger that, what kind of contact?"
"A man with a little girl, both looking Arab-American, films on the way to TA."
"Unknown here, unlikely to be important, next assignment is Hirma Abu Kassis, due in Larnaca in two days from Rome."
"Roger, layla tov (good night)."

Samir waited until the tourist went well past and leaned over to Mustafa. "Does anyone know you are supposed to be here?"

Mustafa was mildly alarmed "No one outside the Islamic Jihad."

"Well, the Israelis know you are here, because we have just been photographed by this one" and he jerked his head toward the retreating jacket.

"In that case we will go out tonight."

"And how is Alia going to deal with it?"

"She will have to tough it out, and better start now, before she sees the Camp."

"In that case, I will warn the boat."

Alia was fast asleep and only mumbled as Mustafa picked her up and took her down to the waiting van. She was so tired that she was not bothered by the rigors of the short trip to the boat, and curled up under the blanket on the bunk. At 15 knots it was only an overnight trip from Limassol to Junia, the fishing port north of Beirut. Once on board the small fishing boat Mustafa changed to less conspicuous clothes, black pants, a once-white shirt, his old worn blazer and a kaffieh, chequered black and white. With his black beard he looked just like the other sailors, whose main transport was not fish, but Hashish and Grass going to Cyprus and cigarettes coming back. Lebanon used to be the Banker of the Middle East, the Monaco and Nice of the eastern Mediterranean, where the rich playboys of the oil-drenched Emirates raced the wind on water-skis pulled by powerful motor-boats in summer, and down-hill ski during the winter. No more. Since the bloody takeover by Hafez Assad in 1975, which had claimed scores of thousands of lives, Lebanon had become one of the major suppliers of Canabis to the Europe and the world. The poppy is grown in the Bekaa Valley, nestled between the snow-capped mountain ranges of eastern Lebanon. It is the major cash-crop of the region. It is harvested openly and processed to the Hashish "Shoe-soles" under the direct auspices of the true ruler, the Assad family. It is transported overland to the coast and from there shipped to Cyprus, Greece, Turkey, to be sold, or further processed to Heroin. For Syria, it is a tremendous source of cash, for Lebanon, the inevitable result of being under the Syrian jackboot. Hafez el Assad and his sons are some of the greatest drug-lords on the planet. That meant that the flow of boating across the eastern Medi-terranean was always thick and heavy. The chance of any specific boat to be stopped by the navy of Israel was slim, since they concerned them- selves with arms, not narcotics.

They were lucky with both the sea and the Israeli navy. The sea was calm, Mustafa was at the bow as the first sight of land came over the horizon as a faint bluish line, almost undistinguishable from cloud. The wind in the early AM was cold, but not freezing, refreshing rather than cutting, as it would be in Wisconsin. His spirits soared as the shoreline solidified and then the high rises of the newly rebuilt Beirut peeked to the south, and the bigger mass of the Schouf mountains behind came out of the morning mists. I am Home, not my true home, because that lay further south, but still Home, much more than America could ever be.

"Daddy, where are we?" Alia was dazed, she had come up to the gunwale and could not really see above it. Mustafa picked her up and settled her on his shoulders.

"That is Lebanon, this is where your grandpa and your uncles are waiting."

"Really, is Grandpa Jeremy waiting for us there where all the ships are?" She referred to Amanda's father, who Mustafa disliked and tried to keep Alia from visiting. That did not stop him, because Jeremy and Linda Carter doted on their granddaughter and came up to Milwaukee whenever they could.

"No, that's grandpa George and your aunties Leila and Fatima and Nadia. Remember I told you about them and they have lots of cousins for you to play with and you are going to be very happy here." He continued to stare at the Junia harbour that rose from the shore, why was everything so old and dirty for God's sake?

They entered the harbor slowly, it was not really a port but a fishing village, and an unlovely one at that. No one paid attention to the fishermen coming ashore. Many took their small children with them for the night fishing and many boats came back not with fish but with contraband, Marlborough cigarettes, stolen VCRs, fake perfumes, you name it. It was a free for all controlled only by the local bosses, who paid their dues to the Syrians so they are not bothered. Mustafa and Alia, dressed for the occasion like a small boy, came ashore without a second glance from any officials. And that's the way Mustafa wanted it.

The old man, his hair wispy white, could not hold himself back anymore, and supported by Fatima pushed himself as fast as his age and deformed leg allowed him. Mustafa took two seconds to recognize his father, who appeared mostly a ghost in his eighties. It was a tribute to George Halim's stamina that he had held on for so long where men half his age were falling apart. Mustafa broke into a run, dragging Alia who was totally disoriented, and fell on his father's neck. They embraced, long and hard, without a word.

Finally Mustafa disengaged and looked at his sister. She looked terrible, she could almost pass for the old man's wife. She was the product of the worst camp, the worst food, and multiple pregnancies. She looked like the fate of the Palestinian people. But she was alive and smiling a blacktoothed smile.

"Mustafa, you are looking wonderful, and where is our dear Alia?"

Alia, disgusted with the smells around her, the dirty clothing and mostly with the horrible smell of the clothes she had been forced to wear, peeked from behind her father and shrank from the old, obese, black-toothed, horrible smelling woman who was bending down to look at her. Mustafa also squatted and said "Alia, this is your auntie Fatima and I want you to say good morning very nicely, in Arabic" and he gave alia his special look, the one the brooked no disobedience.

"Sabah el hir, Fatima" she squeaked.

"And good morning to you too" beamed the old hag and her breath made Alia want to run a way and disappear. Didn't the old woman brush her teeth like her mom insisted? The man who came up was short, and stocky and diffident. Hosny was Fatima's husband and Mustafa had known him before he had left Lebanon as a mere youth. But, as a man placed somewhere in the middle rungs of the Islamic Jihad he knew that his superiors placed a tremendous importance on Mustafa Halim and so he was careful, even if Mustafa appeared American despite the local colors he affected. It was the set of features, confidence without bravado, a can-do kind of attitude, he was back to do a job, something that was too secret for Hosny's level.

"Doctor Halim" George straightened his bent back and looked proudly at his son "I have a car which our comrade Youness Shkaki allocated for you, with a driver, and we should go to headquarters right away."

The car was a luxury Mercedes Benz SL 320. Thousands of cars were stolen in Europe and smuggled to the middle east. Traveling the roads of Lebanon and Syria one might think that the entire production of Mercedes Benz was present in the Middle East. This car clearly belonged to the top echelon, and George was doubly pleased that his son had been so appreciated by the Jihad.

Alia sat very close to her father and tried to not to breath. The stench of people in the car was overwhelming. The flow of Arabic around her just as overwhelming, and she could only understand some snippets. The driver smoked incessantly and Mustafa opened the window to let the fresh sea air in. The road was bad and the driver swerved every few seconds to avoid a pothole, or a donkey or another mad driver, and he leaned on his powerful horn non-stop. She tried to bury her nose in her father's jacket, which was clean and smelled of America. One both sides there were buildings, low-set, all with gaudy green or blue shutters and showing either bare concrete blocks or rough stone finish. It was nothing like the quiet tree lined streets of Milwaukee. Suddenly the sun was blotted out by the dark clouds roll- ing in from the Mediterranean and she could see the sheet of rain falling on the tall skinny buildings not far ahead. The hills and mountains that rose to her left were dotted with houses precariously hanging to the sides, with rutted lanes leading up and it all appeared foreign and foreboding. The buildings on either side were taller now and she could not see the sea anymore. She noticed that many of them had big chunks missing, as if a giant had taken big bites of them, leaving the floors, staircases and columns exposed. She looked up at her father who was stroking his thick, black beard, and he was calm, so she must remain calm until her mother came to get her out of here. She dozed off. They came to a halt a number of times, showing documents to Syrian soldiers, Lebanese police, and twice to less defined armed men. They twisted and turned into the hills finally jouncing over a sharply inclined dirt road to stop in front of a magnificent villa. Two armed men with Kalachnikov assault rifles detached themselves from the booth just inside the ornate gate and one approached the driver side, while the second one covered them from the gate. A third one was watching them from a watch-tower inside the wall and he too was armed. They all appeared identical, young, black-bearded, black-eyed and watchful.

The guerrilla who checked out the driver nodded to the one at the gate. He knew the driver and Hosny, and he knew about the American and his daughter. The massive ornate gate swung open and the luxury car bumped over the flagstones and halted in front of the steps.

Gently Mustafa disengaged himself from his sleeping daughter and stepped outside. The dark clouds did not mar the beauty of this villa and its surroundings. A rich Doctor had this place built, back in the fifties when the Palestinian refugees worked for a pittance and hand-carved each stone for the rich client. The backdrop was as beautiful, mountain slopes covered with cherry orchards, and the occasional copse of the truly magnificent Lebanese Cedar, the noblest of all trees. The rain hadn't reached them yet, it was pelting the city below, which was sprouting new buildings and fixing the damaged ones. PAX Syriana, he thought bitterly, a new prosperity which the Palestinians would never participate in, an airplane was taking off from the new Beirut International, and climbed away to Europe. He turned back to see his host coming down the steps.

Youness Shkaki was the younger brother of Fat'hi, who had been assassinated by the Israelis. He was entirely ordinary, of medium height and thin body, and his strength lay in those glowing eyes deep-set over the aquiline nose. He had not taken the flamboyant leadership style over from his older brother, since he preferred to operate in the shadows. He was not interested in the suicide bombs or the noisy kidnaping of school children. His modus was to undermine the foundations so the building will fall under it's own weight. He ran narcotics into Israel, using Lebanese workers and Israeli soldiers. An Israeli youth on Hashish was one soldier less. He financed covert buying of real estate by Arab-Israeli frontmen. He sent men to cut into major water pipelines, which caused major water loss and loss of agricultural products. One of his special projects was to cut water supplies to poultry-growers during the hot season. The loss of water supply caused thousands of poultry head losses and impoverished the Moshavim of the Galilee for whom that was the main revenue. These actions were less dramatic than a car bomb but they caused a wearying-down effect on the Jewish inhabitants of northern Israel. The Hashish trade also made Youness and his organization rich. Mustafa knew all that, and preferred him for a partner in his endeavor rather than the more flamboyant Refusal Front leaders, those who rejected the Oslo accords and vowed to continue the fight despite the peace treaty signed by Yasser Arafat. Arafat did not represent all the Palestinians, oh no, he was the leader of one faction, the Fatah. Even the so-called democratic elections held in the Palestinian territories meant nothing since the majority of Palestinians, those who resided in the diaspora of the refugee camps, and the world at large, could not vote. Which meant all the other factions were free to continue the struggle to wipe out the Jewish Zionist entity.

Youness was, as usual, flanked by his advisers and bodyguards. He swept down the broad stone steps and hugged Mustafa as the long lost brother he was. Youness was one of the boys who had protected Mustafa from the bullies of the Sabra camp, being a ruthless dogfighter as a kid. They embraced long and hard, until Doctor George Halim exited the car creakily, at which point Youness let go and hurried to help the old man out. He pumped his hand with both hands.

"Thank you Abu-Mustafa for making your son who he is, the spear-point of the renewed struggle." George Halim beamed with pride, then his heart missed a beat, then another, his color changed, the strength left his feet and he collapsed onto the wide steps. Mustafa changed color too, with fright, and screamed at the armed men to call a doctor. They shook their head, the nearest doctor was in Beirut which was close by air and far by ground. The breath of doctor George Halim became labored, then stertorous, but his eyes were on his son, calm and reassuring, His heart went into fibrillation and he was to about to lose consciousness as his son looked on, dumbfounded and powerless. He tried to mouth and Mustafa bent over him.

"Avenge your mother... Avenge Alia..." then silence.

The rain started pelting down, rich fat drops, fast strengthening to a downpour. On the car, the armed men, and the brother and sister who had lost their father at the moment of triumph. Mustafa lifted his head to the black clouds, the driving rain, and howled again, as he did that fateful day when

Alia had died, except this time it was a full blooded roar of anguish, not of the ineffectual youth, but of the grown tiger, who could get hundreds of highly educated men to do his bidding.

"Father, I will avenge you, I will avenge you a thousand fold, and they will know the wrath of Allah."

To: Aman Patzan
From: Shomer rosh
Sub: Shkaki villa
Report: New arrival at villa.
Man, tall, thin, child about six or seven, female.
Welcomed by Youness personally.

persons present: Hosny Abu Hamid, Youness Shkaki, guards and an old man.

Old man apparently died, reason unknown, removed by Ambulance.

Signed
Shomer rosh

Northern command in Safed received the burst transmission, one of many such transmissions from the multitude of observers that Shin Bet   and Northern Intelligence kept in Lebanon. It went to the Kabar, and was duly filed, the child decreased the significance of another person at the Villa. There was no cross reference at this level.

Chapter 11

HIGH WIRE ACT

Karen felt like her head was spinning, even after a good night sleep. Joe had shown her the Cessna 210 at Timmerman airfield, parked with a bunch of other light airplanes "Itsy Bitsy flying insects" She had remarked. He had explained to her, as the early December night fell on the airfield, how the scheme for buying an aircraft and paying for it no more than one would pay for car payments, worked. All through the presentation she had stolen glances at Joe and felt her fascination just growing and growing. Finally, she had made her good bye due to her previous commitment to her mother, she had promised to be there on Sunday night. Even a full night sleep did not resolve the dizzying amount of information and aspects of the situation and the man who had voluntarily taken on it on himself. On Ourselves, she reminded herself, I decided to be involved too.

Her phone rang at 6 o'clock in the morning, Since She was scheduled to work the AM shift, and since no changes could have been arranged, she was already at the coffee machine. It must be Joe, she decided, I know the ring, silly of me.

"Hello?"

"Karen?"

"I never gave you the number, did I?"

"No, but Danielle at the unit did, although she says calling anyone at this time is sexual harassment! We kinda left today open, I am taking it for granted you are still in. Any specific plans?"

The coffee dripper was done and with one hand she poured into the mug and added some milk. "I talked to Amanda last night and she is going to be in today, she said she cannot sit at home and cry all the time. The FBI said they will call her at Children's if anything turns up, so I will do the same, and get a hold of father Wilkins and maybe set up a time with Amanda and the FBI to see if we can get you the list." She took a deep drought; coffee and love that's all I need. Coffee I got, but love?? "What about you?" she queried.

"I am going to fly the Cessna to Memphis." Karen almost spilled her cup.

"What, Fly that itsy bitsy contraption to Memphis? in December? you must be nuts!"

Joe guffawed "yup, that's me, a nut case, but if we want to get Alia out of Lebanon, that's one of the ways to do it! I need some night flying time on the machine."

"Lebanon?! Who said she is there? OK, OK I guess you have that all figured out, go ahead and kill yourself, call me when you get back, and I will work at my end." She plunked down the phone, shaking her head, he is too weird.

Monday AM meeting was different. No jokes, grim faces, the news had leaked out somehow. The nurses came one by one and hugged Amanda who was ashen-faced, blotched with crying. Dr. Kammitzer presented the patients matter-of- fact and asked for input, no one discussed the academic or the esoteric. Staff, nurses, social workers, child life therapists, all craned their necks and searched the meeting room. Where was Doctor Bergman? He had never missed the Monday morning rounds. Nurse Appleby glanced at her colleague's sealed expression, Karen may know, they discussed something together last afternoon, and I wish he would pay her some personal attention and not be so darned professional all the time. But no one else made the connection and the meeting soon ended.

Karen immersed herself in her work at the Oncology clinic. There were five children with leukemia who needed a bone marrow samples taken and intrathecal (to the spinal canal) medications administered. Multiple blood draws and labs to send. IVs placed prior to CT scans and Platelets to administer to other children who were at the nadir of their blood counts between treatments. And so on and so forth, this was the busiest clinic in the hospital and the most complex, and the nurses ran it with precision. Doctor Kammitzer had finished his morning rounds with Doctor Carter and the resident in the HOT unit, and then came down to the clinic to be with Doctor Ziskind, an attending newly recruited to the Service. He was tall, and thin, and possessed a high forehead accentuated by black hair swept straight back. Always severely dressed with a spotless white lab-coat, he had a reassuring manner with the kids and their parents. He specialized in solid tumors but when the pressure was on and he was on service he saw the whole variety of patients.

The Doctors went in and out of the rooms, reviewed the charts, performed the procedures, examined the kids, assessed the labs, and discussed with the parents. They documented everything meticulously and wrote chemotherapy orders, checked and rechecked, and checked again with the pharmacist. This was exacting work. The nurses prepared the rooms and the kids for the procedures, spread the slides, started and stopped IV medications and checked that the flow of patients and doctors and parents and labs matched the inexorable march of the clock. Before you could say "Jack" it was afternoon and time to prepare the clinic for the morrow. A good day was when the kids stayed in remission. A bad day was when you had to tell a mom that the tumor has progressed or the leukemia had relapsed. Karen was so engrossed in charting that she jumped when a pair of small shoes thrust itself at her own. She looked up to see Doctor Kammitzer. He was tired after a long weekend and night and even longer day and he was not a young man anymore.

"Would you come to my office please Miss Fitzsimmons, when you are done? Not here, at the PACC fund building?" She nodded. "See you later." and the diminutive man turned so she could see the Smiley on his white labcoat.

Karen closed the last chart with the nurses notes, little Bill Prescott was in remission and his Is and Os (fluids in and out) were reasonably close. Doctor Ziskind likewise closed a chart and smiled at her.

"Another hard day at the office eh?" He was flirting, just a little. At other times Karen might have been gracious and allowed him the little game. But not tonight, she was not interested. She eyed him coolly.

"Not really, gotta go, good night." She just caught his crestfallen expression. I am sorry, she said to herself, he is just a normal guy trying his luck with a girl, but my mind is set on another, Oy vey, as zeide says, what am I saying. Joe is probably just another cold fish too intent on his medicine and research to share real intimacy. Karen picked her coat and hat from the nurses room and headed out the corridor toward the PACC fund building. As usual they were the last clinic to be done and her steps echoed on the tiles. She wondered what doctor Kammitzer had in store for her. Did anything new turn up with Alia? Probably not because Amanda would have told her. So Joe is an orphan with many talents, but being a lover may not be one of them. He is in his late Thirties and no one had taken a call for him from a girl friend or even a boyfriend. Up this stair case, down this corridor, the empty receptionist desk, there is Doctor Kammitzer's room.

This was a much bigger room then he had at the old Children's but it was still as cramped, with just much more paper and journals and computer disks strewn around. Dr Kammitzer rose from his desk and extended his thin hand.

"Hi Karen."

"Hi Doctor Kammitzer."

"Please sit down" he indicated a tiny settee "and its Abe."

Karen nodded, no way she was going to call him Abe, the man who had tried and tried to save her brother Alex.

Dr Kammitzer answered the last of the E mails. He was the coordinating reference physician for the Aplastic Anemia group, which meant that anyone in the country with queries concerning the clinical trials contacted him. On the one hand, it was much better than the old days with the telephone calls, on the other hand there were many more queries. He shut the Compaq down and looked at Karen. She was so darn beautiful, were the men Blind or something? Or maybe the homosexual community was right and they were 10 percent or more of the population. Ronny did not appear to have any shortage of companions. Well, let's get the dark story out.

"What do you know about our Doctor Joe, Karen?"

Karen was not really surprised. She figured that Joe had some special relationship with Doctor Kammitzer and that her sudden close encounters with Joe under such crazy circumstances might raise some eyebrows.

"Some. He is a very good doctor with the Kids, he knows a lot about nursing, he came from Israel, he was made an orphan by some terrorist activity, and he knows some crazy stuff like karate and flying itsy bitsy aircraft, and now he has decided to save the world, so what's to know?"

Abe Kammitzer grinned. "Nah, that's all nonsense, what about the soul of Doctor Bergman, feelings, emotions? We men are supposed to be an open book to professional nurses."

Karen became more thoughtful, less flippant. "I think he is a very sad man who feels that he has nothing to lose, no emotional commitments, and that no one really cares for him. He thinks he is expendable." Abe nodded slowly throughout this analysis.

"And what would make a person so intelligent and accomplished lower his self esteem so much?"

"In the psychology classes I am taking for my Masters degree they stress that low self esteem is related to the emotional instability suffered during the first year of life. The baby does not get a sense of security and feels unwanted for the rest of his life. But I doubt that about Doctor Joe. He is a very secure person. It just seems that he doesn't really *Care* about himself, or anybody else, except for the sick kids. But that may be just professionalism."

Abe Kammitzer grinned again "are you bothered by it, challenged maybe?"

"Sure, we all are, females that is. So he wears this silly band on his middle finger, but we know he is not attached, and he never ever pays me or anyone any Male interest. Its inhuman, no comments on appearance, no flirting, no come-ons, no soul conversations at midnight. His brain is inured to testosterone effects, although I was lucky his muscles are fully responsive. You should have seen that, he was like a coiled striking Cobra."

Abe Kammitzer prodded some more "how about a deep personal loss?" "Yeah, but for how long? Two and half years here. And usually those who suffer such a loss show it in their work, depression, headaches, crying episodes, fatigue. He does not show any fatigue anytime, not even emotional fatigue."

"So if he is such an emotional eunuch, why did you throw yourself at him and his crazy notion of going after Amanda Carter's husband? Any-one in their right mind would leave this kind of thing to the proper authorities, not join a dangerous pursuit. Do you like him that much? Women in love do crazy things." Karen flushed so deep it reached the roots of the flaxen hair.

"Love?" She stammered, "who, who, who said anything about love? He saved my life maybe, true, but that doesn't mean I fall in love with someone who doesn't ever show he cares for me." She regained her composure and the flush receded. Her fists remained tightly clenched.

"Alright, sit back and relax, do you have time to listen to a long story?" She nodded.

Yossi was fairly tired after a long night in the Intensive Care at the Wolfson Memorial hospital of Tel Aviv. This was Spring break at the Medical school fifth year. It was a month after the reserve duty served in Lebanon and he was sick, like everybody else who had ever served in Lebanon, of the whole military involvement in Lebanon. It was like the American Vietnam with no end in sight and just more and more casualties mounting up every day. It was 0730 and he had just come off duty, taking care of a patient with the new dread disease, AIDS. Now that was like a new version of the Plague, and nobody knew anything about it. The patient was a textbook case of a double life, at home a model family man, and on business trips to Germany and he US, an active homosexual, searching for partners in Gay bars. The patient was falling apart in front of his eyes as Yossi nursed him through the night. His lungs were leaking air into his chest cavity, and seeped around his neck and his eyes so that he looked like a bugeyed frog. He was unable to breath for himself and only the respirator kept him going. And throughout he was conscious and knew he was going to die. Yossi worked on his vacations as a nurse's aid in the Intensive care and since everyone was scared stiff of the dread disease, they gave Yossi full command of his medications, excretions and respirations. Some nurses took time off, or even transferred out of the Intensive Care, for fear of the disease. Yossi did not care, he was invincible, even Lebanon had not killed him, so he had taken this patient on, three gloves, three masks and gowns, and put everything into bright red containers marked DANGER in Hebrew, English and Arabic.

It was a glorious April day outside. His tiredness sloughed off as the main Jerusalem road opened up before the double-cylinder Moto Guzzi he had imported from Italy the previous summer. Yossi was not in any hurry and just enjoyed the wind ripping by his helmet, the open country side, the vines growing on the hills of the Silent Monastery. He was going to visit Peter, the Swiss friend who had accosted him on the shores of Lake Zurich and showed him around the Swiss Alps that last summer. Peter had called him up saying that he had quit his job at the Zurricher Bank and was going to volunteer at a Kibbutz in the hills of Jerusalem. "Just to clear my head" he had remarked. It would be good to see Peter again and show him the less spectacular but not less beautiful Jerusalem Hills and the Soreq Valley.

Yossi found the Kibbutz easily, it was just off the main No 1 road, and up a twisty incline which the Moto Guzzi, being an Italian, loved to gobble up. By then it was already 0830 and Peter would be at work, since early AM and maybe ready for a break. The guard at the gate to the Kibbutz told him where to find the volunteers' quarters and Yossi puttered slowly through the narrow kibbutz lanes toward the low set Asbestos-roofed precast concrete structures. He parked the machine, left his helmet on the mirror and sauntered down the open corridor, shaded by the overhang of the asbestos roof. He knocked at door marked 22.

"Ya, Kom in" said a male voice. The door handle was so loose it almost came off in his hand. The whole place was ramshackle, except for the greenery which was lovingly manicured. Yossi walked in and saw Peter starting the electric kettle.

"Hi Peiter."

"Hello Yozzee, how was the drive, wundarbar jour, nein?"

They spoke in a mish-mash of languages. Peter, as a graduate of a Gymnasium and an accountant, spoke Swiss-Deutch, French and English and some Italian. Yossi spoke Hebrew, American English and high-school French. Peter was a big affable man with a ready smile and a dare-devil twinkle in his eyes. He was in his early thirties. He had treated every road in Switzerland as a private race-track, tearing them up with a little Suzuki. Tried as he could, Joe could never catch up with him, even on a more powerful machine. Peter placed a spoonful of Nestle Mocha in two cups, poured, stirred, and gave Yossi a cup. Yossi settled back on a suspicious looking recliner which had seen better days a generation ago and cupped the hot cup.

"Yeah, it was a good drive, but too slow for you. Especially rewarding after a bad night" and Yossi proceeded to tell him about AIDS. "So stay out of the Wicked Gay bars and stick to the naughty ones."

"Ah, you know me , I am one hundert perzent straight."

"So, what kind of slave job do they make you do here? Milk the cows, Clean the kitchen? Shine the gutters?"

Peter smiled, white teeth flashing, "This is the best vacation I have ever had. No numbers, no bank manager, pretty girls from the whole world, and I keep the pool clean for the guests in the Hotel. They run a gut hotel here, though not up to Swiss standards of cleanliness" and Peter held his nose and smirked "but the old folks who come to relax in the good air are happy. And I get to swim and ogle the girls."

"Now that's interesting" Yossi was languid, the weariness catching up with him.

"I zee, I zee, why don't you catch a nap and I will come back and fetch you for lunch."

"Good idea" Yossi got up and stretched, and heard a soft knock on the door.

"Ya, Kom in, it's open" Peter called.

Yossi turned slowly to look at the newcomer and his jaw hang slack, and his fatigue evaporated, and his heart hammered in his chest. The most beautiful woman he had ever seen was at the door, her lovely figure silhouetted in the door frame by the bright light outside. She was dressed in a loose cotton T shirt, with the saucer needle and SEATTLE emblazoned on it, and skimpy shorts and straw sandals. Joe felt dizzy and his throat constricted, and he was totally mute. She did not see him, because she was looking for Peter, face sleepy and golden curls falling like a halo around her fantastic sensual face.

"Hello Peter, got any of that Swiss Mocha, please, pretty please?" His ears tingled at the slightly raspy, got-up-from-sleep voice. She was tall, almost his height, and perfectly proportioned, she was an angelic figure come to earth to tease the poor mortals.

Peter was unconcerned "Sure, ya, you can have some, kom in, meet my friend Yozzee."

She took another step in and froze, her hand stuck out, they gazed into each others eyed, petrified. She broke free first.

"Hi I'm Helen, pleased to meetcha" she grabbed the proffered Mocha box from Peter and turned and almost ran outside. Yossi sat down heavily on the recliner and almost went through to the floor, he struggled out.

"What was *That?*" Yossi stammered.

"That was a woman, I am sure you noticed."

"Yes but *what* a woman, who is she, what's her name, where is she from?..."

Peter smiled his biggest grin. "Get a hold on yourself Yozzee, we went out on the town in Zurich, and Davos, and I have never seen you act like that. Anyway, everybody here has tried to, to ... hit on her as the Americans say, and they all drew a blank. She plays with them all and sends them to bed alone and aching, so don't make any plans. Go to sleep."

"Sleep, my foot, I can't sit here. Let's go the Pool and I will help you out, is she a volunteer?"

"Ya, she came here three weeks ago from the States and turned everybody on their ear. The girls are green with envy and the boys.... Alors, allez-y."

They walked out to the corridor, Yossi glanced around but she was nowhere to be seen, and Peter led them to the pool. Some geriatric vacationers speaking Yiddish were lapping the pool which was so clear that nothing appeared to need cleaning. Nevertheless Peter gave Yossi some supplies and they both set on the cabanas, and then the shrubbery around the pool and picked up every shred of paper or leaf.

Yossi was inspecting the water trap trough around the pool edge when Helen glided through the low ornate gate and onto the pool deck. She took off her Seattle shirt, folded it neatly on a chaise, and slid off the shorts. Her bikini was iridescent marine blue which reflected the sunlight at every luscious curve. She turned and with three long flying steps jumped high and curved into the clear water. She sliced through like an arrow, reached bottom and swam with long powerful strokes all the way to the other end, 25 meters. Yossi was transfixed at the side of the pool, only his head following the apparition. She surfaced and fairly shot up from the water, settling on the edge with her impossibly long legs dangling in the water. Even the old men looked appreciative.

Yossi woke from the reverie when Peter landed a heavy hand on his shoulder.

"Do not stare and do your verk. She does this every day and then even I go bananas." Yossi knew of the terribly ugly divorce that Peter had gone through, which was part of the reason he had quit the Bank. Liset had cleaned him out. But he could not help himself and glanced in the direction of the Golden Goddess. Her heaving chest slowed and then she appeared to reach a decision. Fluidly she rose and walked in his direction. Yossi buried his face and furiously worked at the gutter to pick up some microscopic algae. The feet stopped right under his nose, and they were perfect toes, the nails painted in shimmering highlights.

"Are you the new pool man?" she asked, sweetly provocative.

Yossi's gaze followed the feet, shins, the kneecaps, the tense quadriceps of the thighs, his breath taken away by the Venus mound thinly disguised behind the blue triangle, concave bronze-on-white belly, the blue-encased breasts, long graceful neck and the most devastating smile. Peter was gesticulating furiously *talk-to-her, talk.* finally, he found his voice.

"Not really" what a croak, like a grey raven at the end of a bad day, "just helping Peter a little." He straightened slowly, drew himself to the full 182 centimeters, her green eyes just a tad below his.

"Well, if you are not too busy, can you give me a ride to Jerusalem? I have to pick up something from the post-office." Yossi thought that her voice was the sweetest of tinkling bells, he nodded, rather dumbly, but then remembered "Er..just a minute, I don't have a car, I only have a motor-bike!!" God I hope she is not one of those I-only-ride-on-four-wheels snobs.

"I noticed the bike has two cylinders" she said sweetly, "pull out that extra helmet." Helen turned and Yossi watched with fascination as she insinuated herself into the shorts, which became immediately wet and stuck to her rear, and the T shirt which likewise cleaved to her bosom. Peter again had to shake him loose.

"Vell, this is a first for her, and you have the biggest idiot grin this side of the Mediterranean. Don't keep the lady vaiting."

Yossi was already astride the machine which was pumping the two cylinders at low revs. Helen was even more striking in tight jeans, chequered lumberjack flannel shirt, low boots and a windcheater jacket. Yossi gave her the black Nava helmet and she buckled it like an old hand. It seemed impossible that the blond curly mane would fit into the confines of the helmet, but then Helen threw a shapely leg over the pillion and placed her hands inside the pockets of his own wind-cheater. Yossi's skin felt overjoyed as the thin hands settled on his hips through the jacket.

"Let her rip" she said, loudly, to carry against the helmets and the motor. Yossi drove timidly at first, through the Kibbutz lanes, the gate and the twisty road. He felt her confidence on the pillion and slowly increased the pace, but never exceeded the speed limits. She did not attempt to speak but he could feel her hands tightening slightly as the road curved and her head turning to watch the scenery. Although it was almost noon, the air was cool, and the motor was beating strongly, seemingly happy to carry the added weight.

The post office was right on the main Jerusalem drag, Yaffo street, an impossibly narrow street for such an important artery. The buildings were finished in Jerusalem Stone, which gave the city its peculiar look. Yossi hopped the sidewalk and Helen stood on the footpegs and swung that incredible leg, to land like a cat on the sidewalk. She unbuckled the helmet and the blond curls exploded out. The divine smile came on again and Joe almost dropped the motorcycle.

"Back in a Jiffy" and she disappeared through the opaque glass door with the Antelope painted on it. The butt of another Israeli joke, the Israel postal service was considered by the inhabitants of the country to be the slowest in the world.

Helen came out with a big box. Yossi hopped off the bike and pulled it to the centerstand, no mean feat of strength. He took the box away and secured it to the small carrier. Meanwhile Helen stuffed her mane into the helmet and soon she was seated behind him again.

"Where to now, Madam?"

"Madam wishes to be driven fast. It's up to you."

I must be dead and gone to heaven, Yossi mused. If heaven means driving the Guzzi into the green hills of Jerusalem with the Goddess Helen at my back then I'm all for it. He took the Herzl route past the National Cemetery, the Yad Vashem memorial halls, and for the first time in his life was not troubled by the agony and death these places represented, but with Life, Glorious Life. He took the Ein Kerem turn off, the Haddassah hospital like a fortress of old guarding the valley and dove into the twisty tiny roads that led into the Jerusalem Forest. This being Israel, none are longer than fifteen miles, but who cared.

"Go Faster" she screamed through he wind, and he complied, though carefully, this package was too precious to be wasted. Every turn brought him a tight hug , and he acutely felt those breasts on either side of his spine, and every uphill sprint was rewarded by those tight hands gripping his iliac crests. He could take this excitement no longer, and he pulled up by one of the numerous picnic spots strewn under the trees. He parked the machine and killed the engine. After the noise generated by the motor and wind the quiet was blessed. On the weekends this place was teeming, but now in the middle of the week it was utterly quiet. The only sound was of the wind sifting through the Jerusalem pine forest.

Helen pulled the package off the bike "let's see if there is anything nice to eat in here." She plunked it on the wood picnic table and tore at the paper. She pulled out a small box of Oreos "I love them and you can't get them here, it's a backward country. No Oreos" and she rolled her eyes dramatically "really backward. Have some" she offered Yossi who was fascinated again by the performance.

Helen separated the cookie and licked the chocolate sandwich filling."Mmm" she said appreciatively. Then she looked Yossi right in the eye "let's cut the Ice, I like you and its obvious you like me. So, let's introduce ourselves, I am Helen Link, I live in Seattle, and I am a student at the Puget Sound University, majoring in Pharmacy. Pleased to meetcha" and she held out her hand across the picnic table.

Yossi took the thin long-boned hand in his sizeable paw and was surprised at the strength in which it was gripped. "I am Yoseph Bergman, of Tel Aviv, currently a fifth year medical student, in a six year program. Overwhelmed to meet you" and he was rewarded by that luminous smile again. It was like the sun breaking through the thick clouds of loneliness, of the loss of both his parents and more recently his grandparents. Here was someone to cherish, even if I only met her this morning.

Helen sat down on the bench and surveyed her surroundings. "You know, this place is kinda nice. My idea of Israel was Camels and Desert and War. There is that too, I know, but there is a nice forest, and a cute picnic table, and even a brook somewhere down there, and cute men too!! Do you mind if I call you Joe?" and she turned towards him, lips turning brown with the Oreo cookie. More than anything in the world, Yossi longed to kiss those lips and make them pink again.

"Joe sounds good to me" he said "when we lived in California they all called me Joe."

"Really, when did you live in California?"

"My dad was a Post-Doc at UCLA so we lived in Westwood for a year."

"So that's why your English is so good, are you involved with any of the Wars?" She was not just sweet or provocative, she was concerned.

"Sure" Joe said, this time his voice was normal, low timbre, very masculine. "I have to be. I'll tell you a little bit if you don't think I'm bragging, or just trying Macho stuff on you." Helen shook her head, the blond curls swaying to and fro. Its just like my heart, bucking inside my chest, and he proceeded to tell her about the Tavassim. Her face withheld nothing, the fear, horror, sadness played on her lovely features as if she was truly participating.

"I don't want to presume" she said slowly, each syllable very clear "but will you show me the scar?"

By now Joe was not surprised. She could see anything she wanted, he was ready to lay bare his soul. Off came the jacket, and he rolled up the right sleeve. There it was, not livid any more, just a stark reminder of a close call.

Helen left her seat and rounded the picnic bench. She extended those long fingers and slowly traced the outline of the scar, very slowly. Joe sat there and aspirated her smell and touch. Take me now Elohim , Oh Lord, maybe there is a God who allows me to be so happy. Then she sat down, naturally, very close.

They talked and talked, about everything, her Jewish father who wanted her to see the Holy land and thankfully paid for the ticket, her mom who was such a boss, college kids, the booze parties she abhorred, and growing up in America, so secure in the future. She had one older sister and a string of dates who tried to get her in the sack ASAP, in a car, out of the car, anywhere, especially after they had had a drink or two. The rape attempt last year by a former rejected boyfriend, right at the dorms. How she loved her classes in comparative anatomy and genetics, and the little dirt motorbike she loved to ride when it does not rain, and even if it does. The decision on a Kibbutz and how she adored the cow-milking early in the morning. Joe talked about his dead parents, his departed grandma, and growing up in a country whose very existence is a daily question. The shadows lengthened as the sun dipped west but they drank each other as if to make for a whole lifetime which had mischievously not placed them together before. It was late afternoon before Joe noticed how dry his mouth was, from talking and not having drank anything since mid AM. The Oreo boxes were empty though.

"I think we better head back and look for some food and drink, it's gonna get cold here."

Helen reconstituted her box, much depleted, and pulled on her jacket and helmet. Joe started the cold, silent Guzzi and it revved happily double-barrel. Thirty minutes later, cold and famished, they were back at her room door step. She stopped at the door.

"I have a room mate here" she warned.

"Warning noted" he said.

Helen turned the handle, the room was unlocked but no one was in. This room was much nicer with photos and rugs and books. She poured some Neviot bottled water into the standard issue electric kettle and soon they had steaming Peter Mocha cups warming their freezing hands. They sipped and gazed at each other, and suddenly the hunger for food was gone and lust, more powerful than Joe had ever imagined, overtook them. Joe was no virgin but his previous sexual encounters were insipid, and sometimes left him with a bad taste and slight self disgust. This was the real thing, his total manhood peaking toward this moment. Fully clothed they fell on the rickety bed, thinly shod with Gummavir mattress, and kissed and explored each others bodies.

An eon later the door opened from without and a chirpy English female voice said:

"Helen, are you in here?...Oh, I'm sorry, I'm sorry, I'm gone!!" and the door closed hurriedly and a peal of laughter rolled outside.

Helen and Joe looked at each other from a distance of two inches and fell apart with laughter.

"Poor Maureen, she is so used to me reading here, she couldn't figure out the dark."

"Doesn't anybody of the male Gender ever visit this room?" Joe was teasing.

"Not if he doesn't want his cojones crushed by a well placed kick" and Joe folded up in a sham pained expression.

"So I need to count myself lucky if mine are still whole" he croaked, "Peter told me there is a line of them willing to take a chance."

Helen became suddenly very serious. She pushed her flannel shirt back inside the jeans and sat across from Joe on a matching rickety chair.

"What are we going to do with ourselves, Joe?"

Joe sobered up in a flash, this was too serious to treat with levity.

"First , we need to stay together."

"Agreed, how?"

"I have a small apartment in Tel Aviv, close to the beach."

"So you suggest I move in with you, 12 hours after we met for the first time?"

"Yes" Joe was simple and direct. He had never wanted any female in the apartment for the morning ablutions, smelly breath, dirty socks, and morning crankiness. Even if it was five o'clock in the morning he would still escort the current date to her home.

"OK, I will buy that. What about school, and work?"

"Let's figure that out later, how long till your break is over?"

"Two weeks."

"Then in two weeks we will figure out the rest of our lives."

Helen smiled her most beatific, it curled Joe's toes. "That was the easiest decision I have ever made, easier than what to wear for the Prom. Let's tell Peter."

"But let's get something to eat first, I'm still a growing boy, you know!"

They sneaked some bread and jam from Maureen who was on kitchen duty out of the Kibbutz kitchen. Then knocked on Peter's door.

"Ah, its you two, how come you steal both my heart and my friend?" Peter wagged his finger at Helen.

"He is still your friend and you can come and visit us in Tel Aviv" Helen rejoined prettily. Peter's eyebrows almost shot through his thinning hair. Joe just shrugged shoulders, to his ears, I-am-not-in-control-here-anymore.

"Yavohl madam Kapittan, but don't go tonight, because Yozee cannot see straight. Stay here, I will move to Bronskie's room."

Helen collected her stuff in the morning and bade the Kibbutz goodbye. Peter promised to send whatever did not fit on the bike to Tel Aviv. An hour later Joe unlocked the door of the small flat, which now suddenly seemed disreputable and not very clean. It was the most wonderful fortnight of his life.

"Helen, you must get back home, and see how you can swing some months here, and I will get as many electives as I can in Seattle."

And they did, Joe was done with his sixth year and graduated, he still needed to do one full year rotating internship in Israel, to be certified. They never broached the subject of marriage but it was not far from their minds. He was Jewish, and she was not, and in Israel marriages are registered only through the Religious authorities. If a person is Jewish he or she must show proof that the fiancé is Jewish too and if he or she is not, then marriage cannot be. There are thousands and thousands of such couples in Israel who are refused the marriage ceremony.

Helen was the first to suggest that she convert and started some lessons through the Tel Aviv Rabbinate. Joe noticed what a great emotional effort she put into these lessons and finally over dinner on the beach he asked:

"You aren't very happy with those lessons are you?"

Helen broke down "I can't take the lies. They keep badgering me about why I want to convert, and I'm supposed to tell them its because I had some kind of illumination. I only want to do it so we can be totally together, because I love you!! I never cared about religion!! And they want me to change my dress and how I wear my hair, telling me that scalp hair is depravity!! Joe, I can't stand this country. I love you but I don't love Israel. Too much pressure, too expensive, too much Holiness, too much dirt, too little courtesy, look at this cab driver, he is slashing both lanes and leaning on his horn at the same time. I tried, God knows I tried, but I want to go home. Please come home with me. We will get married in America, I will even convert in America. Please Joe!" and she cried like her heart was breaking, she is afraid I may say NO, but home is where we make it, be it Israel, America or the South Pole. And every word was true. It was time to show her the good news. Joe pulled out the thin envelope from his fanny pack. He dangled the folded paper in front of her streaming eyes.

Slowly Helen regained her composure. She had told Joe once that she cried easily and not to be flustered. She took both the proffered napkin and the neat paper.

Educational Commission for Foreign Medical Graduates

Dear Dr Bergman

The commission is pleased to inform you that you have passed the FM-GEMS examination dated October 1988.

your scores are as follows

Component one - Preclinical sciences-85

Component two - Clinical sciences -88

English language component-passed

You are eligible for the ECFMG certificate which will be mailed to you in three to four weeks.

"What does it mean Joe?" Helen was coming out of the black cloud as the sun peeks after a day of rain, one ray at a time.

"It means that after I get my License I can get accepted to a US training program. I didn't tell you about the exam I took when you were in Seattle. I didn't want us to be disappointed if I had failed."

the Sun came out all the way. With a yelp Helen jumped across the small table, upsetting the cups and saucers and hugged him so hard his neck felt like it was breaking. He lifted her off her feet and she danced on the sidewalk still hugging him, and cried with relief.

Joe was accepted to the Pediatric program of the State University of Washington, on the merit of his recommendations earned during his electives of the year before, and the fact that Pediatrics was not a very popular choice of American Graduates, so that many programs are filled by Foreign graduates. Helen completed her studies in Pharmacy and entered a residency in Clinical Pharmacy. Many days they even managed to get some lunch together. Helen approached Rabbi Pinsker of the Beth El Conservative synagogue, and they agreed on a plan of conversion.

The Jews in America had created a whole new social and religious structure. Whereas in Israel the local Rabbi is appointed and paid for by the State, in America the Rabbi is hired by the community, to lead the religious and community faith. Whereas in Israel the Kashrut (preparation of foodstuffs according to religious principles) is mandated and therefore has become an enormous cash-cow to the Inspectors, in America it is voluntary, and companies will pay for a Kosher inspector only if they think it is worth it commercially. And many do!! look for the Ou and the K signs on American foodstuffs. Whereas the state of Israel pays enormous sums to keep the religious political parties on the good side of the current government, that would be a complete anathema to the American mind. Secular Israelis are absolutely disgusted by the power of the religious establishment, its total domination of family law, its ability to wring more and more funds using it tongue-of-the-scales position in political life. In fact the main rift in Jewish Israeli society is between the small majority which serves in the armed forces, and the large minority of Ultra religious groups which have used a historical fluke to abdicate that awful responsibility. The majority of Jewish Americans appreciate their Rabbis. The majority of Israelis either don't care about, or don't care for their Rabbis.

Rabbi Pinsker recognized that the major danger facing his community was rampant assimilation. He an his wife Naomi applied them-selves diligently to the task of bringing prospective converts into the community. Ruth, the grandmother of King David was a convert The converts were almost always brought in by their association with a Jewish member. But still, with time, they learned to appreciate and love the faith for its own merits, and sometimes became more observant than their spouses. Helen was enfolded with love and as Joe entered his second year of residency she passed the examination and was renamed Ruth, after the most famous of converts.

They got married at Beth El, Michael Link gave away his most beautiful daughter to his accomplished son-in-law and she was the most absolutely gorgeous bride the Synagogue had ever seen. Michael Link was secretly very happy that his daughter chose to return to the faith of his youth, something he could never get his wife to do. Margie was happy that Helen was finally home, and of all the ruffians with motorcycles she had ever dated she had found a real Doctor. Joe was given away by Irwin Perlmutter, the chief of Pediatric Hematology, who had already earmarked Joe for a fellowship in two years time. Joe was accepted in the family circle and in the Jewish community. He had a family.

Helen woke up with a headache and a little nausea. Joe had to leave no later than 0530 to get to the Intensive Care on time. It was three months since Helen had stopped taking her Pills, and last month, when she had a normal period Helen had cried her eyes out and raved that they will never have any children, and that they should never have waited for the marriage and gone on to have a baby. Joe calmed her down and they tried again. Not that it took any real effort, sex was as joyful an experience as they had ever hoped it could be. But Sex was given an extra zest when they were doing it For Real, hoping that the joy would bring even more joy 40 weeks later, So Joe was happy and full of hope at this nausea, and lack of Period. He did not offer Helen any Tylenol and instead made her some tea, before rushing out to the old car , the empty roads and the critically ill kids in the Unit. later when he called she was feeling much better and she was working on her Masters Thesis. She had made an appointment with Doctor Bloor, an obstetrician favored in the Jewish community.

Joe fidgeted in his chair and looked for the umpteenth time at the door blocking the exam rooms suite. The women came and left, some happy, some not, and then Helen came out, dressed in the blue cardigan he had gotten her for her birthday, and   he braced himself for the flying hug from three steps away. Just like the flying arc into the pool at the Kibbutz.

"We are pregnant, we are pregnant," and she danced him around and round the waiting room. The receptionist smiled with approval. Surely this was the happiest occupation of all, to make a couple happy, and this was the best looking couple this week, the man tall and strong and dark and the woman reedy and full of requited womanhood, with the prettiest curls in the West.

Doctor Bloor, a short black bespectacled man came out and waited for the antics to end. Helen allowed Joe to pump Doc Bloor's hand enthusiastically, blew him an air-kiss, and blew the receptionist an airkiss too. Seattle was a bright place, even if it rained 300 days a year!

The morning nausea got worse and worse. Joe made Helen her favorite dishes but they always ended up in a big puke bowl. It got so bad that Joe brought both the food and the bowl at the same time. The nausea always got better later in the day so that she did not actually dehydrate, but there was no weight gain, and even some weight loss. Doctor Bloor demonstrated a normal heart beat by the 8th week, and the embryo itself appeared to develop well. By the twelfth week it was fully formed on ultrasound, head, and body and limbs but Helen had to be admitted to St Ive's due to HyPeremesis Gravidarum, uncontrolled vomiting due to Pregnancy.

Joe was on Hematology elective and so he was not needed for call that month. It was midnight and he was dozing off at the bedside, while Helen's IV was dripping fluid and hyper-alimentation to sustain his wife and future son. Suddenly he snapped up.

"Joe, Joe, are you here?" Helen sounded frightened, her voice was tinny and far and deeply scared.

" I am here my love, right here, what's wrong?"

"Joe, I can't see, I can't see you."

"I'm here Helen, you are looking right at me."

"But I can't see you, can't see anything, its all dark." Fear gripped Joe's heart, Fear so strong he was paralyzed, he had never feared for his own life that much, not in Lebanon, not anytime. He pressed the light switch and the overhead fluorescent tubes came on so bright that he squinted.

"Now look at me" he commanded. She looked right at him and it was the look of the blind. Joe knew that the nightmares that he had never even dreamed of were rushing at him. He would rather face a fusillade from a dozen machine guns than face that gaze. He turned his face away from the beautiful face with the blind gaze, contorted with overwhelming fear.

"Don't leave me Joe, stay with me, get help but stay with me!" Helen's voice was in complete control. Joe gripped her wan hand and used the other to press the nurse's call button. 10 seconds later a robust nurse rushed in, She slowed as she saw no dire emergency.

" Get Doctor Bloor, right now, and get the Neurologist on call, NOW!"
She didn't even try to assess the situation, this man was all command, and
he looked desperate. She ran back to the nurses station to make the calls.

The CT machine was done and the nurse's aids came into the stark white
room to transfer Helen back onto the gurney. Joe murmured to Helen who
was mildly sedated that he would be right back. It was two o'clock in the
morning, even the busy hospital was quiet. Joe opened the door where the
tech was working the CT controls and was appalled at the grim expression on
Doctor Elkind's handsome face. She could hardly meet his eyes and doctor
Bloor was staring at a microbe on the floor.

Joe turned to look at the screen. The brain was sliced by the machine into
a series of consecutive slices. An ominous mass was pushing and distorting
the posterior brain. A Tumor, an awful tumor, more horrible than any other
apparition. Doctor Bloor's face contorted and the tears welled out unbidden.

"I never saw it, I never saw it, it was just Hyperemesis. I have taken care
of a thousand Hyperemesis . I am so sorry doctor Bergman." Joe eyed him
with pity, the man, so competent, so secure , just dissolved in front of his eyes
and of course it wasn't his fault. Maybe if Helen had been married to
someone more observing, or thoughtful, or rational, or just BETTER, she
might have had this tumor diagnosed before. Joe knew the awful prognosis
of posterior fossa tumors in adults. Being a Doctor himself this omission was
inexcusable. Joe understood what had happened. As long as Helen vomited
she had kept her fluids to a minimum and the pressure inside her head
controlled. Once that self-protective mechanism was bypassed by the fluid
infusion the pressure inside the closed box of the cranium increased and
damage was done . The First Principle of Medicine, *Primum Non Nocere*
(first, do no harm) had been violated , and he was the one responsible. He
turned to Doctor Elkind.

"Is herniation a possibility here?" Doctor Elkind nodded her head,
confirming Joe's suspicion that the brain, under pressure, might push into the
Foramen Magnum and cut its own circulation, meaning instant death "I told
the nurses to rush her to intensive care, stop her fluids and give her Bumex to
make her pee" Joe now nodded, the basic steps in intracranial pressure
reduction "and I called my associate Doctor Hill, Neuro Surgery, for a consult
and possibly immediate surgery, unless you want me to call someone else."
Joe shook his head. Doctor Hill was top-notch, and Joe had taken care of a

few of his patients in the Children's Hospital intensive care.

Joe's eyes were grainy with lack of sleep. Margie and Michael and Alice were tight in a conversation and for the first time in 3 years Joe felt excluded. Helen had been at surgery for 6 hours and occasionally the receptionist passed a message from the OR that things were going well, which Joe did not believe even for one moment. And the baby inside... They knew she was pregnant but the threat of herniation was so great that they had rushed her into the OR by 3 o'clock in the morning. Michael broke off, followed by the eyes of Margie and Alice. Alice shot him a venomous glance. Joe felt what was coming, he was telling himself the same ever since he saw that huge Tumor staring him down from the screen.

Michael Link was very uncomfortable "Mike, just tell me!" Joe said wearily after a couple of minutes had passed.

Michael was even more uncomfortable, he was never good at direct confrontation. He took another cue from Margie and Alice.

"Well, Joe, didn't you tell us this is a really big tumor?" he asked diffidently. Joe nodded.

"So how come, you being a Doctor and all, and looking for a career in Cancer like you told me last week, how come you didn't see any signs before last night, signs that a tumor was right inside her Brain?" Michael would never have thought to formulate such a loaded question. It was Margie, Joe knew it.

"Mike, I ask myself the same question, minute after minute after minute. I don't know, I didn't see it coming. Maybe I should have, but I never did, I am more sorry than I can ever say."

"So if you didn't see it in your own wife, how are you going to see it in a strange kid?"

Joe shook his head "Mike, I have no answer for you. I was not *looking for* a tumor in my wife, the mother of my future child. I have no answers. Helen doesn't deserve this, you don't deserve this, and maybe *I* do. I have killed people and maybe Helen is being punished for my sins. I am talking complete irrational nonsense here, Mike, let's just be quiet OK? Just be quiet!"

Michael edged away from his grieving son in law. Joe held his head in his hands and pressed so hard to make the pain go away, make the pain go away by causing himself pain. But nothing could take away the vision of Helen, face down on the operating table, head being split open, and the Surgeon poking and cutting and burning away parts of her *Brain. She is never going to be the same again.* The person he had loved and cherished for the last five years was gone and in her place-who knows? and the Baby, the baby.... Who is his mother going to be?

Doctor Hill peeled off his mask, time for another difficult interview, and a Doctor's Wife of all things. It was well known that doctors had the worst luck in diseases, or so the legend went. And this was the epitome of the rule. The Link family ganged up on him as soon as he pushed the double doors but he searched for Doctor Bergman, who had appeared to be so much in control at early AM. What he saw was a big figure, huge hands, and a completely deflated face. He is blaming himself, the curse of all doctors. Joe rose with a Herculean effort and finally looked him in the eye.

"The good news is that she is going to live, we removed as much tumor as we could and relieved the pressure on the brain. only time will tell if she will be able to see." The Link family broke into a hubbub, hopeful.

Joe cut through the crap "And what's the bad news Doctor Hill?" the noise was cut with a sword.

"It looks like a GlioBlastoma Multiforme" Doctor Hill was used to giving bad news but even he quailed before the piercing green-brown eyes and those enormous shoulders and huge hands which clenched and unclenched spasmodically. If this man goes berserk then I'm done for. The shoulders went slack and the hands opened slackly and the big man dragged his feet to the corner and sobbed and sobbed and sobbed. Irwin Perlmutter laid his soft hand on the big heaving shoulders and patted ineffectually. Joe hardly noticed.

Three weeks later they had a major conference. Helen was sitting in the wheel chair, cortical blindness giving her open eyes a vacant look. Joe sitting at her side holding the bony skeletal hand. The Doctors were Bloor, Elkind, Hill and Winters, the neuro-oncologist. They waited for the fifth essential component of the team, Doctor Meller, radiation oncology. He bustled in with apologies.

Doctor Elkind led the discussion "Doctor Bloor, can you bring us up to date about the pregnancy?"

Bloor pulled out a series of ultrasound images "the baby appears alive and well, with strong heart pulse, breathing movement, normal internal organs and normal looking brain" he carefully avoided looking at Doctor Bergman or his patient, but he did not notice any signs of blame issuing from the young

Pediatrician.

"Any signs to suggest that he might have been damaged by the anaesthesia?"

"None" he answered with certainty, or maybe I should not be so certain seeing how I mis-diagnosed my patient, so he added "I showed the ultrasound tape to a number of associates and they agree that the baby appears fine."

"Good" said doctor Elkind. She turned to Doctor Hill. "What about the tumor itself?" The dread word was bandied about as if its horrible meaning was lost on deaf ears.

"The MRI carried out last night shows some residual tumor enhancing with Gadolinium. I dare say that if I had this type of imaging modality at the time of the surgery I would probably have taken more out, but at the time the main concern was herniation so the surgery is less than optimal." Joe's face was carved of unforgiving stone, Helen listened, said nothing, but the pressure on his hand increased, he could feel every bone.

Doctor Elkind turned to Winters. "What is the pathological diagnosis and what can you offer us therapeutically?"

SQUAT Doctor Winters said to himself "the tumor was con-firmed to be GBM, GlioBlastoma Multiforme, grade four. The cranio-spinal fluid contained some mitotic cells of the same origin. Currently, there are two clinical trials, one at the NCI and one right here in Seattle. The NCI trial is half way there and they are about to call it off due to disease progression. The trial here consists of high dose combination chemotherapy with stem-cell rescue, either bone marrow or peripheral. Of the ten patients accrued so far, one had progressive disease, two had stable disease and six had partial remission. One patient had a complete cure. It is a woman in her early twenties who had lost her eyesight. Her eyesight is now partially restored. The follow up time is insufficient to make conclusive recommendations."

Doctor Meller put his two cents in. "It seems that prior chemotherapy makes the tumor more radiosensitive so that we have been able to shrink them down later, after blood component independence."

Doctor Bloor was fidgeting like crazy "but this approach would kill the baby!!" and they all fell silent.

"So I guess its up to us" said Granite Face. "What do you say, Helen?"

"Make the baby come" she quavered, her voice a faint shadow of what it had been.

Doctor Bloor was distressed "its too early, in ten weeks time then maybe, you would know, you are a Pediatrician, but now its non-viable outside the womb."

"Helen, I have no use for the baby without it's mother, I say we take the chance we have and that's Chemo, yes, yes, we can always try for another baby once you are cured" lies, lies, *Lies*. Helen held off for a moment and then slowly nodded.

"When shall we start?" Granite Face asked Doctor Winters.

"As soon as Doctor Hill says the wounds are closed." Winters was not enthusiastic at all. This tumor looked especially evil under the microscope.

Helen made it past the Chemo and the marrow reinfusion. The marrow held up and repopulated the space left vacant by the chemotherapy. In a convulsive episode Helen lost the tiny baby. Joe looked at the almost human mess and his face registered nothing. He was dying with his child and wife. The tumor was totally unaffected by the enormous amount of chemotherapy aimed at it. It grew and grew. Helen lost consciousness and after the next MRI Joe signed the DNR order, do not resuscitate, do not ventilate. His face remained impassive throughout, with never a flicker of hope or dejection. Rabbi Pinsker and Naomi came and went, Michael Link hung about like a pale ghost, and cried. Alice came and looked at Joe as if he was a particularly loathsome insect, and Joe remained Granite.

Helen breath hiccuped a few times, a long indraw, and out, and there was silence. Joe was totally unmoved. This was expected. He watched as the nurses pulled up the sheet and cleaned up the implements of useless impotent Medicine.

The funeral was Jewish, a simple gurney, no casket, four men to carry the gurney, the cantor leading. A long queue of people trailing the bereaved, Michael crying, Margie sobbing and Joe impassive, he recited prayers in Hebrew and Arameic, and read from the psalms. Irwin Perlmutter kept a close eye on him, he was too impassive. He should be crying and letting it out. Joe separated himself from the family and started to walk, the constant rain beating on his wide Aussie hat and dripping down onto the drenched coat. Irwin tried to follow but Joe was marching much too fast, arms on the imaginary rifle and butt pumping away like it was autonomous He disappeared from view in the gloom and rain, going nowhere, going nowhere.

Joe appeared back at the Children's Hospital on the first of the month, he still had six rotations to go for graduation. He explained to Irwin that he was not going to join the Hematology service the coming July but since he must fulfill his obligations to the Pediatric Program, he will go through with it. And go through he did. No joy, no smile, no grief, no emotions. Kids lived, kids died, junior residents were excellent or flunked, it was all the same. The nurses could not face Granite Face. He did not change expression at the graduation party as the graduates were given a hearty send off and the new house-staff were introduced.

"I came to Seattle for the ASH conference" Abe Kammitzer continued "and as usual it was rainy and rather dreary. I know Irwin Perlmutter from way back in Cleveland. So when he asked me for lunch I grabbed at it. We took his car and I assumed he was looking for a restaurant but boy was he in the wrong neighborhood. It was all new construction, and it was the new-fangled steel stuff. They get the steel components off a semitrailer and bolt them together into an A shape with braces. Then they tie the construct to a boom and it lifts it up and they place it on some huge screws and they bolt them down. Then they knit them together with Omega shape steel strips. Rather neat and fast, the trick is to screw- knit them together right at the top. And how do you get there?" Karen was blank, so much sadness, so much misfortune, and she understood every bit of it, so steel construction was not high on her priorities of need-to-know. Abe Kammitzer continued   "So Irwin points out a guy, who looks as wide as he is tall, jumping around, wrenching the bolts and securing braces and then this guy ties what looks like a thong to the boom and gets himself lifted over the tops of the A's swinging an electric drill with one hand and one of those Omegas in the other. Looks like a high wire act without the safety-net. He places the omega on one end on the building, screws it down and the boom takes him to the next A, 8 feet away, and so on.

"So I turn to Irwin and say, what's the point Irwin, if I want to go to the circus then I want to see some tigers and ladies too, so he says, you must help me save this lost soul and tells me the story of Joe and Helen, which if you hear it from the end it sounds like a preordained Greek tragedy. First his parents, then his grandparents, then his wife, then his wife's family ostracizes him saying he should have seen it earlier. Gimme a dollar for everytime I should have seen it earlier and I'm ready to retire a rich man. So Irwin tells me maybe YOU can get him away from the grave he visits every day before he goes out trying to kill himself with high flying acts. He also took some flying lessons and skydiving. He figures if God takes away everybody he loves so maybe He should take him too, but Joe does not see that logic dictates that if

God takes away everybody Joe loves, then God will leave Joe who hates himself, to be the oldest SkyJumper in the world!! So we wait for him to finish his act and the boom lowers him down and he sees Irwin and comes to say hello with a smile, all mouth, no eyes, just viewing instruments like Arnold has in Terminator movies. Irwin introduces me and he is very careful not to crush my hand in that paw of his, and Irwin tells about the new Baxter Stem Cell collection machine and that the American Society of Hematology meeting is in town and he ought to go in and just keep up to date and I see he has heard this come-on a bunch of times before."

"So I say, point blank, how long have you been in mourning Joe, and he gives me a sharp look and says 21 months and 5 days. At least he is not totally dead. So I say what is keeping you in this town besides a grave, and he looks like he wants to sock me on the jaw. So I say, Jewish law forbids grieving for more than one year except for Yuhr Zeit, that is a day of remembrance a year, and that I need a good fellow for the coming July because the current applicants are not too good, and I give him my card. It took him three months to call me back and ask if the offer still stands. Now I hear Joe laughing mirthlessly from time to time. Do you really want to be involved with Joe and another convoluted way to get himself killed?"

Karen did not hesitate. "Yes, we are two of a kind."

Chapter 12

Flying Blind

The Cessna series of single engine puller prop aircraft ranges from the tiny 150, a two-seat trainer, through the 172, a 4 place aerial econobox and up to the Cessna 210. The Cessna 310 is a twin engine variable pitch prop aircraft which is half way between a private aircraft and a business plane. The 210 is a 180 knot airplane which means it's the minimum aircraft for cross-country flights. The single engine puts it within the reach of the basic Private Pilot License. The double engine increases the complexity of the aircraft by a factor of not two, but 20. Despite the theoretical safety advantage of double engine, it's the twins that suffer the higher rate of accidents, rather than the singles. Joe had gone for a deal in which he put a down payment on a Cessna 210 with 1000 hours left on the engine, got the First Wisconsin bank to put up the balance, and then rented it out to the Avia Flight School which in turn rented it out to students and the occasional cross country flight. This way Joe could have the airplane almost any time he wished and paid very little for its maintenance. The plane had reasonable avionics, King radios, DME (distance measuring) and 2 VOR's, which gave him direction to radio beacons, and glide-slope, which helped in landing in airfields so equipped. The newest addition was the GPS which was a hand held Garmin, which showed him, to a maximum error of 5 meters where he was on the face of the Globe. This new device was totally independent of radio beacons and of course over the open sea it was the only real choice other than dead reckoning and Loran which was expensive and dated to pre-satellite days. The Sony model was nicer but Joe, even though, and maybe because he was not American, preferred to buy American. It galled him to think that the US air force had spent billions of dollars putting 200 satellites around the earth and then comes along Sony and uses the transmission from those satellites to make money off the American customer. But it was part of the American Way to spread the wealth around because in the end it came back home, as the strength of the American economy showed. Still, Joe bought mostly American.

It was one thing to fly at night at three thousand feet and follow the freeways to major cities. It was completely different to fly at the minimum legal altitude over the least lighted countryside at 500 feet. Although it was not required, Joe kept switching frequencies to let major airports he was in the neighborhood. He was lucky with the weather, there was a high pressure, stable mass of air over the Plains. Joe had prepared his route meticulously with short legs and intermediate airspeed, and checked his position against the Garmin, The Jeppesen map and local VORs which in America almost always worked. It was grueling labour with no time to enjoy the flight itself. His eyes roamed constantly over the instruments, oiltemp, oilpressure, Battery, Airspeed, artificial horizon, Gyro and magnetic compass, Altitude, outside the windshield, identify roads and towns and back to the GPS. The route was marked on the map and tabulated on the clip board as a series of checkpoints and times to reach, and corrections and VOR azimuth. It was essentially a southward route from Milwaukee to Memphis along the Mississippi, skirting the major towns. Joe expected to fly three hours on Monday night and two hours on Tuesday, and rest in a small airport in between. He landed in Centralia, south of the Centralia reservoir at 2230. It was completely deserted, as expected, but the airstrip lights and the two sets of glide-slope indicator lights came on at three and four clicks on the mike, made on the appropriate frequency. This was a luxury he will not have later. Joe admitted to himself that he was not a professional military pilot. Without the Garmin he would still be in the sky looking for an emergency field. In the blue light of the Compaq Armada he read off the names of possible Hotels. He would need a good night sleep after this navigation.

The trains rattled the whole night and Helen rode them and rode him alternatively. Joe knew he was never going to get a good night's sleep as long as he lived. It was already 5 years, and the rest of his life stretched ahead like an endless plain with no destination in sight. No birthdays, no PTO meetings, no holidays, no Friday nights. Just a long dreary death- in- life, of patients, and scientific meetings, and publications. This was the lowest of the low, sitting in anonymous motel, in an anonymous town, with nothing to show for almost 40 years of life. Let's just see if I can get Mustafa before he or his cronies get me. Joe spread out the Jeppessen maps and continued to plot his course to Spain-deWitt airfield.

Joe and Helen had leased an apartment in Renton, south of Seattle. Even after a long day-night-day call, Joe would still take Helen to the Sky Shop Café on the edge of the Renton Municipal airfield and while drinking a sociable afternoon coffee and cheesecake he would gaze at the small aircraft taking off and landing on the airstrip. Sometimes a business jet would swoop down from the north over Mercer Island and sleekly land with a characteristic whine-reverse thrust-whine again. Helen watched the wistful face and the longing eyes and just smiled to herself.

"Joe, let's go."
"And what vehicle would you like Madam, the Old Nova or the new Kat?"
Joe teased.
Helen made a show of looking outside, examining the mild evening sky,
the red edged clouds lit from below by the sinking sun.
"Lets ride into the sunset on the Kat."
"As if I didn't know" Joe grumbled, obviously happy. With so many rainy
days any chance to ride the new Blue Suzuki Katana was reason enough for
a party. And today was his birthday, 32 years old. This current year of his life
had been so fulfilling, so enriching that he could see nothing but bright
horizons and endless love and happiness. He was learning a dozen new things
every day in Pediatrics, his relationships with the other interns were great, the
chief resident Doctor Emily Morgan turned out to be a dear, and Irwin
Perlmutter, head of the Pediatric Hematology and chief of staff encouraged
him to write up and present in Grand Rounds a case of Congenital Leukemia.
He was learning to love Helen some more every day. Her wisdom, her wit,
how she handled people, avoiding pitfalls and not fighting the unnecessary
battles that Joe sometimes fell into. Her fierce arousal at love making, the
nail-marks on his broad back, and her sweet repose afterwards, green eyes
luminous a nose length away. Making love became an art, as they discovered
each others secrets, frailties, sensitive nooks and crannies. Joe learned how
to provoke a tremendous arousal with a flood of lust, or build a long, slow
languid climax, on a magical Saturday afternoon. Helen learned how she
could tweak Joe out of a medical book, make him come after her, and cause
him to explode inside her womb until she had sucked him dry, so a big huge
smile of utter joy and satisfaction softened his hard and weatherbeaten
features. And the longer they were together, the better it became.

The Blue Katana, a powerful 4 cylinder motorcycle started at the touch of
the button and settled into the familiar throaty ricemill sound. They had
bought it from a serviceman who had never really used it so that although it
a was a 3 year old, it was essentially new. Joe drove it out of the detached
garage and Helen closed the overhead door behind them. The Nova, an old
American Boat, was parked outside. Helen then hopped on the machine like
one would jump on a gymnastics horse and cleaved to Joe's back. Joe was
used to these antics and held fast.

"Let her rip."

"Where to, madam Bergman?"

"The Sky Shop."

"Hold on to your hat" but Joe never let her really rip when Helen was on board. Sometimes, when he was alone on his way to Down Town in the early morning he did redline it at freeway on-ramps, for about two seconds in second gear, enough to reach 90 and satisfy his need for speed. But generally he was a sedate rider, there was too much to live for.

The old waitress at the Sky Shop welcomed the handsome couple and winked at Helen as soon as Joe had gone by. A Cessna 152 revved up its small engine, rolled slowly on the runway and like a small overloaded gnat and rose slowly into the night sky. It turned left to follow the pattern and went through the crosswind leg and the downwind leg. Joe watched it wistfully. It was so ungainly and slow and underpowered, yet it flew. They ordered, and discussed medicine, and Pharmacology, and the idiosyncrasies of their teachers and cohorts. Joe guessed Helen might have a birthday surprise and expected a token of love, maybe a disk, possibly a trinket for the motorcycle, something similar to the Aussie Snowy River hat she had gotten him the year before. He did not feel the need for anything astounding or expensive because nothing compared with the real riches of Life and Love.

The old waitress with three other waiters came out of the kitchen with great fanfare and fireworks blazing on the cake. The cashier started singing over the PA system FOR HE IS A JOLLY GOOD FELLOW and in the middle of the Black Forest cake there was a white swath of cream, and stuck at one end of it was a plastic biplane. Helen beamed at the waiters and directed them to place the cake at Joe's side of the table. Joe began to suspect something. The waiters clapped their hands encouraging him to blow the candles out and as he did an envelope appeared by magic, bound with a ribbon. Joe eyed Helen with mock suspicion.

"Is this fissile material?"

"Open it and find out. If it is we shall evaporate together." A waiter flashed the camera. Joe untied the ribbon and opened the envelope. He pulled out the voucher.

Renton Flying School , Inc.
This voucher entitles the bearer
Doctor Yoseph Bergman
to 40 hours of flying instruction

towards the acquisition of Private Pilot License
signed
Phillip Warden
General Manager
Renton Flying school Inc

Helen watched Joe's face carefully. "Are you happy?"
Joe's heart and breath thickened with love. "Yes, I am happy," kind of
choked, "and when I get the license, will you fly with me?"
Helen leaned over the table, breasts enticing under the open vee necked
blouse. "I will fly with you anywhere you want" she whispered, and flushed
at the loud applause from the waiters.

Joe took the flying lessons as a crash course during the three week
vacation he was entitled to as an intern. He had a natural aptitude, and made
his first Solo after only 8 hours in the air. He studied flight theory,
aerodynamics, weather and airspace, radio communications and navi-gation.
A lot of this material was not new to a former infantry officer, which made
everything easier. After 40 hours of practicing long field and short field
takeoff and landing, flying in controlled and uncontrolled airspace, powered
and unpowered stalls and some night flights, he passed the flight exam
without hitch and was encouraged by his instructor, Bill Brown, to do as
much flying as he could afford and make up the requisite logged air time to
advance to non-VFR license. Joe accumulated those hours by flying local and
the occasional cross country flight on a Cessna 172 with Helen. He never
realized his dream of flying with Helen to distant destinations.
Joe shook himself from the reverie, the Black Forest cake, the white cream
swath and the little biplane which he still kept in his flying bag along with the
Softcom headsets, the manual flight computer, the GPS and the Jeppesen
maps, and the Armada laptop which contained the aerial map of North
America on a disk. He was still in a lonely motel, in a lonely town, with a
self-inflicted mission ahead.
The December morning was cold even in these lower latitudes and the
Cessna's battery was sluggish. He had fueled up at the bowser, paid at the
desk with his Chase Visa and took off into the cold morn. He kept to the
major airways and 2 hours later landed in the Spain Dewitt aerodrome north
of the city. He parked the Cessna at the General Aviation section, and
registered his stay at the counter of Spain Aviation. It was certainly warmer

in Memphis than in Milwaukee, but they paid for it with interest during the long hot humid southern summer. He asked the Taxi to take him to St. Jude to find Dr Roger Cohen.

It was always confusing to walk onto the campus of a relatively modern hospital and find in the middle of the campus a pavilion which immediately recalled the Dome of the Rock, the golden Islamic mosque towering over the Temple Mount of old Jerusalem. The layout was so familiar to anyone from the Middle East that Joe was transported, just for one moment, to the great vista which opened up from the Jewish Quarter of The City within the Walls which overlooked the Dome, the El-Aktza Mosque with the silver dome, the huge plaza between them, the tremendous Western Wall which shored up the temple mount, and the thousands of black-frocked bearded religious Jews who prayed at the bottom of the wall. It was ironic that the wall built by Jews before the time of Christ, held aloft the tremendous Islamic structures. The Danny Thomas pavilion was a small replica of the Dome, arched entries and all.

Joe walked into the foyer and asked the pretty black receptionist where he might find Doctor Roger Cohen. She punched the name on the computer, and then a phone number. Joe surveyed his surroundings. Whereas in Milwaukee Children's which was a general hospital for children, only the occasional patient appeared to be with cancer, here everybody was. And what a babel of languages! St. Jude was truly the Capital of Pediatric Cancer and thank God for Danny Thomas and his vision. Only in America could an Arabic speaking group come together for such a noble cause, because back in the Middle East, with all its Petro-Dollars, nothing came even remotely close. If King Hussein needed treatment it was Mayo Clinic and not Riyadh or Cairo. He turned his attention back to the pretty receptionist.

"He is not in the department, they say."

"Is he retired, or at another institution?" Joe was perplexed. Dr Gottschalk would have known.

"Its not that, he is still the head of Genetics, but he is sick" she replied.

"Look, it's very important I speak with him, I came down from Milwaukee especially to speak to him about a problem I have. Here is my card, can you call up that department and ask them how I can get a hold of him?"

She was doubtful "I guess I can ask." She took the proffered card and immediately changed her demeanor "I am sorry Doctor, I will try them right away."

A few seconds later she looked up at him very seriously "he is at the

Cancer Center, and she said he was VERY sick."

"Jeez Louise" Joe muttered, and then loudly "isn't the Cancer Center about a mile away?"

"No, its like 2 or three miles, take a map, are you going on foot, can I call you a cab, Doctor?"

"I'll walk." Joe took the map, grabbed his flight bag and walked out of the campus onto Lauderdale Boulevard. Soon he was warm and took off his rumpled jacket and slung it over his bag. He followed Lauderdale and Mississippi boulevards and the number of churches along the way was unreal. Soon he reached the veritable city of hospitals between Poplar and Lamar avenues with the imposing Van Vleet Memorial cancer center on Madison. This was a post war building, heavier and less airy than St Jude.

Another receptionist, this time a huge matron at the round central console labeled "information" and this one was ready for him.

"Good day" he said "I am looking for a patient, a doctor by the name of Cohen."

"He is in room 479, shall I call up? Shanika from St. Jude called and said a doctor is coming to see Doctor Cohen" she answered his questioning how-did-you-know look.

"Please do" and he gave her the winningest grin. Just like Shanika said, this doctor smiles but his eyes do not, Pity, he is good looking dude.

She called the room and spoke briefly "you can go up, use the left elevator."

Joe set his face to the usual Granite and knocked on the open door.

"Come in, please," a woman said, clear and cultured, and not at all Southern

Joe was not ready for the man in the wheel-chair. Doctor Gottschalk had indicated that Roger Cohen would be in his early seventies. In the late 1990's a seventy year old is a middle-aged man. The person Joe saw was older than Metushelah, he looked 900 years old, with thin skin tightly drawn over the skull, and skeletal arms. His eyes were sunken under a beetling brow which made Joe uncomfortable-something he had seen be-fore but could not place, and they looked discolored, as if someone had given him two black eyes. A middle-aged woman, finely dressed with a Spiegel pin- striped suit sat near the old man and stroked the thinly-clad bones. Her hair was recently styled and her Channel perfume almost overcame the smell of decaying flesh which permeated the room.

"Hello ma'am, I am Doctor Bergman, Joseph Bergman" formally presenting his card, Japanese fashion. He had learned that mannerism from Doctor Yamamoto, one of the Japanese PhD's in Horowitz's lab. It was both formal and informative and allowed one to assess the reader as the card was perused. She read the card and appeared confused.

"Are you the consulting Physician that Doctor Lamar recommended we ask for a second opinion? No offense sir, but a Pediatrician?"

Joe examined the lady who was still stroking the old man's hand. She must be his wife, and a young woman in her sixties, he decided. The old man lifted his head slowly to gaze at the newcomer, as if in great pain, then smiled a rictus of a grin.

"Sit down please" he croaked, and slowly motioned with the arm into which a needle and IV tubing were stuck, "You look tired."

Joe was struck by the ludicrous observation. There is this man, half-way through death's door, and he decides that I am tired. And he is right, another night of nightmares is no rest. I betcha this rictus will enter tonight's nightmares too. Joe looked for a chair and dragged it to sit opposite the Death's head and his comely wife.

"I do not want to disappoint you but I am not a consultant at all. I am a Pediatric fellow in Hematology Oncology and obviously I limit my activities to children only, regards, from Doctor Gottschalk in Mil-waukee."

"That's wonderful" Croaked Roger Cohen, "Peds HemOnc is what I did in St. Jude until this" and he pointed at his black eye "hit me, and no one can figure out what it is."

Joe was really surprised. Occasionally someone on the Pediatric service would come in with a cancerous growth that was hard to define and classify, but that was rare nowadays. The technical powers of Genetics and Immunology and Pathology were such that almost any cell type, normal or tumor, could be categorized and assigned into one of the 200 odd classes of cells in the body. With such assignment came diagnosis and prognosis, and a plan of therapeutic intervention. Without specific classification, the treating physician was flying blind, into a storm, usually into the crash-and-burn situation. The Lady interrupted.

"I am sorry, I did not introduce myself, I am Tammy Cohen, and this is Doctor Roger Cohen, my husband." Joe rose to shake her well-manicured hand with the pianist fingers, and very carefully, the set of bones covered by blotchy film of a skin that was Roger Cohen's hand. "Delighted" he murmured, not very convincing.

"So, what brings you down to Memphis, Doctor Bergman?" she asked brightly, the Social animal reasserting itself.

Joe sat back. although the situation looked grave, the good Doctor could still help. It was unfortunate that he was doing so badly but he was still with all the marbles in place. "I am on the trail of someone you know, in fact someone you recommended highly, a PhD student by the name of Mustafa Halim." Now that's interesting. Doctor Cohen's face lit up, and his wife knitted her brows in consternation. "Have you seen him or spoken to him recently?"

Doctor Cohen wanted to answer but instead a cough racked his thin body, he coughed and wheezed, and it took long moments, despite his wife patting and stroking, for him to get back his breath. Finally he waved his arm at his wife indicating she should answer the question.

"We saw Mustafa about 9 months ago, in March or April. He came for some kind of a conference. That was before Roger became ill."

"Pardon me, Ma'am" Joe observed "but I think you were not very happy to see him!"

"No I was not, forgive me Roger but I never liked that man, even if you did, and I always thought he was a person of bad intentions." Blow me down if it isn't the proverbial Woman's Intuition, Joe thought. Tammy Cohen continued "later he called Roger in the office a couple of times, and called here too, to talk to Doctor Lamar. But he never visited again."

Joe was intrigued, all this appeared related to Mustafa's recent escapade. "And when was the last time you saw him before this?" he queried.

Tammy knitted her brow, making vertical lines where only horizontal lines were slightly visible under the artful makeup. "I think not for a number of years, in fact not since he left town with that fantastic Doctor wife, Amanda, she was such a dear!! And so pretty and clever!! And they had this munchkin of a girl!!" Mrs Cohen's face softened as she recalled the mother and child. Then she was angry again. "And then he turned up, with a big thick, black Islamic beard, and gets Roger to invite him to dinner!!"

Roger Cohen shook his head slowly "Tammy, you are too hard on the poor boy, he had had a hard life and he was going to be a good scientist, and I am happy he found a good mate and a has pretty daughter." And he was out of breath again.

It was time to drop the bomb. "Well, Doctor Cohen, This poor boy kidnaped his daughter Alia and escaped with her to the Middle East, either Syria or Lebanon, and left his wife Amanda Carter to cry her eyes out. And to cap it all he left us this *pretty* note."

Joe produced the page copied from Mustafa's computer.

As for the Zionists, my retribution is almost ready
and showed it to the dumbfounded couple.

Roger Cohen started a new cough, and it became worse and worse and his wife got up and clapped on his once-broad back and he wheezed even worse and his color got worse, and Joe found and pressed the nurse call-button. Red froth started to fleck the old man's lips which were turning purple. The nurse rushed in, she grabbed the mask with the tubing attached to a wall outlet. She turned the Oxygen full on and the bubbles formed in the chamber and gas rushed into the mask. She whipped at Joe "help me get him to bed, Ma'am go back to the desk and tell them to call the Doctor." Joe knew his limits, this was an adult and he had set his limits to kids. Joe supported the head and behind the knees, and lifted the airy bag of bones onto the bed. Flecks of blood spattered his rumpled white shirt and loose tie. A tall black Doctor appeared with a nurse pushing the resuscitation trolley just behind. "Visitors out" he commanded, Joe and Tammy sheepishly bowed out. For Tammy it was not the first time, he could tell, and her lady-like face was swimming in tears.

Roger Cohen was sleeping with the oxygen bubbling, the paroxysm, and the chemotherapy, and the bad news having sapped his meager strength. Tammy and Joe took the elevator down to the nondescript cafeteria. It was late afternoon and Joe who had been inured to pain and suffering was hungry. The food was basic plastic-wrapped sandwiches and Joe took one of the Turkey subs, which was a very tired turkey indeed, and a Coke. Tammy Cohen watched him eat. What a big, sad man. She did with a coffee over which she made a face.

She looked at Joe's big bag. "Are you carrying your house in this thing?"

"Almost, its my flight bag and a change of clothes, I flew myself in."

"You know, Roger was a pilot once, and he kept his license current until his eyesight failed him, he would have liked you" she said it wistfully.

Joe was surprised "you speak of him as if he is already dead."

"Well Doctor, isn't he?" she countered.

"I don't know, I don't have enough information regarding his clinical status, and as long as draws a breath there is hope!!" Joe tried to be emphatic, a hollow effort.

"Not if they don't have a clue as to what this is, and IT has invaded his bones, lungs, kidneys, and gives him so much pain, I dare not look at him when he refuses the Morphine so he can stay lucid and talk to me about the good times we had." Joe pulled out his ever-ready Kleenex, as her eyes brimmed with tears, and then spilled over, without actually crying.

"Thank you" she mumbled.

Joe finished his Coke as she blew her nose. It was time to go to work.

"Is it OK by you if I look into it?" he said, back to Lieutenant Yossi, commanding rather than requesting. That got her attention.

"Sure, maybe a new broom will sweep better."

"What is Doctor Cohen's Social security Number? That may be useful to track down pathology information." he forestalled her question.

"Its 247-01-2280, I had to give this number many times in the last three months."

"Alright" Joe rose and put his hand out "it is a pleasure to meet you Mrs Cohen, even under these circumstances, I will look into this. I have no idea what to look for but they trained me well in Milwaukee, I will be in touch" and he leaned to pick up his bag.

"Now you wait here just a moment, young man." Peremptory, almost like a genteel 3rd grade teacher, thought Joe, and he straightened and looked at the tear streaked face, and the mascara lines, smeared by the kleenex "where are you staying in Memphis?" in the same peremptory inflection.

Joe raised one eyebrow, "I guess in the closest Motel Six."

"You will do no such thing, I expect you at this address tonight" and she scribbled on a napkin with a Gold Parker from the pocket of the Spiegel suit. "And don't be too late either, you look beat as it is!!"

Joe could not help an amused grin "Aye-aye ma'am."

She rose and shook his hand "I promise the food will be superior" and smiled, cracking what was left of her makeup.

"I am quite sure" Joe said and hefted the flight bag.

It was shift-changing time as Joe found the Pathology lab in the labyrinthine bowels of the hospital, and a flood of black faces, joshing and laughing after a long day at the hospital, greeted him as he exited the elevator. It would be a good time to look and ponder at the slides. He walked around the labs until he found the obligatory open room, with a multiple head binocular microscope and the obligatory Pathology resident peering into it. He knocked an the open door.

"Excuse me."

She took her eyes away from the microscope, a typically Indian face, dark smooth features, and straight short black hair, black-within-black eyes. Her name tag said: Dr M Mehta, dptmt of Pathology. She was thin, short and trim, a miniature in Lab White.

"Can I help you?" She said, the unmistakable Indian inflection, slightly British, clipped and precise.

"Yes" said Joe "I wonder if you can help me locate and examine the pathology specimen for this individual" and Joe presented her with the name and SSN of Roger Cohen.

"Probably, are you a consultant?" And she took in Joe's name from the name-tag he had attached to his jacket, issued in Milwaukee "Doctor Bergman?"

"Well" Joe demurred "I am a friend of the family, in a roundabout way, and they asked me to look into his case, even though I am really a Pediatrician, you know how it is in the larger Family" and Joe laughed deprecatingly.

"I suppose that's OK, everybody and their sister have looked at these slides, and could not make heads or tails of them."

Joe raised his eyebrow again, at this rate I need to leave up there all the time. "So you know this case?"

"Who doesn't, its one of those Enigmas, It so happens I'm looking at them right now, why don't you put your bag down and take a look too."

Joe placed his bag in the corner and took a seat next to Doctor Mehta. He raised his glasses and pushed them into his hair, applied his eyes to the double lenses, and adjusted each until the picture was tri-dimensional and sharp.

"Where is this sample taken from?" his eyes were glued to the wide expanse of small, blue-stained closely packed cells, with multiple mitoses (cell division in progress) which screamed CANCER loud and clear.

"This sample is from an open biopsy of the right lung" she replied succinctly.

"Looks like a small round cell tumor, of some kind, where was the primary?"

"We don't know, the patient presented with" and she consulted her clipboard "bone pain, and was found to have multiple lesions, bone, lungs, liver, kidneys. This is a very aggressive tumor." and she shook her head regretfully.

"Did you do Immuno-histo?" Joe referred to the techniques of staining the sample slivers with specific antibodies raised against specific antigens, or markers, present on the cell surface. The biotechnology companies offered the pathologist an endless variety of such stains which allowed pathology to recognize the origin of diseased tissue.

"We stained this tumor with everything that Sigma ever made" Doctor Mehta was bitter, she must have done it herself "and it's positive for a bunch of markers, but nothing specific, it could be Germ cell, Lymphoma, even Neuroblastoma, but who has ever heard of Neuroblastoma in a seventy year old male?? We sent it out to Mayo, and NCI, and Cornell, and so far we received three different answers."

Joe looked away from the microscope, as did Doctor Mehta. She noted the quick exchange of tiny electrical discharges inside that wide, fine forehead, and suddenly the eyes slit.

"Do you have by any chance a Bone Marrow?" Joe asked, quietly.

She was doubtful "I am not sure, with so much specimen around, why would anyone take a trephine biopsy? Ah, but you are a Pediatric Hem-Onc, you always do that don't you? Let me look" and she quickly riffled through the box of slides, each labeled with a neatly hand-written sticker, "No, no, no" she whispered, intensely concentrated. "Ah, there we have it, not a real Trephine, but a bone fragment, with possibly some marrow adherent to it, this is from the Iliac crest" and she expertly placed the slide under the long, times 40 lens, focused on a field, then rotated the objective lens slightly to allow one drop of oil, then rotated the lens again so the X100 lens sank into the oil drop. The sample was magnified one thousand times. Joe applied his eyes again to the double lens of the Olympus Microscope

"This is bone, and in this field, they picked up some healthy bone fragments" Doctor Mehta was in her finest Didactic mode, "and moving in" and she shifted the field, it was like flying at mach 3 over the landscape, the features blurred by the speed, and then stopped the flight in an instant "there is the bone marrow."

"Allow me" said Joe and used his right hand to move the slide under Dr Mehta's microscope. He was flying over familiar territory now, Bone Marrow was what he did for a living. There were the bone spicules, the Erythroid (red blood cell) progenitors, reticulin fibers, primitive Myelocytes (white blood cells), this was the factory where blood elements were formed. Suddenly he froze and retraced his flight to the previous field. He heard a sharp intake of breath from Doctor Mehta. The Malignant cells were like an evil egg-nest, in the middle of the field of normal cells. Anyone could have missed them in a more speedy, blind flight over this blood-scape.

"What do you think?" said Joe.

But Doctor Mehta was off to the other side of the lab and her stool crashed over. She whipped out a big book and she tore through the pages so fast it was a wonder they stayed attached, must be good solid binding. She came over with the book open and a photomicrograph on over which her index finger pressed so hard it turned white against the her dark skin.

"Neuroblastoma, this is a typical nest in the bone marrow. *How could I have missed it ?! And it was here all the time!!* How did you know??"

"I didn't, it is *you* who raised the possibility" Joe pointed out, placating, "I just took it to the next step, being a Pediatrician. But this is not enough. We must verify it, especially in a seventy year old male as you said. And look it up in the Medline, see if anybody ever published Neuroblastoma at 70 years."

"Yes, yes, and we might look again at the cytogenetics, and maybe do some FISH and PCR." She was so excited, she was almost dancing. She was after all in Pathology, she had never seen the sick person in person, this was an Interesting Case. This might be a good Paper. Joe sympathized, but did not join the festivities. If this was indeed Neuroblastoma, then it was a death sentence to the good Doctor Roger Cohen, because Disseminated Neuroblastoma was one of the diseases which had seen the least progress in 20 years of research , and spelled certain death after the age of one year. Doctor Cohen was certainly more than 1 year old.

"Not we, Doctor, YOU, are going to do FISH and PCR. I am only going to keep in touch." Joe said, rising from his stool.

The young resident looked at him incredulously "But Doctor Bergman, if this finding pans out, we can write a really good paper, at least a good abstract to present at ASH or Clinical Oncology!!"

Joe was already at the door, hefting his big bag to his shoulder, he winked. "I'll be in touch, go after all those other studies" and he was gone, a big dark apparition, flew in, and flew out.

The taxi took him out of the downtown to East Memphis and Joe marveled again at the incredible number of churches, and the fanciful decorations for Christmas, the trees festooned with lights, and Baby Jesus at every street corner. The mass of churches thinned out as they left the city towards the suburbs, and eventually the taxi cruised on gracious tree-lined streets with names such as Shady grove and Sweetbriar. They passed the huge and ornate Temple Israel, and finally entered a short circular driveway and stopped in front of the crescent-like stone steps. Tammy Cohen came out to greet him, face wiped clear of any vestige of makeup, looking older but still, beautiful. Joe paid the young black driver and tipped him generously. He had done his navigation on the Armada and noted that the driver had taken the shortest route to the location, and so he deserved the reward.

It was a big house but not a mansion. The oak door was basic rather than ornate. Joe noted the Mezuzah on the jamb. Tammy Cohen led him into a parquet floor hall from which a carpeted staircase ascended to the bedrooms above. From this central hall he could see small corridors lead-ing to a study, the dining room, kitchen, a sitting room and living room. There was a small pool in the yard. Large, comfortable, but not ostentatious.

"Why don't you put your bag right here" Tammy pointed at the foot of the stairs "and join me for a drink?"

"Sure" said Joe, dropping the big bag, he was beat.

"What's your poison?" she asked from the sunken bar in the Great- room. It was big and carpeted, and there were various toys and slides pushed over to the back wall.

Joe eyed his surroundings, noting the details of quality workmanship of doors and trim. "A Miller Lite, I am from Milwaukee now."

"You will have to do with a regular Miller" and she poured delicately into a long flare glass so that a decorative head crowned the light amber liquid.

Joe took a long satisfying draw and felt the tiny bubbles tickle his throat, teasing it into life again "Wow, I needed that." and sank into the nearest sofa.

"Who are the toys for?" he asked, half the glass drained.

"My grandchildren, whenever they come down from New-York with their mother!"

"Did I note a vestige of bitterness?" Joe arched his brow over the glass.

Tammy held a small glass of Dubonet liquor, and sipped it delicately. "Well, I wish they would come more often. That's a neat trick with the eyebrow, you know."

"That's what Helen used to say, in fact I worked on it just so... let's leave this subject, shall we?"

"Oh no young man, now you let something slip. Who is Helen?"

Joe sighed, he hated to sound the bereaved, even if he was. "She was my wife, Cancer got her, just like its getting Doctor Cohen, and incidentally, I know what is getting him."

The glass dropped on the marble counter and shattered, the shards falling all around and the deep brown liquid dripp-dripped to the floor. "*You Know* what is getting him? But how in God's name can you know what everybody here has missed? That's impossible!!"

Joe sighed some more, placed his glass down on the marble end table, gently, he returned the astonished gaze. "Its just luck, I happened to look for something which only Pediatricians look for, and anyway it needs a lot of work to confirm. And if it's true then it gives absolutely no hope for survival, I am sorry, I am really sorry." Her shoulders were slumped and the proud face of a Grand Dame contorted and she turned and almost ran out of the great-room stifling sobs. Joe just looked at his hands, it was the Beer, it had loosened his tongue, I should have kept my mouth shut. He gazed out to the pool, lit blue with underwater projectors, I wonder what it would be like to dive under and just keep diving until there was no air, that's plagiarism, Jack London wrote this one hundred years ago.

Presently Tammy entered the great-room again, composed with hardly a hint of the stormy episode. Joe hung his head.

"It's all right, I am OK now, its hard to hear the truth even if I said it only this afternoon, why don't we have supper, and Gabe will join us later, Gabe is my son."

"Oh" said Joe, noncommital.

It was probably the best dinner Joe had for the last five years. Esmeralda, the housemaid, served them on Wedgewood china with a Caesar's salad, roast chicken and perfectly roasted round potatoes. They opened a bottle of Australian Bordeaux (The Australians have made great strides in their wines said Tammy) and they kept to small talk, weather comparisons, the Milwaukee Bucks, the lack of a major NBA team in Memphis, Clinton's sexual escapades, everything except for the personal and Cancer.

The doorbell rang as Esmeralda was clearing away the plates. Tammy Cohen went to the door.

"Hi mom" and Joe heard a big smack.

Gabriel turned out to be a tall athletic-looking 30 year old, ash-brown hair with a mischievous wave, and blue eyes. Tammy was a head shorter   and very proud.

"Gabe, I'd like you to meet Doctor Bergman from Milwaukee. He came down here to solve Roger's mystery, and he did!"

Joe was somewhat uncomfortable with that assertion. He rose and gave out his hand and was rewarded with somewhat of a limp, short shake, surprising as it came from such an athletic man, it was almost feminine. "Mrs Cohen is overstating it, just a little bit, I don't really have the answer just yet. My friends call me Joe."

Gabriel eyed him up and down, definitely not my type, too straight. Joe was intrigued by this evaluation of his person.

"Delighted to meet you, Joe" he said, "anyone who can help Roger is a friend" He turned to his mom "How is he today? I really couldn't come in the afternoon, it was way too hectic in the office."

"I know dear, don't make yourself guilty just because you have a life, and really there is nothing anyone can do at this point. Roger is refusing any more treatment, and doesn't want to come home so we don't slave over him. He is resigned. Let's take the dessert in the living room, I miss my drink." She was all affection for the overgrown boy, as if she has never outgrown the job of Mother. Joe was getting more curious, but he had his own agenda.

"Madam Cohen, I really need to ask you and Gabe some questions regarding my original problem, Mustafa." Gabe's expression froze, then his upper lip curled with disdain, even disgust. "So if you don't mind I'd like to wash up and then join you, is that OK?"

Tammy was directing Esmeralda with the fruit medley. "Sure, Gabe, why don't you show the Doctor to the guest bedroom? I will wait here and watch Clinton's antics with women" and she switched over to CNN on the big-screen Magnavox TV.

Joe's bag was gone from the foot of the stairs. Gabe led the way, almost dancing up the spiral staircase. Joe followed and kept up with his two-at- a-time step. The carpet was deep and lush, one could drive a Zelda around here with nary a sound, thought Joe. Gabe opened the first door on the right, into a bright spacious room, white painted, with pictures of St Jude and the Danny Thomas Pavilion on the walls. His bag was by the bed.

"See you later" said Gabriel, and almost winked, but held himself back.

Joe locked the door, somehow he wanted his privacy, took some underclothes to the bathroom, and stood in the shower for long moments, savoring the hot water washing off the grime of a long, hard, day. The bed in the room was very inviting, but he wanted some more information before this interlude came to an end.

Joe walked the two steps down into the greatroom dressed simply in black Fliers and a turtle-necked knit white shirt, which was comfortable on his shoulders. Gabriel pursed his sensuous lips to whistle but thought the better of it. No wonder Mustafa aroused such feelings in this man. Gabriel was obviously Gay, and Mustafa, being a devout Moslem, would look at him as a blasphemy. Once this realization was clear Joe became much more relaxed, he knew Ronny and had met his room-mate, before AIDS had gotten him, and he couldn't care one way or another as long as no passes were made at himself.

"Hi" he said to Tammy, who was on the sofa sipping her Dubonet "I feel much better now" and gave her his best smile, reserved usually for mothers to whom he could say that John or Jamee was in remission.

"My, my, you must work out a lot" said Tammy, appreciative, "when do you find the time?"

"No personal life" Joe answered without mirth. He took the Miller from Gabe with a murmur of thanks. "I want to get back to Mustafa, what can you tell me about him?"

"Yes, Mustafa, let me recall" said Tammy Cohen, gazing at the high arched white ceiling "Roger was very keen on helping students of Arab, no, Palestinian origin."

"Why is that?"

Tammy told him the story of Beit Hanun. "He figures that in a way, he was partially responsible for creating the Palestinian Refugee problem, and in his small way he wanted to redress the balance, pay back for the folly of his youth, so to speak. I don't want to presume but you *are* Jewish, are you?"

"Worse" Joe laughed, "I am from Israel."

"Are you really?" Gabe broke in, "I guess you served in the Armed Forces!!"

"Not much of a choice, it mandatory" said Joe.

"Thank God its not over here, and anyway" Gabe snorted, "Roger's notions are total bosh. It's the Arabs who refused to agree to the UN resolution, and ever since then they are the cry-babies of the world!!"

"I guess that depends on whose propaganda is more effective" said Joe, "But back to Mustafa."

"Yeah, sure, but when you mention Mustafa you have to mention the Mideast conflict. He was obsessed by it, and Roger generally took his side. He was a good student and technically excellent, I am quoting Roger here, not that I understand any of this Genetics stuff, I am really a teacher in the Hebrew academy day school. Roger had him over for dinner a number of times, and usually he would leave when Gabe joined us, with some excuse or another. I didn't like him and let them discuss Lab and Arabs and Jews."

"Can you tell me, in detail, about the last dinner you had?" asked Joe.

"I can do that," said Gabe "it was on the 22nd of March, and Roger called Mom to say that he was inviting him to dinner, and I made a point of being early for Dinner. I was surprised as hell how friendly he was. He brought with him the only drink he could have, Japanese Saké, in a cute little china vase."

Joe knotted his brow, then he got it. Saké is made of Rice, not of grape, and with its low content of Alcohol, it was Kosher even for Moslems. Suddenly he had an idea.

"Did you heat the Saké?" traditionally, Sake is drunk warm.

Tammy brought her eyes down from the ceiling, and her legs down from the stool. She was looking at Joe quizzically.

"Why do you ask?"

"Well, did he, or did you?" Joe insisted.

"I distinctly remember that I asked him if he wanted me to do that and he emphatically said NO."

"And why is this specific so clear in your memory?" Joe wondered.

"Because" said Gabe "he was so awfully nice, all of a sudden, he was chatty, and told jokes about people he and Roger knew, showed pictures of his wife Amanda and her darling daughter, and avoided subjects which had to do with the Arab-Israeli conflict, and insisted that we share the Saké with him, very strange!"

Joe was thinking hard "was that the only thing of his that you ate or drank with him?"

"As far as I remember, yes" said Tammy looking hard at Joe "so what is the significance of heating, I am as persistent as you are, you see Doctor?"

Joe curtsied briefly with his head and Miller glass. "Touché, Mustafa's visit and Doctor Cohen's illness are temporally related, and certain mat-erials, especially proteins, are heat labile, but all this is ridiculous since you all drank, including himself, and Doctor Cohen is suffering from Neuroblastoma, a cancer typical to babies and children!!"

"Did you think he poisoned us? Well, we are all here, and he took from the Saké as much as we did!!" Gabe was scornful.

"I know, I realize that, at this point a man who would run out on his wife and abduct his daughter, and leave this kind of a message" and Joe gave Gabe the photocopy with the threat "may be capable of anything."

"Can you be infected with Cancer?" asked Tammy shrewdly.

"Well" considered Joe "indirectly that is possible. People with AIDS frequently contract Lymphoma, which is very hard to treat, and they get a cancer called Kaposi Sarcoma which is related to a human herpes virus" Gabe assented to that, slowly nodding his head "and a dormant virus can cause a leukemia in patients who are heavily treated for cancer, and in animals there are viruses which directly cause cancer such as the Sarcoma caused in chicken by the SV 40 virus."

"And to continue your thought, to it's improbable end" Tammy said "a virus would be terminated if heated, and would survive if not."

Joe looked at his watch, it was 11 PM and he was dead tired, but this conversation with a sharp mind might lead him somewhere "True, but if I take the example of Polio, anyone who takes the Sabin Vaccine by mouth has a 99 percent chance of becoming infected, with the weakened virus, thereby acquiring immunity to the wild-type Polio virus. So a food-born pathogen should hit everyone to some degree. To say nothing of the fact the Neuroblastoma is not transmitted by any virus I know of."

"Doctor Bergman, you will have to be more creative, but not tonight, you have done enough. Why don't we all sleep on it, I'll just call Roger's room and see if he is OK. Gabe, are you staying over tonight?"

"Sure Mom."

"Wonderful" Tammy Cohen exulted "two children at home again, poor Roger , he would have loved being here. Night night, breakfast at 7 sharp, I have to teach tomorrow."

Joe practically fell into bed, but despite being dead tired his brain roamed and tossed, cancer, viruses, Brain tumors, DNA open reading frames.... His sleep was fitful, but somewhere between 3 and 6 AM he got the REM sleep that his brain craved and that allowed him to continue to function.

The Lipjohn Plant in Kalamazoo Michigan is a model of sterile environment and sophisticated manufacture of Pharmaceuticals. The manufacturing halls are spotless, gleaming cylinders discharge fluids into purification columns which in turn discharge fluids into Lyophilisation chambers. The powder or fluid is precisely dispensed into vials. The vials are stoppered, inspected, follow lines into counters, then stream into machines which label them with the names of the product, date and time of manufacture, quantity, units, date of expiry and lot number. The vials continue to machines which pack them into small boxes, also labeled, and into large Tri-Wall containers, and finally to large shipments. All is done in a White, sterile environment, workers selected for their intelligence, cleanliness, and integrity. Supplying Vaccines to the world is a delicate business. Good vaccines save thousands of lives from Polio, Measles, Hemophilus, Diphtheria, Perstusis, Hepatitis, diseases which were the scourge of the world until recently. Vaccines mean healthy live babies and the hopes of mothers to see their children grow to maturity.

John McDermott M.T. had been one of the veterans of the Polio line. This was an especially challenging line because the polio vaccine actually contained three strains of live viruses, which together represented 99.99 percent of all the Polio viruses in the world. These were viruses developed and bred to be similar to the wild type virus in antigenic composition that is their outer coat was similar, but their inherent ability to cause disease was nonexistent. Or, actually *almost* non existent. One in a million recipients contracted the real disease from the weakened virus, so that in the end of the 20th century the number of polio cases caused by the vaccine in industrialized countries was approaching that caused by the live virus. In fact the WHO was considering stopping polio vaccinations somewhere in the beginning of the 21st century, but not just yet. Remote areas of India, Pakistan, Angola and Bangla-Desh still held human reservoirs of the dread virus. Select populations in the United States refused to heed the advice of their doctors and did not vaccinate their children, turning them into potential reservoirs for the wild-type bacteria and viruses. John McDermott saw to it that the flow of Sabin Vaccine to the world never stopped, on it's way to total eradication of the Polio disease.

Today he was showing a new worker his way around the plant. They were dressed in white paper jump-suit, or Bunny-suits as they were known, paper overshoes, paper masks with a transparent plastic shield over the eyes, and paper hold-all caps, all supplied from across the Lake by Kimberly-Clark, the manufacturers of Kleenex. This was the complete clean room attire, as good as any worn in a surgical suite. Dan Leahy, who had worked as Shift Foreman had been badly injured in a hit-and-run accident, and the new man, although obviously not local, proved to be a speedy and receptive student. He had some difficulty stuffing his thick black beard into the mask and John made a mental point to tell him to shorten it somewhat. In fact he was overqualified for this Job. After all he was a full PhD, but he said that family matters prevented him from staying in Detroit, and in Kalamazoo, well, there was Lipjohn, and maybe later, with his foot in the door, he might go on to a research job in the huge company. John sympathized with Muhi's predicament, and anyway, any-one willing to take on the night shift was welcome to it.

John showed him the whole plant, up to the final packaging and destination assignments, and Muhi a Din Shareef, PhD, wrote it all down in a neat scholarly hand-writing on a clip-board, just like he did in the lab. This was easier than it initially seemed, and with some luck, and the help of Allah, in a month or so, when he was totally versed and trusted, he would see to it that the first shipment would go out to Memphis, according to the Plan. As for his good old job at the

Henry Ford Memorial Hospital, well, he was sure the Islamic Brotherhood will find him a position as good or better.

Joe was up as usual at day break and connected his Armada to the Telephone jack. The computer chirped and connected to AOL, and then the Internet and into the USA.Net. He used the ALIA password to see if Mustafa had sent anything to Amanda, but no, not yet. Once he did then one could hopefully find out from whence the message came. He checked his own E mail and answered Doctor Kammitzer that he was making some headway but it was too early yet. At five to seven there was polite knock on the door, and he closed the Armada.

"Its open."

Gabriel poked his head in. "Good morning, I see you are up early, come down at Seven, mom is a real stickler on Time" and he laughed shortly. Joe put the machine away in his bag and followed Gabe down the stairs to the sweet smell of waffles on the grill.

"We have a choice of Waffle or Waffle" said Tammy Cohen "so take your pick."

She was less than truthful because to go with the waffle she had a veritable smorgasbord of toppings. Joe followed Gabe's example and took a seat on the captain's chair fronting the huge buffet, made of highly glossed Cherry. Tammy opened the waffle toaster and extricated a huge waffle for each, perfectly browned and smelling of Heaven. Joe poured a little Strawberry topping and dug in with relish. I haven't been mothered like that ever since Grandma died, and I miss it. Tammy watched the two men wolfing it down with a grin of satisfaction.

"What do you do, Gabe?" he asked, his mouth still full.

"Computers."

"Now that's like saying Medicine, what specifically?"

"I debug software for a small company, clean up glitches and viruses."

"Really, that's interesting, maybe you can help me out."

Wolf, wolf "How?" swallow it down.

The waffle was coming to an end. Joe put down his knife and fork and wiped with a Kleenex. "I have a hard drive from a computer that Mustafa supposedly damaged, and possibly there is information in it that may help us."

Gabe looked at him, hard. "You really think that Roger's disease has something to do with Mustafa?"

Joe was a little uncomfortable at the scrutiny of mother and son. "Let's say I have a hunch, or a gut feeling, or any other word for unsubstantiated suspicion, that it may, and that it may be related to the general threat that Mustafa made against Zionists." Joe creased his forehead. "Did you by any chance get matched with Doctor Cohen?"

Now Gabriel was puzzled "Matched? What do you mean by that?"

"I mean bone marrow matched" explained Joe.

"Would not do any good" Gabe shook his head and Tammy assented "I am not Roger's son."

"Roger was my second chance" Said Tammy, "And I was not even Jewish. I converted at Israel temple, and then I liked it so much that I studied Hebrew and Torah with the Rabbi and then much later became a teacher. We had Rachel two years after we married. Its funny how Gabe, who was already 5 when I married Roger took to him like a limpet" and she fondly ruffled the wavy hair from across the buffet. "Joe, would you like to wait for me here, I only have 2 hours this morning and we can drive to the Hospital, you can use that chirpy machine as much as you like."

Joe's heart warmed to this wonderful lady. "That would be great, I can do some Internet investigation, how about that hard drive Gabe?"

"Sure, bring it down and I'll take it with me and see if I can wring something from it, what's your email?"

"Its helen dot bergman all lower case letters at chw dot edu."

"OK, that's easy, if I find anything I'll mail you."

"Great" said Joe and ran upstairs. He was back with the Seagate rectangle in a jiffy and handed it to Gabe.

Tammy Cohen put everything in the double sink. "Well boys, I'm off. See you in a couple of hours, doctor Joe, call me later, Gabe."

Joe heard both cars outside start and leave. He located the AOL local line and went trolling for markers for Small Round Cell Tumors on the Internet.

Chapter 13

FBI

The Federal Building at downtown Milwaukee is an old and distinguished and imposing structure. There was nothing distinguished or imposing about the room in which Karen and Amanda were sitting. The polite All American kid was grilling Amanda about who Mustafa's friends had been, and tiredly she told him again and again that she really did not know, that Mustafa kept this part of her life separate and had met with them without her. She pointed out again that somehow they were associated with the Mosque, and remembered that a year or two or three ago there was this big meeting in the Lake Geneva area. Karen kept quiet but gave the agent an encouraging smile from time to time.

"Do you know where Mustafa and Alia are now?" Amanda asked Bob Grove plaintively.

"Our sources at the CIA" just saying CIA made him appear self important "say that he took a flight to Larnaca, but there is no record of them leaving Larnaca."

Karen looked at him prettily "isn't there another airport in Cyprus?"

Bob looked at her with obvious appreciation. "No, Larnaca is the main gateway to Cyprus. Doctor Halim and the girl would be a conspicuous couple, we checked and they did not leave from Larnaca. maybe they are still on the island."

Amanda shook her head emphatically. "No, he said that his parents had the right to see her, and they are in Lebanon, he sometimes called them."

"Ah, that's a good piece of information, did he call from your apartment, or previous apartments?"

"I don't think so, I always checked our telephone bills and I never saw an international call."

"Maybe he made those calls from the Mosque." suggested Karen.

Bob was even more impressed "that's a good idea, we can check that out easy enough, although it's possible a bunch of people would call from there."

"So where else are you guys checking?" Amanda persisted.

"We are asking the State Department to check with Cypriot and Lebanese authorities. We passed a request to our representatives in Syria and Lebanon and Cyprus to get their contacts in those governments to look for Alia" Bob spread his arms wide "once she is out of the country our options are pretty limited."

Amanda was getting angry. "So that's all you have to tell me? That the almighty US government can do nothing but ask some bureaucrats to look around if they so please?"

Bob Grove became uncomfortable "that's all the information I have, at this time. The trail stops in Cyprus and no sign of them having reached Lebanon or Syria."

"I want to talk to your superiors, this is ridiculous" and Amanda made to rise, the Agent rose with her.

"Doctor Carter, this will do you no good No one is holding back any information. My superiors don't know anything more, and they are just as mortified as I am at being impotent" Amanda listened, and then relented "We must do as much as we can here to see who his contacts are and maybe we can come with a contact who knows where he is." Bob concluded.

"That sounds reasonable, but let me ask you something, Agent Grove" Karen flashed an enticing smile again, lets curl his toes a little, "do you watch that Mosque?"

"Sure we do... of course not, this is a free country" the agent tripped over his words. Karen gave him more of the same.

"Well if you do, then maybe you can get some pictures for Doctor Carter and she might recognize someone and give you a lead!"

"Wow , that's a GREAT idea, but this will take some time, why don't we meet again tomorrow, and hopefully," he added for Amanda Carter's benefit "we might get more information from out colleagues in the State department."

As they filed out Amanda walked ahead, her step heavy with disappointment. Bob Grove kept slightly back and fell in step with Karen. She was ready for this. She had given the young stud enough signals to go up in smoke, and he was smoking.

"Miss Fitzsimmons?" he ventured.

"Karen."

"Sure, Karen, could we, could we meet later to discuss your ideas about this case, over dinner maybe?"

She stopped and turned full on him, letting Amanda go down the wide steps of the Federal building. "Let me check my calendar" She fished out the little Casio electronic calendar and made a show of searching the date. "We can do that."

He beamed. "Pick you up at eight?"

Karen nodded, "8201 North Mohawk."

"I'll be there" and he almost bounded up the stairs.

Karen felt a little bad. She was not used to this kind of manipulation, but she reasoned to herself, without a little cajoling he is not going to come up with the Lists the Joe thought would be helpful, I wonder how Joe is doing in Memphis. Karen hurried down the steps to catch up with Amanda.

"How did it go?" said Amanda, without breaking her step.

"He swallowed it" Karen was short.

"I really despise these government people. They draw a good salary out of your pocket and mine, and then all he can say is there is nothing he can do!"

Karen felt the need to defend the poor boy "I think you are doing him an injustice" she quickened her pace to keep up with Amanda who was angrily making her way to the parking lot across the street. "Sometimes all *you* can do is tell families that there is nothing you or Science can do."

Amanda whirled on her "There is a difference between an act of God and an act of man. They should send a posse after Mustafa and bring Alia Home."

Karen held her angry gaze. "*We* are the posse, Amanda, and Bob Grove will help us, in spite of the rules."

Amanda Carter gazed at her friend and tears welled up and streamed down unabashed. The cold December air almost froze them on her cheeks. She took a step and hugged Karen and a passerby looked on with dismay and envy, two beautiful women hugging, What-A-Waste.

Amanda disengaged and resumed her quick walk, up the second level to the white Camry. She got in and let Karen in. She started the engine and let it run.

"Karen, why is Joe doing it, and can he do it?"

"He has nothing to lose, and he doesn't care if he loses his life trying."

Amanda was amazed. "But that's terrible, what makes you say that?"

Karen shrugged "Kammitzer says. He knows him, it's a long story. And he can do it. This man is decisive and ruthless, and he is from the Middle East, he know what he is up against!"

"I hope you're right, I wouldn't want Joe to die, even for Alia, even if *he* doesn't care."

They drove back to the hospital in silence. Wisconsin Avenue stretched from down town to Wauwatosa and as they drove past the Great Mosque, something that Amanda and Karen had done a zillion times before, they both looked at the camels kneeling on either side of the wide walkway and the domed Mosque with trepidation and suspicion. Suddenly it was not just a place of worship but a place of secretive and dark machinations.

They separated at the entrance. Amanda went up to the HOT unit and Karen continued to the office of the Chaplain. Donna Fischer was at the desk busily typing away at the computer. She had the apple cheeks of the perfect Wisconsinite.

"Karen Fitzsimmons, how nice of you to come in."

"Hi Donna, is the Reverend in?"

"Sure, he is in there, but there is someone in with him, the Rabbi, you know, from Mount Sinai, they are planning something, for Christmas and Chanuka y'know."

"That's all right, I'll wait" I am lucky, she mused, I can celebrate both. I am unlucky because I celebrate none, because every Christmas I remember Alex, and every Chanuka I remember Grandpa who could not say Kadish on his grave. Life sucks and then you die, she had heard Joe say that once, one bad night, and there is nothing new under the sun, and if a woman has some happiness with her daughter, there is a monster who will take it away from her. Here comes Rabbi Schindler. A young man with a goatee, he nodded at her "Bye ms Fischer" he said to Donna, and went out.

Donna lifted the phone "Reverend Wilkins? Karen Fitzsimmons here for you, you can go in Karen."

Pastor Henry Wilkins had aged in the last ten years, but gracefully, he was still a big man, but he had lost some height. Still, the resemblance to his son was striking.

"Hello Karen, so good of you to drop in, sit down, sit down please" he beamed his most avuncular.

"Hello pastor, how are you doing?" she took a seat opposite the white haired benevolence.

"God's work, I hope" and he laughed, nothing could bring this man down.

"Pastor Wilkins, are you aware of the Doctor Amanda Carter situation?"

He was not laughing anymore. In fact he was angry. "Yes, I know, as if there is not enough trouble in the world, comes a man and inflicts misery upon his wife and his own flesh and blood, any new developments? What's this?" He looked at the paper that Karen handed him, it was the fax to Amanda.

Pastor Wilkins looked up "This is a madman."

"But a clever and dangerous madman, as Doctor Bergman said."

"Yes, I heard from Chris that he met our Doctor Joe at the scene of the crime, and that he was very helpful and resourceful. In fact very resourceful indeed."

Karen leaned forward "Doctor Bergman has decided he is going to go after Alia and get her back" she said softly and seriously.

The pastor leaned back and whistled softly. "Indeed, and exactly how is he going to find them, and where they are?"

"They are probably in Lebanon, because that is where his parents are from."

"And does he know the nature of the threat implied in this letter?"

"No, but we are trying to find out."

"We?" Pastor Wilkins eyebrows were reaching new heights.

"Yes, We," Karen was firm.

"How can I help?" The eyebrows came down.

"Joe told me" The pastor's ears pricked up at her inflection in the name Joe, she cares for him, maybe even fond of him, interesting, "that he had learned from Chris that you were active in various missions around the world, that you had served in Africa and Asia. We thought you might have some contacts with people running missions in Lebanon..." She trailed off, as she spoke, her words became slow and halting, this was getting more and more crazy and improbable. Reverend Wilkins on the other hand slowly nodded, considering the options.

"Yes, yes, I can see where this is leading, and in fact I do know some people who were active in Lebanon, a very unfortunate and sick country that it is. But I can see an acute problem with the whole concept!"

"Which is?"

"Whichever organization lends a hand will forever be barred from Lebanon, thereby harming a multitude of needs. See, Lebanon is different from the rest of the Middle East, because there is a sizeable Christian Maronite minority, which once upon a time had been the majority, and lost it's prominence due to demographics, the Muslims had more children then they did. Slowly but surely they are pushed to extinction by the Muslim majority and the most able ones emigrate or have already emigrated. That means the least able remain, and they need help. Ergo, the benefit to one cannot overcome the damage to many."

"Then we will think of a way to avoid causing trouble, but still get the job done" Karen had regained her resolution, and the Pastor looked at her anew, this was like seeing a butterfly coming out of the cocoon, a new personality was unfolding, very interesting indeed. In fact if I don't help, then she will find some other way, possibly with a thinner cover and even more dangerous. He made up his mind.

"All right, I have an organization and a person in mind. He is a Doctor who had served in UNWRA in Lebanon, and under the Auspices of the Stop the Hunger American Mission, which is non-denominational, and their headquarters are in Chicago. His name is Doctor Harrelson and I have his card right here." Pastor Wilkins leafed quickly through his Rolodex, the old fashioned one with cards, and pulled out the card "Donna" he said into the intercom.

"Yes Reverend" came the cheerful chirp.

"Can you please make us a copy?"

"Sure thing" and she came in and took the card "Reverend, the Duarte family, their 15 year old is in ICU, they are waiting for you."

"Of course, thank you Donna, one more minute."

The pastor leaned forwards to Karen. "You have my cooperation. I am going to call on him and get things arranged. But, I want to be informed of your exact plan, because if it jeopardize's the Mission, this cooperation will be withdrawn immediately and completely!"

Karen rose, and the Reverend with her, a little creakily, "Reverend Wilkins, I understand very clearly, thank you."

He extended his hand, and then grasped hers with both his bony hands "Do God's work and save the innocent."

Karen retrieved the photocopied page from Donna. She cast her eyes on the incoming couple, middle aged African-Americans, with distraught features. She questioned Donna with a look. Donna waited until the door was closed.

"Their 15 year old is in ICU because he sniffed some paint or glue or something, they blame themselves somehow, so the Reverend is counseling."

"Ah" said Karen non-committal, as if there were not enough natural disaster the teenagers had to make themselves sick. She shook her head. Tonight she had to play the seductress for the benefit of the FBI. She shuddered, I wonder what Joe would say if I told him he needs to seduce some woman for information, wouldn't that be distasteful? I'll ask him some time. Also we need to work out a plan of how to become representatives of a Mission, most likely as a doctor and nurse team.

The problem was Joe, she mused as she walked over to the parking structure. Her hands were deep into her pockets, where in her right fist she held the pepper spray she picked up at the Ace. He was an Israeli, and place of birth is an a clearly marked item on a US passport. He had to change his appearance, since Mustafa had seen him before, and that meant medical documentation too, had to be changed. As she drove north on the I-43 Karen thought back to time when her purse had been snatched in Chicago, and the procedure she went through in order to get a new license. She pictured Joe's face and a glimmer of a plan began forming in her mind. What stumped her was how to absolve the Mission from the action of its supposed members. I'll discuss this with Joe when he gets back.

The phone was ringing off the hook as she rushed into the house from the garage. She breathlessly picked it up.

"Karen?" it was Joe, her heart thumped some more.

"Yes, I just got in."

"How are things up in Milwaukee?"

"Sad, Amanda is heart-broken and the FBI are of no help."

"Progress report." Karen took the phone away from her ear and looked at it with astonishment, "Karen, Karen are you there?" the phone squeaked. Karen slowly placed the handset to her ear and mouth.

"Joe, if you want any cooperation and communication, you better talk like a human being, not a drill sergeant, is that understood?!!"

Joe laughed uproariously and she had to distance the set from her ear, the same uninhibited laugh she had heard before, and her heart warmed toward the man who insisted on being so tough and was probably baby-soft underneath. He was still chuckling as he came back on.

"Karen, you did it again, nobody makes me laugh like you do, and you insist on making me a human being again. Let's rephrase. Anything new to tell me?"

"Yes, I am going out for a date with this very nice young man tonight, in an hour in fact."

"Oh?" a hint of jealousy or just my imagination?

"He is the FBI agent on the case and I will try to get him to provide us with lists of the visitors to that mosque."

"Oh!" a definite relief.

"Pastor Wilkins is going to help us but he wants a specific plan so the Mission he represents does not get hurt."

"That's reasonable, do you have a plan?"

"Actually, I think I know how to make you an identity."

"Really? that's great!"

"Now" said Karen "Progress report!"

Joe chuckled again, "I guess I deserved that, I know what Mustafa does but still don't know how."

"What did he do?"

"He can kill people, using some carrier for Neuroblastoma."

"*What*??" Karen was shaken.

"He found a way to transmit Neuroblastoma to Jews. I have to work at it some more, I have to work out how, but I am quite sure. This is scary stuff and he needed to have had a lot of people to help him. Those lists are crucial!"

"All right Joe, I'll do whatever necessary to get them."

"Well, don't go too far, you are no Mata Harri yet."

"I'll keep my hat on, if that's what you mean" she teased.

"Keep everything on, same time tomorrow?"

"Got a phone number?"

"Yes, I am actually staying with the family of a victim, its 901-263-1231, got it?"

"Got it, good luck."

"Good hunting" and he chuckled.

Karen put the phone down, this was preposterous. Or was it? she knew of experiments carried out by the faculty, to replace defective genes such as for ADA deficiency, with normal genes. They did that routinely with mice. Well if one could do that, then one could place a sick gene too, in fact it might be easier, because the cancer genes have an inherent ability to proliferate, how well she knew that having seen the devastation wrought by tumors on the kids. She shuddered some more, maybe a hot shower might take away the chill. The phone rang again.

"Karen?"

"Yes Mom?"

"Are you coming over tonight?"

"No, I have a date."

"Well, its about time, is he a medico?"

"No mom, he is just a nice guy" Karen said, with a sigh, she was never going to explain This one.

"I hope so for your sake, I wouldn't want you to remain an old maid!"

"No mom, and don't expect too much, this is a kind of a business thing, not a real date."

"Oh Karen, Karen, when are you going to get yourself a Life? Alex is dead, long ago, and no amount of slaving in the hospital is going to bring him back!!"

"I know Mom" Karen sighed some more "I just haven't met anyone, except there is this guy... I don't want to talk about it OK?"

"Why not?" Miriam was plaintive "this is the first time I detect a real interest in your voice, anything wrong with this one?"

"Yes and no, its complicated."

"So is Life, nothing is simple and straightforward and untarnished joy. If you think you found a *real* man then go for it , work at it , make him feel it!"

"It will just close him up."

"Then pry him loose, I can't see how a real man can resist you."

"You have a lot of confidence in me, and anyway I don't want to talk about it. I may be absent a lot in the near future."

"What's up?"

"Too early to tell, but possibly I will be joining a Mission of some kind, abroad."

"Karen, are you trying to give your mother a heart attack?"

"No, but you are getting half your wish, about not slaving in the hospital, anyway, I am going to put the phone down 'cause my date is supposed to be here soon."

"I'll have that heart attack tomorrow, Bye."

Mothers, Karen thought as she took her shower, fondly, maybe one day I can be a mother too, she looked down at her flat belly, with the water cascading down from her breasts, and tried to imagine it large and swollen with kid.

She was ready when the door chime came. It was Bob Grove and he looked very nice, the all American Kid, double breasted jacket, neatly pressed chinos and shiny boots. Bob pursed his mouth to whistle softly, she was radiant, her soft flaxen short hair creating just a suggestion of a halo around the fair face, full resolute mouth, and dark-blue eyes. She was dressed in a long white coat that reached almost to the floor and made her appear even taller. That doctor Amanda Carter was a good looking lady but this one was stunning. He adjusted and straightened himself some more.

"Hello agent Grove." That smile, right between the eyes.

"Bob, The FBI is way over there" and he gestured vaguely.

"Your car or mine?"

He was confused at her directness. "Mine of course, if you don't mind a older Continental."

Karen laughed. "Not at all, let's go" and she exited and locked the small house behind her.

Bob drove back down town, to the Sapporo Japanese restaurant that he favored. He made some small talk, about his work, some hilarious incidents, the eccentricities of his boss, who was a secret anti-Semite, about the most notorious criminal Milwaukee had ever produced, the late Geoffrey Dahmer and throughout Karen smiled, and nodded and encouraged, and sipped the Saké from which Bob drank freely.

"You know, the orientals cannot stand as much alcohol as the occidentals, that's why we can drink this Saké like water" he chuckled, bemused by the beauty sitting lotus fashion across the low table.

"How about people from Arab origin?"

"They drink nothing at all, except when nobody is looking" he guffawed. Karen felt herself suspended in the air, watching herself and this young boast playing their male -female games, while Alia was being abducted across the world with a maniac who had found a way to poison people with Cancer. It was surreal. She must get something useful out of this fiasco.

"How do you know who goes in and out of the Mosque?" she asked with a smile.

Bob leaned forwards conspiratorially, "we have a beautiful setup. We have a remote controlled video camera set up in the attic of the Greek restaurant opposite" Karen nodded, encouraging him on "and we just zoom in on the visitors. We have had that camera, and another one watching the side entrance ever since the World Trade Center bombing." and he leaned back with satisfaction, took another tempura shrimp, dipped it in the soy sauce and took a bite.

"And do you know who they are?" said Karen, casually.

"Sure we do, but none of them are active in terrorist circles" Bob concluded with confidence.

"Any unusual characteristics?" Karen asked, suddenly she had an inspiration "any of them Doctors of Science?"

Bob was astonished "How did you know? Steve Kilmer, he is in charge of this operation told me once that at one time there was like a major bunch of them, and when we matched them with INS files lots of them were scientists, from all over the place, New-York, Chicago, Minneapolis, Toronto, you name it. It was a like a conference of Doctors, only they all came in to pray in Milwaukee!!"

Karen leaned forwards, fixed his eyes, and slightly exposed her cleavage through the open topmost pearl button of her white satin blouse. She saw his eyes inexorably drifting, as if against his will, down her face and neck, toward that deep vee. Men are so predictable, except that One man. "Bob, can you get me the names of these people? This may really help Amanda!" Bob Grove pulled his gaze up with a visible effort and fell head-first into the much more troubling dark blue pools of her eyes. "Yeah, I guess, sure. I can get Steve to show me the list, but what are we going to do with them?" his head was clearing up, but only slightly, the double whammy of Saké and overwhelming feminine allure had him smitten.

"Oh, we are just going to look at them together and see which of them might have information about Halim's whereabouts" she said lightly.

Bob nodded, he appeared more business-like, "good idea, when shall we meet?"

"Tomorrow, my place?" she suggested.

"OK, will do" Bob was enthusiastic.

"Great, why don't you take me home now, I really had a long day today and I will see you tomorrow anyway." Big smile again. Bob was lost.

She allowed him to the door and he kept his hands to himself, with an effort. She waved goodbye through the living room window as he started his car. Well, what harm could it do, bend the rules a little, its not as if she was an Enemy of the People, and he would not let the lists out of his sight.

Karen was bright and early into the PACC fund building, to look for a picture of Dr Bergman, which she photocopied off the formal application folder. It was a straightforward Criminal Face picture, passport size, Joe fixing a grim stare into the camera. she made multiple photocopies and took the pages to the library.

From her briefcase Karen pulled out some markers, pencils and Tippex whiteout. She doodled with the photocopies, adding different glasses, a goatee, a moustache, heavier eyebrows, thinner eyebrows, no eyebrows. Then she thought of the Unit. She took the Tippex and whited out the shock of hair and redrew the outline of the head. Then she Tippexed away the glasses, and filled in with light touches of a pencil. She drew a thin moustache, and there it was, completely altered unrecognizable Joe. And of course she knew a place full of people who looked just like that.

The Milwaukee County Medical Complex is, at its name suggests, complex. The different buildings, new and old, are connected with walkways and tunnels. Karen walked to the older county building where the Medical patients were hospitalized and took the elevator to the sixth floor. Julie Collier, who had graduated with her from Marquette, was busy charting at the nurses station. She looked up with pleasure.

"Hi Karen, long time no see, off duty this wonderful morning?"

"Took some time off."

"So what are you doing here, instead of taking a long vacation somewhere warm?" She shot a glance at the light snow which was falling out of the overcast sky, and shuddered theatrically.

"Julie, can you tell me who this is?" and she showed her the picture, which she had copied again so that the Tippex and pencil marks had disappeared.

"Is that someone I know?"

Karen hesitated. "See if this may be one of the patients."

Julie scanned the picture, creased her brow, then said "You know, this may be John Campbell, he is a 36 year old with AML, he had a bone marrow transplant, and he is getting some experimental drug to keep him im remission. He is here right now in fact, hooked up to the IV. Where did you get his picture?"

"I didn't, I made it up."

Julie gaped. "Karen, that's crazy, why would you do that?"

"Can't tell you but I need your help."

"OK what is it?"

"First let's go and look at him."

Julie and Karen walked down the long corridor. It was a big room. A number of patients were sitting in the Lazy-Boy easy chairs, watching TV and each had an IV dripping something into his or her veins. Some had blood, some clear fluids labeled with contents on the bag and some had yellow plasma. Julie walked over confidently to the corner as Karen watched from the door. Julie pretended to check the IV bottle, the IVAC dripper and jotted something on the bedside chart. This was a big man, thin featured, he had lost all of his hair, but he did sport a very thin moustache. Perfect.

Julie was back and they walked back to the nurses station.

"Let's look at the chart" Karen said.

Julie pulled out the chart and Karen copied down all the personal information. She looked up to see Julie give a her strange gaze.

"What are you doing Karen?"

"Julie , don't ask, but it's important."

An even stranger look "All right, I wont ask but one day you'll have to tell me."

Karen finished her note, placed it into her briefcase. "I promise to tell, after this is over" she promised. *If* it's over, she told herself.

Karen left the oncology ward and headed out. She needed a way to copy documents, at home, something that would preserve the document and also allow it to be sent over the Net. She drove to Northridge mall to the Best Buy. There she acquired a simple scanner, the kind that takes pages and scans them a into computer. It was no bigger than a telephone, and the clerk assured her that it required nothing more that a parallel connection to a Windows based computer and the accompanying setup disk. Nevertheless she asked for a demonstration at the repair-shop, until she was certain she could repeat those steps at home.

It was as easy as they promised and the copy she made of her notes was easily retrieved from the computer memory. She sat down and wrote an outline of the plan.

The telephone jarred her. She picked it up.

"Hello?"

"Hi, is this Karen Fitzsimmons?" It was Bob Grove.

"Yes Bob."

"Oh, it's you," and his voice dropped dramatically "I have the complete list, of visitors to the Mosque, you wouldn't believe how hard I twisted Steve's arm to get it. When can we meet?"

"Seven O'clock my place, and don't bother to eat before."

"Sure thing." Ohboy,ohboy ohboy, this woman was HOT.

Karen passed the rest of the afternoon at making a dinner, and preparation of a solution of Sennekot. She was bathed and dressed in a simple jogging suit, closed up all the way, she did not want to give him any ideas. Still, nothing could hide the svelte figure and the proud bust from Bob's scrutiny. He quickly slipped inside, and she noticed he had not parked his car in her driveway, but near the bus-stop at the corner.

Bob took off his Secret Agent coat and Karen hung it in the closet. It was a small living room in a split level house, very much a feminine place with native American rugs on the walls, a small hearth with a mantelpiece, on which there were few pictures, parents, herself in camp, two older couples, and a child, with features resembled remarkably those of the house mistress.

Bob approached the mantle piece, curious.

"A drink?" Karen offered.

"Sure, anything on the rocks."

Karen made it up in the kitchen, dark bourbon, ice, and Sennekot. She came down the steps and handed him the drink.

Bob sipped and examined the picture of the boy "Your son?" he ventured.

"No, my brother, he died of leukemia long ago."

"Oh my, I'm sorry" there goes my chance to make it with this chick, bigmouth, he took a larger sip, this drink was different, kind of chocolate?

"Shall we eat?" said Karen brightly.

"Sure" said Bob and took a bigger sip.

Karen kept bright and made him tell her with giggles, how he had twisted Steve's arm into producing the computer output.

"I even divided it into two tables, the locals and the out-of-towners. I guess the latter are the more interesting" and Karen nodded agreement. They were finished with the salad and Karen brought a two bowls of Chilli to the table. Bob sniffed appreciatively. She was even a good cook.

"Anything new about Alia and Mustafa from the State Department?"

Bob made a sound of disgust. "Nada, they are waiting for someone to tell them which government to question, since nobody knows where they are, furthermore, they say that if Mustafa is Lebanese as Doctor Carter claims, and he went back to his home country, and he can claim his daughter Lebanese, then there is nothing they can do anyway, because the courts in Lebanon will not listen to a claim by an American against one of their own."

Karen watched his face as the cramps started, he tried to hold it, but then he couldn't.

"Excuse me, sorry, where is the bathroom?"

She pointed and he ran, closing the door firmly behind him. Karen had the Copy program all ready. She pulled out the sheaf of papers each marked FBI and SECRET and fed them into the scanner. The sounds from the bathroom were unmistakable, the salad and chilli and Sennekot were a combustible and explosive combination. Poor Bob. It was all done in a few minutes, the papers were back in the brown envelope and safely inside the briefcase.

He came out, white as a sheet, his hair in disarray and his shirt only partially tucked in, then his face contorted again and he beat a hasty retreat back into the bathroom. After the next bout of diarrhea he was better, his color partially restored.

"Gee, I don't know what's going on, what did I have for lunch?"

Karen was at her most motherly "Don't eat that chili, in fact don't eat any thing else, why don't you sit in the living room and I'll make us some tea?" Bob nodded. He took out the sheaf of papers from his briefcase and spread them out on the low table. Karen came down the five steps with Earl Grey, lots of sugar, and they scanned the list.

"See, there is Mustafa Halim, with visiting dates, very often. Not considered of any consequence, very low priority. Shows you how good we really are" Bob sighed, and grimaced some more, but decided he could hold out. "And this is Aziz Sidky, he is the top dog, the Imam, he lives on the premises, I even got a picture of him." From a separate compartment he got a picture, obviously reproduced from video, where a medium sized thin man with a white beard and a white turban, hawkish nose and bulging eyes, was walking down the Mosque steps. "This guy is from Madison, his name is Haled Rafia and we know he is in the department of Genetics at UW." Karen nodded, and then Bob, despite his recent ordeal smiled.

"Remember how you told me to look for scientists? We were tailing this guy, Rashid Hariri, he is a bigshot businessman importing food stuffs from the Turkey, and Lebanon, you know, ethnic foods, olive oil, cherries. We know he finances Hamas through a bank in Detroit. He is real easy to spot with his shiny silver Mercedes. So one day he drives down to Fontana, on lake Geneva. He meets all these Arabs, and Steve dressed up and asked the resort manager what is this meeting, and they said a scientific meeting. Steve got the tapes from the security cameras in the ceiling and he did all the identification later. It was just like they said, a meeting of scientists from all over. It wasn't in Milwaukee like I told you before. Mustafa was there too, he was like the chairman of the meeting."

"And do we know what they were talking about?"

"Don't think so, no recording, but Steve told me the waiters said they spoke in Arabic."

"How long ago was it?"

"Two-three years, but what is the relationship to Mustafa taking his kid away? I mean what's so different about this case from a Canadian or a Filipino having a spat with his wife and taking his kid with him?"

"This man made a threat."

"Oh, that retribution bullshit? They all talk like that in their meetings, except for some real hardliners this is just blowing smoke!"

Karen felt that this meeting was nearing its useful end it was time to make him feel good so he will be inclined to help in the future.

"I am only trying to help Amanda. Lets just put this aside" she said, "are you feeling any better?"

"Yea, I must have ate something bad today." Sure you did, thought Karen Sennekot really cramps you, if only for a short time. She turned on the charm again. He relaxed and sipped his tea. "what kind of a nurse are you?" he asked.

Karen was now in familiar territory. That would make the evening go faster, but it would be better in a public place "How about we go out to the Silver Spring House? my car this time."

"Sounds good to me" His eyes followed her to the upper level, and he was rewarded by the returning figure, sleekly encased in her Guess jeans and adherent sweater. She got the coats out of the closets and they went out to the garage, cold, but not as cold as the exposed outside.

Later, Karen dropped Bob by his car and avoided adroitly from setting up another date claiming work schedule. She hoped Joe would come back the next day.

Chapter 14

BIOINFORMATICS

Doctor Mehta was unsure whether the man who had blown in and out was real, so she found the number of the Children's in Milwaukee and confirmed that a Doctor Bergman was actually on staff, a third year fellow in Pediatric Oncology. Thus reassured she went back to the Medline (Computerized access to the National Library of Medicine, a service that the US government makes available to the whole world at no charge) and reviewed the subject of Neuroblastoma. These days just about any tumor is known to have some kind of a genetic aberration associated with it, that is, the cell that went berserk does so due to a mistake in the arrangement of genes in it so that genes that control replication, or genes that prevent self-death, or genes that prevent normal maturation, are activated. The product of this misarrangement is an RNA molecule that is the blueprint for production of an abnormal protein which exerts these effects, 'good' for the survival of the cell, 'bad' for the survival of the organism. Some of these misarrangement are so gross, one can see them directly on the chromo-somes of dividing cells, so that a piece of one chromosome is attached to the end of another chromosome. Some of these gross translocations have been given eponyms, like the Philadelphia Chromosome. Genetics departments used to be made up of rows and rows of ladies who scanned chromosome preparations, photographed them, cut the prints into little pieces which looked like black-and white caterpillars crawling on the table, pairing them off, and trying to figure out which was a true trans-location and which just a hairpin kink. The last twenty years have changed this practice entirely. A plethora of techniques allow detection of tiny rearrangement that would never be seen on the more crude chromosome preparations. The abnormal RNA, or protein, can be quantitated precisely, the offending genes sequenced, and replicated, and, at least in tissue cultures, precisely cut out and replaced. Doing the same in the living organism was a thousand fold more complex. The understanding of the genes and proteins which cause the malignant transformation allowed development of drugs which could reverse these actions and cause the cells to mature, or commit suicide, or change characteristics so the organism could get rid of it using its own defenses. If 30 years ago most leukemias were a genetic enigma, and cure rate was abysmal, then in the Nineties most leukemia and related tumors had a known genetic marker and the cure rate approached 90 percent.

Neuroblastoma had been such an enigma for decades, but the specific markers for the disease were becoming more apparent, so that most neuroblastoma, a tumor of primitive nerve cells, were related to an aberration on chromosome number 17 and loss of material from chromosome number 1. The cells which were grown from the most nefarious neuroblastoma cases, those that did not respond to therapy at all, were found to have a translocation of material from chromosome 17 to chromosome 1. Thus Doctor Mehta decided that her best chances lay in reviewing the genetic data for the patient SSN number 247-01-2280, who, as fate would have it, was a doctor of Genetics.

As she twisted and turned in the labyrinth, she wondered on the subject of this Bergman, why would he appear out of the blue to solve this medical mystery? The family story did not quite jive, since the patient had been ill for a few months and was going down the tubes. Anyway, there it was, the Genetics lab, headed by Doctor Sundararaman Chandrasekhar (call me Shaker). If there was anyone who could tease out the genetic nature of a disease it was Shaker, he was also from Bombay and they could talk the dialect, but not in front of the Natives.

Shaker was happy to see her "Hi Marten."

"Hello Shaker, can you help me with something?"

"Always."

"Do you remember the case of Doctor Cohen from St Jude."

"Not really, when was it?"

"He became sick with a very malignant grade four stage four small blue round cell tumor a few months back, which was never given a clear appellation."

"That's unusual, what's his number?"

Doctor Mehta gave him the note and he punched it on his computer.

"The report says normal 44XY with no translocations. We did FISH for 8;14 but that's it. It was negative."

"OK this is a strange story. This Doctor Bergman, from Milwaukee, drops in on me out of the blue, and asks about the patient. He knows somehow to look for a bone marrow and in the single bone sample that I have of all the 100 slides, he finds some bone marrow, and in it a nest of tumor that looks just like Neuroblastoma."

Shaker whipped his head back to the screen "But the patient is 70 some years old!"

"That's right."

"That's either impossible or reportable or both!"

"That's right, that's why I am here, we need to confirm."

"Well, do you have any more material?"

"We have some in parafin block, I can microtome some samples. I checked with the tissue culture lab. They plated his cells because of the ambiguity of the diagnosis. What will you do?"

Shaker considered "I can do reverse PCR for the 1:17 RNA product, we can do FISH for the 17 genes and see if they had translocated elsewhere, I can look for loss of 1P material, and if you sit here anymore I will think up many more ways to waste the institution's money on a wild goose chase, so bring me some samples, and start writing it up, and if that Bergman shows up send him here too!!"

Marten smiled, her white teeth flashing, and left the small room. The department was fast outgrowing the facility, which was set up during the times when Genetics was a small and neglected branch of science.

Joe closed down the computer when he heard Tammy's car, a Grand-Am, coming back to the driveway. He had gone through the Medline, the NCI, and the University of Bonn databases to learn some more about neuroblastoma, so that he had a clearer idea of what to look for in confirming that diagnosis.

"Doctor Bergman?"

Joe disconnected the Armada from the electric supply and the phone jack "I am here in the study, coming right out" and he came out to the hallway. Tammy Cohen was glancing through the mail and looked up at him.

"I am going back to see Roger. You are welcome to stay here or come with me."

"Can you drop me off at St Jude?"

"Sure, let's go."

She drove expertly, and soon they were back in the city. She dropped him off at St Jude on Lauderdale and he promised to be back for dinner. This time Joe was dressed appropriately, slacks, shirt, tie and a usable blazer, name tag on. And he had a specific person in mind, Doctor Beverly Kreissman, who he had met at ASH, while she presented new concepts in clinical trials relating to stage 4 neuroblastoma. He found her on the fourth floor, where they had the Solid Tumors. All around him were kids from all over the world, all without hair, wan faces, and all sorts of funny hats to cover their nakedness. It was both depressing and exhilarating, a place where progress was pursued daily on behalf of the sickest of children. Doctor Beverly Kreissman was dictating a note into the house-phone when the faint shadow obscured the bright omnipresent fluorescent light. She looked up and punched the star seven button to stop the dictation.

"Doctor Bergman, what a surprise, It's been only a couple of weeks and there you are." the American Society of Hematology meetings were always held on the beginning of December, before the Christmas rush to the south.

"Hello Beverly, how are you doing?"

"Give me a minute Joe, I'll just finish the dictation."

Joe settled down on one of the chairs and surveyed the familiar disaster zone of children, parents, nurses, assistants, residents, house maintenance, computers, IV poles and even baby swings. It seemed a complete bedlam, but of course it was not. Every child had a chart, the therapy, or follow up, or imaging for the day, scrupulously recorded and performed, and everybody knew their roles. Doctor Beverly Kreissman was the quintessential Jewish female, with long black stresses loosely tied back, smooth, slightly dark complexion, fine nose with just a suggestion of hawkishness, and a full mouth with dark brown lipstick. Her eyes were tear-drop luminous brown and bespoke of keen intelligence and attentiveness. Her earrings were hanging seven candle Menorah and she had a Shield of David golden pendant, should anyone doubt what she was. Try that in Germany, or Poland, or Syria, Joe thought.

Beverly was done and put the phone down. "So, you know I am married and I have two little munchkins, so try your luck somewhere else!" and she laughed a carefree peal, so at odds with the surroundings.

Joe had to smile. "Consider yourself lucky, how is Jerry?" Jerry Stein was a member of the St Jude faculty, and also was Beverly's husband.

"He is fine, fine. What brings you own here, are you out of patients in Milwaukee?"

"Not really, I am after a PhD by the name of Mustafa Halim, he was doing his masters here way before your time, and Doctor Roger Cohen was his supervisor."

"Poor Roger, how come you know about this Mustafa, anyway?"

Joe showed her the letter that was faxed to Amanda. Doctor Kreissman read it with incredulity, her hand went to her pendant and pressed it to her bosom.

"What does he mean by that, and where is the kid?"

"No one knows but the assumption is Lebanon, and I am trying to figure out what he means too."

"How can I help you, I mean all I do here is take care of kids with solid tumors, and I coordinate a national trial for neuroblastoma, you saw my presentation at ASH."

Joe became a little uncomfortable, how do you explain an un-substantiated gut feeling "This Halim fellow was here about 9 months ago, and 5 months ago doctor Cohen came down with a strange tumor."

"I fail to see the connection" Beverly said.

"Cohen's tumor maybe a neuroblastoma."

"WHAT?"

Joe was sheepish, "I need to prove it, but that's what the bone marrow looks like."

"OK, let's say it was, so what?"

"Well, this guy, a PhD in genetics and a whiz in genetic engineering and bioinformatics is threatening the Jewish People as a whole. Doctor Carter told me that he had had some kind of a trauma in Lebanon and I *know* he hates Israel and everything to do with it. I have the feeling he made Roger Cohen sick."

"Joe, that's preposterous, just because someone is a raving lunatic and makes idiotic threats in a letter designed to scare his wife, doesn't mean *you* have to get carried away!"

Joe continued doggedly. "Suppose he is a lunatic, so was Hitler. Suppose for one moment that he found a way to propagate neuroblastoma through some agent. You yourself are treating neuroblastoma stage four with interferon, genetically engineered in yeast!"

"That's ridiculous" Beverly snorted, then her eyes took on a faraway look, examined some star a billion miles away "maybe not so ridiculous" she murmured. Her brown luminous eyes came down to rest on Joe's face, and suddenly her mouth pursed, and she left the chair like a rocket and headed out of the department, she was rather short legged but Joe found he had to almost run to catch up with her.

"Where are we going?"

"Medical records."

Joe kept his peace and fell in step. They descended down the interminable staircases, back to the first floor, until they found the door marked Medical Records. Beverly pushed the heavy door and it flew back despite the slight weight of the woman.

The receptionist was almost hidden behind stacks of folders with patients names heavily stenciled on.

"Can I help you Doctors"?

"I need to speak to Susan Kochar" said Beverly.

"She's here , walk right in."

They rounded the reception desk and walked into the horribly cramped spaces occupied by transcriptionists, folders, secretaries, computers. The last room was marked

S. Kochar, Informatics Supervisor

Beverly knocked impatiently, "Come in" and she entered. A tall bespectacled black lady looked up and smiled at them.

"Beverly, come down to dictate? I'll have them pull out everything for you."

"No Sue, I have something much more interesting, meet doctor Bergman, from Milwaukee?" Joe dutifully put out his hand and the tall woman rose from behind her desk and gave him a radiant smile "Welcome to St Jude Doctor, are you here to stay?" and she shook the proffered hand with vigor.

Joe said nothing and Beverly continued. "Sue, could you pull out of the computer the names of new patients from this year, with diagnoses of Neuroblastoma, Lymphoma, Ewing sarcoma. Could you do that on the screen?"

Sue settled down, all business, and played the keyboard. Lists of names appeared under each of the diagnoses. Beverly and Joe scanned them.

"Can you print for me the names of the kids with newly diagnosed Neuroblastoma?"

"Sure" and the HP printer spit out a crisp copy of the names, twice. She handed one copy to Doctor Kreissman and one to Joe. Beverly sat down heavily into the chair.

"Doctor Bergman, do you see what I see?"

"I think I do."

Beverly turned back to Susan Kochar. "Can you pull all those charts for us, Please."

"ALL of them?"

"Yep."

"It's good you brought help with you 'cause this is going to break your back."

"Right" Beverly said, very heavy sigh, she put her hand over the pendant again "lucky I did."

They waited wordlessly until one of the secretaries, actually an elderly white haired volunteer, came out with a supermarket-like trolley. Joe pushed the trolley into a small dictation booth .

Two hours later, during which Doctor Kreissman fielded multiple pager calls, they had a list of ten patients, all with neuroblastoma, all diagnosed in the last 7 months and all less than 6 years of age. The number was not outstanding except that they were all from Memphis, and 5 of them had obviously Jewish surnames such as Katz and Cowan, and Pomerantz and Spiegel and Le-Vine. Two had already died, and that was highly unusual because they were diagnosed before one year of age, a time in which most neuroblastoma may spontaneously regress without treatment, a fact which made this particular disease so fascinating. In Japan and Quebec there was a program of antenatal diagnosis for Neuroblastoma in newborns, added on to the more established neonatal diagnostic tests for PKU and Thyroid and hemoglobin inherited diseases. This newborn screen detected a large number of neuroblastoma patients, but those regressed spontaneously so that the programs did nothing to decrease the toll of disease past one year of age, where it was lethal.

"What are the chances" said Joe "that five or more Jewish kids out of a total population of 20,000 would acquire neuroblastoma, by chance alone?"

"Infinitely small, and we don't know that the other 5 kids are not Jewish just because their name is not typical. *How* could I have *missed* it?" She wailed.

"Are you on service all the time?"

"No, I am on service 4 months of the year, divided, otherwise I could never get any research done."

"There you have it" said Joe reasonably "not one attending is on service long enough to see a pattern, especially such a bizarre pattern."

"I guess that's true" Beverly said.

"Is it possible that these are not true neuroblastoma but some other blue round cell tumor?"

"I guess that possible, let's look at the Genetics." Beverly leafed through the heavy chart of Joshua Cowan who died at 14 months of age, In Gainesville, Florida, following an unsuccessful purged bone marrow reinfusion. The lab section of the chart was subdivided, and the genetics section was very thin. "Chromosomes are normal, but there are multiple

NMYC copy number. They did PCR for the 1:17 translocation and it was negative."

"Did they do a FISH for the 17 chromosome sequences?"

"No, those are research materials, not routine requirements for inc-lusion in the national trials. I know because I coordinate one of the trials."

"But why not?" wondered Joe.

"Lots of reasons, no one has isolated the *precise* gene in 17 responsible for transformation, second, there is no commercial supplier of the FISH sequence for the suspect gene so that I cannot standardize the test yet, and three, this costs money, and although we are not tight we do not spend routinely on *every* test, for *each* disease entity, especially if the other diagnostic criteria are clear cut."

"But now you will."

"Now I will" she promised "but first I need to find out who has a ready reagent set-up, otherwise this can take months."

"Mehta said they might have it."

"Who did?" Beverly was stunned, this guy had an answer for everything.

"Sorry, a doctor by the name of M. Mehta over at the Van Vleet. when I mentioned FISH for neuroblastoma, she wasn't at all surprised. Let's call."

The operator put them through to the Van Vleet and after a short while Doctor Mehta answered her page.

"Doctor Mehta."

"This is Doctor Bergman, I saw you yesterday about the case of Cohen."

"Sure I remember, you fly in and out so fast you don't need a runway."

Joe chuckled at that. Beverly looked on severly. 10 sick kids were no laughing matter.

"What have you come up with so far"? asked Joe.

"I talked to Shaker and he is going to FISH for neuroblastoma."

"Who is Shaker?"

"He is our Geneticist, sorry, his name is Sundararaman Chandrasekhar but that's too long so he gets the Americans to call him Shaker."

"That's great, how does he go FISHing?"

"He has a probe for the 17 chromosome material, which he gets from England, from Newcastle, and I got him some tissue culture from the lab."

"Wonderful, I knew I could leave this in your hands. Can you tell Shaker not to use up his probe till I bring him some more samples?"

"OK, where are those samples from?"

"St Jude."

"Where else, of course I'll tell him."

"Thanks" said Joe and grinned at Beverly. She was still truculent and continued examining the list of five.

"Do you realize that these are all boys?" she said

"No kidding?" Joe was totally surprised. Being a Pediatrician some-times meant you were gender blind. Sometimes sex made some difference, boys did worse in leukemia than girls, but generally the question of gender did not enter consideration nearly as much as in adults, where the attention to female genital tract and breast cancer became almost a political issue.

"Yes, and in fact 3 of these names indicate they are Cohanim" she continued.

"That's daft" said Joe, flabbergasted.

"*You* are the one who started the daft stuff, I am only pointing out the facts, or the facts that need to be proved."

"And Roger Cohen is obviously a Cohen."

"That's right, and if I go with this material to Stu Berger, he will throw me out like a rag doll!"

"I am sure Jerry will stop him. Why don't we call Jerry and ask him to look this bunch of coincidences over?"

"I would but he is out of town and its already 4:30 in the afternoon and I have to pick up Susan and Moe from the JCC, and I put off so many things that my brain is about to explode. Where are you staying?"

"With Mrs Cohen, Roger's wife."

"Good, be here at 10 tomorrow. I will clear my schedule and get doctor Gibbons to cover for me. This is too important to leave for a mere fellow, no offense." She smiled to take the offense out of the snide remark.

"None taken, where do they keep the tissue cultures?"

"Somewhere in the basement, it's late, do it tomorrow, think of ways to infect 10 Jewish kids with Neuroblastoma, do me a favor, get someone to keep these records together for tomorrow" and in a flash she was gone, her short legs quick as a hummingbird.

Joe took a cab to Van Vleet, got into the elevator for room 479 and made his way there unhurriedly. Tammy Cohen was sitting by the bed and read the skeleton the afternoon paper. She looked up with pleasure at Joe.

"Roger, look who is coming, the Big Man from Milwaukee, or Israel."

Roger Cohen popped his eyes open, a major effort, and lifted his right hand, another major effort "Come in" he croaked "How was your day at St. Jude? I wish they would let me stay there but I'm too old."

Joe considered whether the old man ought to know what his former disciple had probably done. He decided not. This kind of a scientific endeavor was not a single year's effort but a lifetime mission. Some people had missions to bring help and succor to the world, people like Salk and Sabin who perfected the polio vaccines, and Jenner, who tried the Vaccinia on himself. Some had missions of destruction. And it was Roger Cohen who had unwittingly trained Mustafa for his mission of death. He didn't need to know that.

"Oh, nothing much, I met some colleagues and discussed some patients."

"Good" said the skeleton, "so Mustafa did no mischief."

"No" Joe lied.

"Is Gabe coming?" Roger asked his wife.

"Here I am" Gabe said cheerily from the door. He came in and bent over Roger and gave him big buss, and he turned to his mother "Hi mom, see who came in with me."

Tammy turned back to the door and suddenly a cheer erupted from her throat. "Rachel" she screeched with glee. She shot out of the chair and hugged the woman who stood at the door. Joe tried to blend into the corner. this was obviously their daughter. She was dressed very severely, with a long skirt that almost brushed the floor and an odd bonnet on her head. As she took off her coat Joe saw she wore a white shirt with very long sleeves, buttoned all the way up. Now he knew why she lived in New York.

The women hugged some more and two small faces peeked from be-hind her ample behind and skirt. Tammy swept on them too. "Oh you brought my two munchkins, Oooh, do you know how your grandma loves you?" and the two young boys hid further, almost inside their mother's skirt. Joe had to smile, this was as close to family bliss as one could get, *that* should make Roger happy.

And he was. Gabe propped him up in bed and after a while the children, 3 year old twins named Isaac and Yehiel became comfortable with their grandma and the strange man in the bed, who their mom kissed and called Dad. Tammy remembered Joe.

"Joe, come here, I'd like you to meet Rachel and the sons, Rachel, this is Doctor Joseph Bergman, a friend from Milwaukee."

Joe advanced and almost put his hand out. He then remembered that the very religious Jewish women never touched a man who was not their husband. He grinned and said nothing. He felt out of place anyway.

Gabe picked up the kids and placed them on his lap, on the bed, and slowly Roger lifted his arms and put them on both their heads, while they looked on with trepidation at the sick old man. As soon as Gabriel let them go they slid off and started playing hide and seek in the sick-room. Roger laid his head back and smiled happily.

The evening nurse poked her head in and said, with finality, that they must leave, now, visiting hours were over. Joe who had played with the kids pick-up-stick noticed how often Roger had pressed the PCA machine button, that doled out morphine, just enough that he could withstand his excruciating bone pains and still enjoy this rare family get together. Joe rose to leave when Roger signaled him with his eyes to stay behind. Tammy, Gabe, and Rachel with the kids, wished Roger good night, and he smiled back at them, a rictus of pain to Joe's trained eye.

"You lousy liar" hissed the old man.

"Me?" feigned Joe.

"Yeah, what was Mustafa up to?"

"Found a way to infect Jews with Neuroblastoma."

"How?"

"Don't know yet, but I'll find out."

"And I helped him, trained him, right?"

"If it weren't you, he would have found somebody else to teach him."

Silence..........

"Joe."

"Yes Doctor Cohen."

"It's Roger. I had a good life, today was a good day, tomorrow will be worse, the pain is bad, real bad."

"I know" said Joe feelingly "I am sorry."

"Don't be, pull out the drawer, here."

Joe pulled out the drawer "All the way" hissed the skeleton. Joe jerked it out.

"Up side down" and Joe turned it up side down. 10 vials, 2 CC each, were carefully taped to the underside. Joe looked closer.

"Hydromorphone" hissed Roger. Joe drew back. He knew what the sick man wanted. Hydromorphone is 20 times more potent on a milligram basis than morphine.

"Joe, you are an oncologist, I am DNR already, I don't want to suffer any more. I am ready to go."

"Roger, I am not God."

"No, God is not merciful. *You* are . You know what suffering means. I said my goodbyes. Tonight will be worse. Do it. *Please.*"

Joe was transported to another sickroom, the rain outside, the beloved body devastated with chemotherapy, the head swathed in bandages, the blond curls gone, beauty gone, life gone. At least she did not suffer at the end. Roger's bone pains will drive him out of his mind. He stripped the vials in a quick move, picked up a syringe and stepped into the bathroom. With practiced movements he sucked out the vials into the 20cc syringe and hid it in his massive palm. He stepped out. The nurse hadn't come back yet and the sounds of the twins giving Gabe a hard time keeping them quiet carried down the corridor. Joe swabbed the distal port and injected the medicine. Roger smiled and hit the PCA button, and the tiny air-bubble moved down the tubes.

"Now git, go get the bastard" hissed Roger.

Joe popped into the next room just to deposit the syringe in a "HAZARDOUS BIOLOGICALS" yellow round cylinder with the red top. He joined the family at the elevator and rode down, his face revealing nothing, as usual.

They were back at the great room, each with his favorite drink in hand, orange juice for Rachel, the kids safely tucked in bed. Tammy was happy, and Joe wondered why, her husband was just as sick as before. Maybe it was seeing the kids, even though they ate only the foods brought by their mom in disposable utensils. Being very religious Tammy's household was not Kosher enough for Rachel Sodorski.

"How is that hard drive?" said Joe to Gabriel.

Gabe chuckled richly "This guy thought he reformatted the drive, but he didn't really. He reformatted one of the partitions. He had an H and a C and he reformatted only C."

Tammy put up her legs on the foot-stool "And what is on the H partition?"

"A bunch of garbage."

"Garbage? That's unlikely, he used it in the Molecular Biology lab, is it repetitive?" Joe said.

"Yeah, I opened it down to the individual bytes, and it seems to be sections of data of four letters."

"That would be DNA bases" said Rachel.

Joe turned to Rachel, so far she had been exclusively a Mother. "Why do you say that?"

"I majored in Bioinformatics at the Yeshiva University, until I had the twins that's what I used to do, gather DNA data from the sequencers and try to figure out what they were" Tammy beamed some more, she was so proud of her progeny. Joe was very interested.

"So if you get this data you could try and find out what those sequences are, say, with Internet access?" he asked.

"Sure, but I need the program to do that."

"Do you have anything on the drive?" Joe asked Gabe.

"No" said Gabe "that must have been in the partition that he formatted."

"But" said Rachel, "I can download a demo easily enough, and do it anyway!"

Joe couldn't believe his luck. A computer expert and a bioinformatics savant under the same roof. But, of course, this was nothing out of the ordinary in the Jewish population. The Silicone Valley of Palo Alto, and Tel Aviv, were sister cities where most of the Internet applications of the world were hatched. The top echelon of Intel, Motorola, Microsoft, Hewlett-Packard were heavily Jewish. It was up to Joe to get these two to extract whatever useful information they could, out of Mustafa's disk.

"Gabe, can you get us a rewritable CD of the data?"

"I'll do it tomorrow."

The phone rang. Rachel picked it up. "It's for you, she says her name is Karen" she said to Joe. Joe's features relaxed.

"Hello Karen."

"I got the list of contacts for Mustafa."

"How did you get it?"

"Don't ask, it wasn't pretty. Any progress there?"

"Lots, and its bad. There maybe others infected with neuroblastoma."

"Wow, old people?"

"No, children and babies."

"But that's not unusual, it's a baby disease."

"Yea, but here they are all Jewish."

"This is beyond belief" Karen was flabbergasted.

"Tell me about it. I still have to convince myself that this is all real."

"Joe, I know how to get us to Lebanon."

"You are amazing" said Joe, totally enthusiastic "did anybody tell you that?"

"My mom, but I need you here, when are you going to be back?"

"I think on the weekend I'll fly back, unless there is a snow storm."

"Well, if you looked on the news they are predicting the Midwest will get hit on Monday, so do it ASAP."

"All right Karen."

"And don't start any new romance, we don't have time for that."

Joe guffawed "Not a chance, Night."

"Who is Karen?" Tammy made the query.

"She is a nurse at Children's" Joe was evasive.

"A girlfriend?" Gabe arched his brow.

"No, but she decided to join this wild goose chase."

"Don't tell me its *not* on account of your beautiful eyes" Tammy said, teasing.

"Leave him alone" said Rachel "Don't you see he is antsy about it?"

"That's why I am teasing him, because he is not completely frigid, Joe, you were happy to speak to her!" Tammy asserted.

"I was?"

"You can run but you can't hide! Do you like her?"

"Professional relationship only, I am a doctor, she is a highly qualified staff nurse" Joe tried to make it final.

Tammy smirked "I detect a little more than that, why hide it?"

"Let's drop it, shall we? Jeez, you remind me of my grandma. She was on my case to find a girl and get married since I was Eighteen!!"

"We Jewish mothers and grandmothers are all the same. We are not happy if our kids are not happy, cradle to grave" Tammy asserted. Both her kids nodded "And that's true even if I was never born Jewish!"

Joe simply could not get upset with this woman, especially since he had probably just euthenized her husband. I wonder if she will forgive me if she knew.

"Karen is a wonderful woman and a friend of Amanda Carter, so that is the only connection, and that's final, lets get back to the main thing."

"And what is the main thing, except for the fact that my dad is dying of Cancer?" said Rachel, sharply.

"We are trying to figure out if Mustafa Halim" both Rachel and Gabriel sneered at the name "had anything to do with Roger's illness. Joe is convinced he did, that he actually infected Roger with this strange cancer. And now I hear that he has other revelations" Tammy explained.

"A Doctor by the name of Beverly Kreissman..." Joe started.

"I know her" Tammy interjected.

"And myself, looked at new cases of neuroblastoma in St. Jude. We found an inordinate number of cases, all from Memphis, all within the last year and at least some of them carry Jewish names. What is worse is that we found this disease is a bad actor, worse than the typical neuroblastoma."

"How is it worse?" asked Gabe, dismay showing on his face.

"Typically neuroblastoma occurring in the first year of life tends to regress spontaneously. These do not, but inexorably they wipe out the baby."

"That's horrible, but couldn't it be just a coincidence?" asked Rachel.

"It could, but the odds are against it. Doctor Kreissman said one more thing, which sounded incredible, in fact its so daft..."

"What is it?" Tammy pushed.

Joe looked at her with an apologetic face. "She said that three of the names were of Cohanim."

"Well, of course, so is Dad, and any male son he would have" said Rachel.

Joe was about to say that this was nonsense, when it hit him like a sledge-hammer, he had to sit, this was too malevolent even to contemplate, the Males, all the Males, to be thrown into the Nile...

They watched him in silence as his face went through the contortions of disbelief, comprehension, acceptance and resolution.

"Well, this is all conjecture that needs to be proved." He was back to being Lieutenant Yossi, voice assured and commanding "Gabe, you get all the sequences out tomorrow and send it to Rachel. Rachel, you have my laptop, and access to the Internet, with passwords and all. You download the demo, or the complete software package, and work on those sequences. I have some databases already on my favorites but you just get into as many as you need. Do the homologies with all the databases, but I suggest looking at known sequences of Y chromosomes, look at popular expression tools, plasmids, retroviruses, whatever. Mrs Cohen, you are the babysitter, gotta keep the kids happy. Are we all clear?"

Tammy was amused as hell. "And what are you going to do, Colonel?"

Joe was too preoccupied to notice "I am going to examine every chart of the ten, visit with the families, talk to their doctors, I have to find out how whatever this is , is getting spread. I have the help of Doctor Kreiss-man, and the indirect help of some Pathologists at Van Vleet."

Gabe was shaking his head "How did you get so much done, I mean Dad has been sick and getting worse for months, and there you are, in two days you may have it cracked!!"

Joe shook his head emphatically "I don't have anything solved yet. YOU are going to solve it for Roger" and he indicated Rachel and Gabriel. The phone rang, and Tammy blanched. She picked up the phone slowly, with trepidation, fearing bad news.

"Cohen Residence."

Tammy listened very carefully, her face becoming sheet white, then placed it down as carefully as she had picked it up. She looked up at her children, whose faces froze.

"Roger is gone, he died in his sleep."

They converged on her, the princes converging on the grieving queen. The tears rolled down uninhibited but she made no sounds, not a sob. Rachel was not as reserved. Gabe stood over his mother, and cried into her hair. Joe just had to turn away, look through the window, to the street, the graceful trees, the lawns the occasional passing car. Murder, that's what it was. He just *knew* Mustafa had killed Roger Cohen, and maybe many others. If it's the last thing I do , I will get you, he vowed.

"Joe, stay here with the kids. We are going." Joe said nothing, nodded. Tammy Cohen stood up and with both of her children swept out of the greatroom.

Joe opened a second Miller Lite, which Esmeralda had brought, and drank straight from the amber top. I wonder what Tammy would do if she knew. She could easily get his license revoked, get him indicted for murder. Euthenasia was a heinous crime in one book and the greatest of boons in another. Roger was a doctor, he knew what he was going through, he had prepared for a long time and all he needed was an accomplice for something that his physical status prevented him from doing himself. Joe understood the agony of metastatic cancer, and he wished it on no one, well, maybe Mustafa should get a taste of it.

He woke up with a start, and looked at his watch. He had fallen asleep on the couch, it was 2 AM. The car was coming into the drive and parking under the carport. Slowly, painfully, Tammy alighted, and Gabe, who had driven, helped her out. In the bright light of the floodlight Joe watched her move. Suddenly her age caught up with her. He met them in the foyer.

"He died in his sleep" said Gabe. Joe said nothing and watched Tammy.

"They called Rabbi Friedman and he said Kaddish" Rachel said, down cast.

"Well at least he got to see everybody one last time and say goodbye. I think he was happy this afternoon" Said Tammy, and she cast Joe a sidelong.

"I can report that no one stirred here" Joe said.

"All right, let's go to sleep, we have a lot of arrangements tomorrow."

Joe had arranged for a cab and he was out at dark. The charts would still be waiting at St. Jude. He grabbed a coffee and a banana at the cafeteria. In the early morning quiet he arranged himself and the charts comfortably, and started noting the essentials. Name, parents, blood relationships, birth, delivery, food, vaccinations, elimination, growth and development, disease presentation, workup, diagnostic features, laboratory values. They were all noted on sheets connected bannerlike end to end. He was on his third chart, a boy by the name of Zack Chandler, when Beverly Kreissman came in.

"I had a feeling I would find you here" she said.

"I thought I would try to arrange this data before I go looking for cell lines. Roger Cohen died last night."

Beverly was horrified "I didn't realize he was so sick. You know with the work and all I forgot... is this public knowledge?"

Joe shrugged "I don't know, I left before Mrs Cohen had decided how she was going to deal with it. I guess a Rabbi Friedman will help her."

"Alright, let's get to work here, I will read and you take down the notes."

Three hours later they spread the long sheet out and scanned it.

"One girl, nine boys."

"Check" said Joe.

"Eight whites, two AfroAmerican, one of them the toddler girl."

"Check."

"Of the eight, five are under 2 years old, and three are under six year old."

"Check, over 4 years old is unusual."

"Five of the eight are Jewish affiliation, 3 are not."

"Check, but their fathers may be."

"Right" said Beverly "but we can ask them, because all three are in active treatment, that why the chart here is partial, they are on the floor right now."

"All eight with stage 4 neuroblastoma, very aggressive, all negative for chromosome 1 deletions, or chromosome 17 translocations, but multiple NMYC copy number."

"Check, that's really astounding, those two facts are usually related."

"Anything else?"

"They are all either dead or dying despite treatment" said Joe flatly.

"I am going to make some phone calls, and you are going to look for tissue samples" said Beverly "I see you have your Children's Badge on, use it. Conference at two o'clock, at the cafeteria."

Joe was well into his soup and salad when she came in with a small package. She unwrapped the package to reveal a plastic box, which went into the microwave. When she opened it, a smell of goulash wafted out.

"I eat Kosher" she explained.

"I do too, unless there is something else to eat, what have you found?" Joe asked.

"All eight are Jewish, or have a Jewish father, and the five whose parents are Practicing Jews know that the father is a Cohen" and she continued to spoon her food.

"I have 3 tissue-cultures with live cells from 3 of the babies, the techs are packing them up for me to take."

"Do you realize what an impossible odds are there against all this happening by chance alone?"

"Yes, this is no accident. This is murder."

"And who are we going to convince?"

"No one, unless we find out what is going on, and how" said Joe. "How do you get eight babies from different homes, different doctors, all infected with anything?"

Beverly thought for a minute "beats me."

"Lets think through it. Food? impossible, some breast fed, some formula, different formulas. No one got blood products. Babysitter injected them? Rubbish. what do they all get?"

Beverly closed her box, and then she slapped her forehead so hard her earrings danced and jiggled. "Shots, they all get vaccinations" she grabbed the spreadsheet "Here, they all got their shots, DPT, IPV, OPV, tetrammune, and MMR, Hepatitis."

"Well, so do a zillion other kids!!" demurred Joe.

"Yes, but these are a select group, Cohen Jewish Males, oh my God Jerry is a Cohen too!!"

"Relax" said Joe, "How old are they?"

"Sue is Three and Moe is five."

"Uh oh, when is Moe supposed to get his 5 year shots?"

"Shit, next week, oh no."

"OK, don't give it, but we are clutching at straws here." Joe said.

"Like hell, these straws kill, What can we do?"

"Do you ever drive on Shabbat."

"No, of course not."

"Well, saving lives precludes Shabbat. You are going to drive around this Shabbat, put your medical credibility on the line and go to all the Shulls and tell people to stop all vaccinations, and tell all their friends to stop all vaccinations, then go around all the Sunday schools of the reforms and make the same warning."

"They will ask lots of hard questions."

"Let them. Tell them you will have some answers soon."

"Now that's lying" said Doctor Kreissman.

"Maybe, get Jerry to drive you and lend his credibility too!!"

"He thinks I am crazy already."

"Not after this analysis we did today. You said it yourself, the odds are tremendously against this being an accident. I have people working on Mustafa's data, and I will get Shaker to show *you* where his probes attache."

"How come I am supposed to do all the work suddenly?" groused Beverly

"Your kids' life are on the line here, and I took on the responsibility for another kid's life, so I have to go back. I'll give you a cellular number and E mail address." Joe jotted down and strode out, leaving Doctor Kreissman to shake her head.

Joe delivered the package to Doctor Mehta. He refused to meet the Shaker "You are my contact here and you will write it up" he said "tell him to look extra carefully at the Y chromosome" and she said she would. Joe then took a taxi back to the Cohen's place.

Rachel was pecking away at the Armada, Joe looked on the screen and basically was at a loss. Pure gibberish to the uninitiated. Rachel looked up from the laptop.

"The funeral will be on Sunday, will you stay?"

"No, I need to go tomorrow."

"All right, but how am I going to get this work done? The Internet isn't that fast."

"Then you better go to the door, there is a package for you."

"But it has your name on it!!" Rachel was surprised.

"Nevertheless, it's for you."

Rachel went back to the door, to the big box marked Airborne Express, Fragile, overnight delivery. She unwrapped it carefully.

"Wow, Hitachi laptop, with everything, who paid for this baby?"

"Chase did, why don't we start it up."

It was one of those foolproof machines. Very quickly they had it up and running, the Windows 95, set up the America on Line access program that came with it, and activated the TranXit program. after some fiddling they were able to transfer the GeneSearch Demo from the Armada to the Hitachi, and loaded the CD that Gabe had sent by special delivery earlier in the day.

"I really couldn't get much done today because Mom was at the Chevra Kadisha (the Jewish agency made up of volunteers who take care of Jewish burials) and the kids were here" she apologized. Joe waved this concern away.

"There we are" he said finally, "this account is mine and you don't have to worry about it, money- wise, e mail me whenever you have any inkling of what these sequences are."

Rachel was shaking her head. "But this might take days!! maybe more!!"

"Then take the laptop with you to New-York and work on it. Where am I going to find someone motivated enough to go on a wild goose chase just on my whim? And if I give this job to a commercial company, they will stiff me much more than the price of this machine. So take it and keep it."

"I guess you must be rich."

"I am" replied Joe, "it's an inheritance that is finally coming to a useful purpose."

Rachel was still doubtful, its not everyday that you get a brand new computer from a complete stranger. "All right, I'll go ahead with it, what am I really looking for?"

Joe grew pensive. "You are looking for sequences for known retro-viruses which are used for transduction of genes into mice, monkeys and humans. You are looking for known sequences of tumor- promoting genes, especially published sequences for the deletion 1p and 17. Also, known sequences of plasmids used to manufacture vaccinations such as Tetrammune, Acellular DPT. And of viruses used in vaccinations, Hepatitis, Polio, measles, mumps, rubella. That's a lot of work."

"That will cost your account at AOL a lot of money" commented Rachel, while shutting off the machine.

"I know, but I am sure the answer is here in the disk. Mustafa made the effort of trying to erase this data, it must have been important."

"Well, I must prepare for Shabbos. Are you going to fly on Shabbos?" She said with reproach.

"Yes."

"Did you ever think that the troubles of the Jewish People are because of Jews not observing the Shabbos?"

"My parents were observers of the Shabat, that didn't stop anyone from shooting them. That's one argument I don't want to have, especially with the loss of your father just last night. Ah, here is Tammy," and he escaped the study. The kids were throwing things around the greatroom, the plush toys were strewn all over the place. Joe was watching them as Tammy came in.

"So you are leaving us?"

"You have all the support you need, I am only a nuisance."

"Doctor Bergman, you must stop these remarks, a person must know his worth. You did more here in 3 days than all the doctors did in 3 months."

"Roger passed away just the same."

"What time do you want to leave?" said Tammy.

"As early as possible."

"I'll take you, I insist. Tonight we will have a nice Shabbos dinner, and you will make us a nice blessing."

"All right."

The table was beautifully set, the glasses sparkled, the wine was sweet, the kids glowed with health and merriment. Rachel and Gabe were downcast and picked at their foods, and Tammy Cohen kept on a fixed smile, and told funny stories of her life with Roger. Joe said nought about Viruses, Cancer, Plasmids, but encouraged Tammy along and contributed stories about travel to Switzerland, Italy, and getting lost in the Judea desert. From time to times Tammy would gaze at the empty chair, and sniffle, and blow her nose, and continued into another story. It was just like a wake.

Tammy found Joe with his bags packed, staring into the dark morning through the kitchen windows. Wordlessly she brewed them a strong coffee, and offered Joe some danishes. They left the house, closing the door silently, and Joe hefted his big bag into the back and seated himself at the front. Tammy's face was calm, composed, even the careful makeup was on. She must have been up for hours.

There was hardly any traffic and Joe volunteered no conversation. What can you say to a woman who had lost her husband? How to relieve the chasm of the years, the decades to come without her beloved? and it wasn't God-ordained. It was murder, premeditated and perpetrated by a supposed friend, and he was unreachable, likely to escape justice forever.

"I wanted to thank you , from the depths of my heart, for what you did." She said suddenly, looking ahead at the road.

Joe's heart almost stopped, then continued banging away, each beat a tolling bell. He felt short of breath. In his preoccupation with the Neuroblastoma he had forgotten that Tammy could put two and two together. "What did I do?" he stammered.

"Roger had asked me to help him, and I couldn't. Roger collected these vials as soon as he knew where he was heading. You were sent from Heaven to help us."

"Or from Hell" muttered Joe.

"Roger was in terrible pain" Tammy continued unabated "he only waited for Rachel and the kids so he could say goodbye, and you gave him hope that this tragedy can be stopped. I told him to ask you, otherwise I would have, but I knew you would have refused me."

"Damn right I would have refused."

"A close colleague refused Roger, that's why they stayed away the last few days. I am quite sure of it. Here is the aerodrome. Find Mustafa, punish him, stop him."

The car had stopped, Joe gazed at Tammy, she was so strong, so good, she didn't deserve this sorrow. He got out, pulled his bag out, and he came around to the driver's window. It was cold, not Milwaukee cold, but enough to make him draw his trench-coat closer.

"I will do my best, say goodbye to Roger for me." He grabbed his bag and went to the door of the low building. She sat there in the small parking lot watching the big man disappear into the building, the tower directing the early morning departures. Yes, he will do it, and my children will help him nail the killer.

Chapter 15

VIRUS

Nature has come up with lots of ways to distribute DNA. If fact some geneticists have concluded that Life is a solely a system of by which DNA thrives. Taken down to its most fundamental, sexual urge is just an elaborate ruse for the delivery of DNA. Anyone who has ever watched the neighborhood dogs fighting to death for the privilege of delivering their own DNA package to the bitch in heat, knows the power of that urge. Humans, to be sure are no better, and at times of war, when normal conventions are set aside, that urge is unleashed with unequaled savagery, as the victors foist their unwanted sperm on the females of the vanquished. Unlike all mammals, the question of consent becomes moot, and rape is the order of the day.

One cannot really attribute the emotional content of the word 'rape' to viruses, but in fact viruses are tremendously effective means of distribution for DNA, foisting their unwanted genome on the unsuspecting cell. The virus recognizes the cell's voluptuous receptor using a compatible ligand, causing the cell to fold in and encapsulate the virus. Once inside the cell, viruses employ different modes of getting to the cell nucleus, and insinuating themselves into the cell DNA, so that the cell is powerless to rid itself of the invading genetic material. The organism's only option is to kill the infected cell before the inevitable happens.

The inevitable is that the viral genome coerces the cell's life machinery to manufacture thousands of new virions, each containing a copy of the original viral genetic load plus some snippets of DNA it might have picked up. In addition the virion contains proteins which will help it with the next invasion. Those thousands cause the breakdown of the cell, and go ahead to invade the neighboring cells. Under the microscope, the process causes enlarging 'Plaques' in the dish where cells are plated, and the process continues until the cells are destroyed.

Humans have lived with viruses for eons, and natural selection has caused them to develop powerful defenses. No virus, however nasty, has caused the complete decimation of the human population, not even Var-iola, the Pox. But they have caused an awful lot of damage. On the other hand, specific populations which had never been exposed to a certain virus, were decimated when that particular virus was introduced. Such was the fate of the Hawaiian

Islanders when faced with Measles.

The most powerful defense human intelligence has put up involves the use of vaccines. Those viral look-alikes, mutated or killed viruses, present a challenge to the immune system. That challenge is answered by production of antibodies, proteins that specifically recognize the virus, and arrest them before they can invade cells. This is the principle that underlies the action of Vaccinia, the Cow Pox, which was found by Jenner to protect humans from the Black Pox. Polio vaccinations and hepatitis vaccinations use the same principles. This approach has so far been a dismal failure with AIDS. Not that humans do not raise antibodies to the challenge. Far from it, they raise a whole host of them, but, those do not neutralize it and so the AIDS virus goes on to attack cells which show off the pretty CD4 receptor, invade them, and kill them.

Many viruses, instead of killing the animal they invaded, prefer to colonize it, and live in it relatively peacefully, in balance with the host immune system. The Herpes virus colonizes nerve cells, but most of the time it is quiescent, causing only the minor discomfort of the cold sores. But when Immunity fails, even Chickenpox becomes a stormy killer. These viruses, since they have such ingenuous mechanisms to integrate their DNA, and later to reconstitute their viral forms, have taught the virologists fantastic lessons about the cellular machinery. The viral proteins are able to attach to DNA, transcribe specific portions, at a specific order of appearance, and assemble the multiple components into a complete virion. Those proteins have been recognized and the DNA sequences that encode them are known. In fact, they are so universal, that scientists have used them to insert pieces of DNA of their choice into cellular genome, a process called transfection.

Mustafa was not a virologist. He did not have to be. The final common pathway of most molecular biologists leads them to the manipulation of genetic material, regardless of which particular interest started them down that path. Once he had defined the target, a DNA sequence specific to Jews, and a disease-causing sequence, and an agent, a virus to carry the disease, he directed his attention to perfecting the weapon. That meant synthesizing a DNA strand complementary to the published DNA sequence of Cohanim, that was the targeting mechanism. A number of commercial enterprises were able to furnish unlimited amounts of the complementary DNA, for any published sequence. Then he needed a mechanism to insert a DNA snippet into an existing strand, such as that of a cell which already contained the DNA of the Virus. Other biotechnology companies supply kits which allow transfection of DNA snippets into a bacterial plasmids. (Plasmids are small circles of DNA which can transmit genetic information between bacteria, such as resistance to antibiotics). The mechanism of insertion and integration is borrowed from the Herpes viruses. This process of transfection was repeated a number of times, in different laboratories, by members of the Consortium, until a complete plasmid was created, a circle of DNA which contained a targeting section, an integrating section, and a disease causing section. All this work was coordinated by Mustafa and stored on his computer at the Blood Center, a place guarded 24 hours a day. Mustafa chose the Neuroblastoma gene for three reasons:

1. He was familiar with it from his days at St Jude, and

2. It is a relatively common disease for which meant cell lines are available. The cancerous cell display specific markers on their surface which can be demonstrated by staining methods.

3. His target was the young population, those who were expected to be vaccinated two to three times in the first year of life, then again at 18 months and 5 years, exposing them at least four times to his custom-made weapon.

Finally the plasmid was transcribed into RNA and transfected into the agent virus.

The process was long and tedious with many, many failed attempts, but finally, Doctor Munir Saidan from Indianapolis reported to Mustafa that his viruses were doing the job. Mustafa took Rashid Hariri's car, since his own Mercedes was in the shop again, and drove the 5 hour drive to Indy. He found Munir in the bowels of the Riley Children's hospital, observing the 96 well cell cultures through the microscope. Mustafa closed the door and locked it, although it was late in the day.

"Marhaba."

"Marhabtein." the traditional greeting and response.

"Show me." Mustafa commanded, it was a long ride and the afternoon Chicago traffic he had had to navigate gave him a headache.

Munir motioned him to the binocular station, which allowed him to view the same as himself. Mustafa looked at the sheets of cells.

"These are enteral cells which are infected with the with the unmodified virus. Notice the Cytopathic effect, showing that I am using viable viruses." He shifted the view to the next row. "These are modified viruses, they create the same cytopathic effect, which means they are viable too. The next row have the viruses tagged with Green Fluorescent Protein, which will show up only if the NB sequence has integrated. Let me switch on the light." Munir switched on the excitation light. The plaques glowed green. "The rest of the plate is various controls so let's see the next plate."

Mustafa was impressed. He kept nodding and hoping that indeed this was it. His own home situation was so bad he wanted to make his getaway as soon as possible. Alia was ready to go to first grade next year, and he wanted her to study in Arabic, that Arabic would be her first written language. Munir brought out the next plate.

"These are not enteral cells, they are brain cells, but still, the GFP shows up very bright." Mustafa nodded some more. "Look closely at the cells" Munir added oil for the immersion and increased the power of the microscope lens to the maximum. The cells looked somehow different and...

"Those are mitotic figures" Mustafa breathed hard.

"Right, this is neuroblastoma in the making."

"And how do you know that?"

Munir changed slides again "This is a stain specific for the Putative protein. I didn't do that myself of course. This one I sent to Fahed Shukeiri at Nicholinski institute. As you can see the Putative protein is stained in brown and appears to be widely expressed at the Nucleus of the cells which underwent Malignant Transformation, just like this control slide with from an established neuroblastoma cell line." Mustafa had structured his Consortium on the example of the cooperative organizations for the study of cancer such as the CCG (Childrens Cancer Group) and POG (Pediatric Oncology Group). He had established a reference laboratory which would do the expert work for the other members. Protein staining, FISH, cloning, radiography, those techniques had a designated reference person, who was doing the same type of work in his Masters or PhD work. The amount of Data generated was tremendous . Mustafa knew, and kept the big picture, and the best prospects, so he could direct the Consortium members in which direction to go, and which were blind alleys.

"And this is the clincher" said Munir with triumph "I sent Shafiq Khader in Tulane a bunch of slides for Fluorescent In Situ Hybridization, with two probes, one for sequence specific for the virus integration sequence, and one for the Neuroblastoma sequence. The cells are Macrophages, which are the precursors to Brain Glial cells. I infected cells from many donors, including myself, and this is what he sent me over the Net." Munir went to the Mac and showed him a slide after slide. They were all dark. Then one slide showed two sets of pinpoints, superposed on the same place "The Y chromosome" said Munir although he knew Mustafa knew that full well "and look at the name" Mustafa did not have to look hard. It said Sidney Cohen MD, Indianapolis. "And look at the next name" said Munir, an identical slide flashed on the screen. The name was Nichol Schatz PhD, La Jolla. "And what about In Vivo?" Mustafa asked, referring to experiments to be done in live animals. Munir was not the first one to have developed the agent Virus. Other viruses created the described effect in the plate, but when introduced to the live animal, they simply did not develop into viable growths "The reference lab for In Vivo is Mahmoud Fat'hi in Hamilton. I sent him some cell cultures and he injected them into Nude Mice." Munir referred to a strain of mice which lack immunity and are used as hosts for all manners of foreign cells. One could grow five different cancers in one mouse. Keeping such mice alive is a major undertaking in itself, but they are useful testbeds for Cancer treatment drugs. He clicked the mouse again on his Mac and showed pictures of Mice which Mahmoud had sent him. The pink mice had bony growths on their skull, distorting their smooth nude skin. Then followed pictures of gross dissection of an awful looking growth on a leg bone, pathology slides of lungs infiltrated by small round, blue cells, and bone marrow infiltrated by nests of malignant cells. "Aren't they great?" Munir exulted.

Mustafa got up and stretched, then fixed Munir with a baleful stare "Did you write down EXACTLY how to keep and proliferate this virus, the EXACT conditions, broth, temperature, did you put it in a vial, shake it, toss it, then check it for viability?"

Munir was shaken, he was afraid of this formidable leader.

"Ya Sidi, I checked everything, everything was done with multiple controls. I spent night and day on this. My construct is the one that works!!" he said proudly "and I have the complete laboratory manual on this disk." He pressed the button on the Zip Drive, the yellow light winked and the 100 megabyte disk slid out, he gave it to Mustafa.

Mustafa watched the outburst, he was sincere, This was not the Arab Boast of the Six Day war, boast without basis. This was real. They had come up with a weapon of horror so great, with such consequences, that the Jews would run away from Falasteen like cockroaches exposed to light. But he had to do the clinical trial, try it one someone who would be susceptible. It was time for Roger Cohen to pay for his support of the Zionist blasphemy.

"Can you give me some samples?"

"Tiny amounts, but in a week, samples with viral counts the same as

Vaccinations."

"Good, I'll come down again and pick them up, and conduct our own little clinical trial. Would you give this to your own son?" He bored into the shorter man's eyes.

"Yes, Ya sidi, this product is specific."

Mustafa hugged him and kissed him on both cheeks, as is the custom.

"Munir, my brother, you have made me proud, you have made the Islamic Brotherhood proud, Allah will repay you with many sons who will live in our own Falasteen." Munir was bursting with pride, although there was no chance he was going to live with his 'Brethren' in 'Falasteen'. He had visited the newly formed Autonomy in the West Bank. He had seen the killers turned police chiefs, the lolling youth-turned-police, the system of Graft instituted by the new leadership, the sewage running down the Wadis, the dirty streets, the shoe-less children running around, the lousy hospitals crying for the funds which Arafat and his cronies earmarked for weapons, rather than clean operating rooms. He wouldn't mind if the Jews left Palestine but he himself liked America much more then he would ever like another Arab dictatorship, or, even worse, the fundamentalist Islamic regime that Hamas wanted to put up. He returned Mustafa's hug. He would prepare the Virus cultures and hopefully, that will be the last he would see of this crazy scientist.

Mustafa drew away "Do you want to know how this is going to be used?"

Munir shook his head "No, the less I know, the better it is for the organization." Actually, it was not the organization he was worried about. It was his own soul. Sometimes, when doing the cloning and transfection studies, and especially when he had received the pictures of the Mice from Hamilton, he had a glimpse of himself as the Evil Scientist of the children comics and Holywood B movies, concocting Poisons for mass destruction. He wasn't sure he liked that image of himself. This way, if he did not know what was to be done he could shut out those visions and continue with his life. He obeyed the orders of the Consortium, but so had so many others, it was just luck that had made his construct, of which he was justifiably proud, the best one of all. In fact he could use the same vector for something more useful, such as inserting the Insulin code into Pancreatic cells, the thought cheered him up somewhat. It was with relief that he saw Mustafa out.

Mustafa, to be sure, was not blind to the sentiments that the work aroused in some of the Members. But, as long the work was done, and all the strands coalesced into the fabric of the completed Weapon, he did not care. Someday he would deal with those whose heart was not completely as one with the

Movement and the Islamic Jihad. Jihad meant Holy war, Total war, and not everyone was capable of Totality.

Once in his own office at the Blood Center, Mustafa copied the contents of the Zip disk into his computer main drive, made backup copies on the Colorado, and sent the optical disks to two other virologists in the Consortium, with requests to verify the capabilities of the Munir Virus. Actually, it was the Sabin Polio vaccine. It was symbolic, he mused, that the Sabin vaccine, invented by a Jew to help rid the world of Polio, would be used to afflict Jewish children with NeuroBlastoma. With these capabilities demonstrated, they would know that the Islamic Jihad had the power to deliver Death to the Jews in any form or fashion. In the water they drink, the fowl they eat, and even in the air they breath. This would be like the Atomic Bombs on Hiroshima and Nagasaki. If we are pissed, we shall drop the next one on Tokyo, that had been the implied threat.

Mustafa made the trek the next time in the old Mercedes, on which he had spent almost one thousand dollars in genuine German spares. The Germans had known how to deal with the Jews. He collected six small vials from Munir and drove north to Kalamazoo, where he delivered the Zip File and the Virus to Muhi-A-Deen Shareef. In March he made his way south to Memphis. He met with Nadia who had picked up her first supplies. He looked for a liquor shop, and chose one which boasted fine wines from around the world. He bypassed the French, California, Spanish, and Italian vintages, and found the more exotic aisle. There was a display of Japanese Saké and he knew that Roger liked that a lot, and the next case was of wines imported from Israel. He cast a venomous glance at the Gamla, and Carmel, and Barkan wines, until he had another idea. He examined several bottles, and found that Gamla was made in the Golan heights, close to Lebanon, now that was a thought!! he bought a pretty porcelain vase of Saké and headed out to St Jude.

Mustafa found Roger Cohen, now Emeritus, but in the pink of health, free from administrative duties, down in the labs, discussing Malignant Transformation with a small group of students. How fitting. Roger's face lit up like a flare when he recognized his former student at the back of the small conference room. He broke off his talk. "Excuse me folks, a friend just walked in" and he hurried to the back, the eyes of the students following him.

"Mustafa, how are you?!! Long time no see, no call, is Amanda with you?" and he clapped Mustafa on both upper arms. Mustafa was amused with this outgoing old goat.

"No, she is in Milwaukee, working hard and paying the bills, I am in town for the ASCO meeting."

"Right, right of course, I was going to go tonight to the Ball, are you going?"

"No, I would rather visit friends than stuff myself " he added with guile, setting the trap. Roger fell right into it.

"Come for dinner, will you?"

Mustafa made as if considering "Sure, good Idea, and don't buy any non-kosher wines either."

Roger clapped him again, "excellent, wonderful, Gabe will be in too." Mustafa hid his distate at the mention of the Gay son, he often wished AIDS would take away all those abominations.

Roger turned to the small class and announced "Ladies and gentlemen, this is Mustafa Halim, PhD, one of the best Doctorate students I ever had, he is now in Milwaukee, doing excellent research on Major Histocompatibility Antigens, especially pertaining to ethnic minorities, see Mustafa" and he turned to Mustafa with a wink as subtle as a Jumbo Jet "I keep tabs on all my students." Sure, you wish, you have no idea, you pompous old goat.

Mustafa took time to go to a barbershop, trim his thick beard, square it nicely, shave the thick dark hair on his upper neck and under his jaw, and generally to tone down the typical Islamic look. He appeared at Roger Cohen's door with a bunch of flowers, new shirt, new pants and a passable jacket, even Gabe had to admit he did his best and was a good looking bloke. Tammy of course was not fooled by anything, and since Roger promised her this was a one-time visit, she invited him into her home. One vial went into the Saké and Mustafa was careful to ask Tammy not to heat it. During dinner they all quaffed heartily, and Roger especially drank to Mustafa's health, to Amanda's health and success, and to Alia, may she grow to be as beautiful and wise as her mother, and as resourceful and industrious as her father. Guinea pigs, Mustafa thought. No wonder it was easy to develop biological weapons, as opposed to vaccines. One did not have to test them for safety, no first or second or third-phase trials. No FDA approvals, no pesky hospital Institutional Review Boards. It was Fire and Forget, a guided missile right at the heart and Bones of the obnoxious enemy. Thousands and millions of missiles, now homing in on Roger Cohen's Intestinal cells, invading the membrane, breaching the nucleus and homing in on their target on the Y chromosome. While Roger and his abomination of a son were talking and laughing, the viruses were replicating in their dormant Neural cells and the Transforming DNA was integrating into their Y chromosome. Somewhat later, in a few weeks or months, the protein transcribed would impair the cell cycle, and the neural cells will start dividing and proliferating. They would snub the chemical signals of the neighboring cells, and continue to divide and conquer. Once their blood supply runs short, the Malignant cells will start to slough off the main growth and wander in the blood flow, until they soft-land on another beach head, a bone, liver, lung, and they would germinate into new growths, until the organism was completely overwhelmed. So drink up Roger, because revenge is at hand.

Mustafa took his leave at 10 PM, and the only way Tammy could persuade herself to be civil was by telling herself this was the last time. He laughed to himself, the future widow will never know what hit her. He had a few more vials and he wanted to continue his In Vivo experiment That would be tomorrow.

All that had been 9 months before. He had phoned Roger once, gladly heard that he was ill, and had Nadia Lubin inform him by E mail of his victim's plight, as she did for the other guinea pigs. When it became obvious that they were indeed sick he had asked her to go back to her regular life, with a generous payoff. She was a dangerous link to himself, so he thought it prudent to eliminate her. When she came back from the Briarwood clinic after a long day in late October she was surprised that the lights of the garage door mechanism remained dark. Nevertheless, she closed the garage door behind her, secure in the confines of her own garage and home. She turned around to the sudden slithering footstep, much too late and all the lights in her brain went out as the heavy wrench hit her right above the ear, crashing through the thin bone and causing a massive arterial bleed. A few minutes later her brain herniated and she was dead. Her husband, who ran Lubin pest control, when he was sober, found her thus, her head in small pool of blood, an hour later. The police never found the murder weapon and the killer was in Detroit the same night, knowing nothing about his victim. The police never thought to go through the contents of her computer email.

Mustafa had turned the basement of the Doctor's villa outside Beirut into a small factory for the production of the virus. That was the greatest virtue of Biological warfare. His weapon was contained in a tiny vial, and given the right growth medium, that is the right cells to colonize, it could replicate itself to industrial quantities. The dose delivered to the subject was important, because the virus, until it established itself, faced many obstacles. IgA antibodies in the mouth, raised against similar entero-viruses might neutralize

it. Stomach acid might disrupted its envelope, immune cells might recognize
it and render it useless. So, the virus must be administered in sufficient
quantities. This was difficult to do covertly in the US. Lebanon is the Wild
East. While under the patronage and in the manor of any of the war-lords, one
could do anything, distill alcohol, manufacture drugs, bombs, fake CD's, fake
Levies, whatever. Mustafa ordered supplies from leading suppliers of
laboratory equipment and biological reagents to addresses in Cyprus, and had
them shipped overnight on fishing boats whose masters were loyal to the
Jihad. Soon his lab surpassed anything in Lebanon, and he trained lab techs
pulled from various hospitals, those who had studied in France and England,
in techniques of cell culture, centrifugation, elution, concentration. All of
them menial tasks for people who had no idea of the material in their hands
or it's destiny. He had unlimited funds from Younes, who drew them in turn
from the Arab-American fund raising and drug running. Mustafa found it
amusing that US government had directly paid for his education, and
indirectly, through the tax shelter for charitable causes to the Islamic Jihad,
paid yet again for his activities. They were so gullible!! The American
University was flourishing, and attached to it, his own former school, all at
American Taxpayers' expense.

Beverly Kreissman and Jerry stein had parked their cars far away from the
synagogues. Driving around on Shabat was a complete anathema to them but,
Beverly reasoned, if they saved one child from disease, it was justified. Jerry
had spent hours on her data and finally agreed that this coalescence of cases
could not be accidental. He took on the three Orthodox synagogues, which
were mostly Patriarchal and where women never spoke before the
congregation. In each case he approached the Rabbi, and asked to speak
during a suitable pause in the Saturday morning service. He stood as tall as
his 5 foot seven allowed and delivered his message, that due to some
unresolved problem, the vaccinations were unsafe and everyone with small
children should avoid them until further notice. People besieged him with
questions later and all he could say was that the information was preliminary.
Beverly did the same in the Conservative and reform Schulls. They repeated
the same rounds on Sunday, at the Jewish Sunday schools, and asked the
parents to disseminate that information to other members of the Jewish
community. Susan and Moe were very confused at this new activity.

"Do you think what ever it is might have gone beyond Memphis"? Jerry
asked later that Sunday afternoon.

"Who knows, but if this is here it could be everywhere, listen to us talk, it's like we are talking about the Plague" Beverly said.

"Well, isn't it? There is something, and maybe someone, out there, making kids sick with Cancer. Its just like the early days of the AIDS epidemic when I was a medical student. We knew something bad was on the street, but we did not know *what*. And then the addicts started coming in, sick as dogs, and we had no idea. Now this!!"

Beverly was thinking hard "Jerry, watch the kids, I have to go back."

"Why?"

"I want to look up every chart again and see where and how and who gave them vaccinations."

"I'll take them to the mall. They enjoy all this Christmas stuff even though they know it's not Kosher."

Susan Kreissman went back to St Jude, back to medical records. She waited impatiently until the overworked staff pulled the same charts out, those that were not in her own department. Then she went up to the department and looked through those. The answer was not there. Generally, the intern taking history recorded only the fact of vaccination, as reported by the parent, but no other details. Then she sat in one of the dictation booths and started calling.

"Hello, Cowan residence" a female voice.

"Hi, I am doctor Kreissman from St Jude, its about Joshua."

"I remember you, you were the woman doc with the Mogen David."

"That's right, I know Joshua died in Gainesville, and I am very sorry I did not keep in contact, but I need to ask you one more thing."

"He is dead, what does anything matter anymore?" The heart-broken voice was tearful, anguished.

"Please help me Missis Cowan."

"All right."

"Where did Joshua have his vaccinations."

"At his doctor's office, Rosenblatt, on Church and Almond."

"Do you remember anything special about those shots?"

"No, they were just shots, I know shots, come to think of it, Tony, Josh's big brother, needs to have his shots next week."

"Missis Cowan" Beverly said with urgency "Don't give him any shots."

"Why?"

"A visiting scientist we had here said that it was possible something bad was in the shots" Beverly twisted the facts just a little.

"Really? how come no one told us that before? Actually, Jack came back form Sunday school and said something about that."

"Missis Cowan, when I have the answers I will personally call you again, but for now, no shots, and spread the word to other Jewish Friends."

"Jewish? Why Jewish? I have lots of friends, what about them?"

"Trust me on this, I have two kids and they are not going to get any shots till the Expert figures this out."

"OK, so long, and thank you." Beverly was feeling hollow. All these kids, members of the tribe, became sick and died on *her* watch. She called another number.

"Hi, this is the Le-vine residence, we are not home, you know what to do after the beep" Beverly left a message to call her at St Jude.

"Hello" a grumpy male voice.

"Hi, this is Doctor Kreissman from St Jude."

"Yeah."

"Are you Mister Gold?"

"Yea"

"How is Mallory"

"Bad, we moved him to Le Bonheur since you guys did nothing for him."

"I am truly sorry to hear that , and how is he doing now?"

"Worse."

"How worse?"

"Like he is *dying*, are you satisfied?"

"Mister Gold, nothing can make me more heart broken than a dying kid, especially if we screwed up and didn't help him."

"Sorry, I am mad at this fucking world. We waited ten years for Mallory, shots, treatment, Fertilization, finally God listens and sends us this beautiful present. And then he gives him this awful disease.... My wife went haywire. Gone mental. I took him home from the hospital and all I want is to die with him!!"

Beverly was openly crying into the phone, the anguish pouring out right into her ear and brain was devastating. The man regained his grumpiness.

"Why did you call, Doctor, any miracle cures came up?"

"No, but I need some information from you."

"You got all the charts Doc!"

Beverly steeled herself to continue despite the acid "Where did Mallory have his shots?"

"You guys filled him with a billion shots, fat lot of good that it did!!"

"No, I mean baby shots, vaccinations."

"Oh, that, before he became sick, you mean?"

"Yes."

"Uh... Uh... I can't even *think* of the time before he was sick."

"Please mister Gold, try."

"Uh... the East side Pediatrics, Doctor Monroe, she was the one who noticed the big belly. She is a nice doc, but like all of you, **IM-PO-TENT.**

"Thank you Mister Gold, one more question, are you Jewish?"

"By birth, not by choice."

Beverly Kreissman listened, somewhere behind there was a monitor, beeping a baby heart rate. A man, alone, with a dying baby, separated by choice from his brethren.

"My dad was Jewish. His name was Joel Goldstein" came the belligerent voice.

"Do you know if he was a Cohen, a priest."

"Yeah, he was, he tried to make good on marrying out, so he dragged me to Temple when I was little, hey, what's that got to do with my sick kid, my DEAD kid?"

"Mister Goldstein, I mean Gold, it may have everything to do with it. I promise you, my word as a Baby Doctor, when I find out I will let you know!!"

"Maybe that'll get Marilyn out of the nuthouse, bye" and the phone was disconnected.

Beverly Kreissman MD was totally crushed when she finished her phone calls. It was one thing being second only to God on the department, another to talk directly to the afflicted, with what seemed an irrelevant question. She looked down at all the Doctor's offices and health depart-ment addresses. Nothing common to all of them. What a lousy evening. And she didn't even get to play with her own kids! Suddenly, the idea that someone was designing a way to make *her* kids sick overwhelmed her with urgency. She fled the building and drove home at reckless speed. She found Jerry putting them both down to sleep, and she fell on them with hugs and kisses.

"What did you find?" Jerry asked over the Microwave bagels and cream-cheese.

Beverly just picked at her food. "Zilch, Nada, Nothing, just the most

Gawd-Awful miserable parents I ever talked to."

"Show me the Zilch" he asked of her, soft spoken as always.

Beverly pulled out the list "Take a look, maybe you can figure it out."

Jerry Stein scanned the list of offices. There was nothing common to them, just disparate sites all over metropolitan Memphis, more on the East, but that's it.

"All I can think of is that tomorrow you drive around to all these places and ask some questions. Like, who gives shots, who brings in the vaccinations, take the lot numbers of the shots for all the kids, and see what will pan out."

"But I am on service tomorrow" she wailed.

"Take a sick leave, you have *never* taken a sick leave, even when you were *sick!*"

"I was never that sick" Beverly said defensively.

"Yeah right, You had me give you fluids IV so you can go to the Hospital, that one time!"

"Well, I can't get sick with Flu when all the kids I take care of have Cancer!" she retorted.

"Take a sick leave tomorrow, now let's go to bed, and make-believe we want another baby."

"But we *do*!"

"Fine, show me how" and he stroked her neck gently.

Sundararaman Chandrasekhar (Shaker to his friends) preferred not to look at the glass slides directly, but rather to make the photographs using the Kodak Digital camera, and then transfer them over to his Compaq, which had a 19 inch monitor and was SSVGA, the highest resolution available. This way he could display the photos, enlarge, reduce, invert, superimpose, enhance etc...He had received the chromosome 17 probe as a research tool, another marker of Malignant transformation, possibly related to neuroblastoma, but maybe connected to other Neural Crest Tumors. The recent history of Genetics was replete with cases where probes developed for the diagnosis of one disease, turned out to be important in a whole host of others. Using funds won from the NIH for various studies, he had acquired many different probes, DNA snippets attached to a fluorescent molecule, which were complementary to known DNA sequences. It was almost his hobby, he collected the probes avidly, from colleagues, commercially available, some of his own lab's making. In this specific experiment, he used two probes, tagged in Blue and Yellow. One probe was for the chromosome 17 material amplified from 1;17 translocations of Neuroblastoma patients, that was blue. The other was a standard Y chromosome marker, tagged in yellow, complementary to a sequence found only in the human Y chromosome.

First he looked at the controls. Roger Cohen's cells had been induced into Mitosis, cell division, and arrested right when the chromosomes were at their most exposed, right after duplication, and before separating into 2 daughter cells. A number of probes were applied, developed for Lymphoma, breast cancer, primary bone tumors. The cells were dark, the probes had attached to nothing. Then the X chromosome probes. Each and every cell fluoresced a single pinpoint of light, confirming the presence of the X chromosome. The same occurred with the Y chromosome probe. The standard was the Hemoglobin Beta chain locus. That showed up with two bright points, on chromosome 11.

2 Mitoses in Roger Cohens cells fluoresced adequately. The color was Green , even though the probes were blue and yellow. That meant the two probes had complemented sites very close to each other, and since the Y chromosome was yellow, then Green meant was that Chromosome 17 material had translocated to the Y chromosome. This was incredible, groundbreaking. It also needed to be confirmed.

The next set of experiments used the PCR technique, which had revolutionized Genetics in the nineties. It was based on the fact that if the short sequences flanking the gene in question were known then the enzymes which replicated DNA would roll on after starting on the short sequence, and complete the intervening sequence. The process was repeated automatically, and repetition multiplied the sequence of choice. Thus amplified it was easily detected. Shaker had two of his lab technicians do the amplification on DNA taken from Roger Cohen preserved samples. The fact that Doctor Cohen had already died did not matter at all. For his purposes, his genetic material was alive. Using a library of primers from the Y chromosome, generated by the Human Genome Project, he made many sequences, and hybridized each with the chromosome 17 probe. The probe was labeled with a radioactive marker. When Kodak film was exposed to the marker, it showed up as a heavy black band. Thus he confirmed the presence of the Transforming gene located in the Y chromosome. He researched the Medline and other data-bases and confirmed again that this was unique.

The three plates that the Mysterious Doctor Brgman had brought from St.

Jude, and that no one in St Jude had ever heard of, were even more striking, but the data was the same. A new Cancer entity, Neuroblastoma in children and adults, very aggressive, caused by 17;Y translocation/integration. This was not Nobel prize material but still, important. Maybe it will be eponymed the Shaker/Mehta syndrome, like Fanconi anemia, and Nieman/Pick disease? That was the only way to immortality.

Shaker paged Doctor Mehta, she deserved full credit for this.

TO: helen.bergman@chw.edu
FROM: mmehta1@vanvleet.edu
Dear Doctor Bergman
Shaker has conclusively shown me that the putative transforming chromosome 17 derivative is demonstrated in the Roger Cohen Samples. It was translocated to the Y chromosome.

Furthermore, the same translocation was detected in the three samples from St Jude, making this a single disease entity.

Shaker is looking into other Neural Crest tumors, which were considered geneticaly normal, to look for the same translocation.

Are you sure you don't want your name on this publication?
Sincerely

Marten.

REPLY
FROM: helen.bergman@chw.edu
TO: mmehta1@vanvleet.edu
Dear Marten
Great work, but, this is only the beginning.

See if you and your collaborator Shaker can locate the gene published by Katz in Toronto, the one claimed to be unique to Jewish priests. See if your samples happen to express that sequence. Make controls. This might be a special susceptibility gene for this specific disease

Bear with my unusual notions
Sincerely
Doctor Joe

"Your friend must be foux, excuse my French" said Shaker at Marten's message.

"Crazy or not, this is very interesting, and so far he has been on the mark."

"In for the penny, in for the pound, let's go on line for this Katz publication" and Shaker clicked the Netscape button. All those years of poring over the National Library of Medicine huge volumes, and the Current Contents, what a waste of time. Now he could do it all, and much more, from his desk or from his home. Technology was wonderful.

Rachel Sodorski was also on the Net, recovering sequences and comparing them with the data on the disk. One can do a lot of work on four hundred megabytes of information, but of course, she did not to do the homologies herself. The GeneSearch software did it for her. The 698 dollar software package had been delivered to her Brooklyn apartment, and it was much faster than the demo she had down-loaded from the Net while she was still in Memphis. She searched the various data bases, downloaded multiple published sequences for viruses, bacteria and plasmids, and the program compared then with sequences on the disk. Then it presented her with degrees of homology, the percentage of sequence identity, and of course, almost all the time it was very low. She saved the sequences which showed a greater homology and continued to collect more and more data. It was slow work because the download times for the data bases depended on many factors, including the telephone service, Internet speed, The US Robotics modem inherent speed limits, and the servers themselves. Many times the servers were simply not available and she had to try them again and again, until she got lucky. And, of course, she had two small children and a household to maintain while Israel Sodorski was making a living as a diamond dealer on 52nd avenue, traveling frequently to Antwerp and Tel Aviv and Rotterdam on business. One finding was clear though.

From: rachel.sodorski@aol.com
to: helen.bergman@chw.edu
Dear Dr Bergman
I identified one set of sequences. They are variations on a central theme of a section of the Y chromosome. I recall a publication from Toronto by a Professor Katz which proves a Founding Father effect for Cohanim, on the Y chromosome. I will try and locate this sequence and match it with the data.

Rachel

Beverly Kreissman dropped the kids off at the JCC, which was open from seven AM for the benefit of the working couples. An hour later Moe would go on to the kindergarten run by the Day School. The Jewish education deal cost them at least 15 thousand a year, excluding the donations, the fund raising, the special projects, but for every child who was paid for in full, there were two whose parents were unable to pay as much and were therefor assessed a lower tuition, and so it was money well spent.

The East Side Clinic was the closest so she started there. It was a large suburban building, serving a multi specialty clinic. She entered the building from the main entrance and directly ahead there was a big sign, East Side Pediatrics, with pictures of four smiling doctors in a row. Beverly looked for doctor Monroe picture and she saw the face of a young, round, apple-cheeked woman. She went to the reception desk where a secretary was taking the phone calls and arranging the schedule.

"Can I help you?"

Beverly pointed to her name tag from St Jude, "I would like to speak to Doctor Monroe, is she available?"

"She just came in from her rounds. Go right in Doctor."

Beverly went through the door which led to a cheerful corridor decorated with the best of Disney characters. Disney and Pediatrics marched hand in hand. She found the office where Doctor Monroe, a pretty plump woman, was going through her mail. Beverly knocked politely.

"Come in, oh, from St Jude, oh no, it's Mallory isn't it? Did he come back to you?" Her voice quavered, as if Mallory's illness was her fault. "Excuse me, I am Liz Monroe."

"Beverly Kreissman, yes this is regarding Mallory, I am following up on a number of Kids with Neuroblastoma, and I happened to start here."

Liz bent to the intercom "Rhonda, could you please pull the Mallory Gold chart, thanks." She came back to Beverly "he is an IVF baby, normal delivery, no history, got his regular shots on time, his mother doted on him, she had gone through the whole Fertilization rigmarole for 10 years. "Thanks Rhonda" and she opened the chart. "See, nothing special, until at nine months he came in for a cold, and I checked his belly, and it was God-awful distended with a huge something. It could only be a tumor, I was afraid of Burkitt and Tumor Lysis so I sent him to St. Jude, that's it. Here are the weekly letters that St Jude sent back. In fact you signed some of them. After a while it got so horrible I didn't read them anymore."

"He is dying at home now" said Beverly sadly, "his dad took him home when he realized there was no hope, I just wanted to look at one thing, his shots."

"They are here, with the lot numbers, but why the shots?"

"It's just an idea we had" Beverly was evasive. "Who gives the shots here?"

"The nurses, we have wonderful nurses, the kids hardly whimper, sometimes we have a substitute nurse from a temp service, if someone is ill. You know how it is in Peds, we get so sick from the Kids sometimes."

"Whose are those signatures?"

"I don't know, let's go out and look for Barb, she is the head nurse in the Department."

Barb turned out to be a patrician looking lady with bleached shoulder-length hair, probably to hide the grey. She examined the signatures minutely.

"Those signatures are all from the department, I know them. I think that one is Nadia Lubin, she is a temp we get here when we are very busy if the someone is ill, funny, I asked for her from the Holms Agency, but they said she was gone. Anyway, that's her. The four month shots are Tetrammune, and OPV. She was so nice, when we ran out of the shots I asked her to go over to the Health Department and authorized her to get some for us, we were so busy. I wonder where she is now."

Beverly wrote down everything, the vaccinations, the lot numbers, time and place. She took two more days to cover all the Doctors for the babies. Then she tabulated her Data meticulously. Jerry brought the kids with him, and she waited until they had dinner, and bath, and bedtime story, and a short evening prayer before sitting him down, and opening the folded paper.

"What do you see?" She asked.

"Lots of data, under Nurse there is but one common name, Nadia Lubin."

"And what else?"

"The lot numbers for the Hepatitis, Tetranmmune, Acellular DPT, HIB are all different, The lot numbers for the IPV are all different. For the OPV, they are identical."

"So it's the OPV, it's the easiest to contaminate."

"How did this Nadia do it?"

"The story is identical in every clinic. She is a temp, employed by an agency as a fill-in for Pediatric offices. She asked to give shots every time, and the nurses gladly handed over that chore which they hate 'cause it makes the kids cry. She got her own stock from the health department by being sent there , and then for in the next two months she was dripping the tainted OPV into kid's mouths. Disgusting."

"Maybe she had no idea, maybe someone told her it was a Blinded Trial run by the University of Tennessee." Jerry refused to see the bad side of Humanity, he was the kind of Jew who walked into the gas chambers and said it was only a shower. Millions of Jerry Steins thus perished. The phone rang.

"Stein residence."

"Uh, does a Doctor Kreissman live there?" Beverly took the phone.

"This is Doctor Kreissman."

"Doctor, this is Barb Peterson, we met three days ago at the East Side Clinic."

"I remember, you are the charge nurse for the Pediatric service."

"About Nadia Lubin, I know why she is gone."

"Go on."

"My husband is a police captain. I told him about your visit and he mentioned that a few months ago, a Nadia Lubin was killed, murdered, he said nothing was stolen, someone used a wrench to kill her, and disappeared."

"Awful."

"Isn't it? I just wanted to tell you."

"Thanks" She put the phone down.

"Who was that? " Jerry asked.

"Someone murdered the messenger, Nadia Lubin, some months ago."

"Shit. On the other hand it may mean the epidemic may be contained."

"Yeah, maybe, I will E-mail Joe now."

"How did *he* get involved in this mess?"

"He said the same guy who concocted this virus has kidnaped his own daughter from an American spouse and disappeared. The spouse is also a Hem/Onc fellow in Milwaukee. He ran into this by accident."

"I guess he has all the threads so give him another one." Beverly went to her computer and sent off the E mail.

Chapter 16

Identity

The flight back to Milwaukee was technically easier, it was daytime. But it was bumpy as hell, and Joe was happy he had not eaten much before the flight. The Cessna 210 had long-range tanks which allowed him to take the 650 miles in one hop, and it was a bruiser. He took care of elimination just like the astronauts did - by attaching a urine bag with a long tube, available in every hospital supply room. He took some sweet candy to suck on and some chocolate to supply his brain with sugar. His head was spinning as he approached Timmerman just before nightfall. It was windy as hell but Timmerman has two runways to choose from so that the final approach was done into the wind, which made the ground speed so slow that he was able to turn the aircraft out of the runway at the first exit. He parked it on the apron and disconnected the urine bag and tied the tube off. He tied the wings and the tail down securely as the pre-Christmas wind whipped at his coat and his Yamaha ski-cap. Still, the cold sub-zero wind cleared his head enough so he could check the aircraft in, can the fluid trash, and lug his bags to the LeSabre. He almost fell asleep in the car despite the freezing cold, when the door was wrenched open to a blast of icy evening wind, and a lithe figure settled itself on the hard seat. He almost rubbed his eyes. It was Karen, she knew he never locked the doors.

She pulled down her headgear-cum-scarf, and the flaxen hair fairly jumped out. He was transfixed.

"Will it start?"

"Sure, she loves the cold weather" he replied automatically and tried the ignition. No wonder the dome light never came on. It was stone cold dead.

"You chump, you left the main lights on!!" She laughed and she pointed at the knob, which was still pulled out.

"Chump is right, how did you know when I was coming in?"

"I called the Tower, had a nice chat with Bruce whoever, and got him to call me when your call-sign November 46596 was called in."

"Really, they would never do that" he countered.

"You told me to use my female charms, and I assure you, they work just fine."

"Can you use your charms on this car then?" he teased.

"No, she is a hetero, I don't have a chance. But a jump-start might."

Joe sighed, he had met his match as a smart alec "Why don't you bring your car and I will pull the cables outa the trunk."

It took them fifteen minutes of hard charging before the old, cold car would crank over, one cylinder at a time, until all eight were singing. Joe folded the cables and threw them back into the trunk. He scraped the windows until he could actually see inside. Then he settled back behind the wheel. Karen came to his window.

"Thanks." Joe said.

"Just a tiny refund on what I owe you" Karen said, with feeling.

"What now?"

"What does your place look like?"

"Probably cold, and nothing much in the fridge."

"Why don't you follow me to my place, I have a dinner ready."

Joe did a double-take on that "Who is invited?"

"You, if you want to" she said, bravely.

If I don't, I will hurt her bad, and there is no earthly reason to hurt her. "Alright, dinner sounds very good, let's go."

Karen closed the garage door with the Genie remote and opened the front door so Joe, who had parked his car outside, could come in. The little house was warm and cozy. A gas fire with faux logs was spewing heat into the living room. With tired motions he wriggled out of the trench coat, and tucked the ski-cap into the sleeve and gave it to Karen to hang. She held it at arms length, it was like a tent, and it looked like it had seen better days, a hundred years ago. No comment. Joe made it to the couch and almost collapsed.

"Gee, marching 50 miles with full gear was easy compared with this."

"How long ago was this, that you marched 50 miles?"

"Oh gosh, it was about ten, no, fifteen, no, twenty years ago."

"There you are, middle age is fast acomming" she said, already at the kitchen at the top of the stairs, "What will you have?"

"Tea."

"Earl Gray coming up."

"You don't a give a guy a choice."

"No I don't, they make bad choices all the time."

"I guess you must be right, we are at a disadvantage."

"What disadvantage?" She poured the boiling water into the delicate teacups, onto the Lipton tea-bags.

"We have an X missing."

"And all the Y does is make you violent."

He held the steaming cup to his lips and carefully inhaled. "Ahhh, just what the doctor ordered."

"Actually, its the nurse."

"I told you, the X is missing, we don't have our facts right" and he sipped gratefully.

Karen wrinkled her nose "Why don't you wash up before dinner"?

Joe raised his eyebrow as far as it would go. Karen was unmoved and sipped her tea daintily. He brought it down to the straight line "I don't have a change of clothing" he pointed out.

"Let Mama worry about it" she said with authority "no smelly men at the table."

Joe just shook his head with disbelief. He hadn't been bossed around like that since... never mind.

"The bathroom is up the stairs and at the end" she added.

Joe finished his tea with a final slurp, just to show what a barbarian he really was, and trudged up the stairs. Fortunately, they were only 7 steps. The bathroom was one hundred percent feminine, but not overstocked, with a wide counter top. On the counter top, beside the wash basin, there was a neatly folded heap of clothing. Joe was amazed to find boxer shorts, teeshirt and thick fleece Fruit of the Loom slacks and top, all XX large. A large Glad trash bag topped the heap, and fleece slippers number 14 kept it from falling off.

Joe stuffed his clothes into the bag and showered in the hottest he could stand. He sprayed some Arrid before getting dressed with the clothing provided. For a second he felt cared-for, at home, but only for a second.

he was mightily surprised when he came out the corridor, into the kitchen and the breakfast nook. There were TWO women there, the older woman obviously Karen's mother, and Karen herself, distraught and somewhat embarrassed. After missing a step Joe came on right ahead, there was nowhere to hide anyway. Miriam looked him up and down, and if she was impressed she hid it well.

"Mom, this is Doctor Joseph Bergman, he, er, is a doctor at the HOT unit."

"Pleased to meet you ma'am" Joe said, in the least squeaky voice he could manage, and extended his hand across the table.

Miriam shook his hand shortly, he had an impression of an elegant figure, auburn hair with plenty of grey interlaced, carefully plucked brows, brown eyes and a strong nose, firm chin and a generous mouth. No slack yet, and a firm grip. If Karen were to look like that in 30 years then she is in luck. I guess the dark-blue eyes are from her dad. "Nice to meet you too, Doctor Bergman" she said, smooth voice, no cracks, a voice much younger than her age. Karen's voice.

"Mom kinda dropped in" said Karen apologetically. She busied herself with an onion soup which, with the addition of grated cheese, made the kitchen dizzy with smell. Joe, who had not eaten since the early AM had to hold himself back.

"Moms do that, you know" Miriam commented "that smells really good Karen, I think I should come more often." Karen kept her face rigid, and Joe chuckled inside. Let's see how Karen wriggles out of this homey scene. The soup bowls made their way to the table.

"Are *you* here often, Doctor Bergman?" Miriam continued her investigation.

"First time" Joe mumbled between mouthfuls.

"Remarkable" commented Miriam, "I never knew Karen was this well prepared for the unexpected."

"Stop it Mom, Joe, er... Doctor Bergman came back this afternoon with a small aircraft, from Memphis, and I figured he would be beat."

"And...." Miriam prompted, amused by her daughter's discomfiture.

"Doctor Bergman was the man who helped me a few weeks ago at the parking lot." Joe kept his eyes firmly planted in the rapidly vanishing bowl of onion soup. Finally, when it was empty he had to look up. This time the appreciation was very apparent.

"You mean he saved you from being raped and killed?" Miriam said, faux-lightly, holding his gaze.

"Yes Mom."

"And I have to find out about this by accident?" Miriam accused her daughter. Karen was crestfallen, she went back to the range top. Joe twisted the cap off the Miller Lite, and raised his eyebrow at Miriam who shook her head. He poured for himself, very slowly, and watched the frothy head growing. Miriam placed both elbows on the table, rested her chin on her palms and gave him another survey.

"Thank you" she said suddenly.

"You're welcome" he replied. And took a long pull.

The dinner was quite smooth from then on. Miriam did not push to find out what the Memphis trip was about. She was interested in Joe's research efforts. Joe was happy to demolish the grilled chicken-breast and veggies, and the jelly with apple slices. Miriam glanced at her Cartier watch and announced she had to go due to some committee meeting tomorrow. Karen saw her to the door.

"Karen."

"Yes Mom."

"Keep him here."

Karen followed her mother to the car, a newish Caprice. She got in beside her in the car, away from the chill.

"I can't Mom."

"Why not?" Miriam said hotly.

"He is not someone you can push around, and he lost his wife some years ago."

"Listen to me Karen," Miriam was emphatic and earnest "stop living your life in the past, and don't let this man live his life in the past. He likes you, not just the damsel- in-distress. I can feel it, he cares for you. That's what counts, care and love, and neverever leaving your beloved. *Make* him love you and he will!!"

"I don't know mom, he is such a hardshell."

"Pry him loose, gently."

"We'll see Mom, night, I love you, thanks for coming."

Joe was adjusting his shoulders in the coat as she came in. She closed the door, and turned the bolt.

"Where do you think *you* are going?" She said.

"Home, I guess."

"Not after that beer." Karen strode over, pulled the back pillows of the couch, which made it a decent-sized bed. "I'll get you some sheets and a blanket."

"Do I have a choice?"

"Yes, but the basement is colder, its much better here."

"I guess I don't have a choice, at least I have my pajamas on" Joe said tiredly. He took off his coat and put it on the hanger, suddenly that couch looked very inviting. They spread the bedding on it and Karen turned off the light.

Karen woke up. It was completely dark outside, her window looked out to the wide expanse of white that was in the center of the subdivision, where there were no street lights. The phosphorescent hands of the alarm clock said 0235 AM. It was a restless sound, coming from the living room. Karen put on her housecoat and padded softly on the carpet. She stood at the railing looking over the living room and watched the big figure tossing and turning and mumbling. 10 minutes later it slumped into an exhausted slumber, marked by a soft snore. Karen resisted the impulse to go down the steps and smooth that troubled brow. She shook her head sadly and went back to her own bed.

She woke up to the sound of the modem, and the smell of freshly brewed coffee. The Sunday morning light was beginning to filter in, over the dusting of snow on the balcony. Today it was not swirling, in fact there was a complete standstill after a tumultuous night. Karen threw on her Japanese kimono housecoat and padded into the kitchen.

"Good morning" Joe said cheerily.

"Too early, its Sunday for Godssakes" she replied, with a huge yawn.

"Can I get you some coffee?" Joe was solicitous.

"Sure, make yourself useful." She sat down and looked at the screen of the Armada. It was going through the motions of connection. Then it flashed

TO: helen.bergman@chw.com
From: rachel.sodorski@aol.com
Doctor Bergman, the sequence published from Toronto, claimed to be recovered from the Y chromosome of males who are of Cohen ancestry, appears many times in my data. The homology with the published sequence is 90 percent or more. I am working now on trying to establish the identity of the sequences flanking this gene, or whatever this is.

Rachel

Joe came back with a cup, milk and sugar, and placed it in front of her nose. Then he clicked on the reply box.

From: helen.bergman@chw.edu
To: rachel.sodorski@aol.com
Great work. The Founding Father sequence is likely being used to get the transforming gene transfected into the Y.

Sincerely
Joe

"What does Founding Father Effect mean?" asked Karen.

"When you find a specific sequence coding for a genetic disease, especially if it occurs within a closed ethnic group, you can trace that disease to a single individual who originated that mutation and inherited it to his children so that when distant relatives marry that dormant gene comes into play and causes a full-blown disease. There are lots of metabolic diseases where a founding father, or mother, were traced and identified."

"So what's this about Cohanim?"

"Beverly Kreissman at St Jude noticed that most of the new cases of Neuroblastoma were males, whose father is a Cohen. Statistically, this cannot be a coincidence. Let's see if this hunch plays out. Do you know what is a Cohen?"

"No" Karen lied

"The word means a priest. A Cohen is a male, who traces back his ancestry through his father all the way back to Aaron, who was designated by the Lord to be the biblical chief priest. With the loss of the temple the priesthood lost its raison d'etre, but the strict laws governing who is a Cohen, and who he may or may not marry were always observed. I, for instance, am not a Cohen. Lots of Jews go around with names suggesting this ancestry such as Cohen, Cowan, Katz, and others don't."

"Why not a female Cohen?"

Joe shrugged. "I never made the rules. Fatherhood makes a Cohen, Motherhood determines if the child is Jewish at all. If a Cohen marries a non-jew, then his children are not considered Jewish, much less Cohanim."

"Can that be used to target Jews specifically?" asked Karen.

"Theoretically, if the Cohen founding father hypothesis is true, yes, but only the males, can I make you a breakfast?"

Karen leaned back in the chair, squinted her eyes. "Can you make anything more than Methotrexate and Dexamethasone?"

Joe chuckled "Pancakes are much more likely, I see you have the just-add- water-and-eggs mixes. I should be able to handle that."

"Go ahead, make my day" she intoned.

Joe made a short stack for her, and the same for himself. She poured the maple syrup on till it saturated the cakes, and ate with relish. She pushed the plate a way, almost empty.

"Phew, I ate like a pig, did you know that pigs increase their weight by a factor of 70 in three months?"

"If you say so. I limit my practice to humans" he said, his plate empty, "you said something about plans?"

"Yes. I promised Pastor Wilkins that we would present him with a plan to get Alia out without endangering the Mission which sends us there."

"And what about a plan to get me a new identity?"

"I have that all drawn up."

"Wow, you've been busy."

"So have you" she replied, "What happened to Doctor Cohen?"

"I killed him."

"*What*?" Karen almost jumped out of her skin.

Joe leaned back into the settee and laced his fingers behind his head, forehead creased "He and Tammy, that's his wife, set it up. They had been looking for someone to euthenize him for weeks. He was having terrible pains, and his lungs were filling up. He had saved up a bunch of HydroMorphone, all I did was add it to the PCA pump, and he activated it." Joe lowered his eyes to look at Karen. This issue was so delicate. Let's see how Karen takes it.

She took it with equanimity. "Its no different when we push the doctors to upp the dose on a kid we know is going, What did the Widow say?"

Gosh, she is a cool customer. "She said thankyou."

"Joe, that was a brave thing to do, if I were in that same situation, would you do it for me?"

"Now we are getting morbid" Joe said with dismissal.

"Don't duck the issue."

"I don't know" said Joe "It appeared to be the right thing to do that time and place, and it might be wrong another time."

"OK, I won't pin you down, but don't expect leniency another time. Timing is everything, right? Do you want to go over the lists of visitors to the Mosque?"

"Sure, let's take a looksee."

Karen went over to her Dell, located the Paintshop program and found the images. She sent them to the printer and a few minutes later they were looking at the long lists.

"Karen, I am sure these names will help us later but right now I don't know what to do with them. Any ideas?"

"Let's go over the plan for Identity and pick some holes in it."

An hour later they finalized it. Joe got up and stretched He looked his watch and smiled.

"Sunday sure goes fast. Thanks for dinner and the best night's sleep I have had, but I better go."

"Where to?" Karen said jealously.

Joe's eyebrow reached new heights again. "Home, and then Karate class, we meet sundays after the morning services. Interested?"

"Why not?" Karen was brave again. I am *never* that pushy.

"Why not indeed. Put on something warm and I'll start the car. *Assuming* I turned the lights off last night."

The heater was going full blast and Karen seated herself on the wide couch that was the LeSabre's front seat. Joe reversed and drove first to his apartment on Silver spring, and then towards the lake, Fox Point, and Santa Monica boulevard. The huge parking lot served the Jewish Community Center and two Jewish Day Schools. There was a smattering of cars in front of Hillel Academy already dusted with snow. Joe parked and walked around the car to open for Karen, but she was already out. So much for chivalry and courtesy, today's women did not need them. They headed inside, the big clock indicating 11 AM.

They were already lining up for the curtsy as he entered the gym-cum-dining hall. It was an assorted group, young and middle aged men, women and teen-agers. The men wore skull-caps pinned to their hair, however thin they were. They were dressed in the obligatory white pantaloons and laced jacket. Some sported colored belts, yellow, green, blue and brown. The instructor, a white bearded stocky man with piercing blue eyes was a black-belt. Joe joined them in the back, sans glasses. He was the only one without a skullcap, and his belt was blue. Karen sank to the tile floor, knees to chin, off to the side, and watched.

After the initial curtsy the instructor led them, in short guttural commands, through stretching exercises, and Karen noticed how painful the deep knee bend with stretched leg pointing up, and the touch-your-nose-with-your-toe exercises were for Joe and the older men. Joe worked particularly hard at them, seeming to relish the abuse. For the women and teenagers those exercises were a breeze. Then came strength exercises, pushups on the fists and fingers, where Joe was at obvious ease. Then they started punching and kicking the air, with stylized steps, done fluidly, or clumsily, depending on the person's rank and skill. The instructor would walk between the rows, correcting shoulder position, height of kick, and set of fist. Not a word was said between the explosive exhalations which accompanied each punch or kick. Karen noticed the way Joe's body became iron rigid at the punch, and relaxed a millisecond later. Some of the trainees possessed style that was more fluid, but he was unmatched in the combination of style *and* power. A few times the instructor called Joe to use as a mannikin to demonstrate new moves, expecting him to accept some punishment. Joe blocked incoming thrusts, rather than duck them, and the blocks were as powerful as the attacks which he performed.

They went through one Kata, then another, then squared up for Kumite', short stylized "fights" where no one was touched, but points were given for kicks and punches that were deemed effective if continued to their conclusion. Joe was matched with one of the teen-agers, a gangly youth with spindly arms and legs, he encouraged the youth to strike at him in the chest and belly, and took the pounding stolidly. The participants were drenched in sweat by the time the black-belted instructor called it quits. They lined up again and exchanged the formal curtsy. Then the order broke up.

"Shalom Yossi" said the instructor to Joe, and offered his hand.

"Shalom Rabbi Walach" Joe responded, respectfully, and shook the proffered hand. Karen stared. Her idea of a Rabbi was Schindler, a kind, gentle man with white hands and a small voice. This one, although not a young man anymore, was tough and strong and his moves were so crisp that his sleeves snapped like a loose sail in breeze with every punch.

"You missed two sessions this week" said the Rabbi accusingly.

"Yes Sempai, and I am sorry to say that I will be missing many more." Hhe wore his glasses again, Karen marveled at the change those glasses wrought on the face, from a slit eyed fighter to a scholar.

"If you need help, you know where to find it" Sempai Walach said decisively and turned to the teenagers who were having a lively argument.

Joe joined Karen who raised herself from her cramped position, she felt the curious look of some of the participants, especially the two young women.

"Did you enjoy it?" Joe said.

"The question is, did you?"

"Sure, I love getting punched and kicked, its good for the digestion."

"That's not it."

"You are right, its not, if you hurt, it means that you're alive."

"I can think of other ways to show that you are alive" she retorted. The curious looks became more focused. Apparently, no one talked to Joe in this fashion. He was a respected but a distant member who brooked no familiarity, except from the Sempai. Joe grinned again, all mouth, and shrugged into his coat.

"Shall we go?" It wasn't really a request, because he turned and left the hall, Karen following in this unfamiliar territory.

Joe stopped the car in her driveway, after a short, wordless journey. They sat there for a second as Karen waited for him to say, that which weighed on his mind. Finally he said:

"Karen, there maybe other ways, but it's been the only way that showed *me* I'm alive for the last five years."

She looked at him, this was the closest to a confession he could make, and it would have to be good enough for the time being. She pushed the heavy door out, and came around to the driver's side. He rolled the win-dow down.

"Seven o'clock tomorrow." She was laconic. He nodded.

"Thanks for everything."

"Seven o'clock" and she disappeared inside.

Joe drove back to his Silver Spring apartment and spent the rest of the day and evening washing his dirty laundry and mulling over the details.

Rasheed Hariri checked the manifest very closely. He knew this was not the real run but only a demo but he wanted to practice this as if it was real. The manifest was the complete content list of a forty foot container that had been loaded in Beirut with foodstuffs, and since he was running a Middle East specialty delicatessen chain there were literally hundreds of items. There was Hummous (Chickpeas) paste of 15 different varieties, 5 olive oil vintages, 20 types of canned olives 12 wine varieties, canned cherries marked with the Cedar, other cherries in glass containers and a zillion varieties of middle Eastern spices. Lovers of ethnic foods could feast at his shops, which were spread in malls across America.

Of course a lot was fake. The manufacturing conditions in Lebanese and Syrian food plants were generally not anywhere near the requirements of the Department of Agriculture. The food stuffs were actually manufactured in Turkey, Cyprus, and Allah forbid, in Israel, then re-tagged in Lebanon and exported. He chuckled at the joke. If the princes of Saudi Arabia wished to eat Kosher milk products and not get sick, their best bet was Israeli cheeses whose packaging was changed in the West Bank, and transported overnight via the Allenby bridge. Hilarious. He had no qualms about this practice. As long as the bacterial count generated from his products by the random checks of the Department of Agriculture were low enough, he could continue to make the money on the Hummous and falafel.

The cherries though, were the original item, from Lebanon, and Mustafa's contacts had seen to it that the product was manufactured GMP (good manufacturing practices) and so certified. In fact it made business sense to invest in GMP, he wished he could get this concept drilled into his business associates' brains in the Middle East, instead of sticking to their slothful ways, and turning out a half-spoiled product. The glass containers were neatly arranged in boxes, each marked with a lot number, packed on a tray, ready for the forklift. He was standing at the cavernous mouth of the container, and he handed the manifest back to his busty dyed-blond secretary. The forklift picked up the tray and reversed, pulling it out, and deposited the merchandise on the Milwaukee warehouse floor. Everybody was blowing vapour in the cold air, but Hariri's attention never wavered. He held a separate message, taken off his computer e mail with a specific box identification. The burly foreman had another tray deposited by the full one and two men started hefting the boxes from one to the other, in time filling the empty tray. His secretary inspected each box and called out the numbers printed on the side.

"Stop, bring that one to my office" he told the men. The forklift came back and carried the two half-ful trays into the warehouse. I wonder what's so special about that box, it looked just the same as all the other's, thought Jay Reynolds, the foreman. I know its not drugs. Wiley Rasheed had his own men in Beirut and Cyprus to see that no one uses his containers to bring in drugs. He was doing much too good going legit to louse it up with Hashish. He brought the box to the office himself, and all it did was clink slightly, just like all the other glass jar boxes. He deposited it on the mahogany side table, that was better suited to more genteel items.

"Thank you Jay, you may leave now."

Jay Reynolds left, and Rasheed closed the door. He picked up a utility knife, and carefully slit the tape holding the box closed. The jars were stoppered with vacuum seals and they all looked identical. He picked them up and peered at the bottom. The fifth jar was it, marked with a black big J. Hilarious. Mustafa really had a morbid sense of humor. J for Jude, or Youdé, the way the Germans would say it.

Rasheed picked up a UPS box, much smaller, padded on the inside with plastic bubbles, and placed the jar in it. He added plenty of styrofoam nuggets all around and packed them tight. He taped it securely and called his new secretary on the intercom. She stopped her keyboard pounding and bustled in, her heavy breasts jiggling just as he liked them inside the tight black bodice. She knew full well they were her chief asset, rather than her Word 6.0 skills. "Wendy, please have this package delivered by overnight mail to the following address. He is my second cousin and he LOVES those cherries:

Muhi A-Deen Shareef, PhD
Lipjohn Company
7000 Portage Rd.
Kalamazoo, Michigan 49888.

"Will it be premium overnight?" she asked as she scribbled.
"Yes, 1030 AM, report on delivery, Fragile, Glass, you know the drill."
"Yes Mister Hariri."
"And come into the office before you leave for the day."
"Yes Mister Hariri" and she took the small box away.

"Mr Hariri, there's a call for you, from Mister Shareef."
"Put it through."
"Hello, Rasheed?"
"Sabah al hir."
"Sabah al nur, I got it."
"Excellent, next time its for real."
"Yes, I emailed Mustafa and he knows."
"Excellent again, enjoy the cherries." Muhi broke out in a belly-laugh.
Rasheed put the phone down. It was too easy. And he loved those breasts. The idea that he could fondle them anytime he liked gave him another hard on. We will have to go on vacation together after the first   real package is delivered.

John Campbell walked into the County main entrance very slowly, like a 70 year old rather than the 36 year old he really was. The 14 months of fighting off AML wore him down. He was in for another wearying day of blood letting and cell getting. His sister had given her blood cells for him a few weeks before, and he was getting them in small doses, supposedly they were better at fighting off the disease than the cells she had already donated. Well, at least for now, his marrow was clear of the dread Leukemia. Karen watched him pulling his wallet out, to present the receptionist on the ground floor with insurance and identity, and how he tucked it back into the faded leather jacket.

After completing the transaction John Campbell heaved himself up from the chair and trod over to the elevators. The heat in the stuffy old hospital made him take off the jacket, since he was warmly dressed in a thick sweater over a flannel shirt. He swung it over his shoulder and walked the long corridor to the double doors of the Hematology service.

"Hi John" Julie Collier called cheerily.

"Hi Julie" he replied and sat down heavily on his La-Z-Boy.

"Let me take your coat and sweater, its much too warm here" she said solicitously. John pulled off his sweater and gave her both garments.

"Back in a jiffy and I'll start your IV" she said as she took them to the nurses station. Karen took them into the changing room, surgical gloves on, and quickly found the wallet. She pulled out the driver's license and returned the wallet to the same pocket. She came out of the changing room straight-faced and Julie pretended not to see her as she got the IV gear together on the tray.

Joe drove back to the medical complex. He drove up and down the parking lots until he found the Chevette. He compared the license plates with those he jotted at John Campbell's house. The fourth Chevette was it. He looked up and down the orderly rows, no one was looking so he took his cordless drill and removed the cover from the rear indicator. He twisted out the bulb, replaced it with one he had shorted out, and screwed the plastic cover back on. He smiled grimly. Fifteen years of medical training came down to unscrewing bulbs in the cold. Now it was up to Chris Wilkins.

John Campbell trudged out of the County building, slower and even more dejected than usual. Doreen took the kids away for Christmas and he was supposed to join them the end of the week. It was the sidelongs that the residents threw him when they thought he wasn't looking that troubled him. The car was so far out, it was like long-trekking in the woods, something he had loved to do, before the disease hit him.

He was so preoccupied with those dirty looks that it took him time to register the blue-and-white flashing away behind him on Lisbon. He took some more time to convince himself that it was indeed after him, but then he checked himself for wearing a belt, he was, and the lights were on in the early gloom. What the heck... and he stopped the car. Wow, that's one big policeman, he rolled the window down.

"Hello officer, what did I do?"

"License and registration please."

"All right, all right, I have them." John rummaged in the glove compartment, brought out the registration, pulled out the wallet and...

"Here is the registration, but I don't seem to find my license." John stammered. He rummaged some more, through the wallet, the pockets, the compartments, it wasn't anywhere. Finally he looked up to the forbidding figure. The officer wore the expression of I-heard-all-the-excuses-before.

"Officer, I honestly don't know where it is."

"Do you have any other means of Identification?" The officer, whose name-plate read Chris Wilkins, rumbled.

"Yes I do" John said with sudden glee. He found the Sam's Club card and handed it to the officer. "What's wrong?"

"When did you last check your indicators, sir?"

"Uh, I don't know, why?"

"Your left indicator is blown. That also means that your left brake-light is not functional, that is a serious deficiency in the safety features of your car. Your license, sir?"

"I haven't got a clue, I had it this morning, I don't have it now!"

"Wait in the car, sir" The officer went back to the Caprice Blue-and White, and consulted his computer. Presently he came back to the driver's side window.

"All right sir, here are your papers. I am going to write you a probationary citation. You have 24 hours to present your driver's license or an affidavit from the DMV. Call this number" and he gave him his card.

"Thank you, officer." John Campbell said with obvious relief, where the heck was the license?

"Keep this citation in case you are stopped again, and fix that light! There is a parts store just around the corner."

"Yes sir!" John Campbell stuffed the papers into the glove compartment, looked back and saw the huge officer giving him a dismissal. He drove over to the store and got himself a set of bulbs, he will check it out at home, in his own garage.

Chris Wilkins watched the poor bloke drive off. He called the cellular number Karen had given him.

"Hello?"

"It's Chris."

"Was he scared?"

"Thinks I did him a favor."

"Like the story of the goat."

"Goat?" Wilkins was baffled.

"Some other time, thanks" and Joe signed off.

"I hope you wore a thick coat."

"Why?" asked Karen and snuggled further into her down parka.

"Can't sit around with a running car, someone might call the police."

"Oh, this is pretty good, what about you, this leather coat is not exactly warm."

"I am never cold" he said flatly. Karen gave him a sidelong but he was poker faced as usual. His head gear was the Russian cap type, and the thin moustache was evident.

Joe had picked her up at six thirty AM, and they were approaching John Campbell's house on the north-west side. Joe cut the engine and the lights and coasted to a stop under one of the threadbare trees. 10 minutes later the car started becoming cold. 20 minutes later their breath was freezing the windshield, but encouragingly the lights in the house were on. At 715, just as Karen was beginning to shiver, the garage opened and the Chevette rattled out.

"He fixed his indicator" Joe noted.

"Let's hope he is on his way to the DMV."

"We'll find out soon enough" Joe replied. He started the engine and followed the Chevette into the cold brightening day.

It was 0730 and incredibly, a bunch of people were already at the Department of Motor Vehicles doors, beating up their arms until the doors opened.

"OK, stick close to him" Joe said. Karen was already out.

Karen stood in line behind John Campbell, took the Wisconsin Driver Education leaflet and seated herself in the front row. John Campbell waited for his number to be called up. It did not take long, and she changed seats so she could watch his discourse with the DMV clerk. He took off his Russian hat with the fur earmuffs and his scalp shone whitely in the fluorescent light. The clerk asked him for other ID's and he produced his birth certificate, and his army discharge. He showed the clerk the citation, and she nodded with understanding. He paid 6 dollars at the cashier and 5 minutes later was called to be photographed. The smiling clerk gave him the duplicate and wished him good luck. Karen beat him to the outside.

30 minutes later the ratty Chevette rolled into the well-kept police station. John Campbell, ear muffs securely on, went through the doors, and 10 minutes later came out, started the car and disappeared.

Joe and Karen left the Le Sabre and walked in together. Chris Wilkins was at the desk. Joe whipped off his Russian hat for his inspection. Chris had to clap his hand over his mouth to hold his guffaws, he rocked back and forth in his chair.

"Mister Campbell, I presume" he said after a while.

Joe kept a straight face "at your service, Mister Wilkins."

Chris shifted his gaze to Karen, "doesn't this guy ever laugh?"

Karen kept the same expression "Never."

"You two are a couple of rascals, here is the copy. I made him sign it" Joe looked at the official copy of a declaration of lost items, specifically Driver's license and passport.

"I added the Passport bit after he left. I am waiting to hear from my dad what else you guys have hatched up."

"I may ask you to do more than that" said Joe.

"Really, and what may that be?"

"You were in the Navy, right? Navy Seals?"

"Must be that picture on my dad's desk!"

"Those talents may be useful."

"Shucks, they are useful only in the Carribean."

"You underestimate yourself" said Joe.

"Hatch the plan and I'll think about it!!" Chris promised.

Joe stuck the hat back on and held the swing door for Karen. They followed in John Campbell's tracks.

John Campbell was surprised to hear the door chime. He wasn't expecting anyone. The face was slightly familiar.

"Hi there, miss...?"

"Fitzsimmons" she completed the sentence "are you Mister Campbell?"

"That's right."

"Oh goody, my friend Julie Collier at the Hematology Unit asked me to give you this envelope. She said they found it in registration."

"Why, that's great, please come in before we freeze." He opened the storm door, let her into the house.

"Tea?" he asked.

"Wouldn't mind" she said, taking in the small house with the bureau in the corner, and the exit to the garage next to the basement door. The house was cold, set at 60, no doubt to save on heating costs. Pictures of the owner, in uniform, with mousy wife, bright-eyed twins. Being sick with cancer didn't help anyone's finances. He came back from the tiny kitchen with a tray with two cheap glass mugs, sugar and spoons.

"The sick man's drink" he grinned mirthlessly "but its hot, let's see what this is."

He tore the envelope and the laminated card slid out, a much younger man with a full head of hair.

"Jeez, what a waste of time, and what rotten luck with the po-lice" he groaned. Then he brightened, "guess what I did this morning, I made a duplicate! Ain't it ugly?" and he showed her the new license card. Karen just demurred and sipped from her mug.

"I'll just put it away, I like the old one better" he said happily. He went over to the bureau, and placed the new license in a grey accordion-like multifolder. "I hope you didn't wait long for me, I took a little time to come to the door, I'm so pooped."

"Oh no, I was out there for just a few minutes, Julie said this should go directly to you hand."

"Bless Julie for me" Karen cringed a little. She put the glass down.

"Well thank you Mister Campbell, I need to go to sleep now."

He rose too, "Thank *you*, miss Fitzsimmons" and she left the house to the big maroon LeSabre. Her boyfriend was there probably, lucky him, she is such a pretty woman.

Joe started the car up and drove off. "Where does he keep it?"

"In the bureau, right in the living room."

"Good, How did he take it?"

"He was happy to have it back."

"The goat again."

"What goat?" Karen asked, exasperated with the riddle.

Joe kept his eyes on the road to Glendale. "Oh, it's a Jewish story from Eastern Europe. This man in a Shtetle, an tiny town in the Jewish Pale, had a wife and 10 kids, and they were very crowded, and the kids were sick all the time. He goes to his Rabbi and says Rabbi, what can I do? The Rabbi says: You have a goat, right? Bring the goat in the house for one week. The man goes away scratching his head, but the Rabbi said, so he takes the smelly goat in. At the end of the week he runs to the Rabbi and cries Rabbi, I can't take this anymore, its more crowded than ever!! So the Rabbi said; Take the goat outa the house and come back to tell me how things are. The man runs back home and kicks the goat out. He goes back to the Rabbi and says: Rabbi you were right, its not crowded anymore. Here we are, your house awaits."

As soon as John Campbell left his small house the next morning, cursing the garage door which refused to go down, a big man with blue coveralls and the work-belt of an electrician left his battered maroon car and entered the open garage with all the assurance of an invited repair technician. He looked around the garage door and quickly stripped off the tiny wedge of metal which he had inserted late the night before. Once the garage door went down and came up against a resistance, the safety features in the Stanley made it go up again . He pressed the garage door button and it closed down creakily, this wooden door was not new. He took out the Maglight and examined the entry door, took a flat Gauge measure and inserted it between the jamb and tongue. The tongue was only partially engaged due to the piece of Play-Doh that Karen had stuffed in the day before. He entered the small house.

It did not take him long. The birth certificate and the license was in the grey accordion hold-all in the bureau, next to all the other important documents, hospital bills, car insurance etc.. . With the birth certificate were the two certified copies provided by the State. Joe folded one of them into an inside pocket, and the new license. Leisurely he left via the same door, never having taken off his gloves. He left through the garage door, and in full view of whoever chose to glance in this direction, looked on with satisfaction as the door creaked all the way down. Then he was gone. Once in his own yard he wiped off the black marker with which he had slightly changed the appearance of numbers on his license plate so that the 8 became 0 again and the T returned to I.

Joe called up the Passport office at the Federal building. They were accepting applications that afternoon. He donned a white shirt, a dress jacket and drove to Northridge for a set of blue disposable contacts and Passport photos. Then he got on the I 43 down town.

The application process was simple. The license and birth certificate were accepted without a question, and since the reason for renewal of the passport was the loss of the old one, he filled in a loss report, based on the police official report. In a country based first of all on trust, a trustworthy-looking person can get away with anything. He was sure that in old Russia, or present day India, the process would be so much harder. He asked that the passport be sent to his employer, the Children's Hospital of Wisconsin, Pastor

Wilkins' office, since the house, his present address, was on the market.

Karen knocked on the door at seven in the evening. He let her in and the smell of the Chinese takeaway wafted out of the big brown bag. She eyed the apartment, not a typical bachelor's place, neither slothful, nor entirely orderly. A computer corner, laden with peripherals, festooned with cables. Above it, a stunning picture of an even more stunning woman, sitting on a green bench, basking in the sun, leaning her head back, the magnificent curls shooting ricochets of sunlight into the camera. The picture domin-ated the living room. There was a motorcycle behind the bench, and the frame was filled with deep green forest and snow peaks. She was so alive, Karen was sure she was about to step right out of the photograph. Karen stared at the photo, noting the high forehead, eyes closed against the glare of the sun, the lips red, the long neck, the vee of the slightly open blouse, the well-defined bosom, arms languid on the top of the bench, the long legs ending in sporty trekking shoes. A Goddess.

"That's Helen" Joe said drily, as if saying, that's an orange.

Karen took her gaze away from the photo and watched Joe closely. He was, as usual, expressionless, and was placing an official-looking document into the flat-bed scanner.

"She is tough competition, I'll grant you that" she said.

"There is no competition" he declared, in the same flat voice. He was clicking away on the mouse, and the scanner whirred into life briefly, and then the laptop hard drive softly clicked busily.

Karen stole another glance at the magnificent woman, She hadn't moved yet, and anyway, she was two-dimensional, she was the past, however fantastic that past had been.

"We eat before we work, or work before we eat?" Karen asked.

Joe rose from the old brown secretary chair, which looked like a relic from the third hand garage sale. "I am always hungry, and I love monosodium glutamate" and he took out plates and utensils and placed them neatly on the dinette.

"Wine?" he asked.

"What kind?"

"Gamla white."

"What kind is that?" Karen thought she knew most of the French, California, and Italian varieties. Grandpa Toby always thought that being a discerning wine connoisseur bespoke of good breeding and education.

"It's a brand from Israel, grown on the Golan Heights, it's available in the more eclectic liquor shops."

"Why not, let's try, where is the cellar?"

"You have *got* to be joking" Joe said heavily.

"I have to, when this lady is looking down at us" and she pointed to another picture of Helen, showing Helen and Joe smiling at the camera, in a restaurant, with a round dark cake and a little plastic airplane on it. Joe was curious.

"Are you afraid of her?"

"Well, she is quite a presence."

"That she was" said Joe with feeling, then his eyes misted over and he whipped off his glasses and dug furiously into his sockets with both fists. he placed the glasses back on, went over to a kitchen cabinet and brought over a iridescent bottle, which was almost translucent. He uncorked the bottle with a double-winged screw and presented the open bottle for her olfactory inspection. She sniffed and nodded.

"Nice and fruity."

Joe placed a clean white towel on his arm and ceremoniously poured into a wine glass, which, although clean, also seemed to have come out of the same garage sale. Karen lifted her glass.

"Do you buy all of your household at rummage sales?" she asked and sniffed some more.

"Naturally, everything under a quarter, or a dime" he poured into his own identical glass. He lifted it and looked at Karen.

"What shall we drink to?" he asked playfully.

"To life after death" and she clinked before he could react.

Joe stared at the glass thoughtfully, shifted his gaze to Karen who was sipping daintily, shot a glance at Helen, two dimensional on the wall, and brought the glass to his mouth. He snapped his head up and let the clear fluid flood his mouth. Karen tsked-tsked at this display of boorish behavior. He looked back at her, she was really very, very beautiful.

"Agreed, to the afterlife" and Karen frowned at the different interpretation.

She poured the various contents of the Chinese dinner into the plates and they ate in silence. But the silence was not forced. Rather, it was companionable, and Karen started feeling a little more comfortable, despite Helen.

Joe took the plates to the sink and gave them a quick wash. When he came back Karen was looking at the computer screen. It displayed a diploma

The American Board of Pediatrics

hereby declare that

Joseph Bergman MD

Has been certified as a
Diplomate of the American board of Pediatrics

No 0426002   September 25
Seal   President   Chairman

Secretary

Joe made a rectangle around his own name, and then clicked 'cut' which left a big void on the document. He chose the same font and inserted John Campbell's name. then saved the new image. He inserted the Uni-versity of Washington residency completion certification and did the same. He placed a thick yellow page in the HP and printed it, then the other, on a thick white parchment. They came out very crisp.

"Forgery" she said, "and it's so easy."

"It's easy as long as no one checks back, but in our case all we do is create a subterfuge for the Missionaries, and we hope no one checks on them. If we were the Mossad or CIA then we would have the organizational capability to create a complete persona."

"Still, very impressive" said Karen.

"Let's look up the Email" and he logged on. There was one more message from Rachel.

From: Rachel.sodorski@aol.com
To: helen.bergman@chw.edu
cc: gabe.coh@hotmail.com

Doctor Bergman

I am beginning to recognize some promoters and enhancers and open reading frames. This sequence from Katz, the name suggests a cohen

how appropriate, and I am beginning to try and match that sequence
with what I have here

Find yourself a good woman, Doctor Bergman

Rachel Sodorski

Karen laughed at the last sentence "Everybody wants to help you out, it
seems."
"All except me. We are no further ahead but it will do. Let's see what's on
Mustafa's account" He logged onto the USA Net and used Mustafa's
password. There was a message and it was addressed to Amanda

Hello Amanda

We are home and Alia has met her family. She is very happy and
soon I will find her a suitable school. I am writing this to show you that
I am a responsible father and I will not neglect my duties to her. Soon
she will be more Arab than American, she looks very good and
virtuous with the white scarf on. You can reply by using the reply
button, and as long as you write nothing inflammatory I promise to
print it for her.
Mustafa

"Amanda is going to *love* that" said Karen.
"Next he is going to stick her into a Chador, like in Iran" said Joe
disgustedly.
"Do you think Amanda picked up this message?"
"I doubt it, she doesn't get along with the computer" he replied.
"Then let's call her, and you can show her."
"First I want to save this page with these little numbers."
"Why?" Karen wondered.
"I think that someone who knows Internet can figure out the location of
the server, and I know someone just like that."
"Gee, you know a lot of useful people."
"Lucky, Roger Cohen's adopted son is a computer whizz, I am just a

user." Joe saved the page, got back on his own email server and sent Gabriel a short message:

Dear Gabe

Please try and locate this server for me

Joe

Attachment

"Now lets see if Amanda is in, I betcha she doesn't move away from that phone unless absolutely essential" and he dialed her number.

"Hello" very throaty.

Karen picked up the receiver "Amanda, can I come over?"

"Sure, my folks are here, but come on."

"How about Joe, er Doctor Bergman?"

"Him too."

"Alright , 10 minutes."

They drove over silently, and entered the complex. They declined the elevator and walked up to the third floor. The door to 316 was open so they just walked in. It was like a wake, but not an Irish one. Amanda occupied the one seat and her parents occupied the couch. Amanda jumped up to greet them. She was taken aback by Joe's new appearance.

"Hi Joe, Hi Karen, What happened to your hair?"

"Hello Amanda" they said almost in unison "I'll explain about the hair later." Joe added.

"Meet my parents" Amanda presented them and they shook limp hands with Jeremy and Linda Carter.

Karen broached it "Amanda, did you look up messages from Mustafa?"

"No" Amanda said shamefacedly "I am afraid to, and I don't really know how."

Joe seated Amanda in that same computer niche and started it up. He showed Amanda the startup procedure and the AOL icon, and they logged on appropriately.

Soon the message was displayed. Linda hid her face in her hands and ran off to the bathroom. Amanda looked on, features contorted.

"Happy? New Family? Who is he kidding?"

"Nevertheless, I think you must make a reply, something that will not inflame him but let her know you care for her" said Karen.

"I guess you're right. This is so crazy, I can't believe this is *happening* to Alia, to me. How could I have been so blind? He was planning this all along. He *bred* her out of my body as a surrogate sister!!"

Joe looked down at her "Do you really believe that?"

Amanda gazed back at the malevolent message sent for her from across the world. Her shoulders slumped.

"No, not really, we loved for a while."

"You fell in love, you fell out of love, you had different expectations out of life" Jeremy contributed.

"Truth, didn't you think of moving out with Alia during this last year?" Karen asked.

"Yes"

"There you are, you were incompatible, he made the first move and went on with *His* life."

"You are making it as if what he did was right!!" Amanda said accusingly at Karen.

"No, snatching a child is *never* right. I am just rationalizing a little bit so you can write *her* and encourage her, till we come and get her!!"

"Who is going to come and get her?" Jeremy interposed.

"Figure of speech" said Joe smoothly.

"OK" said Amanda, and clicked on the 'reply' button

Dear Alia
I hope you get this letter. I miss you a lot but now you should stay with Dad
Enjoy the new school and make good
Mommy loves you a lot
Grandpa Jeremy and Grandma Linda send their kisses
Mom

"What now?" Amanda asked.

"Just click on the Send button here, but before you do click the Save button."

Amanda clicked Save and then Send.

The screen went blank and then responded.

your message has been sent

"Don't shut it down just yet. Let's see if Gabe is alive." He entered CHW and looked for messages for him. "Yup Gabe is alive and kicking" he opened up his message:

From: Gabe.coh@hotmail.com
To: helen.bergman@CHW.edu

Dear Joe
That server is the American University of Beirut server.
I concur with my sis
Good luck

"Wow, you were right again" said Karen "I might need to get used to it."
"Only with the truly insignificant. On the important things I am DEAD wrong, you can shut it down now" said Joe. He looked at his watch, late, and they had to work on an ingress and egress, without leaving a trace, and without jeopardizing Alia. Impossible.

"Anything we can do for you Amanda?" asked Karen.

Amanda was startled to hear the word WE from Karen. Usually with Karen it was I and Me. Now she talks like she is part of a team. And why not, they should make a good couple, better than Mustafa and herself. She still could not rid herself of the feeling that Mustafa had used her for his purposes, and then dropped her like a dirty handkerchief.

"No, tomorrow is Christmas eve, lots of mopping up to do in the HOT unit although, thankfully, no Marrows" It was standard policy in the unit never to do Marrows on the leukemics before Christmas, so that they did not chance to find a relapse, and ruin another family's holiday.

Outside it warmed up somewhat, but conversely, it began to snow. The flakes came down lazily and covered the buildings, the shrubbery, the cars and the road. The big Lesabre swished through the fresh snow in a hush. Karen's head dropped down slowly until it rested on Joe's upper arm. He felt her body heat slowly filtering through her hair, his coat, sleeve and into his arm. He was afraid to move his arm and so he drove, one armed, to Mohawk. They swished up the driveway and stopped, and still, she did not wake up. His left hand stole, as if of it's own volition, and stroked the fine hair, silky smooth, and smoothed it away from the high forehead. She was like a child, trusting on her father's arm. But I am not her father and I am not trustworthy. He pulled his hand away and she woke up instantly, jerked her head up. He had an sudden feeling of regret, deprivation, something dear was snatched away. She turned her head and gave him a beautiful smile.

"I had such a nice dream" she said, sleepily languid.

"It must be the car" Joe said stonily.

Karen shook her head sadly, the man refused to cooperate with anything pleasant. He insisted on flogging himself. Pry him loose indeed. If I stick my head in this clam-shell, it will snap shut and cut it off.

"What about tomorrow night?" she asked cooly.

Thank God we are back to bristly normal "I'll take the call at the HOT unit, I always do on Xmas Eve. And Xmas day."

"I'll be at home or my mom's place, got the number?"

"Yes."

"I am on for Xmas day AM shift, I haven't changed that, just like last year, if you remember."

Sure I remember. "No" he lied.

Liar, I *know* you remember, that was the first time you looked at me like a human rather than a nursing robot "I'll see you then" and she was gone, her movements as usual fluid and feminine. He felt for the spot on the upper arm where her head had been. It was still warm.

Joe drove to his apartment. For the first time in two and a half years it looked empty. He gazed at Helen who surrounded his lair from every wall. He sat on the decrepit couch and she opened her sea-green eyes, came off the green bench, took three steps and reached for him. He could feel her hands on his shoulders, her lips on his forehead, and they burned like fire. Then she leaned and breathed her fiery breath into his ear "Its all right Joe, I am all right, you can let go, I'll be fine." His eyes smarted and his nose filled up and through the film that covered his glasses he could see her back on the bench, soaking up the sun. and Life.

Joe placed a sheet of paper on the kitchen dinette and doodled on it until the early hours. Finally he put his head on his arms, and slept fitfully.

Chapter 17

Apropo

"Your car or mine?" said Joe.

"Mine, definitely, I wouldn't trust the old jalopy with a trip to Chicago, especially with the snow on the road. It would be safer to *row* to Chicago in the old boat." Karen said. Pastor Wilkins had called her after the Christmas day and said that Harrelson would see them in two days in the Stop-the-Hunger offices in Chicago.

"You are insulting it" said Joe with his mouth full of apple-pie. Karen was dressed in a conservative manner, black slacks, blue blouse with black piping, a black feminine tailored jacket, very nice, very nice indeed.

"No, I am giving it it's due respect" and she stirred her coffee, they met at Tony's Family restaurant on Greenbay Road. Since they had seen Amanda, Joe had avoided visiting her house, and Karen went out on a date with Bob Grove who had called her up. Bob had learned nothing new about the kidnaping, and she did not encourage him along any personal lines. He had been disappointed.

Joe looked at his watch , looked critically at the third of the pie that remained on the plate, and decided that it served a better purpose there, than inside his belly. "In that case, let's leave the old lady here and go off with the Grand Am."

They made desultory small talk during the drive. While on service for Christmas eve and day, Joe had been at his most professional with Karen, and she reciprocated with the same. Doctor Horowitz, who was the attending for the holiday, had not seen Joe that cool and terse for some time, and Karen who rounded with them was no better. Doctor Horowitz reviewed the patients and the orders, and since nothing new had come up, he had left early. Karen worked through the day shift, and from time to time would steal a glance at Joe, who was writing the follow-up notes in the patients' charts. Once she caught him looking in her direction, a wistful look, but he quickly averted his eyes, like a boy with his hand in the cookie jar. She finished her day shift and left almost wordlessly, and Joe, who had brought a huge stack of reprints, took to them, and read voraciously in the dictation room. the HOT unit was as empty as it could get, no routine treatments were given, and so it would remain until after New Year's day, unless a disaster came through the door.

While at her cousin's joyous Christmas dinner, Karen concluded that the relationship with Joe should probably stay the same as it had always been, strictly professional. He did not want to accept any kindness and concern, he was half-suicidal, she will stick it out with her promise to Amanda, and that's it. Then she saw him the next day. He had stayed in the hospital overnight, a 12 year old girl in the bone marrow transplant unit had been sick and bleeding all night. Joe was haggard and his growth was showing in dark salt-and-pepper on his face and his newly shaven head. Despite his fatigue he flashed her a real smile as she came in for the morning shift, and the Smile made THAT resolve dissolve like a snow patch in July.

Despite the heavy snowfall of the day before, the I 94 was clear and the traffic flowed smoothly. Karen followed the instructions and went off the freeway at Winetka Avenue, heading towards the Lake. The Mission occupied a small office building within walking distance from the shore of Lake Michigan. Joe took in the hugeness and the wealth of ChicagoLand. It was so rich and industrious, it could indeed sustain the world which refused steadfastly to accept the American Way.

The wind was as sharp, even sharper than in Milwaukee, and it carried some snow-flakes, After a while, snow does not look so pretty anymore. They hurried inside through the glass doors which proclaimed modestly **STOP THE HUNGER - CHICAGO CHAPTER**, and the street address. There was a small foyer, and a reception desk, with a different-looking young man typing away slowly at the keyboard of an ancient Epson. Joe took off his Russian hat. His scalp was prickly, and his face was smoothly shaven, showing the salt and pepper in the moustache.

"May I Help you" said the young man, laboriously.

He must be a Trisomy 21, Joe thought, immediately assessing the disability. The set of face with a large slightly-protruding tongue was the clue, as were the single-fold palpebrales. A definite Mongoloid. His name tag said Ronald Gilcher.

"This is Karen Fitzsimmons and I am John Campbell. We have an appointment with Doctor Harrelson."

Ronald scanned the computer, which displayed Appointments in large letters, and said, "I will call him first" and punched the phone slowly. He could do things, but very slowly. For this kind of business, the speed was acceptable. For a Doctor's or an attorney's office, it would be intolerable.

"Doctor Heitch, a couple of people are here for you." He put the phone down and grinned, more than anyone should "He will be right down."

The elevator hummed one floor, and a tall white-haired Wild West figure advanced to meet them. He had twinkling blue eyes and a white handle-bar moustache, and a large right hand with which he pumped Joe's hand enthusiastically, and kissed Karen's hand after a show of appreciation for her looks.

"Hello, hello, how was the drive, was it cold? would you like anything hot to drink, Ronald, can you please make us some,,, Tea? Coffee? Soup?" he questioned his visitors.

"Tea is fine" said Karen and Joe nodded.

"Tea it is, excellent, wonderful, and how is dear Henry?"

"Sprightly as always" said Karen in the elevator.

"Unstoppable, I would say, No earthly power could prevent him from getting to disasters. No floods, drought, or even war."

"Sometimes it's a warzone in West-side Milwaukee" said Karen.

"Same here at Cook County. Essentially everybody has enough to eat but it doesn't stop them from raising hell, sit down, sit down. Ah, here comes the tea." Ronald rolled in a tea trolley on which a steaming white porcelain tea-kettle and 3 delicate china cups clinked happily. "Thank you Ronald, how is that manuscript coming along?"

"Fine, Doctor."

"Good, carry on" and Ronald left.

Doctor Horace Harrelson poured, and sipped his tea without any sugar. Karen and Joe used the tongs to add a cube of sugar. The office was beautifully done, with book-cases floor to ceiling, and a view to the lake across the street and park. One could spend a retirement here very happily, thought Joe. Instead, outside the door, there was the constant racket of people going by, telephones ringing and being answered, the trappings of a working office.

Harrelson put down his cup and lifted the crinkly shiny fax paper. Apparently, the plain-paper Fax had not made it to this genteel office. It was the fax that Mustafa had sent to Amanda, as presented to pastor Wilkins by Karen.

"Henry sent me this inscrutable letter. Please explain."

Karen and Joe exchanged glances. By unspoken agreement it was Karen who spoke. "This fax was sent to a colleague who is a physician in training at the Children's Hospital. He took their daughter and disappeared. She went to the police and the FBI and so far all they can say is that trail turns cold in Cyprus. I, er, We, know he is in Lebanon."

"How do you know that?"

Karen showed him the page saved from the last E mail message. She pointed out the set of numbers at the left lower border."This is the server from which the message had been sent. It's located in Lebanon, the American University of Beirut."

"And this note I underlined?"

As for the Zionists, my retribution is almost ready

Karen hesitated "We are not sure yet, but he may have developed some biological means to make people, no, Jews, sick with Cancer."

"And which one of *you* is Jewish?"

"I am" said Joe.

"Do you feel threatened?" asked Harrelson.

"No."

"Why not, supposing that which Miss Fitzsimmons says is true?"

Joe did not answer and held Harrelson's eye. Karen held her breath.

"I can answer that too" said Horace "For the same reason that you are willing to go to Lebanon and risk your neck. Its because you don't really care about your neck. And you, Miss Fitzsimmons? Is it the Whence You Go I Go situation?"

"Probably" said Karen stolidly. Joe's facade almost broke down.

Doctor Horace Harrelson sighed deeply. "What goes round must come round, in a way *I* am responsible for this" Karen and Joe stared.

"I was in Lebanon during the late seventies and the early eighties. This was the most tumultuous time, a time of great horrors and infamy. Especially 1982" Joe kept his face impassive. 1982, Sabra and Shatila, the days that Israel lost the moral high-ground.

" I was the UNWRA doctor in the Sabra camp. After the massacre I was instrumental in bringing Mustafa to the States because I thought that he may be a man of peace, as opposed to the prevailing winds of hatred. I made a mistake. If your interpretation of this threat is true, then this is not just a threat, this is a catastrophe in the making. He was a most able student, and if he has harnessed his knowledge as a means for revenge, God help you" Horace concluded.

"What or who is he avenging?" asked Karen.

"His twin sister, She was brutally raped and murdered by the Phalanga."

Karen was perplexed "But the Phalanga were not Jewish, I read they were a Christian Militia!!"

"Doesn't matter" Joe said, "they blamed us for it anyway." It was Horace and Karen who stared now.

"You *know* about that?" asked Horace, incredulous, naively thinking that he was the only privy to the Lebanon quagmire.

"I was never around Beirut, but I know about it."

"And you want to go *back* there?" Incredulously.

"You said it Doctor Harrelson, I don't care, and If I can Get Alia out and bring her back to her mother, that's something I, we, can care about."

Doctor Horace Harrelson surveyed the strange couple waiting for his word. They should just go home and make some babies, they are a very handsome couple, serious faces and resolve not withstanding. They need help. Alia needs help. Mustafa was his responsibility, and he must be stopped.

"How do you want to go into Lebanon?"

"Doctor and Nurse Team" said Karen.

"How will you find her?" Karen told him.

"How will you get the Mission off the hook?" Joe told him.

"And how will you get her out of Lebanon?" Joe pulled out a some maps of Lebanon he had taken off the US world survey and showed him.

"That's an enormous risk, but so be it."

Harrelson rose from his chair "Leave here all the documentation and I will call Henry when we are ready." Joe shook his hand and this time he did not try to kiss Karen's hand, but shook it with vigour and decision.

Karen studied the road, which she knew well, like she had never seen it before, as if it was route 550 in the Rockies where every turn was hairpin, and each curve a vista. She felt Joe's eyes on her right cheek, no less than if he had been holding two search-beams right onto her skin. The cheek turned red, with embarrassment, but there was no pain associated with the burning sensation. Rather it was the focal point of a warmness that spread to her neck, and chest and belly. Outside it was near whiteout, inside the car it was balmy. They were going by Racine when Joe spoke.

"Did you really mean it?"

"Mean what?" she bluffed.

Joe did not respond, he only seemed to stare some more, increase the intensity of those search lights, until they made scorching holes in the red cheek.

"I meant it."

"Then don't" Joe said forcefully, and turned off the searchlights.

Karen was serene, she had made her decision, it was made for her in that office and she accepted it. Still, she needed to know.

"Why not?" she said, imperceptibly, the car slowed, and the cars in the left lanes were swishing by.

"Because I am bad news, I am a walking disaster zone, because anyone who gets involved with me gets hurt, and dies."

Karen slowed into the Rest Area , drove past the huge trucks which were fast turning into enormous piles of snow, and stopped, somewhere, because the lines were completely obliterated. She shut off the engine, and waited, until the car was shrouded in a cocoon of snow. Within minuted they were in their own igloo, isolated from the world. Karen twisted in the driver's seat and met his gaze.

"Bosh, and you know it."

"I have all the proof I need to say I have the luck of Job, and that the Devil keeps me alive."

"Was it the Devil who sent you to the parking structure at the right time?"

"One time slip-up."

"I am counting on many more slip-ups."

"Do you recognize" Joe inquired, his voice echoing solemnly inside the insulation afforded by the snow blanket "the origin of that quote, 'whence you go I go'?"

"I think I do, but tell me anyway."

"Ruth said that to her mother-in-law after they had lost sons and husbands in Mo'ab. Helen changed her name to Ruth so she could marry me!!"

"And what was the outcome of the Biblical Ruth?"

"She turned out to be the Grandmother of King David."

"See?" Karen teased "all is well that ends well!"

Joe just looked at her, took in the deep-blue eyes, full of candor and courage, the finely chiseled nose, and full pursed lips. She is getting ready to be snubbed, and she is not going to give up. He could not summon up the will to turn her away, he didn't *want* to turn her away. Her hands were in her lap, tightly fisted, giving away the tension, the knuckles white as the snow on the windshield. They were in the snowy cocoon and he could let go of his tension, just a little. He held her gaze and covered her freezing hands with his large warm palms. Slowly the fists relaxed and she absorbed his heat. He felt the urgent need to hold that face, but it was too early, and they had a job to do first. He took the hands and held the fingers to his lips, the nails smooth as pearls, and he kissed them.

Joe was out with the snow-scraper busily brushing and scraping the glass surfaces around the car, so sudden was his exit that she was still hypnotized by her finger nails when he knocked on the driver-side window. The spell broken, Karen rolled the window down "Start the engine and the defroster" he said shortly, and went back to scraping, till the windshield was squeaky clean.

Joe plunked himself down "Let's go" he said, and smiled, this time it was a real smile, his face transformed to carefree gladness, all the way to the roots of the prickly hair. Mom, I pried him loose. She drove off carefully.

Karen drove all the way to her house, without asking Joe, and he did not make any comments. Her driveway had been cleaned by the son of he next-door neighbor who owned a Jimmy fitted with a snow plow, so she owed him five bucks. They swished right into the garage and Karen opened the door and left it open for Joe to close, naturally, as if she had done the same for years. Joe was a little more cautious, and slowly closed the door behind him, and hanged his coat in the closet. Karen was already in the kitchen, raising a racket with pots and pans.

"Can I check my mail?" he called.

"Sure."

He pulled the Armada from his brief case and waited for the machine to start. The kitchen noises continues unabated, and he realized that they had nothing to eat since the early morning. Falling in love makes me hungry, who said anything about falling in love? More like falling into the abyss, but falling together is better than falling alone. Here is AOL.

To: helen.bergman@chw.edu
From:bkreissman@stjude.edu
We did our best so no one gets any shots in Memphis
Without an adequate explanation, people are going to disregard the warning.
I confirmed the victims are male Cohanim.
The disease is spread via OPV, most likely, but the Agent is dead, murdered.
Share any progress you have made

Beverly

Reply

read the attachment, It's a message I got from Van Vleet, Mehta and Shaker are confirming. Keep looking for a delivery means, and other vaccinations.

Joe

To: helen.bergman@chw.edu
From: peter.herzig@swol.co.swiss

Dear Yossi
Don't you have any better vacation spots than Lebanon?
What am I supposed to tell Loise about the trip?
How long will you need us for?
I don't have to shave my head, I already lost almost all the hair I ever had.
I don't want to be stingy but taking a week off for two, is very expensive, especially in Switzerland. Who is picking up the tab?
Your friend
Peter

Reply
To:peter.herzig@swol.co.swiss
From: helen.bergman@chw.edu

I'll buy you some minoxidil after this caper is over.
I am picking up the tab. Finally having money makes sense.

Yossi

"Who is Peter?" asked Karen as she placed two steaming cups of curried rice on the table. Joe inhaled and immediately his mouth was so full of water he could hardly answer.

"Peiter is an old friend of mine from Switzerland" and he dug in furiously.

"How did you meet him?" Karen asked

"I took a motorcycle trip in Europe, long ago, and I met him on the shore of lake Zurich. He was interested in the Guzzi."

"The what?"

"Moto-Guzzi, it's an Italian marque, quite unique, two cylinder vee engine."

"Oh."

"Anyway, we remained friends for 15 years or more, and I always have a place to stay if I get to Switzerland."

"That's convenient."

"Its more than convenient. Peter is the kind of friend, that regardless of the number of years since I had seen him last, it's like we only said goodby yesterday. And, he is willing to help."

Karen was polishing off her cup of rice "How?"

"I have a picture of him at the apartment, it should be self explanatory."

"Let's do that after dinner."

Joe finished his cup too. "Any more of this stuff?" he asked hungrily.

"Tut, tut, hold on, we have other foods too."

They ate companionably and then Joe said "I have an idea what we should do with those lists, many of them are supposed to be scientists, right?"

"Yes, that's what Bob said."

"In that case they will have publications and email addresses and we can see where they came from, and where they work."

"Before you do that, we will need some strong coffee, let me make some and you get connected."

"Teamwork."

"Traditional teamwork" Karen said and went off to the West Bend dripper. Joe connected again. With the coffee mugs full they looked up the Medline and Email finder for each of the names, Starting with Mustafa. And indeed, they were all molecular biology doctors, from all over North America. Just about every major city was represented, and the scientific work they had published from all those labs was enough for a textbook.

"Wow, what a bunch of talent Mustafa put together" Joe marveled.

"But to what awful purpose" Karen said with disgust.

"There are a few names here that we can't locate. Like this Rasheed Hariri."

"Bob Grove, the FBI agent told me he is a business man in Milwaukee, he is a big contributor to the Mosque."

"Let's find him on the Yellow Pages" Joe said, and a few seconds later he did, as Hariri Fine Foods Import, Milwaukee.

"Bob told me that he drives a conspicuous vehicle, a silver Mercedes."
"How close did you get to Bob for all this information?"
"What's it to you how close I got?" She asked archly.
"I guess nothing."
"I'm teasing, you chump, he was just a little drunk and moon-struck."
"I'd say" said Joe heavily, but he was also relieved.
"And here is another one who does not get published, Muhi A Deen Shareef."
"Let's see if we can find him on the Email look up" they came up with lot of Shareefs, all over the world. "Let's try the Ameritech white pages" and they drew a blank . "Looks like someone who doesn't want to be found. Its getting late, I still have a small hang-over from the Unit, how about taking me to the Boat?"
"Alright, go to the car, I'll come in a minute."
"Thanks for dinner."
"You're welcome, off you go."
Joe was somewhat perplexed at this quick sendoff, he picked up his coat and went out to the garage, checking that no one had put any Play-Doh in Karen's door. The garage door opened by remote and she put something into the trunk, having exited through the front door.
Karen did not drive to Tony's. She drove straight to the Silver Spring apartment, and up the driveway into the small yard, Joe was getting more perplexed all the time.
"Thanks" he said, and hefted his briefcase.
"You're welcome" she said as she got out and went back to the trunk. She pulled out a sizeable gym-bag. Joe was bewildered "What are you doing, Karen?"
"Don't you want to go inside? it's freezing out here."
Joe had no choice. It was obvious Karen did not intend to get back into her car and it *was* freezing. He opened the door with the latch key and in the darkness they climbed the narrow stairs to Joe's apartment. He switched on the lights, and there she was, waiting for them from every wall, almost alive, but not quite. Karen plunked down the gym bag and looked around defiantly, as Shrines went this one was not clean enough, and the windows were too bare.
"Where is the bathroom?" she asked Joe, in her most no-nonsense voice.

Joe just pointed at the appropriate door. She grabbed her gym bag, and went into the bathroom in her most haughty manner, as if she was going to a ball. She doesn't even look tired, and I am beat, Joe remarked to himself.

She was out 20 minutes later, face scrubbed clean, hair shining, and pajamas, really they were scrubs with Children's Hospital emblazoned on them.

"A thief, too" he remarked.

"Part of my female charms, where is the tea?"

"Above and to the right of the sink, I made your bed, over there" and he pointed to the threadbare couch, beneath another picture of the Goddess, this time standing near the propeller of the Cessna. "And this is Peiter" and he showed her a photograph, Peter standing by the little Suzuki, snow-caps behind.

"Looks good, and the tea-cups?"

"The next cabinet over."

"Off you go then."

She likes to boss me around, doesn't she. Joe took a long shower, putting off the time he must come out and face...What? An execution squad? The mother of a dying child? A beautiful woman who had decided singlehanded to save him from himself, so what was he so afraid of? Joe looked at his own body in the mirror, a little fat here and there but not excessive, passable for an almost 40 years old. 40 years old??!! He put on the Fruit of the Loom fleece Karen had gotten him, they still looked new.

Karen was siting at the ricketty dinette, rocking back and forth on the chair whose one leg was shorter than all the others. Not a very good buy for a buck. She was sipping the tea and exchanging glances with the other ethereal occupant of the apartment. She appeared perfectly comfortable and at ease. Joe pulled up the other chair and eyed her with just a little trepidation over his cup. The couch had been remade into a setee.

"Tell me about your grandmother?" Joe felt a lurch in his stomach.

"Karen, why are you doing this?"

"It's time to let the Bad Spirits out."

"Aren't you afraid the same Bad Spirits might take possession of you?"

"I am afraid of Cancer, I am afraid of Bad People, I can deal with Spirits" said Karen easily, as if she delivered this kind of assertion every day of the week.

Although Yossi wanted to, Fella did not want him living with her, even though the Sackler school of medicine was closer to her apartment than the little apartment by the beach that he rented from her, at least in name, he paid a sheqel a month for the sake of a contract. She took care of his grandfather Shimon, whose Alzheimer became more and more severe, until one day he decided that climbing ten stories of the twelve in the Tel-Aviv high-rise apartment building made more sense than taking the elevator. By the time the medics arrived on the tenth floor the old man was dead. The funeral was small, Shimon's family had been decimated in the Holocaust and so had Fella's. Yossi had offered to move in with her, but she refused, saying that no self respecting girl would ever stay overnight at a grandmother's house. Yossi had to admit she was right, and that the downtown apartment near the Tel Aviv beach was potentially a much better love-nest, except he never made it one. Anyway, physically, Fella was a tough old nail likely to survive to a hundred, she volunteered at various charities, and kept active. Yossi worked hard at his studies, worked nights as a nurse's aid, and went on Army reserve duties when he had to. He told Fella that if he passed the first three years of Med school, then he was surely on the right track. Many evenings, after school, he would ride the bicycle to his grandmother's apartment, climb the 10 stories at a run to beat the elevator, and huff and puff his way to a lovingly prepared dinner. The conversation always came around to women, and when was he going to get himself a real girlfriend and get married. Fella was acutely aware of the fact that Yossi was the only survivor of the Wars, the World wars and the local wars. Yossi would good-naturedly parry those inquiries, and refused to get into the blind dates that she was willing to arrange through her friends, whose eligible grand-daughters were very, *very* nice girls.

He relented one time though. It was his birthday, he had just finished his third year, in the top third of his class, and was feeling both magnanimous and confident. Fella set up an rendezvous with her friend from WIZO charity whose granddaughter was also to be there, and she was a *very, very* nice girl, whom Yossi was sure to like. The café was Apropo, a typical TelAviv open air café, with its own little gazebo in the back, open to Dizzengof street to the front.

The bus service in Tel Aviv is excellent, and really the only reason to own a car in Tel Aviv is the weekend. Due to the power of the Religious Political parties, bus service stops on Friday afternoon, and resumes only on Saturday night. This was a Thursday evening, favoured by Tel Aviv dwellers because Friday is a day off for many. The cafés on Dizzengoff were bustling as pretty waitresses were rushing around the people who were out to enjoy the evening breeze which came off the Mediterranean to cool the September heat of the day. Yossi and Fella alighted from the No. 5 bus and sauntered to the Apropo. Yossi was in blue slacks and white collared short sleeve shirt (Don't you *dare* show up with your ratty shorts and tee shirt, Fella had admonished him) which showed off his splendid physique, and Fella was all dressed up with a lacy blouse and a pleated skirt, and she looked as proud as any peacock to walk around with her handsome Doctor-to-be grandson.

The waitress showed them to the flag-stoned back-yard, where an old lady and a young woman were already sitting. The young woman was indeed quite an eyeful, long straight auburn pony tail, high brow and almond eyes, and her body, lithe as a cat, as she rose and shook Yossi's hand. The old ladies introduced the young grandchildren to each other. Yossi had to admit that Fella had chosen well.

Michalle Greenberg turned out to be a gymnast, she was currently in the top 5 of the country in a certain branch of Gymnastics which included wizardry with balls, and hoops and throwing sticks. She was reedy and her hands were quick and precise. She smiled easily and very soon they were deep in a conversation, as the old women chuckled and approved. The nearby tables filled up, and the waitresses were busier than bees. Yossi was absorbed and did not notice the two men who were sitting two tables away, one of whom had a briefcase which he placed under the table.

After the second coffee he had to go to the restroom. Yossi excused himself and went back into the café to look for one. He looked back to ascertain where their table was in the crowded yard and the two men were just leaving. Something bothered him about them but his full bladder clamored for attention so he looked for the restroom sign which pointed to the other side of the café.

Yossi came out, and stood at the doorway leading from the interior out to the pretty yard. It was well lit with white globes hanging from the gazebo and fixed to the wood posts. The major portion of light came from a couple of floodlights mounted high on the brick wall. Their table was right there, both grandmothers were talking and Michalle was looking idly around. There was a briefcase under the next table, a briefcase which to Yossi's suddenly telescoped vision appeared as big as a house. No one leaves briefcases unattended in Tel Aviv. Unless....

The bomb blast hurled him back like a rag doll and his back actually broke through the cupboard behind him. Despite the pain his vision remained clear, his spectacles remained on his nose and the glass around him broke to shards. Bodies flew in the air and were deposited everywhere, against the posts, on the upturned tables, pieces of flesh spattered on the white-washed walls, and on the wooden lattice of the gazebo, which was torn and allowed the floodlights to penetrate. Mayhem, Pandemonium, screaming, which sounded tinny to his blast- shocked ears. Yossi picked himself up and raced to where their table had been. Half way there he stopped as if he ran into a wall. Fella was propped up against a chair, which had been stopped by a post. Her skirt had blown off showing vein-lined old legs, and she was strangely peaceful. Her face somehow was not hurt, but her abdomen which had taken the blast, blew open. Yossi, supposedly hardened by innumerable autopsies and Anatomy classes, retched, the coffee and cake rushed out and emptied on the bloodied flag-stones.

He looked around. Bodies were beginning to move. Michalle Greenberg's body did not move, her neck and face was shredded by the crockery and glass, and she was in a pool of blood. Her grandmother, Gilla, was dead. A waitress was groaning and bleeding in spurts from her arm. Yossi whipped off his belt and tightened it on her upper arm so tight the bleeding stopped. Other people were coming out of the café, coming right through the frame where glass had once been, looking bewildered. Yossi started recalling his CPR classes, Airway Breathing Circulation, he was an officer, he took charge of situations. The wails of the ambulances and police filled the air. Soon the yard was full of Emergency personnel.

"I was lucky, I wasn't even scratched. Grandma and Gilla and Michalle took most of the blast. Another woman, mother to a two month old baby also died" Joe told the story impassively. "Lots of injuries, lacerations, broken bones, cuts from flying glass. This was a small bomb, relatively. Looking back, what bothered me was that I had *seen* the men leaving, and I could *see* the briefcase peeking from under the table cloth, from where I stood. It didn't register just because I needed to go to the bathroom. If I had stopped for just *one* minute, cleared everybody out, called the bomb squad, done *anything,* Fella would still be alive, but she is dead because I needed to *pee,* for Godssakes."

"And what about Hitler, was that your fault too?"

"Come on Karen, that's not funny."

"It's not meant to be funny, just because something bad happened does not mean it's your fault!!"

"Yes it was, I should have paid attention!!"

"Pay attention Now, what's done is done, other people should have paid attention, someone should have guarded Rabin's back, someone should have stopped David Koresh before the Waco disaster. You have to stop blaming yourself and get on with Life."

"What for?" said Joe, coldly.

Karen refused to be cooled "because you have a job to do, children to cure, disease to disarm, and you have people who appreciate you and love you!"

Joe hung his head, he was ashamed. This proud woman poured out her heart and all he could do was squirm.

"All right , I'll stop lecturing" said Karen, strong and confident, "what happened after the bombing?"

"Big funeral, big chiefs talking down to poor Orphan, condolences. Lots of legal stuff, my grandma made me the sole heir, gave me her apartment and bank accounts and what not. That made me relatively rich. That also gave me a big sense of self-disgust" Karen shook her head again and curled the corner of her mouth, that made her even more desirable. "They wanted me on the news, They said I did CPR and maybe saved someone from bleeding to death. They made poor Michalle my girlfriend, her mother wanted to strangle me, I was so busy I couldn't see straight. I was actually happy the Army was so blind they called me to action in Lebanon. I asked the Dean for a year off, and used the money to shoestring around the world. Europe, the US, Canada, Japan, Australia, New Zealand, on and off motorcycles. I slept under bridges in Australia, and got kicked out of Yellowstone for sleeping near the bike outside the Camping Designated area. Now that was hilarious. Those Park rangers pointed a gun at my nose and couldn't believe that I wasn't scared, I laughed in their faces. After about a year I hoped everybody had forgotten and flew back home. You see, I have restarted my life once before, and it was no good, all I did was hurt another woman" and he looked at Helen, who was still, and smiling, on the wall.

"So today you are a miserable chicken, afraid of getting emotionally involved?"

"Yep, that's me, chicken, yellow-bellied chicken."

"OK chicken, let's go to bed, it's late." Joe was shocked, his head jumped as if he had touched a live wire. The glass tipped over slowly and the remains of the tea spilled out on the plastic table cloth. "What did you say?" he stammered.

"Let's go to bed, what is there to explain? Late-Bed-Sleep-getup the next day!"

She made it sound simple, and clear , and logical, without any loaded sexual import. Karen went back to the bathroom, brushed her teeth with lots of gusto, came out and headed into the bedroom. Joe stayed rooted at the table. He gazed longingly at the couch, as if it was the only haven from the storm, and then, very heavily, went about the same ablutions. He tip-toed into the bedroom, and his nightmare materialized, a sleeping figure was just when Helen would have been. Gingerly he lowered himself into his side of the bed and tried to make himself small and inconspicuous. Karen did not budge, he knew she wasn't sleeping, and slowly her warmth invaded his side of the bed, the kind of warmth, and smell, that he had deemed forbidden to him forevermore.

He woke up with a start, a hand was smoothing his prickly hair, which was wet with perspiration. He was hot beyond belief, the smooth hand and cool fingers were on his brow, his cheek, neck and shoulder. He froze.

"You were having a nightmare" Karen said very softly, as she would say to a child whose mother had gone home, alone and frightened in the Hospital.

Joe sat up suddenly and threw off the fleece top, so that he night light shone on his enormous shoulders, suddenly bare, shiny with sweat. Karen was looking up at him, perfectly serene, angelic. Slowly he leaned closer and diffidently tried to kiss her lips. The sensation shot through his whole body which was tight as a string on a hunting-bow. A groan tore from his throat and he collapsed on the bed, and cried, and sobbed, the vision of Helen on the operating table with the skull split open, the evil Tumor rising from it, superimposed itself on the face of the woman who wanted desperately to give him comfort, and return his self- respect. Karen just hugged him and rocked the big body which was convulsing with sobs, and murmured words of comfort.

They lay together, hands exploring each other's outer features, never wandering to anatomical landmarks of sexual arousal. He stared into those deep blue pools, and felt himself falling further and further into the realms of caring, fondness, protectiveness. The awful visions of his nightmares receded till they became insignificant.

He woke up very early, it was pitch dark. It was not a dream, Karen was still there, he propped himself on one elbow and watched her child-like guile-less features. Yes, I could learn to love this woman. This was not the wild, stormy, lustful, fiery, all consuming love he had had for Helen, returned in full measure with equal love and lust, this was a different sort, the kind, that would bloom with careful tending.

If I can do that without killing her first. The thought pierced his chest. He swung his legs down and left the bed. Karen turned over sleepily and hugged the blanket, which now held his body heat and smell, it was just like a baby holding on to his favorite blanky or plush bear, it was touching, and gave the bedroom a sense of Home.

The smell of freshly brewed coffee wafted into the bedroom and tickled her nose. Karen stretched luxuriously, even though that was not her bed. Finally she got up, put on the gown that was hung on the door, and walked over to the bathroom, sleepily acknowledging Joe who was sitting at the breakfast table. His hair seemed to have grown overnight.

"Morning" he called after her.

"Morning, I'm still asleep."

She looked in the mirror, her hair tousled, I look like Baghdad after a Tomahawk raid. She brushed and washed and passed a comb through her hair. Thank God I cut it short, and I need a little more dye for the roots. After New Years. She exited, and landed on the chair that rocks.

"I could sleep for another year" She said.

"I slept like the proverbial baby" said Joe and poured her a cup of strong coffee.

"Me too."

"What are we going to do, Karen?"

"Go back to bed?"

"BZZZZZZZZZZZZ, wrong answer, we still have a job to do."

"I haven't forgotten," and she took a big mouthful. The cell phone rang. Joe picked it up from the charger.

"Joe here."

"Hey, doctor Joe, did you leave your car in front of Tony's family restaurant overnight?" It was Chris Wilkins.

"I did."

"It's in the pound now, Glendale police."

"I guess I deserve that."

"Come and pick it up and we will call it quits."

"OK" the connection broke.

"My fault" said Karen, the booming rumbling voice carried well.

"You know," said Joe "in one of the surveillance reports about Ra-sheed Hariri, the agent noted that it was not Hariri who was driving the conspicuous Silver Mercedes but a different man whose description fits Mustafa."

"I am listening."

"This was an unusual trip, because it was in the beginning of the year, and the agent followed him all the way to Indianapolis to Riley Children's Hospital."

"Government gas."

"Why would Mustafa drive in the dead of winter to Indianapolis?"

"Because,,, because,,, because he needed to talk to someone."

"There is phone, he is an E mail kind of guy" Joe objected, over his third cup of coffee, the copies of the surveillance reports, well thumbed, back and forth, spread on the table.

"Do you have anything to eat in this place?"

"Cereal and milk."

"Good enough, I saw the bowls somewhere, there they are, not too clean, Mustafa drove there to talk to someone about whatever that someone was doing, or making." She poured the Cornflakes into the bowls and added milk.

"Go on."

"You assume he was trying to make a biological means to make Jews sick with cancer, and we know he succeeded because an old man and ten kids already got sick and died. He used a big organization with lots of scientists, and they met, at least once, and maybe more. Maybe the one in Indianapolis was a key figure?"

"Brilliant" Joe said and pointed at a name on the list "Munir Saidan, We found six citations in the Medline in his name. He is a virologist, working at Riley."

"Now what?" said Karen.

"Back to bed , didn't you say that before?"

"We can do that in Indianapolis."

"You need a big teddy-bear, what are we going to do with, or to, Mister Doctor Saidan?"

"Ask some questions, maybe scare him into telling us what is going on?"

"Scare him?" Joe retorted incredulously "The next thing he will do is E mail Mustafa and then the element of surprise is over, and Mustafa will disappear into Syria, or Lybia or God knows where, anyway how will you scare him?"

"I am running out of ideas, let's get the dear old Le Sabre outa the pound, finish your cereal and milk."

"Karen, I am almost forty years old for heaven's sakes."

"And you want to reach at least two times that number so listen to your Nurse" she chuckled.

"That does it" Joe put the bowl to his lips and slurped it down in one gulp. He set the bowl down with a thump. "That's a good boy" Karen approved. She got up and went past him to the bedroom, and as she passed by, she strummed her hand through his growing black-brown hair, playfully, sending shivers through his whole body. She is playing me like a guitar, and I like it. Helen looked on happily from the pillion of the Blue Kat. Joe waited for her to get dressed, and traded places. He had already shaved, leaving the moustache on, and pulled on his blue jeans and turtle-neck. Outside it was bright, sunny, and cold.

Chris Wilkins was waiting for them at the station. The same thought occurred to both of them as the huge man rose to meet them, chuckling as usual.

"Back to being Doctor Bergman, I see, your beauty is over in the lot." Joe pulled out his keys and strode outside.

"Officer Wilkins?" said Karen.

"Yes Miss Fitzsimmons."

"Karen."

"Chris."

"Chris, how good are you at scaring people to death?"

"Pretty good, I guess, but I don't think the good Doctor can be scared by anybody, try feminine allure instead" and he chuckled again.

"You men have a single track mind. We need to scare someone else, one of Mustafa's colleagues in Indianapolis."

"Why him?" the sound of the old V-8 started out as two then four then 8 cylinders all together in a cacophony, it was a very quiet police station. Chris regarded her with amiable curiosity.

"He may know what Mustafa was up to. Mustafa took a special trip to see him a year ago." Karen replied.

"Sweet Hesus, and how do you know so much about Mustafa from about a year ago? Share with your friendly police officers who are paid to serve and protect!!" Chris looked accusingly at Joe who had returned, twirling his keys.

"The FBI told us" Joe said blandly.

"You two are amazing, Jim!" He called out, a young gangly police officer came out of the back, and took off the Walkman headphones. "Mind the store, I am out on patrol, come-on, I need to hear more about this."

Chris drove the cruiser around, and got the story from Karen, Mustafa, the scientists, Hariri's car, old man and babies dead or dying with cancer, he took it in while patrolling his neighborhood.

"One thing you forgot to mention, how did you get those lists of scientists and surveillance reports?" Chris said quietly.

"You don't want to know" Karen said.

"I guess I don't, how is Amanda, that is Doctor Carter, holding up?"

"Desperate, but holding on."

"When's the last time you saw her?"

"Before Christmas" Karen said, suddenly concerned "come to think of it, I haven't heard from her, no messages on my machine, and she wasn't in on Christmas day, Joe was on call."

"You're Jewish" Chris said, as he turned the big cruiser onto Green-Bay Road.

"Yeah."

"On Christmas, all the doctors on call, at County, Children's, Sinai, St. Mikes, they are all Jewish. Figures. Here is Doctor Carter's complex, I am going in."

"Shouldn't we call her first?" Karen said.

"Go ahead" and he parked the cruiser.

Karen called Amanda's number on the cell phone. She was answered by the 10th ring.

"Hello."

"Amanda, what happened to you, you sound terrible."

"Who is it?"

"It's me, Karen."

"Who?" Karen covered the mouth piece "you guys go on up right now, she sounds terrible." "It's Karen Fitzsimmons, from the HOT unit."

"Go away." and the phone dropped and banged against some furniture. Karen closed the flip-phone and raced after the men who had already gone through the door. She met them at 316, and Chris was banging on the door with his stick.

"Doctor Carter, this is the Police."

"Go away."

Joe's multi-tool was out, and he got a nod from Wilkins. It was easier now because he had done this door before, and it was never fixed. The wood gave and the door swung in. Karen went in first, and from the sharp intake of breath Joe knew it was not a pretty sight.

The apartment was a mess, it was cold, it was thick with the smell of liquor, and some bottles were rolling around, the carpet was stained. Amanda was slumped in the couch, near the phone which was hanging down, emitting that repetitive screeching beep off-the-hook. The blond hair was plastered to the haggard face, and the eyes opened blearily, "Go away" she croaked again. She was dressed in the same clothes as they had seen her before Christmas. Karen knelt by her friend and held her hand.

"Amanda, what's going on?"

"Go away."

"The fridge is absolutely empty" Chris came back from the kitchen.

"And look at these liquors, Chivas, Crown Royal, Curvoisier, things you might keep around for guests" Joe said.

"The computer is on" said Chris. Joe came over "Its still online, and look at this message."

From: Mustafa@USA.net

Amanda
First: When I said non inflammatory message I meant just that. Alia has NO American grandparents, only Palestinian.

Second: Someone has been snooping at the blood center. This is your fault.

Since you disobeyed me yet again, this channel of communications is closed and sealed. You will never see Alia again, and in time, she will forget you exist, and good riddance.
Allah-Hu Akhbar

"Son of a bitch, son of a *bitch*" Chris Wilkins banged one huge fist into the other enormous palm, impotently. He looked over to Amanda, who was beyond reach, she was almost out. Karen snapped out of the shock first.

"Joe, Chris, help me get her to the bathroom, and leave. Look for some clean clothes, get some real food in here." Joe and Chris, two big men, lifted the featherweight Amanda and dragged her limply to the bathroom. The stench of alcohol was overwhelming. They deposited her gently into the tub, and left her to Karen.

"I'll get the food" offered Joe. Chris nodded, it would be unseemly for a police officer to be doing his shopping while on duty. He went into the bedroom and gingerly, rummaged through the female underclothes and sweatshirts. He felt as if he was invading her privacy by going through her intimate apparel.

"And a towel" Karen called from the bathroom. Chris found the bathrobe in the cupboard opposite the bathroom door. He knocked gently on the door, and although he tried hard not to look, for an instant he saw Amanda sitting up in the bathtub, naked, painfully thin, but cleaned up, and she was more beautiful than he could ever imagine. Karen took the towel and the clothes and banged the door shut. Chris went back to the living room and stared at the malevolent message. He had been a soldier, he was a police officer, a crime had been committed, and he was powerless to defend the innocent, or apprehend the guilty.

Amanda came out of the bathroom, under her own power, and looked around the dismal apartment. She realized how Karen and this big policeman had found her, and she was deeply embarrassed. Total loss of control, what a Doctor, what a Mother. She doubled up with pain from her screaming cramping stomach and sat down heavily on the couch. Joe came in huffing, carrying a SuperAmerica convenience store brown bag. Karen jumped at him.

"What did you bring?"

"Milk, eggs, cottage , mac and cheese, coffee, sugar."

"Put some milk in the microwave, she is having hunger cramps, Chris, get a blanket, she is beginning to shiver, I'll make the mac and cheese, she needs something hot, Chris, push the temp up, will you?"

An hour later Amanda was looking much better. Her shiny hair was tied in a pony tail, the smell of liquor was gone, and she had some calories in her. The bottles of liquor were secured in a nylon bag, and Joe vacuumed up the major stains. Chris was fussing around like an old woman. Joe printed the message, saved it and shut the computer down. It was already past noon on the Friday, and a big weekend was coming on.

Karen brought the original subject forwards. "Chris, can you help us?"

"Anything you want."

"OK" said Joe. He called information and got Riley in Indianapolis.

"Whitcomb Riley Children's Hospital, how may I direct your call?"

"I need the faculty office" the call was put through.

"Faculty."

"Hi, I am Jon Campbell, INS. I need to find out who deals with the Visas for foreign trainees."

"Cheryl Lodinski does that, let me put you through, it's busy, can you hold?"

"Holding"....

"Hello, this is Cheryl."

"Hi, My name is Jon Campbell, INS, we seem to have a slight problem with the Visa status for one of your foreign PhD's."

"Really? which one is that?"

"Munir Saidan, we have him as a J-1 and we have no sponsorship affirmation for him from your institution."

"Let me check, Siadan,,Saidan,, Saidan, here he is. We have him on an H-1 visa. He is here already five years and in fact he is applying for a Green Card!"

"Wow, what a screwup, Something is really wrong here...Ma'am, please don't do anything at this time, I have to check what the heck is going on here, I apologize, happy new year!!"

"You too." The connection was broken.

Chris was looking at Joe and holding his mouth. Even Amanda managed a smile for this performance. Karen was smiling widely.

"We have our Achiles-heel" Joe announced.

"What is it?" Chris was eager.

"This specific scientist had recently applied for a Green Card. That means he wants to stay in the States, and he is unlikely to jeopardize his application and future residency."

"Tuesday, after New Years, take a few days off, Chris"said Karen.

"Will do. Doctor Carter, are you OK?"

"She is going with me to my place" Karen said with finality. Joe concurred.

"No Karen, I don't want to put you in a spot" Amanda protested weekly.

"If you refuse, I'll have Chris arrest you and ship you over anyway!!" Chris nodded forcefully.

"Amanda, there is nothing to wait for here, he is not going to phone, or fax, or mail. It's up to us, and in the mean time you have to get yourself back in shape!!" Joe added his argument.

"Oh all right, its so messy here, I got so lonely..."and her eyes watered again, but just for one moment.

"Get some stuff together and follow the cruiser" Chris was soft spoken, and adamant.

"Chris, when are you off duty?" Karen asked as Joe and Amanda carried the suitcases into her house.

" 'Bout Four, unless something happens."

"Come round to my place a little later, OK?"

"Sure" he was perplexed.

"You have a calming influence on her, she is not out of the depression yet."

"Sure, I'll come."

"Great, six-thirty" and she planted a quick kiss on his cheek, almost jumping to get up there.

Officer Wilkins drove the cruiser away rubbing his cheek. This must be my lucky day, he mused.

Joe came out of the house and was followed by Karen to the car.

"I want you to come for Dinner, Joe."

"Got any wine?"

"Some, I guess."

"I'll bring some."

"Where to now?"

"Some exercise, then Temple, Beth Israel."

"About Seven?"

"OK."

Karen reached up, forced his face down, not too much resistance there, and kissed him full on his freezing lips. The moustache tickled her. Before his arms could complete the sweep to a bear-hug, she pushed him away. Amanda almost rubbed her eyes. Doctor Bergman? Kissing? the Ice-Man from Seattle? But then it was Karen, whom she always thought should be irresistible. Karen came in just as the raucous V-8 roared off. Amanda wagged her finger at her playfully. Karen's fair skin reddened from the neckline up.

"What are you smirking about?" asked Karen, feigning ignorance.

"Anyone who can get Doctor Joe to Kiss, deserves the Congressional Medal of Honor!! How did you do it?"

Karen took it quite seriously "I made him talk."

"Nobody made him talk, *ever,* except about Work."

"Come-on, help me make dinner, once he saved my life, it wasn't as hard."

"Joe makes a habit out of saving lives" Amanda remarked "I like to peel potatoes, where are they?"

"Lower cabinet left to the fridge, he doesn't think so, he thinks his Karma is to be the cause of suffering and death to anyone who loves him, especially women."

"I know someone who does that on purpose!!" Amanda said, her hands trembled but she concentrated on the simple task of potato peeling.

"You know what I think?" Karen was cubing the onions and her eyed stung and watered, "I think he was attracted to me from the start, ever since he came on the Service two and a half years ago, but he repressed it so it would never show. At gut level I knew that, but he was smooth as glass and endearing as cold tuna fish!"

"What a waste of time!!" Amanda remarked, she was dicing the potatoes.

"No, I don't think so, he was in mourning, he had to work it through that tough system, he needed to do enough good before he could put the self-blame behind him."

"And is it behind him? Where do you want me to put those potatoes?"

"Pyrex is in the corner cabinet, no, it's not, but I am working on it." She flashed Amanda a big smile.

"This is for the long haul, am I right?"

"The longest." Karen placed the onions in a big saucepan and fried them and added the potatoes.

"What a stack, who are you feeding?"

"I asked Joe to come for dinner, and we may have guests."

"Guests?"

"Oh, my Mom likes to pop in sometimes" Karen was evasive.

"What shall I wear?"

"My Nursing diagnosis is that you are fast on track to recovery, can you open the oven for me? If there is nothing in the suitcases we'll find something for you in my closet. Are you a size six or an eight?"

"Eight mostly, but now I can fit into a six long. I think this mac and cheese was the first food in three days. I haven't been drunk since the first year in college, I swore it would never happen again. But that e mail, it was so final... all I wanted was to Lose it. Can I have that banana?"

"Don't ask, eat."

Amanda peeled it quicker than a monkey, and gobbled it down.

"That's better, I'll make the salad."

"Lettuce in the fridge."

Joe cleared his living room space, and stretched his joints. He proceeded with his own karate class and went though the punches, blocks, kicks, whirling in all directions, but taking up very little room in these cramped quarters. When he had worked up a good sweat he went down to the freezing garage in the yard. He placed three planks on the blocks, concentrated, and broke them with a SHUTO delivered straight down with the edge of the hand. Then he loaded three planks onto the posts set up in the garage. With an explosive Exhalation he punched them hard, his sleeve snapping. Two broke, the last one didn't. He repeated the punch with his left, and the last one broke, as did the skin on his two knuckles. The sweat was beginning to freeze up on his body. He ran up the stairs, showered, shaved, band-aided the knuckles, and changed into his only good suit. Then he drove, first to the Kohl's and then to Temple for the Friday night Service.

At seven o'clock sharp he parked the Le Sabre in front of Karen's house. The driveway was full with two other cars, Amanda's white Camry, and another, a red old Mustang, restored with a power bulge. That's not Mom's car, thank God. He knocked on the door politely, and almost got knocked off his feet.

Karen looked devastating, she took his breath away, standing at the elevated doorway she was taller and he had to look up. The flaxen hair reflected the porch-lights, cheeks shining clear, full mouth, a thin black choker, a shimmering black blouse closed with a butterfly pin, her bosom well defined in the shimmer. He was rooted to the spot. Three weeks ago he would have ignored this display of female attraction, let it flow over him like water over a duck. But now, he was fully susceptible, and therefore powerless to resist. Who wanted to resist anyway?

"Come in Joe, you look very nice" This time everything was in place, the jacket sitting squarely on the muscled shoulders, the white collar, the solid blue silk tie. He took a step up and they were on a level, and Karen pecked him quickly, on the mouth, and for half a second they looked into each others eyes, deep blue into the dark brown-green, it was another kiss, of the souls and brains behind those eyes. Karen stepped aside and let him through the doorway, Joe handed her the Kohl's plastic bag.

"I believe you know Chris Wilkins" and Chris who had been holding a Pabst shook his hand. That was the first time Joe had seen him out of uniform, and he was a fine form of a man. Amanda appeared from the top level, and she was a completely different Amanda from the miserable broken drunk he had seen that morning. She was Doctor Carter, an accomplished, beautiful woman who will take her life and set it right again. Chris was also looking up those stairs, and he was bewitched.

"Dinner is ready" Karen announced.

The table was festively set, this was after all New Year's weekend. The silverware and wineglasses sparkled. Joe was impressed, Karen had put some real effort into this family dinner. In fact they were four strangers, tied together by hate for one criminal, and the concern for one child. Still, the feeling of Family was strong.

"Is it OK if I say a Grace? It's called a Kiddush in Hebrew, designating the holiness of the Sabbath?" Joe asked. Amanda and Chris nodded, why-not. Karen nodded decisively, "go ahead" she said.

Joe pulled the cork off the bottle of sweet Herzog wine and poured for Chris and Amanda. He filled his glass and stood up, and delivered the Grace with a lilting song. Chris and Amanda were interested, uncomprehending. Joe noticed that Karen mouthed some of the words, as if she knew them by heart. When he was done he sipped and gave her his glass, naturally, as he had done on a hundred Fridays with Helen, as Naftali had offered his glass to Deborah, on every Shabbat Eve of his childhood. Karen took the glass and sipped, as if she had done that too throughout her life.

Chris exchanged a glance with Amanda, and she shrugged slightly as if to say, Beats-Me. Joe used a bread-knife to cut one of the loaves of Challah bread, said something over it and handed each one a slice. He sank his teeth into the slice and smiled at everyone.

"I hope you will excuse this rigmarole, just a little tradition."

"Fascinating" said Amanda, "and this bread is great, where did you get it?"

"Kohl's, I have a standing order for Friday, who says "fascinating" on every TV show, at least once?"

"Are we playing Trivia?" asked Chris.

"Just a little trivia."

"It's Spock, on StarTrek, the old generation."

"And the name of the actor?"

"Leonard Nimoy" said Chris.

"And what's his other famous quote? Or blessing?" Joe persisted.

"I'll give the girls a chance to answer."

"OK, you bring the salad." Chris got up and stepped over to the kitchen island. The girls were silent, apparently they were not Trekkies. Karen glanced at Amanda and she just shrugged her shoulders even higher, how-should-I-know.

Chris brought down the big blue bowl and set it in the middle of the table. "Live long and prosper" he said.

"Ah, I remember now" breathed Karen.

"Do you remember the exact hand motion?" Joe probed.

Chris went blank. Joe showed them, both hands, four fingers split into a vee, thumb spaced apart "Live Long and Prosper" he intoned, and Chris broke down with a guffaw. Joe smiled but remained serious.

"Any idea where he took this from?"

"Tell us" said Amanda, noticing the lack of levity.

"This sign, and very similar words, are made over every Jewish congregation by the resident Cohanim, priests, at prayer. The only function of the Birth-right Jewish priests is to perform a vocalized blessing of the community and the world. I have no idea if Leonard Nimoy is a Cohen, but he must have seen it, and incorporated it, in the most positive manner. Mustafa is out to kill people whose function in life is to bless other people!!"

"And I married him" Amanda said despondently. Then she sat up "How does he do that?"

"He is using a DNA probe complementing a unique sequence as a means to transfect a transforming factor into a targeted population."

"Wowowo there, Doctors, speak American please." That was Chris.

"Joe, please stop right now and let's eat, Amanda is about to pass out."

"Sorry Karen" Joe was sheepish. Amanda was amazed, the bit was in the mouth and the Stallion was reined in.

The meal was as good as anyone could have wished, and it was over so quickly!

"I am stuffed" said Chris, and patted his belly, "Karen, are you available?"

"Nope, I'm taken."

"Lucky boy" said Chris and leered.

"Come-on Chris, let's load the machine" said Joe.

"What machine?" asked Karen.

"The dishwasher, it's right there!!" said Joe.

"It aint working."

"How come?"

"I don't know, one day it stopped and that was it!"

"Let me take a looksee" Chris offered and got up, "Got your Gerber?"

"Sure." Joe handed it over. Chris took off his jacket and tie, and draped the jacket over a chair. It swept the floor like a gown.

"Doctor Carter, help me here, OK?" Joe and Karen exchanged looks, and Karen's was especially conspiratorial. Joe and Karen cleared up the table and stacked the dishes, pending the washer repair. She headed downstairs, leaving Chris and Amanda together.

Joe joined her on the sofa.

"It worked" Karen breathed.

"What worked?"

"They are like magnets, put them close enough and they will stick!"

"Oh, are you a matchmaker?"

"It's a Mitzva."

"Where did you learn *that* word?"

"You met my Grandpa, didn't you?"

"I guess, five minutes two and a half years ago."

"He says those kind of words."

"How is he doing?"

"OK, he is a tough survivor."

"l think it's time for me to split."

"Fine, your car or mine?"

"Are you coming with me?"

"What did you think? That last night was a one night stand?" Joe was flustered "I didn't mean it that way, I just didn't want to presume."

"Ta-Da, It's working, load it up!!" Chris was crowing like a child.

"Keep up the good work, good night!" Karen called.

Chris was alarmed, "Where are you going?"

"To Joe's place."

"But... but.."

"You babysit till I come back in the morning" Karen said cheerily and grabbed the same gymbag, freshly loaded with clothes. Joe lifted his arms in a show of total- loss-of-control. Chris was thunderstruck.

"All the bedclothes are in the cupboard in the hallway, come *on* Joe" and she swept out, leaving the door open so Joe had to hurry up and close it behind them. She wrenched open the Le Sabre heavy door and sat up smirking like the cat who drank the milk, her breath forming a white cloud in the car.

Joe started it and backed out "I didn't know you were so crafty."

"You have no idea."

Chapter 18

SHARPER IMAGE

"Do you think the Sharper Image will deliver on Sunday?" Joe asked over breakfast. They had spent another night of talking, and stroking, but no sex, both afraid that a blatant show of lust might somehow ruin a love relationship in the making. Joe woke up more refreshed than in years, the nightmares retreating before the presence of Karen in his bed.

"I can't imagine what you would want to buy at the Sharper Image. Looking at this furniture, Goodwill is more your store."

"The furniture reflects what I think of myself, cheap and utilitarian. A mug for a dime does the same job as a Wedgewood porcelain cup."

"I hope the same value system is not applied to humans."

"In dollars and cents, the amount of material that goes into a human is probably less than a dollar. It's the *information* that's worth more wealth than Bill Gates. From my point of view, the crystal goblet contains no more information than a wineglass for a quarter."

"You just defeated your own argument. *You* are worth more than the wealth of Bill Gates, and occasionally you can show it by acquiring tasteful accouterments for Living. The Sharper image will deliver anytime, if you pay enough. What are we buying?"

"Are you chipping in?"

"Whatever I can afford, which ain't much."

"How can you pay the mortgage if you are not working?"

"Beg, borrow or steal, but later."

"I can make you a loan" Joe said carefully, ready for a rebuttal.

"I'll take that into consideration, but I'm fine for the time being, I don't waste any money on Boys" she teased.

"We need some spy stuff, for our meeting with Saidan."

"I thought Chris was going to do the talking."

"He is, but he doesn't have enough background for a thorough investigation. He needs to appear all knowing and omnipotent, otherwise a PhD in molecular biology will eat him for breakfast."

"Speaking of breakfast, you are hardly eating."

"After last night's dinner? I need a week's hunger strike" said Joe and patted his thin Michelin tire.

"Try another tack."

"OK, they usually have brunch at Temple, on Sabbath, and if I'm in town and not on call, I like to make it to services, then Brunch."

"Aren't you going to invite me?" Karen fluttered her eyes, playfully hurt. Joe was taken aback "Well,,, I,,, Jeez,,, I didn't think about it!!"

"When are you going to get it through your thick skull that I may be interested in things that you do, and that you should be interested in things I do? The least you can do is **ask**, invest some thought and consideration in your Partner!!" And Karen jabbed her finger angrily at his shoulder to make her point.

Joe did not answer, he just kept looking at the mobile features of the lovely Presence, the flashing eyes, the tumultuous personality, emotional, logical, a complete woman. She finished her finger jabbing and looked at her nail. "See what you made me do? It's broken. And don't think what you are thinking. I am *not* going to die just because we go somewhere together."

"Karen, will you please come to Temple with me?"

"Can I say No?"

"Sure."

"Then its Yes, what shall I wear?"

"Something conservative, elegant is OK, eye-gouging is not." Joe went back to the Armada and started clicking items into the Shopping basket in the Sharper Image site. E commerce was growing by leaps and bounds. The final sum was stiff but Joe entered his Chase number into the Secure Site, and specified overnight Sunday delivery.

"Is this OK?" she asked.

"Lovely, much too good for me."

"I have to band-aid your silly mouth" she said "Is it really all right?" She asked anxiously.

"I swear it's fine and I'll be honored to be seen with you. How did you know to bring this along?" She was smartly dressed in a pearl gray knee length suit, a white blouse with a black bow at the neck, with white-pearly buttons. The shoes, matt black , gave her some additional stature, but not excessive.

"Girls are ready for anything. You look very nice too, Haven't I seen that jacket before?"

"It's one of the only decent jacket I have."

"Why so many jackets?" She teased.

"Like the car, it does the job."

"Were you that stingy with Helen, as you are with yourself?... Sorry, sorry Joe, that was mean of me."

Joe remained unaffected. "Different days Karen, I was as happy as a human can bear to be, we spent freely and we didn't spend that much. A night in Motel Six, or a night in the Ritz, it didn't matter. After the baby died, and she died, I realized that the lowest of the low was too good for me." Joe shut the computer, and stood up. In those heels, he was just a tad taller.

"What baby, you had a baby?" Karen said, tremulous.

"A fetus, it never had a chance."

"I am so sorry Joe, so sorry" and she came into his arms and buried her face in his neck. Joe placed his big hand on the soft hair, which were tickling his face and nose, and stroked longingly. Over that hair he could see Helen, smiling, as alive as the woman in his arms.

"Come-on Karen, let's go."

The Temple was large and airy, and well-appointed, testament to the fact that the Jewish communities of Glendale, Fox Point, and River Hills, were both affluent and involved. Mostly, the patrons were couples, dressed in their best, flanked by their children. Joe showed Karen the books of prayers, which were translated to English, and transliterated so that those who did not read Hebrew, could still say the prayers. Joe was called once for a short participation in the Service, and she noticed immediately how his Hebrew prayers were enunciated with the confidence of a Mother-Tongue speaker.

The whole thing involved a lot of standing for certain passages, and sitting at others. The Rabbi gave a short sermon recalling the War of the Maccabees. Occasionally some words recalled fleetingly the same words as uttered by Grandpa Jacob, especially on that terrible night when Alex had died. She shivered, and Joe sent her a questioning look.

The brunch was a wonderful little affair, carried out in the Social Hall. Kids dressed in their best scooped up food and raced around screaming. The little girls flounced, the adults filled their plates with herring-in-cream and salads, and sat around in loose groups, discussing the events of the week. Rabbi Lowel Kantor, a young tall man recently recruited from New-York, went from group to group, answered questions, imparted a piece of lore, and the whole scene was very comfortable.

"Hello, Doctor Bergman, we needed you last week, we were a little short."

"Hi Rabbi. Sorry."

"Please introduce me to this lovely lady."

"Karen, this is Rabbi Kantor, Rabbi, this is Karen Fitzsimmons."

"Enchanté" said the Rabbi, "if its due to your presence that Doctor Bergman made it, then you should come every Sabbath!!"

"Why not? This is a lovely service and great company, I think I recognize a few Doctors from Children's here, but I won't point" she added with a peal of laughter.

"Good to see you, Yossi, and you too Miss Fitzsimmons, I shall continue my Rounds."

The old man was squinting his eyes at them for some time, and Joe wondered why. He was Desmond Fried, a retired businessman, and he was sitting by his wheel-chair-bound wife, who was talking, animated, with another older lady. Joe watched him push himself up on his cane and slowly tap his way to them. He stood over Karen, and pointed his finger at her, jabbing in the air.

"I know you, I am sure I know you."

Karen was slightly embarrassed, but yes, there was something vaguely familiar about him, the fog of time was lifting very slowly.

"I know, you are Jacob Lifshitz's grand-daughter, I remember those eyes! I was at your brother's Brith, right here in Temple! Not this hall, this one is new, the old little Social hall!!"

Karen smiled uncertainly "I was very little."

The old man continued unrelenting "and Jacob used to brag that he had delivered him by hisself, and that you had helped him."

"That's right, I remember THAT" Karen said warmly to the old man.

"Where is that young man then? He should be twenty, twenty five by now."

"He is dead."

The old man lost his balance and Joe shot out to steady him and help him into a chair.

"Dead?" Desmond Fried croaked.

"He had a kind of cancer, he was just 8, and he died."

"I am real sorry to hear that, I remember he was such a good baby, and a good kid, Old Jacob brought him to Temple sometimes."

"Yes he was." Joe was eyeing Karen in an entirely new light. She wasn't just sweetness and light, happy and secure. She was a person who had been tested by disaster and sorrow, and she came out of it a better person. And she was as closed mouth as he had been. Thank God for this old man, and his fantastic memory.

"Dad, are you OK?" A fortyish balding man came over, concerned, to see why Desmond was so distraught.

"Nah, I am fine, what happened to Jacob and Esther? We moved away to Tampa for a few years, and when we came back he wasn't here"

"They moved to LA, to be close to his younger sister, on the west coast. That was years after Alex had died... anyway, Esther didn't last long in the Smog." Another loss, Joe noted to himself, the way she speaks about her, she was a very dear Grandma, just like Shimon and Fella had been.

"Dad, we better go, Mom is tired" said the son "Excuse us, maybe we can catch up on the reminiscence next Saturday." Joe helped the old man rise, and then let them go.

"Drive me home Joe." Joe took her to Mohawk. Her clothes were elegant, but she was not. Some of the fire and happiness were out. The red Mustang was gone, Chris must be on duty. Joe drove up the driveway and stopped.

"Are you OK Karen?"

"I'll be OK tonight. Will you come over?"

"How about Amanda?"

"Don't worry about her, we will arrange things to suit everybody. Please come, I'll need you."

Joe leaned over and met her for a long lingering kiss. The separation of the lips was almost painful.

"About eight?" he asked

"Eight is fine" and she exited and went to the door, dejected.

The telephone rang.

"Joe here"

"Mister Bergman?

"Yes"

"I am calling from the Sharper Image. Can you read for me your confirmation number?"

Joe rummaged around the table for the number he had scribbled that morning.

"4215667."

"And your address, sir."

"1215 east Silver Spring Road, Glendale."

"This is an unusual order sir so we had to confirm."

"OK with me."

"Thank you Doctor, Fed Ex will deliver at 1130 at the latest, please have someone there to accept the package."

"Doctor Gottshchalk?"

"Yes, who is it?"

"It's Joe Bergman."

"Joe, did the earth swallow you? And Doctor Carter too?"

"No-no" chuckled Joe "but I wanted to ask you a question."

"Academic?"

"No, remember I came to see you Sunday because of Mustafa disappearing?"

"Sure I remember, you know the bastard took the main computer memory out with him?"

"Oh wow, anyway, Mustafa is in E mail contact with his wife, and he mentioned that someone had been snooping at the Blood Center."

"Why we had the FBI here like a swarm of locusts, asking questions and poking at things."

"I don't think that's what he meant. Who saw us, specifically, while we were looking around?"

"God knows, a bunch of techs were in at the time. No, wait a minute though, there is someone specific, Francine Dobbs."

"Who is she?"

"She is the busty blond tech that we talked to that day, the one who said that Mustafa had left with his briefcase."

"What's special about her?"

"It's ugly to say it, but after Mustafa I became more antsy about Middle-Eastern types. Monday after Mustafa ran off I saw Francine being picked up by a guy in a Beemer, a black Beemer, and he looks like Mustafa's brother. The same guy drops her off at work the next day. Just put two and two together."

"I am sure Francine has no idea she is being used, he is just a boyfriend or a lover."

"Nice Beemer, I couldn't afford one" Gottschalk chuckled.

"Doctor Gottschalk, can I ask you to lie? Just a little."

"If it's to help Amanda, yes."

"It is. Tell Francine that the big guy who was snooping around gave up and decided to mind his own business."

"I dearly hope that's a lie, I know Roger Cohen is dead."

"I promise you I am lying to beat the band."

"Good, I'll lay it on thick for her."

"Don't forget , she is probably a victim of her physique."

"Keep me posted, good luck Joe."

Amanda had made a complete recovery. She was unloading the dishwasher, and except for a small cloud on her brow, she was back to normal. She was surprised to see Karen come in, downcast.

"What happened, did you fight with Joe?"

"No, no, Joe is a dear, I just had a nasty reminder of the past."

"Dark secrets?"

"Dark, but no secret. You know about Alex, my brother?"

"You told me one night when we were working over the kid with CMV pneumonitis, I forget his name."

"Jim Eling, anyway, Joe told me a horror story how his grandma was blown up in a terrorist bomb attack in Tel Aviv, something he could have prevented if he had been more vigilant. Alex died of Varicella Zoster coupled with CMV, in the days before Zovirax and DHPG. For years I told myself it was inevitable, and I lied to myself over and over again!"

"Karen, you're shaking!"

"I feel like freezing to death. I saw that kid with the pimples on his skin *before* he came to play with Alex, and I never stopped him from going in!"

"How old were you then?"

" 'Bout fifteen, sixteen"

"How could you have known? For heaven's sakes Karen, you can't blame yourself for something you knew nothing about!!"

"I know, I know," Karen said miserably "I can rationalize till doomsday, I thought I got over it, until this old man shows up today and reminds me of Alex all over again."

With a mighty effort Karen lifted up her head, rubbed her eyes and cleared her brow. "How was the Babysitter?" She asked with a smile coming through her wet eyes.

"Chris?" Amanda blushed "I forgot that men can be so nice. After the last three awful years with Mustafa, he is like a cool shower in the Mojave in July."

"Are you interested?" Amanda blushed deeper.

"Yes, maybe, he is like a huge Tigger, ferocious form, all plush."

"Aren't you bothered by him being, let's say, not very highly educated?"

"Who cares?!" Amanda retorted "what did education ever do for my happiness? Look at Mustafa, he is highly educated, and a liar and a cheat, and he took my baby away, I tossed away the best years of my life on him, and the only good thing that ever came out of it, he took away too, I hope she is all right, he could be so mean and cruel sometimes!!" Amanda remained dry-eyed throughout, as if her source had dried up.

"Did he ever use force?"

"No, worse, he looks at you, as if you were a tick that came off a dog, that one needs to crush and throw in the toilet, totally contemptuous. Alia was so afraid of his eyes when he did that. And of course he physically ignored me for at least a year."

"How did you survive?"

"Work and Alia, and friends, like you. I am dying for a real close Man hug, the kind that makes you feel wanted and cared for, and protected, its silly."

"Me too" said Karen.

"But you have Joe now!"

"Joe is so fragile, touch him the wrong way, he will blow apart."

"Joe? Fragile? I thought he was made of cold rolled steel" Amanda was amazed at her friend's observation.

"Emotionally I mean. He covered himself with layers of self-protective shells. It takes work to get him to Do something!!"

"Is it because he may be, ah, unable? Men can't take that!"

"I don't know, he lives in a Shrine to his former wife, it's eerie, she looks at you from every wall, and I have to admit, she was something special."

"Take her off the wall" suggested Amanda playfully.

"If I do that, I can call it quits, Joe will go back to being Mister Cold Granite and I will be Alex's sister."

"We are a sorry bunch, aren't we" observed Amanda, "one married to a hateful child kidnapper, and one tied to an emotional fiasco, anybody happy up there?" She directed her query to the ceiling, and the sky, and whoever was beyond it.

"I believe our luck is about to change" Karen asserted. "First we will get Alia back, then we can get our men to love us."

"That's if you don't get killed first" Amanda said "You mean to go with Joe, right? That puts you at tremendous risk. I am not sure I want you to do that for me."

"Amanda, I am not doing this just for you, I am doing this for me too."

"How come?"

"If Joe and I get through this, then I shall have him forever, I am his last chance of getting a Life, and I am pretty sure he is mine."

"I think that qualifies as a commitment" Amanda said quietly "is he going to make the same commitment?"

"He better. I want to go shopping for some food, wanna come?"

"Why not, maybe we will see Chris on patrol, do you know he restored that old car, the '67 Mustang, all by himself?"

"Too much free time, take some off his hands."

"Hello?"

"Deenah?"

"Yossi, is that you?"

"Yes."

"Yossi, its 1 o'clock Sunday Morning, go to sleep!"

"Deenah I am still in the States, it's Shabbat afternoon here."

"No wonder you sound so clear, it's he local lines which are worthless, I paid the rent on time, this month."

"Yeah, Shai told me you did, and you made up for the month that you didn't."

"See, I told Attorney Carmel that Rami would come up with it."

"Deenah, I want you to do something for me."

"Since you are such a nice landlord, I'll do it."

"Take the cordless phone first."

"OK, it's a real nice 900 meg phone you sent us, you know it's illegal in Israel?"

"Still? Idiots. Go to the old radio in the living room" Joe instructed. He heard Deenah, who rented his old apartment in Tel Aviv, rustle off the bed. A male voice said something like "who is this schmuck on the phone?" behind her.

"That was Rami, don't mind him" Deenah said "I'm in front of the radio."

"Reach behind the old radio, and bring out the nylon bag." He heard the breath and groan of exasperation and finally the rustle of nylon.

"These look like old maps."

"That's right, I want you to put them in a big heavy envelope tomorrow, and bring it to Shai's office. If you do that first thing tomorrow morning, I'll forgive you a month's rent."

"Yossi, you are an angel, 'course I'll do it."

"I knew I can count on you, Deenah, on the other hand, if it doesn't get there, I'll have to double the rent effective February."

"All you landlords are mean, mean, mean. I have some new Geraniums on the veranda."

"I know, they cover the cracks in the stucco, I'll be seeing you."

"When?"

"Soon" and he clicked it shut.

To: Shai Carmel, Attorney
From: Yoseph Bergman MD
Dear Shai

Deenah will deliver to your office a package. Old maps we used to use. Please forward it, Flying Cargo, to my address.

How is Rivi? And the kids? E mail me sometime you lazy bum.

See you soon
Yossi

Joe faxed the message to Shai Carmel, one of the lieutenants from 801. He had a lively attorney's office in Tel Aviv and was doing very well.

The mobile Motorola rang stridently. Joe picked it up from the charger.

"Hello."

"Joe, I got an idea" It was Chris.

"Are you on patrol?"

"No, I am back at the station, except for one Wife-Beater, there was nothing else."

"What happened to the Beater?"

"His wife chickened out, she didn't press charges."

"So?"

"I called him outside, asked Dorland to talk to his wife, and while he was freezing his miserable cojones I hinted that next time we get called he will have to say goodbye to those cojones."

"That's dangerous, Chris."

"Fuck dangerous, anyone who beats up on his wife while the kids are looking on should have the urge removed. Did you see one of those Shaken

Babies ever Doctor Joe?"

"Unfortunately, I did."

"A doc at Children's told me once that looking into their eyes is like seeing the Angel of Death."

"I agree" said Joe, the vision of the White eye grounds and dead look flashing to the front of his mind.

"Those are wife-beaters first, and baby-beaters later, There is nothing lower in the Jungle."

"What's the idea you had?"

"We should get Saidan on Monday, New Year's day, not the next day like we planned."

"Why?"

"It's scarier to have the Police on the Holiday, it means the situation is bad. Also that way we find him at home and get his family to understand something bad is happening. This way he doesn't have access to Lawyers, and wants to get back to normal ASAP."

"Do you know where he lives?"

"Leave that to me, I am the police, right? And I know some guys in Indy."

"OK, can you make it to my place tomorrow at 1130?"

"My schedule says OK, what for?"

"To set up the gear."

"What gear?"

"You'll see."

Joe busied himself with some house chores, and wondered why the apartment felt so empty, despite the music from the boombox (another 80's relic). He had an hour to kill so he read up some articles he had downloaded two weeks before and hadn't gotten around to reading. He prepared an overnight bag, and wondered what he should do with this nightly see-saw. She had good intentions, but those may lead to Hell, again.

He was disappointed to see Amanda's car still there, somehow he fancied having Karen to himself, call it jealousy, he wanted her undivided attention, even if he didn't really deserve it. It was Amanda who opened the door.

"Hi Doctor Joe."

"Hi Doctor Amanda."

"We were just coming out" and Karen came out and locked the door. His heart jumped again at her beauty. It wasn't the same leap-into-the-throat he had experienced with Helen every time she had walked, or took off the helmet, or stepped out of a car. It was more sedate, appreciative. Joe wondered if he would ever recapture that adrenaline and testosterone rush. Probably not, it was a once in a lifetime thing, and he was 10 years older now.

Amanda headed for her car, her step light, blond hair loose "I am on call in the Unit tomorrow, so I should get a good night sleep" she explained and drove out. Karen joined him in the Le-Sabre, and Joe watched each movement, waiting to see if the magic would happen again. Karen laughed and passed her hand in front of his face as if he were blind "let's move, I am hungry."

Back at the Mohawk house, Karen closed the curtain and blinds, and offered him a tea, and they sat, close together on the sofa, and watched a James Bond movie, rerun for the umpteenth time. The impossibly narrow squeaks out of trouble made Joe laugh every time. Slowly Karen slid closer, leaned her head on his chest, and draped his arm over her shoulder. He did not resist, but did not initiate anything either. Finally, with a sigh, she took his large warm palm and placed it carefully on her breast. She felt his whole body react as if to a galvanic current, and then relax, and the big hand made slow stroking motions on that breast, and then moved over to the other breast, the middle finger slowly circling, and stoking her desire. She twisted suddenly, quick and slippery as an eel, and faced him, pushing him down on the sofa and leaning her elbows on his wide pectorals.

"Do you realize how difficult and embarrassing it is to seduce a Boy so directly?"

He was very comfortable with her bantam weight on him, except that one place where it became very uncomfortable, "Probably as difficult and embarrassing as it is for the Boy, anyway, why embarrassing?"

"It's the fear of rejection, withdrawal, turning the cold shoulder on the advances."

"I am not rejecting."

"Nor are you doing anything positive."

"That's because I am not sure it's the right thing to do" said Joe, anticipating the hurt in her eyes. His huge arms locked on her back before she could jump up, and regardless of her struggles she could not break free. She gave up a few seconds later. That place was *acutely* uncomfortable now, and Karen felt it too through their clothes.

"I am not totally unresponsive, am I?" He smiled in her face, and she relented and assumed her former position.

"Why are you making it so difficult for me then?" she asked plaintively.

"It's so damn serious, that's why."

"What's wrong with serious?"

"Getting serious with me gets women dead."

"That's not why you are making it difficult."

"Are you second-guessing me again?"

"Yes, you want to scare me away, because you love me *and* you don't want me to die like Helen."

"Maybe."

"Maybe you love me or maybe you don't want me to die?"

"Maybe to both."

She dug he elbows into his pectoral muscles, till she got a reaction of pain. "You are trying to make me give up" she said.

"Give up on what?"

"Give up on going to Lebanon."

"What's wrong with trying to stop you from getting yourself hurt or killed?"

"Nothing, except you are willing to get yourself killed."

"Its me, my body, and I can risk it, its no one's corporeal existence but mine."

"That's where you are wrong."

"How am I wrong?"

"You saved my life, you own me just a little bit."

"I don't own you, and if you think I do, you can take it back."

"I don't want it back. By owning, you assume responsibility for me, and that means you can't just go and get yourself killed."

"Is it better that we both lose our lives?"

"Our lives have meaning to each other, you just said you loved me."

"You are a crafty one, aren't you?"

"You have no idea." Karen laid her head into the hollow of his neck. "Joe?"

"I am here."

"I want you to make love to me."

"Karen, why are you doing this to me?"

"Because I have wanted you for two and a half years, this is my first opportunity."

Joe held her head between two palms and slowly forced her head up and stared into her eyes. "*Two and a half years*?" He asked with incredulity.

"Ever since you came on the unit with a stone-cold face and the laconic 'good morning' that sounded like a prelude to a funeral." Joe broke up into a massive guffaw that rocked them both. Karen laughed too, he looked so much younger, and innocent, and free, when he was laughing.

"Was it that bad?" He asked, still chuckling.

"Worse, because it never changed. No meanness, no anger, no friendliness, no hostility, not even if I badgered you enough to drive someone else round the bend! You were like a Medicine Robot with an inexhaustible battery."

"Poor Karen, Beautiful Nurse ignored by Doctor."

"Do you honestly think I am beautiful?"

"You *are* beautiful. If I were a man I would ravish you on the spot!!"

"But you *are* a Man" she beat on his chest, ineffectually.

"Physically, I am. Emotionally?..."

"Then let me help you be one" Karen said forcefully.

"And what shall be your reward, milady?"

"Your undying and everlasting gratitude."

"That's what I am afraid of. *My* undying? I wished I were dead many times, and I tried hard!!"

"Its time to stop trying. I wont permit it!!"

"You sound worse than my Grandma, I wont permit you this, Motorcycles are bad, stay out of the Sayeret Golani. I am not the issue here. People who love me getting killed is the issue!"

"Is that why you don't want to make love to me?"

"Yes."

"All right, you are so stubborn, I wont take NO for an answer, but I can put it off, can we sleep together?"

"I love sleeping with you."

"That's good, can you imagine yourself saying this a year ago, or even two months ago?"

Joe saw her point "No, not a chance."

She rose on her elbows again, her breasts hanging enticingly right in front of his eyes "See? We are making progress" and she fell on his lips and extracted a real response, from all over that big muscular body.

"Joe, Joe wake up."

He was bathed in sweat again, the nightmare devoured his sleep, and he was in an adrenergic rush, pupils dilated, heart beating hard, sweat pouring, muscles clenched, mouth dry. Karen shook him some more and he woke up with a start. Recognizing the room he was in he fell back exhausted. Karen reached up and snapped the light on. It was two AM.

"Joe, what is it?"

"It's the same thing all over again."

"What thing, say it , tell me."

"Do you remember that scary movie, Aliens? Where this monster rips through the crewman's belly and later kills everybody on the spaceship?"

"I remember."

"I can see Helen on the operating table, face down, with her skull split open, and the Tumor is rising out of the skull, and assumes this awful toothy slimy monster face and then jumps out of the skull, and it's after everybody, my dad, my mom, my grandma, and Raffi, and I keep chasing it and it keeps getting them."

"Who is Raffi?"

"He was a friend in Officer Training school. He was canned for the second time, and he couldn't take it, 'cause his dad was a Major General or something, so he put a Galil into his mouth and pulled the trigger, his room in the barracks was two rooms away from mine."

"Don't tell me anymore, I have to get you out of this wet pajama, come-on, go, go to the bathroom."

Joe allowed her to push him out of bed, into the bathroom, and into the shower. She helped him strip off the sodden top and turned her back as he stripped off the bottoms. He remembered his mom doing the very same when he was a five year old with the night-terrors typical of that age. His fondness for Karen kept growing and growing, he could not stay impervious to the emotional investment she was sinking into him. Resistance was futile, as the Borg said.

She held the unisize bathrobe for him, eyes still averted, and he took her in his arms, close to his naked body, and he could feel her almost dissolving into his skin through her ridiculous scrubs. He kissed her hair, and forehead, and eyes, and cheeks and mouth. Not with lust, not yet, but with sheer gratitude.

The nightmares stayed away for the rest of the night. It was cold and bright again when she woke up, unrequited, but still, companionable. She found Joe leaning his head on his hand, and examining her features closely, his glasses off.

"What?" she said.

"You are still beautiful in the morning" he said.

"Yeah, right , like Hiroshima after the Bomb."

"No, I was at Hiroshima, it's actually very impressive, but not beautiful. More like awful."

Karen jumped up and headed to the bathroom. She brushed her teeth with vigor, then she came back to bed. "That's what I meant, awful" she said.

"*You* are beautiful. Have you ever seen the shadow of a man?"

"Of course, sometimes we have the Sun visit Milwaukee."

"No, I mean the shadow remain when the man is gone."

"Like Peter Pan?"

"Yes."

"Only in Peter Pan books."

"In Hiroshima they show a set of stone stairs, which used to lead to a bank. On those stairs the Bomb left only the shadow of a man."

"How is that possible?"

"The Gamma rays hit the man who was sitting on the steps, waiting for the bank to open for business, and bleached out the stone around him. The Infrared heat rays vaporized his flesh and the air blast picked his bones up and scattered them to the four winds, one thing followed the next in a twinkling of an eye. Only the shadow of the man remained."

"Oh wow."

"For years I felt like the shadow of the man."

"And now?"

"Better, *much* better."

"And what is my reward?"

"Breakfast at the Bavaria Inn. They have Sunday Brunches which are positively sinful."

"You're cheap, aren't you!"

"You have no idea."

Karen placed her hand on his chest, and slowly passed her hand under the cloth of the pajama. She felt the response in those pectorals and tiny nipple. "You'll pay, one day, and dearly."

"Do you want to see the Gadgets?" Joe asked over the half finished ice-cream.

"Those I didn't pay for?"

"Yup, FedEx promised by eleven-thirty, I guess we should get there before."

"Good. Because if I eat any more of this Lemon meringue you'll have to scoop me off the floor." Contrary to her words, Karen rose from the dining table as if floating up and let Joe admire her flat bellied profile, and proud bust.

"It's a waste of money to take you to one of these places, where it's a free buffet. You hardly ate anything."

"It's not the quantity, it's the variety."

"Is that what you do with Men?" They were heading out the door, and it was very cold and bright. Karen rounded on him, eyes flashing.

"Listen you, for the last two and a half years I did not let a man get near me, just because you were around, and believe me plenty of them tried." She whirled around and stomped to the Grand Am. Joe was left rooted. She was even more beautiful when she was angry. He followed at a safe distance.

She drove very carefully, wary of the ice patches.

"Don't blame me Karen, I did absolutely nothing to make you avoid men. You could have gotten married, and had three kids by now."

"You were there, that was enough."

It began to dawn on Joe that the relationship Karen had with his person was rather like the one he had had with Helen, except it was a one way street. Karen had loved him from a distance, across the bulwarks of his dead affect, professional behavior, and total lack of recognition. The depth of her investment was incredible, it was a mistake, he could not be the one who aroused such feelings in a woman, not after he had failed the women in his life, young and old, so miserably. Karen drove to his apartment in silence. In silence they mounted the steps, and in silence she looked at Helen. Joe took the chair-that-rocks, and straddled it so he could face her.

"Karen, please give me a chance, You have been having these feelings for a long time. I am just waking up to the possibility of the *existence* of such feelings. Go slow, you have been patient or so long..."

Karen shifted her deep-blue eyes to him, twisted her mouth in a rueful grimace. "Its like the Nationals. You worked so hard to get there, to get to the final race, you can't believe you still have to *run* that race, the prize is so close, and it can still repudiate you, and snuff out everything you worked for, and there is no second chance, 'cause the next Nationals are two years away, and you just can't repeat the same effort again, I was a champion skater once, 500 and one thousand meters." So that's how she got these fantastic legs and body, Joe thought.

"Am I such a prize?"

"Like the medal, it's a piece of metal to one, a lifetime achievement to another. I am the 'another'."

"I don't know what to say."

"Say nothing, do something, actions speak louder than words."

"And I always thought I was a man of action."

"You are, I have seen you in Action, throw some my way, I ain't asking for much."

"Wrong, you are asking for everything" Joe said.

"Maybe, let's start with something."

Joe got up from the chair, went on his knees to face the proud eyes, and buried his face in her lap "I don't deserve you" he said, voice muffled by the cloth, she noticed the slacks were getting wet. She ruffled the black-brown hair, the occasional white one, and said "Let me decide what you deserve" and it was as tender a moment as they had ever shared. The doorbell rang from below. Joe lifted his face up, then jumped up.

"That is either Chris or FedEx" He pressed the intercom button.

"Hello, who's there?"

"FedEx, delivery to mister,,, doctor Bergman."

"Coming" Joe smiled at her, sitting mute and prim on the threadbare sofa. "Now you will see how stingy I am" and clattered down the stairs.

He came up, holding a big package marked FRAGILE all over. He set it on the ratty coffee table and peeled off the paper carefully. Half way through the peeling process another ring came.

"That's Chris, he is the user" said Joe, and pressed the buzzer. The stairs creaked heavily as the big man came up, off duty jeans and flannel shirt and black bomber jacket.

"Hi Karen."

"Hi Chris."

"And what have we here?" Chris nodded at the box.

"Mission impossible" Joe said.

He unwrapped each item carefully, and kept the manual for each. Then he connected the battery chargers to the mains, and inserted the single use batteries into their receptacles. Karen found the invoice at the bottom of the box and whistled softly, the man knew how to spend on baubles, electronic ones. Then they tried them, one by one, and went to the other room and tried again, then Joe put on his coat, and walked out of the apartment, and walked until the reception faded, which was half a mile away, and came back, his face frosted up.

"I assure you that Milwaukee County Sheriff office doesn't have this kind of quality hardware" Chris informed them.

"That's because they pay the police personnel too much" Joe said.

"Really think so?" Chris said belligerently, "let me show you my paycheck."

"Let it go Chris, he is just pulling your leg" said Karen" and anyway, his paycheck as a senior fellow is not much to look at either."

"Yeah, let's fight who is poorer" said Joe, and grinned at Chris, who relented immediately.

"When are we going?" Chris asked.

"Going where?" Karen queried.

"To Indy, Joe and I are going to Indy today, I have Saidan's address, he has a number of unpaid parking tickets" Chris grinned.

"Slight change of plan, Chris" Joe said, "Karen will be coming with us."

Chris frowned "No offense Karen, but what for? I am going to question him and Joe will teleprompt me."

Joe shook his head "Karen and I are a team, and we work together. You do your part, Karen and I will do our part" and he was rewarded by the most luminous smile he had ever seen her flash, the hopes were back, and in force. She had finally driven that nail through that thick skull, she had finally made him understand, finally pried him loose enough so she could enter that shell safely. She stood up, gracefully elegant, and confident.

"When are we going?"

"This afternoon, we spend the night at Indy, and hit him at the early AM, when he is most vulnerable."

"Where did you learn that AM tactic?" Chris inquired.

"When we were in Lebanon, facing the Syrians, and Amal, and Hezzbola, and God-knows-who-else, we knew that was the time the energies are the lowest ebb, and surprise is most devastating. The routine was to get everyone up at dark for battle-stations, no one in the cot regardless of when they went to sleep, and stay at battle-stations until full light. They learned the hard way we were ready for them!" Chris looked at Joe with new respect, he was a vet too, and probably an officer. Chris had no special respect for officers, unless they were truly superior in Tactics and paid their men the proper respect.

"In that case, I'll make me an overnight bag" said Karen.

"How is Amanda?" Chris asked.

"Ask her yourself, she is in the hospital today, did she give you her pager number?"

"She did."

"There you are, she wants you to call her."

"You really think so? Does she like me that well? I am no Doctor, or Lawyer, or Engineer. I am just a veteran and a police Sargent, though Chief said he is putting in a recommendation for me to go back to Academy to make Lieutenant."

"You men. Amanda doesn't care a hoot about suffixes, MD, PhD, ATTY, those mean didley. It's Decency, Honesty, Care, and a good strong back" and she winked at him raffishly.

"So you think I have a chance with her?" he asked eagerly.

"More than a chance, just stay yourself and don't pose."

"All right, I'll call her. It's one thing catching her when she is low, and on the rebound. It's another when she is with it and in her element."

"See you Joe, come pick me up" and she smacked him a good one.

They drove in the Grand Am, the consensus being this was the newest, and likely, the most reliable car of their little pool. Karen drove as far as the I-65 turncff, then Chris took the wheel and Joe opened up the Armada and located the address, which was on the north-west side of Indianapolis. Strange, that was where the bulk of the Jewish institutions were, according to the Sierra Streets disk, the JCC and the Day school and the synagogues. Guided by Joe, Chris went off the freeway on 78th street, and continued till they saw St Vincent. Adjacent to it was the Marten House, a motel which was part of the hospital system. Joe had reserved for them two adjacent rooms, it was ridiculously inexpensive, relative to the amenities.

"These are the keys Doctor, and they also open the rear entry doors to the pavilions, welcome to Indianapolis."

They deposited their bags in the rooms, Karen and Joe took one room, and Chris, the other.

"Let's case the joint" said Chris. He was the professional now, and he took charge.

The street lights in Indianapolis left something to be desired, but Chris carried the powerful Maglight, long as a baton, with which he scanned the tree-lined streets, with the wide snow-dusted lots, all decorated festively with Christmas lighting, a tree in most windows. Although that section of town was heavily Jewish, still, they were but a minority. They found the small brick house fairly easily, it was as unremarkable as a house can get. A garland with a red bow was on the door, and a Christmas tree was visible. The houses on each side did not display those outward signs of Christmas, and their door jambs showed Mezuzas, something that Joe could ascertain from the car using the Russian Army Starlight Amplifier bino-culars he had acquired from the Sharper Image. Joe was intrigued.

"What's wrong Joe?" Karen was finely tuned to his facial expressions by now.

"I was wondering, this looks like a regular house of a regular married couple."

"Well, maybe he is married."

"But if he, as a foreigner, was married a Christian American wife, why does he need the H1 visa, or apply for a Green Card? His spouse can just apply for citizenship."

"Maybe the information is wrong."

"Perhaps, but that Cheryl seemed to know what she was saying."

"OK, I have it" Chris interrupted, "that's a good spot to park, I am going out, check the equipment." The huge man exited the car laboriously and walked away, singing to himself "Oh what a beautiful morning" in the gloom of the 10 PM suburban night. Joe let Karen follow him with the binoculars long after he had disappeared in the gloom, and when the display started fading, he called.

"Chris, can you hear me?"

"Loud and clear, Lieutenant Doctor."

"Stay where you are, we'll come and pick you up" Karen drove the car for about half a mile again, and let Chris into the back.

"We have 6 hours, let's make the best of them" Joe said and Karen chuckled to herself, I wonder what he has in mind.

"I am going into the shower, or do you want to go first?" Joe said.

"You go first."

He was just washing off the soap and shampoo, kindly provided by the Marten House, when he heard the knock on the bathroom door.

"I'll be done in a minute" he called.

"Can I come in?" Karen asked diffidently.

"I am buck naked."

"That's fine with me."

"Door's open."

Karen padded in, pulled the shower curtain aside, and assessed the view. She was clad in a large bath towel.

"I am at a disadvantage here" Joe pointed out, pointing the shower stream into his own eyes. Karen let the bath towel fall and stepped into the bathtub. He tried, unsuccessfully to control the sharp indraw of breath. Body-wise, she was Helen, although not as tall and willowy, she was more toned and robust. The neck and head was all Karen, unabashed, but ready to be rebuffed, despite her splendid form and offer. His corporeal response was immediate, his brain screamed 'How can I deal with a woman who gives herself so Completely.'

"Turn around" she said, like a mother telling her child, her beloved child. He did.

Karen poured some soap onto the bath-sponge and rubbed his back, hard, with the rough side. Joe shivered with pleasure. To complete the torture she raked four nails on either side of the spine, raising eight wheals top to bottom over that wide expanse.

"Turn around" and he did again, still holding on to the shower head, his eyes closed. "Open your eyes" she commanded, and he did, taking her wet hair, the deep-blue eyes, the mischievous smile, the perfect breasts, right just slightly lower than left, and the flat belly, taut, all the way down to the bushy dark-blond triangle.... Enough to drive a man mad with desire, if he were normal. He was approaching normalcy, but not yet. Karen poured more soap on the sponge and raised some lather on the broad chest, well-defined pectorals, covered with a rather fine fuzz of hair. She was intoxicating .

"Feel clean?" she asked.

"Very."

"You can go now, I'll finish up in a minute."

"Not so fast, turn around" She did.

He soaped her back, and pressed the balls of his thumbs into the para-vertebral muscles so hard that she squirmed, with pleasure. The flare of her hips was fantastic and he passed both hands over the tightly clad iliac crests, stopping short of the triangle.

"See you in bed" he said, she nodded, still bemused by the sensations evoked by those powerful fingers.

She came to bed, completely naked, total lack of embarrassment, and laid her head on his outstretched arm, feeling the large biceps contract as he flexed him forearm to turn her head towards him.

"That was very brave of you" Joe said quietly.

"I have dreamed this shower scene for weeks now, it was just like repeating the dream, every step preordained."

"I am still not ready, Karen."

"I am, and I'll be waiting."

"Can you sleep now?"

"If you can, I will."

"Good night Hel... sorry,, sorry, Karen."

"Don't be sorry, she was your first and only love, it's a good mistake."

Joe didn't trust himself to speak. He flexed his arm to bring her closer, and kissed her forehead and eyes, so gently, it was the touch of a butterfly wing, and so it was on the lips.

"Happy new year" he said.

The Armada squealed a chirping alarm, and Joe was awake instantly. He covered the machine with his pillow and swung his legs out. He tried to go to the bathroom without a light and stubbed his toe.

"Ouch" he said, through clenched teeth.

"You can put the light on" Karen said from the bed.

"Good, did you get any sleep?"

"Some, what time is it?"

"Four AM."

"A good time for bad things to happen."

"That's what we are counting on." He went quickly through the necessary ablutions and while Karen did he knocked on the adjoining door.

"I'm awake" said the muffled gravely voice.

They were out the door at five fifteen AM, the majority of the time was taken by setting up the equipment on Chris. The button camera was in his front pocket. The earphone stuck to his mastoid, the microphone to his other pocket, the transmitter in his waistband on one side and the battery packs on the other. The voice and visual monitors were set up in the car.

"I look like a an ad for I Spy" Chris grumbled.

Karen was less critical. "You look like a very authoritative policeman."

The drive was short. The streets were deserted, and poorly lit, it was not as cold, but instead the snow was coming down, gently.

Chris strode to the door and used his Maglight to bang on it. He banged three times before the porch light came on. Joe and Karen watched on the monitor.

"Who is it?" A male voice.

"Sargent Wilkins, Glendale police, open up."

"*Police*? *Glendale*? where the hell is Glendale?"

"I repeat, for the last time, POLICE, is this the residence of Munir Saidan?"

There was some kind of an altercation behind the door, but then it opened up carefully, and Chris shoved his Shield into the man's face.

"Can I come in, please!" His voice made it obvious this was not a request.

"All right, all right, you can come in, mind the door." Chris almost had to duck.

They were two men, both clad in identical silk pajamas and silk housecoats, one shortish, thin, with a wire-thin moustache, glasses askew on his face, meek. The other bigger, dark auburn shiny hair, wearing a truculent expression, positioned a little forward. With a little imagination one could see how the smaller one was hiding behind the big one.

"They are a gay couple" said Joe.

"That's right" said Chris.

"What's right?" asked the big one belligerently.

"It's the right place" Chris covered up, "Who of you is Munir Saidan?"

"That's me" said the short one, retreating further from the threatening presence.

"Mister Saidan..." Chris started.

"DOCTOR Saidan, if you please, sir" said the big one.

"Of course, Doctor Saidan, I need to speak to you in private, this is an official police investigation regarding a Federal Felony which was perpetrated in *my* jurisdiction." Munir was almost hurled back by the weight of the words, Federal Felony. Chris continued, unrelenting "I suggest we sit down and Talk, or we can go in the car and go to Wisconsin, right now" Munir reeled at the word Wisconsin, and cringed.

"You can't talk to him like that" protested the big one, not very convincing.

"What is your name, sir?" Chris turned his full glowering attention to him.

"George Moniz."

"You will notice, Mister Moniz, was that all I asked of Doctor Saidan was to talk to him, I said nothing about arrest. On the other hand, refusing to do this basic minimum will constitutes an Obstruction of Justice, which in a case of Kidnaping, is very serious."

"Scary" said Joe.

"You bet I am" said Chris.

The couple was totally bewildered, it was the time, the Power this man exuded...

"George, George darling, let's just sit down and talk" Munir beseeched. he turned to Chris, "Can George stay? He's family, I would tell him everything later anyway, please?"

"Let them" said Karen, "he will feel less intimidated, less lies."

"All right" said Chris.

"This way" said Moniz and led them into the small comfortable living room dominated by a large green well-decorated Xmas tree.

Chris sat on the edge of a recliner, took off his coat. The men sat on the love-seat, a family in distress.

"Doctor Saidan, are you familiar with Doctor Mustafa Halim?" Saidan cringed again, like a blow he had expected for a long time, like a nightmare coming true.

"Yes" he said, almost in a whisper.

"Doctor Halim kidnaped his daughter from her home and fled to the Middle East. We suspect this was the final part of a bigger conspiracy."

"What conspiracy, what does Halim have to do with Munir?" George asked.

"Hush George, this is Big trouble, is the child all right?" asked Munir.

"We don't know. What we *do* know is that a year ago, Doctor Halim came here to see you at Riley, twice in as many weeks."

"We feel you may be a part in the conspiracy and kidnaping" said Joe

"And the proximity of events implicates you in a conspiracy and Kidnaping."

"Me ? Kidnaping? I never knew he had a child!!" Munir cried "I am a scientist, a virologist."

"A molecular biologist" Joe said.

"Molecular virologist" Chris said, the man cringed again, this police-man knew too much. "What was the purpose of the visit, Doctor Saidan?"

"I developed a virus for him" said Munir, in a small voice. George Moniz twisted in the love-seat and gave his spouse a startled look.

"What kind of virus?"

"A mutated virus."

"What was the basic virus?" Joe prompted. Chris was jotting things down, buying time. "What disease does this virus cause?" Chris asked.

"Its not a disease, it's a vaccine, the Sabin vaccine, the live one."

"Shit" said Joe

"Shit" said Chris, and jotted furiously.

"What was the mutation?" Joe said, and Chris repeated.

"Actually it was not just one but a number of Mutations." Doctor Saidan warmed to the subject, he was on firm ground, and this policeman understood, and maybe the Kidnaping spectre would be lifted, and his Green Card application would stay, I hope he doesn't know about THAT "Mustafa got me, and a bunch of others, two main sequences, and I transfected them into the viral genome, with the appropriate promoters and LTR's and so on."

"Is one of the sequences used to Target a gene on the Y chromosome?" asked Chris.

"How did you *know?*" Munir was almost stupefied.

Chris stared at him malevolently. "We know a Great Many Things, Doctor, Go on." Chris was a Star Wars fan, as well as a Trekkie.

"OK, the target was a sequence, found, so Mustafa said, only in one ethnic group, something Jewish, but I don't know what."

"And what else?"

"The other main gene is a malignant transformation gene" Munir was getting quieter, George was looking at him with more and more disgust, and was edging away from Munir.

"Bingo" said Joe "Do you know what kind of malignant disease this gene represents?" Chris repeated verbatim.

"No."

"Press him" Joe said.

Chris stopped jotting and skewered the poor Munir "Doctor Saidan, so far you have told me enough to implicate you in a conspiracy, and a wide scale conspiracy, with a known felon, you better go on, maybe you can climb out of the hole you are in. "

"It's the gene found in 1:17 translocations in certain neoplasms. I know Mustafa personally decided on this gene. Its probably Neuroblastoma" and Chris jotted some more.

"Look, Officer... officer..."

"Wilkins."

"Officer Wilkins, this was a just a mental exercise. Mustafa got me the funding, the collaboration, the help, the materials, to do something I could never attempt otherwise. It was a Molecular Biology achievement, to design a virus that could target a specific gene, integrate, and express the gene product taken from another organism. I wasn't the only one. The same thing was done in a bunch of other laboratories." George got up and went over to the door. "George, don't leave, I need you now." Munir pleaded.

"How *could* you, Munir?"

"It was a challenge, a scientific challenge!!!"

"FUCK Challenge" screamed George "don't you realize what you have done? You made a *virus* that targets *people*, and gives them a *disease*, a *malignant* disease!!"

"George... I... I didn't think he would use it, and it was only in cells, petri dishes... please George, don't leave... " Munir was piteous.

George became cold, cold as Ice. "What would you say, Munir, if someone could target Gays, find out what makes Us, and Target Us, like Roaches, or Pests, is THAT a worthy challenge?"

Munir was crushed, his hands went to his eyes and he wept, and wept, Chris waited him out. "Are you getting all this?" he asked quietly.

"Its all on tape" said Karen, in charge of recording.

"We called it the Jewish Genome Project, and initially we were looking for Chromosome 6 similarities, you know what I mean?"

"Say yes" said Joe, and Chris nodded emphatically, although he had no idea, whatsoever.

"And we met at ASH, as a group of Arabic speaking PhDs. This Doctor from Toronto came up with it, a sequence that was specific to a large Jewish group, like a Hamula, a big family, that was absolutely specific for them. Mustafa was the head of the organization. He was the one that assigned responsibilities, tasks and funding. I just did whatever I was doing anyway, except with the material and data that he provided. My construct worked. It targeted the Y chromosome in cells taken from Jews and did not do that for any other Y chromosome."

"Where did you get the cells?" Chris asked that of his own volition.

"Each member of the group solicited blood from their Jewish colleagues." Munir's face was working, his hands clenching and un-clenching.

"OhmyGod" said George with horror.

"The virus, where from?" Joe prompted "What was the source of the virus?" Chris repeated.

"The virus? That was the easiest part of the whole thing, it was the regular Sabin vaccination any Doctor can buy from the Health Department, that's how I got it, and everybody else too!"

"How long did you work at it?"

"Four years, at least, two before the Fontana meeting and two after."

"All of our life together" George said with wonder "And I didn't know."

"What was there to know?" Munir cried with exasperation, "it was just lab work, clone this, PCR that, the cycler broke down, do it again, set the temp up just right, sonicate the cells, purify, hybridize, transfect, illuminate, microscope, send pictures, get mail, fail, try again, it was *just Work.*"

"Yeah, work that kills" George said.

"Ask about Mustafa" Joe prompted. "What did Mustafa do with the product?" Chris asked.

"First he confirmed that my construct actually worked, I know he sent a vial each to two other virologists, but he didn't tell me who, and I didn't ask. He came back two weeks later for some more virus cultures and I gave him my stock."

"Did he know what the viruses were for?" Karen prompted.

It was as though George had heard her. He faced Munir, still standing at the doorway. "Did you know what the viruses were for, did you ask this Mustafa?"

"He wanted to tell me, I didn't want to know" Munir had his eyes on the carpet, the spot was very minute, and he wanted to disappear into it.

"Because you knew!!" George accused venomously.

"Samples, ask for samples" Joe prompted.

"Doctor Saidan, did you keep any samples of the mutated virus?" Chris asked, very officially.

"One vial."

"In the lab?"

"No, it's in the fridge."

"In the Fridge? *Our* fridge?" George almost choked with horror and fear.

"Why not? it's perfectly safe, we are immunized to Polio, and anyway, we are not Jewish."

"*We* are not Jewish? You fucking asshole, my Grandmother was Jewish." George exploded, his face was red as a beet.

"Uh, sorry to hear that, I didn't know" Munir apologized innocently.

"*Sorry to hear that?*" George almost hissed "She was a wonderful woman, she was the only one who didn't try to force me straight and loved me!"

"But I love you too, George, believe me, I , , I would never put you at risk!!" Munir stammered.

"Get the sample" Joe prompted.

"Doctor Saidan, show me the evidence" Chris. Commanded. Munir rose, like a 90 year old, he could hardly put one foot in front of the other, and trudged heavily, each step a minute, to the small kitchen. He opened the Amana, and pulled out the veggie drawer. He closed the Amana and went over to the island, and turned the drawer over. Joe, who was watching on the monitor was transported to another room, a sick old man, drawer inverted, Death taped underneath. The cucumbers and tomatoes rolled out and the vial was taped to the drawer in a groove. Saidan peeled it away and suddenly his face turned into a snarl and he hurled the vial to the sink. He didn't get far. The iron fist caught his in midair, vial safely inside, and the other iron hand forced the clenched palm open, his resistance was puny against the huge strength that Chris Wilkins brought to bear. Chris took the vial and placed it in his shirt pocket. Munir looked at his crushed hand, what a useless gesture.

"Go to the living room and wait for me" Chris commanded. George was at the kitchen door, his face was ashen, like someone who sees his entire life crumble before his eyes. Chris gave him a reassuring clap on his shoulder and went past. George followed him weakly.

Munir was back at he love-seat, occupying the same side, waiting for George to take His place. But George wasn't coming.

"Ask about other contacts of Mustafa" Joe prompted.

Chris pulled out his notebook and faced Munir. "Tell me about Mustafa's other associates."

"I don't know much, I saw colleagues at the Fontana meeting, after that it was E mail only, Shafiq Hader for instance, I never saw him. The Muslim brothers don't look kindly on Gays."

"That's why we rented the place here, between two Jewish families, so your bigoted friends don't come to visit" George retorted "Didn't you know what this Virus was for?"

"No" Munir cried "all I did was make a genetic engineering construct."

"That's like saying the makers of Zyklon B were making a Pest Chemical" George sneered, "that's what the Nazi Chemists claimed, a Pest Chemical to kill Jews and Gays. I can't believe I lived with you for four years while you were making an agent of Ethnic Cleansing!!"

"Hear hear" Joe said.

"And what have you got against Jews, anyway?" George continued. Chris just twisted his body this way and that, to let Karen have a good recording.

"They took away our Homeland" Munir said sullenly, inadequately.

"*What* Homeland? You live here in Indianapolis for Pete's sakes, next to a bunch of Jews! And what about Jean Markowitz who dressed up the cut you had last week, did *she* steal your homeland too??" suddenly he turned on Chris. "Did this Virus kill anybody yet? That you know of, that you are *sure* of?"

"One man and 6 kids, that we know of" Joe said.

Chris nodded at George "Seven persons, that we are aware of, maybe more." Munir seemed to involute into his sofa, to escape the burning stares of the men facing him.

Suddenly George turned, and ran upstairs. Munir, his face mad with anguish shot out of the seat and rushed after him. Chris stayed in the recliner, he too was spent by the emotional discharges.

"What now?" He asked.

"I think we have all we need right now, we can always get to him another time" Joe said. Chris took his coat and walked out into the early morning, the bare trees, the light just beginning to show. He crossed to the side street and into the parking lot of the small complex. Chris settled into the back. Karen twisted to look at him.

"They might think it strange if you don't conclude this interview in a Police-like manner."

"If I go in there again I might snap his scrawny neck, did you see how he tried to destroy the vial?"

"Partially" Karen commented "there was a lot of violent movement, but the sound-track says it all."

Suddenly a man came out the house across the street, holding a small suitcase, and tore open the car door. The other, obviously Munir, was holding on to him, to his hand, then to his coat. The bigger man shook him off violently and Munir fell down on the frozen grass, and tried to scramble up, and slipped and fell heavily on his face. George started the engine, gunned it violently and the little Sunfire jumped in reverse and a violent swerve, scraping the post of the carport. Munir tried to get up again, and his slippers slipped again. George changed to Drive and the little car spun its wheels and then caught traction and surged forward, and away, down the street. Lights were coming on in the adjoining houses. Munir picked himself up, slowly, and whimpered his way back to the house.

"Chris, it's very important you talk to him, tell him, warn him, not to talk to Mustafa or anybody, make it gentle and decisive" Karen said urgently.

"Right, right" Joe chimed in, "if he talks then Mustafa will can this plan and will start another one." They could see the second floor light dim and brighten, as Munir was moving inside that room. Then the movement stopped.

"So you want me to warn this miserable turd not to talk?" Chris was flexing his huge hands.

"Yeah, be careful, don't harm him, otherwise we become as bad as he is."

"OK, although it'd be better if you tied my hands." Chris was almost out of the car on Joe's side when the shot rang out, clear and crisp in the early morning cold air, Chris was about to run when Joe hand locked on his arm, with tremendous force, that checked the big man.

"Don't, we can't show ourselves, we can't help, the neighbors are awake, they'll call 911." Chris collapsed back inside. Karen shut off the recorder. Joe started the engine, and very slowly he drove the car to the far side of the complex, came out the other side, and carefully drove away, accelerating very slowly. They could hear the Paramedics coming full tilt on the parallel road across the trees, and there they were, going Ninety

"Poor George, they are going to grill his ass" Chris said. They were sitting in a small diner, each with a coffee.

"And then they are gonna grill *your* ass" Karen said "we didn't plan that, at all."

"Who knows where he went, and anyway, let them. If we had gone for this information in the Ususal Way, we might still be at it next Xmas" Chris concluded.

"What are we going to do with this vial?" asked Karen.

"We have to confirm Munir's testimony." Joe replied.

"How?"

"I will give this to Bev Kreissman. She will take it to the CDC and get them to sequence the whole damn genome. It's only a virus, they can do that, and look for the elements of Promoter, Enhancer, malignant transformation, and so forth. And they will compare it with the original."

"What original?" Chris was baffled "I thought this was the original."

"It is, but what I mean is, we know which vaccination is used, and a sample of the Lot Numbers are kept in every Health Department, in case of trouble. We got trouble."

"Memphis?" Karen asked.

"Yup, I'll rent a car, somewhere."

"What is my job?" said Karen

"Find out who supplies the Sabin vaccine, could be one, or two, can't be that many, and then look for employees, off our lists, maybe we'll get lucky."

"And me?" asked Chris.

"Go make Amanda happy, no really, if there is something I need you to do I'll find you, or Karen will. Take care of all the gear. Karen, I'll give you a call tonight."

Chapter 19

Joe's Trial

Karen drove them to the closest rent-a wreck in the yellow-pages. Joe knew that no one would rent him a general aviation aircraft on the weekend. The grizzled black mechanic had taken the red Camaro with a busted transmission due to severe abuse from a young man who had agreed to the estimate but dematerialized when it came time to pay. After much paperwork the Camaro joined his little fleet of rent-a-wrecks, by which the mechanic sought to recoup the costs of unpaid work and parts. The mechanic loved his cars and made the Camaro better than it ever was, a fine mount for a man in a hurry. Joe paid for the car for one week in advance, and left the imprint of the Chase Visa with the owner who was mightily surprised to make a buck on New Year's day, so he filled it up and threw in a small Igloo refrigerator for no extra charge which connected to the lighter jack and hummed softly. Karen and Chris drove North, toward the colder weather, and Joe drove to Memphis, an eight hour trip.

About thirty miles north of Memphis Joe stopped for gas and food and put the Irridium phone to use. This was an inadequate trial because in the presence of local repeaters the transmission was carried locally rather than by satellite. Outside the range of local repeaters, the 77 satellites around the earth were supposed to pick up the call and transfer it to the recipient. Joe hoped fervently that theory would translate into practice when he needed it.

"St Jude."

"Hi, can I speak to Doctor Kreissman?"

"Let me page her for you.".....

"Doctor Kreissman" said an irritable voice.

"Beverly, its Joe."

"Where are you calling from, you sound weird" she said.

"I am thirty minutes away, can I see you?"

"If you must, I am finishing up in the Hospital, fourth floor."

"Fourth floor, see you" Joe signed off, wondering about her decidedly uninviting comment, as he entered the city on the freeway, the roads as clear as one can get, he wondered if he had said or done anything to annoy her, personally.

Beverly was in he usual place, dictating a note into the phone. She saw Joe come on the floor and signaled him to sit. Joe sat down and observed the pile of charts in front of her. Her beeper beeped, the phones rang, the residents scurried, the nurses went in and out of rooms with medications, blood bags, fluids and charts. It was thirty more minutes before she direc-ted her attention to Joe

"What a day, this has been a disaster weekend, kids crashing, new diagnoses, what brings you back here?" She said this with the shortest of tempers, Joe could understand very well, this was already the evening, and she had been on call for twenty four hours at least and she was not an eager-beaver intern anymore. Still, Joe had expected less belligerence.

"I have the infecting virus, we need to go to the CDC" Joe said and showed her the vial.

"I am not going with you anywhere. All you have is a vial with some amber fluid in it. Somehow you have been able to take me off the logical path and spin me out of control." Beverly retorted angrily. Joe was dumbfounded by the ferocity of the attack. He had expected an ally, not an enemy.

"So what about the eight children with Neuroblastoma?" he queried.

"Coincidence and chance, nothing else. I can't believe you were able to make me and Jerry go around the city and make fools of ourselves, on Shabbos too, and scare the Jewish community to death without any credible basis." She closed the chart in front of her with a resounding whack.

"All right, alright, will you watch a movie with me?"

"Doctor Bergman, if I want to watch a movie I will go speak to Spielberg, not you." and she got up to leave.

"Bev... Doctor Kreissman, please, give me one more chance" Joe pleaded.

She considered him for five long seconds, it was so uncharacteristic of this big man to plead..."What kind of a movie?"

"A confession."

Beverly positively jumped at the sound of the distant gunshot recorded by the camcorder. The screen clearly showed the date, the first of January, early AM. They were sitting in one of the conference rooms which possessed a video recorder and a TV. Presently she got up to switch the lights on, and Joe busied himself with popping the cassette from the VHS recorder, and rolling up the wired connections he had set up between the camcorder and the video recorder. He stowed everything in the capacious black bag, while Beverly regained her seat and held her face in her hands. Joe waited

"Doctor Bergman...."

"Its Joe."

"Joe, I don't know what to say, no, I *do* know, I apologize deeply for my..."

"Don't apologize" Joe cut her off "If I were you I would think the same too, but we MUST go on from here."

"What do we do?"

"We have some evidence but it's not scientifically conclusive. I suggest I go after the evidence worked up by the people in Van Vleet, the Genetics and the visual, and you go after the source of the virus, namely the Health Department. Then we go together to the CDC and present the evidence, and hopefully get some action. If we leave tomorrow midday we can be there tomorrow night and make our pitch the next day."

"But the CDC is in Atalanta and we are in Memphis!" she wailed out of the depths of her bottomless fatigue.

"I have a sports car."

Joe checked into the nearby Ramada Inn. After hauling his stuff inside he called Karen on the Irridium.

"Joe?"

"Yeah, how did you know?"

"You are the only one likely to call me at eleven PM."

"I guess that's good. How was your trip?"

"Having a policeman at the wheel is very useful. How did it go down South?"

"Doctor Kreissman was full of doubts, the tape convinced her, tomorrow we go on with the collection of evidence and the next day to Atlanta, how about you?"

"Taking a shower is awful lonely. Tomorrow I think I will try your phone tricks to get information about employees in the pharmaceutical companies, and match them with the lists."

"Which companies?"

"The PDR says there are only two, Lipjohn in Michigan, and Artour in Pasadena."

"Good idea."

"I miss you Joe."

"Me too."

"G'night."

To:helen.bergman@chw.edu
From:rachel. sodorski@aol.com
Dear Doctor Bergman
I think I am done with the annotation /identification of the sequences in the data from the disk.

The main sequence is of the polio virus, the Sabin mutated form. This virus is an RNA virus and contains the reverse transcriptase, the mechanism to revert to DNA once the virus has gained access to the cell nucleus plus all the elements needed for integration.

Within this sequence there are stretches which are not native to the virus RNA genome.

a sequence complementary to the published Katz sequence on the Y chromosome.

LCR (locus control region) with the DNAse hypersensitive configuration. The presence of this sequence means <u>extremely high transcription</u> of the ORF which follows.

Enhancer, from the CMV (CM virus) genome.

Open Reading Frame of a sequence presumed to be <u>tumor-promoting,</u> found within the 1;17 translocation.

38 percent of the sequence I could not annotate from the GenBank and other repositories

What shall do I with the computer?

Reply
Keep it

Joe was surprised to have slept well, with none of the usual nightmares. Despite the long days before and the hard days ahead he felt better rested than anytime in the last five years. He met Beverly in the usual place, the St. Jude cafeteria. Joe was on his second coffee. Beverly put down her small suitcase and looked at him curiously.

"What is it?" Joe verbalized her inquiry.

"You look different, somehow."

"Same glasses, same face, hair is shorter."

"I noticed the hair, that's not it, You look happy."

"That's overstating it."

"Don't duck, something happened in the last week to make you look and sound alive, and it sure ain't kids sick with Neuroblastoma, it must be a woman, who is it?"

Joe shook his head with amusement "talk about chauvinism, can't a guy be happy with a good book and a good night's sleep?" Beverly looked at him searchingly, she was right, he sounded free and happy. She fetched herself a coffee and came back.

"You can't fool me, OK, what's the plan?"

"I looked up the map. The Health Department is on Jefferson, pretty close to Van Vleet. I will stop at Van Vleet and you take the car to the Health Department. When you are done you can call me at this mobile number." He showed her the Iridium and she copied the displayed number.

"Nifty" she said.

"Expensive too."

"Come to think of it, how are you paying for all this out of a fellow's salary?"

"My grandmother is paying, let's go."

The city was chockerblock on the second day of the year, with much standing traffic. Joe exited the Camaro at the entrance and waved Beverly on. He headed for the bowels of the hospital to look for Doctor M. Mehta.

Doctor Marten Mehta was in her usual place, at the multi-head microscope, but this time she had two students to teach about the morphology of the intact and cholestatic liver. Joe put his big bag down and waited for her to look up.

"Doctor Bergman" her dark face lit up with true pleasure, I wonder what's going on today with all the ladies "You fly in quieter than a stealth fighter."

"Your radar is off, how are you doing?"

"Great, great, I have the paper all written up, a seventy four year old with Neuroblastoma, and I really wanted you to put your name on it."

"I hate to dampen your enthusiasm, but before we write anything up we have to talk to Shaker" Joe cautioned.

"Sure, let's do that right now, before he goes into the interminable teaching sessions in the afternoon, you guys" she addressed the students "I want you to read up on hepatic Pathology and review the slides in the box, I'll be back in an hour or so." She upped and left the lab, her short feet clicking away along the corridors. Joe grabbed his bag and followed closely.

Shaker was also at his usual place, in front of the 19 inch screen, facing away from the door, setting up a presentation. Lab workers flitted in and out of the nearby rooms, this was a busy department. The secret of American success lay in the ability to extract the best from people, regardless of their background, and reward them handsomely for their efforts, be it in tangibles, or intangibles such as prestige and recognition. Marten knocked on the open door and walked in, motioning Joe to follow. She took a seat and waited. Shaker saved the files and turned to them.

"Shaker, this is doctor Bergman, he directed our attention to the case of the Neuroblastoma in the seventy four year old" Joe extended his hand and was rewarded with a warm enthusiastic shake.

"Aha, the stealth fighter has landed I see, that's how Marten calls you, great case, GREAT case," Shaker went on with the same enthusiasm, "it is truly unique, and what's more, we are now beginning to recognize related cases. Let me show you, I have it all arranged for presentation in a album file." He swivelled the screen so they had a good view, Joe noticed the Compaq was hooked up to a Zip-drive, which allowed the exchange of voluminous files of 100 megabytes.

"This is the first slide, what we can see is a small round cell tumor, closely packed cells, with many mitoses, screaming Cancer." Shaker's voice slipped into presentation mode, clear, precise and didactic. "This sample was taken from a lung biopsy but it is representative of this very aggressive tumor." The fact that an aggressive tumor meant a dead patient did not bother Shaker in the least. This was not a person, this was a scientific challenge, and so it has been since medical science began, one person's tragedy was another's scientific achievement and triumph. "The cells were stained with a variety of specific stains, Sudan black, Neuro-enolase, none of which are positive enough to make a diagnosis. These slides are courtesy of doctor Mehta" and he inclined his head to recognize the young pathology resident.

"We come now to the Genetic analysis. This is a standard karyotype which shows a normal 44XY pattern, no overt duplications, translocations or deletions. The next slides demonstrate FISH analysis. The fluorescent marker shows up only if a selected DNA sequence is complemented by a probe. This is the control probe for Beta Globin chain residing on Chromosome 11. It shows up as bright red. This is a Y probe, which shows up as yellow. This is a new proprietary probe which I received from Newcastle, it's a probe for the putative Tumorigenic gene created by the juxtaposition of chromosome 1 and 17. This probe shows up blue in this control Neuroblastoma slide. I combined the two probes in the case in question, and as you can see, the color is green, meaning both probes segregate to the same location on the genome."

"At the same time, Doctor Mehta sent the slides to doctor Archibald Hohner at St. Jude, he recently presented evidence that the protein coded by the 1;17 translocation can cause malignant transformation. Doctor Hohner stained the cells for us with a monoclonal antibody, which, as you can see, stains the nuclei of the cells in deep brown."

"Finally, I subjected the DNA culled from the index case to PCR amplification, with intent to find the sequence published by Katz et al in Science two years ago...'

"Two years?" Joe interrupted "That's impossible, it's too short of a time!!"

"By the time a paper of such import is published the information is at least a year old. All these probes and antibodies which I presented are in the process of being reviewed and refereed by the scientific magazines. To continue, this autoradiograph shows that the said sequence can be amplified from the index case, but not from the controls."

"These findings were essentially the same in patients two through nine, who are male, and negative in patient 10 who is a female and patient number eleven who is an African ancestry male."

"To conclude, we have demonstrated a new pathologic entity, Neuroblastoma associated with a translocation of a malignant transformation gene which translocated to the Y chromosome. The Katz sequence is probably a susceptibility locus. It is not unusual that a ethnic entity may have a genetic traits which make it susceptible to certain kinds of cancer, such as Anaplastic Stomach Cancer in Japanese and BRCA 2 Breast Cancer Gene in North European females, still this is a fascinating entity which calls for further investigation and review of previously published series." Shaker finished his presentation with a flourish.

"Doctor Chandrasheker" Joe asked formally, just as he would have done in a scientific conference "can you think of any other explanation for this coalescence of events?"

Shaker concentrated on the slit-eyed investigator, then closed his eyes and folded his legs into the lotus position, back straight, a Buddha, and meditated. Marten looked at him with appreciation. He could have been a Guru somewhere, preaching sweet nothings to the adoring masses. Instead he utilized his heritage and teaching to crack scientific puzzles, to provide the basis for diagnosis and cure. Suddenly the black lashes flew open, and horror looked through.

"You think someone made this on purpose, that the susceptibility gene is in fact a targeting mechanism?" Joe nodded emphatically. Marten lost her color, became white as a sheet under her deep-olive natural pigmentation.

"But why?" Shaker was plaintive "why would anyone want to do such a thing?"

"Ethnic Cleansing." Joe said.

"Ethnic cleansing?" Marten echoed, her lips quivered.

"Yes, the Serbs cleansing Kosovo of Albanians, the Turks killing the Armenians, the Catholics ridding Ulster of Protestants, the Indians ridding Kashmir of Pakistani Moslems, Deutchland Uber Alles, it's all the same, just the means keep getting more sophisticated."

"How is it spread?"

"Sabin vaccination, genetically modified" both Indian scientists nodded. It all made sense now.

"But you are going to stop it?!!" Marten said, question and a fact rolled into one.

"Yes, this material can still be presented, with the appropriate proof, but not now, maybe in a year. Doctor Shaker, can you make me a copy of your excellent presentation?"

"You mean awful and hideous, don't you, certainly I can, in fact I have it already backed up into the zip drive." He popped out the thick diskette and gave it to Joe.

Joe placed it carefully into his evidence black bag. He got up to leave.

"Doctor Shaker, Doctor Mehta, thanks a million, I'll be seeing you" and he left.

"Flew in, flew out, with a bang." Marten said after a while "But you know what?"

"What?" shaker said, while backing up the file into a new diskette.

"He looks much happier then he did the first time he came by."

Beverly had a lot of trouble with the Camaro. She was used to the high seat and the unobstructed view afforded by the Chevy Astro minivan which was the vehicle she used for the day to day chauffeuring of the kids to and from the JCC, and the general commuting. The Camaro, with it's long snout and laid-back bucket seat scared her. She was certain that long power snout was going to run into vehicles, posts, and trees. Fortunately, she had only a short way to go from the Van Vleet to the Health Department on Jefferson.

She found a convenient parking spot across the street and ascended the steps slowly, rehashing her cover story.

"May I help you?" said the receptionist.

"Yes, I am looking for the person in charge of the vaccinations in Shelby County."

"That would be Missis Barkley, she is in room 206, who shall I say is coming?"

"Doctor Kreissman, from St. Jude."

Lea Barkley turned out to be a clone of Barb Petersen, an older lady of the Public Service, in bleached shoulder length hair. The ladies shook hands.

"We don't get many visitors from St. Jude, none in fact" Lea commented. "This is LebonHeur territory, we are scared to come cross this turf."

Lea Barkley laughed politely "My daughter is an intern at Lebonheur, and she has black bags under her eyes all the time. How can I help you?"

Beverly launched into her rehearsed pitch "I am following up on a set of vaccinations given to children after bone marrow transplant, they have to be revaccinated from scratch, you know" Lea nodded vaguely, she didn't really know, which encouraged Beverly to continue to expound. "A num-ber of kids received a vaccination from this lot number, with weaker-than-expected titer response. We are unsure if it was the kids or the vaccination itself. It was my understanding that you keep a sample of each lot that you distribute to the clinics."

"We do that. Was that OPV?"

"Yes." Beverly said, hoping that the good lady will not call her bluff. She would *never ever* give children who had had a Bone Marrow Transplant a live virus, even a weakened virus, especially when the killed virus, given by injection was a safe alternative. The OPV was generally preferred because it raises a better antibody response and promotes herd immunity by competing with the wild-type, disease-causing virus. But not in BMT kids. Their immune system was so weak, the OPV caused full-blown Polio.

"In that case you have to speak to Mister Altman, he is responsible for the warehousing and distribution of the shots, he knows everything that goes in and out of here. He is in the basement."

Walter Altman was nearing retirement age. But he was not counting the days because he was very happy at his present position which he had held for thirty years. He had been there when the OPV was new, when no one even thought of a shot for Hemophilus Influenza, the dread Meningitis bacteria. He wanted to be at his post to ship out the long-awaited AIDS vaccine. He was intrigued by the call that informed him of a visit by a Doctor Kreissman.

"Walter, how are you?" Beverly greeted him, she recognized the balding head, the silver fringe, the bifocals wedged on the bulbous nose, he was one of the community members, a regular who never missed a Saturday morning service, and could be counted on for every function.

"Doctor Kreissman? I always thought you were Doctor Stein!"

"That's Jerry's name, but I was a Doctor before I married, so my diplomas are all Kreissman."

"Ahuh, now I get it. What are you looking for? Lea told me it was a funny OPV?

"Correct."

Walter lowered his voice "does it have anything to do with the warning that Doctor Stein issued in Shull? I can tell you I was very surprised to hear Doc Stein say something about the shots, that I know nothing about, seeing shots is what I been doing for thirty years. I was even more surprised when I saw the Doctor leave the Shull and go into his car on Shabbos ! Me and Marcy, we always figured you to be very frum."

"We are" said Beverly quietly.

"This must be serious then, let me have that lot number." Beverly handed him the crumpled note. Walter scanned it quickly.

"Something fishy 'bout this lot," he clicked the computer "No, no recalls, no complaints, but I remember something fishy anyway." He punched the phone.

"Doug, oh Dougy" he called on the intercom.

"What is it Walt?"

"Take down this lot number and bring me the vials. Please."

"Why don't you send Ricky?" the phone screeched, a young voice.

"Cause you need the exercise, also I need your brains."

"That's better, read it out."

Beverly arched her brow, Walter just grinned and tapped the desk with his pencil. They waited for a while. Soon she saw why Walter thought the young man needed the exercise, Doug was a hugely fat, young black rolly-polly pack of bonhommie. He brought with him a small box which he handed to the older man. Walter compared the numbers printed on the label with the lot number that Beverly had shown him.

"That's it" he broke the box open, there were six red vials in it, entirely innocent, he held one up to the light, as if he could divine their misdemeanor by X ray vision. He looked back at the screen.

"Lipjohn, manufactured about ten months ago, no allergies, no side-effects, no recalls, so what is wrong with it?"

"Lemme see that number again" said Doug, he looked long and hard at the numbers.

"It's that nurse" he said finally.

Walter whacked his forehead with a mighty slap, which resounded like a gunshot in the confines of the small room.

"Yeah, Yeah, that wacky nurse, hand me that file box marked January, the one at the top." Doug stretched up, he was tall as he was round, and brought it down. Walter rummaged through it turning the pages furiously, "There, there," he almost drove his index through the page. Beverly and Doug craned their necks over it.

Walter was animated "usually the nurses who pick up shots for the Pediatric offices don't care about the Lot numbers except to sign them out. But this one" he jabbed again "asked for this specific lot number, weird." The signature on the slip was identical to the signatures at the Pediatric offices, Nadia Lubin.

"And she came back again, every time for anutha office" Doug added "an she asked for the same lot agin and agin."

"Me and Doug we remember *everything*, we don't need the damn computers which are gonna crash January One anyway" Walter chortled and held up his open palm for a high five, which Doug slapped. Doug turned and left, his huge buttocks rippling underneath the yards of cloth encasing them.

"Can you pack 2 vials for me?" Beverly asked of Walter .

"Gotta keep'em cold but not frozen" Walter said as he packed the vials in a small box with Styrofoam nuggets. Beverly remembered the small humming box in the cramped back seat which Joe had said to leave connected. Walter handed her the box.

"I noticed you kind of expected that name, Lubin" he said, his hand shaking just a little "anything special about her?"

Beverly took the box "she is dead, murdered." The hand remained in the air, but the tremor increased.

"Nobody knows why and how, so don't ask me" the hand dropped.

"I have to go now" Beverly said gently to the old man "When I know things better I will have Jerry tell everyone."

Walter recovered "Godspeed Doctor Kreissman" Beverly left quickly.

Beverly was out of the building before she recalled that she was supposed to call Joe. She was about to turn back when an ear-splitting short whistle cut the sounds of traffic. The reflex turned her head towards the source of the sound, and she saw Joe waving to her from the parking lot across the street. What a relief she doesn't have to drive that thoroughbred with the throaty motor anymore. The day was magnificent, the sun was out, the air was dry and Memphis flourished in the good winter air.

"What did you get?" Joe asked, observing her over the long magenta hood.

"Two vials, that need to be kept cold but not frozen." She unlocked the door and placed the small box along-side a similar box. She clicked the auto-lock open. Although the inside of the car was warm, a greenhouse effect of glass, the Igloo was cool. Joe got in at the driver's side and with a groan pushed the seat back to accommodate his much longer legs. Beverly seated herself and secured her seat belt. She opened the window, just a crack. As a religious woman she was not supposed to be in an enclosed space with a man not her husband, so the open window was a symbolic gesture. Beverly gave Joe the keys and he drove off. Joe stopped in front of a Radio Shack and came out with a small package in two minutes flat.

"And you?" she said as Joe drove the powerful machine onto the Seventy Nine and headed East.

"Nothing, nada, zilch" he said matter-of-fact.

"Nothing?" Beverly was incredulous, Joe smirked.

"Nah, just pulling your leg, those Indians gave me the works, lock stock and barrel."

"What Injuns?"

"Not Native Americans, real Indians, Bombay, Madras, who knows, Pathology and Genetics, I have a complete presentation on disk of the malignancy and how it is targeted at Cohanim, with FISH and PCR and the rest of the alphabet."

"So what's missing? There is always something missing" the traffic thinned out.

"Where is the mutated virus manufactured?" Joe asked.

"Lipjohn, assuming the chain of events is as we presume" she replied.

"Call Karen" and he gave her the phone number and the Iridium.

"Hello Joe."

"Just a second" Beverly said and passed the phone.

"Hi Karen."

"You sound on the road."

"To Atlanta, with lots of evidence."

"It's Lipjohn, right?"

"How did you know?"

"Muhi a Deen Shareef is employed there as a supervisor, for about a year, I played the Feds on the phone."

"Crafty." Joe laughed.

"I have a good teacher."

"I'll call you tonight, in the meantime get Chris to make us a false bottom in a medical case, for the gear."

"Love you."

Joe felt his face flushing "me too" and flipped it closed, tucked it into the leather jacket.

"I was right" Beverly said happily.

"About what?"

"It's a woman and I will pry no longer."

"Good, call Jerry, tell him where you are."

"On your airtime?"

"I told you my grandmother is paying, she doesn't need it anymore in this world."

Beverly shot him a glance of I-am-sorry and punched in the numbers for Jerry's office.

"St. Jude."

"This is Doctor Kreissman, can you please page doctor Stein?"

"Please hold."

....

"Hi bubby."

"Jerry, we are on our way to the CDC, in the reddest lowest sports car I ever rode in, tell me I am not nuts."

"Bubby, I told you a hundred times, you are the only sane person in an insane world!"

"Flattery will get you nowhere, who is our contact?"

"Doctor Corey Baille, she was an intern with me in Kansas, I emailed her that you were coming."

"Don't forget Moe has a music lesson at the JCC today."

"I wont, listen, Corey hates any waste of time, make your point and drive it to the hilt, and don't look anywhere under her neck."

"Jerry!"

"Don't say I didn't warn you, and doctor Bergman, Bye Bubby."

"Kisses to the kids."

"Take one yourself" and Joe could hear the prolonged smooch, he kept his face rigid. Beverly flipped the phone closed smiling to herself, Jerry was such a dear.

"He always does that, even if he knows the phone is open to the public" Beverly explained "in fact I think he does it on purpose when everybody and their little brother can hear!"

"Lucky you" Joe said.

"What about you? Any kids somewhere? That Karen sounded nice."

"She is a nurse at the HOT unit, and we are kinda at the beginning of a relationship."

"That's not what I asked."

"I almost had one, once, but I failed it too, and this is the end of this tack."

"You expect me to sit for seven more hours with you in a car no bigger than a matchbox inside and be quiet?"

"Talk about something else" Joe said, gripping the wheel tightly.

"I don't want something else, when I said 'kisses to the kids' you had a pained expression, fleeting, but I know what I saw, what happened to your kid?"

"Why should I tell you?" Joe said bitterly, the visual memory of the almost-human mess welling up from the recesses of his subconscious, vivid as if it happened the night before.

"Because I am a mother, I am a doctor, and I need to understand why you are willing to throw your life away for a stranger's child."

"Amanda isn't a stranger" Joe objected childishly, holding on against the onslaught on his personal self-inflicted pain.

"Neither is she some kind of a bosom friend, she is a colleague and no more!"

"How do you know?"

"I talked to Kammitzer last night, briefly, about you."

"He thinks I am finally off my rocker!" said Joe, almost with relief, the only person who trusted him also turned his righteous back on him, confirming his low self-esteem.

"Of course not!!" Beverly retorted "he said if he were younger by twenty years he would join you right now, but I asked about Doctor Carter and he said she was a Fellow, a colleague, and naught else."

"All right, I killed him" Joe said with explosive anger, his knuckles tightening and turning white on the wheel, the speed crept up, to seventy five, eighty, eighty five, ninety, the engine sound changed imperceptibly from a relaxed hum to a throaty snarl, they were too wound up to notice.

"Killed who?"

"My kid, I killed my own kid, with my own hands , my own brain, my own *stupid, vain decisions.*"

"That's bullshit, that's pure Bull-Shit, you wouldn't kill the Devil's kid, and *slow down*, I want to get back to mine." The speedo reeled down from 105 to 55, Joe still had the wheel and visibly relaxed his grip on it, his Granite mask was back on.

"Nevertheless, I did kill my own child" he said flatly, each syllable a hammer on the coffin.

Beverly took a little time to answer "I must say I am not impressed with the show of intelligence here, on the driver's side of this car," Beverly said matter-of-fact, "why don't we have a mini-trial right here, you are the prosecutor, God will be defense, I will be the Judge, Jury and Executioner."

"Since when is God on defense counsel?"

"Since forever, look up Noah, Court is in session, prosecutor, you have the floor."

"Ladies and ladies of the Jury, have you reached your verdict? Bailiff, hand me the verdict!" They were running in the dark, the headlight had popped up and pierced the darkness ahead, Atlanta 127 miles. The recess in the trial had taken place in a truck-stop which featured Kosher Jewish National hot-dogs, try *that* on the German Autobahn, Joe thought as he filled up on the gas for the guzzler, and drove off.

"And the verdict is:" Beverly continued sonorously...

"Count one: Self mutilation-Guilty."

"Count two: Inability to recognize human limits - Guilty."

"Count three: Illegal prolonged bereavement - Guilty."

"Count four: Death of wife and child, also of grandmother, mother and father, also of every other woman who ever died due to acts of Man or God - NOT GUILTY."

"Sentence to be given forthwith."

"The defendant, who is also the accuser, is given a life sentence of rebuilding his life, making a family, and fighting childhood disease."

"This is a life sentence without parole."

"Ladies and Gentlemen, the court will now stand down."

"Please drive carefully" Beverly finished breathlessly.

"You should have been a lawyer, you are a lousy, biased judge."

"So what, you agreed to the trial, now abide by the sentence,'cause the defense counsel is watching."

Joe stayed quiet for the next hour.

Atlanta 58 miles

"Do you remember the concept of trial by the hand of God?" Joe asked suddenly.

"Like Ivanhoe?"

"Yes, I have my own trial, in Lebanon. If I get out of there alive, again, then I will accept the verdict you handed down."

"You are really *hard* on yourself. I should have put it into the counts."

"Start looking for Motel signs, Tell us something nice about Moe and Sue."

They met in the Ramada Inn restaurant, where Beverly chose the fruits and vegetables, and Joe tried something of everything. They made minimal small talk and were out to make it to the CDC complex at eight thirty.

Doctor Corey Baille was waiting for them in the guard-house, It was just as well that Jerry had warned them, because she was enormously fat, a big woman who had lost all will to keep normal body proportions, and succumbed to the ravages of a high-calory diet. On top of the ungainly body resided a wholesome face and a ready smile and intelligent eyes behind the simple glasses. Beverly forced herself to look only above the neck, and soon forgot about the rest of the body. Joe found himself feeling some discomfort, which surprised him somewhat. A month or two ago he would have been untouched, having trained himself to disregard any female attributes, be they comely or ugly. I guess that means I am alive, and his mind flashed back to the shower at the Marten House.

"Hi, I am Corey, You must be Beverly Kreissman" she acknowledged Beverly first.

"Thank you for meeting us here" Beverly said, "this is doctor Joe Bergman, from Milwaukee, he carries the Big Bag." Joe extended his hand and was rewarded by a firm no-nonsense handshake.

"Jerry sounded very mysterious, I must say" said Corey as she arranged for them to get visitors passes to the huge complex. The guard was dumbfounded by the contents of Joe's big bag. The CDC is the US government agency which deals, among other issues, with infectious diseases.

The breadth and the scope of this assignment is mind -boggling because the CDC does not limit it's activities to the US. It is concerned with the whole world. Any epidemic, anywhere on the globe, whether a known or an unknown quantity will see CDC investigators. The laboratories are of the highest security and maintain stocks of the deadliest bacteria and viruses, anthrax, botulinum, Ebola, HIV. These killers are under intense investigation aiming to find ways of mitigating their effects or abolishing them altogether. The CDC keeps tabs on all the vaccinations and their side-effects, and long before the Internet it provided faxBack service, free of charge, for the vaccinations or medications needed fort travel anywhere on the Blue Planet. It's the kind of scope and service that only the USA, the benevolent Global Power can provide. Despite her size Corey strode quickly and soon they were in her office. Joe quickly assessed the Gateway computer and pulled out the new Zipdrive.

Corey seated herself comfortably on the executive chair which groaned in protest and surveyed the unlikely pair.

"So what is the big mystery?" she asked Beverly.

"Doctor Baille, before I begin I must ask you to keep an open mind about all this and to hear it to the end."

"I see Jerry has already warned you I have a short fuse for cowshit, I'll try" Corey chuckled.

"He did. Doctor Bergman came to see me the end of December with a suspicion that the cancer that afflicted a colleague in St. Jude was Neuroblastoma, the colleague was over seventy years old. I happened to recall that an inordinate number of Neuroblastoma diagnoses had been seen at St. Jude and rechecked the medical records. We found an impossible coalescence of cases, all Jewish, all male, almost all with Cohen ancestry." Corey was about to say something but recalled her earlier promise. "One of the unusual aspects of these cases was that children under one, whose tumor is expected to regress, went on to die, regardless of the treatment. The tumor in all cases was highly aggressive stage four, no overt translocations or deletions with multiple NMYC copy numbers, let me show you the clinical data" Beverly pulled out the long banner of tightly tabulated raw data and spread it on Corey's neat desk, end to end

"Looking through this data we found one common fact. These children, apart from their common genetic heritage, all received OPV from the same nurse, from a single lot number, and developed Neuroblastoma 4-5 months later. I went ahead and got 2 samples from the health department of the same lot number."

Corey could contain herself no longer "Doctor Kreissman, are you suggesting that Oral Polio Vaccine can cause malignant transformation in a selected population? That is the most absurd statement I have ever heard. Ridiculous!" she concluded angrily.

"Unless someone made it on purpose" Joe interjected.

"On *purpose*? That is even more outlandish, did you tell Jerry what you are telling me now?" Corey rounded back on the diminutive Beverly.

"Yes I did" Beverly did not flinch.

"In that case I better listen some more, 'cause one thing for sure, Jerry was never a cowshitter" she settled back.

"Would you like to watch a movie?" Joe asked innocently.

"In for the penny, in for the pound."

"And while the movie is running is it OK if I install a Zipdrive on your Gateway?"

"Any viruses on it?" Doctor Baille asked suspiciously.

"Plenty" Joe chuckled, "Especially Polio" he pulled out the camcorder, flipped out the miniature screen, gave her the walkman earphones and played the original tape.

Joe had the zipdrive all ready by the time the final shot rang out. Corey was shaking her head with disbelief. She clicked the recorder shut.

"Fine set of actors you found."

"At five AM on New Year's day?"

"I guess that's a little hard to arrange unless you tweaked the machine somehow."

"He would rather tweak kid's noses, doctor Bergman is a third year fellow at Children's in Milwaukee" Beverly said.

"I need a little more proof that this is real" said doctor Baile.

"Do you have Internet connection here?"

"Naturally."

"Why don't you look up the Indianapolis Sun for the second of January?"

The story was told in a graphic way, with police accounts, neighbors, interviews of the Riley faculty, and the search after George Moniz, who had rented the house under his own name. Moniz was originally from California. the police concluded suicide as a cause of death, but wanted to question him anyway. Beside the speedy getaway of the Sunfire prior to the fatal gunshot there was no other mention of a vehicle leaving the arena.

"*Excellent* actors" concluded Corey "Doctor Kreissman, you did not tell me what prompted doctor Bergman to start a new career?"

Joe handed Beverly the sheaf of faxes and E mail messages from Mustafa. Both women exchanged horrified expressions, doctor Baille finally cracked her crusty demeanor and stole a glance at the photograph on her desk. A short thin dark man, leading two miniature ponies, with two children, a boy and a girl, laughing into the camera from their perch. Joe followed her glance.

"That's Dan, He is not a Cohen, thank-God, with Max and Emily. I need some scientific proof of these allegations." Joe inserted the disk he had received from Shaker. He reeled the same presentation, although not with the same pride of a job well done but an account of murder in the making.

"In case you think I made this up, you can call on doctor ChandraShaker in Van Vleet and also on doctor Marten Mehta who did the pathology work on the Roger Cohen case."

"Is he dead?"

"You can call on Rabbi Friedman of Temple Israel."

"OK, OK, I am past the point of disbelief, I am into the realm of how to convince the higher ups and get some action."

"I have one more piece of evidence, Doctor Halim....."

"You are so formal, aren't you?" remarked Corey "what's your angle in all this?"

"He wants to get himself killed" volunteered Beverly.

"I thought the trial was over" said Joe drily.

"What trial? the kidnapper is in Lebanon you said" Corey was bewildered.

"Sorry, what I meant was that doctor Bergman intends to follow Halim to Lebanon and pull the kid out, somehow, and he doesn't care if he dies in the process."

"Can we get back to the problem at hand?" Joe said with asperity "Alia's fate, or mine, are tiny peripheral features of this issue. This is a Mass Murder issue and, Doctor Kreissman, by now you have intimate knowledge of the victims, so let's get on with it."

"Touchy, touchy, I am all ears" Corey said.

"We were lucky to find Moustafa's records in his hard drive. I had a bioinformatics expert analyze it and let me show you he results." Joe had the armada open and showed the analysis to both the Doctors.

"The final   proof to tie all this information together is that the virus in this vial, taken from Munir, and the Sabin vaccinations collected at the Health department this morning, will match the sequence in the attachments, and that is something I can't do."

"How come there is something you can't do?" teased Corey.

"Doctor Baille," Joe said formaly "the work you see here represents the concerted efforts of scores of geneticists, virologists, computer mavens, all intended to come up with a weapon targeted at My People. The effort to decipher and expose this plot involved the intense effort of a dozen individuals. I just happened to be at the pivotal point."

"I am also of the same People, let me remind you, and we use humour as a weapon. What you have done is truly remarkable, looking at the timeframe, it is almost supra human. Why are you so intent on getting yourself killed?"

"Let's say it's my penance."

"I hope I don't do any penance after I show this material to Will."

"Who is Will?" asked Beverly.

"William Corchak, chief honcho."

"Any relation to the great Yanusch Corchak?" Beverly was curious.

"So the legend goes, I never asked. Leave me the disks and the names of every person who collaborated on this investigation, and a copy of that confession tape." Doctor Baille concluded.

"I suggest a little preemptive strike on Lipjohn and an employee by the name of Muhi A Deen Shareef" said Joe, "don't mention my name in all this, use Doctor Kreissman and Stein."

"Why is that?" asked Beverly

"If word gets out with my name Mustafa will put two and two together and will disappear, so Bergman is dead."

"I hope God doesn't listen to this" said Corey fervently.

"Don't worry, he never does" Joe said, resigned, and Beverly shook her head, sadly.

Beverly was unable to keep her eyes open during the long seven hour drive back. It was 10 PM when Joe woke her up and asked for directions. They lived in East Memphis, not far from Temple Israel, close to their own synagogue. Jerry came out to greet them.

"I am done for" said Beverly as she exited the low car.

"How did it go?" Jerry asked.

"She bought it, they will sequence the viruses and if it all pans out then they will pull the plug on production. The only caveat is they wont do anything overt without doctor Kreissman's approval" Joe said as he deposited the small suitcase on the driveway.

"Yeah, I am the kingpin, the queen-pin, how are the kids Jerry?"

"Believe it or not, they had a whale of a time without you bossing them" Jerry informed her lightly "Wanna come in doctor Bergman?"

"Just for a quick phone call, my Iridium is dead, I forgot to plug it in."

Joe called Tammy, he felt he owed her.

"Cohen residence" he heard her sweet voice.

"Mrs Cohen, this is Doctor Joe, I wanted to...."

"Where are you?"

"Close by actually, in East Memphis."

"Then come over here!" peremptory.

"Mrs Cohen, really..."

"It's Tammy, Joe, if you don't come here I will personally call every motel and hotel within two hundred miles and tell them you are a fugitive from justice, your Miller Lite is waiting in the fridge!!"

"I guess I have no choice" Joe was happily resigned.

"You betcha, no choice!" Joe put the phone down. He was actually very happy. He turned to Jerry, Beverly had already gone up to kiss the kids "Got to go, orders!"

"Tammy Cohen?" Jerry shook his head sadly.

"Yep"

"Pass our most sincere."

"I will" Joe promised and exited back to the cool January air, it was almost eleven PM.

"Did you actually expect to drive to Indy tomorrow? Then to Milwaukee??!" Tammy inquired after she had extracted the update from the half-dead Joe.

"Well yeah, I owe it to the owner of the car!!" Joe protested mildly.

"Your brain must be fried with all this thinking and planning, before you go to sleep call that lady of yours, Karen? Let her know you're OK, she must be worried sick."

"But I called her yesterday!"

"That's 24 hours of worrying, women worry about their children and their men, who are nothing but grown up children, you know what? I don't trust you, what's her number?"

"Oh gosh, I can't believe it, Fella all over again, its 414 226-2120." Tammy punched in the numbers and waited for the ringing to be answered.

"Joe?"

"Just a second, here comes the lazy bum" she passed the cordless.

"Joe, who was that?"

"Tammy Cohen, she made the call."

"Lucky for you she did, I was worried sick!"

"Nothing ever happens to Bergman" Joe was flippant.

Karen refused to be mollified "Don't do that *ever* again, use the phone! are you OK?"

"I am fine, just too tired to talk."

"When are you home?"

Joe was amused, and touched, by this domesticity. "Don't know, depends on the road etc... I will use the phone."

"Kiss me goodnight Joe" Joe blushed under Tammy's keen observation and smooched the phone shortly.

"We will have to discuss your kissing skills, g'night" and she smooched him a long and ringing one. Joe put the phone down.

"Didn't that do you good?" Tammy asked him archly.

Joe drained his glass "Yes it did."

"There you are" she beamed "Go to sleep, you know the room."

Joe had been up for an hour, laying on the bed, with nothing pressing to do. Everything was out of his hands, and he was waiting for things to happen. At seven o'clock sharp he made his way to the kitchen, guided by the smell of coffee and pancakes.

Joe seated his behind on the captains chair and regarded the work. Tammy ladled him the pancakes which made his mouth water, and poured them the coffee.

"I wish Roger were here, I wish it a hundred, a thousand times a day, he would have liked you, hell, he *did* like you" Joe looked curiously at a piece of paper with numbers on it. While he waited for Tammy to explain he imbibed the coffee and demolished the pancakes.

"Where is Gabe?" he asked after a while.

"San Jose, with the rest of the computer freaks, some kind of a meeting."

"You realize of course that without him and Rachel we would still be in the dark."

"I realize it and I am proud of it, what can I do to convince you that you have done enough?"

"Nope, I still need to get Alia out."

"Or die trying?"

"Or die trying" Joe conceded with equanimity.

"What would your death prove for Pete's sake?" she was almost gnashing her teeth.

"That I was right all along."

"Right about what?"

"That I do not deserve to live."

"Idiot" she banged the counter so the cups jumped. Joe finished his coffee and she collected the crockery into the double sink. Then she came back to face him.

"And if you don't?"

"The verdict is that I should try once more."

"That's better, because this Karen sounds like someone you should cherish."

"I don't really deserve her."

"But if you get Alia out, then you have paid your debt to whoever?"

"Yes."

"In a twisted way I suppose that's a fair deal. The numbers are a confirmation for a flight from Memphis international to Milwaukee via Cincinnati, that's the earliest connection, it should bring you there in early afternoon."

"But what about the car? I promised this man I'll bring it back!!"

"Show me the rental" Joe produced it from the fanny pack. Tammy took it and folded it into her ample apron pocket.

"It's my problem now, I'll ship him the car by train."

"But that's gonna cost you, and the flight, let me write you a check..."

"One more word young man, and I will make you see stars" Tammy snatched one of the burnished copper skillets and waved it threateningly. Joe put his hands up. "That's better" she lowered the skillet "Get your stuff ready, the flight is at nine."

Joe hefted his big bag out of the trunk, and Tammy came out to bang it down shut. He put the bag down and extended his hand. Tammy threw her arms around his neck and pulled his head down.

"Come back alive, you hear? Otherwise I will have to come after you!" and bussed his cheek. quick as a cat she let him go, before he could see the mascara and makeup falling apart and drove off.

"Joe" his head snapped up with surprise. After so many years and so many flights with no one to care if he came or went, just hearing his name called at the exit gate was a tremulous surprise. Karen's flaxen halo showed up in the crowd and he headed for it. He was not prepared for the big hug and the kiss that came with it, but his response was immediate. They stood there as if they had been separated for a millennium and tried to force a corporeal merger.

"How did you know?" although he was sure he knew the answer.

"Mrs Cohen called and gave me the itinerary."

"Bloody unfair world, he did not have to die" they headed for the luggage claim.

"You know a thing or two about the unfairness of the world."

"You look wonderful" Joe said with wonder that indeed she cared for him, that it was not just another dream to wake up from into the aching solitude, that she was real, and radiant with love.

"And you looked like a bedraggled cur, that requires lots of TLC and I still love you." and she quick pecked his cheek, already prickly since the early morning shave.

It was a replay of the first time in her house, the bathroom, the clothes, the feeling of being pampered, of almost domestic bliss, and finally the spectre of Mother waiting at the kitchen table. This time he did not break step.

"Hello there Doctor Bergman."

"Hi Missis Fitzsimmons."

"Miriam will do, and how was your trip?"

"Difficult" and he buried his face in the chicken soup. After the food on the road it radiated Home to his brains and belly and loins all at the same time.

"Does it have anything to do with the fact that Karen is going to leave for unknown parts for an unknown length of time?" Miriam asked sharply when he was forced to look up and meet her piercing gaze.

"Most likely, yes" Joe admitted.

"I must say I don't like any of this, in fact *none* of this mystery, especially not dragging my only child to some unknown territory for some wildass mission, at the risk of her life." Karen was blanching and flushing alternatively as her mother leveled her fire at Joe.

"No one is dragging her" Joe said quietly.

"*You* sir, are a dangerous man" Miriam voice was getting stronger and she was pointing her index between Joe's eyes "and I will not stand for it if you put my only daughter in jeopardy."

"I keep telling her that" Joe remarked in the same quiet, infuriating voice. "Stop it, stop it stop it Mom, *you just stop it*" Karen was almost shrieking and crying at the same time "Joe didn't make me do any thing, he demanded *nothing*, he asked for *nothing*, *I* made him take me, *I* forced myself on him, and I will not allow you to ruin my *life* with these false lying accusations." The force of the words rattled Miriam. Karen was al-ways quiet and reserved and respectful, now she was shaking with anger.

"Maybe your Mom is right" Joe said in the same tone as before.

"And you, *shut up.*" Karen turned her anger on him "we are in this together, we have a job to do and we will do it together for better or for worse" Joe gazed into the flashing blue flames, hotter and more scorching than the Sun, resistance was futile. "And Mom, I expect you to apologize to doctor Bergman" She concluded, her voice under control.

Miriam was looking at her daughter with new respect, the girl knew what she wanted, and she went out and got it, and woe to the one who crossed her. Look at the big man, he was completely under her spell. So be it. Maybe the fearsome one in this pair was Karen. She decided to make her peace.

"Doctor Bergman,..."

"It's Joe" he said politely.

"Joe then, I apologize for my earlier remarks, and I hope you realize that I am just a concerned, no, terrified mother."

"Did you know she has such a temper?" Joe asked playfully.

"No, not really."

"She scares me half to death" Joe said and shivered theatrically.

"Alright, alright, smart alec" Karen said, her anger evaporating "but what I said still stands, anyone for lasagna?"

The fireworks were off for the rest of the meal and Miriam made a point of inviting Joe to dinner ASAP. They went to bed together and explored their bodies and feelings. Despite his obvious physical need he did not feel ready yet and they slept together, Joe with a deep low ache, and Karen unrequited, but hopeful. Every day and every night together brought greater understanding, and at some point the big body beside her was sure to follow the mind. The best sign of all was the relative lack of nightmares, and the increased time of deep sleep designated by a snore. In fact Karen found out she liked that snore, it meant a tranquil sleep of the Man at Home.

Unlike Joe, Karen was not a natural early riser, her sweet morning sleep was interrupted by a phone call which Joe fielded after the first ring. She stretched languidly, maddeningly desirable to Joe's eye as he came into the room.

"Who was that?" she mewed.

"Chris, he just finished the case and he wanted us to come by the station."
Joe leered at her. She stretched her arms out playfully and he took them
both and heaved her out of bed like a hooked fish out of the lake - twisting
and squirming but powerless to resist. He kissed her lightly to sweeten the
rude change of habitat.

"Are you working today?" he asked.

"Evening shift."

"Good, it's coming on eight, let's see where Amanda is."

"Why do you need her now?" she queried after morning ablutions and a
first taste of coffee.

"We need her to be a movie-star."

"She looks like one anyway."

"Not that kind of a movie."

They met Chris at the station. As before he pulled out the gangly youth
and told him to mind the store, and showed them to an inner office. From
under his desk he fetched out a large boxy aluminum suit-case stenciled with
bright red letters:

AMERICAN RED CROSS - MEDICAL SUPPLIES

He opened the case which was neatly subdivided into a number of
compartments. It was empty.

"Pick it up" he invited Joe. Joe closed the case and tried to pick it up with
an effort commensurate with a light empty aluminum. A grunt of surprise, it
was heavy, as if the case had been made of safe-grade steel. Chris whooped
with laughter, and Karen with him. Joe launched his mobile eyebrow sky-
high.

"The old double wall false bottom trick" Chris explained. He inserted a
thin watchmaker screw-driver into a small recess hidden by the handle, and
pushed, then opened the case and pulled at the compartment wall. The whole
tray swung up and underneath were Joe's toys, the GPS, the nightsight, the
button camera, the transmitters, battery packs. He replaced the tray and it was
as if it had never been. Joe was ecstatic.

"Did you make that yourself?"

"Not a chance, too professional. This is a left over from a big drug-bust in Detroit, years ago. The hoods are in the slammer, this was item number twenty four. It was sitting around in the storage. Frank Wallace is a friend so this is on loan. I just got it stenciled nicely" Joe nodded happily, he couldn't ask for anything better.

"Where is Amanda?" Karen asked.

"In the HOT Unit" Chris informed.

"How do you know?" Joe countered.

Chris turned red as a beet "I am picking her up to early dinner today."

"That's wonderful" Joe enthused and Karen beamed, "We will see her lunch time and pass your regards" Karen continued.

Joe nodded in confirmation.

"I picked up your messages from your machine, Joe. Apparently both the passport and the Pastor are waiting anxiously for your return" Karen said sweetly.

"She got you there!" Chris was amused at Joe's surprise.

"And here are the maps" Karen continued to spring the bunnies, pulling the FedEx package from her capacious bag, slit open to reveal the old nylon.

"Even the mail ain't holy anymore" Chris whooped it up.

"Information is Power" Karen declared "Daddy is expecting us at Eleven o'clock."

Karen tsked tsked at the mounted passport photo.

"Somehow I imagined you more handsome" she said. Pastor Wilkins ears pricked up, this was a new tone. He had met Karen a thousand times, both casually and professionally on both sides of the fence, as a bereaved, and as a care-provider, he had never heard a fond, nay, loving voice. And doctor Bergman, the coldest fish in the frozen lake, lo-and-behold, a new man, with a real smile and a confident air of a well-loved man. *What* a change in three weeks. Pity the circumstances were so dangerous, this couple were heading willingly into the lion's den before their relationship had a chance to bear fruit. Together they made a formidable team though.

"Horace called me this morning. How soon do you want to leave?"

"A-S-A-P" Karen spelled it out.

"Plane leaves Chicago Friday night, Zurich at early AM, Beirut late afternoon, with a small group. Will you be ready?"

"Yes" they said, almost in unison. then looked at each other in surprise at the unity. Henry Wilkins smiled his most benevolent.

"Then God save you from yourselves, and bring the child home."

The snow was falling silently on their hair and coats. Joe insisted on shooting the video outside, and having their faces exposed. They all smiled at the camcorder and the winking red light which indicated it was working until Karen pressed the Stop on the remote control. Then they repeated the show on another cassette. Joe stowed the camcorder in his Big bag and the cassettes in two different compartments.

They made a short raid on the Hospital pharmacy. Joe and Rodney Lindley, PharmD, looked for meds which were close to expiration or expired and put them into the Medical Supplies suitcase, antibiotics, Steroids, fever and pain relievers, ointments, muscle relaxants, Broncho-dilators, circulatory drugs, everything a doctor might need in adverse conditions. Karen went into her shift, and Joe went to his apartment to get his traveling needs together.

"After work I'll go to my Mom's place, she needs a little reassurance" she told Joe on the phone. The little apartment had never looked so empty, even with Helen's ethereal presence. Joe shaved his head closely and slightly trimmed his moustache .

They boarded the Swissair flight, two doctors and two nurses. For the benefit of the Stop the Hunger crew Joe acknowledged Karen in the same distant tone as he did Nurse Laura Brown and doctor Jim Dworeck who was going back to the mission and filled the novices on the country and the work. Beirut terminal was partially new, with all the signs that work to refurbish it completely was in progress. Doctor Neal Strickland, who was the head of the mission greeted them on arrival and, aided with some dollars in Baksheesh, got the suitcases and supplies out to the loud street and the old Volkswagen Transporter. The most dangerous part of the journey turned out to be the cavalier way in which the driver handled the chaotic traffic. Joe came to the other side of the looking glass, looking out from within.

Chapter 20

TARGET ACQUIRED

Mustafa had thought hard about where to place Alia. A regular school for the girls of the Sabra Camp, where his sister still lived, was unthinkable. He had been horrified to see where his own childhood had passed. The American University system went all the way to first grade level, and catered both to foreigners and to select locals. He had gone, under an assumed name (The Islamic Jihad could provide him with any passport he could ever require) and even though it was the middle of the school year he finagled a spot for her, with the aid of some Green-backs. Alia was totally subdued at first. Her stilted Arabic made her a stranger and quietly she pined for her mother. She rarely laughed, and she preferred to pass the time doodling a house, and trees, and snow. Mustafa was too busy to pay attention to her moods and admonished her when she got into crying episodes. Slowly she got used to the new routines of life. There were no females in the villa, If the Men wanted some time with their wives they waited until they rotated with other troops. Mustafa assigned her a beauti-ful room, indeed, it was the room of the daughter of the former owner (Actually, still the legal owner) of the house, before he had fled Lebanon in the late seventies. It was opulently appointed, a four poster, white dressers, soft lacy window shades, a pretty desk, even some toys. All that had been prepared in advance for the arrival of the Great Avenger. In this room, she was totally alone. Every day the green Mercedes would drive her to downtown, in the company of two truculent guards who thought that guarding the baby of this upstart American Palestinian was below their dignity, and the same car would pick her up in early afternoon, to take her back to her lonely room and surely father, who was always too busy to play with her because he was down in the labs in the basement. Even when he was with her, any number of technical people would interrupt them with a question.

The exception to loneliness was her aunts, who brought their many small children with them for visits, carefully chaperoned by the soldiers. She couldn't stand her cousins though. They were dirty, and stinky, dressed in rags, patched and repatched, and their Arabic was incomprehensible. Mustafa had taught her the Written Arabic, a high lofty form of the language, the language of Naghib Mahpouz, the great Egyptian poet, the language of King

Hussein when he addressed his parliament. Their language was gutter jargon, with more swearwords regarding female parts than regular words. Their games were war games, exactly the kind her mother had frowned on. On the one hand, she pined for the company of children, like the first grade she had attended in Glendale. On the other hand, the smell of her 'cousins' made her puke. She grew less responsive, and more listless by the week. Her only solace was the TV. The Middle East Channel ran old series such as the Little House, and Bonanza, and in those programs she escaped back to America. Fatima noticed it, most acutely. Although her life had been in the miserable gutter of poverty and fear, although she knew she was Gross and ugly, her heart went out to the poor lovely kid who had been dragged to this hell-hole. She envied her not the comfortable room in the big villa. Children had no idea if they were rich or poor. They only knew if they were loved and cherished. She tried, as hard as she could, to steer her teeming older male children from the games of hate, the Gangs, the Shabiba, but , she had no chance against the awful environment. When she visited the Villa, she sat down cross-legged on the Persian carpet with Alia and played with her, and let her vent her loneliness and anger.

First grade in the American University school meant catch up on all the tools needed for first grade, which had not been provided before. The disparity in education level was dramatic, some children having educated parents who were already reading, and some, from the Shiite households especially, who needed such basics as "What sound does the cow do?" they should have mastered at two or three years old. The teachers, many of them graduates of the system, some from other arab countries such as Jordan, struggled to bring them all to baseline for second grade.

The same was true of vaccinations. UNWRA, and the WHO provided the vaccinations. Many of the kids would come to school without evidence of a single vaccination for any of the major killers, Polio, Pertusis, Diphteria, Tetanus, Hepatitis, and therefore were both likely victims, and infection reservoirs for susceptible kids. The American School vaccinated everybody in first grade.

"Children, Children, please listen carefully" cried Nadia. The teeming classroom, shabby by American standards, luxurious with books and an old IBM PC for Lebanese standards , slowly piped down.

"Children, this week, we will all get shots." a hubbub broke out, some children stared in fear, some in trepidation, some cried, some were brave.

The bravest was Alia, she knew her Mother was a Doctor and she gave shots that made children healthy. She wasn't afraid, and in fact she felt contempt for those who were afraid.

"Before you get any vaccinations, we want everybody to be examined by the wonderful Doctors that are here to see you today'" the whole class swivelled their collective head to stare at the Doctor at the door. He was a very big man, totally bald, watery blue eyes, with a thin moustache, dressed in a white coat, with all the paraphernalia of a Real Doctor, lights, otoscope, tongue depressors, pens, all neatly arranged in his pockets. With him was a heavy-set nurse, also American, and the third was Fat Doha, she was the interpreter, and she was wider than the big Doctor.

The children sat on the mat and a makeshift partition was erected in the class-room. A thin mat and a white sheet logoed WHO - STOP THE HUNGER, spread on the teacher's desk, served as an examination table. Each child was called by name, weighed, measured. and examined, all the data was noted on a sheet marked in English and Arabic, they worked at breakneck speed, one hundred and twenty, one fifty a day. Most of the problems were concentrated in the children of the Shiites, the pinworms, the Giardia, the Anemia, the Thalassemia. He marked the page for vaccination or not, pending absolutely essential investigation,   and Joe jotted down what further investigation he wanted, blood or urine or stool cultures. He remembered to sign a flowery 'Campbell' every time. This was the tenth elementary school Joe and Laura had visited, and in fact it had been both his first choice, and the least problematic, since it was out of the camps and a scion of the American University. He had submitted to the schedule imposed by Strickland because he did not want to disclose his true interests. He also agreed to be assigned a nurse other than Karen so as to obscure the association between them.

"Alia el Haq" the 6 year old girl came into the partition and took off her white scarf. Joe recognized her immediately. He took in the curly black hair, the startling dark-blue eyes and the fair-under-olive skin, and he had no doubt. She was obviously the healthiest of the lot, having lost her front teeth and otherwise having a perfect dental survey. All the others had terrible carries due to bad food, lousy hygiene, no fluoride, and ignorance. She looked at Joe and for an awful moment he though she might recognize him, but she addressed Laura Brown, who was less intimidating.

"Are you *really* from America?" she asked innocently.

"Yes" Laura smiled at her.

"I was born in America too" she announced happily, the first happy moment she had since she had arrived in this place, "do you know my mother?"

Laura shook her head, she realized that for the child America was no bigger than her own neighborhood, she had no concept of size. "No" she said "Now lay down on the mat here, Doctor Campbell will check you out" what a relief to speak directly to the child rather than use the interpreter. She helped her onto the makeshift exam table, and Joe continued his examination, stone faced.

"My mother is a Doctor too" she said to Laura, while Joe was listening to her heart "but she is much nicer." Joe almost guffawed. The little girl continued conspiratorially "can I tell you a secret?"

"Sure" said Laura, placing the measurements on the percentile nomograms. Alia was the 75th percentile for height and the 50th percentile for weight.

"My Mom is going to come and take me back to America, but don't tell my Dad"

"BAAS, That's enough" said Fat Doha in Arabic and she grinned an awful grin at the hateful American pair "She does not know what she speaks, a little crazy" and she twirled her finger around her ear, crazy. Alia looked at her, stupefied with Anger but she was careful not to say anymore. Her father had warned her not to say anything abut America, and if he heard.... She sent a beseeching look at Doha. Joe made a grimace of impatience, as if this whole discourse was wearisome and said loudly "Next." This was Monday, and Vaccination day was Thursday. The delay was enough for the Mission lab to complete the basic studies he ordered so that with the vaccinations he could dispense necessary medication such as Iron supplements, and Vermox for the worms, and Flagyl for the Giardia. It was an effort to continue to be so disagreeable to Laura who was really a good nurse and a comely woman, in a big and busty way.

They were done when school was done, Joe had an afternoon clinic to go to, in the Shatilla camp, but that could wait for an hour. He told Laura he had a meeting and winked heavily and she took it for whatever her fancy was, registering some dismay. She didn't like this Doctor because he was the most taciturn she had ever seen. He wasted not a motion or a word, just worked fast. He disappeared down one of the dirty back streets and she wondered how he had the courage to do that in this city of soldiers, factions, criminals and drug-runners.

Joe mounted the little Suzuki 125 he had bought from one of the street punks and paid in Greenbacks to keep from being stolen. He watched the vehicles coming to the school wrought iron gates, and then Alia came out, accompanied by Doha, who was giving her a piece of her mind. Alia was submissive, but not cowed, she *knew* that somehow her mother will come to bring her Home. A green Mercedes drove up to the gate and one man, dressed in jungle greens came out and held the door for Alia. He slipped Doha a little something, and she gave him her Godawful grin. The soldier retreated hastily into the car which drove off with a screech of tires and loud honking. Joe started the little engine with a kick and followed.

Following a car in Beirut is the easiest thing in the world. The lanes are ignored, traffic lights, however few there are, are a source of mirth, people cross without a warning, chaos and bedlam, a society without rules. Joe knew how that was, Gazza, and Rammala and Nablus were the same. No one could spot a tail in this chaos. He was unobtrusive, dressed in grey rain outfit, helmet on, with a million mopeds and cycles milling around. The Mercedes was easier to spot, and he tailed her in town, and going out to the Schouf hills, and all the way to the Villa. The fact that rain began to fall heavily was even more helpful. He killed the engine and stopped behind a house that was half destroyed, and bullet ridden, and watched the Mercedes stop at the gates, identify, and drive in. The gates were closed but his tiny binoculars allowed him to see the tall figure waiting for the girl on the top of the wide stairs. Mustafa. Target acquired. He looked around and committed the place to memory, then pushed off without the engine, down the dirt track, down the hills, and back to the city. He knew the City to a certain extent, the Lonely Planet books and maps were very useful and showed main arteries and highlights of the city. Joe hurried back, he was sure he had a zillion patients waiting in the UNWRA clinic. I hope Laura dislikes me as much as I want her to dislike me.

To: Aman Patzan
From : Shomer Rosh
Sub: Shkaki Villa
Report: A man observed watching the villa. Late afternoon, single man, on motorcycle, followed the green Mercedes in the rain, and observed the villa through pro binoculars. The Mercedes delivered the child, as noted in previous report. The observer returned to the city.

**This is very unusual
signed
Shomer Rosh**

"What do you make of this report?" Omri Nitzan, Pazan (Northern Command) representative asked Ron Shivek, Shin Bet representative to the Alert meeting. Since the October 73 war, when Israel had been caught with the proverbial pants down despite adequate Commint Elint and Humint, Aman convened an Alert forum daily to evaluate the various threats facing the embattled country. Each Service sent a representative with the current Alert signs and together they came up with a daily statement. Those meetings allowed the services to correlate Info which was not necessarily Alert quality.

"Someone watching the watcher" Shivec snickered, then sobered, "we had a report from Cyprus some time ago about a man and a child who arrived at Larnaca and were met by an Islamic Jihad operative. The man appeared Arab American, and the child more occidental. Then they disappeared. Next a report about Youness having in his Villa a man and a child, and then excessive activity at the villa, lots of people and lots of equipment. Laboratory equipment, our operative sneaked a look at the garbage. Thermal Cycler, what the hell is Thermal Cycler?" Shivec was thinking aloud. "Now, we have someone else watching the villa and the child, I think we need to watch the place more closely!"

Joe and Karen walked hand in hand to the waterfront, it was dirty, breezy and cold. They found the only decent faux-English pub, the Yorkshire Boar, and went in for a non-alcoholic malted beer. A group of Norwegian UN troops were whooping it up at the next table. Joe took the drinks from the bar and joined Karen in the corner. He was more than a little nauseated by the powerful cigarette smoke the pub stank off. Lucky Strike and Marlborough were ubiquitous, and Joe thought that if there was one thing he did *not* appreciate about America, it was the powerful Tobacco industry which spread it's putrid wares around the world. Karen was even more disgusted by the clouds of smoke and beer fumes wafted by the Nordic Soldiers, accompanied by raucous noise. At home they would never do that. Joe set the glasses on the non-too-clean chipped Formica table and gave her a big, big smile. The major advantage of talking in the bar was secrecy. It would be virtually impossible to listen in on their conversation.

"You found her." she said with conviction.

"Yup. Her name is Alia El-Haq now."

"How did she look?"

"She was ridiculously happy to see Americans, she told me her mother is a doctor and that she was coming to get her."

"I hope Mustafa wasn't listening."

"Yeah, I hope the fat cow who was chaperoning everything doesn't report to him. I pretended non-interest and went on to the next kid. I found Mustafa too!"

"Where is *he* skulking?"

"He is not skulking, he is in a big villa out of town, surrounded by soldiers, or militiamen. Well guarded. How was your day?"

"Horrible, the clinic was awash with sick kids, asthma, diarrhea, osteomyelitis, draining ears, malnutrition, and Doctor Dworeck is a total washout. He's been here too long."

"Why malnutrition? UNRWA brings in tons of food."

"Distribution. The Henchmen control it, it goes to the black market, the bigwigs get the money."

"Figures, got to go, sit tight." he headed for the bathroom, which was passable by Middle Eastern standards and pulled out his Irridium tele-phone.

"Hello."

"Amanda?"

"Joe?"

"Target acquired, go go go."

"Yah."

"Peiter?"

"Yah."

"Its Yozee."

"Quand?"

"Tuesday in Wednesday out."

"Yavohl."

"Bev?"

"Joe?"

"Make you gambit Thursday."

"It all matched, Joe."

"Great."

"Good luck."

Joe stuck the phone into the pocket inside the waist-band, which he noticed, was getting slack. He was losing weight. He came out of the back and could not see Karen at all. The table was obscured by the bodies of two Norwegians who were towering over her. Joe made his way there quickly but unobtrusively.

She was sitting and trying to appear calm, they were Europeans after all, but then one of them sat down, pushed his butt closer, squeezing her to the wall. A look of fright crossed her features.

"Gentlemen" Joe said in his most reasonable voice "Please, the lady wishes to leave." The one who was standing turned around and assessed the threat. He was the proverbial Viking, tall, crew-cut blond, his face flushed with too much beer.

"Screw you" he said, too much American TV, thought Joe. The soldier turned his back on Joe and said something to his companion, who placed a paw on Karen's hand, and squeezed her even further to the wall. They wafted beer fumes. The three other UN soldiers at the next table started paying attention.

It was a trick Joe had used many times with children who could not be subdued for a bone marrow aspiration, but this time it came with a twist. Joe's hand sneaked out from his long coat pocket, and with a swift jab he stuck the Epipens into the man's thigh. The mechanisms tripped and ran the Ketalar into the quadriceps. The soldier jumped with surprise at the bee sting, coming from unexpected quarters, and turned on Joe, then his eyes drooped, his muscles gave way and he collapsed heavily on the floor. His companion stared with disbelief at the fallen tower, then at Joe's male-volent stare, and Karen used the delay to violently push the Formica table away and scramble out. Karen and Joe backed out of the pub which remained noisy and uncaring, all except for the 4 Norwegians who stared, stupefied and drunk, at their fallen comrade. Karen and Joe escaped out, into the rain that came in from the Mediterranean, and soon disappeared.

They took a taxi to the Ambassador. The small lobby, with it's own active bar was mainly full of UN troops trying to get laid with the Le-banese girls. The front desk gave them a cursory glance. Joe took to the stairs, which were stark concrete, and ran up the five floors. Karen kept up with ease. His room was 558, and the corridor was poorly lit, every second bulb was blown, it had seen better days. Joe locked the door behind them and switched the radio on, loudly. Karen was about to say something but Joe put his finger to her lips. He pointed at the telephone and mimed a man with headphones on. Karen nodded understanding. Joe placed the blaring radio which was tuned to a Cypriot Rock'nRoll station and pushed volume up. If the device was indeed connected, the person listening would turn deaf. Joe took his sodden coat off and placed it on the chair. He looked out of the window into the narrow Shiffa boulevard, full of people, cars, with no resemblance to an orderly flow of traffic. The wind was cold and he closed the shutters and the single pane iron-framed window. She snicked the overhead light, a bare bulb, off. The lamp in the corner, with it's ancient cloth shade, she draped with her own coat. Soft light escaped the cover.

She went over to Joe, and pulled at his tie, and unbuttoned his shirt, button by button, from the top. she continued al the way down to his pants, then pushed him back on the bed, which responded with a cacophony of rusty springs. Resistance was futile. She took off his shoes, and socks, and tossed them in the corner, and pulled his pants off. She surveyed her handiwork, there wasn't much left to do. He was thinner, the four weeks of constant work, travelers's diarrhea and scant edible food thinned his skin, so that the abdominal cubes were visible, and the muscle fibers of his great shoulders were visible, one by one, and they slithered like snakes under his skin. The slit eyes were challenging her. She waited. So far she had been the one to make all the moves, this time it was his turn.

He rose, only the Fruit of the Loom boxers to his skin, and pulled her down on top of him, on the creaky bed, then he smiled his big smile again.

"Did they scare you?"

"Not really."

"Come-on, they were big and drunk."

"And you were sober and fast. Did you use the old trick?"

"Yup, I put Ketalar in the Epipen, I stuck him with three lashed together."

"Good for an elephant."

"He was big, he'll sleep well."

"The other guy was really afraid."

"It kept him from having his face bashed in."

"Thursday is the big day."

"Yes."

"Are you scared?" Karen asked.

"Shitless."

"Are we going to make it?"

"I give us a 30/70 chance."

"That's not generous."

"That's realistic" he pulled out her blouse from the waist band, and slid his hands up her back, kneading the tense muscles, slid his finger under the strap and stroked the shell of her spine.

"You can undo it" she said, he fumbled a little until the little hooks came undone. Her hand dove into the front of her blouse and came out trailing the bra, which she slowly brushed over his nose. "The color of your eyes is so weird" she said.

"I am dying to get my glasses back on again."

"Is that *all* you are dying for?"

"I am dying to make love to you." Finally, he said it at last.

"Are you sure?" she asked.

"Yes"

"Are you ready?"

"So many questions."

"Don't move, if you move I'll kill you" She rolled off him, stood up and slowly unbuttoned her blouse until it fell aside, catching on her nipples, revealing the tight curves. She took off her slacks, and he devoured her with his eyes, which had adapted to the low ambient light. Then she took up position again on top of him, with only insignificant pieces of cloth separating them. Her breasts touched his chest and she wriggled a little to make then swim through the fuzz. Both Joe and Karen watched the nipples rise out of the deep brown areolas and brush is own. Their eyes met , and suddenly she broke loose, and sat up straight, pressing down with her pelvis right where it hurt.

"I can't stand them" she announced.

"Can't stand what?"

"The contacts, its not you."

"I'll take them off." She jumped off him and he took off the contacts, they were such a pain. When he turned back his vision was not as acute, but Karen was totally naked.

"I am at a disadvantage here" she pointed out. The last piece of cloth came off and he stood there, the man she had pictured in her mind a thousand times, and in the flesh he was a thousand times better. He leaned over her and covered her completely, eyes to eyes, mouth to mouth, chest to chest, belly to belly. He weighed a ton, ten tons, and she welcomed every ounce of it, then, effortlessly, he spun around and she found herself on top again and he threw the bed cover over her bare buttocks.

"Hold me Joe, as hard as you can" and he pressed her to his body, the Manhug she had always craved materialized, the big palms encompassing her back, spanning it side to side, and crushing her breasts and chest against his tense pectorals. She felt her juices flowing and wetting her cleft, and she wanted him inside her so bad, so bad. She wanted his sperm, his essence, she wanted his baby. She could move her pelvis, so she did, and like a bolt sliding into the breech, his penis slid into the waiting womb and locked home. The same groan broke from his throat, and before he could change his mind she locked her legs on him so was immobilized. They gazed at each other, eye to eye, the deep blue into the brown-green, past the irises, into the choroids, the optic nerve and the back of the brain. They tasted each other's mouths, and the urgency of the intercourse lent an extra zest to the rush of the tongues. It was as if they were drinking each other up, to the last drop, and she did not allow him to move, or even think of withdrawal. She had her quarry, and she was not going to let it go, notwithstanding the fact that with his superior strength he could break free anytime he wished. It was the total Female Attraction that kept him in the tractor beam. Joe was being devoured.

Still in a deep kiss she began to move her pelvis, extracting more of those groans from his throat, faster and more urgent, arching her back to create pressure on her own sweet spot. The tension in their opposing muscles grew and grew, the pressure in their brains increased to a pitch level, the world contracted, they were transported to a realm of intense concentration, the blood roared in their ears, hearts beat faster and faster, they clenched to a pinpoint in space, and then the supercoiled springs snapped and the releasing spasms came together and they bucked against each other, beat themselves raw at each other and released the pent up breath, the pent up sperm and juices, and the pent up tears, again and again and again, till nothing was left, and they were sucked dry. Inside the womb, millions and millions of sperm began to beat their tails spasmodically and swim up the primordial waters of life, like salmon swimming up-current and over the rapids, driven by the Force to complete the deed of reproduction. It took time for the heaving chests and the sweaty bodies to calm down to tolerable levels. Karen released the mouth and kissed the watering eyes, tasted the salt that kept coming and felt the pressure on her back slowly being released. She could breath again. but she did not withdraw, she still wanted him inside her for as long as she could.

"Karen?"

"Joe."

"Do you love me?"

"Yes, I have been in love with you for a long time."

"I love you too Karen."

"I know."

"Are we going to have a baby?"

"My pills say no."

"Pity."

"I am counting on many more slip-ups."

Silence....

"Am I crying?" Joe asked.

"Yes. "

"I am crying for Helen, for a moment there, you were Her. That's not fair to you, because you are YOU."

Karen kissed him another deep one "do you still love Helen?"

"Yes."

"Then I love her too, she is part of you, she makes you what you are, and *you*, is what I want."

"So logical."

"I must have read it somewhere."

Incredibly, he was getting hard again, and she felt it. This time they made love slowly, carefully goading each other into a higher and higher pitch of excitement, speeding up, and slowing down, slow exploration of hands, and mouth, fingers and nails, until they could hold it no longer, and they succumbed to the climax, and subsequent let-down. Karen, un-willingly, finally, relinquished her hold on him.

"Are we doomed to do this for the rest of our natural lives?" he asked.

"Not a bad sentence."

"Consider that the end of our lives may be in three days."

"In that case we must do it again."

"You are asking too much of this old man" he chuckled.

"Let's get cleaned up, and then we'll see."

"Lukewarm water, at best"

"In *winter*?"

"This is the Middle East. You can get the Ritz, but the basics do not filter down well. We missionaries must share the plight of the recipients of our benevolence."

the water was as lukewarm as he had promised, and Karen shivered and held his warm skin.

"I know why we should stay together" she said, her shivers mollified.

"Great sex?"

"That too, but really for the heat you produce."

"Finally I am good for something."

"I refuse to be drawn into this self-deprecation mode, just hold me tight again."

"Joe?"

He woke up "Yeah."

"I have to get back to the Maronite house, we still need to obey the rules."

"OK, we'll walk there, got your gear all ready?"

"Yes, fresh batteries and all, and the epipen."

Beirut, under the Pax Syriana was beginning to regain slowly it's former glory as a city that never sleeps, like its southern neighbor, Tel Aviv, so the couple walking in the streets around midnight was not out of place. The Maronite school for girls whose dorms served the Stop The Hunger miss-ion was walled and gated, and the guard accepted Karen as he did the other UNWRA and missionary volunteers.

"See you Wednesday" he said, and looked longingly as she passed un-der the stone arch.

The next two days were the same, a busy clinic, sick kids, mothers to twelve who had already lost three, whose complaints needed to be translated, and since most of the time the info was suspect, it came down to direct examination. The consanguinous marriages produced a plethora of inherited disease, Thalassemia, a blood disease which necessitates life long blood transfusions was rampant. It was so unnecessary, but the Palestinians and Shiites were Moslem, and they refused to be informed of abortion, assuming one could do prenatal diagnosis, another joke. The refugees were forced to stay in the camps, they were not allowed to leave and prosper. In the old days of the Arab oil power many of the men would leave to the oil fields and send money. After the Kuweity debacle, where the Palestinians backed the wrong side, they were sent back to the camps. They never achieved Lebanese citizenship, and the new prosperity held nothing for them. So they waited for Yasser Arafat to establish his Palestinian State in Israel, that is Palestine, and call them back, except there was no way that Israel would agree to such a demographic shift. The refugees served as an attractant for resources. The UN poured millions of dollars in through UNWRA and they disappeared into thin air, or rather war-lord pockets, leaving the teeming majority mired in the dumps. Joe worked a punishing 12 hour day, until the mission workers closed the iron gates and told those who still waited that tomorrow was another day.

Joe drove the little motorcycle to the Intercontinental. Now this is a hotel, a real four star.

"S'il vous plait monsieur?"

"I am Doctor Campbell. I have a meeting with Monsieur Herzig. I believe he should be registered here."

"Just a moment, yes here he is, room 886, and he instructed that you should go right up."

"I'll take the stairs" said Joe, and received a weird look from the Reception. Joe took the steps , two at a time, just like he did at Children's, except now it was easier, he was trained and thin. He exited into the corridor. At least here the light fixtures worked. He found 886 and knocked on the door.

"Ya, qui est ce?" Peter must be practicing his French.

"Yozzee."

The door opened from within and his breath was knocked out by the bear hug. Peter rocked him side to side and pulled him inside. The woman inside took a sharp indraw of breath.

"Loise, meet Doctor Yozzee, he is paying for this trip."

"And he is paying the hairdresser too" said Karen from the door, Peter assessed her up and down as she closed the door, and he was very serious suddenly.

"Yozzee, is this Helen all over again?"

"Not a chance" Karen said cheerfully.

"I am sorry, shouldn't have said that" said Peter.

"Are you sure you two are not Twins?'" said Loise, she was a tall athletic woman in her thirties, black haired, shoulder length.

"That's what I thought too, when I met Yozzee trying to mesmerize the ducks on lac Zurich. Doctor Yozzee, meet Loise, we haf been together for 4 years."

"She must be good for you" Joe said with a laugh "except for the hair loss, you look better than you did 5 years ago."

"Yozzee, you are laughing again!!" Peter was amazed he turned to Karen "I came to zee Yozzee after Helen was gone, God-rest-her-soul. He was like a stone obelisk, only with less humor. After a week even *I* couldn't stand it."

"And he stayed the same for the next five years" Karen attested.

"But now, better, much better" Peter said with glee, and gave Joe another hug.

"Let's go to work, folks" Karen said, and led the way to the bathroom. Loise followed meekly. The men sat on the settee, and Joe repeated the same trick, bringing the radio near the telephone, turning up the volume.

"This is dangerous, Yozzee."

"No worse than going one hundred and sixty over the Susten pass" Joe teased.

"That was a long time ago, since I am with Loise I am very careful. I really do not understand why You haff to do it for this girl." The noises of clipping and the buzz of the clipper were very distinct through the paper-thin door.

"Initially, it looked like a good attempt at dying" Joe said with a straight face, Peter cringed. "Then Karen came out of nowhere and the whole thing changed, but I was committed and she committed too."

"What do you mean, out of novere?"

"Well, actually, she has been working in the same unit as I have for the last two and half years, I just refused to notice."

"You must haff been blind, she is Fantastique."

"I was, but not any more."

"And is she really committed to you?"

"I checked last night, very thoroughly" Joe smiled widely "she is."

"Vundarbar, it's time your luck changes, mine already did."

" I feel alive again Peiter, we'll get through this madness, and then we'll go home and make some babies!!"

"Invite me for the Brith, is she Jewish?"

"I don't know, her grandpa is, I know that for sure, but does it matter?"

"Of course not, but it vill be easier!!" Peter emphasized.

"One thing at a time, first the Job, then we'll see, there is another aspect to this caper but I will tell you about it another time."

"Gut, there *vill* be another time."

"Here we come, ready or not!!" Karen announced, and led Loise out, her hair covered in a tall turban of a bath-towel. Dramatically she yanked off the turban, and the hair came into view

"Twins" said Joe, and Peter nodded. Loise's hair was cut short, identical to Karen's and her colour had changed to flaxen blond.

"I like it so much I think I vill keep it" said Loise.

"Don't I haff an opinion?" Peter feigned hurt.

"Of course my darling" Loise came over and kissed him "but only as long as it fits *my* opinion" and she sat on his lap, happy as a lark. Karen and Joe smiled too.

"I hope you don't let *her* boss you around like that " Peter said.

"Worse" Joe declared "Much worse" and had his nose tweaked. Then he became serious. He extracted his passport, stamped by the Beirut International and handed it to Peter "the flight is at early AM."

"In a few hours? I hope they vill be gut and tired." Loise and Karen exchanged passports too. "Yozzee, that was a very generous sum you transferred. It was excessiff." Joe stopped him with a trivializing motion.

"I never worked for it, it was never mine, call it hazard pay, invite me to Davos sometime."

"But you *are* invited, and you too Karen, and we live in Davos anyvay!!"

"Then buy something nice for Loise, she has just sacrificed her hair for us" Karen said.

"Oui, oui, bon idea, I agree" Loise said.

"We are off, good luck" Joe said, rising from the settee.

Peter gave Joe another bear hug, bussed Karen cheeks, and his eyes were slightly wet.

"Don't worry Peiter, we'll make it" Karen said and they left.

"I need to make a telephone call" Joe said. He used the hotel payphone to call Strickland's satellite phone. He was the only one in the mission who had such an expensive piece of communications.

"Doctor Strickland?"

"Yes" a lugubrious voice.

"This is Doctor Campbell, I am sorry to tell you that sir, but I will be leaving tomorrow, on Swissair" he verified the ticket "809, out of Beirut International."

"Sorry to hear that, will you be coming back?"

"Small family matter, I hope I settle it quickly."

"Goodbye Doctor Campbell" he signed off.

"Nice little machine" she said.

"Isn't it? pity we have to leave it behind, hop on."

"Don't I need a helmet?"

"You got it" and gave her the helmet.

"What about you?"

"This is Lebanon, no rules, Death and Depravity just round the corner, but, I'll strap it. hold on" and he whizzed through the narrow streets and alleys.

"How do you know where you are?" She spoked into the mike. There was no need to scream over the wind.

"I learned the tourist map."

"Gifted."

"I'll have to do much better than ride the streets, tomorrow."

"You better, St Mary's awaits" Joe drove on to the Maronite house and let her off. She took her helmet inside, and he left his helmet on, and waited. A few minutes later he heard the crackles in the earphone.

"Joe, how do you read."

"Five by five" he said into his helmet, a heavy hand landed on his shoulder. Joe jumped, the bike between his knees, with an explosive breath. His field of vision was restricted by the helmet, and he had not seen them coming.

"Joe, Joe, Joe" Karen was pleading but he had a bigger concern. They were fully armed, on either side, two men in Jungle green, one placed a hand on the bike and twisted the throttle, and the motor screamed wildly. They laughed, and said something in Arabic. Joe did not comprehend. One of them motioned him to get off the bike and the other covered him with a gun. Joe released the bike and let it fall over on it's side. The engine continued to tick over. The helmet weighed on him, despite their guns he took it off. The gates were locked, the guard was either gone or hiding and there was nowhere to run.

The men were startled to see a foreigner. Joe went back to his reasonable voice.

"Gentlemen, I don't want any trouble, if you want the bike, you can take it." One of them, at least, understood.

"You American?" he said in the heaviest Arabic accent .

I wonder what he would say if I told him I am an Israeli. "Yes" that's not even a lie, Helen made me an American.

"I Syrian"

"Mister Syrian, I am a Doctor and I help people." Maybe they like Doctors, maybe they don't.

"Doctor, on Motorcycle?" and he laughed his head off. Then he stopped and said something to his friend who pointed the Kalachnikov at Joe, the motor continued to put-put.

"Go" he said and as Joe turned to go he swung his rifle and hit Joe, on the shoulder, where, years ago, a bullet had sliced through. That spot was numb, so Joe hardly reacted. Enraged, The soldier swung again, this time higher, to the head. Joe was ready. He ducked, and as the barrel whizzed over his head the soldier lost his balance and almost fell on Joe. Joe hit the exposed head with the helmet, and heard a crack, either the helmet or the skull. The other soldier was trying to cock his weapon. Joe grabbed the Kalach from the lifeless hands of the fallen, and used it in the same way except he held the barrel, and hit the soldier with the wooden stock, across the temple. Another crack, there were two bodies in the alley. Shit, that's all I need.

"Joe, Joe, I am coming out" crackled the tinny voice in the helmet.

Joe grabbed he helmet and spoke into the microphone he had taped to the chin protector.

"No, stay where you are."

"What happened?"

"Two goons tried to jump me."

"Are you OK?"

"They're not, they saw my face."

"We are gone tomorrow, leave Joe, leave now."

"OK" Joe assessed the Kalachnikovs. One was the metal folding stock type. He folded the stock, that made the weapon short, stuffed it inside his coat, together with an extra banana clip. He disassembled the other Kalach, as he had done before in training a thousand times, in the dark, extracted the sliding mechanism, and hurled it away, and threw the useless stick down. Then he stepped over the bike, which was still running, lifted it up, gunned the engine, the wheel slithered in the dirt and he was gone. The two soldiers did not budge. It would be hours before they would, and then how to explain being overpowered and having their weapons snatched and destroyed by a Doctor? Hopefully they would opt to go AWOL.

Joe secured the little bike to a railing and walked into the Ambassador again. The UN troops were still at it, although it was a different group. He waited for the receptionist, who doubled as a barman at this late hour, to be busy, then slipped inside and to the staircase, his grey waterproof still on. Once on the his own floor he waited quietly, and when he was sure no one was about, he strode quickly to 558. The black hair was still in the door jamb, so the room was probably safe. He turned the old-time lock and went inside.

Only when he was securing the door and window did he recall that last cryptic remark. St Mary's was Milwaukee's busiest Maternity center. Maybe the next time she will be off her pills.

Chapter 21

AMBULANCE

Karen adjusted the tiny earphone, the throat mike behind the heavy polo necked sweater, stuffed as much as she could into her gym-bag and went down to the gate. Another overcast day, who said there was no rain in the Middle East. It was a wet, cold morning, and she hunkered down into her down Parka. Thank God for Joe, if it wasn't for his insistence I would have taken just a blouse. Joe had warned her that Lebanon, especially in the mountains, was cold. At seven AM it was even colder, and she could see the heavy clouds rolling in from the Mediterranean. Laura, Jean and Sarah joined her presently, looking cold and miserable. Their coats were obviously inadequate.

"Brrrr, they never told us it was so chilly here" Laura complained and her heavy bosom quivered, "where is that driver? he is never on time, and what's with the dark glasses today?"

"Allergic Conjunctivitis. Hey, Laura, who are you working with today?"

"Campbell, we are giving shots today, so dull, and I did it so many times."

"How is this Campbell?" Karen asked innocently

"A pain, a cold fish, he never talks to you, or looks at you, just gives orders in a dead voice. You know, there was this sweet little girl whose mom is apparently American but her Dad is here, and she said something about going back, and he just said 'Next' and pushed her off the exam table."

"He *pushed* her?" Karen sounded amazed.

"Well, not really *pushed*, but he's so short-tempered, if a kid cries with the shots he will probably spank her, who are you with today?"

"Kevin Kelley."

"Wow" Laura rolled her eyes "Now that's a real Doctor, not a square block of Ice."

"You want to switch?"

"Sure" Laura jumped at it, "but why should *you* want to?"

"I gave him a try, and he laughed and said I was not his type, he likes the Big Mama type better. It's a little uncomfortable now, working together."

"Really? here comes our driver, fifteen minutes late, OK, you got it, all the shots are in this box, and the top tray is the basic crash cart. Doha, the interpreter, has all the sheets, she's done this before, she'll tell you how." The

Volkswagen Transporter screeched to a halt, and the driver, a middle aged paunchy man opened the front door with a long metal handle.

"Hi Farouk" said Sarah as she climbed in.

"Good morning to all the American Ladies" said Farouk happily. He had been working for the Mission for 20 years, fair pay, pleasant people, sometimes a perk, he could raise his five children without grubbing, and now his wife was working at the Mission too, at housekeeping, and they treated her nicely, not like dirt, unlike the Lebanese nouveaue-riche. Farouk was a happy camper, and reliable, except he couldn't read the time. The nurses climbed in, and he drove on.

"Next stob, the Ambassador" he called. Dworeck and Kevin Kelley climbed aboard.

"Where is Doctor Cambbell? " asked Farouk.

Dworeck replied "he called me last night on the housephone and said he was coming separately and not to wait." Farouk closed the door and drove on, the Transporter jouncing over the potholes, swerving around bikers and men with trolleys, and honking his excellent German horn.

Farouk stopped at the iron gates of the American School, and let Karen off. Doctor Kelley was wedged in by Laura, he had no idea why she was suddenly so interested and close, but again, why not, this far away from home... Farouk helped Karen with the big box and her gym-bag and climbed up to the transporter. The guard at the gate helped her into the school, and into the primitive gym. The first children were beginning to filter in. Karen used the time to make some changes and waited for the school principle. Presently Nadia Haliff, dressed severely in black as usual came into the Gym. Karen rose to greet her. She was a benevolent lady who had married a Lebanese Moslem businessman while still in college. She had converted and lived in Lebanon for the last 30 years, and had seen the balance of power shift from the Maronite Christian minority to the Moslem majority.

"Are you from the Mission, for the vaccinations?"

"That's right" Karen said, and gave her most radiant smile, her shoulder-length black hair swinging freely, her eyes made up to look slightly oriental.

"Is there a Doctor coming too?"

"Yes, a little later, we can start the shots with the healthy ones, and leave the sicker ones till later."

Nadia pouted, thought and finally acquiesced "I suppose that's OK, getting them rounded up is so hard, I wouldn't want to do that again. Doha will help you" and she went outside to the gathering melee.

Doha and Karen set up the desk, the mat, the screen, and Joe listened to everything from without, clad in his grey waterproofs, hidden in the alley. Then Doha started calling the kids one by one. Karen consulted the sheets and gave the kids the OPV, sabin Polio, and the DPT, Diphtheria Tetanus Pertusis, and finally Engerix, the hepatitis B vaccine. They screamed, they squirmed, they cried, they froze, it took all types.

"El-Haq," Alia came in, without fear, she was going to show the bullies, that even though she was a soft American, she can take the shots. Karen smiled and gave her the shots, and proudly, even though her Gluteal muscles were sore, Alia went back to her group.

Two minutes later there was a commotion among the children, and milling about. Karen finished the last poke and came out from behind the screen, a small circle formed in the middle of the pack, children were standing around a child who was on the floor and staring at the small figure, they were bewildered, because she appeared to be sleeping. Doha bustled out and Karen had her stethoscope and blood pressure cuff out. The children parted before the fat interpreter and the black haired nurse they did not know, and a hubbub broke out in Arabic.

"Ask them what happened " Karen said with authority.

Doha did, and she was perplexed "they say she just fell asleep."

"What's' her name, get the sheet" Karen commanded.

"Her name is Alia El Haq, where is the Doctor?"

"Lets see, her pulse is 76, write that down, and her respiration is 20, and her blood pressure is...." the cuff deflated "90 over 60. Stable. I don't know where is the Doctor. Call an Ambulance from the University Hospital."

"Yes, yes, right away" Doha jumped up and rushed outside, to the office, and grabbed the only phone from the dumbfounded secretary. It was the old type rotary phone, and she dialled at it 9, and it clicked laboriously back, 9, and again 9, interminable ringing, and a sleepy voice said:

"Marhaba."

"Marhaba, we have a sick walad at the American School, quick, quick, send an ambulance."

"Marhabtein to you too, I will send you one now. No Doctor, just a driver, the Doctor is busy."

"Allah-hu Akbar, we have a nurse here, send the ambulance quick, her father is a very imbortant man at the Islamic Jihad" and she put the phone down. What was his phone number? They never told her that, it was secret. Now what will the secrecy do? Thank Allah, the Hospital was only one kilometer away. She huffed and puffed outside to the gate and told the guard to open it wide so the Ambulance could enter.

The wail of the siren waxed quickly, and the white-and-red Transporter with the red crescent-moon came into view, it was inscribed in Arabic and English 'Donated to the people of Lebanon by ALSAC, Cedar-city, California'. The driver changed from wail to wow, with abandon, and turned the ambulance neatly inside the yard, with it's front facing out, and the back doors facing the school. The driver ran to the back, and jerked out an ancient gurney, which, miraculously, still rolled, clicking away busily.

Karen in the meantime had shifted the sleeping Alia to a comfortable position, established an IV, taped it, and made her ready for transport. She had Nadia, who was aghast at this situation, and Doha, help the driver in loading the thin body on the gurney and kept listening to her heart. "Move in now" she said loudly and Joe moved quickly. He took off the grey rain-suit and revealed the doctorish get up, and moved up to the gate. The guard was mightily surprised and spoke to him in Arabic. Joe replied in English.

"There is a sick walad inside."

The guard's English was only enough to nod, he understood the 'walad'. Joe strode to the front of the Ambulance and climbed into the front seat, hefting a big bag in. The guard's attention was taken up by the procession that came through the school's green-painted iron door. The driver, pulling the gurney, two women behind, and a nurse holding the fluid bag, a bunch of hysterical teachers trailing. He rushed to hold the back doors open and Joe hunkered down so as not to be seen from the back. The driver loaded the gurney, Karen climbed in with the sleeping child, and the driver closed the double doors. He rushed to the front and almost jumped out of his skin at the sight of the Doctor who had materialized out of the thin air.

"Go, go" screamed Karen with urgency comprehensible in any language "She is having seizures, Doctor come and help me" The driver stepped on the pedal and engaged the gear. Joe used the momentum to move to the back, and winked widely at Karen.

The driver concentrated on the narrow roads and lousy drivers who were jostling him for road space even though he was The Red Crescent Ambulance Driver. He decided to take a short cut, through a side street and as he did, he felt the cold steel circle of a rifle barrel at the nape of the neck. His blood seemed to freeze in his veins and cold sweat suddenly stood on his face.

"Arretez le voiture." Joe said in his most venomous. The driver obeyed,

He had seen enough violence on the mean streets of Beirut..

The Doctor, a blue eyes individual, with a blond shock of hair, blond brows and smooth shaven face clicked the siren off. "Raus" he said in a thick German accent. The driver knew that too, and he slowly opened the driver side door. Karen gave Joe two epipens lashed together and Joe stuck them into the drivers deltoid. His eyes turned sleepy and he collapsed. Joe pulled him into the back and laid him on the bench. Alia was beginning to move groggily. Joe got into the front, gunned the engine and engaged the first gear. The Transporter surged forward and Joe pulled off the wig and snicked on the wail. He took off the driver's French Kasquette hat and pulled it low over his forehead and eyes. He went back on the main Shari Dunan thoroughfare and headed south, the American University to the North and the Mediterranean to his left. Shari Dunan was one of the few wide unobstructed roads and he soon passed the Shari Kurie, and the Lebanese university and Unesco buildings. The peninsula got narrower and he joined the main road to Sidon, only 43 kilometers south, bypassing Beirut International to his left at the foot of the mountains. As was the custom he used the siren and leaned on his horn liberally.

Mustafa was very satisfied. Three shipments of the virus had gone out to Rasheed, and had made their circuitous route to Muhi-a-deen-Shareef. Muhi had incorporated them into the production of the Sabin virus and the first lot had been sent on it's way to Israel. Fat'hi el-Hadir, Hariri's body-guard, who cultivated that Francine from the blood center relayed the information that whoever had been snooping around the blood-bank the day after he was gone, had not shown up again, only the FBI types stayed. Mustafa was not worried by the FBI. He knew of their abilities. He also knew how hampered they were by red tape and procedures. They could look around if they wished. Pity he did not have time to physically destroy that hard drive but he did erase it.

His newest ploy was very ingenious. His laboratory had just produced a crop of Virus which had been taken to southern Lebanon. The Jezzin region, which abutted the Israeli proclaimed, so-called Security Zone, was completely infiltrated by the Shiite sympathizers of the Islamic movements, including the Jihad and Hezbollah, the Party of Allah. They had recruited a Christian Lebanese woman who had a permanent job in Metullah, the northern-most Jewish town, whose city limits was the Good-Fence, as the stupid Israelis named that section of the border. Their allies in Lebanon, the Antoine Lahad forces , who were Christian Militiamen paid by the Israelis to do the dirty work for them, and who were in reality the last remnant of the old Lebanese Army, were completely corruptible, and for money would smuggle anything over the Fence. This woman, whose husband was a low-ly sergeant in that motley army, made the acquaintance of a Druze from Mas'ade, a village near the Hermon mountain in the Golan Heights, a village which retained it's ties with the large Druze minority in Syria, and was therefore anti-Israeli. That did not stop them from participating in the relatively booming Israeli economy, which meant they were strong in the construction industry in Metullah, and in the Wine cellars of that new-fangled brand, The Golan Winery. Again, just as Hasheesh was smuggled into Israel over the Good Fence, Youness had been able to establish a route into the Israeli wine-makers cellars. The automatic machines which filled the bottles after pasteurization still had to be dealt with, but he was assured that it was only a matter of time before he could introduce his virus into the wines.

He had to admit though that the situation with Alia was much more difficult. Mustafa was happy at his work and milieu. Obviously Alia was not, and he was troubled by the report from that goat Doha, that Alia was talking about her Mother out of his presence. It was the American School, he decided, he must find her another school, maybe an all Girls Islamic institution that will bring her into line. A soldier, one of those Jungle Green bozos came into the lab office, carefully.

"I am busy."

"Ya Sidi."

"What is it?" Mustafa said testily.

"Ya sidi, telephone call from the school."

Mustafa got up and followed the soldier upstairs, the only phone line to the basement was dedicated to his computer.

"Marhaba."

"Marhabtein, Doctor El Haq?"

Mustafa took a moment to readjust.

"Yes."

"Doc-Tor, your daughter is sick, we sent her by ambulance to the Hospital." Mustafa felt as a if a jackhammer hit him in the chest, and his breath whistled in and out.

"What Hospital?" he croaked.

"The American University Hospital, in an ambulance with a nurse and a doctor. It was right after the shots."

"What shots?!!"

"We give all the children shots at first grade."

"Kuss Ommac" blurted Mustafa, the gutter language reasserting itself across the gulf of adulthood and education.

"Doctor el Haq!!"

"Sorry, I will go there right now" and he threw the phone down. "Suleiman, Suleiman" he screamed. The soldier reappeared.

"Get the car, take me to the hospital, the American University." The soldier shook his head.

"I cannot do that, orders!!"

"*I* am giving you an order, you imbecile!"

The soldier shook his head. "Youness says...."

"Fuck Youness, listen, if you don't take me now, I will personally concoct a virus that will make your balls fall off, and pour it down your **EAR**." The soldier, a child of poverty, ignorance and superstitious fear , blanched, who knows what this crazy Doctor will do, see how Youness Shkaki treats him with kid gloves. He turned and ran outside, with Mustafa in close pursuit.

"Al sayara, the car" Suleiman called on the guard outside, and that one ran off. The green Mercedes was brought out of the posterior garage and made it to the gate. Suleiman held the door for Mustafa, and jumped in himself, he was armed, and he had a bunch of VIP cards which enabled him to go past road blocks manned by the Syrian Army, and the Lebanese posts. Money talked, and Youness knew how to spend it wisely. Behind him a new detachment of soldiers took up the guard duties.

As befits a leader, the leader's car had a cell phone. Mustafa, who was being bounced around crazily as the car negotiated the track down from the villa to the more civilized streets, called 999, and waited interminably. The car crossed the Bayrut river and still he could get nothing, the car turned north and the driver took chances and close calls nonstop up Tariq Ash-Sham and the National Museum, and all the way to the congested Cornice of the peninsula to the American University and Hospital. The Mercedes came to a screeching halt in front of the Emergency Room doors. Mustafa threw the Mercedes door open violently and was out like a shot. This wasn't Chicago or Milwaukee but it appeared adequate. He grabbed an orderly.

"Did you see an ambulance come in with a child?" the orderly shook his head. Mustafa pushed him aside and ran to the reception behind the windows. There was a long line of people waiting at that window. Mustafa, with the aid of Suleiman pushed them aside roughly. The people protested mildly till they saw the Kalachnikov.

"The ambulance !!Did the ambulance come with a child, a girl?"

The receptionist, frightened, heavily made up to look like a French film actress, shook her head "no, it went out with a driver but it's not back yet."

"When was that? and what about the Doctor on the ambulance?"

"I apologize, but there was no Doc-Tor on that ambulance. Our Doctor came back with an old woman."

"No Doctor?? What about the nurse?"

"Just the driver, it was not an emergency."

Mustafa was about to vent his frustration at this dumb bitch when the realization hit him yet again, with a massive blow to his midriff. No Doctor, no Nurse, She had been Kidnaped, taken forcibly, or by trickery. Who could it be? The Israelis? they had done some daring deeds in the heart of Beirut but that was in the Seventies, since then they had lost their audacity and were shaking in their boots. The Americans? impossible, they took months and years to make a move, and none of Youness' informants have told him about any CIA coming through Beirut International. A rival faction? but who knew that Alia might be important. It must be Amanda, but that was impossible too, the same watchers and paid Border Police had been notified, and Amanda could not be missed. Then who?

Mustafa recovered and talked to the girl more reasonably. "Look, I am her father, and I am worried sick, can you call the Ambulance on the Radio?"

The woman opened the door to the reception area "go back there to Samir, he is taking emergency calls, he can call on the Motorola, but this one" she indicated Suleiman "stays out." Mustafa rushed in, and ran head-long to the room marked 'RADIO.' He burst in. Samir El-Kader was hunched over the Motorola, calling.

"Red Crescent two, red Crescent two, do you read?"

"Is that the ambulance you sent to the American School?" Mustafa huffed.

"Yes, who are you, no one is allowed in here."

"I am the father of the child in that ambulance."

"There is no reply, he said he was at the school, then he was gone from the air."

Mustafa grabbed the mike "Red Crescent two, Alia, are you there?"

"He is on to us" Joe said, he had turned off the siren and was riding sedately along the coast road, they had passed Damur and the horrible camps to the west, and sign said in Arabic and French 'Sidon 10km.' Alia was awake, but not quite, and she had no concept yet of what was going on. The driver was still out, the day was overcast but the cloud cover was thinning and the sun was coming out.

"How do you know, it's all the same Arabic?"

"I know his voice, and he said Alia, who else would know? Let's switch. You drive."

"I have never driven a gear-shift."

"Now is the time" Joe turned into an orange grove, one of many which appeared on the side of the road and stopped. The radio kept the urgent messages, and Joe grabbed the driver under his arms and pulled him out, obscured from the main road. He laid him down in the dirt, and jumped to the passenger side. Alia, her eyes huge with terror, was staring at Karen, and then at him.

"Uh-Oh" said Joe and as Alia gathered air for a really big scream Karen whipped off her black wig and said:

"I am American." And the scream never came.

Joe rummaged in the big duffel bag and came up with a camcorder, a Sony with a flip screen. He fiddled with the controls and opened the flip-screen to Alia. He stuck the jack of the Walkman earphones into the receptacle and Karen gently placed it on Alia's ears.

Amanda's face came into view.

"Alia, my sweet darling, don't be afraid, these are my friends and I sent them to bring you back" the view zoomed back to show Joe and Karen, smiling on either side of herself.

"Mommy, mommy, where are you?" sobbed the little one.

"Don't be afraid Alia, I want you to trust them, and go with them. Their names are Karen."

"That's me " Karen said.

"And Doctor Joe."

"That's me" Joe smiled at her.

"Your father took you away from me and from Linda and Jeremy, and I want you to help Karen and Joe to bring you back to America with them. Do you understand Alia my darling?" Alia Nodded forcefully at the screen. Karen and Joe exchanged a sigh of relief.

"I know you would, I'll be waiting" Amanda beamed at Alia from the screen, and waved goodbye, and faded out. Alia looked intensely at the screen, as if sufficient concentration could bring back her Mama's face.

To: Aman Pazan
From: Shomer rosh
sub: Shkaki villa
urgent urgent urgent
The man under observation code named Zefa left
the Villa in a major hurry going to Beirut. With
Guard and driver. Looked like a disaster.
Signed
Shomer rosh

"OK, you have three pedals, gas, brake, and clutch. Before you do anything you depress the clutch, that neutralizes it." Joe stuffed the camcorder back into his duffel-bag.

"OK."

"You depress the gas lightly to get the engine to move, and you ease out the clutch, as you feel the van moving you add more gas and continue letting out the clutch till it's all engaged."

"Like this?" the van jumped and stalled.

"Keep the clutch in and restart it" Joe said. The engine secreted in the back woke up again, "Try again." This time it moved very slowly and Karen drove it around the trees and back to the main road.

"Stop and depress the clutch" and she did, with confidence. Joe waited for a stream of cars vans and trucks, mostly the round-fronted Mercedes, to go past, at least they had a consensus of riding on the right, otherwise the traffic was chaotic with vehicles joining the road and cutting the opposite lane with abandon. "NOW" he said and with a lurch they rejoined the main road. The radio stopped squeaking.

"That's it, this ambulance is hot property, they are going to alert everyone and their sister to this ambulance." He looked at the map, which he had picked up from the Lonely Planet book, supplemented by one from the Anastasia travel agency, "Go as fast as you can to Sidon then we will turn left, faster."

"I can't"

"Yes you can" he operated the siren "Go, now" and she drove on and got into the habit of cutting the other traffic. The traffic thickened and they crossed the bridge over the Awali. They were in the outskirts of Sidon, a pretty fishing port from Phoenician times.

"Turn left now." She crossed the lane and up the narrow road, which started as a street with scores of turnoffs, then thinned out and ran along a small brook. The brook was running water and on either side there were more orange groves, and lemon and apple, if it wasn't for their predicament this could have been a pleasure ride into the bountiful countryside.

"Youness!"

"What is it Mustafa?"

"Someone grabbed my daughter from her school."

"By the Prophet's beard, how?"

"I don't know, it was an impostor Nurse and an impostor Doctor, they snatched the ambulance she was in."

"I am here with the chief of Police and the second in command of the Syrian Seventh Division. Give me all the information."

Mustafa rattled off the descriptions he had gleaned from Doha. "The ambulance is the Red Crescent two, it's a Volkswagen transporter number 4528, it's very conspicuous. Who could have done it?"

"We will ask after we catch them."

"But they might hurt her!!"

"If they went to such lengths to get her, they are not going to harm her now."

"Go with Allah, I will go back to the school and ask more questions."

"Allah-hu-Akbar."

Youness replaced the phone in the cradle, and looked at his troops, the chief of Police and the lieutenant commander of the Seventh Division were both in his debt, one for house he lived in and one for the bank-account he possessed in Switzerland. It was time to call in the debts.

"Gentlemen, the daughter of a brother had been abducted. It's noon now and in a few hours it will be dark. The Sayara is a Red-Crescent transporter, a man and a woman, both Western, the man blond, the woman black haired, the child is a six year old girl, black hair, blue eyes, very pretty. Do what you do best, we will finish out business another time. GO, NOW!"

To: Kaman Pazan
From: Kabar Moran
Sub: Islamic Jihad activity
In the last hour there is increased activity in Radio

networks identified as Islamic Jihad.
The activity is down to platoon level. They are
actively seeking a vehicle designated red crescent.
The field units are called to identify and follow but
not apprehend. The units which confirmed are
triangulated to Jazzin, Junia, Bikkfayah Alayh
Ba'abdah, Shta'urah, Nabatiyah, We are not aware
of any of our activity.
Advise.

To: Kaman Pazan
From: Kabar Horan
sub: Syrian seventh army activity
In the last hour, increased activity in Syrian
Seventh Division radio networks, especially Military
police posts. They are to report and follow a red
crescent   ambulance. The seventh division   is
primarily deployed in the Beirut environs and south
as far as Sidon.
We are not aware of friendly activity.
Advise.

"Who gives the vaccinations?" Mustafa interrogated the distraught school
master, Nadia Halif.

"Its UNWRA, but they use the Missions who bring in charity doctors,
from all over, France, Germany, the United States. The Doctor who was here
on Monday was Campbell, from the United States, the nurse was Laura
Brown, of the same mission, Stop-The-Hunger. But the Doctor did not come
in today, and it was a different nurse too."

"Who is your contact with this lousy mission?" They had the whole
conversation in English. Nadia was after all, an American, conversion or no
conversion.

"The chief of the mission is Father Doctor Strickland."

"Get him."

Nadia searched her little book and came up with a phone number. The
slow turning of the rotary phone infuriated Mustafa beyond belief, he raged
at this country and the antiquated infrastructure.

"Father Strickland?"

"Yeeeees" Strickland was as slow as the phone, no wonder they kicked his ass to Lebanon, Mustafa thought.

"One of the parents of a child here at the American School says that one of your doctors is involved in kidnaping his daughter."

"Is he mad?"

Mustafa leaned over and grabbed the phone, he was getting used to grabbing phones. "Listen, Doctor, or Father, I am not one of the primitive Islamic natives you guys look down on. One of the doctors you sent over here for the vaccinations has taken my daughter, and I know his name, It's Campbell, where is he? I want to know right now."

"Mister...."

"It's doctor, Doctor Halim." Nadia was perplexed, he had registered his daughter in the middle of the year as El Haq, and paid in advance. Halim?

"Doctor Halim then, I find the accusation ludicrous, and Doctor Campbell had left the country to go back home, if anyone has taken your daughter I am deeply sorry, because a child is not a game to be toyed around with, but I suggest you look closer to home before blaming one of MY doctors who are doing God's work here!!!" Strickland was furious, and Mustafa felt the sting of the words. It was better to get this man's cooperation rather than antagonize him

"Doctor Strickland, I am sorry, I am just very very concerned."

"I understand, please give our esteemed Nadia a means of communicating with you, and I will ask around our cohorts, I hope you find your daughter sir."

"We will have to dump this machine very quickly" Joe said scanning his 1;50,000 IDF Army topographic map. Karen was driving very slowly, this asphalt covered donkey track made it impossible to drive in a straight line more than 10 yards. She was negotiating potholes and debris, and going down to the narrow shoulder every time another car came in the opposite direction. "Turn up this track coming up on the right," Karen slowed and changed gear to first, and drove up the steep incline. A small village was spread out at the top of the hill. "Turn into this grove now." She turned and a second later the wheels sank down into the soft earth and the engine stalled.

"Break out some bandages, I want to use them as ties" Karen was very quiet, this was the real thing. They were in enemy territory, everyone's hand may be against them, and she could not picture how they could get out of this foreign intimidating land.

"Stay in the van till I call you" Joe said. She looked at him. He had the Kalachnikov across his belly, and he looked like a warrior, not a Doctor at all. He is my man and he is gonna get us outa here. Alia was dumb-founded with terror as she watched Joe leave the van in a crouch.

Joe slunk away, under the cover of the orange grove, to the track, and waited for a likely victim. An ancient Toyota pickup, it engine badly in need of attention, heavily loaded with firewood, lumbered up the incline, he let it go. Another ancient Mercedes, with eight or nine people stuffed inside, went up the slope, and 20 minutes later came back down, similarly loaded with other passengers. Another 15 minutes passed. A diesel engine turned at the main road and lumbered up. This was an old Mercedes truck, with the green rounded front and the blue piping that the Arabs preferred. The engine sounded good though. Joe checked his weapon, and chambered the round, and sneaked a quick look, there was only one driver, no one else was coming. He sprang to the middle of the narrow track and pointed the gun at the driver, aiming from the shoulder. Then, before the driver could make any assessments, he fired one round at the cabin. A hole appeared to the right of the driver, and the windshield starred. The heavy vehicle stopped, and Joe ran to the passenger side and wrenched the door open. He jumped up the three steps and pointed the gun at the terrified driver. The driver, a thin rake of a man with a thick moustache and a red Keffieh was trembling.

"Raus" said Joe and pointed outside. The man understood , opened the door and Joe followed closely, so that the driver will not run. He quickly pulled the parking brake handle. He followed he driver down the three steps and pointed him to the van. The bewildered man did not resist even for one second as the incredibly pretty woman tied his hands with the bandages, and the child looked on with trepidation. They left him tied to the benches in the Ambulance and ran back to the truck. Karen picked up Alia and urged her into the tall cabin. Joe threw all of their belongings into the cabin and climbed up. The engine was still turning over so he released the handbrake, engaged the clutch and continued the uphill drive as far as the first turn-off. He drove inside, and used the steep grade to turn the truck back, and then back down the track to the main road, which was at least, asphalted. He almost ran down a Syrian Army Gaz jeep which was going by full tilt. He followed the jeep at a distance, sticking the Keffiyeh on his head.

"You didn't hurt him, did you?"

"I frightened him badly" Joe said "he will get his truck back tonight, I guess, this is probably his livelihood" and he continued negotiating the narrow road and the oncoming drivers.

"Where did you learn to drive these trucks?"

"Right here in Lebanon" Joe chuckled. "The guerrillas stuck their Katyushas on anything that could move. They hid the pickups and trucks in schools and mosques, and then would pull them out to the outskirts of town or near a UN post, and shoot the Katyusha over in the general direction of a town or village in Israel. The Armistice border doesn't stop anything that flies. Then they would drive right back and hope that the Israelis would triangulate the direction and shoot back. If the Israeli artillery hit a village then viola, an instant public-relation coup, the Israelis are the bad guys again, pictures of wounded kids first page everywhere and Hezzbolah.com full of new fodder. If the Israelis hit a Katyusha truck, so what, there is lots more where it came from. We learned to steal those trucks so they don't get a chance to use them."

"You have had a hard life Joe" Karen shook her head and screamed over the raucous motor.

"And now you have it too."

"That's right, and don't you forget it, where are we heading?"

"Nabatiyah, then the Beaufort."

Karen looked down at the detailed map "I see Nabatiyah, where is the Beaufort?"

"Look for a major river and look for a sharp knee bend, its right above it." Alia was getting used to all this and she was sitting forward and looking over the truck's rounded beak. Karen found it.

"Why there?"

"This is the Northern-most Israeli outpost in Lebanon."

"How do you know it's manned?" Karen yelled.

"I logged on to Hezzbolah.com, they are saying the fight to liberate it is still on."

"Shit."

"Got a better Idea?"

"You got us in, you get us out."

"Didn't anyone tell you Joe goes around with a death wish?"

"Do you?"

"Not anymore."

"I love you Joe" and Karen leaned over Alia and kissed him on the stubbly cheek.

"Youness!" Youness Shkaki was back at the villa, in the communications room. He was monitoring all the activity, the telephones, the cell phones, the radios. He got all the troops of his relatively small organization alerted. He called on Nassralah, the Chief of Hezzbola in Lebanon and personally asked for help in locating the ambulance. He called on the Ahmad Jibril group and the other Refusal splinter groups to keep their eyes skinned, and the Seventh division was doing it's own road blocks. He was worried by the time, and by the fact that the darker sky were coming back, and sheets of rain on the horizon, closing in on the coast. Mustafa was sitting in the back of the room, knuckles rubbing at the white teeth, his jaw moving spasmodically.

"Yes."

"Message from Halil Mansour" Youness grabbed the phone, this must be important, Mansour was the second in command of the seventh Division.

"Youness here."

"Its Mansour, one of our patrols found a man who said he was the ambulance driver, north of Sidon."

"Any description?

"Man was big, Blond and spoke in German , woman black haired, tall, spoke in English. The driver had been drugged."

"Location?"

"Five kilometers north of Sidon on the coast road." Youness whirled and poked a baton into the map.

"Make a perimeter around Sidon, get into the harbor, stop all the fishing vessels, commandeer a boat, check any boat which left since 10 AM..."

"Youness, you forget who you're speaking to."

"Sorry, brother Mansour, but the father of the abducted girl is staring at me, and he is a dear childhood friend."

"All the jeeps are scouring the countryside, and all the fishing boats are being ransacked as we speak."

"Thank you Mansour, if you catch this man and woman there will be an extra reward for you and your battalion commanders." Youness put the phone down. "Prig" he said to no one in particular, "just because he was given command of a bunch of lazy pricks with all the guns and armor in the world he thinks he is above us, if we had half of what they have we could have rolled down all the way to Tel Aviv." he turned to Mustafa, who seemed to contract before his eyes, drawing his long legs up and biting, to self mutilation, on his knuckles.

"Mustafa, brother, what's with you, we will get them" and he held

Mustafa's shoulders and shook them, trying to bring life and decision into him. Mustafa's job was not over. Youness had many more plans of biologic destruction to wreak upon the Jews.

Mustafa took time to look up.

"They will hurt her, rather than give her back, I am so afraid, first it was my sister Alia, you knew her, didn't you?"

"I was in love with her, as a kid, why do you think I fought for you?" Youness smiled at the forlorn man, Mustafa didn't register.

"And now Alia will be mutilated and defiled again, and I caused it to happen" Mustafa wailed.

"Wrong, you did the right thing, she was being defiled by the American environment, free sex, free drink, free to help the Jews kill us. You saved her from it. Now they, whoever they are, want to destroy our scheme, destroy us, and give her back to this abomination of freedom. You can't give up, come, we'll go and talk to this driver, maybe we can come up with something more" Mustafa unfolded slowly and followed Youness to his Land-Rover.

To: Aman Patzan
From: Shomer Rosh
Sub: Youness Shkaki
Subject is leaving the Villa in his command car, followed by 4 guards in green Mercedes. He is with the tall thin individual, code named Zefa, (rattlesnake) no sign of Child which usually accompanies Zefa.
Signed
Shomer Rosh

To: Aman Patzan
From: Kabar Horan
Sub: Shkaki
report: Transmissions from Shkaki command vehicle. Shkaki is on the air himself, calling on units throughout southern Lebanon. Replies from Damour, Rashaya, Nabatyia, Marj-Ayoun. This is highly unusual. Shkaki prefers to stay off the air.

To: Rosh Aman

From: Aman Patzan
Sub: Islamic Jihad
Unusual activity in radio nets and other communications system in the organization. Youness Shkaki has left the roost and the whole organization has been mobilized for a search for an unknown vehicle code named Red Crescent. Activity in Lebanese Police networks, and Seventh division networks, regarding the same subject.
  Request correlation with other sources.
Signed
Amir Katz
Aman Patzan

Joe stopped the truck just before the top of the hill, and ran ahead. He whipped out his binoculars. Right where the map showed a narrow bridge and the junction with the north-south Bekaa road, there was a road block, two jeeps, soldiers around the junction. Once the truck was over this ridge there would be no way back without being seen. He ran back and climbed into the cabin.

"What is it?" Karen asked, she was busy opening a can of tuna for Alia. She had already cut some slices of the bread she had bought the day before. It wasn't great but it was food.

"Road block, we have to turn back, and cross the Zahrani somewhere else."

"What's the Zahrani?"

"A deep river gorge, the last one from here to the Litanni." Joe reversed the truck laboriously, the power steering had all but failed long ago, and drove back for one mile, then took a dirt track south, which wound it's impossible way across the hills. The traffic here was non-existent, and the truck was the best possible vehicle to cross the deep ruts and the flowing brooks, this area was sparsely populated, and even the map said the track was a secondary one, connecting god-forsaken villages to the main Sidon road. The fact that the old map was still good showed how little development occurred in southern Lebanon is fifteen years. The actual distance traveled was a few kilometers but, an least, this track lead to a bridge on the Zahrani. Alia, despite the jouncing, munched into the tuna sandwich, and Joe bit into his. The rain from the west was coming up fast and the afternoon was making the hills dark and forbidding. Joe drove on, thanking the hapless driver who had filled up, probably in Sidon.

The ambulance driver was not helpful at all, he was scared stiff and the great number of senior and intimidating officials, and, worse, non-official guerrillas, terrified him even more. All he could say was that the man spoke German, but understood the English that the Oriental-American nurse spoke, they had a gun but he didn't know which, and that he was drugged, and found himself wet and shaking in the rain a few meters from the main road, which he knew well, having traveled there daily. They were standing around the situation room of the Sidon Police Station. The Lebanese Police official nodded at Youness and Mustafa. His Motorola chirped.

"Red chief, red chief, this is Hosni Four, can you hear me?"

"Go ahead Hosny four."

"We found the Ambulance, Red Crescent two, eight kilometers east of Sidon, a local called in a gun shot."

"When was the gun shot?"

"Two hours ago, over."

"*Two hours*?" Ra'ed Al Ganem exploded

"Only one phone in the village, and the Moukhtar demanded payment for the use of the phone, a man was found with the Ambulance, over."

"What man? Over."

"Owner of a Mercedes truck, Green, mark five, long bed. He says a man shot at him with a Kalachnikov and made him give up his truck, and he saw a woman and child go with him."

"Bingo" said Mustafa, turned to the large map of southern Lebanon pinned to the wall. Youness joined him.

"Where do you think they are heading?" Mustafa asked. Youness followed the road east, which led to a major intersection north and south. Mansour Joined them, he was the military expert, he had fought 15 years before in the Bekaa valley against the might of the IDF and had seen that the invincibles can be defeated, or at least held back. The Jews had no stomach for losses.

"We have road blocks set up at this intersection, also all the way to Naqura, and on all the roads leading to the Zahranni. I could bring a chopper but it's too dark already, and this truck is the most ubiquitous type of truck in Lebanon. I'll get my men to check with all the patrols and road blocks." He went out side to his own command vehicle, festooned with antennas. He thought about radio eavesdropping, but this was not a military operation, this was just a favor he was doing Youness Shkaki, and an even bigger favour to his own Swiss bank account.

"Hafez one, hafez two, hafez Three."

"Hafez one, loud and clear."

"Hafez two, 3 by five."

"Hafez three, five by five."

"All Hafez units, this is Chief Hafez. Target is changed, green Mercedes truck long bed, man, woman, child, all Western, call all patrols and check position and road block set up."

"Hafez one, wilco."

"Hafez two, all after call all patrols."

"Hafez three, wilco."

Mansour repeated slowly for the benefit of Hafez two, they were the furthest, at Al-Quirwan . He listened in on the secondary nets as the patrols called back one by one.

"Hafez one two and three, recheck every 30 minutes" and he signed off. What a miserable day, instead of being in bed with that sweet babe he had stashed away in Beirut, he was stuck here in this lousy fishing port, and lousier police station yard. Youness will have to pay for this lost day. The fact that he sitting in a comfortable closed heated Range Rover while his soldiers were either in open Gaz Jeeps, or worse, on foot, bothered him not in the least. If you were born to the Alawi minority elite of Syria you became the Lieutenant General or better. If you were born to the majority Sunni then you were an enlisted man grubbing in the trenches. That's the way it always was since the Revolution. It made governing Lebanon much simpler. The down-trodden Sunnis could play high-and-mighty in Lebanon.

After an hour of riding walking-pace, Alia suddenly announced that she had to go. Joe stopped the truck, and allowed the girls to go out. In fact he needed to go himself. He left the motor running and jumped outside, where fat drops were beginning to wet the earth. He took the Kalach with him, product of a long habit. You ate, and pissed, and slept with your weapon. He crossed the dirt track and disappeared into the cherry grove. What a relief.

The Russian Gaz jeep crested the hill and came down fast onto the stationary truck that was blocking the route. The men had orders to set up a road block on the Zahrani, and check for a foreign couple and a child, totally weird, but the orders were clear, stop them and separate the adults, who were armed and dangerous, from the child, who was the daughter of some-one high and mighty, so instead of being in the warm barracks south of Damour they were running around looking for an Ambulance or a truck. This truck was in the way. Ranem, the driver, was about to beep his horn, when he noticed figures climbing into the truck, from the passenger side, a woman, in pants, and a child. A child? Ranem killed his engine and coasted to a stop behind the truck. Ranem stayed with the Gaz, and Moukhtar Zuabi and Mahmoud Halfi approached with caution. Joe, who was hidden behind the cactus fence agonized what to do. He crouched down and slunk along the fence to the Gaz jeep.

Karen almost jumped out of her skin when the ugly snout of the Kalachnikov was shoved into her face, followed by the bearded face of the Jungle-Green clad soldier. Alia screamed "Mommy" and made to flee out of the other side. Another Kalach made her retreat. Moukhtar said something in Arabic.

"He wants us to come out" Alia translated.

Moukhtar yelled some more, and waved his gun, Karen nodded, and descended slowly. Alia followed suit, and the soldiers prodded both of them back along the truck, to the stationary jeep. There was something strange about Ranem, the driver, but Moukhtar couldn't figure out what it was. Anyway, it was beginning to rain in earnest now, and Moukhtar wanted to get inside the jeep, and call company HQ. Suddenly he realized what was wrong, Ranem's gun was gone from it's slot.

"Karen, lay down" Joe screamed and Karen, already used to Joe's uncanny ability to materialize out of thin air dove at the dirt track pulling Alia with her. Joe appeared from the back seat of the jeep and loosed a short burst from the Kalach. The bullets zoomed by Ranem's ear and it began to bleed. The two soldiers stared dumbfounded at the menacing Kalachnikov, at the huge figure which towered over them from the back seat of the Gaz.

"Lie Down" Joe screamed, in Arabic, it was one of the phrases he did know, and the soldiers dropped their weapons and hit the deck. Karen, quick as a cat, picked the guns up, and ran to the jeep. Joe motioned Ranem to leave the jeep, the radio started squawking, calling the jeep no doubt. The threesome were on the ground, pelted with rain, and dark was only one hour away.

"Karen, tie them to the truck fender" Joe said.

"With what?"

"Use the gun straps, they're tough, Alia, go in the jeep, stay at the back."
Alia jumped into the Gaz, into the third seat.

"Just a minute, Ishlechhu, Ishlechu" Joe said. The trio looked up beseeching but Joe was implacable. Under the gun, one by one, Moukhtar, then Mahmoud, then Ranem, took off their coats and let Karen tie them to the truck fender.

"Joe?"

"What? put on one of those coats."

"They'll freeze to death."

"Yeah, I see some ponchos in the back of the jeep, throw over them." The soldiers could not believe their own eyes, as the beautiful woman opened the ponchos and gave them protection from the rain. The radio squawk continued.

"That's it. Let's go." Karen gave the tie one last heave and they hopped into the jeep, which was wet everywhere. Joe started the Russian engine, and then released the straps that held the canvas top and pulled it over the shivering women, then he swung into the driver's seat and gunned the engine. It was not very powerful, nothing like the four liter straight six, but it moved better than the truck.

"Thank you" Karen called as the truck was left in the gloom.

"Why thank them? They would have shot you if they thought you were dangerous."

"The only guy doing any shooting here is you."

"Did I hit anyone?"

"No" Karen conceded.

"Shooting first means they are shocked for long enough we can move before they realize we have only one gun, and one person capable of using it."

"Says who?" challenged Karen. She took one of the Kalachnikovs, released the clip, opened the breech, it was empty, then pushed the clip in and slapped it home. Joe who was driving as fast as he could, was amused.

"Annie Oakley?"

"I had a boyfriend who was a gun enthusiast."

"I hope we don't have to put your skills to the test."

"Me too, I have never made a shot in anger." Joe drove quickly through another motley hamlet, with no electricity, oil-lamps dancing in the windows, the rain eased off, it was going to be an on again, off again affair all night.

"The question is, where are they heading?" Mustafa repeated "that Syrian prig had no answers."

"He is just a military Bozo, he and his troops will do the leg work for us, for a fee" Youness said. "Let's think who they are, and then we will know where they are heading. Could your former wife have hired someone, like mercenaries?"

"I don't think so, she is just a Doctor, and she doesn't have the money."

"I thought Doctors make good money in America."

"They make good money and they have to pay big school loans, this man is a professional soldier, he doesn't kill if he doesn't have to."

"If it's not a Merc, and it is not a competing Arab organization, what could he be, and the woman too?" Youness wondered.

"Israeli, maybe they are following you, and thought that Alia may be a soft spot. They abducted Sheikh Obbayed, and Sheikh Yassin of the Hamas, fat lot of good it did them, but still."

"So why break East? Why not go to Sea where they have those Dvora patrol boats all the time?" Youness argued.

"I don't know, let's look at the map again, look in the general direction they are heading, This is Jazzin, lots of Maronites there, they are in cahoots with the Israelis."

"Possible, but Mansour has that route all covered, all the back roads too, he has more men and Jeeps than he has sperm" Mustafa grinned at that. Then his eyes wondered back to the map.

"Where is the Northern-most Israeli outpost?"

"That's easy, the Beau-fort. That's an old Crusader fort that overlooks the Litanni knee bend. We made them bleed for that Fort many times, Hezbollah is giving them hell every other day, but it's important, they wont give it up" Youness concluded.

Mustafa was looking at the point on the map, trying to give it some substance.

"If we get any additional data that points us in this general direction, I say this is where He is trying to go, with Alia, whoever He is, Allah-damn-him."

"I have some forces in the area, just at the foot of the fort there is a village, see it? Arnoun, they are supposed to be farmers, but during the day they are farmers, and during the night they are freedom-fighters, some of them are willing to be Shahid. If, as you said, they are heading for the Beau-fort, Arnoun will be ready for them."

Chapter 22

AHMAD

One of the headlights was blown, and Joe was taking the hairpin turns very slowly as they descended into the deep gorge, rattling and jouncing. The seats of the Russian Gaz were nothing to write home about, and the shock-absorbers were non-existent. It was like riding a stiff pogo-stick. Joe wondered how Alia was taking it, but he left that to Karen. Finally they made it to the narrow wood-planked bridge, and rattled over the rickety structure. Now came the laborious task of driving the sharp incline, and the hairpins up the other side, while the wheels spun in the dirt and mud. Painfully they made it up, up to the hilly plateau between the Zahranni and the Litanni, a rough land of huge boulders, which Joe knew well. Geologically, this was just an extension of the Upper Galilee of Israel. He stopped for a minute, doused the lights and used his small Maglight to review his old Army map. The orange printing which was so distinct in daylight was very faint in the artificial map of the Maglight. He confirmed with the GPS reading It was getting cold. Karen was shivering, and poor Alia was shivering even more.

"Joe."

"Yes Karen."

"We have to find some shelter, we can't spend the night outside, she will get sick and die of exposure."

"I know, we will find shelter."

"Where, who? Not some kind of a cave, I hope, we have to feed her, warm food." He could hear Alia's teeth going castanets.

"Ahmad."

"Who is Ahmad?"

"Long story, I'll tell you when we get there."

"If there a chance he will turn us in?"

"Yes, but I don't think so."

"Why not?"

"He owes me his life" Joe said.

"Another one? I thought I was the only one."

"First I almost got him killed, then I saved him, the goat story all over again."

"Whatever, let's move, she is freezing to death, the coats are wet through."

"Here, take this" Joe took off the Syrian coat, then his own, and draped it over Alia, her small face was pinched but she stayed brave, thanked Joe with her eyes.

"I know, you are never cold" Karen said with a chuckle.

"I wish to God you were right, keep that Kalach handy" Joe gunned the engine, he wondered when the radio people, who had been calling every few minutes, will alert their superiors. He had only six or seven miles to go to the village, west of Nabatiyah. Joe engaged the engine and continued the arduous task of driving the hell-road, shivering in the cold night air.

"Hafez Chief, Hafez chief, this is Hafez three" Mansour's radio man jumped and took the mike. Mansour was snoring in the front seat, he was fat and he snored loudly. Walid Jumbalat, the intelligence officer rolled out the map, switched the light on.

"This is Hafez chief, Go ahead."

"From Hafez three, one of the patrols is off the air, for at least one hour, you wanted to know."

"Lieutenant General, listen, one of the patrols is off the air." Mansour woke up with a start, it was mid-evening, but the dark sky made it midnight. he took the mike.

"Hafez three, elaborate."

"Patrol number 3, D company, does not reply."

"Where is he supposed to be, over?" Demanded Mansour.

"Coordinates 33815 north and 34995 east, bridge on the Zahranni."

Mansour's Intelligence officer located the point on the map, "its deep in the gorge, transmission may be difficult."

"Hafez three, could it be the location, over?"

"No sir, we have a repeater at the top, if he were on the air we should hear him."

"Hafez three, this is Hafez chief, close in on that bridge from both directions, use caution." Mansour lumbered outside, into the police station and found the threesome, Raed, Mustafa and Youness examining the map. He took out his pointer and slapped it on the Zahranni bridge.

"That's it, they are trapped, a Jeep is gone which was supposed to be going down this track to the Zahranni. They are trapped on the plateau between the Zahranni and the Litanni." Mustafa and Youness exchanged glances, Mustafa's hunch was playing itself out.

"Do you have any detachments in Nabatiyah?" Youness asked the Syrian

Lieutenant general.

"Of course not, that's too close to the Israelis, we can't give them an excuse to attack us from the air." It was a sorry fact, that despite the enormous effort Syria put into the Airforce and the air-defence, it was the IAF, the Israel Air Force, that ruled the sky, bombing with impunity wherever. For the Guerrillas, the airforce was not a factor. For the Syrian Army, it was a major deterrent. If the Syrians ever made a suspicious move, the Israelis raided the Syrian controlled Bekaa valley, or the main Beirut- Damascus road, and the Syrians backed down. Actually, it was a source of embarrassment to the Syrian Commanders vis-a vis the Palestinian and Islamic guerrillas who were lobbing Katyushas over the border on Jewish villages and towns. They could, but the Syrians could not. "I am going back to my Command car" Mansour said and backed out. He hoped his limited forces south of the Zahranni would catch those rascals before the Lebanese or the Palestinians or even Hezbollah.

"I have a sizeable detachment in Nabatyiah" Raed al Ganem said. He lifted the phone and asked the operator to get him the Nabatiyah Police, while he was waiting he grinned at the others "When the Israelis left it in '85, it was cleaner than when we left it in '82."

"Nabatyiah Police."

"This is Raed al Ganem, I want to speak to Halil Jubran."

"He is gone for the day, the officer of the watch is Sabah Nimri, here he is sir."

"Sabah al hir Nimri."

"Sabah el nur, Al Ganem, sir."

"Sabah, we have a situation here. A bunch of brigands kidnaped a little girl, and are heading in your direction, probably in a Syrian Army Jeep."

"Did I hear correctly, Syrian Army Jeep?" Sabah was laughing his head off.

"Most likely, and the Syrians are pissed but helpless, if the Israelis see Syrian vehicles south of the Zahranni, the F16's and the Apaches will blow them apart, that's the unwritten agreement, so its up to us. Get some men on the roads, and off road."

"Now? Its raining cats and dogs."

"Yes now, your next appointment is coming up isn't it? You better earn it."

Mustafa and Youness drove south, to Az Zahranni, and turned left, east, into the dark hills. The driver was very careful, and the Mercedes behind him was even more careful. These roads needed daylight, and there was very little traffic on the narrow bitumen. This was the main road to Nabatiyah, and it stank. Mustafa found himself looking back with longing to the wide dependable roads of America, He had heard that the Jews built roads just like the American roads, wide and comfortable. Soon, once the virus was out and their babies started dying like flies, they would realize that the Middle East will not tolerate them, that Palestine was Arab, just like Syria, and Lebanon, and Jordan. I hope this man is not molesting my Alia, because if he is, I will tear him apart, bit by screaming bit.

The hillock at the end of the track was a few hundred meters short of joining the pavement that led to Nabatiyah. Joe stopped the jeep, jumped out, and slithered up the slope, to the top of the hill overlooking the road. This was a main artery, and even at night there was some sparse traffic on it. There was a bigger glob of light, which was moving, and his amplified Russian binoculars showed him a sizable convoy of identical headlights, which was moving slowly in their direction. He ran back to the jeep. Karen was not even speaking, she was just trying to keep Alia and herself warm. Joe gunned the jeep savagely and careened down the track, swerving violently to avoid potholes and boulders revealed by his meager light, and then they hit the asphalt. Joe turned on the asphalt, east again, towards Nabatiyah, and decked the gas. The wind tore at the canvas, luckily the rain had stopped, but the cold air froze them even more. The mouth of a tiny ribbon of Asphalt appeared on the right and Joe took it like a rabbit down a hole with the fox in hot pursuit, drove up about two hundred meters and suddenly killed his engine, doused the lights and coasted to a stop. The night was utterly quiet. The gas gauge was lit, and showed almost empty. Behind them on the main road, the convoy of cars and jeeps went by. At the turnoff to the north the convoy dropped off two vehicles. Joe heaved a sigh of relief. We are famous now, or maybe notorious, they don't dare send just one vehicle.

"What now, Joe?" Karen's voice was unrecognizable, a sick frog with Laryngitis.

"How is Alia?"

"Can you believe it she is asleep?!"

"I can, we have to dump the jeep and walk."

"Walk!!!? how far?"

"Just over one hill."

"These are mountains, not hills."

"This Jeep is hot property, we wont be able to use it anyway."

"Don't worry, I'll walk, what about Alia?" Karen asked.

"I will take her, she is lighter than many loads I have taken, right here in these hills."

"But that was years ago."

"This is my last hurrah, after this I will retire" Joe said.

"Me too."

"We'll retire together, we have one more mile to go, then we walk." Joe checked again, the map against the GPS, started the Russian engine, and read the kilometers precisely. He knew exactly which hill it was, it was the hill of the Cherries, where long ago, a life-time ago, he had been served a steaming cup of coffee by Ahmad Abu Rabia.

"Slow down" Youness ordered the driver, a convoy of four jeeps were coming in the other direction on the main road going east-west, "Stop" and he got out and waved at the police jeeps that were coming up.

"Marhaba, where is Sabah Nimri?"

"I am Sabah, who are you?" said a shadowy figure in the lead jeep. This was an old US army jeep, bought as surplus, and it sounded surplus too. Nimri eyed the new model Land Rover and the matching Mercedes with envy. Those murderous Palestinian factions knew how to live, and even now he was getting the runaround due to one of their numbers. Like most other Shiites Nimri wished the Palestinians begone from Lebanon, they were an unwanted pest, which brought on Lebanon the double pests of Syria and Israel. But Al Ganem told him to cooperate, and in view of his upcoming promotion, he would. Nimri knew who Youness was, he just wanted to make sure.

"Youness Shkaki, and in the Land Rover is he father of the kidnaped girl, this is a friend, I am doing this for a friend, and You are doing it for a friend and comrade."

"Of course" Nimri said, not at all convinced. Youness pushed on.

"Did you search all the roads and tracks from the Zahranni?"

"I left a two-vehicle unit each with a corporal at every north turn, there are not that many, but he may cross between them. It would be better at daylight."

"I am sure this man thinks the same."

"But he is bogged down with a woman and child!!"

"This man has been able to overcome three Syrian soldiers, and take their vehicle. The soldiers were found tied to a truck he had stolen earlier. The woman with him is as dangerous, she handles guns as if she knows how to use them. Don't underestimate them."

"Alright, I wont, but I don't have the manpower to search this whole block of territory, 15 by 15 kilometers, the hills and valleys and houses."

"First we look for a Syrian Gaz on a dirt track, then we narrow the search down, and call all of the Seventh Army to help us. I am going to Nabatiyah to get my forces out on the road."

Mustafa exited the land Rover and came over. "Captain Nimri, do you have any children?"

"Four" said Nimri proudly, "two boys, two girls."

"What would you do if your female child were taken from you by force?"

"I would tear the world to find her."

"Then do it for me. One day you may need a favor from the Islamic Jihad."

Nimri nodded, unconvinced. Having the armed Militias around cut into his Policeman's soul. No one should be able to carry arms in public except the Police, and these people represented the opposite, an untamed militia, who strutted around and flouted the law. The hell with Al Ganem, he was probably collecting graft. Why did no one say anything about the mother of this child, where was the Crying Mother? This whole thing stinks. He nodded and drove off. Youness shook his head.

"This policeman is of no help. We will have to play out our hunches and wait for them in Arnoun."

Nimri called up his men and told them to do a slow, methodical job, and drink lots of coffee.

Joe drove the Gaz into a tiny side track, behind some trees and cactus. He reviewed the place and at least from the track no one could see it. The clouds were rolling away but the cold was getting worse, the temperature rapidly approaching Zero celsius. Alia was totally bewildered and disoriented, she wondered about until Karen caught her and held her still.

"Where are we?" she asked Karen, her voice very tiny.

"Joe knows" Karen replied.

"And he always knows?" asked the little one.

"Almost always" Karen replied, Alia was too tired to say anymore.

"Take one Kalachnikov, I'll take one, and the bag with all the electronics, you take some food, and water canteens." He slipped his arms into the handles of the big bag and loaded up."Now you" he said to Alia. Karen helped her up on Joe's shoulders, and she lay there like a sack of potatoes, and

Karen covered her with a Syrian coat.

"It's about one and a half miles" Joe said and began to climb up the hill. Karen slipped into her bag the same way and followed. It was the hardest hike of her life. It was quiet, and strange, at least she was not cold anymore, in fact after a while she was compelled to take off her coat. Joe stomped on like a machine, but when she caught up with him she heard the breath whistling in and out, the heaving chest, the bowed back. The ambient light increased as the clouds rolled away, and the vapor wafted out of his steaming mouth. Joe stopped one time for a short five minute rest and a drink, but then loaded up again and continued up hill. They were crossing terraces, and the ground between the terraces was soft and clingy. Slowly and painfully the incline became less aggressive, and then they crested the hill. Joe stopped and gently went down on his knees to let Alia down. She was shivering uncontrollably. Karen opened her coat and covered the poor waif top to bottom.

"Here it is" Joe said pointing at the shadowy hulks strung along the narrow blacktop , "it's the last house with the flat roof, keep her warm, I am going down there."

The village was on a road, there were electricity poles, and some of the houses showed electric lights. Ahmad's house was the last, as it has always been, the population of south Lebanon did not increase by much, owing to the pressures on all sides. Whoever could emigrate and move North, did. Beirut was enjoying a renaissance, Junia, Tripoli, even Zahle and Riak and Baalbek were doing OK. The South, where all the factions were waging war against Israel and each other, where the main type of teacher was a Shiite Iranian fundamentalist Moslem, remained backward. Nabatiyah had exactly one hotel, or Inn, and no visitors. Only the Cherry and Apple and some other fruits brought some income.

Joe approached with caution, placed his Kalach just behind the terrace and hopped over it. Twelve years ago it had been much easier. He came up to the back door. Gently he knocked at the sheet-iron door, then again, and again, until he heard movement and talking inside, a man and a woman, arguing.

"Ahmad, Ahmad" Joe called, quietly. The bolt was with drawn and the door opened a crack. "C'est Capitan Joseph" there was a sharp indraw of breath, and the door was opened all the way, the tall man, his beard white, but his face still as guile-less as before, held the old oil lamp to Joe's face.

"Monssieur le Capitain, c'est vous, vraiment, entrz, entrez."

Joe moved in and closed the heavy door, the woman, old, lined, tired of life, crouched behind. Joe stopped Ahmad from asking questions by raising a finger to his own lips.

"Ahmad, I have a woman and a child up the hill, they are half-dead, I need shelter and hot food for them, I would not put you in danger just for myself."

"Je sait, I know" Ahmad replied in the same whisper "bring them in quickly" and he doused the light.

Joe exited carefully, then jumped over the terrace and ran uphill as if the jets of hope were charging his feet. He could not see them, his night vision was destroyed by the lamp. "Karen, Karen" He whispered fiercely, and a tree split in two and became a figure.

"Here."

"Let's go, he is waiting." Joe gathered Alia in his arms and headed down, Karen dragging the bags behind her. This time Joe was careful, the little body was shivering in his arms, and the heart was beating very fast and he did not want to lose his footing. I hope she isn't sick with anything. They reached the back door and before Joe could call it opened and Ahmad pulled them in. This time the Kalach came into the house.

Karen and Joe were sitting on the rug, on soft pillows, in Ahmad's sitting room, sipping the hot sweet tea, of which there was plenty in the pot. Joe relaxed, and draped his arm on Karen's shoulder, drawing her close, and she snuggled even closer. Latifa, Ahmad's wife, was transformed into a mother instantly as she saw Alia, she had taken her from Joe, waved Karen away, made a hot bath for her, and plied her with rice and dumplings. The little one took a little time to revivify, and Joe was amazed to look at his watch, it was only eleven PM, but then the actual distances they had traveled were short, and night began early in a country without daylight savings in winter. Ahmad poured them some more tea and they conversed in French and English, which Ahmad had learned in the intervening years. Joe was looking fixedly at the one picture in the whitewashed bare room, a picture of a young, raven haired, bronze-skinned beautiful girl, the girl on the roof, the girl who had sworn spitefully in his face more than a decade ago. Ahmad followed his gaze, and his eyes clouded with wetness.

"Sura, my beautiful Sura, c'est magnifique, le photo, n'est pas?"

"Where is she?"

"Upstairs. She will not show her face to strangers."

"I am very sorry, I watched her once, she is so full of life" said Joe with real sorrow, Karen was amazed at the emotions expressed. Joe took some time to tell her about that day when Ahmad was wounded.

"She thought I was responsible for the shooting, and of course, that was partially true."

"I keep saying Joe, that you take too much of the world's miseries on your shoulders, however wide there are. Let it go Joe, you are not responsible" Karen said with compassion. Her man would not be consoled, but he gave her shoulders a hug, transmitting his acknowledgment for her effort.

"C'est vrais, you did not let me die, you control what you can, and the rest is up to Allah, who is the child?"

"She is the daughter of a friend." Karen replied "her father kidnaped her forcibly and we decided that we should bring her back."

"Comme toujours, Capitain Joseph to the rescue" Ahmad smiled, just for a moment.

"Yeah right" Joe said, deprecating, "what happened to Sura? You never wrote me the details."

Karen was taken by surprise again and again, as the multiple lives of the man she had chosen were being revealed, like the peels of an onion. "Have you two been in contact over these years?"

Ahmad leaned back to the wall. "Once a year, on the anniversary of my shooting, Capitain Joseph writes a letter, addressed via an Swiss intermediary, and I answer to the same address. Peter Herzig, but in the last five years, nothing, until about a week ago. Voulez vous les details?" Joe and Karen nodded.

"The military ambulance took me to the military clinic, I was badly wounded but stable, that's what *you* told me later. They did some first aid, then they took me by helicopter to Haifa hospital, Rambam. They treated me very well, just like they treated the Lahad wounded. You came there to visit me, at least three times. That was very important for me, because I was all alone in that huge Hospital. Then, when I was out of danger they took me with a military ambulance to Mettulah, and then by a Lahad forces ambulance to Marj Ayoun. Only then did I understand how low Lebanon was. Cross the border, and I was in a different continent. But I needed only nursing, and I was twelve years younger, and Latifa came to visit. Sura stayed with my half-sister in the village."

"When I came back to the village, it was like coming back to Iceland, but colder. I opened the café, but no one came. I sat alone day after day, after day, and no one came to the café. I polished the pots, and cleaned the cups, and collected the cherries, but my buyer in Nabatiyah would not buy, nor did anyone else. When the Toyota broke own, the shop wouldn't fix it. And Sura, my beautiful Sura, who was a the age for matrimony, not a single boy or man would talk to her."

"They came one evening, four men and the Kadi. They knocked on the door and asked to come in, to discuss the Café. I let them in, they all live in the village, and I thought that if I explained to them that I had had no choice, that I had been taken by the Israelis unwillingly, they might reconsider and lift the boycott. They said that the village council was waiting for us, all of us, so we went to the Mosque.

"You realize in this kind of village, we are about four Hamulas, with just a few strangers thrown in. We know everyone, everyone is a distant cousin. I was one of the few who had ever left the village for studies before the 1975 war, and I came back here for ma chere Latifa," Ahmad stroked, with his eyes only, his old wife, who came in to replenish the teapot and bring Baklawa sweet cakes. By Arab tradition, the woman never sits with the men, but rather retires to the back room with other women, and Latifa was of the old tradition. "This house was my father's and my grandfather's. My six children were born here, three died young, probably because Latifa is my first cousin, and three lived. The older two are boys, Hani lives in the village, and Omar, the clever one, emigrated to Germany, and sends money. Without his support we could not survive."

"Mukhtar Mahdi was sitting in the center, and the Kadi took up position to his right. It was a trial, and I was accused of collaborating with the Enemy, the Israelis. The Kadi read it all out, the coffee, the acceptance of the coffee, they had me under observation for a long time because I resisted the way the Islamic fundamentalists took over the village. They read out that an Israeli officer helped me, that an Israeli ambulance took me away to the Division head-quarters, that I had been to hospital in Israel and in Marj-Ayoun, which is Maronite, everything was an accusation. These at least were facts, but then they read out complete fabrications. The Kadi wrote that I had turned in Islamic brothers to Shabac, that I signaled from the top of the hill to the Israeii watchers with a mirror, that I had a radio for communications."

"All that was just the beginning. Then the Kadi continued to read from a second scroll. Now the criminal was Sura. She refused to wear a chador, she displayed her beauty in public, she displayed herself to the Israeli soldiers from the roof-top, she was in fact a Zionist harlot and she had the Zionist soldiers in her bedroom, with my encouragement, and so on and so forth. Sura, my beautiful Sura blanched, and cried, and made herself small, and lowered her kerchief over her face, but the Kadi was implacable. It was a very long scroll, and it was all lies, lies, lies. The friends, and neighbors, and the young men who had asked me for her hand innumerable times hooded their eyes and said nothing. And of course there was nothing they could say. In the shadows of the back wall sat a figure, long black beard and a turban, surrounded by a dozen fearsome men with guns. They said nothing, they did not have to say anything. I and my family were to become an example."

"Then the Kadi asked if I had anything to say."

"I looked at all the people, cousins, customers, friends, neighbors, and no one would look back at me, their eyes were hooded and they were afraid."

"I stood up, and said that it was all lies, that I had served coffee to the men because they were in my orchard and Arab custom decrees that if a man is in one's house, or field, then he is a guest, and must be treated with respect. I said that after the shooting I had no control over my body, and that I had never had any relations to the Israeli soldiers. I challenged them to find a radio or any other means of communications. And I pleaded with them to place any blame on me that they wished, but that Sura was blameless, all she did was hang laundry in the privacy of the roof. I pleaded that she was pure and had never revealed herself to anyone. I could see that the sentence had been set, and that their hearts were hard, or fearful, or both."

"Finally I could hold my tongue no longer, and I said to my friends and neighbors and Hamula that they were lower than sheep. That they knew who had shot me in the back, and that only an Israeli was man enough to save me from bleeding to death in the street, like a dog."

"One of the men, a distant cousin, rose and asked the council to speak. The Kadi allowed him. He turned to me and said: "It would have been better if you had bled in the street like a dog, rather than take help from those curs, the Israelis, and cast a curse on the whole village" and he sat down. The black-beard in the back nodded agreement. There was nothing else for me to say."

"The Kadi asked the council if anybody wanted to speak in my favor, no one did, no one wanted to be singled out by the Hezbollah. They made a show of a conference, then the Kadi read the sentence:

"36 flogs to the Traitor Ahmad Abu Rabia, and

Boycott, everlasting ,of the café and the house. No one to build a house nearby, and.

Imprisonment to the village, I may never leave the village, on pain of death, mine and Latifa. She is their insurance. And

24 flogs and disfigurement to Sura, Harlot, daughter and collaborator of the Traitor."

"When I heard the last part I hurled myself at the Kadi and Mukhtar, but the men in the back were quick and they had me pinned down. The Kadi announced that since I resisted Justice, my sentence would be doubled. The sentence was to be carried out immediately."

"They tied Sura's hands around a post, they tore her dress to reveal her young unblemished skin, and the evil man in the back produced a fearful whip, with nine tails, and one of the younger bearded men flogged her, slowly, so that every scream cut into my heart. I tried to burrow into the soil, I tried to eat dirt, but they wrenched my face up so I had to see and hear. Every time she collapsed they threw a bucket of water on her back, which became a living, livid bloody mess with the little muscles showing, and bone peeking at her shoulders. They counted exactly 24. They poured more water on her, and then the evil man stood up, had two men hold her up, and used a ceremonial dagger to cut twice on her face, eye to chin, thick, ugly cuts that would never heal. Latifa cried and screamed and they let her take Sura away."

"Then they tied me, the same way, and flogged me, but it did not hurt anymore, I was weak anyway so I lost consciousness." Joe sneaked a look at Karen. She hid her horror well, she was getting inured to the savagery of this country.

"The women helped Latifa nurse us, and I wanted to get better for Sura. Her back healed slowly. Her face never did. All the bandages and poultices could not close those fearful cuts. There is no Doctor in the village and they did not allow Latifa to take Sura to Nabatiyah. The wounds healed badly and remained as red, then white scars, on my beautiful Sura" and he looked back to the photograph, Sura as a vivacious 16.

"Two months later Hani took her to the Doctor. The Doctor shook his head, the wound was set. That was the last time Sura left the house. That was more than 10 years ago."

"Ahmad, I want to see her" Joe said.

"She will not see you."

"Nevertheless, I want you to bring me to see her. I am not Capitain Joseph. I am Doctor   Joseph Bergman, I am a Pediatrician. This is Karen Fitzsimmons, she is an expert nurse. The least we can do is see if the wounds can be helped."

Ahmad regarded Joe with a new gaze, a new hope, he rose with a groan from his pillow, he was only 55 years old but his body had been badly abused, He led the way up the worn stone steps, leading with his oil lamp. He knocked on the green door.

"Sura."

"Go away" she replied in Arabic.

"I have a Doc-Teur to see you" and he pushed his way in. Joe pulled out his Maglight. Sura was sitting on the mattress, her face covered with a kerchief and incongruously, the room was full of bookcases and books. Joe, who was used to the bare walls of the typical Arab or Beduin abode was speechless. Ahmad noticed.

"Omar sent her these livres, the postman says it's a sin to carry books to the house of the Traitor, but he is also a distant cousin, so he brings them anyway." Joe played the light on the books, Arabic, English, German, French, and back to Sura, who was holding Shakespeare.

"Sura, viens ici, le Doc-teur est la" Ahmad commanded. Without a word Sura stood up, she was tall and still reedy, at the age when an Arab woman was already heavy with childbearing and feeding, and slowly she took off her kerchief. Karen inhaled sharply at the ghastly scars, Sura, at the recognition of Joe. Joe remained impassive and got closer to examine the scars. Sura lifted her free hand, and, in a flash, slapped Joe as hard as she could, a sharp stinging blow, which resounded on every ear. Ahmad and Karen recoiled at the ferocity of the slap. Joe said nothing, he retrained his flashlight on the scars, resettled the glasses on his nose, as if his left cheek was not on fire. Silence ensued.

Joe gave Karen the flashlight. She pointed it at his face, it was no worse than a bad case of a sun burn, and every finger could be seen.

"Next you'll say you deserve this" Karen said.

"Look at Sura, I am whole, she is not."

"Your fault again, I suppose" she was facetious.

"If not me, then who?"

"Whoever *did* it to her, you knuckle-brained idiot, you are not responsible for every goddamned sadist that ever walked the earth. Now do something positive!!" Karen almost hissed.

"Like what?"

"Like take them outa here just like you want to take *us* outa here!!" Joe smiled, and then his smile widened, until it encompassed his whole face. he turned to Ahmad.

"Listen Ahmad, listen to Karen, come with us, this can be fixed, given enough time, and money. I have a distant relative in Beverly Hills California. He is a plastic surgeon, he does the noses and chins for the Hollywood stars, he can fix this. Leave this miserable hell-hole, we will go to America, we will fix Sura's face, she could start a new life." Ahmad shook his head.

"Non, mon Capitain, I am too old, too set, and Latifa, she will not adjust to anything new, but if you take Sura with you, I will be eternally grateful. This place , this house, is living hell for her. Sura, will you go with Capitain Joseph and his Wife to America?"

"Avec Lui, avec le Soldat Israelien? Vous etes foux, Papa" she spoke with disdain, in French, so that Joe would understand.

"He is *not* an Israeli Soldier anymore. This was his past life. He is an American Doctor now, taking care of children with Cancer" Karen spoke slowly and clearly, the books in English made it possible that Sura was likely to understand, and she did. "We are here to bring a child of a friend Home. She is here now, would you like to see her?" Sura nodded. Karen turned and led the procession down the worn-smooth-with- a-dimple steps. Alia was sleeping peacefully, her curly black hair fanned on the pillow, her face angelic in repose, her chest rising and falling gently to the rhythm of breathing. Sura knelt and passed her hand over the raven curls, regarded the trusting face. She turned to Karen.

"I shall come with thou" she said in halting English. Lightening lit up the sky without, thunder followed a few seconds later, and a new rainstorm hit the village, obliterating any footmarks, tire-spoors, and dampening any wish by Nimri's and Mansour's men to continue the search.

The UN forces are spread thinly throughout the Middle East, trying to guard the fragile peace, and generally recording the infractions of loosely worded agreements. They were once in the Sinai peninsula, between Egypt and Israel, but since they were pulled out by the secretary U Tant at the behest of President Gammal Abd-el-Nasser, Israel refused to see the UN responsible for that territory and preferred the MFO, which, although Multinational in name, is American in everything but the name. The Syrian demarcation is overseen by UNDOF and the UN presence in South Lebanon, UNIFIL, has been continuous since the Litanni operation of 1978. The command headquarters is in Naqura, a sea side spot where the white cliffs negotiate the Mediterranean with a series of caves carved out by the waves, and the long border is divided into sectors manned by battalions. Each battalion is drawn from a different nation, the longest serving of which are the Norwegians.

They are lightly armed, and in fact never use their arms. At one time, when a French Battalion prevented Fatah from moving arms and ammunition, it was severely punished by having half a company slaughtered in a firefight, just to teach them who was the boss in Southern Lebanon. The UN learned quickly that if they wanted to survive in this hostile place, then they should turn a blind eye to the Guerrillas, and complain loudly about the Israelis, who always wanted to be on the good side of the member nations. Complaining about Israeli infractions was much safer, because typically, complaints were answered by letters and explanations, not with bullets and RPG rockets. The war in Lebanon raged on and the UN dully reported it, by telephone, by radio, the reports making their way from the Post, to Company, to Battalion, all in the native language of the soldiers, and then on to headquarters in Naqura in English. As long as they did not actually intervene to enforce peace, the Soldiers of Peace were unharmed. After 20 years it was a merry game where everybody knew the rules, Israeli soldiers and Hezbollah Shahids died in fierce skirmishes and the UN forces reported. And of course everybody and their sisters listened in to these reports, as an adjunct to their own intelligence efforts. The game was so transparent that on Christmas eve, the drunken Irish, or Norwegian, or French soldiers, wished everyone who was listening in , be it Palestinian or Hezbollah, or Israeli, a Merry Christmas and a lousy new year.

The Norwegian battalion headquarters was just south of Nabatiyah. Company number 1 shared the same location. The sky blue command car with the two sky blue-capped soldiers left at first light to bring some rations to the outpost number 12 which was situated overlooking the intersection of the main Zahranni-Nabatiyah road, and the secondary blacktop which wound its way through the hills to the smaller villages. It had been relatively quiet for the last few days, although the night before saw a lot of police and irregular activity on the roads, it seemed they were looking for something. A routine report went out. Jonas Gundersen rubbed his eyes and looked again, this time through the binoculars. It must be fata-Morgana, but it was still true. A woman, a Western woman, short blond hair, clad in an army type coat, was waving them down frantically. What in the blazes was a single woman, and a Westerner, doing here in the wilds of Lebanon at this ungodly hour? Eric Andersen who was driving was just as amazed, and of course he slowed down, and stopped the vehicle.

"Who are you, what are you doing here?" Jonas asked in English, she appeared American.

"Hi, I am Karen, my vehicle broke down just half a mile from here, can you help me?" She was American, as far from home as one can imagine.

The whole scenario was so incongruous that the soldiers could do nothing but fulfill the request, as it came from a beautiful woman with a mellifluous voice. After the harsh Arabic they heard all day, the hooded women and the crafty eyes, this was a blessing. Karen climbed into the rear of the command car and gave them the benefit of her most devastating smile, the kind that curled their toes and sent a shiver right to their cojones.

Eric engaged the gear and Jonas went back to watching the narrow empty road, for the supposedly disabled vehicle. They were just coming up on an ancient Toyota pickup when Karen stuck the Ketalar into the muscular neck under the blond hair. Jonas tried to slap the sudden wasp-bite, and then slowly collapsed. Eric looked on with bewilderment. The last thing he could think of was that the woman might be responsible. He stopped the command car, and called on Jonas to wake up. Karen gave Eric the benefit of another Ketalar. Joe came out from behind the Toyota and assessed the fallen soldiers. He turned to Karen.

"I see your female charms work just fine, this guy looks big enough, I'll take him, you drag the other one."

They dragged the soldiers behind the Toyota, Joe and Sura and Karen stripped them of their NATO sky-blue coats and sky blue caps with the UN emblem, they laid them asleep in the pickup and covered them with the Syrian outer coats. The morning promised to be beautiful and sunny, the rain had exhausted itself the night before, and the birds were singing to beat the band. A wonderful day to be alive, a lousy day to get shot at. Sura and Alia went into the command-car's bed, among the eggs, milk and preserves. Karen climbed into the driver's seat, and pulled the UN cap low over her forehead, Joe took up position on the passenger side. Now they were heavily armed, with Ingrams and Kalachnikovs, and Joe dearly hoped there will be no call to use either.

Ahmad left the Toyota and looked in at the girls in the back.

"Au-revoir Sura."

"Au-revoir Papa."

"Clutch in, light gas, first gear, release clutch slow, add more gas" Joe intoned and Karen performed. The command car started moving and Ahmad walked, then tried to run behind, until it was too fast for him. He turned and walked back to the Toyota, and got behind the wheel. Sura was gone, and there was nothing they could threaten him with. He started the ancient motor, got in and drove back to the village, paying attention to his human cargo. Capitain Joseph had promised him Amnesia, so that even when they woke up and walked about, they would remember nothing of his vehicle. For the first time in twelve years Ahmad was Happy. Sura was not free yet, but she was in the best possible hands, and she had a fighting chance of having a Life.

Chapter 23

CROSS HAIR

Karen drove like a pro, upright and confident. Joe spread the map on his knees, noted the kilometers reeling on the odometer, consulted the GPS, and called changes in direction. The VRC-77 was standard issue NATO, most likely manufactured by Tadiran under contract for NATO, Joe was utterly familiar with it. It was beginning to squawk in Norwegian, They had skirted Nabatiyah with the utmost of bravado, hubris and chutzpah, and the Beaufort was only five miles away, with the village of Arnoun intervening.

He clicked the mike and spoke in Hebrew. He hoped the code names for the Israeli listening posts had not changed over the years.

"Nevo, Nevo, this is 2298178 calling" he was using his military ID number, a number he had written and signed innumerable times, a number branded on his brain.

Limor Aharoni was one of the prettiest girls on the base, her father was a Yemenite Israeli, and her mother a Norwegian volunteer, who, 19 years before, had fallen in love with the chocolate-skinned lieutenant, and married him, and stayed on the Kibbutz. Limor retained the best of those disparate lineages, with fair skin that bronzed easily, straight blond hair, and startling brown eyes, and the propensity for singing that the Yemenites are famous for. Her mother had insisted on speaking Norwegian, so she could converse with her grandparents whenever they made a summer visit to Trondheim. When Limor was eighteen she was drafted into the IDF and soon found herself in Commint unit, that listened in on the Norwegian battalion. This was a quiet Winter morning, the only traffic so far was Norbatt 452 which had left Company One, and failed to report in at no12 watchpoint. Limor had been at her post for one hour when her earphones jangled with Hebrew. This must be a practical joke, one of the Israeli soldiers has decided to get onto the UN net and garble up the works. Anyway, where or who was Nevo?

"Nevo, Nevo, I know you are listening. This is 2298178, call the KABAR." Limor jumped a mile, only an insider knew the meaning of Kabar. So she did, she twirled the handle of the field-phone whose other end was at the Kabar station.

"Kabar station?"

"Yes Limor, are you in love with me this fine morning?" That was Ami

Cohen, the Kabar on duty.

"Ami, get off your ass and come over here, someone is calling on the Norbatt radio, and in Hebrew."

"Limor, it's a prank, anybody can get on this frequency" Ami said.

"Ami, he is calling for Kabar, this guy knows who he is calling, he is calling us, listen, there he goes again" she switced to the external monitor.

"Nevo, Nevo, this is 2298178, get the Kabar right now."

"Shit, Nevo was the old call name for the Base, and the number is a Zahal , IDF ID number, must be 20 years old. Keep listening Limor, good work, what frequency is that?"

"78 point 95 megahertz." Limor read. Ami left the phone and raced over to the corner where the spare PRC was, he switched it on, and tuned it to 78.95 and routed the output to a high gain antenna.

"2298178, get off the air, over."

"Kabar Nevo, listen carefully, in ten minutes I am going to be at the gate of Lincoln Three. Don't fire, I repeat do not open fire, women and children in the blue vehicle."

Ami made a series of quick phone calls. He called on his superior Kabar, then the base commandant, then on the Personnel sergeant to identify the ID number, then on the triangulation units, which usually never bothered with UN transmissions, and finally to Aman Patzan, because he knew his own superior, he was s-l-o-w. Now what the hell was Lincoln Three? Ami rummaged through the outdated map box. This ID number was an old-timer, and Nevo was an old-timer name for the Horan Base. Anyone over 25 was old timer to Ami, who was only 20 years old.

"Commander Shkaki, commander, listen to this." Youness and Mustafa had spent a sleepless night in Nabatiyah, monitoring the search conducted by the combined efforts of the Islamic Jihad, Raed Al Ganem, Mansour and sheikh Nassralah's people. It was as if the earth had swallowed the Gaz and its occupants. Mansour's forces had found the three men tied to the truck, and beat them to pulp, as befitted men who were taken by a single gunman and a woman, a *woman,* by the prophet's beard. Obviously the Gaz had gone over the Zahrani, but after that, it was gone. On the map, the territory appeared small and well defined. On the ground it consisted of myriad tracks, thousands of haphazard houses, caves, terraces. The spoor was washed away by the rain, and the men were unwilling. Before daybreak Mansour pulled back all of his Syrian vehicles and troops. Nimri's men went to sleep. Mustafa and Youness stayed awake at the Islamic Jihad HQ, which was really the basement and ground floor of one of the four-story buildings in Nabatiyah. The three upper stories were full of ordinary citizens. Youness knew that the Israelis would never risk another Kafr Kana massacre by targeting a populated building, even with a smart bomb.

The radio operator who called was Nassir Yihya, who had been a waiter in Oslo for some years. His job was to monitor NorBatt, sometimes Israeli infiltrators were not as careful with the UN as they were with Hezbollah, so that UN reports revealed their whereabouts. Youness approached that radio station. Nassir had a monitor for each company frequency, and one for the Battalion frequency.

"What is it, Nassir?"

"Someone is speaking Hebrew on the Company One frequency."

"So what, the airwaves are free. How many times did I pick Hebrew transmissions even in Beirut?" Youness was contemptuous.

"Commander, I know this radio, it squeaks a certain way, it's a NorBatt vehicle that is always on the road at this time."

"Anyone understands Hebrew?" Youness inquired of the HQ personnel. no one did, they were all known to Shabac, and had never been inside Israel.

Yihya lit up "I know someone in Nabatiyah, she is a Maronite who married a brother, years ago, she worked in Israel."

Youness turned to Suleiman "Take Rassem with you and bring her." The radio monitor called Nevo, Nevo again, but the rest of the transmission was not understood.

To: Aman Patzan
From : Kabar Horan
Extremely urgent, extremely urgent
Sub: Islamic Jihad
In the last 30 minutes, a complete mobilization of Islamic Jihad networks from Nabatiyah, They are disregarding radio silence and calling all vehicles on the road, searching for a UN vehicle.

NorBatt is also looking for a vehicle, which has not responded in the last hour. Vehicle is Mobile 452 from Company One, based outside Nabatiyah

We intercepted transmission in Hebrew on NorBatt 1 frequency, calling himself 2298178,

calling kabar Nevo, and heading for Nitzanit. We triangulated the transmission to the Nitzanit vicinity. Says in Hebrew he has women and children in the vehicle
My assessment is a friendly who is heading for home.
Advise.

"Who is 2298178?" Ami screamed down the lousy phone line at Central Personnel in Ramat Gan. Seren (Captain) Doron Sartena, the base commandant, was standing at his desk, scanning the message Ami had sent to Patzan. The Base had in fact two top figures. The chief Kabar who was responsible for the Commint and Elint output and initial intelligence assessment, and the base commandant who was the military and administrative commander, responsible for the day to day running and the security of the Horan Base. The chief Kabar was on vacation so Ami was running the show.

"Name is Lieutenant Yoseph Bergman, formerly Sayeret Golani, last Miluim eight years ago, now abroad" said the girl in Ramat Gan.

Captain Sartena spoke into the mike "2298178, name, rank serial number, over."

Silence....Norwegian traffic....

"Lieutenant Yossi Bergman 2298178. over, we are close to Lincoln Three" Joe tried to be calm. The Beaufort castle, the crusader strong-hold was in view, on the promontory overlooking the Litanni river gorge.

Mustafa turned white under his dark skin, a pallor so ghastly Youness was sure he was having a heart attack. The color drained away from the lips, and suddenly they were pinched and dead. The last transmission occurred in the middle of a litany of Norwegian, and to his knowledge, Mustafa knew even less Hebrew that Youness himself, so what hit him so hard?

"*Bergman, Bergman*," Mustafa hissed, "I *know* that name, from Milwaukee, he works with Amanda, but he was from Seattle. Amanda had him for lunch once and *he knows Alia.* This cannot be a coincidence. He followed me here and now he has Alia" Mustafa said in a thin, dead voice, lips moving, eyes frantic in their sockets."*Bergman is a fucking JEW.*" He jumped up and grabbed Youness "yallah, go go, he is about to get to the Beaufort, get the men." Youness yelled at his men and they ran outside to the vehicles, the Land-Rover and the Mercedes.

"Move, move" he screamed at the driver who was napping at the wheel. Two seconds later the small convoy was tearing down the narrow road to the Beaufort, which commanded the only useable road leading south of the Litanni.

Seren Sartena knew he was making a crucial decision, he was cutting the red tape of the order of command, which dictated that Patzan make a decision, route the order to Yakal, then Yakal to the Nitzanit, the Beaufort code name. The name Bergman tolled a distant bell, of the Tel Aviv student who had survived the Apropo blast more than a decade ago, when Doron himself had been a teen-age waiter at the café named Cherry, one block away from the Apropo. Gilead, his younger brother by one year, was lieutenant commander of Nitzanit. Gilead was there and forewarned is forearmed. He called on the secure 32 line wireless.

"Nitzanit" said the bored voice.

"This is Seren Sartena, get me Gilead, right NOW."

"Hey, Gilead, Fancy Doron wants to speak to you" the phone changed hands. Sartena was always Spit-and- Polish, and everyone in that loose army made fun of him.

"Hey bro, what's up?"

"Gilead, this is important. Look around the fort for a blue UN vehicle coming your way, don't fire even if he comes close, ask the occupant who he is, and if he says 'Bergman' open the gate."

"Are you all right Bro, or did you drink too much Vodka with the new recruits?"

"Gilead, as I am your brother, if this caper turns out bad, I will tear you to pieces right in front of Mama."

"OK, I'll keep my eyes skinned."

The radio monitors tuned to the Islamic Jihad networks were going berserk.

Aman Patzan, this is Kabar Horan, Youness Shkaki has mobilized all Jihad units to Arnoun.
Advise advise advise

Karen drove slowly into Arnoun, dirt muddy roads, haphazard houses, right angle turns, Joe just kept telling her right and left, Sura and Alia hid in the back, under a canvas shroud, they drove through the teeming center of the village, and out the other side. The forbidding Beaufort, a huge ruined castle, looked like the promised land. A donkey laden with firewood crossed her path and she slowed down some more. The donkey halted, the child riding it kicked at his sides to no avail. "Keep going, push it" Joe whispered while grinning, teeth only, at the populance, Karen engaged and drove. They heard the sound of vehicles driving at high speed, the rending of metal as one of them scraped stone just behind a blind alley "Move, now" Joe hit the horn, and Karen, the gas, the donkey scampered, a Toyota 4 Runner careened behind them, the passenger side window opened and a gun barrel was poking out. "Go, go go" Joe yelled and loosed a short burst in the direction of the Toyota. A tire went flat, the Toyota swerved and hit a wall, the vehicle behind it was stuck. Karen was not taking prisoners anymore. She floored the gas and shifted up, the command car surged forwards and the thinning crowd, those who did not flee the gunfire, fell aside. There was about a mile to the fort, and Karen stepped on it.

"I want the Sagger out" Mustafa shrieked.
"Mustafa, if we hit them with the Sagger, Alia will die too."
"I don't care, If I can't have her then Amanda can't have her either" in the same awful voice.
"Get the Sagger out" Youness ordered.

Salim Al Houss was the best man with Saggers Youness had ever seen. The Sagger is an old Russian anti-tank rocket, guided by wire, good for up to two miles in the hands of a good operator. Guided Anti-tank missiles fall into 3 generations. The older generation requires the operator to follow the target and guide the rocket manually. The second generation requires only that the operator keep the target in his sights, the computer then guides the rocket. The third generation is fire and forget. Once the target is acquired, the missile homes in on it. This is the safest and most expensive way. The Sagger is a first generation missile, success depends on the skill of the operator, and Salim was good. Youness had led the convoy not into the village but to a hill which overlooked the last section of the road to the Beaufort, while his troops dove into the village narrow mud streets.

The sky-blue command car was racing along the track, but it had to slow for the turns and boulders. Salim opened the case, set the Sagger up, unhurriedly, settled down to the side with the joystick, sighted, and fired the rocket. It would take just a few seconds.

Joe's head snapped to the north, there was a hill overlooking the road, and two vehicles had just appeared there. A flash of smoke erupted and a small object hurtled away, right at them. Sura peeked out of the canvas, and was looking wildly around, but she kept Alia under wraps.

"Tillim (Missiles)!" Joe cried with alarm.

"We are almost there" Karen called, not comprehending.

Joe said nothing, and placed his hand over the parking hand brake, he counted 21,22,23 and pulled the handbrake so that the command-car dove on its shocks, and Karen was thrown forwards onto the wheel. The rocket whipped past them and exploded harmlessly on a boulder, throwing a shower of rocks and pebbles that rattled their windshield and engine grill. Joe released the hand brake and Karen was thrown back, and she shot a glance at Joe, who remained impassive.

"Go like hell" Joe said conversationally. Karen floored it again and the tortured engine screamed in protest, but the command-car leaped ahead. The Beaufort was looming over them.

"The Rifle" Youness commanded. Salim, chagrined at being outfoxed, handed him the Anschutz. Youness was an expert marksman with the rifle, and the 7.92 Austrian Anschuz was the most accurate marksman rifle in the world, with a punch. Youness placed his elbows like a tripod on the engine-hood, put the crosshair on the vehicle and awaited his chance. The way it moved and bounced and swerved, he couldn't hope to hit anything, but it was bound to slow or stop somewhere. As long as it was not within the fort, they had a chance.

Karen slowed down, Joe released the canvas top and stood on the seat and screamed at the Fort, in Hebrew "Open up, move the Zelda" over and over again. The fort used the APC as a moving gate, and in order to open it they had to start the engine, and drive it forwards, like a rolling gate. That always took a little time.

"Who are you?" boomed a voice from a megaphone.

"Yossi Bergman, Yossi Bergman, they are shooting Saggers. Move the Zelda."

Youness had the standing body in the crosshair. He took a deep breath, held it, and slowly depressed the trigger. The vehicle jumped, and the body jumped down as the round was capped, the explosive ignited and the bullet went on it's way, Youness knew he had missed.

Gilead was ready for that answer, and in fact the Zelda's diesel engine was already running when he called on the megaphone. The driver caught his signal and pushed both handles, and the Zelda rolled forwards. Karen gunned her engine, Joe slid down and the command car leaped the intervening yards and rolled into the yard. as soon as they had passed, the Zelda driver shifted back and rolled the Zelda to close the gate. Joe pulled on the hand brake. He was back in the fold and no one was hurt. The men in olive green were pointing their Galils at them. He knew those men, or boys really, they would never shoot unless they were threatened. He let out a huge sigh of relief.

"Capitaine Joseph." That was Sura, her voice tiny.

"Oui."

"Il y a beaucoup de sang ici."

"**Blood**?! What blood, who's bleeding?"

Karen's head lolled back, she was Sooooooo tired, she just wanted to sleep, forever sleep.

"Nitzanit, this is Yakal."

"Yakal, Nitzanit."

"Nitzanit, this is Kodkod Yakal, a blue vehicle is heading your way at high speed, do not admit, do not admit, vehicle maybe booby trapped."

"Yakal from Nitzanit, too late, the vehicle is already in the compound, two men, one women, one child, man severely wounded, will need to evacuate soonest."

"This is Kodkod, what the *hell* are you talking about?"

Joe spun in his seat, Karen's face was white, whiter than the snow on Mount Hermon, whiter than a frozen Wisconsin lake in midwinter. Joe's heart froze too, and the beat slowed down to a crawl, each beat a double whammy in his ears, and intestines, tolling on, and on, even though he willed it to stop, once and for all. He wished to die, there and then, more than anything in the world, he wished that someone will finally do him the favor and release him from his miserable, excruciating, stinking existence.

Karen could not feel the bullet. But the need to breath was more powerful than any other instinct. The need for oxygen was the greatest imperative, she was drowning in her own fluids, and no one was helping her. She opened her mouth to breath but that made it no easier, so instead she opened her eyes, and what she saw was a dead face, a face which had been drained of all expression, all emotion, all hope. She had to save that face because this was her man, and he was dying.

"I am not dead yet, Joe" she whispered.

"Get the Medic" Lieutenant Gilead yelled. For two seconds after the command-car had driven in, five seconds after the sound of the distant rifle shot had died, the "thunk" as it hit something, after the Zelda shut off the engine, there was a Silence. The man in Sky Blue was frozen, the child was staring up, the woman in the back was staring in horror at the pool of congealing blood, and the driver, who was a slight figure clad in the UN blue and a UN cap, was slumped in the seat. Blood, bullet, someone had been hit, this was not any booby trap. The driver moved, and suddenly the man in front was galvanized, and jumped out of the seat, over the driver, and picked up the driver as if he was the lightest of straws. "Hovesh, Hovesh" he shrieked in a voice mad with anguish, and the Fort knew he was one of them.

The Galil rifles all pointed down, and the soldiers moved purposefully. One helped Joe by holding the feet, one helped Sura out, and one picked the child and shielded her face from the gruesome specter of the blood. Something tore through the air, a high-pitched whine and an explosion rocked the outer walls.

"Patzmar (Mortar), take cover" Gilead yelled, but not in any panic. The mortar attacks were a daily routine of Hezbollah, and they were as expected as the electric bill. Gilead, a tall muscular nordic type, hustled Joe with his charge into the underground shelter, and the infirmary. David Bitton and Vladimir Lev were ready for them and Joe laid Karen on the exam table. Joe stripped off her cap and opened the bloody coat. The soldiers were shocked. The UN soldier was a woman.

"You, get an IV line!" Joe said to David. "Take the pulse and blood pressure" he barked at Lev. Bitton did as he was told and only later recalled that he was the chief Hovesh, but this guy knew what he was doing, and Bitton was trained to help the military doctor.

"Strip off the coat" said Joe, he whipped the stethoscope off Lev and listened. Karen's face was even whiter, if that were possible, her pulse was thin and thready, and her chest was heaving and gasping for air.

"No air entry on the left, good breathing on the right, Pneumothorax or Hemothorax, what's you name?" he demanded of David

"David Bitton."

"I am Yossi, get me the trocar NOW, what's her BeePee?" Joe whipped at the other.

"Its sixty five over nothing" reported Lev, who had gotten himself another stethoscope.

"Got the line?" Joe pressed Bitton

"No veins, she's collapsed."

"Get me a big line, you, lieutenant blondie, what's your name?"

"Gilead."

"Take the scissors and strip her pants off."

"Her *pants?*"

"Yes and be quick, I have to get a central line." Gilead held the scissors with trepidation and started cutting up from the bottom. The female leg became exposed and he slowed down, the further he got up.

Joe took a hold of the khaki blouse and tore it off. It was all bloody underneath. He tore off the teeshirt and the bra, so she was all exposed, "Trocar ready, gloves, Venflon 16" Bitton was handling it like a pro, now that the initial shock wore off, this woman was heaving away ineffectually, and her lips were turning blue, her eyes remained open, though. Outside the Patzmars kept coming.

Joe slipped the venflon into the chest wall and withdrew the stylet, air under pressure escaped from the exposed chest, the heaving decreased and the blue color started fading away. "Knife, Trocar and holder" Joe said curtly, this was not Karen, this was a wounded human with a torn lung, with air trapping in the cavity, preventing the lungs from expanding and breathing. He was the Doctor and this was the Trauma patient, just like the ATLS course he had taken six months previously. He made the incision, drove the trocar in, withdrew the big, ugly, bloody metal stylet, and pushed the clear perforated plastic tube into the cavity. Bitton connected it to a water-seal and immediately the bubbles came out. The heaving regressed some more, and some pink returned to the pale cheeks. Lev clapped his hands with glee, Gilead finished cutting the pant leg, and now the inguinal fossa was showing, and the panties, Gilead was embarrassed and turned his gaze away. Joe made a quick purse stitch around the trocar. Bitton used a cloth to cover up the exposed breasts and set about dressing the wound Joe had made. New sounds were heard outside, the IDF artillery was returning fire, the mortar hits dwindled.

"Good work," said Joe, "Give me the intracath, what's your name?"

"Vladimir Lev."

"Lev, prep me that inguinal fossa, Karen, are you with us?" She nodded, weakly.

"Your BeePee is down, you need volume, femoral is the quickest route." She nodded some more, closed her eyes in anticipation of the pain.

"Hold that leg Gilead, Syringe, Lev." Vladimir handed him the syringe, this was looking just like practice, except the patient was prettier. Joe palpated for the femoral pulse, then jabbed medially, the leg jumped, weakly, and he was in the vein. Practice paid off. He left the thick needle in and slipped in the plastic catheter, pulled back the needle and secured both metal needle and plastic catheter with the tough plastic 'book'.

"Give her a liter of Hartman, open the cock all the way" he instructed Lev, who was making the connections. "Stitch" he ordered and Bitton gave him the needle and holder. He stitched the contraption to the thigh. "Its running" said Lev.

"Blood pressure" Joe snapped.

Lev pumped it up, and released, a big smile broke on his youthful pimply face. "Ninety over sixty" he said. Karen's chest was settling into a more normal rhythm.

Joe wasn't satisfied. "Secondary survey, Bitton, Lev, help me turn her over." The two men, their skills confirmed, rolled her over and Joe snipped off the rest of her clothing. There it was , a single entry wound, no exit, left lower posterior chest. That bullet could be anywhere, it could be endangering her heart, her aorta, she could still die, Joe's energies left him and he sat heavily on the metal stool, she could still die, still die...

Karen turned her head to Joe, whose head was bowed, his ear close to her mouth.

"I am not going to die, Joe" she whispered.

"We had better get away now" Youness said. His vehicles were clearly visible from the Fort, and once the Israelis lifted up their heads, they would call the artillery on them. One by one the Mortar crews of Hezbollah picked up and rolled away, except for one crew who were unlucky enough to receive a direct hit, and blow up together with the Ammo.

"No, bomb them, kill them, where are the other Saggers?!" Mustafa was furious, and illogical, the Fort had withstood thousands of attacks over a thousand years, and the Israelis had fortified it some more. It was impregnable, except for the determined kind of commando attack that even the Hezbollah were incapable off. Mustafa was pacing around the hill top raging and kicking. Youness' men waited for him to bring his mad scientist to heel, before the next artillery salvo.

"Mustafa, *Mustafa, we have to save the lab*, we can still take our revenge, but we have to save *the lab.*" He grabbed Mustafa by both shoulders and shook him, like a dog shaking a kitten, until the blaze of rage and madness left his eyes, and he sat heavily on a stone. Two men grabbed him and hustled him into the Land Rover. The driver gunned his engine and raced down the hill, away from the line of sight of the accursed Fort.

"Listen Gilead" Joe said tiredly, they were speaking in Hebrew "the story is too complicated, tell Yakal whatever you want, I have to watch Karen."

"OK, so who are the woman and the child? If I ask for a medevac I have to tell them something."

"Alright, alright, the child is Alia, she is an American kidnaped by her father. The woman is Sura, she is the daughter of a collaborator."

"Did *they* do her ghastly face?"

"Yes"

"Savages, and you are a lucky sod."

"Think so?" said Joe.

"They missed you with the Sagger, and the bullet."

"I'd rather the bullet got me" Joe said tiredly, then perked up, "Gilead."

"What?"

"I want to speak to someone senior, someone in Patzan."

"You have some chutzpa, don't you, first you bust into a military installation, you use IDF maps, you put my soldiers and me at risk, you get my brother in trouble, and now you want to speak to the Aluf?"

"Yes."

"Tell me first."

"The father of this child is named Mustafa Halim. He is a biologist who is making biological warfare agents directed at Israel. He has a lab, he must be eliminated before he moves his lab."

"Oh boy, oh boy, this is rich."

"It's true Gilead, I swear it's true." Joe slipped inadvertently into English.

"Gil" Karen whispered, the lieutenant jumped, so far Karen had been a trauma victim, not a person.

"What?" he bent over her.

"How is your English?"

"Fair" he said, in English.

"Listen to Joe, you have only one chance to do good" she whispered, then faded into exhaustion, the fluids were dripping into her system. Joe had no way to know if she was bleeding inside, but at least, there was no blood froth. Gilead retreated from the dying woman.

"OK, medevac, and Kaman Patzan" and he turned and left. Sura came into the underground, whitewashed vault, trailing Alia, and a hesitant soldier, who appeared to have no clue as to how to handle a woman and a child.

"Comment est elle?"

"If the helicopter takes too long..... he left the sentence incomplete.

"I am telling you that if you do not send that chopper right away, we are going to have a dead American on our hands, and I will be the first to say, that she died due to your slo-mo" Gilead was exclaiming angrily over the secure scrambled phone, the electronics robbed voices of all inflection, it sounded mechanical and slightly garbled. He was speaking to Gideon at Yakal.

"Gilead, keep your temper, it's Patzan, they are the slo-mo, they need to determine if the risk is worth the benefit."

"I don't want a dead woman in the Fort, that will demoralize the men, if you can't get a Hello for an injured woman how are you gonna get it for an injured soldier?"

"I see your point Gilead" said Gideon "hold on" there was a hubbub in the back ground. "Good, good" and back to Gilead "the Hello from Gibor is on it's way, the Doctor will talk to the medic from the air."

"This Bergman is a Doctor, he did all the work, I wish we had him last month when Yuri stepped on a land-mine."

"Tell me again about biological warfare."

"Bergman insists he wants to talk to someone high up in Patzan or Matcal because he has information about a biological warfare effort in Lebanon. Sounds like bullshit to me except he is no bullshitter, he was a cool customer, used all the emergency equipment and seems to have no loose marbles. The American, even though she is half-dead, she said I should listen to him, that got my attention."

"It sounds too important to mess up, I'll get Motti Shneior to meet him in Gibor."

"Thanks Gideon."

"Hold on Karen, the chopper is coming, hold on, squeeze my hand, please, hold on" Joe pleaded, as the eyes closed, and the pressure on his hand dwindled to nothing. "Get the Epi ready Bitton" he said to David, referring to the adrenaline shot. Gilead burst into the infirmary. They had already fitted her with an oxygen mask, and her breath was making it mist up. As long as it misted it was still OK.

"That's it, ETA five minutes, Lev, Bitton, on the stretcher and up." They moved Karen, with all the bandages and the fluids, gently onto the stretcher, and walked on eggs through the ancient ruin.

"Wait here" the thwap-thwup of the venerable Bell 212 reverberated and suddenly the helicopter came over the walls and landed on the makeshift helipad, before it touched with the skids the Doctor was out and running, he was a young one, this may be his first or second evac, and he was nervous as hell. Gilead did not wait, he knew that the newcomer did not have much to contribute.

"Go!" and they ran awkwardly with the stretcher and loaded it up, as the Doctor checked the lines, Sura and Alia ran behind and climbed into the 12 place craft. The soldiers on the ramparts kept a sharp eye for Stingers or Strelas, but the previous bombardment had sent the Hezbollah into their own shelters. Joe climbed in last, dragging a small medical bag into which he had stuffed his Armada, and GPS, the Irridium phone, the rest would have to stay. He turned to Gilead and yelled "thank you, you did good" and slid door closed in front of him, it was just like old times, but instead of the giddiness of going to battle, it was the anguish of Time, every minute took a life-time, might mean a Life. The chopper increased power, the cyclic control went forwards and they were away, first up, then down into the deep gorge, hiding from the threats of guns and missiles. They stayed close to the ground all the way to the border, then gained altitude.

"Where are we going?" Joe yelled over the racket.

"Gibor."

"No, go to Rambam, she took a bullet in the left chest cavity."

"We use Gibor first." The young doctor insisted.

"Don't do it" Joe pleaded "she needs blood, O negative, she needs a CT and the OR, if she dies in Gibor....." The Doctor leaned forward to the pilots and they changed course, it was his call.

"Call them ahead, full trauma team on the roof" Joe yelled.

They waited for her on the roof. It was a beautiful winter day, the air was cool, the sun was shining, the Mediterranean sparkled, and the Bahaii temple radiated gold. The chest was heaving again, her color was bad, she did not even get blue, somewhere inside her chest she was bleeding to death. Alia was so tired she fell asleep in Sura's arms, despite the noisy bucking machine. They touched down and the sliding doors flew open. The trauma team took over. Just before the stretcher was taken away Joe felt one more tiny squeeze "I am not going to die, Joe" the squeeze said. Joe was dead tired, he stumbled on the concrete roof and they had to hold him up and drag him outside the perimeter of the chopper. The pilots made a quick check, and they were off.

Joe remained on the warm roof, he could not move a muscle.
"Capitain Joseph?"
Joe took a lifetime to answer. "Oui Sura."
"Thou hast fulfilled thine promise."
"Not yet, the girl's mother does not know she is free" with tired motions Joe pulled out his Irridium and switched it on.
"Information."
"North Star Hotel in Mettulah."
"06-5597250." Joe dialed that number.
"North Star Hotel."
"I am looking for a Doctor Amanda Carter."
"Carter,,, Carter,, it's ringing."
"Yeah" the gravely male voice.
"Officer Wilkins I presume."
"Doctor Joe!! Its doctor Joe Amanda, its Joe, where are you?" Chris was yelling so that Joe had to take the phone away from his ear.
"Chris, put Amanda on the line."
"Right, right."
"Sura, bring Alia over here," Alia was captivated by the panorama of the Carmel mount and the sea. She took the phone hesitantly. Suddenly her face lit up, as only a child's can. "Mom, Mommy, where are you, I missed you so much, mom, I knew you would come to take me home, where are you?" and she cried and kissed the phone, the closest she could get to Mom's face. Sura gently pulled the phone away and gave it to Joe. Amanda was sobbing at the other end.
"Amanda?"

"Joe, how is she?"

"She is fine, she survived this crazy caper better than anyone. Take a Taxi, ask the Taxi to take you to Rambam Hospital in Haifa."

"Hospital, oh no, is she hurt? are you hurt?"

"Alia is fine. Its Karen, she got shot."

"Oh no, dear God no, what,,how,,,?"

"Amanda, it's out of my hands now, tell the Taxi to go slow, I will be waiting at the OR."

Motti Shneior thought this was the stupidest thing Gideon Degani had ever made him do. Drive to Haifa, to Rambam, talk to an Israeli who busted into the Beaufort in a UN vehicle, claiming he had information about a biological warfare threat. This topped the list of stupid assignments. He went to Information first.

"Shalom, do you know anything about the Hello which came in an hour and a half ago?"

Rambam is used to this kind of questions, since 1978, when Israel became embroiled in Lebanon, Rambam University Hospital had been the recipient of thousands of casualties, Israeli, Lebanese, UN, and the chopper visits were frequent as the visits of the honey-bees to the orange groves in flower season.

"One casualty, gunshot, in the thoracic surgery fourth floor" said the volunteer to the army Major. Motti made his way through the throng of humanity that always crowded the hospital to the elevators and the fourth floor. Next to an open air market, the Shouk, the busiest place in Israel is the Hospital. People just love to visit their relatives, friends and neighbors when they are sick. There was a bunch of people milling about in the waiting room of the fourth floor, but he picked out the biggest, meanest, scruffiest looking of them all, who was accompanied by the ghastliest scarred beautiful woman, and an angelic child with black curls and blue eyes, who was staring at the door with fixated expectation. If this was not the weirdest trio of humans he had ever seen then his name was not Motti.

"Lieutenant Bergman?" The man who was slumped on the chair looked up slowly, painfully, his face grim and stony, the slit eyes blood-shot behind the incongruous round glasses.

"Yes, I am Yossi Bergman."

"I am Motti Shneior. Aman Patzan sent me." Motti could see how the call to duty made Yossi gather up the remains of his strength and determination, determination for what? he wondered.

"You made a big impression on the young and impressionable Lieutenant Sartena" he said accusingly, as if Joe had in some way suborned him.

"He is a gem, you ought to give lots of credit for being cool under fire." Joe said tiredly

"Lieutenant Bergman...." Shneior started.

"Doctor Bergman, Milwaukee USA" Joe said in English.

"Milwaukee? where the hell is Milwaukee?" Shneior replied in heavily accented English.

"Check item Golda Meir in your book. In short, a Doctor Mustafa Halim, a Palestinian from Lebanon, who had trained in the US in Genetics, used the combined talent of scores of Arab-ancestry scientists to mutate a virus to transmit a cancer to Jews, in a selective manner. He is the father of this six-year-old with us here. He is connected with an armed organization in Beirut, and set up the ability to manufacture the virus vaccination in commercial quantities. You have to get him and his laboratory before he moves them to another location and do it now, because he knows the game is up."

Shneior was shaking his head, he couldn't believe someone had sent him to hear this story, his face registered complete disbelief. Joe got the drift.

"Alia, what is the name of your father?"

"Its Mustafa, Doctor Joe."

"And where did you live for the last two months?"

"I don't know, it was a big, big house, with lots of scary men with guns, and they let Fatima see me, and she was the only one who was nice, but she stank so bad, yech, I can say that can't I, Doctor Joe?" Joe had to smile, she was so true, so genuine.

"And what was your dad doing in the big house?" Joe persisted.

"He had lots of men, in white coats, and they kept asking him questions and when is Mom coming Doctor Joe? she said soon, and it was a long time ago, and where is Nurse Karen, why did all the doctors take her away? My mom once took me to the Hospital, but it wasn't so crowded." Alia took another breath but Sura shushed her, Alia was the only person who was not appalled by the double hideous scar, but rather intrigued by it, and she formed an instant friendship with Sura, taking her for an older sister. They spoke in Arabic, and Major Shneior who understood Arabic followed the childish conversation as Alia complained about the house, the loneliness, and her father who was too busy for her, after the long plane ride. The disbelief left his face. The door at the end of the corridor opened yet again, and as before Alia's attention flew to the door. The big man held the door, and Amanda

Carter came in, her eyes searching and probing. With a yelp, Alia leaped, and flew to the door, into the arms of her mother, whose eyes brimmed with tears of relief, and whose mouth worked speechlessly.

"Mom...."

"My baby..."

Chris wiped away a tear or two, the populance, Jews and Arabs, and Druze, who were waiting for their loved ones, looked on with approval. No one could remain indifferent in the face of such happiness.

"The mother" Joe said quietly, in Hebrew to Shneior, "Mustafa is her husband, and she is my colleague in Milwaukee, now do you believe me?"

"Yes, I am going back to Patzan to do some correlations, an airforce attack will require approval at the highest levels, how do I keep in contact?"

"I will be here, Karen is my wife."

"Sorry, I heard she got shot pretty bad, I hope she makes it."

"If she doesn't, you will have no one to speak to."

Shneior did a double take on that, but he could not read Joe at all, he let it go. "One last thing, who is the scarred woman?" he asked.

"She is a daughter of a friend in Lebanon, he was accused of collaboration."

"So she is your responsibility?"

"Yes." said Joe.

"Then you will have to stick around, regardless, because you cannot abdicate your responsibilities, this is what got you here in the first place, right?"

Joe froze, then released his breath. "Right, I am not going anywhere."

"Good, I will find you " Shneior upped and left, a quiet unobtrusive man who needed to convince a hesitant command and Matcal, and Cabinet, to commit to a dangerous course of action, on the basis of one man's warning.

Chris waited for Major Shneior to leave before he came and took the vacated seat. Amanda and Alia were still hugging, and touching, and making sure that they were real. Chris did not join in the merriment.

"How is she?" Chris said quietly in his gravely voice.

"Bad."

"How bad?"

"High velocity bullet in the left chest, lost lots of blood, I did what I could in the field, but I had no blood replacement, I didn't go to look at the CT."

Chris draped his arm on the bowed back. "You are from here, aren't you?"

"Tel Aviv."

"You're a good doc, I expect them to be as good."

"I hope they are better" said Joe, exhausted.

"She'll be fine, the Taxi driver said this was the best trauma hospital in the country, and he ought to know with the number of crazy drivers on the road here." Amanda and alia separated so they could come over, a nurse came out the door leading to the OR's and called in a bored voice, a voice which had seen it all.

"Family of Karen Fit, Fit, Fitzsomething" Joe pushed himself up painfully and went over.

"That's me."

"You can come in to Recovery, put the gown on first." Joe threw a look back at the Chris and Amanda and they both gave him thumbs up. He followed the nurse through the corridor and into the large recovery room. A dozen beds, some empty, some filled, and there she was. His heart missed a beat at the sight of a tube, and the respirator and multiple plastic lines which led in and out. The machine was breathing for her, this was not recovery, this was a disaster, the Doctor was still in green with a mask, and as he came close he was transported to another place and time, the same place and time, when another green-clad man told him Helen was doomed. His steps slowed to a crawl, he felt like folding his ears, to hold off the disastrous news, but he had no choice. The monitor showed she was still alive.

"Are you Mister Fitsimmons?" the Doctor asked in Russian-tipped English, struggling with the unfamiliar name.

"Yes" Joe said, it was so much simpler to keep the non-truth.

"She is very lucky, we recovered the bullet, see?" and he pointed at the side-table, at a small plastic dish. "You should go back and thank the Doctor who treated her in the field, without his intervention she had no chance of survival, are you OK?! Nurse, nurse, help me, sit down, sit down, didn't I just tell you she is doing OK?" Joe collapsed heavily on a bedside chair, the overwhelming relief draining away his last reserves of muscle control. His head swam, his ears burned, his heart beat the drum, she is alive, alive...Really alive. He steadied himself and became professional again.

"Why is she on the respirator?" The doctor was surprised at the fluent Hebrew uttered by this scruffy-looking big American.

"We had to crack open some ribs, to get at the bullet, that's why she is paralyzed and sedated, but she will recover consciousness shortly."

"How do you know she will?" Joe persisted.

"Cause we had to put her down before surgery, once she got the three units of blood, she was conscious, and she asked about a Joe Bergman, who is that?" Joe nodded and cracked a smile, then a laugh, then a belly laugh, she was alive, and the world was bright again, for once in his life he had not screwed up. The doctor regarded him curiously and one of the nurses twirled her fingers behind him. This man was sitting in a recovery room, his wife sick with a breathing tube, and he was laughing his head off, weird.

Joe controlled himself "I am going out to tell the family." He slipped his hand under the blanket, found a hand and squeezed it. Then, stepping lightly, he went back the way he came, and smiled at everyone, nurses, doctors, orderlies. He pushed the swinging doors and met Amanda and Chris' eyes. The looks of concern changed to relief, Chris stood and whacked him a good one between the shoulder blades.

"Told you" he said.

"Is Nurse Karen alright?" piped Alia.

"Yes, she is going to be fine" Joe said "and you were GRRRRReat" he tweaked her nose "she really was" he said to Amanda. Amanda let her daughter go and fell on his neck, and hugged till her own ribs cracked. Chris beamed.

"Thank you Joe, thank you for,,, for everything" his shoulder became wet, it was embarrassing, in front of all these people.

"Chris, take her away from me, I can't breath" Joe said, this time mirthfully, and she cracked her ribs some more. Sura grinned too, it must have been her first in twelve years.

Finally released Joe became serious. "Look, the authorities here are stunned, but they will recover and start asking questions. I want you to go to the Dan hotel, and take Sura with you, I don't want a sudden arrest for illegal entry or anything. I'll wait here, and they will start with me first."

"What do you need to do, besides waiting for Karen to recover?"

Joe called her to come close and whispered in her ear, so that Alia does not hear, Mustafa was, after all, her father. "I want them to take Mustafa and his gang out. As long as he is alive, he is a danger to you, to me, to Karen, and to Jews in general." Amanda recoiled with horror.

"You mean *Kill him*?!!" She hissed.

"Amanda, when we were escaping he had his men shoot a rocket at us. It would have killed Alia" he said that in a normal voice. Amanda was shaking her head with disbelief.

"C'est vrais" Sura said " t'was a rocket, Capitain Joseph was wiser than the rocket."

Amanda reached a decision "then do what you must, he is a monster, and should be treated as such, let's go, Chris, Alia, Sura, I bet you a hundred to one you are hungry and thirsty and can use a hot bath, am I right or am I right?" and she led the girls out, followed by Chris. Not a moment too soon, five minutes later 4 Military Police, 3 boys and a girl, so they seemed to Joe, came into the fourth floor waiting room and scanned the humanity. They locked in on Joe immediately, but they had obviously been instructed to look for others too.

"Lieutenant Bergman?"

"Doctor Bergman" he corrected the sergeant, who was the girl, she was in command of the detachment.

"Where are the woman and child?" she reexamined her papers.

"What woman? What child?" Joe was the picture of innocence.

"Uh, they told us there was a woman and child who came in with you in the helicopter."

"It's only me here, as you can see" Joe was laughing inside. He had always liked to confound the authorities, even if they were represented by such a comely youth.

Then girl recovered "fine, we will deal with them later, but you must remain here under guard."

Joe laughed some more, this time openly "Any charges?"

"No, orders."

"Relax sweetheart, my girlfriend is in there , I am not going anywhere, except to get me some coffee. Actually, I don't have any money, will you get me some?"

"You have some Chutzpah, don't you?" She said angrily, her authority undermined.

"Well, if I am your prisoner, then you have to keep me in good shape. If I am not mistaken, in 30 minutes we are gonna have lots of high, very high ranking officers here, and I will have to tell them you kept me thirsty!!"

"Benny, get this pain the neck some coffee from the cafeteria" she shot Joe an angry glance. Joe got up, and one of the MP's got up with him.

"I am going back into the recovery room, call me when the coffee is here, or the officers" and without a by-your-leave he took the opportunity of the door swinging open to slip into the OR suite.

Now that he was confident of Karen's chances he assessed the monitors more carefully. The respirator, the monitors, every piece of equipment, even the room, had been purchased with the financial aid of North American

Jewish fund-raising, each with it's own plaque. Incredible, a whole country built on Schnorr, fund raising in Yiddish. Karen's heart rate was steady, her color was good and sometimes her chest did it's own effort at breathing, tripping the respirator. In fact it was only the fentanyl which kept her under. Good, this looked real good.

Joe was wrong, it only took them 20 more minutes. Israel is a small country, and the helicopter from Tel Aviv flew fast.

"Who is Doctor Bergman here?" the orderly asked.

"I am" said Joe to the orderly at the door. The Russian anaesthesiologist's head snapped up with surprise, then understanding and appreciation for a job well done.

"A bunch of officers are looking for you in the waiting room."

Joe went over to the anaesthesiologist "got an extra tooth brush and paste in your call room?" he asked, colleague to colleague.

"Spasiva" said Alexei Dachis, and led Joe to a small room, unmade bed and a wash basin. He pulled a disreputable toothbrush and Zebra tooth-paste tube and shrugged, "that's it."

"Harasho" Joe said with a smile. He also found a single-use Bond shaver, about ten years old, in the far recess of the same drawer, and carefully set about shaving and brushing with scalding water. However contaminated this stuff was , it was better than being dirty, scruffy and with halitosis. As for the clothes, the cupboard yielded some clean scrubs, Joe was getting comfortable. Throw him anywhere in the world, hospital scrubs and a call room were home away from home. He went back to Doctor Dachis.

"What's the word?"

"I will move her up to the respi-intensive care very soon, seventh floor."

"Watch her for me, will you?" Joe grinned.

Joe went right past the gaggle of officers, who were sitting uncomfortably in the waiting room, to Shneior, who was now the most junior of the heavily epauletted officers. There was also a civilian, and they all paid him great deference. They were not expecting a doctor who looked like a Doctor, but rather a scruffy refugee.

"Motti Shneior, what do you know" Joe clapped his thin shoulder.

"Elohim, it's *you*!!" Motti exclaimed.

"Introduce me, won't you?"

"How is your wife?"

"She is not officially my wife, but who cares, she is doing OK."

"Where are the scarred woman and child?"

"Sura and Alia. Gone with Alia's mother."

"Where?"

"That information stays with me, back to work."

"OK, they can't be far." The four visitors waited for the exchange to end.

"Rabotai, gentlemen, this is Doctor Bergman. I suggest we look for a more secure location." Shneior led the way to the Ram 2, the military sub-section, where the girl-corporal found them a small, secluded office. She also brought coffee and cookies from the cafeteria, and Joe, who otherwise would have stayed away from the lousy coffee, slurped with relish.

"This is Amiram Levine, adviser to the Prime-minister," Shneior introduced the civilian first "this is Omri Nitzan, Patzan, Ron Shivek of the you-know-who, and Nahum Machness from Aman Matcal. Doctor Bergman is a former Sayeret Golani, and has the history of having lost his parents in Savoy Hotel, and his grandmother in the Café Apropo explosion." The eyes of the four riveted on the big green man, who carried such a big load of misfortune. Israel is replete with such examples, women twice widowed, sisters whose brother and boyfriend were felled, but still, meeting someone with this kind of ill-fate sent a shiver through the collective back. The history of Sayeret also made sense because Sayeret meant Scouts, the soldiers with the most motivation , highest fighting skills, and field craft, survivors of hardships. The legacy of Sayeret stayed with the fighters long after they were old, paunchy and bald.

"Doctor Bergman has an interesting story to tell us" Shneior concluded his introduction.

Joe took his time to explain his peculiar role in the unlikely intersection with Mustafa. In a way, it was the most singular bad luck that juxtaposed the most carefully laid scientific plans with the unlikely obviator of these plans. The Religious would find in such occurrence the proof of the hand of God. The Logician would only find 'blind crazy luck' , to quote Tommy Lee Jones.

Joe figured that if Mustafa was left alive and unaccounted for he would come after Amanda and himself. The Sagger proved that Mustafa had failed the Solomon trial - he was willing to cut the child rather than give it to the real mother. That put him outside the Pale, and the only logical outcome of this reasoning was elimination. The persons to whom he was making his plea possessed an enormously big stick, and the greatest aversion to using that stick un-necessarily. He had to convince them it was necessary, and right, despite the risks.

"We need some corroboration for this story" said Levine.

Omri Nitzan pulled out the transmissions and assessments which were related to the Islamic Jihad activity, and arranged them temporally. Nahum Machness pulled out the Shomer Rosh reports. Ron Shivek - the Cyprus reports. Suddenly, put together, they all made sense.

Joe read the Shomer rosh reports upside down. "You had someone watching the Villa?"

"Of course. Tell me what kind of vehicle did you use to stake out the villa?"

"A single-cylinder Suzuki motorcycle" Joe replied.

Machness underlined it for Levine's benefit.

"We still have it under surveillance, daily, since you came into the picture" Machness remarked dryly.

"What about the American side of the picture?" Levine asked.

"That will be a little more difficult to corroborate. What you need to do is get someone to call on the CDC..."

"Excuse our ignorance, CDC?" Amiram interrupted

"Pardon, the CDC is the American government Agency that oversees the national health status in terms of communicable diseases, and is responsible for the safety of vaccinations. My associates in the States called them to raid the Lipjohn plant and stop all shipments of Polio vaccinations. You may be able to confirm that. If this has not happened I am advising you, very strongly, to stop all Polio vaccinations in Israel which originate in that plant, and submit lot samples to Nes Ziona, or the Hebrew university for genetic analysis. I suggest you do it *now*." Joe concluded in an even voice.

"Do you actually suggest that the plan was to cause cancer in a significant portion of the population, especially babies?" Amiram repeated slowly. Joe nodded emphatically.

"I am a Cohen" said Shivek, his voice breaking up "Amir is four months old, he got his shots last week." Silence settled over the officers, the last comment made it close and personal.

Amiram Levine got up "Doctor Bergman" he said officially, "where are you staying?"

"In the hospital, until Karen is ready to go."

"One last question, in fact two" Levine continued "One, who financed you, Two, why did you do it, why risk yourself?"

"Fella financed me, as for the other question, I guess that's between me and the Almighty. I will talk to him again on Yom Kippur." Shneior whispered something into Levine's ear, Levine nodded.

"Yossi Bergman, I believe I represent the Prime Minister if I say Thank You on behalf of all of us. Shneior will keep you informed." Amiram Levine strode out, and the three satellites with him.

"I think you made a strong impression on Amiram" Shneior commented. The day was drawing to a close, the sun was sinking into the west, a big huge red ball, sinking into the Mediterranean . Friday night was coming, the eve of the Sabbath."Wanna eat something real, like Shawarma on Atzmaut street?" Shneior referred to the Haifa downtown main drag, where the food-pits were close, noisy, and smelled to high heaven of middle-eastern delicacies, 20 hours a day.

"Like this?" Joe indicated himself, dirty, smelly, green-clad.

"My sister lives in Haifa, her husband is your kind of size, we will find you something to wear, actually, they will have us for dinner."

"Major Shneior, you have a deal, I'll check on Karen and come back here."

"I'll wait."

Amiram Levine arranged his features suitably before he went into the Chamber. He had asked that the PM convene the security cabinet, the heads of Aman, Nes Ziona Biological station, Chief of Staff and the Airforce, on Friday night. This has not happened before in this administration. This Prime-minister had great oratorical powers, he was excellent in organizing his own political power base, he was fantastic on TV, he was *not* as good in making decisions, and the recent Mossad fiasco made him skittish about Special Ops, even though he had been Sayeret Matcal himself once. The data that Amiram had was also thinner than usual, but the window of opportunity was so narrow, and the consequences of dallying so far-reaching, that Amiram staked his whole standing and reputation on this issue.

"Shalom Amiram, come in" said the Prime Minister "everybody knows everybody and it is late, go ahead and start."

"Gvirty and rabotai, (my lady and gentlemen)" Amiram Levine began "today I met a remarkable man, who together with an American woman saved a kidnaped child from Beirut and using their own devices and manipulations forced their way into the Beaufort, and were later evacuated to Haifa. The American is severely wounded, but I am told she is out of danger. The child is safe with her mother who is American too. This man whose name is Yossi Bergman..."

"I know that name" said the PM, searching back into his prodigious memory.

"I will get back to that in a minute" promised Levine "he claims to have evidence that the father of the abducted child has developed a biological weapon directed at us, at Jews, which he aimed to introduce into the country."

"That's impossible" snorted Emanuel Anati, head of Nes Ziona.

"Why impossible?" queried the PM.

"Because there is no way to target Jews specifically, we are not that specific" Anati replied with conviction.

"Doctor Bergman told me that this is untrue, and that Mustafa Halim has found a way to target Cohanim, based on a genetic trait inherited by Cohanim only." Emanuel blanched. Yigal Cohavi, the internal security Minister watched him closely.

"Furthermore, Doctor Bergman said that this biological agent had been tried by the this Doctor Halim on a number of Jewish babies in the city of Memphis, with very serious results. By serious I mean these babies are *all dead.*" The listeners moved about uncomfortably. This was outside their realm of understanding. They all understood bullets, and bombs, and missiles. They did not understand Bugs.

"What exactly did they die of?" asked Anati

"A cancer, called Neuroblastoma, I was told by Doctor Haroosh from Haifa this is a very malignant baby cancer, rare and lethal." Amiram replied, looking through his notes.

"To go on, we have a number of reports from agents and commint which give credence to the Bergman story. He said that he got involved because Halim kidnaped his own daughter, whose mother is a colleague of Bergman in the States. His description fits exactly a man noticed and photographed by an agent in Cyprus in December, identified with a child, and of activity reported from Shomer Rosh, which are operatives observing the Islamic Jihad headquarters in Beirut. The same observers reported the Bergman himself had been there on Monday, and in the last two days the Islamic Jihad had gone nuts, essentially going after Bergman and the child, which he managed to steal, apparently from her school. The Jihad used every possible means, including mobilization of Syrian Army, Lebanese police, and Hezbollah, to track him down and stop them. He managed to evade them. We have received this from Shomer Rosh

To: Aman Patzan
From Shomer Rosh
Sub: Shkaki Villa
Urgent Urgent Urgent
Since early this evening intense activity at the villa.
Subject Shkaki and Subject Zefa are overseeing
major dismantling of the equipment which had been
installed in the last three months.
They are moving out
signed
Shomer rosh

"Doctor Bergman warned me that this is likely to happen and that we should stop it. He says that all this equipment is related to the manufacture of the Biologic Agent."

"So what is the Biologic Agent?" Zehava Livni, the only woman on the security cabinet asked. There was no getting around it, most of the cabinet ministers were men, and used to be high ranking officers. Zehava was a tough campaigner, and she beat a bunch of other Generals to her present position, Minister of Communications.

"It's a Polio vaccine, altered to cause cancer" Amiram Levine said shortly.

"Corroboration?" said the PM.

"Bergman referred me to the CDC, an American agency," Levine continued "I asked Doctor Vered Sahar, who is the head of Virology in Tel Hashomer hospital, to make the call. We are lucky. The Head of the CDC is Doctor William Corchak, who is a great friend of Israel, on the private front. I asked Doctor Sahar to come with me, She has been vetted by Shabac and she has the highest security rating. She agreed to come even though it is the Sabbath, she considers what she heard a major threat to life."

The PM nodded. Doctor Vered Sahar, a petite woman wearing a hat came in. Her long blue skirt and white long sleeved blouse closed at the neck were almost the hallmark of the Modern Orthodox. These women raised half-a-dozen kids and still managed to be active in medicine and research.

The PM rose and greeted her, he knew better than to extend his hand. "Thank you for coming, Doctor Sahar" he said "I realize that your coming here on Shabat means something by itself. We are listening."

If Vered Sahar was impressed by being called to the PM and Security Cabinet chambers, she hid it well, and she got right to the point.

"This afternoon I spoke with Doctor William Corchak, head of the CDC. We know each other from my previous academic work at the CDC. He was very surprised because my call preceded an announcement from the CDC, which was to out by all possible means of communications including the Internet, of total recall of all Oral Polio vaccinations in the United States. Doctor Corchak confirmed that following a report from a Memphis Doctor by the name of....Kreissman, confirmed by a team led by a Doctor...Baille, the CDC had seized some lots of polio vaccinations, which had been genetically tampered with. He said that *all* Oral Polio vaccinations in the United States had been stopped, until the source of tampering is found, and all suspect lots taken off the shelves. To explain this action they are coming up with a story of a tainted preservative, Thimerosal. He told me, off the record, that one of the two companies manufacturing the Sabin vaccination in the United States has been raided and now they are going through the whole process to find out how, when, and who is responsible for introduction of a mutant live virus. Some of the suspect lots were already earmarked for export, and some are in transit."

"Export to where?" Amiram asked.

"Export to Israel!!?" Livni said , not really asking.

"To Israel." Doctor Sahar confirmed.

"What kind of tampering?" asked Anati, who was a master of Tampering.

"William did not want to commit, except for one thing. He said that the same Doctor Kreissman presented evidence of integration of a human cancer gene into the virus, a gene known to be related to NeuroBlastoma, a pediatric cancer. Baille's lab then ran specific tests which confirmed this hypothesis. The presence *of Any* human origin genetic material means tampering, but a Cancer gene - that means intent to kill." Doctor Sahar concluded.

"I assure you, that I did not discuss any of Bergman's story with Vered, in fact this is the first she is hearing the name" Amiram said.

"Who is Bergman?" Doctor Vered Sahar asked Amiram.

The PM took upon himself the dismissal.

"Doctor Sahar, Please accept my sincere apologies for bringing you on Shabat, Yoel " He called the Shabac secret service who were outside . Yoel, tall, thin, short spiked black hair, ear-piece plugged in and Berretta always ready, and always on the alert, poked his head in.

"Please escort Doctor Sahar to the Moriah, I think she will prefer to walk" Yoel nodded, Amiram had already briefed him, and he had the men ready.

"What do we know of this Bergman? we seem to be putting an awful lot of stock into his report, or story" said the PM after the Doctor had left.

"First" Amiram said "he is a first rate doctor, according to the medics in the Beaufort, and the doctor on the chopper. Second, he was an Officer in Sayeret Golani, before going on to Medical school in Tel Aviv. I don't know how we ever allowed him to enlist, because he lost both parents in the Savoy Hotel. Possibly because he later lived with his grandparents."

"*That's* why I remember the name" the PM broke in, "I was on the unit that came in the second wave. One of the victims was a Bergman, he feigned a heart attack on his own initiative, he and his wife bought it first from Marzouk." The security cabinet nodded. Bergman was not a name anymore, it was part of the gruesome national reality.

"Like father like son. Yossi Bergman served in Lebanon on Miluim, and was reported to be an exceptional leader, as expected of Sayeret." Levine said that proudly, he himself, long ago, had been the commander of Sayeret Golani. "He is familiar with the Nabatiyah territory, to keep it short, any report from this man is relevant and likely to be true and accurate."

"Sum it up for us" said the PM.

"I suggest that we are facing a new threat, we are lucky to be given an early warning, that the threat now is concentrated to one single location, and that we should use our capabilities to take it out, NOW." Amiram concluded.

"How serious is this threat?" Kohavi directed the question at Anati.

"I don't have enough data, but I am familiar with the technical challenge of creating a mutant virus which can be a vector for disease. If someone had been able to address the question of specificity, then we are facing a major, MAJOR crisis, because once you have the technology, you can apply it in a thousand different ways, use another vector, another genetic trait, Hell is the limit. This can be worse than the Osirac atomic reactor Begin took out in 1982." Anati concluded.

"Feasibility?" asked the PM. Everyone turned to Yair Biran, Rosh Aman.

"Lights out" said Aluf Biran. His aides had collected from Aman archives slides of every conceivable target in the of the Islamic Jihad in Lebanon, ground photos, air photos, satellite imagery, the works.

"First slide" said Biran "to orientate, this is the Beirut Cornice, very pretty, this is the port, this is the Beirut international, this is the main road to Tripoli, and these are the foot hills of the Schouf mountains. Let's take a closer look at the Shkaki Villa."

"Shkaki as in Fat'hi Shkaki?" asked Livni

"His brother, Youness, he is not as flamboyant as his late brother, but he is as dedicated to the replacement of Jews with Palestinians" said Amiram.

"This is the villa, seen from the F-15"Yair Biran continued "it is rather isolated, and it commands it's surroundings. One can clearly see vehicles in the front yard, and unloading. We were prompted to look by Aman Patzan who said that technical equipment was being unloaded and set up. Shomer Rosh are usually hidden in one of these three structures" and he indicated them.

"These are ground photos. This is Youness Shkaki, on a rare occasion when he shows himself."

"Just for corroboration" Amiram said, "we asked Bergman to make a drawing of the surroundings. Rav-Seren Shneior, who is keeping tabs on Bergman sent us this Fax." The transparency of a crude drawing was placed on the overhead projector, together with the slide. "The similarity is unmistakable. Bergman was there."

"Doesn't Bergman have his own agenda?" asked Kohavi, always on the alert for assassins. Since Rabin's murder, the internal security minister had to be on his toes.

"I am sure he does, but in this case his agenda goes hand in hand with ours" Amiram said.

"Back to feasibility" said the PM.

"If we had someone on the ground who could designate it for us, we can slip a bomb into each and every window, one hour from now" Shalom Rosen, commander of the IAF, said that with utter conviction.

"You can do that, at night, without touching any other buildings in the vicinity!" asked Zehava Livni, just to make things clear.

"With ninety-nine point nine percent accuracy."

"The question is, do we want to?" Shaul Yitzhaki, Minister of transportation said. "For years now, we have stayed out of Beirut, we have examined this question again and again, do we want to make the Beirut government accountable for Hezbollah activity in southern Lebanon, do we want to escalate the conflict, which, at this time is mainly local."

"Local for you, not for my youngest son who is in Lebanon right now" Livni countered, she was the youngest, the most comely , and the fiercest minister on the Security Cabinet, someone had once remarked that like Golda in her time, Livni was the only minister with Balls.

"Zehava, don't make this a personal issue" the PM cautioned, "to sum it up, it's feasible, if you had a designator. Ronen, do we?"

"Every operative in the field has one, it's really just a laser pointer like the one we are using. But, if we use him, we burn the operation and we have to plan on evac." said Rav Aluf Ronen SimanTov, Chief of Staff.

"Knowing you, it's all arranged" the PM grinned wolfishly.

"The evac is all set up. It's always on hold, and waiting for activation."

"Do we want to escalate the war in Lebanon? I don't think so" Yitzhaki persisted.

"We should make a decision" Amiram prompted "if it's to be done, it has to be done now, in a few hours the building will be an empty shell."

"I agree" said the PM, "Siman Tov, you have been very quiet, I want your input."

"Like Anati I don't have enough data to go on, but as my grand-daughter's pediatrician says, sometimes you got to make a decision on insufficient data. Shkaki has been running a nasty operation for a long time, drugs, arson, small arms, maximum damage with little risk. I say we upp his risk, and any other terrorist, this is a good opportunity."

"Livni?"

"Give him some of his own medicine. My son says they are eating Patzmarim everyday, I say hit them with the big stick."

"Kohavi?"

"I am not as impressed with all this biological voodoo. The Syrians and Iraquis and Iranian have been devising Biologicals since Ben Guryon's time. I think the Palestinian Authority is going to scream if we bomb their brethren in Lebanon, and we are going to have a resurgence of Intifadeh. I don't want to be a hair trigger. I want to see more data and make a slow, cool decision" Kohavi concluded.

"I wish Michael Yanai was here" the PM said wistfully, he was referring to the Foreign Minister who was visiting Thailand. "This conference does not leave this room, I don't want to make threats but lately I feel the CNN and ABC and my grandmother know as much as I do. This is a Black operation, which means that nothing will indicate the source of the blast, is that understood?" he addressed Siman Tov and Rosen. The decision was political, they were the executors, the rules were clear.

"Merde, and merde again" Noam Bohbut said to Alon Mizrahi, they were still watching the villa from a deserted building a mile away. It was a clear night and the lights were on and the trucks were coming in to be loaded. Zefa was jumping about like a hooked fish. Bohbut had just deciphered the burst message.

"What, what?" Alon Mizrahi was suddenly terrified.

"They want us to designate, after that our ass is in the sling."

"Figure that has anything to do with that Motorcycle Dude?"

"Yeah, they should have made *him* designate, let's get the stuff ready. Mama, here we come, sweet Natanya, Bohbut is coming home!!"

The F15 and F16 fighters climbed with tremendous afterburners, the F15 double, the F16 single, and made their way West from Nevatim. They streaked across the coastline at Ashkelon and continued to increase alti-tude. They knew exactly what they were looking for. The A14 airway was the aerial highway that led to Tel Aviv. The A-15 was north of that, and all aircraft inbound for Beirut International followed the same Radian to Beirut. The fighters were looking for a likely Jumbo to piggyback them to Beirut. Since the major international carriers scheduled routes were public knowledge, the controllers at Meron knew exactly when and how those carriers are coming, altitude, direction, even the names of the pilots. The Israeli fighter pilots knew that route by heart. They made bets that they could land an F15 in Beirut, and take off, without anybody being the wiser, not even the American Sixth Fleet.

The Lufthansa 747 began losing altitude inbound for Beirut. The fighters, bunched in close formation, joined him from below, the F15 who was Tail listened in on the Beirut Approach, to forestall sudden changes, not that a Jumbo could *make* sudden changes. The F16 maintained formation, and checked the Smart Bombs. He had trained on the simulate target many times before, and so far this was just like practice, no opposition, easier than Oded Kattash shooting from the line. Easier because Oded, the new Basketball whizzkid, did not have maneuverable balls. The only unknown in this night raid was the designator. No designation - no bombing run.

They followed the landing Jumbo almost all the way in to runway 130 then veered left under the radar, the F15 using the ECM to make them invisible. Israel did not posses the tremendously expensive stealth fighter, and whatever could not be achieved with hardware was achieved with software. The sensors looked frantically for the designator wavelength, because they had only one run

The beep alerted Rimon Hod that he had picked the designator up. The Villa appeared in the cross hair. Insistent beep of Lock and he released the bombs and banked hard into the ravine in the looming mountains. His night vision was perfect and he needed only the minimum of night vision enhancement.

Rimon double clicked 'bombs away', streaked out of the ravine and made a low getaway back to the sea.

Mustafa was all wired up, jumping into the trucks, directing the men, yelling at them to hurry up, lending his back into the effort. The centri-fuges and thermal cyclers, the boxes of culture media, the shakers refrigerators and heaters. Youness was also evacuating, although not in such a tearing hurry. This was after all Friday night, the coming morning was Saturday, the Jews were slow, not as slow as the Americans and Russians, but still, hampered by the demands of Democracy. Their responses to the repeated attacks on their strongholds in southern Lebanon were laughable. If he had the kind of firepower that they possessed he would have pulverized every stone in response for a single mortar shell. The Zionists were trying to fight a clean war, ridiculous, but of course it played into his and the Hezbollah's hands. With every retaliatory shelling they could display a child with an amputated leg and arm in cast, and make the Zionists ashamed of their own existence.

Suleiman approached him cautiously. He did not want to bother the Chief but the red dot bothered him. It had appeared on the side wall of the building, the size of penny, and it was very intense. Could it be something from the Mad Doctor? he wanted Youness, whose bodyguard he was, to see.

"Chief"?

"What is it Suleiman?"

"I an ashamed to say that there is something I do not understand."

"What don't you understand? we are leaving this place for the time being for the Bekaa."

"No, come with me."

Youness knew not to pooh-pooh anything Suleiman said, he followed him around the marble villa. Suleiman looked expectantly, but it was gone, as if it had never been.

"Ya Sidi, it was here, really, it was, a red dot."

"I know, wait a minute."

They waited in silence, the first truck in the convoy started it's engine, a jet was approaching the Beirut International, except for the frantic urging and surly responses at the front of the Villa, it was all quiet.

"There, there it is" Suleiman said excitedly "a red dot."

Youness gazed at the red dot which reflected brilliantly from the marble, and felt a great peace descend over him. His life had been of strife, and fighting, and connivance. Leading the hopeless, and hoping to kill the Invaders. Now the Invaders were saying the last word, catching him, and his most prized project, his greatest effort, out in the open. This blow would tear the heart out of the military wing of the Islamic Jihad, because, let's face it, if the organization is a one man operation, then it falls with the man. Youness Shkaki was the man, because he could trust no one.

The two half-ton bombs homed in on the designated target, one with immediate fuse, the other, delayed. The delayed fuse bomb smashed through the walls as if they were paper, and buried itself in the basement. The touch fuse of the second half-ton tore up everyone and everything in the yard, threw the trucks like toys and toppled the columns and walls down, sealing the building. The perimeter fence was brought down and the iron fence wrapped itself around the flying vehicles. Most of the men, among them Mustafa, never felt the airblast that concussed their brains in an instant. Youness and Suleiman who were standing closest were blasted apart. Then the buried bomb exploded, pulverizing everything from within outside, spewing concrete and earth in a round perimeter, creating a huge crater in the middle of the compound. Windows were broken for half a mile around, the nearest buildings lost some mortar and stucco, but the amount of damage to the surroundings was minimal. The bombs did not leave any traces. The explosive was generic and the casings were Black Composite, which combusted to carbon dioxide in the intense heat, disappearing into the blast.

The F15 cameras took some quick photos in the intense light produced by the blasts which came two seconds apart, infrared imagery of the burning vehicles, and then headed west again, underneath the AirMaroc tristar which was taking off right after the Lufthansa. The Syrian radar registered, but far too late, and not very clearly. They were not ready to switch on the locking radar, because, in the past, it meant a Shrike missile homing on the Radar.

The PM was in the IAF Bor (The Hole, Air Force command) with his aides, Siman Tov and Rosen and Levine. They waited for what seemed like hours, but really was only long minutes. The air strike, in a way, was the simpler operation, Israeli aircraft have been operating in Lebanon like they owned the sky for 15 years, ever since the great aerial Victory over the thickest Russian SAM network in the world, 1982. Syrian aircraft never ventured into the air over Lebanon, and the pilots had practiced every possible scenario and target, including the Shkaki Villa. The more hair-raising operation was getting Shomer Rosh (headguards) out, once the heads did not need to be guarded anymore. The full resources of the Army and Navy and Air force were brought to bear, and as SimanTov had indicated, those plans were also pre-laid and only needed to be activated. Still, the PM, who had suffered two major setbacks in secret operations, one in Lebanon when 10 commandos, the pick of the Navy 13th Flotilla, were massacred by an ambush, and a second one, when a biologic attack on a Hamas operative ended in ignominious failure in Jordan, fretted, and drowned his worries in endless cups of Black coffee and chewed up cigars. This kind of operation was Black if it succeeded, and Brilliant Red to the eye of the raging Press if it failed. The problem was not in not getting the target. The problem was the public-relations fiasco if civilians and Israeli soldiers were somehow injured.

"Double click" Meron control reported

"Double click" Rosen said, this was his show, and he was running it personally. Secretly he envied the pilots who were up there tearing the sky. But, time waited for no one and he knew he did not have the razor sharp reflexes of the younger pilots anymore. He had had his kills in the Yom Kippur war, 1973, and in Sheleg, 1982. "That means bombs away" he translated for the PM. The waiting just became more tense, the seconds dragged the minute was an hour.

"Target destroyed" Rosen said quietly, and a cheer broke out from the surrounding soldiers, each in his or her station.

"What about damage to the periphery?"

"Later, when we get the imagery from the F15, and the satellite in the morning" Siman Tov said.

"Now we wait for the Hello signal."

"I expect Noam and Alon to be on their way to the airport beach. They have underwater SCUBA equipment, located clearly by the airport runway lights. The Hello will pick them up, we practiced this getaway a million times" said Meir HarZion, the 13th Flotilla commander. He knew each man intimately, including the ten who had perished a few months before. They waited some more.

"Hello away" said Rosen referring to the helicopter which had taken off the Satil, the missile boat. The first light was coming on, and with it, the risk to the helicopter, interminable minutes passed, the distance were short, but the chances of radio beacons malfunction, pilot error, opposition intervention, those risks kept mounting and mounting.

"Hello collected them both" Rosen took off his ear phones, just in time to receive a whack on the back from SimanTov. The PM smiled tiredly as the Bor erupted with cheer, another long night in a series of long nights. Sleeping was *not* one of the most frequent chores of the PM.

The cellular phone rang. He fumbled for it, pressed the wrong button, then the Send.

"Who is it?" said Shneior sleepily.

"Its Amiram, find your favorite Doc and tell him Mustafa is out."

"So the PM agreed?" Shneior asked in wonder

"The deed is done, Shkaki and Zefa are dead, all without the usual fiasco. I am going to sleep now, I can't believe that at my age I still work these crazy hours."

"Thanks, good night."

It was six thirty in the morning of Saturday, light was just coming up. Shneior looked through the window, as always, the vista was breathtaking, the Carmel mount, the harbor, the Mediterranean, it was a good morning, which repaid you for plenty of bad ones. I wonder if the Islamic Jihad can retaliate in anyway.

Chapter 24

EPILOGUE

Joe had fallen asleep on the bench in the waiting room of the Seventh floor intensive care. After Friday night dinner at Motti's sister, dressed in borrowed pants, shirt and coat, he had made it back to the Rambam. At midnight the Respi Unit quieted down somewhat, the respirators making their blowing sounds and the monitors beeeping mournfully. Karen was stable, and her spontaneous breathing tripped the respirator machine-regular rhythm. Her colour was good and the best sign of all, the doctors were not hovering nearby, they were near the bed in the corner where an old man with lung cancer was fighting the vent.

He woke up with a start, a hand was on his shoulder, shaking him awake, it was early morning, the waiting room was empty, early morning light bathing the drab walls. Karen, Disaster, something must have happened while I was asleep, Alexei was grinning at him, a tired grin, someone who had not slept all night.

"She is coming round, still intubated but not for long" Doctor Dachis said. Relief, *what* a relief. Joe got up, his whole body aching from the hard bench and the previous days' beatings, and followed Dachis into the Unit.

The deep blue pools enticed him from a distance, Joe forgot about the tube, the plastic lines, the monitors, he desired to dive into the cool blue and stay there forever. Instead he came over, fumbled for the hand under the cover, and squeezed. The squeeze was returned, with strength, vigor, with promise of Life. Joe just stood there, drowning in the Blue, and let the tears run. The morning shift changed, the nurses let the lovers have their tiny private cocoon.

Thus Shneior found them, the big man weeping soundlessly leaning over his wife and gazing into her eyes. He waited, then waited some more, then he cleared his throat. The blue eye pools shifted in unison, and Joe had to break away.

"Shalom Motti."

"Hi Yossi, I have some news for you."

"The Villa is gone."

"The Villa is gone" Motti confirmed.

"Are the Watchers safe?"

"They were recovered safe and sound."

"The CDC?"

"Locked down on all vaccine production, no more bad shots."

"So it's over?"

"Yep, until the next diabolical plot."

"Don't count on us, we are out of the hero business."

"God will come up with another savior, that's what my name-sake said to Esther two and half thousand years ago."

"I got to tell Amanda. Should I, should I?" he asked Karen, still mute with the tube. She nodded slowly, winked with one eye.

"Shneior, take me to the Dan, will you?"

The Dan Panorama is majestically situated on top of Mount Carmel. Elegant rooms overlook the city, the golden Bahaii temple, the magnificent gardens, the harbour and the Mediterranean. The lobby, the facilities, the dining rooms, the accouterments, and the price, are second to none. Shneior, dressed in civies, and Joe, in second-hand, slept-in clothes early Saturday morning, were out of place, as the receptionist's face indicated.

"Doctor Carter, she checked in yesterday."

"Room 454, Adoni (sir)."

They waited for the elevator, The Shabat elevator was completely automatic, that is, it stopped in every floor, and the buttons were useless. Slowly they made it to the fourth floor, and the adjoining rooms.

Chris, in jeans and checkered flannel opened the door, cautiously, and then threw it wide.

"Joe!" Joe braced himself for the hug. For a Midwesterner Chris was uninhibited.

"You met Shneior yesterday, he is my very own Army representative" Chris was careful with Motti's hand.

"Hi Joe, look at this view, its breathtaking" said Amanda, her eyes were clear, her hair brushed till it shone, in Levies and black knit, "we were just going down for breakfast, coming?"

"Amanda, where is Alia?"

"In the next room, with Sura."

"Mustafa is dead, Amanda."

Amanda just stood there, her arms dropped, her shoulders shook, and she wept, silently. She turned to the veranda, and walked out. Chris, alarmed, followed her, and placed a big comforting arm, and slowly drew her to him and she sobbed into his shirt.

"I loved him, once, and then I became afraid of him, I loathed him, hated him and then I wanted him to die." she said quietly "I never knew one could wish and it could come, and Alia has lost her father." They were on the Dan Veranda Restaurant, and the view was undiminished in its grandeur

"I don't think so" said Joe, "if anything I think she gained one."

"I accept the role" said Chris, and directed his gaze at Alia, who was playing table hockey with Sura using forks and a piece of bread. The girls giggled.

"You'll have to do better than that, Chris" Joe chided.

"Here?" Chris asked.

"Why not?" Shnieor got the drift, Amanda looked puzzled at all this male cipher, what were they talking about? for goodness sake!

"Alright, here goes" Chris got up, stretched his huge frame and then folded down, knee to the floor. He took the chair legs, and turned the chair as easily as if a butterfly was the sole occupant. He faced the amazed woman, the one he fell in love with ever since he had seen her in grief, so far away.

"Amanda Carter, will you do me the honor of becoming my wife?"

"Hear, hear" Shnieor commented and jumped as Joe's hand clamped on his knee like a vise-grip.

"In a twinkle, yes, yes, I will" Amanda said, Chris did not move, thunderstruck, fossilized.

"I think that was a yes" said Shneior, conversationally.

"YES" Chris yelled and jumped into the air, like a wound up spring, finally released. He grabbed Amanda and danced her around, while the rest of the breakfast- takers whose collective head had jerked at the joyful yell, went back to their food. Joe and Motti clapped their hands politely, while Alia and Sura looked on with amazement.

"What are you going to do now?" Asked Amanda, they were in Ben Guryon airport. The Israeli government officials were happy to get rid of the Sura problem. Chris had gone to the Embassy in Tel Aviv, and ranted and cajoled until they had allowed her a special permit, on his passport, at his responsibility. Sometimes, being a police officer and a Veteran helped.

"I rented a small apartment in Nahariya, it's a sea side resort north of Haifa, we will stay there for a little while until she is strong enough to go" Joe said.

"So we will see you in Milwaukee, in a few weeks?" Chris asked.

"A couple of months at least, we'll see" Joe replied.

"Tower Air flight number zero-zero one will be boarding in fifteen minutes" the overhead PA system said, in Hebrew and then in English.

"That's you, and you still have customs to clear, Bye Alia, Give-us-a-kiss" Joe bent down and the curly headed angel gave him a big wet kiss.

"See ya" Joe said, and retreated from the gate, he hated long goodbyes.

"This is it" Joe said, and stopped by the grave, in spring, nature was all green and blooming, the Cemetery in Rehovot was well kept, and Joe had seen to it, with small donations, that the graves be well cared for.

"Thank God we took the bus" said Karen, still leaning heavily on Joe, the weeks of shortness of breath and minimal activity had wasted her muscles. Even the short walk from the entry to the grave-site was a major effort. But things were looking up. The week before she had hardly been able to take two steps. "The drivers here are *awful.*"

"The more things change, the more they remain the same." The country was richer, newer cars, faster buses, the congestion was worse, as the Nation contracted into it's pre 1967 size, and the noise and pushing and shoving were not better, except there was much more Russian added to the general noise. In the cemetery it was quiet, with the occasional Kadish being heard.

"Well, I am the last of the line" said Joe, the Graves reaffirming, "so I better say Kadish too." He brought a Yarmulke out, a small prayer book and recited the Kadish for his parents and grandparents. Karen joined him in the last Amen.

"You don't have to, you know" she said as they walked away from the Cemetery.

"Have to what?" Joe inquired.

"Be the last of the line."

"But I am."

"But you don't have to, it's up to you."

"I will hold you to that promise" he promised.

"What happened to your Dad?" asked Joe "we keep hearing from your Mom, but nature dictates you have a Dad, somewhere." They were on the red eye from Chicago to LA, Sura was napping by the window, her lovely silhouette grotesquely marred by the scar. It took some time for her to start going out in public, but she was taking Driver's education and she was assisting in Arab translation for students of Mid East studies at the UW Milwaukee.

"Irreconcilable differences. First he left while mom was pregnant with Alex, then after Alex had died he started getting into the Middle Age routine of chasing younger women. He left the house when I was in college for a girl my age. She jollied him for a while, then cleaned him out and dumped him. After that we never wanted to see him again."

"Men" Joe said "Vermin, don't trust'em."

"Some of them, I guess that was one reason I was wary of men, as relationships go. I was always the monogamous type."

"And now you are living in sin, how come?"

"We don't have to, you know."

"Know what?" Joe retorted, he knew where this was leading.

"You chump, you always make me work hard for everything, live in Sin, I mean."

"Uhuh."

"We are going to see Zeide."

"We are?"

"Sure, maybe he has another car for you." Karen teased

"No thanks, the old one works just fine."

"Mom told him to look for the Ketubah."

"Whose?"

"His and Esther, my Grandma, she got the Lung Cancer, a few months after they had moved. Zeide can't stand the cold so he stays in LA for the winter and comes back to Milwaukee in Spring, depending on his health. He is eighty but Grandma's death aged him terribly."

"What is a Ketuba?"

"You know!!"

"Tell me anyway."

"It's the Jewish marriage contract that the groom signs in front of the Rabbi and two witnesses, written in Arameic."

"OhmyGod."

"Rabbi Kantor told me."

"Are you seeing other men behind my back?" Joe knitted his brow, trying hard not to laugh.

"If I leave things to you I will be waiting until doomsday. The Ketubah means that Miriam was born Jewish, and that means I am Jewish too, and that

makes things *much* easier, like Peter said."
"You are a crafty one, aren't you?" said Joe with wonder.
"You ought to know by now."
"Did I ever tell you I love you very much?" Joe said softly. Sura shifted slightly.
"Yes, but you can repeat it as often as you like. Me too."
"You too what?"
"Love you, you chump."
"Its nice to hear it again."
"Go to sleep, you two" Sura said.

"What do you say Dan?"
"Its fixable, I have done worse" said Dan Sanderson, his usual customer was a Hollywood actress looking to hide the ravages of the years or enhance a lip or a curve. A day a week Dan did Charity surgery, fixing floppy ears, receding chins, burn scars, and cleft palates of children who could not afford Plastic Reconstructive Surgery.
"How much?" said Joe.
"That depends on who's paying."
"Me, and Fella."
"So you are paying with *my* money?" Dan joked, he was a third degree cousin, he knew of Fella and Shimon but had never seen them.
"That's right" said Joe.
"Then we will split the overhead, I am still making more in a year than Fella made in a lifetime."
"The more the merrier" Karen said.
"Shucks, Joseph, how come you bring along a woman who needs absolutely *no* improvement?!"
"You have it all wrong, *I* am bringing him, not the other way round" Karen said.
"Sura, Doctor Sanderson will fix the scars, so take lots of pictures now" Joe said
"I thank thee, O Master."
"Too much Shakespeare, come-on Joe, Zeide is waiting" Karen said.

"Don't I know you?" said Jacob Lifshitz, wagging his spindly finger at Joe. They were outside, in the hot So-Cal June sunshine, and Jacob was in a wheel chair. His body was slowly coming apart, but his faculties were still there.

"I bought the old LeSabre from you, three years ago" Joe reminded him. The old man was a shadow of himself.

"Gott-im-Himmel, my head is going to rot. But you vere a very sad man."

"Not any more" said Joe cheerfully.

"The Ketubah is in my room, New-York, Ellis Island, that's where I met my lovely Esther. We fell in love and Rabbi Jonah married us, all in three days. The Rabbi's wife wrote the Ketuba. Esther always kept it on her side of the Bed. You can have it Karen. Up there the good lord know we were married for fifty years. Be a good boy and push."

"From one cemetery to the next, are you scared?"

"Told you once, I ain't scared of Spirits, and this is a Good Spirit anyway" Karen replied. It was raining, as usual, the cemetery was lush, dark green, and the plaques were sunk in the lawn, marked with Mogen David.

Ruth Helen Bergman nee Link
Beloved Wife and Daughter
1964-1992
May her spirit be enrolled in life everafter

Karen laid a wreath on the plaque, and retreated.

They stood in the rain, hats dripping, coats dripping, the trees dripping, endlessly weeping.

"Goodbye Helen" said Joe. He squatted and placed his ring on the grave, into the wet earth.

"Goodbye Helen" Karen added, choking.

They turned and walked away together, hand in hand.

In Memphis, Beverly Kreissman and Jerry Stein and the rest of the St. Jude Faculty maintained their vigil for new neuroblastoma cases. Beverly took upon herself each new case and followed it personally from diagnosis to grave, berating herself for each and every setback. Six more Jewish babies died during that year. Each death caused immeasurable heartbreak and community-wide consternation. Finally the Plague abated, and only when the Millennium turned did they all heave a sigh of relief.

"It's a girl, and she is perfect" Doctor Bartell chortled. Joe squeezed

Karen's hand and mopped her forehead with the other, with a last heaving effort she had pushed the baby out, and now the little bundle was filling her lungs with air, raising the roof, just a little bit.

"Do the Honors" said Doctor Bartell. Joe took the scissors and cut the Umbilical Cord between the clamps. The doctor placed the whooping bundle on Karen suddenly deflated stomach and Joe held them both, eyes brimming, and nose smarting.

"I need to do some repair work down here, go to Grandma."

The tiny face was rooting so Joe put his pinkie in her mouth, kissed Karen and went out of the delivery room, stepping on air. His heart was light, he could hardly breath, Miriam jumped at him.

"Let me look, let me look."

The baby opened her eyes, so deep, so blue. Miriam and Joe gazed at the little wonder, and she gave them just a hint of a smile.

The Social hall was full of people milling around. Karen was in the middle, the baby swathed in white, her eyes slowly scanning the many faces. Jacob made it from LA, Miriam was the queen-mother, Amanda and Chris showed off her growing belly, Alia was radiant. Abe Kammitzer and Irwin Perlmutter rubbed hands with joy, exchanged bottoms-up with Pastor Wilkins. Gabe and Tammy had made it too. They were all stuffing themselves with bagels and Lox and cream cheese, cheese cakes and Seattle Cappucino coffee, and wines galore. Rabbi Lowel Kantor was walking around like a peacock in heat, this was a great day, *a great* day. The whole community was as one with joy to greet the newcomer. It was as though they knew that a curse had been lifted, and somehow the happy couple, married less than a year ago were responsible for lifting the curse.

Rabbi Kantor rang his glass, slowly the hubbub receded, some of the kids were still arguing loudly and they were shushed by the adults.

"This Sunday morning brunch is hosted by the Parents of the newest addition of out community, and by Miriam, and Jacob Lifshitz, whom we welcome back after a long, long absence. We will not do any surgery despite the inordinate number of Doctors here" everyone laughed politely, they would have laughed at any attempt at humor, spirits were so good. It was spring again and the leaves were coming out, hinting of the green to come, the right time for young ones to come into the world.

"This is a naming ceremony, on the Eighth day of her life" continued the rabbi.

"And the name she will be known by will be..."
"Ruth Helen Bergman" Karen and Joe said in Unison.
Helen let out a cry and started rooting for the breast.

THE END